I0763319

Secrets and Spellcraft

Art of the Adept

Volume 2

By

Michael G. Manning

Cover by Amalia Chitulescu
Map Artwork by Maxime Plasse
Editing by Keri Karandrakis

Printed in the United States of America

ISBN: 978-1-943481-36-1

For more information about the Mageborn series check out the author's Facebook page:

https://www.facebook.com/MagebornAuthor

or visit the website:

http://www.magebornbooks.com

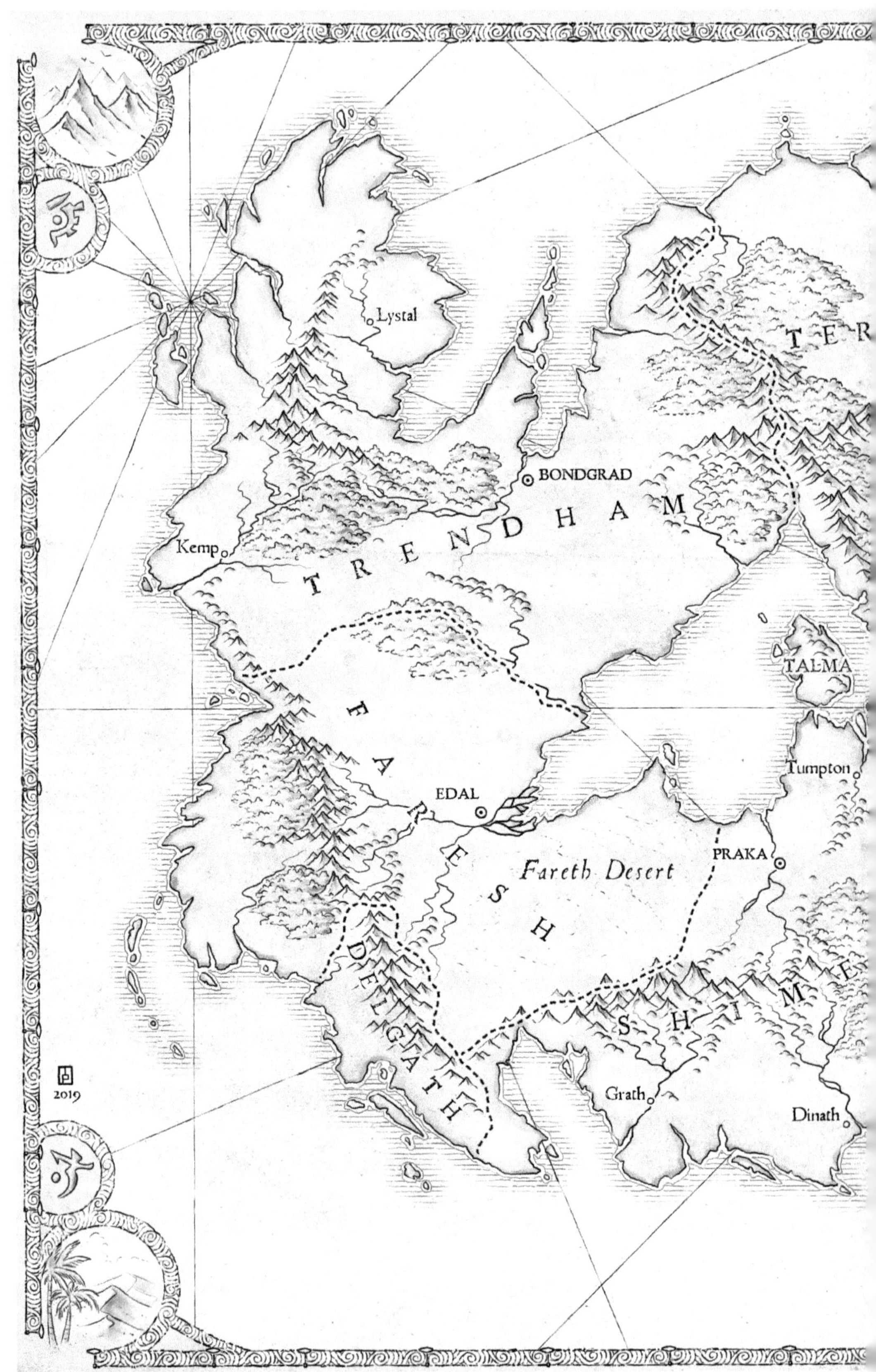

Lystal
BONDGRAD
TRENDHAM
Kemp
TER
TALMA
Tumpton
EDAL
FARESH
Fareth Desert
PRAKA
DELGATH
SHIME
Grath
Dinath
2019

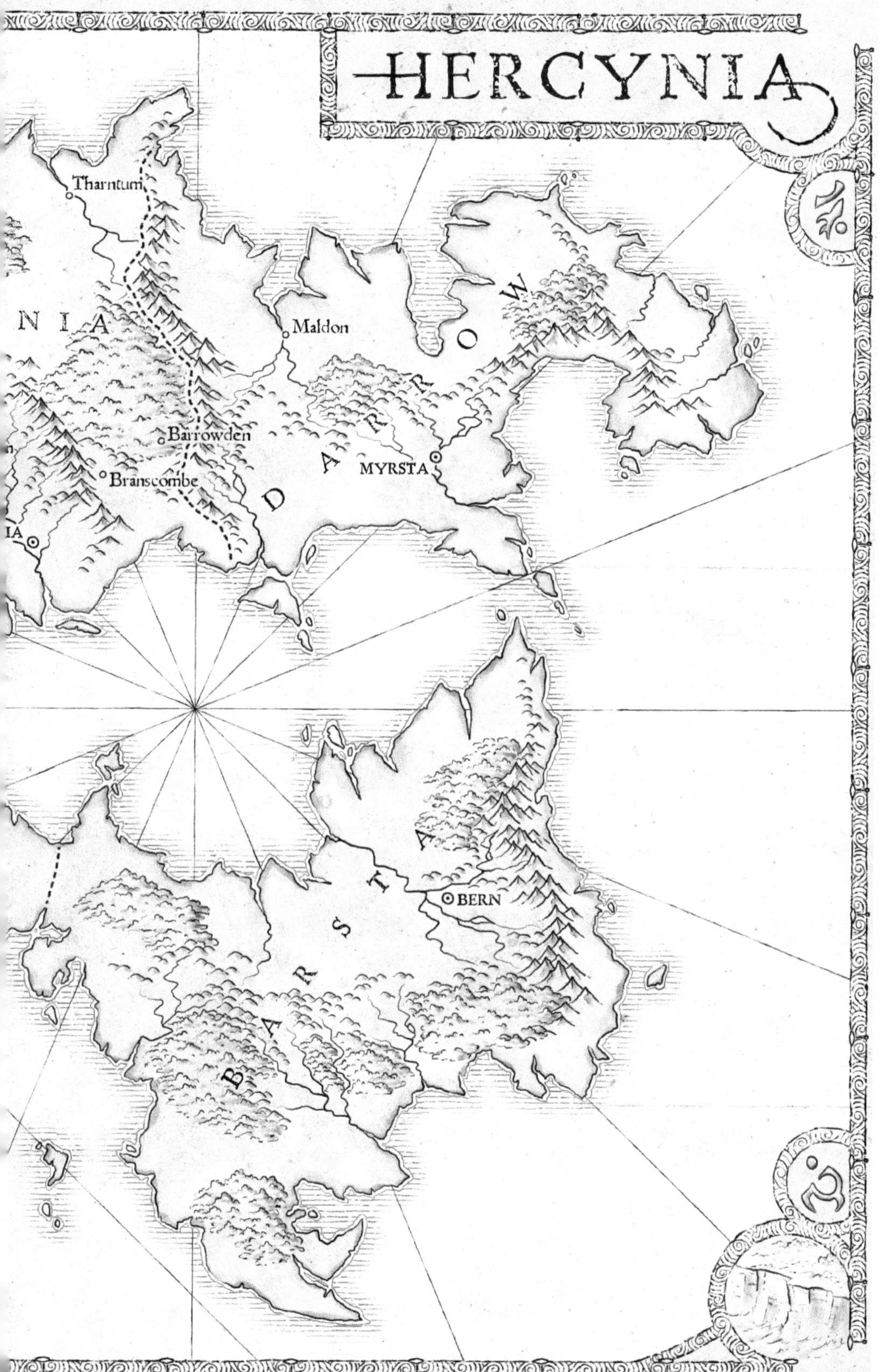
HERCYNIA
Tharntum
N I A
Maldon
Barrowden
Branscombe
MYRSTA
D A R R O W
IA
BERN
B A R S T A

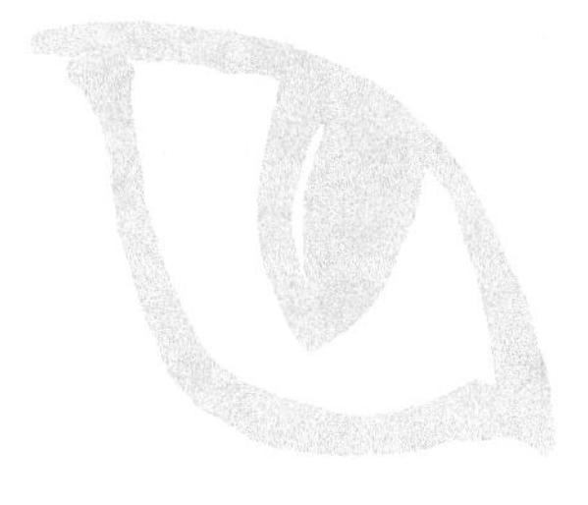

Chapter 1

Will had never been to school, any school, so he wasn't sure what he had expected. It certainly wasn't what he saw as the king's carriage drove past the guard station at the college's main entrance. The gate nestled securely within a formidable wall that rose thirty feet in height. He felt as though he was passing through a boundary into an entirely different world.

As they passed under the high arch and through the wall, he expected his view to be dominated by looming stones structures, but instead his eyes were greeted by green lawns with sculpted bushes and centuries old oaks shadowing a neatly cobblestoned lane. In the distance there were numerous large buildings clustered together here and there, but there was no fortress as the wall had led him to expect. Later on, he was forced to learn a new word to describe the wide layout of ancient buildings and landscaping: *campus*.

And yet there was more, for the entire thing took up more than a thousand acres of land. On every side—surrounding the academic buildings, the chancellor's manse, the student dormitories, the masters' dwellings—was a rolling landscape of trees and fountains, sculptures, and even a heavily wooded park.

It was an entirely different world, encapsulated by the great city of Cerria. *Bloody hell,* thought Will, but even his inner voice was subdued with awe. He felt as though he had passed through a congruence point, emerging onto a new plane of existence. From the way Arrogan had once described the wizards of Wurthaven, Will had expected to find them in a grubby and poorly maintained single building.

The carriage proceeded to the center of the campus, where four tall buildings soared toward the heavens. The road passed between two of them and then entered a lane that circled the interior courtyard between the four. It stopped in front of one, where the driver indicated Will should get out.

"Thank you for the ride, sir," said Will.

The driver tipped his hat and lifted the straps, urging his team to pull away. Will was left standing alone. He hoped that the building he stood before was the correct one, and plucking up his courage, he walked to it and tugged open one of the broad oaken doors. Once inside, he discovered that the exterior was deceiving. The first two floors were actually one floor with vaulted ceilings and two wide staircases on either side that led up to the higher levels.

There was a variety of people moving about, and as Will took in the scene, he couldn't help but mutter, "Fucking hell." He had never been in such a building. A man passing by him glanced oddly in his direction when he heard the words, then hurried on.

He wandered aimlessly for a few minutes, circling the wide, central space and reading the carved stone signs chiseled above the entrances on either side. He stopped when he found the one labeled 'Registrar's Office,' which was the one he had been told to look for. Passing through another set of tall doors, he found himself facing a long desk with several men seated on the other side. Two of them were talking with others that he assumed were students. The third seemed to be free, so Will stepped up to greet him. "Hello."

The man glanced up and then returned to whatever he was reading.

Will thought that was rather rude, so he persisted. "Hello, my name is William Cartwright. I'm here to see the registrar."

The fellow looked up, his eyes widening in faint surprise. "I'm sorry. Are you a friend of Lord Doster?"

He'd never heard the name before. "I was told I need to see him to get settled for classes here."

The man behind the desk frowned, then pointed at a small, wooden plaque in front of him. It was labeled with the words, 'Closed. Next window please.'

Will nodded toward the next window. "Is that Lord Doster, then?"

The clerk sighed. "Temarah save me, are you an idiot? Lord Doster doesn't personally handle registrations."

"I'm in the wrong place?"

"No, hayseed, this is the place. This office handles student registrations. Wait for the next *open* window and they'll take care of you. I'm on break."

Will's cheeks colored. He stared to move on, but he didn't leave without a parting shot. "Asshole."

The clerk stiffened, sitting up straight and a malicious light filled his eyes. Pushing aside the 'Closed' plaque, he smiled. "My break is now over. How can I help you?"

Will repeated himself, "My name is William Cartwright. I was told to register for classes here."

"Have you been admitted to Wurthaven?"

Uncertain, Will answered, "Um, I'm not sure? How does that work?"

The unnamed clerk smiled. "I'll check the list for your name." He got up and went to a massive ledger, where he casually leafed through the pages. The man returned with an artificial smile. "I didn't see it. You'll have to go to the vice-chancellor's office and see if you can be admitted."

"Where's that?"

The man pointed upward. "Seventh floor. You can't miss it."

Will left. The stone stairs leading up were wide and well maintained, so it was only a matter of some effort to climb them. Thankfully his time in the army had gotten him into excellent shape, so it was only a mild annoyance having to climb to the top floor.

Once there, he found it was much smaller than the lower floors, and a single hall led him to a well-appointed office. A secretary waited behind a private desk when he entered. "Do you have an appointment?" she asked, glancing at him over slender glasses.

"For what?"

"To see the vice-chancellor."

"No, ma'am. I was told to come here to be admitted.

A look of amusement flitted across the woman's face. "I'm afraid you've been misinformed. We don't do that here. You need to visit the registrar's office on the ground floor."

He'd been had. Will's brows lowered like looming thunderclouds. "The man down there told me I had to be admitted here." He started to leave.

The secretary took pity on him, however. "Wait." He turned back, listening. "While it's true you can file for admission, it generally takes months. Do you have a sponsor?"

Will thought for a moment. Originally Lord Nerrow had offered to sponsor him, but King Lognion had said it was a bad idea, since it might eventually get to the ears of the Arenata family. The king had offered an alternative. "Yes, ma'am. King Lognion."

The secretary froze in place for a moment. "Are you putting me on, young man?"

Will shrugged. "No, ma'am. Should I return and tell him I still need to be admitted?" He was beginning to feel a bit of malicious pleasure.

She frowned, still unsure whether he was playing a prank or being serious, but she decided to err on the side of caution. “One second.” She disappeared through another door and returned a minute later. Then she held the outer door for him. “Let me take you downstairs and see if we can sort this out.”

When they arrived at the registrar’s office, the secretary, whose name he had learned was Dorothy, walked completely around the long desk and consulted the massive ledger herself. The unfriendly clerk who had turned Will away initially watched her anxiously. Will gave the man a smile when their eyes met, and he saw an icy seed of fear settle in the man’s heart. *You’re so fucked,* he thought.

Dorothy turned around, her cheeks having noticeably reddened. “Which one of you sent this young man up to the vice-chancellor’s office?” she asked in a cold tone.

None of them answered, but Will pointed. “I believe it was him.”

“Stanley,” hissed Dorothy. The worried clerk started to rise but she waved him away, then marched through another door. Will’s sharp ears picked up the shrill tones of her voice as she made her complaints to Lord Doster, the registrar, personally. He was also delighted to hear her mention ‘that idiot Stanley’ in one sentence.

She emerged a few minutes later, her stride brisk and her expression cold, ignoring Stanley’s apologetic looks as she left. Stopping beside Will, she told him, “If you need anything in the future, don’t be shy. My name is Dorothy and I work for the Vice-Chancellor of Education.” With a nod, she was gone.

Stanley was shooting daggers at Will with his eyes.

“I just did what you told me to do,” said Will calmly.

A new figure emerged from the office Dorothy had gone into, a man with an aristocratic bearing. He rounded the desk and offered Will his hand. Will took it. “You must be the new student King Lognion sponsored,” he said, pitching his voice louder so everyone in the room could hear him clearly. “I’m sorry for any confusion. My name is Garett Doster.” He glanced over his shoulder. “I’ll have a word with you after I get back, Mister Fyfe.” Stanley’s face paled.

Will gave Stanley a wink as Lord Doster put an arm around his shoulder and let him out of the office and into the main atrium. “Don’t I need to sign something?” asked Will.

“All that’s been taken care of,” the registrar assured him. “If there’s anything else that needs doing, I’ll take care of it when I return.”

“But classes—”

"Those have already been set for you as well, considering your unusual circumstances." Lord Doster spotted a familiar face and called out to a young man who was passing by, "Mister Burwood!"

The student he called to turned and stared at them in confusion for a moment before he realized who was speaking to him. "Lord Doster," he answered, bobbing his head. "What do you need?"

Will had already noticed that some of the norms he had come to expect of interacting with nobles were somewhat blunted here. The students and staff treated Lord Doster with respect, but none of the fawning obedience that noblemen usually required.

"William, this is Robert Burwood, a second-year student here at Wurthaven," said the registrar, introducing them. "Robert, this is William Cartwright. He's starting here tomorrow on the recommendation of King Lognion."

Robert's eyes widened with surprise. He extended a hand. "Pleased to meet you. Just call me Rob, everyone does."

"I go by Will."

"William needs to get his bearings, Robert. I'd appreciate it if you would take him under your wing and help orient him. Could you take him to the dorms and help get him settled? I'm sure he'd like to unpack his things," said the registrar.

Will coughed. "Actually, all I have is what I'm carrying." He wore the clothes the king had given him, and he carried the oiled leather bag that held his mail and gambeson. Aside from those and four silver clima in his coin pouch, he had nothing else.

Lord Doster and Robert gave him a surprised look, but the registrar recovered first. "Well, I'm sure you can buy whatever else you need in a day or two. You'll certainly need a change of clothes, at the very least."

"And paper, pens, journals—" added Rob. "But there are shops here on the campus. I'll show you."

Will was beginning to have serious doubts. Four clima had seemed like plenty of money to him before, but he doubted it would suffice to buy clothes along with expensive items like paper and books. "Let's see the dorms first," he suggested. "This bag is heavy."

"I'll carry it for you," offered Rob. He started to tug at the strap and stopped when he felt the weight. "What do you have in there?"

"My armor."

Rob seemed confused, but he gave a quick wave to Lord Doster. "I'll take it from here, sir." As they walked away, he glanced at Will. "Did you say armor?"

Will nodded.

"Why did you bring armor?"

"I'm a little attached to it," said Will honestly. "It's saved my life several times now."

"Are you a knight?" Rob's tone suggested he would be surprised if such was actually the case.

"No. I was a private contract soldier in Branscombe before I came here." He paused for a moment, wondering if he still was. "The king said I had to come to Wurthaven, though. Do you think that means I'm out of the contract, or will I have to serve the rest when I finish in a year or two?"

Rob seemed stunned. "I don't know, but nobody comes here for just one or two years. Most stay for at least five, more if they join the academia or take jobs in research."

"Five years?" It seemed like a lifetime to Will at seventeen years of age. If his military contract was stacked on top of that, he wouldn't be out until he was closing in on thirty. "Is there that much to learn?"

"That depends on you," said Rob with a chuckle. "Some people devote their lives to this place."

"Like the registrar?"

Rob shook his head. "I suppose he has devoted himself to Wurthaven, but I mean the academics and engineers—the researchers."

Will gave him a blank stare.

"People like Master Courtney," clarified Rob, as though the name should mean something to him.

"Who's he?" asked Will.

Rob's jaw dropped a little. "You've never heard of Lord Alfred Courtney, the metaphysicist?"

"Meta-what?"

The second-year took his elbow, urging him to continue walking. "You have a lot of catching up to do. Where have you been until now, under a rock? Master Courtney is the head of the research department here and one of the largest contributors to our modern understanding of turyn and the underlying principles of magic. He's so famous everyone in the city knows his name."

"Oh," said Will, as though that answered everything. "But what is that metafizzy thing you mentioned?"

"Metaphysics," corrected Rob. "It's the study of the principles of magic and how it interacts with the regular, mundane world we live in."

Hearing the description, Will thought it sounded like a fancy term for wizardry, and he said as much. "That's wizardry."

Rob laughed. "Well, yes, but there's a lot to learn here so it's divided into a number of categories. What would you call the design and construction of new spells?"

"Wizardry."

"It is, but here it's taught with the label of spell engineering. We have an entire department devoted to just that."

"And Master Courtney runs it?"

"No, he oversees most of Wurthaven's research projects, so he doesn't really belong to a specific department. The Engineering Department is headed by Master Dugas." When Will only looked more confused, Rob went on, "The engineers do their best to create and perfect new spells. They work closely with researchers, though, since they're often trying to turn new theory into something practical and useful."

That sounded much more pragmatic to Will than metaphysics, but he refrained from saying it. Rob's words had implied there were more departments than just Engineering, so he asked, "How many departments are there?"

His new friend began counting on his fingers, "Let's see, Divinatory Arts, Alchemy, Artifice, Engineering, Healing, and—" he paused. "What was the last one? Oh! Psyche."

"No Department of Sorcery?"

Rob waved his hand. "That doesn't qualify as a subject of study. They inherit their elementals and any research into how elementals were originally tamed is strictly prohibited. The nobility prefer to keep their secrets to themselves."

Will found that interesting. From what Arrogan had said, the secret was lost. "So some of them still know how it was done?"

"Not as far as I know," said Rob. "Otherwise we'd probably have a lot more sorcerers attending the college."

"They study here?"

Rob nodded. "Of course. Aside from the elementals, they're just like us. They need to learn spellcraft too, if they're to make the most of what they're given." The young man stopped then, gesturing to the buildings that rose up in front of them.

They had left behind the four central buildings that surrounded what Will later learned was called the 'Quad,' and stood now in front of two impressively large square buildings connected by a covered stone walkway. "These are the dormitories," explained Rob. "The one on the left is the women's dorm. We're not allowed in there. The one on the right is for those with testicular endowments."

Will's head was already swimming with new terms and information, so he failed to recognize the word 'testicular' even though he was very familiar with anatomy. "Where will I stay then?"

Rob began laughing hysterically. "You've got balls, right? Do we need to have Master Morris examine you?"

Will grinned, belatedly realizing his mistake. "I suppose not." He found himself growing to like Rob. The young man seemed solid and certainly wasn't above rough humor. He assumed that Morris was the head of the Department of Healing.

Rob led him in through the center of the covered walkway, taking a right to enter the men's dorm. The front door opened into a large space dominated by couches and chairs of a sort that Will had never seen. They bore resemblance to some of the furniture he had seen in the palace, but they lacked the ornamental features he had seen there, making up for the lack with an excess of cushions and padding. He immediately wanted to try them out, but Rob pulled him along to meet a woman sitting beside a table.

The woman had a strong figure, though age had added some extra padding here and there. Her gray-white hair was piled up on her head in an impressive bun and when she looked at him, he was taken with her warm brown eyes. "This is Dianne. She's the resident assistant here, but we all call her 'Mom,'" said Rob affectionately.

Setting aside her tea, Dianne stood and offered Will her hand. "Dianne Young," she said briskly.

She's anything but young, noted Will, immediately chiding himself for his uncharitable thought. To make up for it, he took her hand in his, but instead of shaking it as was expected, he bent over it and brushed his lips across her knuckles, a gesture he had learned at the palace. "William Cartwright, milady," he said with a grin.

Dianne blushed mildly and gave Rob a surprised look. "This one is going to be trouble."

"Don't look at me!" exclaimed Rob. "He's your child now, Mom."

"As if I could give birth to so many unruly boys," said Dianne. "Come with me, William. I'll give you your room key. I think there are some packages waiting on you as well."

"Just Will, please," he begged.

"Will, then," agreed Dianne. "Call me Dianne."

She turned away, already starting toward the desk that served as her duty station. Rob gave Will a wink and mouthed a word silently. Will took his cue and called out, "Sure thing, Mom."

The resident assistant kept walking, but she cast a stern eye on Rob. "How long are you going to keep that going?"

"Until you finally agree to marry me, Mom," said Rob with a roguish grin.

"Hmmph. I'm more than twice your age, you scoundrel. Don't think I don't know what you're up to, with your unorthodox comings and goings." She leafed through a book on her desk and then turned to open a door behind her desk, unlocking it with a key that hung around her neck. She went in and returned a moment later. She handed Will a brass key. "You're in 407 with Seth Gabet."

Dianne pointed at Rob and snapped her fingers. "There's a box in there for him. Be a dear and carry it since he's already got a bag."

Rob emerged a moment later carrying a heavy wooden crate, then led Will to the stairs. Will took pity on him. "I'll switch with you." Despite his brief tenure in the dungeons, he was still fresh from his time in the army.

"No, I'm fine," protested Rob, but by the time they had climbed the fourth flight he was red-faced and panting, while Will wasn't even breathing hard.

"I offered," said Will as he stepped into a long, wood-paneled hallway. The building's interior was old, but well maintained. He passed several doors, noting the numbers on them, until he came to 407. "Here we are." Keys were a relatively new thing for him, so he fumbled with it for a full minute before finally getting the lock to turn.

Inside, the room was positively palatial by Will's standards. His one week in the palace notwithstanding, he had spent a significant portion of the past few years sleeping on the ground. This room held a massive, wood-framed bunk bed that dominated the right wall. A narrow window was set in the opposite wall, and he was shocked to realize it held actual glass. On the left-hand side were two study desks separated by a pair of tall dressers.

He was drawn immediately to the window, dropping his armor bag on the floor and staring outside. A view of the well-manicured lawns of Wurthaven greeted him, and he stuck his head outside to inhale the air. *I've died and gone to heaven.* Far below, he saw both male and female students walking, and he was unable to restrain himself. Sticking his arm out, he began waving.

Rob quickly pulled him back in. "They'll think you're off in the head if you keep doing that."

"I don't mind," said Will. "This feels like a dream."

"You are living the dream, my dear fellow," said Rob, looking out the window. He swept his arm wide. "Below you will find a field of choice fruit, ripe for the taking."

"Fruit?"

Rob winked. "Girls, my friend, girls. Half the student body is of the feminine persuasion. Merchants' daughters, well-fed and well-dressed, daughters of noblemen, they lie before us like a banquet waiting to be supped upon."

Will frowned. "Daughters of noblemen?"

His new friend held up his hands in a placating gesture. "All right, I'll admit, most of those are not to be trifled with, but you never know. Some are third or fourth children of lesser gentry. Besides, you don't necessarily have to *marry* them." His lips split to show pearly teeth.

"I didn't come here to chase girls," said Will disapprovingly.

"You should. Many profitable matches begin with a chance meeting at Wurthaven. Play your cards right and you could even move up the ladder a step or two. Personally, though, I simply revel in the chase."

"I have a friend you should meet," said Will, thinking of Tailtiu. His aunt would make short work of someone like Robert Burwood.

"Oh really?"

Will shook his head. "Never mind. Let's see what's in the box."

CHAPTER 2

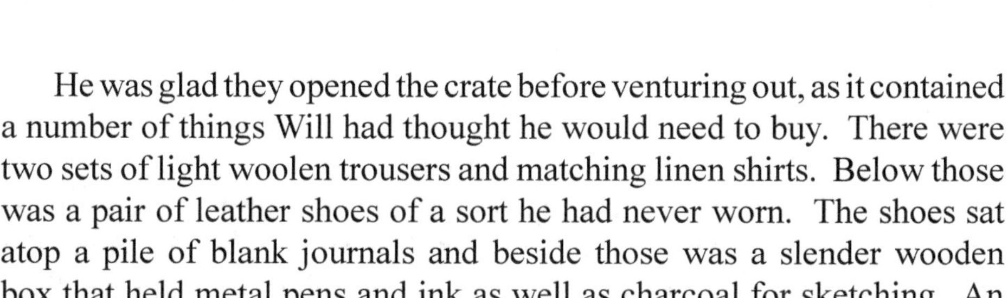

He was glad they opened the crate before venturing out, as it contained a number of things Will had thought he would need to buy. There were two sets of light woolen trousers and matching linen shirts. Below those was a pair of leather shoes of a sort he had never worn. The shoes sat atop a pile of blank journals and beside those was a slender wooden box that held metal pens and ink as well as charcoal for sketching. An envelope had fallen down on one side and Will retrieved it.

Within were two sheets of folded paper. The first was a note:

> *William,*
>
> *Despite the nature of our last meeting I would like to congratulate you on your entry into Wurthaven's halls of learning. I still think fondly of my own time there and wish you the best in the coming years.*
>
> *I regret not being able to sponsor you directly, but as Lognion has advised, that would probably not be the best course for either of us. Therefore I am grateful to him for giving you this opportunity. I have included a number of items that I am sure you will need over the coming year, and for those things which I couldn't foresee I have included an allowance. Take the note of credit enclosed with this letter to the Bursar's Office and they will see you paid.*
>
> *On other matters I would tell you that the campaign against Darrow has gone remarkably well, thanks in large part to your efforts. Barrowden is once again in Terabinian hands and the Crown is investing resources to rebuild the area. A fortress will be raised to prevent similar disasters in the future.*
>
> *Best of luck,*
> *M.*

"M?" asked Rob, leaning over his shoulder. "Who's that?"

"Someone who feels guilty," said Will in a neutral tone. He glanced at the note of credit and after a moment he spotted the bottom line. "Ten crowns?"

"Not bad!" said Rob. "That'll keep you in beer for the semester at the very least."

That wasn't what was on Will's mind. That amount was three times what he would have made in a year if he had stayed with the army. It seemed like a ridiculous amount of money. He pocketed the note. "Let's go see the bursar."

"I can give you the grand tour along the way," said Rob magnanimously.

The trip to the bursar was uneventful, as was the tour, although the peaceful and scenic campus continually amazed Will. He hadn't even imagined such a place existed, so everything was a surprise. Robert left him to his own devices after a while and Will returned to his room. On the way in Dianne caught him and told him he had a new letter waiting.

It turned out to be a notice that he was to meet with his advisor, Paul Wattle, in the morning to confirm his classes. He took it with him and when he got back to his room, he met his roommate, Seth Gabet.

Seth was possessed of dark curly hair and a pale almost deathly white complexion only partly offset by the moustache and patchy beard he was trying to nurture. He glanced up nervously as Will came in and raised one hand in a silent greeting.

Will strode forward, putting out his hand. "I'm Will Cartwright. Good to meet you."

"Seth," was all his roomie could manage in response.

"Are you a first-year student too?"

Seth nodded, his eyes darting to the side as though he was uncomfortable. "Would you like the bottom bunk?" He asked the question as though he assumed Will would take preference, even though he had obviously already been using it.

Will frowned. "You were here first. Plus, I rather like being up off the ground."

The other boy stood up, moving as though he would strip the sheets. "I'll move up top. It's no trouble."

He put his hand on Seth's shoulder and felt the young man flinch at his touch. "It's all right. I prefer the top anyway. Why are you so nervous?"

Seth stared at his feet. "I didn't think I'd be rooming with a young lord," he answered after a moment. "We can probably find someone to switch rooms if you want."

"Lord?" Will began to laugh. "I'm from Barrowden. My mom is a village midwife. I don't even know my father. You don't have to worry about me looking down on you!"

"Oh." The tension in Seth's shoulders began to fade.

"Besides," said Will, "I was told that all the students here are treated equally. Even the teachers and administrators prefer their university titles to whatever social rank they have." Rob had explained the custom to him during their tour.

"Sure," agreed Seth, but it was obvious that he didn't really believe it.

From the other things Rob had said Will also had gathered that most of the students were from modestly wealthy families, while a smaller percentage were from the gentry. With that in mind, he asked, "What does your family do?"

"Dad's a cobbler," said Seth quietly. "But he's done well."

It took an hour to coax more out of the nervous young man, but Will eventually learned that Seth's father was one of the most successful cobblers in Cerria. Seth himself had shown little facility in his father's trade, so his dad had taken an apprentice and hoped that his son could find a better place for himself as a wizard. Will wasn't sure what the tuition at Wurthaven cost, but he gathered that it was only barely within Seth's family's means.

So, he's at the bottom of the ladder, realized Will, *and here I am being sponsored by King Lognion. No wonder he was fearful.* He was happy he could put his roommate at ease, since they might potentially be sharing a room for years.

Later in the day they went to the dining hall and had supper, sitting at a table by themselves. Will studied the students that sat at the other tables but didn't find any opportunities to introduce himself. He knew no one other than Rob and Seth, but he hoped that soon that would change.

He went to sleep that night feeling optimistic.

***

Will was running. He had left his advisor's office with a list of classes and the knowledge that he would be late for the first of them if he didn't hurry. The class he was rushing to find was Composition, located in Room 302 of the General Lectures building, which was one of the four buildings on the central quad.

Two of his other classes were there as well, History and Mathematics. His others were all in separate buildings. In the afternoon he had Spell Theory at the Magical Theory and Divination building, just across the quad. After those he would have his last class, Alchemy, in a building that was well separated from the main buildings of the quad. His next class after that wouldn't start until the next day, at the crack of dawn. That was his physical elective, for which he had chosen Fencing.

When he finally found the classroom, he was definitely late, but he opened the door anyway. He didn't expect to see forty pairs of curious eyes looking down upon him as he entered, though. The class took place in a small auditorium with seats that angled up on a slope so that everyone could see, while at the base was a small platform and a podium.

The lecturer, a woman named Jennifer Conrad, turned out to be far younger than he had expected. She was clad in a long, black robe from which emerged a white collar with an aesthetically pleasing hand-tied bow. Her form was entirely hidden by the robe, but from the face alone he could tell she was a stunningly lovely woman.

Professor Conrad's eyes were hard and unforgiving, however, as she stared at the late arrival. Will felt himself begin to wither under her glare. "Name?" she asked coldly.

"William Cartwright, ma'am."

"Take a seat. Arrive late again and I'll have you ejected."

He walked up the side aisle, but rather than go all the way to the empty rows in the back he spotted an empty seat in the third row and crossed over to sit there. A girl with mousy brown hair looked at him briefly and then studiously pretended he didn't exist. Will whispered to her in a convivial tone, "Will, nice to meet you." He turned his head to the right and repeated his greeting to a pale-haired guy who promptly put his hand up to prevent eye contact.

This is going well, thought Will sarcastically.

Glancing around, he soon realized he should have brought pen and paper, for everyone else was rapidly taking notes as Professor Conrad talked, while he was empty handed. Will's stomach sank as it occurred to him that even if he had, he couldn't possibly have written fast enough. His penmanship was more than just crude—it was also far too slow.

Free from the labor of note taking, Will did his best to remember everything the professor said. Despite his grandfather's constant criticism, he had come to realize early on that his memory was pretty good. Hopefully, he could find someone later willing to share their notes.

Since he was able to devote all his attention to listening, he also had some extra time to try and understand what the lecturer was trying to achieve—the purpose of the topic. It all came down to one simple thing; Professor Conrad was hoping to teach them to write and communicate effectively with pen and paper. For the foreseeable future, his life would be preoccupied with a fair amount of reading and a much larger amount of essay writing.

For someone who still struggled to write legibly, it seemed like an insurmountable task, but he didn't let his fear drive him. He'd known fear on the battlefield, he'd survived the constant scathing criticism of his grandfather, what was the worst that could possibly happen? *Humiliation, or possibly being expelled,* he decided. *Until then I'll learn as much as I can.* He kept his eyes and ears open, trying to absorb everything Professor Conrad said and wrote on the board behind her.

When the class finally ended, he relaxed. The students were exiting rapidly, and the fellow on his right was gone before he could say a word. He addressed the girl to his left again, since she had to get past him to exit. "Sorry for interrupting. I'm William Cartwright." He stood and made room for her to get by.

"Janice," she said quietly. "Janice Edelman." Then she was gone. The hall emptied, and he sat back down, closing his eyes for several minutes and letting his mind drift and assimilate what he had heard. That done, he rose and headed for the dorm. He needed to pick up a journal and writing materials for his next classes.

Mathematics was a relief, as he was easily able to write down what he needed, and the material was all comfortably within what he had previously learned. In History, he found the topic familiar, but it was rapidly apparent he couldn't take notes fast enough. He gave up before long and resumed listening.

Will sat alone at lunch, unable to find anyone he knew. He was picking apart a piece of fish he couldn't identify but that would probably have been excellent if the cook hadn't overcooked it—when a stranger stopped and pulled out the chair across from him. "Hello," said Will, flashing a smile.

"I hear you came in on a royal sponsorship," said the young man sitting across from him.

He studied the newcomer for a moment, taking in the high quality of his jacket and noting the gold ring set with a wide ruby that was carelessly displayed. The other boy had long brown hair that appeared to have been curled or styled in deliberate fashion. A fire elemental hung in the air above his right shoulder. "I'm William Cartwright," he said, offering his hand across the table.

"You didn't answer my question," said the young noble.

Will stared back evenly but kept his expression calm. "You made a simple statement. Was I supposed to interpret it as a question?" He waited several seconds without blinking, then added, "If so, then yes. King Lognion sponsored me."

"You've got some spine, Cartwright. I like that. Dennis Spry." The young noble held out his hand in a duplicate of the gesture Will had made a few moments before.

Will didn't move. "You wouldn't shake my hand a second ago. Why now?" Dennis had managed to set his teeth on edge. The young man reminded him of a younger version of Dave, full of repressed anger and a sense of entitlement, only Dennis hadn't had the experience of a world that refused to accept his demands. Dave's personality had been tempered in the school of hard knocks, while Dennis had been encouraged in his every whim.

Dennis gave him a smile of smug superiority. "I didn't want to dirty my hand if you didn't have at least a bit of merit." His hand was still out, hanging in the air.

He knew the wise option would be to quickly take the other man's hand, but his pride wouldn't allow it. Instead, he replied, "I have always assumed everyone has some merit, but you've changed my mind."

Dennis's face clouded with anger and he sat back, crossing his arms. "That's a shame. I thought perhaps we could have been friends." He stood, looking down at Will. "No need to be enemies, though. There's a party at Malview House on Friday night. You should come." He dropped a small envelope on the table. With that he left.

It was only then that Will spared enough attention to realize the dining hall had gone silent. He tried not to look around, but he could feel that all eyes were on him. *What did I just do?* he wondered.

Chapter 3

His next class was Spell Theory, and Will arrived early enough to get a seat in the second row. Will leaned forward with interest when the professor entered, an older man named Dulaney. This was the one class on his schedule that he thought would be the most interesting. *Today I'll begin to learn the things Grandfather never got to teach me,* he thought with anticipation.

Professor Dulaney stood behind the podium and gazed at the class without saying a word. Unlike the previous teachers, he didn't bother calling roll. He simply stared at them for a long minute until the students began to shift nervously in their seats. Then he turned and picked up a piece of chalk and began to draw a diagram on the blackboard.

A cross with arms of equal length appeared first, and the old man labeled each of the ends, putting a 'P' at the top, an 'N' at the bottom, an 'O' on the left, and a 'C' on the right. Then he stepped a few feet to the left and wrote the word 'turyn.' "Forget everything you think you know about turyn. In fact, it might be better for you if you haven't learned anything." He set the chalk down and stared at the class, appraising them. Finally, he asked, "Would any of you like to venture as to guess what the labels on graph represent?"

Will had no idea, so he kept his mouth firmly closed. No one else volunteered either. After a short time, the professor sighed. "All right. Perhaps I'm moving too quickly. Would one of you like to tell the class what you think turyn is?"

"Energy," someone said in the back.

"Yes, but that doesn't begin to cover it. Who else?"

"Magic," offered someone else.

Dulaney rubbed a hand over his face in frustration. "Single-word answers only supply a different label. I want a description, something with some meaning—an answer that attempts to wrestle with the question. Would someone else like to try?"

Once again ignoring the instincts the army had taught him, Will volunteered. "It's the vital energy that all living beings produce—humans, animals, and plants. It's the energy that catalyzes our motion and enacts our thoughts and will upon the material world, whether through physical motion or magical effects." He felt rather proud of himself for remembering Arrogan's lesson.

Professor Dulaney studied him intently for a second. "Excellent answer, Mister—what is your name?"

"Cartwright, sir. William Cartwright."

The teacher nodded. "I applaud your effort to meet my expectations. You are only half correct, however."

Will frowned. He was damn well certain he was absolutely right.

Dulaney smiled faintly. "Would someone like to give me names for the ends of the graph? The letters are place holders. What do you think they represent?" When no one answered, he urged them on. "This will be a very boring lecture if no one steps up. I'm perfectly happy to stand here and have a staring contest for the rest of the hour."

Finally, a girl in the front row made an attempt. "The elements, fire, water, earth, and air?"

"No," said the professor smugly. "But thank you for helping move the lecture forward, Miss…?"

"Rebecca Swafford."

"Very good. No, the axes of this graph represent a continuum that runs between positive and negative, chaos and order." He pointed at the letters. "The primal elements that you've been so conditioned to think about are actually general areas found between these extremes." He pointed to the top right quadrant. "Fire would be here, falling in the area between positive and chaotic." Next he pointed at the bottom right, then the bottom left, and finally the top left quadrants. "Water, earth, and air, respectively. From what I have shown you so far, Mister Cartwright's answer is fully correct, but there's more."

Professor Dulaney drew a diagonal line across the cross. "For those of you with enough math experience, this represents the z-axis, making this a three-dimensional graph. Think of it as extending out toward you, and back through the blackboard away from you. This axis represents the polarity of turyn. Coming toward you, the turyn becomes more vital, more in tune with life. Past the center and moving away, turyn takes on qualities of the void, the antithesis of life.

"Mister Cartwright, can you tell me now why your definition wasn't complete?"

Will nodded. "Because the only turyn I referenced was turyn of the vital sort. I wasn't aware of the other sort."

Dulaney nodded. "Actually, this graph oversimplifies things. The vitality-void axis isn't a gradient. It's an either-or shift. Turyn can only be of one type or the other. The two don't coexist. To be candidly honest, the positive-negative axis is similar in that regard, but the two types can coexist. In the case of the positive-negative axis what we are describing is the overall mixture of positive or negative charge."

Some of the students' eyes had glazed over, but Will was rapt with his attention. *If only Arrogan had explained it like this.* Of course, back then he still hadn't learned anything about graphs, so perhaps it wouldn't have helped.

The professor continued, "Turyn has three basic properties, which we can show on this graph, but a better way to describe it is as a wave." He drew several wavy lines on the board. The top line had wide peaks and valleys, while those beneath it were closer together. The bottom line was a frenetic scrawl. Then he marked two peaks on the broad, top-most line. "The distance between two peaks or two valleys is called the wavelength. Turyn on the order side of our graph has longer wavelengths and less overall inherent energy." Then he pointed at the squiggly bottom line. "Turyn with very short wavelengths is on the chaotic end and possesses a higher inherent energy.

"The positive axis represents the fact that turyn can have a positive charge or a negative charge. Whenever someone produces turyn from their inner gate, it is usually a mixture of positively and negatively charged turyn. The overall ratio is represented by the y-axis on our original graph." Dulaney paused to take a breath.

"Would anyone like to take a stab at what the vital-void differences are?" After several unsuccessful attempts, the professor explained. "A wave also has a quality called polarity. Imagine the lines that I just drew. All of them go up and down. If those are of the vital-type, then the void-type waves move back and forth at a ninety-degree angle."

Rebecca raised her hand. "If the only type of turyn found in living creatures is of the vital type, how do you know the void type exists?"

The professor smiled at her. "That is an excellent question. Would anyone like to guess?"

Without thinking, Will answered, "Demons. They have black turyn."

The teacher stared at him for a moment in surprise. "Where did you learn that?"

"I saw a demon in Barrowden," he said sheepishly, realizing how ridiculous it sounded. "It had black turyn that burned whenever it touched someone."

Dulaney gaped. "You saw a demon? How do you expect us to—"

"I was in the army, Professor," interrupted Will. "There was a Priest of Madrok in Barrowden when we entered the village."

The professor blinked. "Oh. Very well, I'll accept your statement as fact, incredible as it is. However, I have to inform you that turyn doesn't have colors."

"But it was black, sir."

"Could you actually *see* its turyn?"

"Yes, sir. It wasn't anything like the turyn other people have," said Will.

"I'll need to see you after class, Mister Cartwright," said Dulaney. "As to colors, I can explain that for everyone's benefit now. While it is true that once your ability to see turyn is awakened it appears to have colors, there is a reason we don't rely on color to describe it. Humans are not ordinarily born able to see turyn, so our brains haven't developed a regular system for experiencing it as we have for our other senses. Where one person might see black or green, for example, someone else might see yellow or purple. This is one of the main reasons we developed other methods for studying and describing its properties."

The teacher pointed at the back, where someone had raised their hand. "Yes. You have a question?"

The class continued, and while Will listened eagerly, he couldn't help but wonder what the teacher wanted to see him about. Hopefully it wouldn't be because of his remark about demons. He had left his description of the circumstances deliberately vague, since he doubted anyone would believe he had gone into Barrowden with only one other person.

When the bell finally sounded and everyone filed out, he stopped in front of the podium anxiously.

Dulaney spoke once the auditorium was empty. "You're not in trouble, Mister Cartwright. I merely wanted to enquire about your ability to see turyn. Ordinarily, we don't take students through the ritual to open their eyes until the end of the first year. How did it happen?"

Unwilling to talk about his first meeting with the fae, Will simplified the story. "My mother is a midwife. I was searching for herbs and mistook diviner's sage for regular sage. When I tasted some, it made me hallucinate. Afterward I started seeing turyn."

The professor nodded. "Unusual, but not unheard of. Normally a person has to be exposed to several such events before the sight fully manifests."

Will said nothing. He definitely didn't want to talk about his near-death experience.

"About this demon you saw. You're very lucky to be alive. What happened?"

"There was a sorceress nearby who slew it, but she was wounded. I saw the black turyn beneath her skin. It seemed to cause her a great deal of pain," said Will.

"Dying is usually painful," said Dulaney. "How long did she survive?"

"I don't think she died," said Will. "I think someone helped her."

The professor scoffed. "Trust me, young man. She's dead now. Demonic turyn is invariably fatal."

"But I saw her get up," argued Will. "She even fought some more after that."

"How long did you observe her after that?"

Not long, thought Will. *A half an hour, maybe?* "She disappeared a little while later. I'm not sure where she went."

"Then she died somewhere else," said Dulaney. "Void turyn isn't compatible with living creatures. Even a small amount will continue to damage a person over time until it eventually kills them."

But I pulled it out of her, thought Will. *I converted it. She has to be fine.* "Couldn't her body have transformed it into normal turyn?" he suggested.

The professor shook his head. "People can't change turyn. That's why we make transducers."

"Transducers?"

"You'll learn about those in your classes on Artifice next year. For the time being I will have to see about having you take an additional class. Since you've already got the sight you can go ahead and start learning spellcraft once you've been typed."

"Typed?"

The older man nodded. "As much as I dislike using elements to describe turyn, they remain an apt description of the various mixtures people produce. It's different for each person, which affects how efficiently you can create and cast various spells. All spells require different types of turyn, so if your gate produces only a small amount of that type you wind up spending more of your overall turyn to get enough to make a particular spell work. By determining your type, you can avoid trying to use spells you aren't suited for and focus on those that are better aligned with what your type of turyn is."

"Seems like a lot of trouble."

"Not when it helps you to live longer. If you go about using spells that don't match your type, it costs you a greater amount of turyn, and that means you'll be wasting your life needlessly."

Lost in thought, Will didn't reply. Everything the professor had said about types and affinities was in direct opposition to what he had learned from Arrogan. His grandfather had said nothing about affinities. He wasn't sure that meant it wasn't true, though. Intuitively he felt that perhaps the nature of his early training had made such distinctions irrelevant. He knew he could change turyn from one type into another. He did it when he pulled it from another person into himself, otherwise he would be stricken with nausea. He had done it when he drew the demonic turyn from Selene, otherwise he would have died.

In fact, he was probably doing it even now, since his source was kept reduced to a level far below what was ordinarily necessary to sustain life. He drew turyn from the environment around him and converted it into whatever mixture he needed to live.

Without that ability, the wizards of Wurthaven were literally burning their own lives to produce spells and create magical effects. Given that circumstance, it made sense that they would employ every possible advantage to make the most of what they spent.

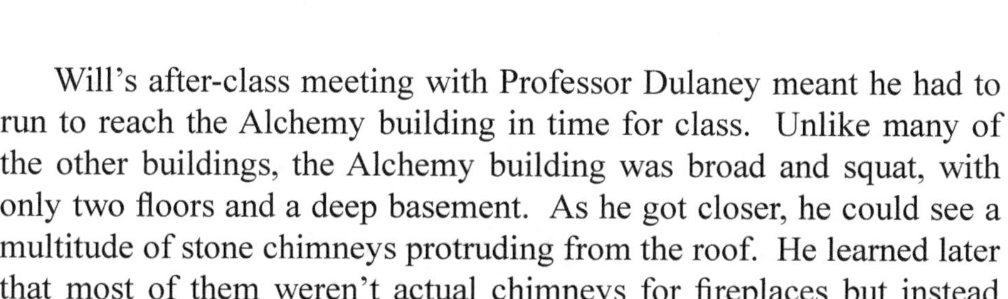

CHAPTER 4

Will's after-class meeting with Professor Dulaney meant he had to run to reach the Alchemy building in time for class. Unlike many of the other buildings, the Alchemy building was broad and squat, with only two floors and a deep basement. As he got closer, he could see a multitude of stone chimneys protruding from the roof. He learned later that most of them weren't actual chimneys for fireplaces but instead ventilated fumes from the workrooms.

Once he found the classroom, he immediately noticed another major difference. Rather than an auditorium, the Alchemy class was in a large room with heavy, blacktopped tables spread evenly throughout. The tables had two sinks set within them at either end, and several shiny metal objects stuck up from the center, as well as a few mysterious small holes.

The holes made sense. Arrogan's workshop table had them as well, places where he could mount metal rods to support glassware at varying heights. The other metal protuberances he wasn't sure about. They appeared to have handles, which meant they could be opened to allow either a liquid or a gas to flow from them. Will wasn't sure which.

The instructor made it clear, though, during his introductory speech. One of the valves opened to supply clean water, the second provided a flammable gas for use with burners, and the third supplied a vacuum, or more accurately a negative air pressure. Will understood the concept, but he'd never had access to something like it before. Arrogan's workroom was much more primitive by comparison.

Their teacher was a man in his thirties named Aaron Karlovic, and he was notable for the fact that his attire was simple and neat. Unlike the other professors, he wore no robe, no necktie, and the sleeves of his shirt were tightly cuffed around his wrists. He began his lecture by explaining his attire.

"As you may have noticed, my clothes have no loose ends or voluminous elements. Beginning tomorrow, make sure you emulate this. Also, I would advise you not to wear anything you feel any personal attachment to. In the closet to the left you'll find aprons, gloves, masks, and eye protection, but there will inevitably be accidents.

"Anything you wear into this class runs the risk of being stained, bleached, or worse. If you get something particularly nasty on your clothes, you may even be forced to remove them and have them burned. For this reason, you should consider keeping a spare set of cheap clothing here in the classroom. I will be assigning personal lockers for that purpose at the end of class.

"Today will be entirely devoted to orienting you and explaining safety procedures," continued the instructor. "You'll also be assigned a partner, so if you have any preferences be prepared to present them to me when we get to that point."

Instructor Karlovic then began demonstrating the emergency shower and wash stations they would use in the event of an accident, along with a warning that in certain disastrous circumstances water should also be avoided. "On days that we deal with substances which you *do not* want to come into contact with water there will be specific instructions given, so always make sure to pay careful attention to the warnings given at the beginning of every class.

"Before we start assigning partners, are there any among you who already have some experience with alchemical procedures? I ask so that I don't inadvertently pair up two students who both have good working knowledge. I prefer to match experience with inexperience to help you all to learn faster."

Will raised his hand.

"Name?"

"William Cartwright."

"How much experience have you had?"

"My mother is a midwife, so I learned a lot about herbs and medicine from her. I also spent some time with my grandfather who had a small workshop," answered Will.

"Are you familiar with a balance scale?" Will nodded. "Units of measurement?" The questions went on and began to get rather detailed as the professor asked him about titration, measurement, and a host of other basics. When Will answered all of those to his satisfaction, he ended by asking, "Have you learned stoichiometry?"

"Yes, sir."

"Meet me after class, Mister Cartwright. I won't be assigning you a partner."

Consequently, Will was forced to stand by quietly while the instructor spent the rest of the class quizzing the students and matching them up into pairs. Once again, he felt the eyes of his classmates studying him with barely disguised curiosity. When the class was finally over and they had all filed out, he wondered what Professor Karlovic would tell him.

"You won't be coming to this class anymore," said the instructor without preamble.

"Sir?"

"It would be a waste of time. I don't doubt there may be a few holes in your knowledge, but the majority of this class would bore you to tears. Instead, I'd like you to work as a lab assistant for me on Tuesdays and Thursdays. You could earn a few coins and gain some experience."

Will's only response was a blank stare.

Professor Karlovic rushed to add, "Of course, you'll also get credit for the class. Depending on how skilled you are, I might exempt you from the second-year Alchemy class too."

"How much time will you need me in the lab?"

"Two hours twice a week. In the beginning it will be drudge work, cleaning glassware, that kind of thing, but once I've gained confidence in your work, I'll put you to more gainful tasks." The instructor smiled.

A wave of relief washed over Will. Not only would he gain an extra free hour each week, but he would be paid. He had a feeling he would need the time to survive his Composition class. "Thank you, Professor. I'll do my best."

"Good. Be here at six in the evening tomorrow and be sure to bring an extra pair of work clothes to keep here. You're almost certain to need them eventually."

He left in a daze. His first day had been a mixture of disaster and triumph. Will still worried about his Composition class, but it appeared that Alchemy was already in the bag. He hoped the rest of his evening would be quiet. He'd had enough surprises.

Supper began at five, so he went and claimed a tray of food. After spotting Seth sitting by himself, Will went over and took a seat. The other boy didn't have much to say, so they ate quietly until Robert Burwood happened by and joined them with his usual infectious grin.

"How was your day?" asked Rob, his eyes hinting at something.

Will shrugged. "It was fine." Seth said nothing.

Rob leaned forward. "Are you *sure* you don't have anything to tell us?"

Seth glanced back and forth nervously between the two of them. "Did something happen, Will?"

"I'll be working as a lab assistant at the Alchemy building," confessed Will. "It looks like Professor Karlovic is going to exempt me from the class."

Surprised, Rob sat back in his chair. "I hadn't heard that, but I guess I'll be seeing you. I work there in the evenings as well."

The tension eased out of Will's shoulders. He wouldn't be alone.

"But that's not what I was talking about," announced Rob. He gave Seth a serious look. "Will here is a war hero!"

Will choked and almost spit out the meat in his mouth.

Seth's eyes went round. "What?"

"It's all over the campus," said Rob, satisfied by their reaction. "Apparently our friend here is an army veteran with demon blood on his hands. It all makes sense now. *That's* why he got sponsored by King Lognion. Isn't it, Will?" Rob took a moment to stuff a roll in his mouth, chewing languidly while he waited for a response.

Will ground his teeth in frustration, quietly wishing he could throttle his new friend. "I was in the army, and I did see a demon," he admitted. "What are they saying?"

Rob put his arms behind his head and continued chewing, gradually drawing the rest of the roll into his mouth. Once it was all inside, he began talking, though his mouth was still full. "All sorts of things, old chum. The jealous ones are calling you a braggart and a liar, while those with more imagination are dreaming up stories in which you slew the demon with a magic blade and saved a princess."

Will choked again, and this time his tea came up through his nose. That had been a little too close to the truth. "That's ridiculous," he said evasively. "I didn't kill the demon, the sorceress did. I just happened to be there."

"And of course, that sorceress was King Lognion's daughter, Selene," pronounced Rob with a chuckle.

Glaring, Will demanded, "How did you know that?"

Now it was Rob's turn to be shocked. "I was making a joke." His head turned from side to side to see if anyone nearby had heard him. The dining hall was suspiciously quiet.

"Oh!" said Will, laughing nervously. "My mistake."

"Sweet Temarah of the Heavenly Tits!" exclaimed Rob. "You really saved her, didn't you?"

Will put his face in his hands. His cheeks were burning with embarrassment. "We fought together, but if anyone was saved, I'd say she had more to do with it than me."

Seth's face was white as a sheet, and the boy sat utterly still, as though he had been carved from stone. Meanwhile Rob couldn't contain his excitement, he pushed back his chair, stood and paced in a circle before sitting back down. "Holy shit!" said Rob. After a moment he relaxed and held his hand out, palm up. He wiggled his fingers. "Fess up. We need details."

"Not here," said Will. Whispers were spreading across the dining hall, and he saw many of the students sneaking furtive glances in his direction. "Let's eat. We can talk in my room."

They finished their meal and headed upstairs, but Will refused to say anything until they were inside, and the door was firmly closed. He gave Rob a withering glare. "Who knows what they'll be saying about me tomorrow!"

Rob was abashed. "Sorry, Will. I only meant to tease. I had no idea I was anywhere close to the truth."

Surprisingly, Seth broke in. "So, what exactly did you do in the army?"

"I was a private contract soldier," said Will. "Most of it was pretty ordinary, except for constantly fearing I'd catch a spear in the gut." He gave them an abbreviated version of the battles he'd fought in, leaving out the parts that involved him taking on sorcerers.

"But what about the princess?" insisted Seth. Apparently the quiet-spoken young man had a keen interest in romantic tales.

"I didn't know who she was," Will admitted. "She worked with the medical group and somehow we got to be friends. At one point I decided the only way to stop the war from dragging on forever would be to burn the enemy supplies in Barrowden. She wouldn't let me go alone, so we wound up going together."

Rob's breath hissed as he inhaled. "The two of you went alone, against all odds?"

"I probably wasn't thinking too clearly at the time," offered Will.

Seth hugged himself, whispering, "He really is a war-hero." Then he stared up at Will from his bunk, his dark brown eyes deadly serious. "Did you kiss her?"

Will turned red. "No! Of course not!" *She kissed me,* he thought silently.

Rob was pacing. "Now I see why the Patriarch's offensive dried up so quickly. No one knew why when the news came in. How many people know about this?"

"You, me, Seth, the king, and Selene, I guess."

"He calls her by name," mumbled Seth. "Not 'Her Highness' but Selene."

"Well, we went through a lot together. I doubt I'll ever see her again anyway, so it doesn't matter." Even as Will said it, though, he hoped it wasn't true.

"So officially, you aren't a hero," said Rob with a sigh.

"At first they thought I was a kidnapper. I spent my first few days in Cerria in a dungeon."

Seth was up and moving to his study desk. "I need to write this down."

"What? No!" Will protested. "Nobody can know about this."

"It's for my book," said the pale young man.

"You're writing a book?" asked Will.

Seth nodded. "It was going to be a different one, but I've changed my mind. Now it's going to be *The Adventures of William the Wizard*."

Rob began to laugh.

"What is wrong with the two of you?" said Will, exasperated. "No book, no adventures, and if you keep writing I'm not going to say another word."

Seth turned two woeful eyes his direction. "This is my life's work, Will."

"I thought you were here to study wizardry?"

"That's just to get my dad to leave me alone. I'll learn enough to make a living. Writing is my passion," said Seth firmly.

Until then, Will had thought his roommate was merely a timid and nervous fellow, but he was beginning to see a different side of him now. He couldn't help but admire Seth's conviction, but that didn't mean he had to participate in it. "I'm going to sleep," said Will, looking pointedly at Rob.

"What are we going to tell everyone tomorrow?" asked Rob.

"I was in the army. I fought in some battles. I met Selene and I saw her take down a demon. That's it. Good night." He began pushing his friend toward the door.

"Fine, fine," said Rob. He waved over his head to Seth. "Night!"

Will shut the door and ignored Seth's gaze as he climbed into his bunk. He was tired, but he lay awake thinking about the day's events for some time, until sleep finally claimed him.

CHAPTER 5

Morning came early, as it always did, but Will was already up and moving. His time in the army had left its mark on his sleep cycle, and he had gotten into the habit of waking up before dawn, even when he didn't have to. Consequently, he arrived at the gym for his first Fencing class almost a quarter of an hour early.

The instructor turned out to be a neatly groomed man named Valentine Rhodes. The teacher had a pencil-thin moustache with waxed ends that curled up. His hair was trimmed too short for the man to have been part of the nobility, but Will later learned that Rhodes was actually a squire who had been granted a small farm, so technically Squire Rhodes was a part of the landed gentry, if just barely.

As the other students appeared, Will noted that most of them had elementals and all of them bore the unmistakable marks of gentle birth: longer hair, finer clothing, and an air of superiority. He began to feel out of place. Some of them were staring openly at him, but there was only one face he recognized, that of Dennis Spry.

Perhaps I should have been friendlier, Will thought regretfully. The other young men stood in small groups, with the largest one around Dennis, who seemed to be exceptionally popular. The young lordling glanced at Will for a moment, flashing a smile as he said something else to his peers, who began to laugh with him. *Just great.*

"All right, gather round, lads!" shouted Rhodes. "Is there anyone here who hasn't had at least some experience with the saber?"

Will held up his hand. He was the only one to do so. Several of the others laughed as they glanced over at him.

"What's your name?" asked Instructor Rhodes, pointing at him.

"William Cartwright, sir."

"Everyone separate into pairs and warm up. Mister Cartwright, you'll be with me so I can acquaint you with the rules."

While the others began doing simple calisthenics, Instructor Rhodes took Will aside. "Over here is where we keep the equipment." He showed Will a long rack that held long, thin, blunt-edged swords. They were far different from what he had seen in the army. Most of the swords used in the military were far shorter and thicker, built for powerful chopping and savage thrusts. From what Will could see, these weapons would be nearly useless against a soldier, even if he were only armored in a gambeson.

Rhodes could see his confusion. "What? Spit it out, lad."

"Do people fight with these, sir?"

The instructor laughed. "Quite often, why do you ask?" Then he paused. "Are you the lad that just left the army?"

Will nodded. "Yes, sir."

"Then I understand your confusion. These aren't the sort of weapons you'd see on the battlefield, although they are similar in some regards to what the cavalry uses."

He had seen cavalry sabers—they were a little longer with heavier blades. "Then what are these for, sir?"

"These are the weapons of a gentleman," said Rhodes with a smirk.

"Wouldn't a gentleman want to be able to defend himself?"

The instructor began to laugh. "You're thinking about armored combat. These are meant for dueling. Generally speaking, if two men are fighting with these, they aren't wearing armor, nor do they have shields or helms."

"But still—"

"In that situation, these are far superior weapons, Mister Cartwright. They thrust and cut quite well, and their speed is unrivaled. Also, most duels end with first blood, so there isn't the same necessity for men about town to go around wearing armor."

Will's eyes widened, glancing at the others who were still warming up. "Will we be dueling?"

"I doubt the college would look kindly on me if all their well-bred students were regularly injured. No, I'll be teaching you the sport, but it will be good practice in case you ever *do* wind up in a duel. Come over here." Rhodes led him to a long set of cabinets. Inside were heavy, long-sleeved jackets, similar to the padded gambeson Will had worn in the army. At one end were curious helmets with faces composed of wire mesh. "You'll be wearing these during practice to prevent serious injury or disfigurement. Let's get you suited up."

The instructor helped him into the jacket, head gear, and gloves, before going over the basic rules. It turned out that the sport of saber fencing was meant to teach and replicate the fundamental nature of what happened in a true duel. The blades were lightweight with rounded guards to protect the hand. The opponents were allowed to cut and thrust and a match consisted of multiple rounds in which the first to land such a blow was awarded a point.

The idea was that this blow was similar to first blood in a real duel. The big difference, of course, was that a real duel ended with the first cut, which might or might not be lethal, whereas a saber match involved a scoring system that ended once fifteen points had been scored between the two of them. The swordsman with the better score, eight points or more, won.

If both opponents scored a point at the same time, a judge made a call to award the point to whoever had been in possession of the 'initiative.' Initiative was a subjective concept, but generally it meant the swordsman who was moving forward, rather than retreating, at the time the two points were scored.

The contests took place on a long, thin strip marked by two lines. If someone backed all the way to the end and stepped out, that also gave a point to the opponent. The instructor went through a few rounds with him, during which he made a startling realization. If two saber fighters were to actually duel, it wouldn't necessarily be the best man that won. While Rhodes scored the majority of points, Will managed to score a couple of his own. In a real fight, that meant that out of fifteen duels with a man obviously far superior to him, he would have potentially won twice.

It was a sobering thought. It meant that even a great duelist was taking a terrible risk any time he made a challenge, assuming his opponent was reasonably quick and fit, which Will certainly was. *Why would anyone ever think that was a good idea?* he wondered.

While he was taking a breather, he watched the other young men sparring, noting their scores. Even in the most mismatched sets, the loser usually managed to score at least a few times. Having recently survived a battlefield, the entire thing seemed ridiculous to him. Every 'point' scored was symbolic of a man taking a wound, fatal or otherwise, and yet the fighting style was outlandish and suicidal from a soldier's point of view.

Fighting without armor? Why? No shield? Who would give up such a defense?

Compounding the silliness was the fact that the game held no real risk, yet it was meant to simulate a situation with real risk of death or serious injury. As a result, the best tactics were lighting-quick strikes and hyperextended lunges meant to take the opponent off-guard.

Unfortunately, if the hit failed to land, the defender usually struck the one making it. Will couldn't imagine an actual human, facing naked steel, doing something so inordinately risky.

After his short break Will was paired up with another student, a first-year named Chris. He had more experience than Will, but their skill levels were closer. In their first match, Will managed a respectable six points to his opponent's nine. He learned a few more things as well.

Unlike the instructor, Chris didn't vary his speed or flow, making it far easier to predict his movements. While resting after their matches, Will paid close attention to the others. Those with better scores all showed some ability to suddenly change the speed of their attack and defense, and the instructor was the best at it.

It reminded him of something his grandfather had once told him after he had learned to increase his speed or strength using his turyn. *"Just because you don't see ordinary people casting spells doesn't mean they don't depend on it. Athletes, warriors, people that train themselves to be the best at what they do, they're doing something very similar with their turyn. And on top of that, they're building their physical capacity at the same time. You can use your magic in a large variety of ways, including to give yourself a physical advantage, but don't ever make the mistake of underestimating people who train hard at fighting, or you'll learn a painful and bloody lesson."*

Did that mean he could use his gift to improve his score? *Probably.* He had already considered doing so, but he had held back because of another lesson he had learned in the army. Don't stand out. If he immediately started scoring as well as the better, more practiced fencers, it would only bring attention, and with attention came trouble.

When class was over, he went back to the dorm to clean up before his next class, History. Arriving early, he found only a few students in the auditorium when he stepped in. Will made a quick decision and found a seat in the second row, next to the only person he recognized, Janice Edelman, the girl he had met in Composition.

He lifted a hand as he sat down beside her. "Hi."

Janice ran her fingers across her forehead, nervously pushing her hair out of her eyes, which she kept firmly on the book in front of her. "Hello," she answered quietly.

He wondered if she was shy or if it was just something about himself that made her nervous. Opening his journal to the first page, he set out a pen and made sure his inkwell was ready. From his previous experiences, he doubted he would be able to keep up and take notes, but he figured he should at least be ready in case there was something important he absolutely had to write down.

"Hey," said Will quietly.

Janice's eyes flicked toward him briefly, showing him a flash of hazel, but she said nothing.

Pretty eyes, he noted. "You probably noticed last time, but I'm terrible at note taking."

She pushed her hair aside again without looking at him, but gave an almost imperceptible nod.

"It isn't that I don't want to, but I write too slowly. I can't keep up with the lecture and write at the same time," he added. "I only learned to read and write a year and a half ago."

That provoked a response. Janice's eyes went wide and she stared at him for a full two seconds, blinking once. Then she looked away again, her cheeks coloring. "Oh."

Her shy face caused a stir of uncertain emotions within him, though he wasn't sure if it was attraction or just a feeling of protectiveness. *She really is cute,* thought Will, *and more importantly, she isn't a princess.* Mentally, he reprimanded himself for that thought. Rob had been a bad influence on him. Gathering his courage, Will pushed on. "What do you think about studying together?"

Janice visibly shrank, making herself as small as possible.

Damn it. What did I do wrong? Hastily, he added, "I don't take notes, but I listen very well. I know you probably don't need help, but I—" He stopped, afraid the girl might jump up and run out of the room. With every word she seemed to flinch.

"Sorry," he said after a moment. "It was just a thought."

More students were filing in now and he saw another face he recognized, Chris Burnham, from his Fencing class. The other boy nodded at him but took a seat in another row, though Will noticed a strange look pass across Chris' face when he noticed Janice. *What was that?* wondered Will. *Do they know each other? Why didn't he say hello, then?*

The professor made an appearance then, introducing herself as Melinda Fontenot before continuing, "Today we will begin our journey through the past, exploring the history of our nation. In order to do that we will start with what came before the War for Independence to give you all a frame of reference.

"Since many of you won't have any further exposure to Terabinia's long and interesting history, this class will attempt to paint antiquity in broad strokes and give you a basic understanding of what Terabinia emerged from and why we occupy the unique spot we do today. I encourage those of you with greater interest to consider signing up for some of my advanced courses next year if you'd like to enjoy a greater depth of understanding. By the end of this semester you should know whether you fall into that category or not.

"We will begin with Stephen the Great, who after the conquest of the Kingdom of Trendle, found himself in possession of all of what we now recognize as Darrow, Terabinia, and parts of Trendham. Although the kingdom he ruled at that time was known as the Darrowan Empire, we will be referring to it as simply Greater Darrow to avoid confusion with the smaller states that we are familiar with today.

"As most of you know, the Darrowan calendar begins with the year of Emperor Stephen's birth, although it wasn't officially adopted until late in his life. Since this gives us a simple method of tracking the time of different events, we will be using the Darrowan calendar for dating events that occurred before our own War for Independence. If any of this confuses you, remember that you can always convert Darrowan dates to Terabinian years by simply subtracting three-hundred and twelve from the Darrowan year."

Professor Fontenot went on, covering the first three hundred years of Greater Darrow's history in a very abridged manner. All of it was new to Will, though, so he listened with keen interest. It turned out that while Stephen the Great had been a skilled strategist and general, he had been woefully inadequate when it came to governing the vast territory he had claimed. Fortunately, the man had died in his middle years, and his son, Flarian, had been born with a knack for governance that was equaled only by his aversion to war.

It was near the end of the class when Will heard a name that caught his immediate attention. "In 283, Emperor Laernan took on a new advisor named Arrogan Leirendel. I only mention this now so you'll have the date for context since that advisor will become extremely important in later discussions of our own War of Independence," said Professor Fontenot.

Will's hand went up. "Excuse me, ma'am. Did you say Arrogan Leirendel?"

"I did. Are you having trouble hearing me all the way back in the second row?"

"No, ma'am. I just wanted to be sure. Do you know how old he was when he took that position?"

Something about the question seemed to give the professor indigestion, judging by the look on the woman's face. "What is your name, young man?"

"William Cartwright, ma'am."

"Mister Cartwright, if you have an interest in mythology please indulge yourself at the library. My class is for the more serious pursuit of truth."

Will was bewildered, but the bell tower began to ring a second later and Professor Fontenot dismissed the class. Unable to contain himself, Will turned to Janice. "It was just a simple question. Did I say something wrong?"

His classmate stood and gathered her things quickly. As she left, he heard her say, "No. Excuse me."

For the life of him, Will couldn't figure out why she seemed so scared of him. With a sigh he capped his ink bottle, packed his pen and journal, and followed her out with the last of the students. As he stepped out into the hall, he heard a familiar voice. "Janice. How good to see you!" He spotted Dennis Spry, who looked to have been waiting for the girl.

She gave the young lord a weak smile, but Will noticed a slight flinch when Dennis casually draped his arm over the young woman's shoulders. Will frowned.

Dennis lowered his voice as they walked away, but Will's sharp ears could still make out his words. "You haven't forgotten our study date, have you? I need that essay by tomorrow." Janice shook her head.

Is he making her do his work? Will found it hard to believe, but as he thought back to her previous reactions it got him to thinking. *Did she think I was trying to do the same?* It was a ludicrous idea from his perspective, but from hers it might seem entirely plausible. He was tempted to approach them and give Dennis a piece of his mind, but he didn't know enough to run around making accusations.

He'd already done enough damage to his reputation by being rude to the young lord. There was no need to make it worse when he didn't actually have any proof.

His next class was Composition, but he didn't see Janice there when he arrived. She showed up at the last minute, barely in time to avoid being late. Will waved to her and offered her the empty seat next to him, but she ignored him and sat in the back. He watched her walk by, taking note of her hair, which was in a mild state of disarray. He caught a glimpse of her eyes even though she kept her head down. They were red.

What happened? Will felt an angry spark run through him, mixed with guilt. Had Dennis done something to her? Was it his fault for not intervening before? Professor Conrad entered and class began, so he was forced to stay quiet.

CHAPTER 6

Lunch passed without anything of note happening, and Will's afternoon classes were likewise mundane, until he got to Spell Theory. Professor Dulaney started speaking as soon as the class began. "Please get up and come forward once I begin calling names. Today you'll all have your turyn typed so you can start planning what you'd like to do in the future. Knowing your type will help you focus on information that may pertain to you in particular and help you plan your coursework for the next year."

He began calling out names, and those called lined up in front of the podium. The teacher stopped after ten names to avoid having too many people at the front of the class. Will was the fourth student called, since his name was close to the beginning of the alphabet.

Dulaney resumed his speech as they formed a line. "As I showed you with the diagram yesterday, everyone produces a variety of different types of turyn and every person's individual mixture is unique. The one thing that we all have in common is that if you average the different types and wavelengths produced by any given individual, they will always average at the zero point on the graph. Does anyone know why this is?"

One of the students who was still seated answered, "Is it like body temperature, sir?"

"An excellent analogy, Mister Holmgren. This is very similar. Just as most people have the same body temperature to within a few tenths of a degree, the turyn produced by different human beings also averages out to almost the same figure. There is a tiny bit of variance, though. Next question, if everyone's turyn averages out to the same zero point on the graph, how are there different, so-called 'types'?"

No one volunteered to attempt that one.

Dulaney stepped up to the blackboard and drew another cross, then he marked the four quadrants. "Fire, water, earth, air—again, these are oversimplifications, but they are useful for our purposes. You type is defined as which of these general types of turyn you produce the most of. You will almost certainly produce turyn of the other types as well, but if there is an excess in one area, balanced by smaller amounts in the other three, then the graph still sums to zero. The important thing is that we then know that if you have a larger degree of one particular type of turyn then you'll be able to create spells using it while wasting less of the other types."

"Couldn't a person just produce the type of turyn needed without making the types they don't need?" asked Will.

The professor grinned. "If only that were the case, Mister Cartwright!" He then drew two parallel lines on the board. "Think of this as a pipe. Turyn is the water flowing through it, although unlike water, it comes in many different flavors. Is everyone with me so far?"

Dulaney waited a moment until the students began nodding. Then he shaded in a thick portion of the bottom of his pipe. Above that he drew another portion, but rather than shading it he marked it with crosshatch marks. He continued until the pipe was full with four different types of turyn, each denoted by a different pattern. "As you can see, this hypothetical person is producing a larger amount of what we'll call earth turyn." He pointed to the thicker, shaded portion. "But they don't control what they produce. The turyn is always produced by his gate or source in a fixed proportion. So if he needs 'x' amount of earth turyn to cast a certain spell, he has to keep producing it until he reaches the desired amount, but the entire time he will also be producing these other types, which are wasted.

"As a result, if someone with a low production of earth-type turyn wants to cast a spell requiring earth turyn, they'll have to produce a much larger overall amount of turyn to reach the amount needed for the spell. Does this make sense?" Dulaney glanced around the room, then continued, "The reason this is important is that you have to increase your turyn production when casting a spell. The more you increase it, the faster your gate degrades."

"What is a gate, sir?" asked Will.

"The source," said Dulaney. "We think it is similar to a congruence point between different planes. Every person's life comes from such a gate, and we produce turyn for magic by manipulating our own inner gate. The more you consume, the sooner you'll die."

Will couldn't help himself. "If being a wizard shortens your life, why does anyone want to be one?"

The teacher gave him an odd look. "Well, a large part of what we learn here is to help you avoid foreshortening your life too much, but there is no doubt that *any* exercise of magic will decrease your lifespan by some degree. Let's ask your fellow students. Why do you want to be a wizard?"

Rebecca Swafford raised her hand. When the professor pointed at her, she responded, "I plan to become an artificer, so hopefully I won't affect my lifespan very much."

Another student called out, "For the money!" Several students laughed at that.

Professor Dulaney nodded. "In case you hadn't noticed yet, Mister Cartwright, most jobs involving wizardry require only a minimal amount of spell casting and turyn expenditure. Alchemists work to concentrate and harness the turyn found in organic and inorganic materials to produce their products. Artificers work to produce enchanted objects and devices that won't require much of their own turyn in the making. Spell engineers design spells that are more efficient and practical, but they generally try to avoid casting them unless absolutely necessary. The main exception to this rule would be healers, who are presumably driven by their need to help others. Incidentally, it is also why they tend to command the highest income of all wizards."

Will frowned. "If artificers are making devices for others, and spell engineers are crafting spells they don't want to cast—who are they making these things for? Surely someone has to use them?"

Dulaney gave him a look he knew well from his time with his grandfather. It was the 'how dumb can you possibly be' look. One of the students in the back called out, "Sorcerers, idiot!" The professor smiled and indicated the line should start moving. "If you'll step up to the device one at a time, we will get the typing over quickly."

Will was stunned. He should have realized it already, but it still came as a surprise. *All these people are learning magic, how to make spells, how to enchant items, just to give them to sorcerers.* None of them were actually learning magic for their own sakes. Arrogan's words suddenly made perfect sense. *"Most of them spend their time bowing and scraping for the sorcerers, hoping to be given scraps."*

As he was thinking, the boy in front him had just finished. The machine they were using consisted of a simple glass ball mounted between two metal plates. Each student would place their hands on the plates and then wait while the enchantment engraved on the inside of the device measured their individual turyn wavelengths and then reported the results by causing the glass globe to show different colors.

The fellow in front of him, Shawn Campbell, was excited because the glove was showing two colors instead of one. "A dual type," announced Professor Dulaney. "Lucky for you! It appears to be earth and fire."

Dulaney addressed the class, "What this means is that Mister Campbell's turyn is narrowly confined to two opposing quadrants on our graph while he produces very little in the other two. His turyn still sums to the zero point, but since he produces almost nothing in the air or water quadrants, he should be able to more efficiently produce spells that require either earth or fire turyn." He looked back at Shawn. "Congratulations!"

It was now Will's turn, but he felt a sudden urge to create mischief as he moved to stand in front of the device. He was already fairly confident in manipulating his own internal turyn, and while he wasn't entirely sure which types corresponded to the different quadrants on Dulaney's graph he wondered what would happen if he tried to skew the results. Thinking of Selene's elementals, he tried to replicate the feeling he had gotten from her water elemental.

A moment later the globe turned a vivid blue. "Water," announced the teaching assistant standing close by, but then the young man frowned. "Hang on. This isn't right." Dulaney came over, and the two of them spoke together quietly for a few minutes.

Will smirked as he picked up the professor's words. "That can't be. It doesn't average out properly. It's almost entirely high frequency and negatively charged. He'd be dead." The professor turned to Will. "Try it again, there was some sort of interference."

Will nodded, and this time he tried to emulate the turyn from Selene's earth elemental. A few seconds later, the globe turned a dark brown.

"Earth," muttered Professor Dulaney. "But it's still not averaging correctly." He glanced at the teaching assistant. "Paul, are you sure the machine was calibrated?" After another quick discussion, they urged Will to try again.

This time he attempted a mixture of fire and water, and he was rewarded when the globe turned equal parts orange and blue.

"Fire and water?" exclaimed Dulaney. "That's not even possible. There's no way for them to zero out." He stared at Will suspiciously. "Have you tampered with the machine?"

Will smirked. "You mean this?" He put his hands back on the machine and began changing his turyn from moment to moment, causing the globe to cycle through all four colors. "That's why I was curious about types. Can't a person just shift their turyn to produce whatever type is needed?"

The professor blinked, then grabbed onto Paul's arm to steady himself. "Are you seeing this, Paul? Am I imagining things?"

"No, Professor," said Paul. "I'm seeing it too."

"He's a natural transducer. Is that even possible?" muttered Dulaney. The professor struggled to regain his composure. "Go back to your seat, Mister Cartwright. We'll talk after class. The rest of you, line up again. I want to retype you just to make sure the machine is still giving accurate readings."

Will sat quietly, observing the proceedings. Everyone else's results fit the standard pattern—they showed either a mild affinity for one of the elemental quadrants, or in a couple of extraordinary cases they produced a dual type, either fire and earth, or air and water. One unfortunate student, Arlen Morelli, had no type at all. The globe remained clear, indicating an almost perfect split between all four elemental types. Dulaney explained that while this meant she could perform almost any spell, she would have a poor efficiency with any sort of magic she attempted.

When the class was finally over, Professor Dulaney gestured toward him. "Come with me." Will followed the teacher out of the room and down the hall. At one end was a door with a name plate attached with the professor's name on it. "Do you have much time before your next class?" asked Dulaney as he unlocked the door.

"I would have Alchemy, but Professor Karlovic is taking me on as a lab assistant so I don't have to report until after supper," said Will.

Dulaney's brows lifted in surprise, then he waved a hand toward a leather-bound chair. "Have a seat." Moving around the massive wooden desk that dominated the room, he sat down and faced Will. "So, you impressed Aaron with your knowledge of alchemy, then?"

"I guess so, sir."

"You told me before that your mother was a midwife skilled in the use of herbs, correct?"

"Yes, sir."

"And she was the one that taught you alchemy? Did you have any other teachers?"

Will wasn't sure what to say, but given that the king already knew most of his secrets, he didn't think it would do him much good to lie. The professor might send a request for information to the Crown. "My grandfather was an unlicensed wizard," Will admitted. "After my accident with the diviner's sage he taught me a little before the war started."

Professor Dulaney frowned. "Where is he now?"

"He died when the Prophet's army invaded."

"And you're here because the king sponsored you. Does he know all this?"

And more, thought Will. "Yes, sir."

"Then I suppose I don't need to worry about any legal issues. How much did your grandfather teach you?" asked the professor.

"I only know one spell," said Will. "The one for linking to someone's source."

"Demonstrate it for me."

You asked for it. In the blink of an eye, he manifested the simple spell construct and linked to Dulaney's source. He felt a brief resistance, and then the link firmed up. On a whim he tried to separate the professor's will from his source and he was surprised when he succeeded.

Professor Dulaney sat rigidly in his chair, only his eyes moving as the rest of his body was paralyzed. Will released him a second later. "How was that, sir?"

His teacher took a deep breath, visibly attempting to calm himself. Leaning over, he opened a drawer and pulled out a tall, brown bottle and a glass, pouring himself a drink. He took a long sip before answering. "Your will is extraordinarily strong for someone who only awakened his sight a few years ago. Do you mind if I return the favor?"

Will nodded. "Go ahead." The professor's spell was so quick he never even saw the construct appear before a green line shot toward him. It vanished a moment later as his body absorbed the foreign turyn. "Oh," said Will, shutting down his reflexive absorption. "Try again. I wasn't ready."

Professor Dulaney blinked, trying to process what had happened, then he repeated the spell. Will was surprised when it connected. His teacher was obviously skilled, but when the man attempted to paralyze him as Will had just done, he fought him. Beads of sweat broke out on Dulaney's forehead, but after a few seconds he lost control. Working through the connection between them, Will paralyzed his mentor once again. Then he dismissed the spell.

Dulaney let out an explosive breath and took another sip of his drink. "What on earth? That's the only spell you learned? How long was your grandfather teaching you?"

"A little less than two years," said Will. "But almost all of it was focused on learning self-discipline, though I didn't understand that at the time."

"How *exactly* did he teach you that?" said the professor slowly.

Will hedged. "Meditation? He used a spell to link my source to a candle. I had to carry it around for months."

"And what else?"

"That's it," Will lied. "I thought he was crazy at the time. He would yell at me if I forgot to keep the candle with me."

Dulaney rubbed his chin. "We still use the candle exercise, but only for a week or two. I can't imagine how that would make your will as strong as it is now, much less allow you to transform turyn from one type to another."

"He was surprised by that as well," Will temporized. "One day I got bored and changed the color of the candle flame and it shocked him."

"You're suggesting you were always a transducer?"

Will shrugged. "Maybe? I didn't even know that's what I was doing until you told me today."

The professor sighed and finished his whisky with a final swallow. "I really don't know what to make of you, Mister Cartwright. This is uncharted territory. I'll tell you what we will do, though."

"What's that?"

"Since you no longer attend the Alchemy class, I'd like to devote some of my time. Every day, after this class we'll spend some time working on your spellcraft. I'd like to see what you're capable of."

Will groaned inwardly. He had just gained some time from being exempted from Alchemy; now he'd lose that time in private lessons. "How much time?"

"Half an hour of one-on-one. The same amount of time we've spent here today. If you do well, I'll give you credit for your first semester of Spellcraft. Ordinarily you wouldn't get to take it until next year."

"Do I have to keep coming to Spell Theory, then?"

"Learning spells is one thing, but you need a good foundation in the underlying principles," said the professor firmly.

Will sighed.

CHAPTER 7

"What is all this for?" asked Will. He was in a lower basement laboratory within the Alchemy building. Unlike the classroom lab he had seen the day before, this area was divided into discrete portions with large metal vats, tanks, and a variety of glassware.

"This," said Professor Karlovic, "is how we pay the bills. What do you think the number-one product of this facility is?"

Will had no idea. All he knew how to make was ink, glue, and herbal tinctures, and none of that involved such oversized pieces of equipment. "Ink?" he answered tentatively.

His teacher laughed. "No. What do you think the main purpose of alchemy is?"

"Making potions for specific purposes?"

"Yes, and no. We can indeed make a variety of potions, but that is not what we mainly do. Alchemy is the art of taking raw ingredients, herbs for example, and distilling from them their vital essences, the turyn they possess. Using various formulae, we can then take those concentrated essences and create magical potions, *without*—and this is key—without needing a wizard to burn his or her own life to do so."

Will stared at him. "Huh?" None of that sounded remotely like what Arrogan had taught him.

Karlovic nodded. "The old recipes call for base ingredients and then use turyn from the creator to empower them, but that method has all the same drawbacks of spellcasting. Honestly, when I look back at the work of the Founders, I cannot help but think they were a little insane. They wasted their lives. What we do here is take those old recipes and find ways to recreate them without forcing the alchemist to burn up their own turyn.

"In order to do that, we work with large amounts of raw materials and distill them down—concentrating them to get the full amount of turyn required to empower a potion." The professor waved a hand. "But I digress. The purpose of my initial question was to get you thinking about what our main product is. Which potion do you think people need the most?"

Will tried again. "Glue?"

"Good guess. That is one of our more favored products, but what I am referring to are healing potions. I'm sure they've covered this in your Spell Theory class by now. Once wizards graduate, they go into a number of different occupations, but one of those jobs requires more of the practitioner than the others. Healing."

He made an 'o' with his mouth. "I see."

"To help keep from overusing their powers, one of the most demanded products are healing potions for use with minor problems. We make elixirs for fever and sickness, tinctures for wounds, and even minor healing potions that can close wounds and mend broken bones. We make these things without spending our own lives, and we sell them to healers to help them avoid spending *their* lives on any but the direst of injuries. Do you understand?"

Will nodded slowly. "That makes sense." More and more, he was beginning to understand how the practice of wizardry was crippled by the fact that magic users were forced to burn up their own lives to create spells. He was also interested in seeing those old recipes the professor had mentioned, since he obviously didn't suffer from the same restriction. It would be far simpler to just make a potion with base ingredients and empower it himself than to concentrate or distill essences from large quantities of raw materials. "So what will I be doing today?"

The professor smiled. "See that vessel there?" He pointed to a massive metal tank set above what appeared to be a burner. "Grab a shovel. You'll need to load it with pennyroyal from that bin over there. Once it's full, we'll add water and start the first phase. Have you ever done fractional distillation before?"

He blinked. He had, but it had involved a small glass setup in Arrogan's workshop. "That's for fractional distillation?"

Karlovic pointed to the top of the tank, where a long, vertical pipe emerged. "That's a fractioning column. The part you see coming off the side is where the condenser begins. Over here is our thermometer…" the professor went on, naming and describing each component of the system until Will could understand what was happening.

The scale of it awed him. Then the professor pointed to a rack. "Get the shovel. I need you to load the distillation tank."

An hour later, Will was sweating as he rested on a stool. *Is this what I'm here for? Manual labor?*

It was then that the professor motioned him to come over to a small desk at the corner of the room. "Now that the hard part is over for tonight, let's see if you can work through these calculations. What you see here is a list of the raw materials we are starting with, along with a table of yields we have gotten from similar materials in the past. I've already done the calculations several times, but you can get some practice working through it again and double-checking my work. I'd like you to calculate our likely yield given these raw materials.

"Once you've done that, see if you can tell me what step we will be using next to further purify the azeotropes that emerge from tonight's process."

Will stared at the ledger. He had learned the principles from Arrogan, but he had a lot of questions to ask before he could begin to do what the professor asked. It seemed he would be learning after all.

***

When Will finally got back to his room Seth, was already there. His mild-mannered roommate sniffed the air as Will entered. "What have you been doing? You smell like you've been rolling around in a mint haystack."

"Close," said Will. "Pennyroyal."

"Lucky you," said Seth, reclining on the bottom bunk. "If you keep working around that stuff you might be able to stretch your laundry to two weeks."

Will had already heard that the dorm offered a laundry service, and that most residents availed themselves of it at least once a week. "How much does it cost?" he asked curiously.

"What, the laundry? Almost everything is a penny each, a penny for a shirt, a penny for trousers. But if you want to get your fancy dress clothes done that costs more since they have to starch and iron them. That's six pennies."

He only had one set of clothes. The expensive linen clothing the king had given him. "What would my clothes count as?"

"Six."

"Uh…" Will realized he had a problem. Between the clothes his father had sent and the clothes the king had given him, he had three sets. If he changed them every day, he would wind up spending almost two silver clima a week. At that rate he'd spend more than three gold crowns just getting his clothes washed during the first term.

Of course, in the past he had worn his clothes for up to a week at a time without changing them, but that had been in the army, and even there he'd been expected to wash himself daily. The standards at

Wurthaven were considerably stricter. He hadn't come across anyone yet that didn't appear to be wearing fresh clothing.

If he was to wear freshly cleaned clothes every day then he would also have to bathe at least every other day. *Correction, every day,* he told himself when he remembered that he had Fencing class every morning. The bathhouses behind the dorms cost a penny each time, which would add another crown plus change to his expenses for the term. Adding it up, he arrived at a total close to five crowns.

Then there was food, incidentals, and probably other expenses he hadn't even learned of yet. "Are there any extra fees we have to pay?" asked Will.

"There's a lab fee for Alchemy," said Seth. "But since you've been taken as an assistant, I suppose you won't have to pay that."

"True," said Will. He had forgotten that. Professor Karlovic was also paying him two clima a week for his help in the lab, so that would help keep him solvent.

"Have you paid your library fees yet?" asked Seth.

Will leaned over the edge of his bunk and looked down. "There's a fee for the library?"

Seth nodded. "Five crowns each term."

He groaned. There went his surplus from working as an assistant. Worse, that put him down another two gold for the term. If he was very careful with his money and there were no surprises, he might make it through with a few coins left over, but he didn't like not having anything extra to cover emergencies.

Lying down, Will pillowed his head with his arms. Having an actual pillow would have been nice, or bed sheets. Unlike Seth, he was still sleeping on a bare mattress. How much would those things cost? *Damn,* he cursed silently. After he bought bedding, he'd have to pay to have it laundered as well. He started to ask Seth what the cost for washing sheets was, but he heard a soft snoring beneath him. His roommate had fallen asleep.

Will wasn't sleepy so he stared at the ceiling, which, thanks to his elevated position, was only four feet away. Thinking back over the past year he found it difficult to believe all the things that had happened to him, that had led to him being there. He lifted his right hand and stared at the ring he wore. He still had no idea what it was or what it could do. His life was full of mysteries.

Turning his hand over, he looked at his palm and thought of the limnthal, causing it to rise and hover in the air above his hand. It was yet another mystery. What it could be used for, what it meant, he still had no clue. Not long after he had received it, Aislinn had given him a gift, something she had stored within it, but what that might be was also an unknown.

"Sometimes I think I know less about myself than I did about Selene," he mumbled.

"Who the fuck is Selene?" asked a cranky voice that clearly did not belong to Seth.

Will bolted upright in the bed, dismissing the limnthal. "Who's there?"

Silence was his only answer. Leaning over the edge of the bed, he searched the room with his eyes. There was only a dim light coming from the window, but that was no hindrance to his sight. He adjusted his vision until the room seemed as bright as day, but there was no one there. Will backed up until he was sitting with his back against the headboard, his head resting in the corner of the room. *I'm not crazy,* he told himself. *Someone spoke to me.*

He studied his hand. *Was it the limnthal?* With a thought, he summoned it again. "Were you talking to me?"

"No. I was talking to your ass. Who the hell else would I be talking to?" said the voice.

Will stared at the limnthal. "You can talk!"

"Yeah. I'm starting to wonder about you, though. Moron."

"I didn't know the limnthal could talk," said Will slowly.

"Of course, it can't. Were you always this stupid?"

The voice was extremely familiar, and with every insult Will became more certain of who it belonged to. "Grandfather?"

"Who? Kid, you are seriously deluded."

"You're Arrogan," insisted Will.

"Sort of, but I'm afraid there's a good chance he wasn't your grandfather."

"He told me he was."

"Then he lied. He lost track of his descendants within a couple of generations. I'm starting to think you're a few cards shy of a deck," said the voice.

Will shook his head. "You're wrong. He told me I was his grandson. *You* told me that."

"First, I'm not Arrogan. Second, I know everything he knew, and he most certainly didn't know anything about any of his descendants. It's even possible that they all died off."

"What are you then, and how would you know everything he knew if you aren't him?" asked Will.

"You're wearing a ring, aren't you? Probably with something weird mounted on it, such as a bone or something."

Will stared at the ring but didn't say anything. *Is it the ring talking?*

"Well, am I right?" demanded the voice.

"Yes."

"I knew it. What does it look like?"

He frowned. "If you're the ring, shouldn't you know?"

"How the hell should I know, you moron? I can't see."

"Why can't you see?"

"You really are dense, aren't you? Do you see any eyes on that ring? No. I don't have a body. I'm just a disembodied intellect, bound to a piece of fucking jewelry," answered the voice, then it snorted. "Typical. You still haven't told me what the ring looks like."

"It's gold, with a tooth mounted on it. I think it's a wisdom tooth."

Will heard the ring begin to chuckle. "That's Aislinn for sure. She always did have a warped sense of humor. Let me guess, did she tell you it was a ring of wisdom?"

"No. She just said it was an object of vile and unspeakable knowledge and power." As he said the words, he couldn't help but think his grandmother's label was more apt than he had realized.

The ring paused. "Oh. I rather like that. Let's just shorten it to 'Ring of Vile and Unspeakable Knowledge.' I don't really have any power."

"Are you Arrogan's spirit, his ghost?" asked Will, feeling hopeful.

"No, you nitwit. I am not. Nor do I feel inclined to tell you what I am. Knowledge should be held by those who are responsible, not by dim cretins who can't even figure out what sort of ring they're wearing."

Will closed his eyes, taking a deep breath to calm himself. "You sound just like him. I was his apprentice. You can trust me."

"That's just what a sorcerer would say. I'm not falling for your tricks. I was old before you were even a gleam in your daddy's eye," said the ring.

"I was his apprentice," insisted Will. "I can prove it."

"No, you weren't. I—I mean he—he killed all of them."

"If you know everything Arrogan knew then you should remember me. My name is Will, William Cartwright. And you just said 'I,' so you really *are* Arrogan."

The ring growled. "No, I'm not. Listen, it's confusing, especially for me. I'm just his knowledge. The technical term is a spirit of intellect, but even that's confusing since there's no spirit involved. His spirit is long gone. How did he die, anyway?"

The words triggered the memory of a conversation. What had Aislinn told him? A mage, or any human, consists of three things: the mind, the will, and the soul. She had also said that death wasn't the destruction of those things either, merely their separation. Had she somehow bound Arrogan's knowledge to the ring, while letting his will and soul go their separate ways?

"I asked you a question, fuckwit," reminded the ring.

Will took hold of himself. "He died protecting me and my mother. Soldiers from Darrow invaded Barrowden. Why can't you remember that?"

The ring sighed. "I call bullshit. He didn't care enough about anyone to throw his life away. And the reason I don't remember is because the last few years of his life were lost. Recent events, recent knowledge, they don't remain with the intellect after death. Only memories that have had time to mature are kept. What was your mother's name?"

"Erisa."

"I remember her, pretty young thing, though her mother was a self-righteous fool. She stayed with him for a while. You're saying you're her brat?"

"Yes."

"Nice try. You really did your research, but I still don't believe you—*sorcerer*!"

Frustrated, Will tried again. "I'm not a sorcerer. Why haven't you spoken before now?"

"Hmm. You haven't figured out much, have you?"

"It's the limnthal, isn't it?" said Will. "I haven't looked at it since Aislinn gave me the ring. It wakes you up somehow."

"You mean since you stole the ring, and the limnthal."

Will scratched his head. "How would a sorcerer steal your limnthal? They don't even know what a limnthal is. I barely do. You gave me the limnthal."

"Good point," agreed the ring. "But I still don't trust you. If you were really his apprentice, tell me something only an apprentice would know."

He thought carefully for a minute. "There was a cat, he called it 'the goddamn cat.' He said it was our landlord."

"Not bad, but not enough."

"He hated the Lord of the Hunt. Aislinn was his wife, before she became one of the fae."

The ring growled again. "Now you're pissing me off. Still not good enough."

"He was a tailor before he became Aislinn's apprentice. He gave her a pillow he made as a gift. I returned it to her with his body after he died," said Will.

"He wouldn't have told you that. You're trying too hard."

"No. Aislinn told me, after I returned the pillow. All he ever told me was not to touch it. He was as mean as the day is long." The ring remained silent, so Will asked, "Now do you believe me?" Still no answer. "What are you thinking?"

"How sad," said the ring.

"Well, he had to deal with a lot of hardship during—"

"No, how sad that he was forced to scrape the bottom of the barrel and take a simpleton like you as an apprentice."

Will's eyes began to water. "It really is you. You don't know how much I've missed you."

"Don't get sappy. I already told you I'm not really him. Most emotions arise from the soul. Don't expect me to reciprocate your feelings," said the ring.

He still had hope, though. "You said *most* emotions. That means you have something left, right?"

"Certainly. I'm pissed off and angry. Is there any chance you'd be willing to have the ring melted down? I don't think you have much chance of accomplishing anything useful, and you'll probably wind up losing me to some pinheaded sorcerer. Better to just nip disaster in the bud and get rid of me."

"Seriously?" Will was aghast. Even Arrogan hadn't been quite that dark. *Or maybe I'm just remembering him at his best.* "I'm not doing that, so you might as well make yourself useful."

"How?"

"Can you teach me some spells? My teacher never got very far with that."

"Not really."

"Why not?"

"First, I can't see. That means I can't observe and advise you as you try to learn. Second, me trying to teach you by reciting the order of runes for a spell isn't going to get you very far. Third, I only remember the spells he used regularly. Arrogan had forgotten more than you're ever likely to learn. If he needed something particular, he looked it up. Fourth, I don't have to do a damn thing I don't want to do. Talk to me when you're less ignorant and slightly more useful. Maybe I'll feel like sharing something then."

Will ground his teeth in frustration.

"Putting me in a slag pit is starting to sound better and better, isn't it?" observed the ring.

"Don't tempt me," said Will sourly. Then he thought of a different question. "Aislinn gave me another gift. She put something in the limnthal. Do you know how I can figure out what it is?"

"Try looking at it? Are you really this slow?"

He ignored the insult. "What do you mean look at it? The limnthal looks the same as it did when you gave it to me."

"Didn't he show you how to open it?"

"Open it? Is it like a container?"

"Every limnthal connects to an extradimensional space. Wizards use them to store all manner of small items. That was part of the reason they were so useful," answered the ring.

The possibilities of such a thing struck Will like a thunderbolt from the sky. How often he could have used such an ability! It also cleared up a few other questions. He had figured out that Arrogan made regular trips to Branscombe to buy supplies, things like butter. But he hadn't found any perishables stored at the house after his grandfather had passed. *And he was my grandfather,* thought Will stubbornly. *Whether we shared blood or not.*

"How much stuff can be stored inside one?" asked Will.

"It varies, but Arrogan's limnthal could hold quite a bit. The interior dimension was roughly the size of a wardrobe or closet."

There could be anything inside! Will's eyes became round as he imagined all manner of valuable and arcane materials that might be held within. There might even be gold. He could be rich! Or there might be long-forgotten magical artifacts. "How do I open it?"

"The limnthal has a built-in conjuration function that connects to the pocket dimension. On the left side there are two runes that serve as control points. They're right next to each other. Senket is the rune that summons, and raylin is the rune that stores. You just touch senket with your other hand and imagine the object you wish to call out. It will appear in your hands," explained the ring.

"But I don't know what's inside."

"Then you simply have to think 'empty' when you touch it. That will eject everything at once, but be warned, you'll have a mess if you do."

Chapter 8

Holding out his hand, Will prepared to follow the ring's advice, until he heard a warning. "If you're planning to empty the limnthal you may want to make sure you have plenty of room. Where are you now?"

"In bed."

A low chuckle issued from the gold band. "Go ahead. Forget I said anything." The ring's tone did nothing to inspire confidence.

Will glared at the sinister piece of jewelry adorning his finger, which accomplished nothing since it couldn't see his expression. "Thanks for the warning," he said dryly. He eased out of the bed and climbed down the ladder. Seth was still snoring steadily, putting his mind at ease.

He moved to the center of the room, and after a moment's thought, sat down. If any of the items were breakable, he didn't want them falling to the floor. With his left hand he touched the senket rune on his limnthal and formed the thought, *empty*.

His ears were assaulted by the sound of dozens of heavy items falling to the wooden floor. It was immediately obvious that his decision to sit was a good one. He was surrounded by boxes and clay jars, large and small. In between the containers were a variety of smaller items. Will's head swiveled as he looked behind him and to the sides. The floor of the room was littered with flotsam and jetsam. *Holy hell.*

Afflicted by a sudden onslaught of paranoia, he studied his roommate. Incredibly, Seth was still snoring, though Will couldn't imagine how the noise hadn't woken the other boy. *Priority one is putting everything back before he wakes. All I need to do is look at it, remember it, then put it away again.* In future, assuming the ring had been truthful, he could recover any individual item without needing to create a chaotic mess as he had just done.

The large clay pot in front of him had a lid. He opened it and was instantly caught by the smell of freshly baked bread. Looking inside he could feel warmth rising from the loaves piled within. *It's almost as though they just came from the oven.* Making note of the clay pot's exterior, he saw the word 'bread' written across the lid. Putting his hand over the pot, he touched the raylin rune with his thumb and sent it back whence it had come.

The next pot was filled with fresh cuts of meat: lamb, pork, beef. There was enough to cook a feast for thirty men or more. The flesh was still pink, as though a butcher had just cut it. He stored it as well. *And that cheap bastard forced me to make do with carrots and turnips,* thought Will ruefully.

He moved on, discovering jars filled with water, salt, peppercorns, and most notably, a vast supply of butter. Will counted the small butter jars. *There must be twenty pounds of butter in those, and that jerk used to punish me by not sharing.*

That was the end of the jars, so he began opening crates and boxes. The largest crate held a collection of wine bottles. Will knew nothing of wine vintages, but he had a suspicion that some of them were probably valuable. The next box held carrots, and the one after that turnips, all of them looking as though they had been freshly harvested and washed. A heavy burlap sack held onions. *Was he obsessed with food?* Will shook his head. He knew better. The old man had definitely been passionate about cooking.

A slim wooden case with hinges contained a variety of knives, from paring knives all the way up to an enormous butcher's cleaver. All of them were honed to a keen edge. A smaller case held whetstones.

There was definitely a pattern emerging.

The collection of pots, pans—and a complete set of fine porcelain plates, cups, and bowls—confirmed his hypothesis. Will stored them away, feeling disappointed. If he was willing to sell them, he could probably finance several more terms. The silver tea set and cutlery cinched that idea, but he couldn't bring himself to consider it. *I bet those are from Aislinn's dowry when they got married.*

Even more valuable, he discovered a wide case filled with smaller square compartments. It was a spice box, and as with everything else, the contents were still fresh and fragrant. Thus far, Will had found everything one might need to prepare a meal for a prince. The old man had been rich. *But where's the money?*

A tall pile of neatly folded blankets, sheets, and two pillows appeared once he had put the boxes back in storage. Will smiled. He was saved from purchasing bedding. Moving those aside, he found a collection of vials sitting loose on the floorboards. They were labeled 'elixir of turyn,' and when he counted them, he arrived at the number twenty-three. He couldn't imagine why Arrogan had stored so many, though. Elixir of turyn wasn't that useful unless you were starved for turyn, and that was something his training had ensured wouldn't be a problem.

Near the door to the room, Will found something he was intimately familiar with, his grandfather's antler cap. Near it was a modestly sized tent, something he had frequently dealt with in the army. Beside it was a large coil of rope. He stored them both away and surveyed the empty room, feeling somewhat letdown. While he wouldn't have to worry about starving for a very long time, and all of the items were useful, there hadn't been any magical artifacts or money.

He found a neatly folded item of clothing on the floor underneath where the tent had lain. It was dark in color, though since he had adjusted his vision for starlight he couldn't be entirely sure what color it might be in the light of day. Unfolding it, he saw that it was an elegantly made robe. The material was soft and smooth, and the edges were decorated with silver embroidery. Will saw no sign of magic, however. He admired it for a moment, then stored it.

What the hell had Aislinn given him? He seriously doubted it was a clay jar filled with meat. Perhaps it was the porcelain? Then his eye lit upon a small object in the corner of the room—a book.

Will grinned. He picked it up and read the title, *Practical Magic.* "Yes!" he exclaimed.

"What did you find, your virginity? Never mind, a bumbling blockhead like you would never manage to lose that," said the ring.

"A book," whispered Will. "*Practical Magic*."

"Oh, that old thing," said the ring. "You might find that useful. He wrote that back when he was just getting started. It's full of simple spells, though most of them have the potential to get you tossed in prison if they catch you using them."

Will frowned. "Why's that?"

"Thumb through the pages. Even an idiot like you will see what I mean."

He dismissed the limnthal. He was getting tired of the ring's constant criticism. Will then climbed back into his bunk and opened the book. There was no title page or preamble. The first page was blank, and the second held a detailed diagram and description for a spell that was titled 'Silent Thief.' From what he could see, it was identical in function to the spell that Selene had used to keep his armor quiet when they had raided the camp in Barrowden.

The next page held a spell for light, with two variants. One produced normal light, but the other created a mage light, meaning it gave off light in the same manner turyn did, so non-mages wouldn't be able to see it. Neither version interested Will much. The trick Tailtiu had taught him for adjusting his vision was superior in most instances. It might be useful if he wanted to provide light for others, though.

He began to chuckle when he turned to the third page. It was titled 'A Universal Spell for Unlocking.' *Was Arrogan a thief when he was younger?* Given how firm the old man had been about debts and obligations it seemed unlikely, but then again, a person could probably change a lot over the course of six-hundred years. He decided he would ask the ring tomorrow.

Tucking the book underneath one of his newly acquired pillows, Will drifted off to sleep.

***

"Will." Seth was shaking his shoulder.

He opened bleary eyes and stared at his roommate. Dawn was just beginning to filter through the window, blinding him. Will closed his eyes and returned his eyesight to normal, making the soft light bearable. "What?"

"Did you go somewhere last night?"

"Why?"

Seth held something up. "I found this on the floor."

Once his eyes focused, Will realized it was a large and somewhat bloody steak. His mouth fell open as he struggled to think of an explanation that his roommate would accept. "Uh—"

"Do you think someone's playing a prank on us?" asked Seth.

That's a damned expensive prank, thought Will. *Who would waste a prime cut to play a joke?* He didn't say that, however. Instead he replied, "Probably."

"Do you think it's still good?"

Will sat up and shrugged. "It's been on the floor overnight, and who knows what they did to it before that. You should get rid of it." It hurt him to say. The cut of beef weighed at least two pounds and he was sure if it was still good, a few hours on the floor weren't enough to spoil it. A quick rinse and it could easily be made into a stew or pie.

Seth stopped beside their small trash bin, uncertainty in his eyes.

"Don't put it in there," snapped Will. "It'll stink up the whole room."

Unsure what to do, Seth eyed the window.

Channeling his grandfather, Will found himself swearing internally, *Fucking moron.* "Don't you dare toss it out the window. Put it in the chamber pot."

"Then what?" asked his roommate.

Will smiled evilly. "Today it's your turn to empty it."

"I didn't even use it!" protested Seth.

"Sorry. Them's the rules. I just abide by them." Will pulled on his trousers and ran out of the room laughing. He didn't want to be late for fencing practice.

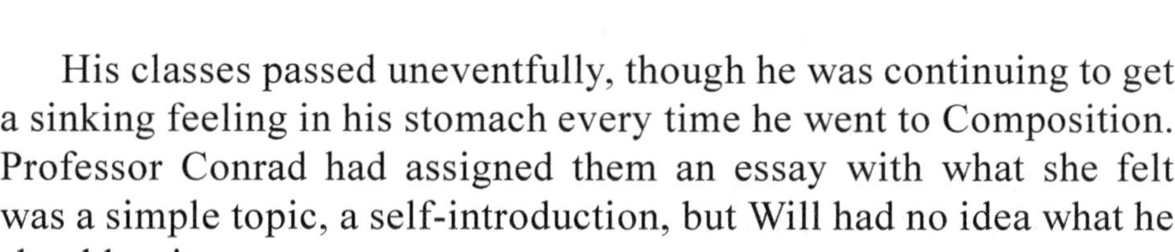

CHAPTER 9

His classes passed uneventfully, though he was continuing to get a sinking feeling in his stomach every time he went to Composition. Professor Conrad had assigned them an essay with what she felt was a simple topic, a self-introduction, but Will had no idea what he should write.

After Spell Theory, he was interested to discover what Professor Dulaney would start him on, but he was disappointed when it turned out to be a spell for changing colors.

"No! What are you doing?" interrupted the professor for perhaps the tenth time. "Keep your runes thin and delicate. If you put that much turyn into them you'll not only be wasting your life but you'll also color far more than the vase you're working on."

Will kept his eyes on the vase. "It's a temporary effect anyway. It doesn't matter if I color more than the vase."

"You'd still be wasting your life. Besides, this spell is a preliminary for a spell that is permanent. Mess that one up and you'll ruin my desk. Hell, you might even permanently stain me some hideous shade of purple," argued the professor.

"You could just overwrite it," suggested Will.

"No. *You* could. I wouldn't waste my life on something like that. Besides, do you realize how hard it is to match skin tones? How would I explain that to my wife? 'Sure, honey, I've gotten a permanent tan,' or 'No, dear, I love being the color of milk.' I'd prefer to just stay the shade I was born with."

Will couldn't help but chuckle.

"You may think it sounds funny, but it would be far better for you to just learn to do the spell properly."

"I thought you told me the color change remains limited to the object I define during the casting," countered Will.

"It *should*, but if you put that much power into it it's almost guaranteed to bleed over. A bucket can only hold so much water. Even if you don't care about wasting your life, you still need to learn finesse or your spells will only ruin whatever they touch," lectured Dulaney.

He sighed and started over, doing his best to keep the runes small and fine. He still failed to satisfy the professor. "Maybe if we start with something simpler."

Professor Dulaney shook his head. "This is a first-order spell. They don't get much simpler than this."

Will furrowed his brow. "Order?"

Dulaney waved a hand dismissively. "I'm not talking about order versus chaos, I'm referring to the complexity of the spell. Every spell is graded according to its complexity and difficulty. Spells like 'light' or the source-link spell are the simplest, so we don't classify them, though some people call them zero-order, or cantrips. Most spells are at least first-order, such as this one."

"What are higher-order spells like?" asked Will. "Are they things like battle magics?"

The professor scoffed. "We don't teach battle magic. No, high-order spells are things that require complex rules or that produce complex and subtle effects. For example, a few years ago one of our better students produced a new cleaning spell that completely eliminates the need for all the simpler, single-purpose cleaning spells. Her spell was classified as eighth-order, meaning it requires a very high degree of skill to successfully cast."

"Selene," muttered Will.

"Her Highness," said Dulaney firmly. "Don't let anyone catch you referring to her with such familiarity. And yes, she was the originator of the spell."

"So, what were the simpler, single-purpose spells like?" asked Will, ignoring the rebuff.

"Suppose you wanted to clean a rug," said Dulaney. "There's a spell for that, but it's only good for rugs. You can't use it for wood floors, or even fabrics like clothing or sheets. Or maybe you want a spell to polish your shoes. There's a spell for that, but it's only good for leather shoes. If you want to clean cloth shoes you have to learn a different spell. Most of those spells are second or third-order, which means they're much easier to learn and use."

"Then what's the use of her creating a much more difficult cleaning spell?"

"Well, although it's much harder to learn, it does it all. You can define an area, and anything within that area will be properly cleaned, polished, washed, dusted—whatever is appropriate. Conversely, if you limit the area to a single object, perhaps the shoes from my earlier example, it will perform just that task but with only the minimal amount of turyn required. The princess purification spell is hard to learn, but once you've mastered it, it's the only cleaning spell you would ever need to know."

"Princess purification?"

The professor smirked. "That's what we call it, though she hates the name."

"How long before I can learn it?"

Dulaney laughed. "That depends on you. If you apply yourself, maybe two years, but we don't teach that spell."

"Why not?"

"Haven't you listened to anything I've said? Casting spells requires the expenditure of your life. Do you think any wizard would want to burn a day or two of his life to clean a room or do his laundry? We have a separate class for sorcerers who want to learn utility spells like that, but few of them bother to put in the effort. It's easier just to have a servant do it.

"Remember, as wizards, we only use magic to do things that are impossible to accomplish in a mundane fashion. Anything else is foolishness," finished the professor.

Speak for yourself, thought Will. *I'd love to save money on my laundry, and it doesn't cost me my life to cast spells.* He couldn't say any of that, however, so he simply nodded.

"Back to your practice. Try again, and don't even think about releasing your spell unless I say it's been done properly."

Will didn't manage to meet the professor's expectations before their time came to an end, so he returned to the dorm. Since he had been exempted from the regular Alchemy class and it wasn't a day he had to report for duty as an assistant, he had quite a bit of free time looming over his head. Naturally, he decided it would be to his benefit to continue his practice.

Back in his room, he tried assembling the color change spell. He had gotten quite good at this, although the runes were still too thick and turyn-infused to make the professor happy. *What the hell,* thought Will. *Let's see what happens.*

He focused on the chair at his desk and released the spell. Within seconds, everything in the room turned a lurid shade of purple. This included Will himself. His clothes, skin, fingernails, hair, all of it had gone purple. "Oh, shit," he exclaimed. He began to hyperventilate before remembering that the color change was temporary. *What if I had used the permanent version?* The consequence of that was too terrible to think about.

Even the book on his bunk, still hidden under his pillow, had turned the color of a ripe plum. Will opened it and thumbed through the pages. There was no writing to be seen. Every page was a perfectly uniform shade of nausea-inducing purple. He could only hope that when the spell wore off the writing would again be visible.

"I wonder how long that will be?" muttered Will. "Did he say one hour, or was it two?" Then he groaned. Supper would be served in less than an hour. "I can't go down there like this!"

It was then that the door opened, and Seth walked in, whistling a simple tune to himself. He came to a sudden stop, staring wildly around him, then at Will. "Sweet Mother Temarah! What the fuck happened?"

Will grinned, flashing shiny, violet teeth. "Well, it's funny you should ask."

Seth shivered. "Gods! Close your mouth. You look like a demon when you smile." After a second, he added, "Actually, you look like a demon with it closed. Can you even see? Your eyes are a solid color, there's no iris, white, or pupil."

"What color would you like to be?" asked Will, feeling malicious. He let the runes begin forming above his palms.

His roommate backed out of the room at speed. "No, no, no!"

He dismissed the spell. "Do you think you could bring me some food from the dining hall? This is going to take a while to wear off."

"We can't take plates out of the dining hall."

"Then you'd better run!" Will raised his hands threateningly. Seth was gone in less than a second.

Left alone, Will continued his practice, turning the room and himself every imaginable shade and hue he could imagine. While Professor Dulaney had refused to let him finish the spell, probably because he thought it would be a waste of his life, Will found it more helpful to be able to see the results of his mistakes. The amount of turyn it cost wasn't enough to faze him in the slightest, and he absorbed enough from the environment to replace it almost as quickly as he could cast the spell.

In the span of an hour he attempted it more than a hundred times, and by the end he finally had a good grasp of what Dulaney had been attempting to teach him. He had to keep the amount of turyn he invested in the spell minuscule to avoid it overflowing and coloring more than just his target.

Feeling more confident, he experimented with changing the color of individual objects. He changed the glass in the window to an opaque black color. *That might be helpful if I ever want to sleep during the daytime.* He restored his clothing to colors that resembled what they had originally been, though he failed to match them perfectly. The professor had been right, getting a hue to match the original was incredibly difficult.

He tried to get his own skin tone right and failed repeatedly, although at least he no longer looked like a monster. A multitude of ideas occurred to him. He could make his hair different colors or change his eyes. *Or I could turn my teeth red if I wanted to scare someone.* Will grinned at the thought.

"Or I could change my clothes," Will said aloud. The possibilities were endless.

He grew bored after a while. He'd mastered the spell and he needed to stop if he wanted the room to return to its previous state. Sitting down at the desk, he used the limnthal to produce a loaf of bread and some butter to slather it with. Once he had finished that, he lay down on his bunk and took a nap. In future he would keep the book inside the limnthal. Accidentally coloring it had made him realize how vulnerable the valuable tome was if he left it out.

When he opened his eyes again, he realized he had slept through the night. Looking out the window, he guessed that dawn was still several hours away, so he pulled the book Aislinn had given him out from under his pillow and adjusted his eyesight until he could read it. He was relieved to see that it had returned to its former color and that the writing within was once again legible.

Will opened it and studied the first few pages again. 'Silent Thief' wasn't extremely difficult from what he could judge with his limited experience, but it was still a bit more complicated than he felt comfortable attempting. The unlocking spell was definitely out of reach for him, so he turned to the light spell. It was even simpler than the color spell he had already learned. Glancing over the page, he recited the runes to himself. There were only five required to form the construct, so he quickly assembled them and turned the spell loose.

The world went white, and pain shot through Will's eyes. His vision was still adapted for maximum sensitivity. He pulled his pillow over his face and dismissed the spell, though he continued to see a purple afterglow behind his lids.

"Will? What was that?" came Seth's tremulous voice from the bottom bunk.

"Sorry," he apologized. "I was just experimenting. Go back to sleep."

"Please don't kill me in my sleep," begged Seth, his voice entirely serious.

Will chuckled. "I won't. Don't worry. It was just a light. I'll be more careful."

"Don't dye me purple either," Seth pleaded. "I'd die of embarrassment if I had to go to class like that."

"I won't. I promise." Will switched to the mage light version of the spell. It was just as easy, and since Seth hadn't awakened his sight yet, he didn't think it would bother his roommate's sleep.

This time he returned his eyesight to normal first, but the spell was still blindingly bright. He would need to learn to adjust the amount of power he put into it, just as he had with the color spell. Another idea came to him then. *Can I adjust my sensitivity to the light produced by turyn, the same way I can for normal light?*

He left the light burning and began experimenting with his vision. It turned out he could indeed adjust his sensitivity. Could that be useful? Will dismissed the mage light and created a single glowing rune above his palm. Then he adjusted his eyesight until it seemed to burn brightly. With practice, it might make it easier for him to see faint traces of turyn. Whether that would be useful in the future or not, he had no idea.

Will practiced with the light spell until he had it down pat. The amount of light it provided could vary greatly, depending on how much turyn he pumped into it when it was cast. *I bet Dulaney never uses more than enough to make it glow like a candle,* thought Will wryly. *No, scratch that, he'd save the turyn and find a candle.*

He shook his head. Arrogan was right. Modern wizardry had fallen into dark times, whether they had refined the science of it or not. What good was a wizard who wouldn't use magic?

Chapter 10

His classes went smoothly over the next couple of days, though Will still felt a stab of existential dread every time he went to his Composition class. The only thing that made him feel better on that front was that Seth had promised to give him a hand writing his first essay over the weekend.

At lunch time on Friday he encountered Rob and the two sat down to eat together, so Will brought up a topic that had been on his mind. "Do you know Dennis Spry?"

Rob's mouth was full, so he nodded as he chewed. After a second, he answered, "Of course. He's the son of Reginal Spry, the earl."

"He invited me to go to a gathering at Malview House tonight."

Rob's eyes went wide. "You're moving up in the world!"

"Maybe," said Will sourly, then he recounted the circumstances of his first meeting with Dennis.

"Wow. You must have a death wish. Why do you think he invited you after that?"

Will shrugged. "That's what I don't understand."

Rob waved his fork in Will's direction. "There's only two possibilities. Either he thinks you're important because of the king's sponsorship, or he wants to humiliate you."

"I don't trust him," Will observed. "I heard him saying something to Janice Edelman about her writing his essay for him."

His friend snorted. "Nothing new there. She ought to write it. His father is the one paying her tuition."

"Huh?"

Rob nodded. "She's not the only one. There are a number of students here who have been sponsored by this or that nobleman. Most of the time it's when they have a son or daughter here. They sponsor a commoner and then their precious children have someone they can order around. I guess it helps them adjust to having to live here without servants."

"That's awful," said Will.

"Maybe," replied Rob. "There'd be fewer commoners here if they didn't, though. Not many families are wealthy enough to send their children here. On the other side, if the nobility didn't do that, there wouldn't be enough wizards graduating to fill all the jobs. It's a win-win. The college gets more students and money, some poor kids get opportunities to better themselves, and the nobles get more wizards to serve them."

Will could imagine Arrogan's foul response if he had heard that line, and Will felt much the same. "Don't a lot of the graduates stay at Wurthaven?"

"A few do," said Rob. "Most take service with this or that lord for twenty or thirty years."

"Twenty or thirty years?"

"Until they die."

Will gaped. "They die that young?"

Rob nodded. "Haven't you been listening in Spell Theory? Few wizards manage to forego using their magic enough to live a normal lifespan. Most of those that do are academics. It's not all bad, though. Those who take service with the nobility usually die with money. It makes a big difference for their families."

"What about you?" asked Will. "Are you satisfied with that?"

His friend grinned. "That's why I'm focusing on alchemy. Who do you think helps Karlovic out on the days you aren't there?"

"Oh, right, you're one of his assistants too."

"Yep. I work the days you don't. Although unlike you, my lucky friend, I had to spend a year worming my way into his good graces to get the job."

Will returned to his original topic. "What do I do about the invitation?"

Rob mulled it over. "If you want to make sure he dislikes you, ignore it. If you want to mend your fences, go, but be cautious."

He made a sour face. "Caution hasn't really been a strong point of mine for a while now. Maybe you should spell it out for me."

"Go, don't drink much, and leave early. In fact, make sure you have a good excuse to leave before you get there. That way you won't have to make one up on the spot when things start getting ugly." Rob grinned. "I mean *if* things start getting ugly."

"You're really boosting my confidence," said Will.

"Just trying to be realistic." Rob stopped suddenly as something occurred to him. "Oh, be sure to bring a gift. Dennis probably doesn't expect you to, but he could embarrass you if you don't have something."

"What sort of gift?"

"Something to drink maybe," offered Rob.

That made Will feel better. Nothing like a solid plan of action, and he already had a gift. There were quite a few bottles of wine stored within the limnthal.

***

Malview House was small compared to most of the college buildings, but as houses went, Will found it rather impressive. It was a wood-framed structure that stood three stories tall with broad windows and columns supporting two balconies above a wide porch. The house faced a green lawn, across which stood a complementary building named the Primrose House. The two buildings served to house students of noble birth who were deemed too valuable to be rubbing elbows with regular students in the dormitories.

As a result, there were only twelve boys living in Malview, though the place easily had room for twenty. Dennis Spry and his housemates were also sorcerers, as it would have been unthinkable for people of their standing to not have been granted elementals.

Will had never been to a party before, unless one counted the annual harvest festival in Barrowden, but he had put on his best clothes and used the color-changing spell to dye them in a bright shade of red with white accents at the collar and cuffs. It had been Rob's idea of course, and he felt rather conspicuous wearing them.

As he approached the front of the house, he saw that a fair collection of the party-goers were on the second-floor balcony. Whistles went up as they spied his bright clothing and one leaned over to call out to him. "You're looking smart today, Cartwright!" The voice belonged to Chris Burnham, who Will knew from his Fencing class.

He grinned and waved. "Thanks!"

The front door was open, and a student he didn't recognize greeted him, though guessing by the fellow's clothing he was one of the resident's sponsored commoners. Will handed the other boy the bottle of wine. Then he turned as someone's hand descended onto his shoulder.

"Will!" said Dennis loudly. "I hoped you would come!" He looked past Will to the bottle. "You brought wine? How thoughtful. Let's see what it is."

Will didn't detect any sign of animosity in Dennis' voice, but he wondered what the young lordling would say if he didn't like the wine. "It was just something I had lying around," said Will modestly.

Dennis took the bottle and turned it over in his hands. "A Movelli Red from Darrow," said Dennis with surprise. "From 751? This is older than we are! You've outdone yourself, William."

Was that good? Will had no idea, but from Dennis' expression it seemed that he had brought a decent gift. He shrugged. "I didn't know what to bring, but I figured I couldn't go wrong with wine at a party."

"I'm not even sure if we should open this here," admitted Dennis. "I'm not an expert, but I believe this is a valuable vintage."

Will smiled. "Well, it's a gift, so you're welcome to do whatever you please with it." His eyes roamed across the front room, examining the faces. Some of them were familiar, but he couldn't put names to them. Then he spotted Janice Edelman standing on the opposite side of the room, chatting with another boy. She met his gaze briefly, then looked away.

Dennis leaned in and whispered in a conspiratorial tone, "You've got a thing for her, don't you?"

He shook his head. "I wouldn't say that. She's in a few of my classes, but I haven't had much luck getting her to talk to me."

"Play your cards right and she might do more than talk to you tonight," said Dennis, giving him a wink.

Will wasn't sure what to make of that statement, so he kept his face neutral. "I should meet some of the other guests," he said, to deflect from the topic.

"Feel free. The drinks are in the kitchen." Dennis pointed toward an open door that led off to the right. "You should arm yourself with a glass before you start carousing."

He took the advice and met another fellow in the kitchen who introduced himself, "Mark Townsend. I'm a third-year so we haven't met before. Want some wine?"

"Will Cartwright."

The other boy grinned as he poured a glass of wine. "Oh, I know."

"You do?"

Mark nodded, handing him the glass. "Everyone has heard of Wurthaven's war hero, not to mention you're sponsored by the king.

You're big news lately." He leaned closer. "They even say you've met Princess Selene. Is that true?"

Will had no idea what to say. "Well, I was at the palace for a week." He hadn't seen Selene there, but it seemed a more reasonable response than to break open the topic of his time in the army.

"Even that is remarkable," observed Mark. "She doesn't appear in public very often. I met her a few times, though."

"You did?"

Mark sipped his own glass. "Mmm-hmm. She was finishing her last year when I started. She was rather famous on campus, and not just because of her father. If she hadn't been a royal, she would have had a bright future as an academic."

"I had no idea," said Will diplomatically.

"Most of us just enjoy ourselves while we're here," Mark told him. "We get by, doing the bare minimum just to finish our time, but she was a role model of academic success."

"She probably had a lot of pressure on her," suggested Will. "Being the daughter of a king, she wouldn't want to make a poor showing."

"Perhaps," said Mark noncommittally. "You should go mingle."

"How about you?"

Mark smiled. "Don't worry about me. I like pouring drinks. It makes me feel important. Plus, this way I get to see everyone at the party." He swung his arms out in a dramatic fashion. "Everyone comes here eventually."

Will returned to the common area and began to circulate, introducing himself and promptly forgetting the names of most of the people he met. The conversations were short and superficial, and almost everyone asked him about his time in the army, which only served to give him the impetus to move on.

At some point someone began playing on a harpsichord that sat in an adjoining room, giving the party a strange yet whimsical air. Will nursed his first glass of wine for nearly an hour and he still had a few sips left when he eventually found himself standing beside Janice.

"Are you enjoying the party?" he asked her, feeling more confident after an hour of socializing.

There was a certain wariness in her eyes when she answered, "As much as I can, I suppose." She sipped at her drink, which appeared to be simple water.

"You don't like wine?" asked Will.

Her expression hardened. "It wouldn't be wise for me to drink here."

Will laughed, trying to lighten the mood. “That’s why I’ve been stretching this one glass out for an hour.”

“I don’t think our reasons are quite the same,” said Janice sourly, then she spotted Dennis heading toward them and her face changed. She smiled brightly and pointed at Will’s coat. “You outdid yourself. That fabric must have cost a fortune.”

“Not as much as you might think,” said Will, giving her a wink. Then he studied her dress. Unlike some of the noble ladies in attendance, her dress was a simple affair of dark green with a minimal amount of lace at the cuffs. “Personally, I think you’re the belle of the ball tonight.”

Janice raised a brow and nodded in the direction of a girl wearing a brilliant yellow gown with matching earrings of gold and topaz. “Surely you jest.”

“You can dress a pig in ribbons and bows, but it’s still just a pig,” said Will softly.

She put a hand up to cover her mouth as she laughed, and then Dennis arrived, carrying two full glasses of red wine. He offered one to Janice. “No, thank you,” she demurred.

“I insist,” said Dennis. “You must have at least one tonight.”

Will didn’t like the young nobleman’s forceful manner, but he kept his opinion to himself. As he had learned from Rob, Janice’s situation was complicated, and he wouldn’t be doing her any favors by interjecting himself into it.

The young woman accepted the glass, but she held it without taking a sip. Dennis casually draped his arm over her shoulder and Will saw him run a finger along the edge of her ear. “Have you been enjoying the party?” the young lord asked her.

“Yes,” said Janice, but her tone said the opposite. Watching Dennis’ overly familiar actions had the hair on the back of Will’s neck standing up.

Dennis turned to Will, forcing Janice to turn with him. “Did you know that Janice has an incredible talent?”

Will’s throat felt dry and his shoulders were beginning to ache from the tension in his shoulders. “No, I didn’t.”

There was an evil gleam in the young lord’s eye. “You should guess what it is. I’ll give you a hint.” With his free hand he touched the young woman’s lips, then ran a finger down her throat. “It involves this, and this.”

Janice had gone scarlet, while Will’s mind was blank. The world around him seemed to beat in time with the loud drumming of his heart. He was too angry to even speak.

"Don't look so serious! She can sing!" Dennis exclaimed with laughter, then his eyes narrowed. "What did you think I meant?"

Janice's eyes held desperation as she looked at Will, but he wasn't sure whether she was pleading with him to keep the peace or start a war. He looked down and saw that his fists were clenched, so he made a conscious effort to relax.

"You should sing a song, Janice. This is a party after all," said the young lord.

"I'd rather not," she replied quietly.

Dennis smiled. "But you should! Otherwise my new friend here will think that I was just being crude. You need to prove otherwise. Besides, I'm sure your *father* would be proud to hear that you shared your gift with such an esteemed crowd."

The way the young man emphasized the word 'father' seemed to unsettle Janice. She lifted the forgotten glass in her hand and took a long swallow. "I don't think I know anything suited to a party."

"Doesn't matter. Sing that aria you sang last year in the Great Hall. Father loved it. He wouldn't stop talking about it for days. I'm sure it was a large part of the reason he sponsored you," said Dennis. Then he turned and cast his eyes about, searching the crowd. "Chris!" He pointed. "You can play Lord Mallow's Ballad, right?"

Chris nodded and went to the harpsichord while the others cleared the center of the common area to make room for Janice's performance. The young woman drank the rest of her glass and set it aside before smoothing her skirts.

Will found himself nervously standing on one side of the room. His anxiety was on her behalf, but when Janice raised her head and gazed at the crowd her shy demeanor was gone, replaced by calm confidence. The harpsichord began playing a gentle melody, and when her lips parted the sounds that issued from them silenced the room as every student turned their attention to her performance.

Will had little experience with music, but it would take a fool not to realize that what he was hearing was something beyond the ken of ordinary men and women. Janice's voice rose, soaring to the heavens before trickling downward like rain to grace the grateful earth. He stood in awe, and while there were certainly words to her song, he was too stunned to comprehend them. Reality fell away, replaced by an aural experience of celestial glory.

When she finished, the crowd remained silent for several long seconds before breaking into a tumultuous round of applause and cheers. Dennis walked over to Will. "See what I mean?"

Stunned, Will nodded.

"You probably thought I was bullying her but trust me, she loves to shine. She just needs a bit of coaxing to get her out of her shell."

Will still didn't trust the young lord, but he wondered if perhaps he had misinterpreted things. Was his own prejudice coloring his vision of Dennis in much the same way that it had his perception of Selene? Certainly, the young man was privileged, self-important, and overly assertive, but perhaps he wasn't as malicious as Will had thought.

Janice was surrounded by admirers, but after a few minutes she made her way back to him. "Did you like it?" she asked, her eyelids drooping slightly.

"I've never heard anything like it," said Will honestly. "With a voice like that you could perform anywhere."

"That's what my mother always said, but it landed me here," replied Janice, who emphasized her response with a quick twirl.

Something was off. Being enthusiastic after a performance was one thing, but it was too big a change from her usual personality. Janice's eyes were impossibly blue as she stared back at him, but it seemed as though they weren't focusing properly. *Would one glass of wine do that?* wondered Will. *Is that why she didn't drink, she can't handle alcohol?*

She lost interest in him almost immediately and wandered away, a mild sway in her steps. He watched her go, wondering if he should worry, but another woman approached and distracted him.

"I don't believe we've met," said the young woman, extending her hand. "Stephanie Beresford."

"William Cartwright," he responded, bowing over her knuckles for a second without quite touching his lips to them. "It's a pleasure."

"I've heard a lot about you," she responded. "Do you like my dress?"

It's horrible, thought Will, studying the pink and lavender concoction that draped her figure. "It suits you," he replied. He entertained her questions for several minutes, but quickly tired of describing how sweaty and muscular the men in the army were, which seemed to be the only thing she was interested in. As soon as he got the opportunity, he excused himself.

Will made a slow circuit of the room, but Janice was nowhere to be seen, and after a minute he realized that Dennis and a few others were also notably absent. Finally, he stopped by the kitchen.

"Another glass?" asked Mark.

"No, I'm looking for Dennis."

"I think he went upstairs," said the other man without inflection. After a moment's hesitation he added, "You should go up too, if you're interested in that sort of thing."

Confused, Will headed for the staircase and started up. At the landing for the second floor he saw nothing but empty hallways, but he could hear voices coming from the third floor above. "Five crowns if you want a turn, Chris." It was Dennis' voice.

Something clicked in Will's mind then and he remembered Janice's eyes. They hadn't been simply blue, her pupils had been tiny, almost pinpoints. *Tincture of opium,* he realized. He'd seen the effects in his mother's patients many times. *That bastard put it in her wine!*

"Five is too much," countered Chris. "Maybe if I was first, but not for third."

"Too bad," said someone else. "I paid seven for second."

Will felt paralyzed. There were at least three people on the third floor, and it wouldn't do him any good to start a fight with any of them. They were obviously wealthy, noblemen, and utterly lacking in any sort of morality he was familiar with. His heart was pounding as fear and anger fought a short, vicious battle within him.

The moment passed, and a calm settled over him as he began climbing the steps to the third floor. When he reached the top he spotted Dennis, along with Chris Burnham and another student he had met only a short while ago, Brett Conn.

Dennis called out when he saw him appear. "There he is, our number one!"

"Why is he first?" complained Brett.

Dennis ignored the question. "Will! Mark told me that wine you brought is worth at least fifty crowns. Did you know that?"

Will walked toward them slowly. "No. I didn't."

"That's why I decided to give you a special gift in return," said Dennis, nodding toward the bedroom door behind him. "Would you like to have a little time alone with Janice? I promise, she's in an excellent mood."

Chapter 11

The leering grin on the other man's face filled Will with fury, but he kept his features blank. He wanted to be close before he started swinging. If he could put one down quickly, he might have a chance with the other two. There was always magic, of course, but all three of the other men were sorcerers and even if he succeeded, he knew there were rules against using magic against other students.

As it was, he would likely be expelled anyway, simply for angering three of the wealthiest and most important students. Another thought occurred to him as he came abreast of them. Without thinking, he began to talk. "You'll really let me go first?"

Chris and Brett gave him frustrated looks, but Dennis positively glowed. "Of course! Anything for my new friend."

"How long can I have?" asked Will, hoping his acting wasn't as poor as Selene had so often said.

"Half an hour," returned Dennis, "though I doubt it will take you that long."

The bile was rising in his throat, but Will managed to continue. "Is she tied down or anything?"

"Not necessary," said Dennis, flashing a small glass vial from the inside of his coat. "She's as docile as a lamb." He opened the door and gestured for Will to enter. "Be gentle, my friend. You're her first."

Will stood still as the door closed behind him, trying to collect his thoughts. Janice was still dressed, lying on a small but elegant bed that sat on the right side of the room. He thought she was asleep, but after a moment he saw the light reflecting from her eyes as she stared at him glassily. He approached slowly. *I've got half an hour,* he reminded himself. "Are you all right?" he asked softly.

Her gaze followed his movements, but the only sound that emerged from her throat was unintelligible. Will saw a small line of drool trailing from the side of Janice's mouth. The sight made him furious all over again. He put a palm against her cheek, noting the cool, clammy feel of her skin. *He gave her too much,* Will noted worriedly, moving his hand to hover beneath Janice's nose. She was still breathing, but slowly.

Surveying the room, he could see only one way out other than the door, which was obviously not an option. A small window, barely wider than his shoulders, faced the back of the house. Will opened it and looked out, making note of the long drop to the ground below. It was much too far to jump, not that Janice was in any condition for such a feat. Glancing from side to side, he saw no pipes or other features that would enable a climb.

I'm screwed, he thought. A sudden inspiration came to him, and he called up the limnthal so he could talk to his ring. After a quick description of his situation, it gave him a short answer. "Make a rope with the bedsheets and climb down," suggested the testy ring. "Then get the fuck out of here."

"How am I going to climb and carry her with me?"

"Forget the girl. Just run," said the ring. "None of this is your fault, so unless you want to cement your relationship with young lord needle-dick out there by taking advantage of the girl, your only option is to run."

"You're suggesting I find someone in authority and report it," said Will hopefully.

"Grow up. The only way that would work would be if the girl on the bed was one of the ladies from the Primrose House you mentioned. Why do you think they chose a peasant? The daddies of these rich little bastards own the place and everyone out there knows it. No one is going to stick their nose into this shit show. Just get out," advised the ring.

"Shut up," ordered Will. He wasn't about to leave Janice alone, but the ring had given him an idea. There was rope stored inside the limnthal, and the bedsheets could be put to a different use.

He summoned the rope, then went to the bed and carefully lifted Janice and laid her down on the floor to one side. Removing the heavy, quilted coverlet, he spread it out on the floor at the foot of the bed, then moved Janice, putting her on one edge of it. That done, he rolled her up in the quilt so that only her head was visible, sticking out at one end.

Using a filet knife from the limnthal, he cut several lengths from the rope and tied the bundle in four places, at her feet, knees, waist, and below her shoulders. Then he tied short sections from each of the four places together and used an ugly knot to put the whole thing together at the end of the rest of the rope. Sergeant Nash would have been disappointed at his display of poor ropework, but when he tested the joins they held.

Picking up the feminine bundle, Will returned to the window and discovered that pushing a human-sized object out of it was easier said than done. He fumbled for several minutes, grunting and wheezing, before getting Janice outside, whereupon he promptly lost his grip. She fell several feet before he caught hold of the rope and managed to bring her to a stop by slamming his head and shoulders into the window frame.

He froze, listening to see if the men outside the room would come bursting in, but no one entered. Then he began lowering Janice to the ground, feeling the coarse rope burn his hands. It was a relief when she finally touched bottom and the line went slack.

Will went back to the bed and tied the other end of the rope to the leg of the bed. Pulling it taut, he worked his way back to the window and tossed the rest out of the window before easing out and walking his way down the side of the house. Once there, he reached as high as he could and cut the rope, then he did the same close to the point where it attached to his bundle of Janice.

All told, he had probably lost around forty or fifty feet of his once impressive piece of cordage, but he felt it was more than worth it. Storing the rest in his ring, he considered the bundle at his feet.

Janice was completely unconscious now, and Will panicked for a moment until he confirmed that she was, in fact, still breathing. Even though she was probably of an average weight for a young lady at her age, carrying her would still be a significant burden. He would have preferred to carry her over his shoulder, but given the drug in her system, he worried she would stop breathing completely. Squatting down, he slipped one arm beneath her knees and the other behind her back and stood up. Then he began to walk, heading away from Malview House in a straight line.

He couldn't afford to circle around to the front until he had gotten well away, otherwise he would risk being seen by the partygoers. That would add a considerable distance to his journey, but it also had the advantage of taking him in the direction they were least likely to search. The back of Malview House faced east, away from the center of the campus, away from the dorms, away from any reasonable destination he might have chosen.

Another advantage was the lack of lighting. By the time Will had covered thirty yards, darkness covered him. There were modern gas lamps on the campus, but those lights were only located near the larger buildings. Fortunately, light wasn't a problem for him. Will adjusted his eyesight until the half-moon and starlight provided ample illumination.

After a hundred yards, his arms and back were burning. He focused his turyn to improve his stamina and kept going until they were close to the wall that separated Wurthaven's green lawns from the rest of Cerria. Will found a large laurel hedge and deposited Janice beside it. He checked her breathing again.

That done, he untied the knots around the quilt and gently extracted her from the bundle. He wasn't comfortable letting her lie prone, so he lifted her by the shoulders and pulled her with him until his back was to the wall, then he sat down and propped her up against his chest. His mother had always cautioned him that people with breathing problems should never lay flat.

Then he waited.

Aside from the stone wall digging into his back, it was peaceful. Using his foot, he managed to pull the quilt close enough so he could grab it, then he settled it over Janice's legs and torso to help keep her warm. *Five or six hours,* he told himself. *It should start wearing off by then. If she can make it that long, she'll be fine.* He wasn't entirely sure of the time, but at a guess that would be somewhere between midnight and dawn. He was glad he didn't have class the next day.

With nothing to do, his thoughts quickly began to drift. The night was cool, but the warmth from her body soon had him sweating, though not unpleasantly so. He might have slept, but for the stones digging into his back. After a while he rested his chin on the top of her head, noting the pleasant smell of her hair.

It was at that point that his body began to take notice of Janice's feminine charms. It had been a long time since he had been so close to someone of the opposite gender. He wasn't truly tempted, though. Instead his mind began to think of the past, when he had shared a cloak on a cold night with a certain sorceress. *Selene.* He wondered how she was getting along. He hoped her father hadn't been too angry with her.

Looking up, he saw the moon peeking at him over the wall and he wondered if she might be seeing it as well, wherever she was. What would she think if she could see him now? After a moment he decided she would likely approve. Despite her background, Selene had never approved of those in power abusing their privilege.

"I bet she would have torn that house apart if she'd been there," Will said, chuckling lightly. Or would she have? He also remembered her counseling him to leave the comfort women in Barrowden behind. *It would probably depend on the situation,* he decided. *Selene's a pragmatist first and foremost.*

Did that make her good or evil? If someone only chose the good when it was practical, did that count as good? It was certainly better than not choosing to be good at all, but it wasn't necessarily virtuous. Then again, Selene had frequently chosen to spend her free time feeding the poor and treating the sick. Those actions hadn't necessarily been practical, not for a woman in her position.

Hours passed, and eventually, Janice began to stir, seeking a more comfortable position. Will took that as a good sign. "Wake up," he told her. "Can you hear me?"

"Huh?" she asked fuzzily.

Will tried explaining the situation to her, but the young woman was still addled from the tincture of opium. Dawn was still hours away and he didn't want to spend the rest of the night outside, so he decided to head back to the dorms. Will helped his companion to her feet, where she swayed, drifting gradually from side to side. Bending down quickly, he recovered the quilt and draped it over her shoulders then stood with his back to her and bent his knees. "Put your arms around my shoulders."

She didn't understand, so he was forced to reach back and take her hands so he could draw her arms around him. Once they were in place he leaned forward, put his hands behind her thighs, and lifted her up. Her reflexes took over then, and she held tightly to him to keep from falling. Carrying his classmate piggyback, he began the long trek back to the dorm.

It took him half an hour to get there, whereupon he discovered that the doors were locked. He didn't know the resident assistant for the female dorm, nor did he want to risk Janice's reputation by waking them and leaving an obviously intoxicated girl on the doorstep. Instead, he parked his companion by the door to the boys' dorm and walked around until he spotted his own window.

Will spent ten minutes or longer throwing pebbles at the window before Seth finally woke and poked his head out. "Will?"

"Let me in!" Will hissed, his voice half whisper and half yell. Seth nodded and disappeared. A few minutes later, he met Will at the entrance.

"You're not supposed to come back so late," whined his roommate. "They lock the doors for a reason."

"So I've discovered," said Will dryly. Then he went and got Janice back on her feet, maneuvering her into position for another piggyback ride.

"What the hell?" exclaimed Seth. "Is that a girl?"

Will nodded. "I know you've never seen one before, but this is indeed a girl," Will answered sarcastically.

Seth's eyes bugged. "You can't bring one of those in here!"

"One of *those*?" asked Will. "It's a girl, not a desk or a chair. I believe you're supposed to say, 'one of them.'"

"Whatever! It's against the rules."

"Well, I'm not leaving her out here to sleep on the bench," countered Will. "She's drunk and someone's already tried to take advantage of her."

His roommate stared at him suspiciously. "Was it you?"

"Really?" spat Will. "Do you think I'm wicked or stupid enough to rape someone, then carry them back to my dorm? Does that make any sense?"

Seth shifted from one foot to the other. "Well, I suppose when you put it that way, maybe not. You still can't bring her in here."

"I am," said Will firmly, "and you're going to hold the door for me."

"And if I don't?" said Seth rebelliously.

"I'll knock you down and lock you out. You can try sleeping on the bench. If you keep arguing, I'll have her sleep on your bunk."

"I'll get the door."

The two boys went through the lobby, wary lest they be caught. "Where's Mom?" asked Will.

"Probably sleeping in her room," offered Seth. "As sane people usually do at this hour."

They got to the stairs and Will went first, carrying his semi-conscious charge on his back. His legs began to burn fiercely after a single flight of stairs. Then he heard a strange sound from Seth. Will stopped at the landing and looked back. "What?"

"Sk—skirts," stammered Seth. "Her skirts."

"Yeah? She wears them, I know."

Seth pointed at Janice and made a few more unintelligible sounds. After a moment Will realized what had the other boy so flustered. The girls dress had ridden up, exposing most of her legs and some of her derriere. In fact, his hands were now holding her by her bare hips. Will's face flushed. It was a chore putting her down and getting her back up, so he simply grimaced at Seth. "You go ahead of us."

The next three flights of stairs were sheer torture, but they finally reached the fourth floor. Seth checked to make sure the hall was empty and then led them to their room. He balked when he saw Will settling Janice into the bottom bunk. "What are you doing?" hissed Seth. "That's my bed!"

"You can sleep up top," said Will with a sigh. "I'll take the floor."

"But she's in my bed!"

"I promise, you won't catch anything," said Will dryly. "Didn't you have sisters or cousins?"

Seth shook his head.

"What about a mom then?"

His roommate pointed at the girl. "That is *not* my mom."

"True enough," said Will. "If she was, she'd have smacked the stupid out of you by now. Climb the damn ladder and shut up. We'll sneak her out in the morning, don't worry."

"But my sheets—"

"Seth. You won't get pregnant from sleeping on the same sheets a girl slept on. Trust me. If you're that worried, I'll pay to have them washed for you. Stop being a baby."

"Pregnant?" huffed Seth. "I know that."

Will pushed his roommate to the ladder, placed his hands upon it, then landed a resounding slap on the other boy's buttock. "Up you go! Oh, toss me the extra pillow, the floor's hard enough as it is."

The pillow flew at his head a moment later, but Will caught it deftly. Then he lay down and made himself as comfortable as he could, given the circumstances. He was tired, and sleep came quickly.

CHAPTER 12

He knew something was wrong as his mind slowly surfaced, returning to the waking world. Streamers of sunlight were shining around him, their brilliance blinding him until he realized he needed to return his vision to normal. As the vast sea of white retreated, he saw two eyes filled with animosity staring at him from the other side of the room.

It was Janice, sitting in one of their desk chairs, which she had moved over by the door. Off to the side of the room, Will saw Seth huddled on his bunk against the wall. The expression on his roommate's face was easy to read, for it screamed, 'save me!'

Will sat up, groaning as the muscles he had abused in his arms, legs, and back made their grievances known to him.

"Would you mind explaining to me how I got here?" asked Janice's stern voice.

His eyes darted toward Seth. "Didn't he tell you anything?"

Seth shrank even farther back, whispering, "I tried."

"The only reason I didn't run out of here yelling bloody murder is because he said you could explain," replied Janice. "That, and the fact that this is the boy's dorm."

"You don't remember anything?" asked Will.

Her eyes narrowed. "I remember talking to you. I remember singing, and I remember getting sleepy. After that it's all a blur. Did you give me a piggyback ride last night?"

"So, you do remember a little," said Will. "Yes. I carried you back here late last night. I couldn't leave you there."

"You know if they catch me here, I'll be expelled," accused Janice. "And hopefully you too. Should I thank you for that?"

"Dennis drugged you last night," said Will, jumping straight to the point.

She blanched, then a look of puzzlement stole across her face. "I didn't drink. I never do."

"He gave you a glass of wine, right before you sang. Remember?"

She did. "If you knew, why didn't you stop him?"

"I didn't know, not right away," he explained. "I didn't realize until after you disappeared. I found you upstairs in one of the bedrooms. Dennis had a line forming outside the door. They were paying him—"

Janice held up her hand. "Enough. I get it." Then she shivered, crossing her arms tightly across her chest. She closed her eyes tightly, and her hands balled into angry fists. "That bastard." Will saw a trickle escape from the corner of her eyes.

"It's all right," said Will. "I got you out before anything happened."

"How?"

"He said that since my party gift was so expensive, I could have the first turn. Dennis said I'd have half an hour, so after I went in—"

"Stop! I don't want to know. That's enough." She had her hands over her face by then.

"No, no, no!" said Will. "Nothing happened. It was a ruse. After they let me in, I tied you up in a blanket and lowered you down from a window. Then I climbed down and carried you away."

Seth broke in, "You tied her up and kidnapped her?"

Will turned on his friend. "You aren't helping. I didn't kidnap her. She was comatose. I prefer to think of it as an involuntary relocation."

Janice was openly crying now, which perplexed Will. "You're safe," he told her. "They didn't get a chance to do anything to you."

"He's going to be furious," Janice said quietly, tears still running down her cheeks.

"I'd like to think if it was me, I'd say 'thank you,'" suggested Seth.

Will glared at his roommate. "You're *still* not helping. Can't you see she's upset? Besides, she shouldn't have to thank anyone for *not* being raped. That's just human decency." He turned back toward Janice. "What's wrong? If you're worried about Dennis, don't be. I won't let him bother you."

She shook her head. "You don't understand. His father is Count Spry. My parents live on his estate in Lindham. They work for him. What do you think will happen when he complains to his father?"

Will studied his hands. He'd thought he was doing a good thing, but had he? It had to be. He refused to believe a world existed in which the best option was letting an asshole like Dennis Spry abuse someone like Janice. "Listen," he began, "You didn't do anything. It was all me. I'll make sure he knows. If he's going to take revenge on someone, he can come after me." It helped that no one could find his family, but he didn't mention that.

"Do you think he cares?" said Janice. "He's been humiliated. He'll find a way to punish both of us. You don't know him like I do. My life is over. I don't even care if they stop paying my tuition. His father will toss my family into the streets, or worse."

"Surely his father can't be that unreasonable," suggested Seth. "The truth is that you didn't do anything."

"Dennis won't tell the truth. He'll say whatever he wants until he gets what he wants, and his father will believe him."

Will listened, his mind blank. How could the world be so unfair? Then a stray thought came to him. What would Tailtiu have done? *Stupid question,* he told himself. *She'd have tied herself to the bed. Then afterward she'd have murdered them all, if they survived the act to begin with.* "Oh!" he exclaimed.

Seth and Janice both looked askance at him.

"I'll take care of it," said Will with quiet determination.

His roommate began shaking a finger in his direction. "I don't like that look. That's the same look you had last night when you threatened me, so I'd hold the door. See where that got us?" He waved his hand in Janice's direction.

"Don't worry about it. It won't involve you," Will assured him.

Janice had dried her cheeks with her sleeve. "What are you going to do?"

"Count Spry won't do anything to your parents if he doesn't hear about this, right? It's only a problem for them if Dennis starts feeding lies to his father."

Her eyes narrowed with suspicion. "And?"

"I'll just make sure he doesn't tell any lies," finished Will.

"How?"

Will gave her a faint smile. "You're innocent, but you won't be if I tell you. Let's figure out how to get you out of here instead." He asked Seth, "What time is it?"

"Almost time for lunch."

"You can take the front and make sure the stairs are empty once everyone goes to eat," said Will. "We'll throw a cloak over her and if Mom is near the door you can distract her while Janice gets out."

They waited, and when the time came Janice's exit was even easier than Will had hoped. No one was on the stairs or near the door. As soon as they were outside, they turned to the right and headed for the corner of the building. After checking to make sure they were unobserved, Janice removed the cloak and handed it back to Will.

Her face was a mask, behind which hid a multitude of conflicting emotions. "Thank you," she said. "Whatever happens, I know you were trying to help." Then she headed for the women's dorm.

Will watched her go. He had gotten the full message. *Thank you, but you probably fucked up my entire life.* It wasn't his fault, though. "Never accept blame for the evil actions of others," he told himself. Janice might be right about the consequences, but it wasn't her fault, or his. The blame belonged to those who chose to punish good people for nothing more than refusing to quietly accept being violated as their lot in life.

He went to eat lunch. The long night had left him hungrier than ever. Once his stomach was satisfied, he took a walk, heading toward the main gate. He needed money.

Along the way he recolored his tunic, restoring its crimson glory. If Dennis happened to spot him because of the bright color, all the better. The sooner he could begin the groundwork for his plan, the easier it would be.

Will was destined to be disappointed, though. No one approached him during his half-hour walk to the entrance, and he was able to leave the campus without trouble. Once outside, he made a mental inventory of what he had stored within the limnthal.

The wine was probably the most valuable, but he had no experience with it. He'd likely be ripped off if he tried to sell any of it. Some of the bottles predated the Terabinian War for Independence, meaning their price might be more a matter of historical value than taste. Trying to sell it would bring unwanted attention.

Fortunately, he knew the price of salt and pepper, both of which were extremely valuable. Summoning the jar of peppercorns, he hefted it in his hands, trying to judge the weight. *At least ten pounds,* he estimated. Spices could be worth more than their weight in gold, and while pepper wasn't *that* valuable, he figured a pound or two would provide more than enough coin if he could find an honest buyer.

He walked on, and within an hour he was hopelessly lost. Cerria was vast, far beyond his experience, and he had little knowledge of its streets. Luckily, the quality of his clothing made most of the people he met uncommonly helpful, as they assumed he was either a nobleman or someone of some importance, which made getting directions easy.

Along the way he sold several ounces of pepper to shopkeepers and tavern owners, making a few crowns. He was confident that even if he didn't find the market, he could raise enough money, so he continued onward. The directions he received eventually got him to the place he sought, a large, open-air market where all manner of goods and staples were bought and sold: meat, flour, beans, and more. It only took him a few minutes to find the spice seller.

Will had considered continuing to sell the pepper directly, but that would only engender ill will between him and those who made their living in the trade. When he saw the old woman who managed the spice stall he felt justified in that decision. The old lady appeared competent, wrinkled, and potentially vengeful. Given the value of her wares it was possible that upsetting her would have caused him even more problems, for she was likely wealthy, despite her ragged appearance.

"What do you need, sir?" she asked politely, measuring his clothing with sharp eyes.

He tried to appear non-threatening. "Hard coin, madam, but I have spices to trade for it."

The woman's eyes narrowed, and she waved a hand. "I'm a spice *seller*. If you aren't buying, I don't have time to play."

"How much are your peppercorns?" he asked.

"Five clima for an ounce," she responded instantly.

"And salt?"

"Two."

Will leaned in. "I have several pounds of both and I'm willing to sell for half that. I'd rather sell it to you and be done with it, but if you're not looking for a bargain, I can afford to spend my days hawking it here in the market."

The old woman snarled, showing yellow teeth. "Are you threatening me, young man?"

He put his hand over his heart. "My dear mother would curse me if I were ever to do such a thing. I'm merely desperate for money. So desperate I'm willing to make a bad deal if it will preserve my life."

She thought for a moment, then spat on the ground. "How much do you have to sell? Let me see it. I'm not interested if the quality is poor."

Will summoned the jars of salt and pepper directly in front of her, which caused her to draw back in alarm. "You're a sorcerer?" There was fear in her eyes.

"A wizard," he corrected. "Deal fairly with me and I'll deal fairly with you."

They haggled for several minutes, but the spice seller had been impressed with the quality of his peppercorns. Will had never had a doubt about that. Arrogan had been a stickler for quality, and the limnthal had kept everything as fresh as the day he had purchased it. The price they settled on was four clima for two ounces of pepper, and two for two ounces of salt.

"I'll need to sell three pounds of each if you want me to go that low," cautioned Will.

The old woman grinned. "Deal."

"Do you know where I can find a decent weaponsmith?" asked Will as they weighed the goods and she counted out the coins.

"Follow the lane south past three streets and you'll find several," said the spice seller. "Tell them Magda sent you and maybe they won't overcharge you too much."

Will touched his brow, tipping an imaginary hat to the old woman. "Thank you." Then he set off down the lane, feeling the heavy weight of gold in his purse. Magda had paid him close to twenty-nine crowns, and combined with the money he'd had already, he had just over forty-six gold crowns to his name. Feeling self-conscious, he stepped to the side of the lane and quietly stored his coin purse inside the limnthal.

With his money safe, he continued onward, keeping a watchful eye on the road behind him. Given how much she had paid him, there was always the possibility that Magda might send a few enterprising freelancers to waylay him. Even if she had to split the money, it would still make her profit from him even more extraordinary.

No one seemed to be following him, and soon enough he smelled the distinctive odor of forge-fires coming up ahead of him. The first place he found turned out to be an ordinary smithy, but the man there was kind enough to direct him to a weapon-seller. "Tylan makes the best blades, but he doesn't sell them himself," said the smith. "Take a right at the next street and then a left. "There's a shop where Tylan's son works. He's the one you want to see."

Will followed the directions until he saw a shop with a sign bearing a painting of a sword and axe. He stepped inside and saw a young man in his twenties sitting on a stool.

"Can I help you, sir?"

He jumped straight to the point. "I need a dueling saber."

The man nodded. "Are you thinking of something ornamental to wear to court, or something more practical?"

"Practical."

"Then I have several you can look at over here." The shopkeep rose from his stool and led Will over to the right side of the shop and unlocked a large case. He lifted the lid, and Will saw seven slender swords laid out on velvet within.

The blades were almost straight, with hardly any curve. Will had seen cavalry swords before, and those were heavier, and slightly more curved. These weapons were designed for dueling, much like the practice weapons they used in his fencing class. Their lengths varied by an inch or two. "May I?" asked Will, reaching toward one of the hilts.

"Let's see your coin first."

Will summoned his purse and gave it a shake.

"Are you a sorcerer?" asked the shopkeeper worriedly.

Will shook his head. "Just a slightly paranoid wizard."

The shopkeeper held out his hand. "I'm Lawrence. My father is Tylan, the bladesmith."

They shook hands, and then Will lifted the sabers one by one, checking their heft and balance. Unlike the falchions he had used in the army, the weapons were light and elegant with ring guards to protect the hand and knuckles. He didn't think they'd be much use against an armored opponent, but against someone in nothing more than a tunic or doublet, they were absolutely lethal.

After a few minutes he selected one of the longest sabers. The hilt was simple, with a leather grip, but he liked the false edge at the tip, which gave the weapon the ability to perform effective back cuts. He tested the edge with his thumb and found it lacking, though. "I like this one," said Will.

Lawrence noticed him feeling the edge. "We only put the final edge on after they sell, and only if the owner requests it."

"Why's that?"

"An edge starts to dull as soon as you put it on," said the dealer. "So no one sharpens them unless they intend to put them to use in the near future."

"I'll need it as sharp as you can manage," said Will. "When can you have it ready?"

"Ordinarily, we'll put the edge on for free, but if you're in a hurry—"

"I can pay a little extra if need be," Will reassured him.

They bargained for a while and eventually settled on twenty-four crowns for the sword. The price included having it sharpened and ready for Will to pick up in the morning. It also included a sword belt and sheath.

As he was leaving, Will asked, "Is there an armorer you recommend?"

Lawrence gave him an odd look. "Are you taking an officer's position in the army?"

He shook his head.

"What sort of armor are you looking for?"

"Nothing substantial," said Will. He ran his hands over his chest and belly. "I just need something to keep a knife out of my vitals."

"A breastplate?"

"No, something less conspicuous—maybe a mail vest?"

Lawrence nodded. "I know who you should talk to." He gave Will quick directions and sent him on his way.

The next shop was a few blocks away and was run by a fellow named Byron Waters. Will stopped to appreciate the armorer's impressive beard for a moment when he stepped inside, for it stretched from the shopkeep's chin almost to his waist. "I'm told you sell armor," he said, introducing himself.

Byron combed his fingers through his beard, which appeared to be something of habit. "Depends on what you're looking for."

"Something small and inconspicuous," said Will.

"A mail shirt then?"

"I have one. I need something I can wear underneath a tunic."

Byron frowned. "You worried about being stabbed on the street?"

He nodded.

"You'll have to wear something under it, no matter what you choose," said the armorer.

"What do you suggest?"

"How about brigandine?"

"Show me what you mean."

Byron took him to another room where a number of articles were hanging. They looked like vests covered with rivets. The man opened one to show Will the metal plates underneath. "Ordinarily you'd wear at least an arming jacket under this, and a lot of men wear an arming jacket, a mail shirt, and then put this on top."

"I need something to go under my tunic," said Will.

The armorer resumed combing his beard. "That's not easy. Maybe if you had a custom padded vest sewn inside the brigandine. That'd keep it from tearing up your skin, but without the mail shirt or at least a larger jacket you'd be vulnerable to all kinds of attacks."

"I'm not going to war," explained Will. "I just need something to keep a point out of my belly or back."

"And you're going to wear your clothes over it?" asked Byron doubtfully.

He nodded.

The armorer clearly thought he was crazy, but he finally agreed. "All right. I can make something like that. I can do a modified brigandine jack that will cover your ribs, belly, and back. We can sew the padding inside and try to keep it slim enough that your tunic will go over it, but I wouldn't recommend it if you think someone is planning to put a blade in you."

"Concealment is more important to me than maximizing protection," said Will.

Byron shrugged. "Well, it'll be better than nothing, but even if it's slim enough to go unseen they're going to hear it. Brigandine is noisier than mail." Reaching over, he grabbed one of the vests and flexed it slightly so Will could hear the sound of the plates rubbing against each other.

Will had to agree, but he had a possible solution for the noise. "I can deal with that. How long will it take you?"

"Two weeks, and it'll cost you fifteen crowns."

"If you can do it in one, I'll pay twenty," said Will.

The armorer frowned. "Can you pay in advance?"

"Half now and half when it's ready, less one crown for every day it takes past a week."

Byron hesitated a moment, then nodded. "Let's see your money and then we can start measuring."

CHAPTER 13

He found himself taking a different route to get back to the school, and when he eventually found the road that led to Wurthaven's entrance he was coming from the other direction than the one he had taken that morning. Consequently, he walked past the entrance to the royal palace on his way. Will stopped after passing the gate and studied the wall. It was even more impressive than the one that surrounded Wurthaven's neatly trimmed lawns, standing almost forty feet in height.

Selene's in there somewhere, he thought. *Probably.* He wondered if he would ever have a reason or opportunity to see her again. The wall seemed like a perfect metaphor for the distance between them.

"Except I could climb a wall," he said to himself. "I'll never be able to close the gap in social standing." After a moment, he corrected himself. "All right, maybe not that wall. Anyone would struggle with that."

He wondered if there was a spell for scaling walls. "Not that I would," he reminded himself. "That would be foolish. Besides, there's every chance I won't live past the next few days."

Will hadn't shared his plan with anyone, but he knew it was tantamount to suicide, and even if he succeeded, he might well be murdered afterward. His only consolation was that it would almost certainly keep Janice's family safe.

He glanced up and down the road, making sure he was alone, then summoned the limnthal so he could talk to the Ring of Vile and Unspeakable Knowledge. "I need your advice," he began.

"Fuck off," said the ring. "I'm not in the mood."

Will found himself grinning despite his dark thoughts. "Too bad." He launched into a description of what had happened the night before and what he planned to do about it, only pausing once he had finished.

The ring said nothing.

"Well?" prodded Will.

"What?"

"What do you think?"

"You're a blithering idiot. Happy now?"

"Got anything more specific?"

"Not really. I'm sure having several feet of cold steel rammed through your belly will communicate my thoughts better than any words ever could. Good luck."

"That's the worst case," argued Will. "I'm interested in what you think will happen if I don't die."

The ring snorted, despite lacking a nose. "That's the *best* case, jackass! You'll really be in a pile of shit if you don't die. You must be aware that Little-Lord-Pus-Dick has friends and family. What do you think they'll do afterward? The best you can hope for is a knife in the back. More likely, they'll find some way to put you somewhere dark and damp where they can take their time making you properly miserable."

"But I'm not going to break any laws," he countered.

"Someone needs to slap the teat out of your mouth so you can grow the fuck up," snapped the ring. "Those people don't give a damn about laws. They *write* the laws, and people like you are only useful to provide the blood they use as ink."

"I already told you what I'm going to do. That's done. Give me some advice on what to do afterward. You've been there before."

The ring produced an audible sigh. "Arrogan's been there before."

"You have his memories, just tell me what he would say."

"He'd say not to do it."

"What would he have done in my place, then?"

"Probably the same damn thing, if he was as powerless as you are! You want his advice, fine! If you're going to start down this road, don't look back. You're going to paint a giant target on your back and a lot of people are going to be taking aim at it. So, if you do this, don't apologize. Show no remorse, no weakness. You're going to have to pretend to be ten feet tall and made of nothing but balls and spite."

Will squared his shoulders. "I think I can manage that."

"You think that because you're angry. But that's today. The next day, you'll be tired. The anger won't last, and after it's gone, you're going to find yourself alone and without friends. This won't be the first time. You'll have to do it again, and even if you get good at it, sooner or later all of it will catch up with you. One of these days you'll wake up dead, and there won't be anyone crying over you. Trust me."

"You're wrong there."

"About what?"

"I cried over you after you died."

The ring didn't respond.

"Can you teach me something?" Will asked. "Arrogan had a trick he used when we practiced. I think I've got the basics of it, but he was a lot better."

"What was it?" asked the ring.

***

Will felt better after their talk was finished, and he enjoyed the fresh air as he walked toward the boys' dormitory. He had a day and a half to prepare, but he felt as though he had a fair chance.

He spotted a familiar figure waiting for him outside the dorm. It was Dennis.

Of course, Dennis wasn't alone. Chris Burnham and Brett Conn had come along for the show. Will let his eyes drift to the sides, searching to see if there were any other people nearby. He spotted several students loitering between the two dormitories.

Better than nothing, he thought.

"William," said Dennis as soon as he had come within ten feet, his face emotionless.

He took a deep breath and projected his voice as he answered, "Rapist! I can't believe you decided to show your face. Are you looking for more girls to drug unconscious?"

Dennis' face turned an ugly shade of red and Chris and Brett moved forward threateningly. "I was going to suggest we could put this behind us if you'd apologize and accept a few bruises," said Dennis, "but it seems like you don't have the brains to know when you're in trouble."

Will noticed that some of the nearby students had moved slightly closer in order to hear better, while inside the boys' dorm someone had run off to either notify the resident assistant or bring others to listen. He didn't particularly care which. "Before you sic your dogs on me, I have a question," said Will, stalling for time. The bigger the audience, the more effective his ploy would be.

"I'm feeling less inclined to talk to you, Cartwright. Why don't we skip to the part where you bleed on the ground and kiss the soles of my shoes?"

"But I'm really curious!" Will said loudly as he danced back a few feet to maintain his distance. He could see people looking out the doors of both dormitories now, and some of the windows had opened. A lot more people were listening.

"I want to know if you drug girls for sex because you don't know how to talk to them, or is it the fact that once they see your tiny dick, they run screaming?"

Chris lunged at him and Will stepped forward, planting a fist in the other boy's stomach, causing him to double over. Then he dodged sideways to avoid a grab from Brett.

"Are you afraid of me, Dennis?" he yelled. "Is that why you brought so many friends? Or is this how you normally operate? I guess you need at least two friends to hold girls down for you to rape, don't you?" Brett started running toward him, so Will turned and broke into a sprint, heading for the corner of the building. Chris was still trying to get his breath back.

As soon as he turned the corner, Will stopped and turned back. He caught Brett with a surprise punch as he came around the corner and followed it with a knee to the head when the other boy doubled over. Then he started back toward the entrance.

Dennis stared at him as he advanced, backing slowly away. "Don't even think about it, Cartwright!" he yelled.

"Or what?" demanded Will. "You'll bleed on me? Why don't you tuck tail and run, you goddamn coward?" He kept coming.

Dennis might have held his ground, but Chris broke and ran. Lacking support, Dennis followed suit.

"You're a fucking rapist, Dennis Spry!" screamed Will, doing his best to keep his voice loud and clear. "And I'm going to make sure everyone in this school knows about it!" Having made his point, he turned and glanced around, making sure his audience had stayed until the end. He felt pleased by what he saw.

A few students approached Will before he went inside. "What was that about?" asked a girl that he recognized as Rebecca Swafford.

"Be careful if you go to any parties and Dennis is around," said Will. "He's not above drugging girls to get what he wants." With that, he left them and went inside.

Rob was standing just inside the door. "Are you insane?" he exclaimed. "Why would you do that?"

"Because it's true," said Will. "I've got nothing to be ashamed of. That bastard tried to drug a girl and sell her to his friends." He kept his voice loud enough that everyone in the vicinity could hear him clearly.

Rob's face went pale. "You can't just go around saying—"

"I can," said Will. "I was there. He offered her to me first. That's how I know what a despicable asshole he is. If I hadn't said something then and there, I can't imagine what would have happened." That was stretching the truth, but Will didn't care. The bigger and nastier the rumor became, the better it would be for him.

"Who was it?" asked someone behind him.

Will turned and saw a student he didn't recognize. "I'm not going to say, since I don't want to drag her into it. Dennis knows what he did, and I was there to catch him out. Ask him and see if he dares own up to the truth!"

He started for the stairs, but another voice stopped him in his tracks. "William! Come here." It was Dianne Young.

Will went quietly, and the resident assistant led him to her office and closed the door. "Do you mind telling me what that was all about?" she asked.

"Dennis Spry invited me to a party at Malview House yesterday evening," said Will plainly. "While I was there, I saw him put something in a girl's wine. I followed him upstairs after she passed out and he offered to let me sleep with her. He had several other guys offering him money for turns with her."

Dianne's face blanched at his directness. "Who was the girl?"

"I'd rather not say. She's got enough trouble already."

"With you shouting about it, do you think her identity will remain a secret for long?" demanded Dianne. "You're not doing her any favors."

"If I don't say something, he'll try to do it again."

"And if you're not willing to give names or she doesn't step forward, that rich asshole will have you expelled, or worse. He could take you to court for slander," warned the resident assistant. "Do you think that will help her cause?"

Which is exactly why I have to make him so mad he can't see straight, thought Will. He lowered his head and tried out his acting skills. "I don't know what else to do! It isn't right!"

Her face softened. "If you'll give me her name, I can pass it along. Some of the faculty here care more about this sort of thing than you might imagine."

"Enough to kick that jerk out of Wurthaven?" he asked pointedly.

Dianne shook her head sadly. "I wish, but no. At the very least some of them will keep an eye on her and try to help if he starts trying to bully her."

Will glanced up, giving her a hopeful look. "And they won't tell everyone? If her name gets out, she'll be embarrassed beyond belief."

"I'll only tell those I trust to keep it quiet," she answered. "The vice-chancellor and the proctors take this sort of thing seriously. They'll do as much as they can."

He wanted to smile. That was better than he had hoped. Seeding the administration with the news in advance might help his case when the time came. "It was Janice Edelman," said Will quietly. "I got her out of the house before they could do anything to her, even though Dennis had her drugged to the point of unconsciousness."

"Do you know what drug it was?"

"I think it was tincture of opium," said Will. "He had a vial of it in his coat pocket."

"How do you know what it was? Did he tell you?"

"My mother is an herbalist," he answered. "I recognized the symptoms."

"Thank you for telling me, Will."

"What else should I do?" he asked, affecting an air of uncertainty.

Dianne leaned back. "Nothing. You've caused enough of an uproar already. If Dennis tries to approach you, you should stay calm. It won't help if people think you're spoiling for a fight. Let the proctors handle it."

"I'll do as you say," said Will meekly. *Until Monday,* he added silently.

CHAPTER 14

Will spent that evening practicing the 'Silent Thief' spell, though he didn't try to cast it. He needed to improve his skills before he would try that. Instead he just attempted to complete the construct since it was a bit more complicated than anything he had done before. He wouldn't have the brigandine in time for Monday anyway, so the spell was more of an investment in the future.

Once morning arrived, he ate breakfast and made the trip to the weapon-smith's shop to collect his sword. He was pleased with the edge when he inspected it. The forward-facing edge was nearly razor sharp, as well as the first six inches of the back side of the point. After his time in the army, he had a great respect for the damage sharp steel could do to a human body, and he wouldn't have wanted to face a weapon like the saber without armor.

But that's what I'm going to do, he told himself, suppressing a shudder.

He belted the sword on and walked back to the dorm, taking a roundabout path to make certain that at least a few of Dennis' friends saw him wearing it. *A lot of anger and a little bit of fear,* he told himself. *I have to get the mixture just right.*

A few of the male students asked him about the weapon. Generally speaking, the only students who wore such things were the sons of nobles, and even they usually only wore them as status symbols at certain social events, or if they went into the city. No one walked about the campus with one. It simply wasn't done.

Will's general response was to feign surprise. "Oh. I'll put it away then. It's just that he threatened to kill me. I didn't know what else to do."

Selene would be proud of me, thought Will after he got back to his room. *My acting has improved considerably.*

He spent the rest of the day in his room, practicing the technique that the ring had described. His roommate wasn't pleased, however. From Seth's perspective, all he saw was Will continually lunging back and forth across the room, which made it impossible for the other boy to study, write, or even think.

"Please, Will, will you stop? You're driving me to nervous exhaustion," exclaimed Seth.

"Imagine how I feel," Will countered. "He threatened to kill me!" In actuality, Dennis had never said those words, though Will didn't doubt the young lordling would have if he had had the opportunity. The important thing was that he repeat them to as many people as possible before the next morning arrived.

A knock at the door interrupted their conversation. Will opened the door to find a young man he didn't recognize outside the door. "Mom says to come down. Someone wants to see you."

Will went down, and Dianne directed him toward the cushioned chairs in the common room. "She wanted to talk to you."

Janice Edelman was sitting in the direction she pointed. Will went over immediately. "Hey," he said, giving a small wave.

His classmate appeared visibly upset. "What do you think you're doing?" she asked.

Will took a seat across from her. "Drawing a boil."

"Huh?" She stared at him as though had grown two heads. "What does that mean?"

"When you have a boil on your skin, you have to use a salve to draw it out, such as coal tar. It makes the boil angry and red, until it festers to the surface. Once it rears its ugly head, you can lance it," explained Will.

Janice shook her head. "You're only making things worse for everyone. People keep asking me if I know who the girl was. Not only that, but Dennis is beyond angry. I thought maybe he'd calm down, but you've injured his pride. He's not going to let this go. Do you realize the things he could do to you?"

"Not really," said Will, playing dumb. "List them out for me."

"His father could convince the chancellor to have you expelled, for starters. They could take you to court and have you locked up for slander. You could go to prison! And those are the nice options. They could hire men to wait for you in town."

He nodded, relieved that she hadn't named anything that he hadn't already considered.

"Not to mention me," she continued. "I'm almost certain to lose my sponsorship. If you make things any worse, he's bound to do something to my family."

"Lindham is more than two weeks from here," said Will. "Dennis will have to send a letter to get his father involved."

"And your point is?"

He's not going to get a chance to send a letter, thought Will. *And by the time anyone does, I'll be the only one they mention.* He remained silent, lacking a good answer since he couldn't share his plan.

Janice leaned forward intently. "Are you doing this because you think it's brave, or that I'll like you? Do you have some demented idea of chivalry in the back of your head? All you're doing is ruining your life, and quite possibly mine along with you."

Will returned her gaze evenly. "I'm not doing this for you."

"Then why?"

It was something he'd given a lot of thought to over the past couple of days. "I wasn't even sure myself," he admitted. "Not at first. But I understand myself better now. I'm doing this for me. I'm doing it so I can look myself in the mirror. I don't want to live in a world where people like him get to do whatever they please and damn everyone else, and one way or another, I won't. I'm also doing this for all the other people that little turd might hurt in the future."

"Well nothing you're doing is going to help any of that," said Janice in exasperation.

Will shrugged, then stood to leave. "He threatened to kill me," he added at the end, seeding his lie in one more pair of ears.

Janice watched him go, but he picked up her last words as he reached the stairs. "You're an idiot, William Cartwright," she muttered to herself.

***

Monday morning arrived after an interminably long night. Will had tried to sleep but with only limited success. Nevertheless, his nerves were wound too tightly for him to feel sleepy as he headed to fencing practice almost an hour early. Under his arm he carried a long, slender bundle wrapped in his cloak.

He was the first to arrive at the gym, but he had no doubt someone else would show up soon. *He'll want to confront me before practice,* Will told himself, hoping it was true.

Making use of his time alone, he went and stowed his bundle in one of the equipment lockers, then did a few exercises to stretch out his muscles and use up some of his nervous energy. It wasn't long before his prediction came true. Dennis Spry appeared, accompanied by Chris Burnham.

"Look who it is," challenged the young noble.

Will looked his enemy up and down, noting the sword on Dennis' hip. "Feeling brave now that you're armed?" he asked.

"I heard you were carrying one," said Dennis. "As violent and deranged as you are, I didn't want to get murdered coming to class, so I took precautions."

"And I heard that it's in poor taste to carry weapons around Wurthaven," said Will, "but then, a dog like you wouldn't know anything about taste, would you?"

"You're a lying braggart, Cartwright," said Dennis. "A churl like you wouldn't even own a saber. You were probably walking around campus with a kitchen knife yesterday, trying to scare the other underclassmen."

Will met the other boy's gaze calmly. "I'm not carrying a sword, but that doesn't mean I don't *have* one—you pus-ridden little rapist." He spotted movement then, and saw Matthew Holmgren arriving through the side door. *Finally, a witness,* he thought to himself.

"Take it back and apologize this instant!" commanded Dennis, his hand falling to the hilt of his weapon.

Will leaned in, pitching his voice just loud enough that both Dennis and Chris could hear him. "Or what? You'll offer me a glass of wine? No, thanks."

Dennis snapped. Whipping out his saber he screamed at Will, spittle flying from his lips. "I'll gut you like a pig, Cartwright!"

Will retreated. "Are you challenging me to a duel, Dennis?" he asked loudly, making sure Matthew was listening.

Dennis froze, sanity returning for a moment. Glancing around, he saw Matthew and Chris both staring at him with keen interest. "Well…" he started to fumble his words as he realized he had backed himself into a corner.

"So you just bared your steel to threaten me?" asked Will calmly. "I knew you were spineless. I can't wait to tell everyone once class starts." He could see a couple more students entering the gym already.

"I do challenge you!" shouted Dennis boldly, then he added. "Too bad you don't have a sword, otherwise I'd spill your blood right here."

Will grinned. "Oh, but I do have a sword. One moment." He walked over to the equipment lockers and retrieved his bundle, then removed the saber in its sheath. "This should do," he announced.

Dennis' eyes bulged. "I didn't mean we should duel right this minute," he said, backpedaling.

"Why? So, you can find a way to back out of it? Or maybe you think you can have some of your friends catch me alone somewhere?"

Will turned to the others. "You heard him. He challenged me." Then he looked back at Dennis. "We don't have to do this if you don't want. I understand if you're too scared."

"Instructor Rhodes will be here in a few minutes," offered Dennis. "We should probably wait."

"It's early," said Will. "He won't be here for at least a quarter of an hour. How long do you need?"

His opponent clenched his jaw. "Fine. You asked for this."

Will shook his head. "No. I didn't." He waved his hands at the other students. "And these are my witnesses. You challenged me, not the other way around." He raised his voice. "Does anyone dispute that?"

Matthew Holmgren spoke up. "No. I heard him. He definitely challenged you." The others nodded.

Unsheathing his blade, Will bowed slightly in Dennis' direction. "How do you want to do this, to the death, or just first blood?"

"First blood," said Dennis immediately, his body tense to the point of making his movements jerky.

"Fine with me. Matthew, will you referee for us?"

Matthew readily agreed and moved to stand midway between them, lifting his arm in the air. Meanwhile, Will contracted his turyn. He had expanded his personal boundary a few minutes earlier, allowing him to absorb more than usual. Drawing it in, he could feel his heart speeding up as his muscles grew hot. It almost felt like his very bones were vibrating.

Extending his arm, he pointed the tip of his saber at Dennis, keeping the point low. His opponent did likewise. From the past week everyone already knew that Dennis was the best fencer in the class. *But we aren't sparring,* Will reminded himself. *Someone's about to get hurt, and he's never stared down a sharp sword pointed in his direction before.*

Will had never tried to stand out in the class. He might have been close to the top of their rankings if he had, but he still wouldn't have been as good as Dennis Spry. The young noble had been practicing the sport for years. What Will had done, however, was pay attention. He already knew a few things about the way Dennis liked to spar, and he had little doubt the man would try to repeat what usually worked for him.

Matthew's arm dropped and Dennis leapt forward, his point dipping down for Will's thigh, much as he had expected. Rather than retreat, which was the normal response when someone else had the initiative, Will lunged forward as well.

The world seemed to slow as he brought the point of his saber up. Arrogan's trick for increasing speed worked, but it wouldn't be enough to overcome the difference in skill between the two of them. But it didn't need to overcome that gap, for they weren't in a match. It was a duel.

The point of Dennis' blade entered the middle of his thigh a split second before Will's blade reached him. In a match that would have meant that Dennis had won a point. Will continued forward and his blade continued upward, slipping under Dennis' chin and through his throat until it was stopped by a bone.

Will felt a jolt as Dennis' sword shuddered to a halt against his femur, then he flicked his sword out and sideways, ripping through the side of his enemy's neck to be sure he finished the job. He hobbled back a second later, bleeding profusely from his wounded thigh.

Across from him, blood was spraying from Dennis' ruined throat and the other man fell back, collapsing to the ground. He was dead within seconds, his blood pooling on the hardwood floor of the gym.

Gritting his teeth, Will tried to keep his expression calm as he looked at the referee. "Did his point strike first or mine?"

"I think it was his," stammered Matthew.

"Damn!" swore Will. "That's too bad." He hobbled over to Dennis' corpse. "It appears you drew first blood. Since I lost, I retract my words. I apologize for calling you a pus-ridden little rapist." Reaching into his tunic, he pulled out a short length of rope he had brought for the occasion and tightened it around his leg above the wound. He winced despite himself as he cinched it taut before tying it off.

The other students stood around him, stunned into silence, their faces pale. Will wiped the blade of his sword clean on his already ruined trousers, then hobbled over to his sheath and put it away. Addressing the others, he said, "Would anyone like to help me to the Healing and Psyche building? I don't think I'll be fit to participate in class today."

It was then that Instructor Rhodes walked into the gym. The older man knew something was off as soon as he entered. "What are you lads doing?" he asked loudly, then his eyes fell upon Dennis' body and the spreading pool of blood. "Sweet Temarah's tits! What the hell happened?"

"Dennis challenged me to a duel and won, so I apologized," said Will, feeling woozy. Lack of sleep and loss of blood were taking their toll on him. He leaned on Matthew. "They'll tell you," he added, his head beginning to sag.

CHAPTER 15

"He's waking up," said a man's voice from somewhere nearby.

Will rolled his head to one side, searching for the source of the voice. After a moment, his eyes came into focus and he spotted an older man standing nearby. The man's hair was white—what remained of it, for he was mostly bald. He stared down at Will over a belly that had a distinctly rotund shape.

His head was pounding and his breathing was too fast. Will could feel his heart racing in his chest, which only exacerbated the throbbing headache that was beginning to make itself known to him. He stared up at the unfamiliar face. "I hope so."

"What's that?" asked the man.

"I hope I'm waking up," said Will breathily. "Otherwise this is a shitty dream. I have higher expectations for my dreams than this."

"Young man, do you know where you are?"

The world swayed as his eyes rolled in a circular fashion. "No," Will answered faintly. How many people were in the room? He could see several other shapes standing off to one side, and he struggled to focus his vision on them.

"You're in the main operating room of the Healing and Psyche building," said the man. "Be grateful they got you here in time."

One of the figures was definitely female, though her figure was obscured by a loose gown. An odd-looking cap covered her head, hiding her hair.

"One of the large veins in your leg was torn. You almost bled to death."

"Which one?" asked Will curiously.

The man frowned. "Excuse me?"

He wheezed as he tried to clarify, "The saph—saphenous vein, or the femoral vein?"

"Does it matter? I'll explain everything when you're feeling better," said the old man.

Will turned his head toward the woman. “Is there someone smarter I can talk to?” he asked drunkenly. “This fellow’s a fucking idiot.” He tried to laugh but couldn’t catch his breath.

The balding man stepped back. “He’s delirious.”

Will heard a familiar voice respond. “His mother is a healer in the village he comes from.”

“I guess that explains his questions on anatomy,” said the man.

“Thank you for everything you’ve done, Doctor Morris,” said the woman. Her voice was agonizingly familiar.

“It was probably a waste,” said the doctor. “The Spry family will be asking for his head on a platter.” He walked away. “I’ll be back in a little while.”

The woman turned to the others. “I’d like a few minutes alone with him.” The other figures filed out. Then she came closer, leaning over until Will could see her face. “Will, do you know who I am?”

He blinked. It was Selene, and the first thing that popped into his mind was the line King Lognion had given him. *I know who you are,* he thought, but he couldn’t say those words. Instead, he tried to shake his head. “No,” he rasped.

“You’re probably confused. There’s barely enough blood left in you to keep your heart working, much less your brain,” she responded gently.

Reaching up, Will pulled on her cap, causing it to come off. A cascade of dark locks fell forward, framing her face and tickling his cheeks. “What did you do that for?” she asked.

“I’m sorry.”

She held up the cap. “For this?”

“No. For the things I said—before.”

Selene leaned closer, studying his eyes. “So, you *do* recognize me.”

Will muttered something unintelligible.

“What was that?” She turned her ear toward him and moved her head until it was close to his mouth.

“I said, ‘no,’” he repeated, then he raised his head slightly and kissed her cheek.

Selene pulled away and gave him a stern look. “I didn’t give you permission to kiss me.”

He smiled weakly. “There’s money in my purse. Is six clima enough?”

Her features softened, and she blinked several times to clear her eyes of excess moisture. “What am I going to do with you?”

He tried to shrug but his position made the gesture difficult.

"You've been here a little over a week and you've already murdered someone," she chided him. "Do you think that's normal behavior?"

"He was an asshole," said Will. "He tried to—"

She put a finger over his lips. "I heard the story." Her expression grew thoughtful. "Who was the girl? No one seems to know."

"Her parents work for Count Spry," said Will. He still couldn't catch his breath. "Need to keep her name out of it."

"Who else knows who she is?"

"Chris Burnham and Brett Conn," he answered. "They were going to pay for turns with her. If they say anything—"

Selene nodded. "I'll make sure they know better." Then she added, "You should be more worried about what's going to happen to you. Lord Spry will want your blood when he hears you killed his son."

He looked away. "I had to do it."

Her hand gripped his chin, turning his face back toward her. "No, you didn't." A few seconds later, she asked, "Is she pretty?"

Will nodded. "Yes." He saw a hint of anger in her eyes when she heard his answer.

"Are you in love with her?"

"No."

"Why not?"

He kept his eyes firmly on hers. "There's someone else."

"Who?"

"I don't know her name," he answered.

Selene's face was a picture of conflicting emotions. "I know you recognize me."

"I don't," he said stubbornly.

"He knows I'm here," she said, her voice tense. "He'll ask me what you said. Just say it, damn you. Get it over with." Her eyes were welling with tears.

"No."

"You have to say it," she told him fiercely. "Everyone does."

Will turned his head away, closing his eyes. "Get out. I don't know who you are." *Please leave, so I can keep loving you.* Something wet landed on his forehead and a moment later he felt the light brush of lips against his cheek.

"There. We're even," she said. The only sounds he heard after that were her footfalls, as she left the room.

***

Chapter 15

The next day Will was propped up in bed, supported by several pillows. He was eating steak from a bowl. Someone had generously cut the meat for him, so all he had to do was navigate the task of getting the pieces to his mouth. He washed them down with watered beer from a clay mug that sat on a table beside the bed.

"Someone needs to castrate the jackass that cooked this," he complained around the overcooked piece he was chewing. "It's blasphemy what's been done to this meat."

Rob shook his head. He was sitting in a chair not far away. "I can't believe you have the audacity to complain about the food. You nearly died yesterday."

Will gave his friend a hard look. "Your point?"

"You whine about food the way a nobleman complains when he's brought the wrong vintage to go with his roast duck. You should just be grateful someone's feeding you."

"Just because I'm a peasant doesn't mean I have to enjoy bad food," Will said sourly.

"Most people would be happy to be on a strict red meat diet for two weeks," observed Rob.

"I would be too," said Will, "if they let me do the cooking. When I can get out of this bed, I'm going to find the man that did this and punch him in the nose."

His friend started laughing, but he stopped when a knock came from the door.

"Come in!" called Will.

Rob rose from his seat and headed for the door. "I should get going. I'm already taking my life in my hands just visiting you."

The man that entered was of average height with grey, speckled hair, a clean-shaven face, and an intense gaze. He walked over to the bed and gazed at Will over the rims of his thick glasses. "I've heard a lot about you, Mister Cartwright."

Putting aside his irritation over the state of his steak, Will decided to be diplomatic. "Then you have an advantage over me, sir, for I don't know your name." He offered his hand.

The man shook it. "Alfred Courtney. I'm the head of Wurthaven's Research Department. Professor Dulaney has described your unique ability to me at some length."

Will was surprised. He had expected another lecture or more threats about his violent behavior. "I didn't realize I was so unusual."

Professor Courtney's expression was friendly, almost whimsical. There was an air about the man, almost as if he didn't quite exist in the same mundane world everyone else was forced to live in. "Oh, but you are!" he said. "I wonder if you could be persuaded to help me with my research."

"I don't know that I would be much help," Will replied. "My only talent seems to be causing trouble."

"I'd like to study you, if you're willing," said the professor.

"That depends," said Will.

"On what, if I might ask?" said the researcher mildly.

"On how long I can continue breathing. I'm told there are a lot of people who are very upset with me."

Professor Courtney nodded. "I've been talking to the chancellor and vice-chancellors about that. I believe there's a good chance we can keep you out of harm's way, for a time at least."

"I'm interested to know how."

The older man rubbed his hands together, warming to the subject. "Well, as I understand it, you've broken no laws. As barbaric as the custom of dueling is, there are still no laws against the practice. King Lognion has resisted every effort to reform the laws in that regard for the past twenty years. As misguided as I think that is, it means you can't be charged with the crime of murder. Several of your classmates have already come forward stating that Dennis Spry issued the challenge and that you merely accepted it."

"So, everything is fine?"

"Not quite," said the professor. "As you know, the duel was not a duel to the death, but rather to first blood. To make matters worse, you've already admitted to losing, which means your opponent's death occurred after the duel should have officially ended."

By a fraction of a second, thought Will dourly. "You just said I wasn't guilty of murder, though."

"You aren't," agreed the professor. "But you're still open to a claim of wrongful death. Once the news reaches Count Spry, he is almost certain to demand a blood-price."

That didn't sound very reassuring. "What's that?"

"When someone is found to be at fault for the death of another, the victim's family can demand compensation," explained Professor Courtney. "You'll have to pay a hefty penalty."

"How much?"

"It varies depending on the status of the person who died. For example, a healthy laborer is valued at a hundred crowns, while a woman or child only incurs a debt of seventy crowns—"

"How much for Dennis?" insisted Will, irritated by the professor's lengthy explanation.

"A thousand gold crowns," answered the man. "The good news is that it will take at least another ten days for the news to reach Lindham, and another two weeks for a response, which gives you almost a month. So, if you're recovered enough to leave in a week, then—"

Will held up a hand. "Wait. A thousand crowns? I can't pay that! What happens if I don't have the money?"

"Oh, you'll be put in prison, of course! Lord Spry will likely ask to have custody as well. I understand he's a very vengeful man, so it will probably be quite unpleasant. But, as I was saying, it will take at least three weeks for him to make the demand, and you'll have a period of time to respond as well. If you'll start working with me as soon as you're better then I can probably gather the data I need before they haul you away," said the professor happily.

After a moment he noticed the look of dismay on Will's face and hurried to add, "I realize that you may be upset, naturally, but it's important to think of the good you could accomplish in the time you have left."

Will stared at the man as if he had gone insane. "I've already done enough good just getting rid of that sick bastard. You expect me to smile and help you with your research when I'm going to be put in prison and tortured?"

Professor Courtney held out his hands placatingly. "I understand how overwhelming it must feel, but Professor Dulaney and I have already done as much as we could for you. Did you know they were going to have you expelled? It was only our dogged determination and endless requests for leniency that convinced the chancellor to keep you on at Wurthaven. Surely that must count for something."

He's mad, thought Will. *This whole damn world is mad.* He struggled to contain his temper and probably only succeeded because his extreme fatigue made it difficult to summon the energy to scream. Sighing, he leaned back into the pillows. "I appreciate your efforts, Professor," he responded, his voice dripping with unappreciated sarcasm, "but I'm tired. I'll think about your offer if and when I find a way to come up with a thousand crowns."

The professor nodded, stepping away. "We'll talk more after you've recovered." He quietly exited the room.

"The hell we will," muttered Will acidly.

Chapter 16

Will spent a week in bed at the Healing and Psyche building before he was sent back to the dorm. Aside from Rob's one visit, he had surprisingly few visitors. One of the proctors, a man named Blake Grim, stopped in to explain his situation once again, though he did little more than restate the same facts that Professor Courtney had outlined. He was given a stern warning not to repeat his behavior, and most especially not to consider wearing his sword on the campus grounds, even though there wasn't a specific rule against doing so.

All in all, he felt strangely unchastised. Even though everyone told him he'd done something terrible, no one was going to do a thing about it. He was free to return to classes on Monday. It felt surreal when he smelled the fresh air outside as he walked back to the boys' dorm.

If not for the fact that he would probably be thrown in prison in a month or two for not paying an astronomical blood-price, it would have been completely unbelievable.

As he walked, he noticed people staring at him. If they happened to be along his path, they quickly found other places to be, and those at a safe distance whispered to one another. It was ironic, since he had tried his best to be friendly from the beginning, with the exception of Dennis Spry. "You stab one asshole through the neck, and suddenly you're a pariah," he told himself with a dark chuckle.

He hadn't made friends, but he had found infamy. He wondered if they avoided him because they feared him, or if they feared being associated with him when Count Spry's inevitable vengeance arrived. Either way, he would be alone to face it.

He spotted the resident assistant as he entered the boys' dorm. "Hi Mom," he called out amiably.

The glare she answered him with was cold and unforgiving. "Do you have business with me today, Mister Cartwright?" she asked.

Brought up short, he replied, "No, ma'am."

"Then I'd appreciate it if you didn't speak to me." She returned to the book she was reading, dismissing his existence from her reality.

"But—"

She glanced up sharply. "Do you remember our last conversation?"

He nodded dumbly.

"Then you understand why I don't trust you or wish to associate with you."

Her rejection hurt more than all the lectures he had received put together. "I understand," Will said quietly.

He made his way up the stairs and opened the door to his room. Seth looked up in alarm as he entered. "Will."

"Seth," he replied. His roommate hadn't visited once during his recovery, though he didn't blame him. Seth's situation was precarious, and the boy couldn't afford the sort of attention that being friends with Will would bring. Will climbed up to his bunk to lie down. He was out of breath from the short walk.

The saber he had used to kill Dennis Spry was sheathed and laying on the mattress. Will sat down and unsheathed it, examining the edge. There were still spots of blood on the steel, along with traces of rust. The edge still felt sharp, but his thumb detected a few rough spots. It would need some honing to get it back in perfect shape again. *Later,* he thought, storing it inside the limnthal.

He made himself comfortable, then asked, "How've you been?" There was no reply. After a few minutes, he spoke again. "I understand if you don't want to talk to me. Everyone seems to hate me now. It won't do you any good to be friends with me. I'll make sure to keep my distance outside the room, so people won't get the wrong idea." He closed his eyes.

"I don't hate you, Will," said Seth a few minutes later. "I'm scared of you."

"I hope you realize I would never hurt you, Seth."

"I'm not so sure about that."

Frustrated, Will tried to explain, "You know why I did it. You were here when I brought her back. You know what he tried to do. You heard what she said about her family. How else was I supposed to keep them from suffering for my mistake? That asshole deserved to die."

"Probably," agreed Seth, "but I don't think you understand why I'm scared."

"Explain it to me then."

"Normal people don't just murder someone in cold blood."

"It wasn't cold blood," Will argued. "It was a duel. He challenged me, not the other way around."

"No, it wasn't," said Seth quietly. "I was there when you made up your mind. You wouldn't tell us what you were planning, but you went right ahead. You decided he needed to die and then you executed your plan with no more remorse than a fisherman shows when he guts a fish. No sword? You went and bought one. Then you made certain he knew it, and you also made sure he couldn't afford to ignore you. And you were so *calm* about the whole thing. Sure, you were yelling and making a scene when you were in public, but you were completely composed when you came back to the room.

"Regular people don't do that. They get upset. They make mistakes. Most of the time they're afraid and they just swallow their pride. But you didn't do any of that. You made a decision, then you made a plan, and two days later—you shoved several feet of sharp steel through his throat in front of your gym class."

"That doesn't mean you have to be afraid of me, Seth," argued Will. "I'd never—"

"How do I know that?" interrupted his roommate. "It's like when you have a dog and it bites someone. Sure, maybe you know why the dog did it, but can you be sure they won't do it again? You're a killer, Will."

"You don't seem that afraid," countered Will. "If you really thought I was that dangerous, would you tell me all that?"

"I'm not brave, Will," said Seth. "I never have been. I've been nervous and scared my entire life. But I'm tired of living in fear. Maybe you're right. Maybe I don't think you'd do anything to me, but violence follows you. There will be more to come when Dennis' family decides to punish you for what you did.

"Maybe I didn't have any friends after coming to Wurthaven, but I felt safe. I don't feel safe anymore. Not around you."

Will sighed. "I won't argue. Everything you've said makes sense."

"Mom says I can change rooms in a few days. One of the guys in 311 is moving out," Seth informed him.

"All right." Will swallowed, trying to clear the lump in his throat. He couldn't even call Dianne 'Mom' anymore.

***

Chapter 16

Will returned to classes the next day and discovered that if he had thought he was something of an outcast before, he had been badly wrong. He'd merely been the new student. *Now* he was truly an outcast. No one talked to him directly, and whenever he passed near anyone, all conversations that were underway immediately ceased. After he was out of earshot, though, they resumed and generally the focus was on him.

With his improved hearing, he was able to pick up snippets, however. "They say he was a black scout in the army."

"What's that?"

"They're the ones who go behind enemy lines to take out important targets."

"What kind of targets?"

"They kill people, dummy. Dennis never had a chance. He was dead the minute he caught that one's eye."

"He looks too young."

"I heard that the king's daughter came personally to make sure he lived."

"King Lognion didn't want to lose his best assassin."

"Someone said he fought a demon."

"He didn't fight it; he's possessed by one. You should have seen the cold look in his eyes when he sliced through Dennis' neck. I was there."

Will just ignored it all, but day by day the rumors got more outlandish, as though his fellow students were trying to outdo one another with their tales.

Thanks to Seth moving out, he had a room all to himself, so he didn't have to worry about timing his conversations with the ring for periods when he was alone, or Seth was asleep. A few people heard him talking through the door, however, and more rumors sprang up regarding his conversations. Most said he was unhinged, while others claimed he was talking to the demon that had supposedly possessed him.

Worried that someone might break into his room, he took to keeping all his possessions in the limnthal. He polished away the rust on his sword and restored the edge to perfection, but when he returned it to storage, he left it unsheathed. Objects inside didn't spoil or rust, and he figured if he needed it suddenly in the future it would be best to have the blade bare and ready for action. He even took some time to practice retrieving and storing it again, until he could perform the action so quickly that an observer would be hard pressed to realize he was using the limnthal rather than casting a summoning spell of some sort.

The teachers in his classes stopped calling on him, and he never volunteered to answer questions, since that seemed to make it easier for everyone involved. He continued his work as Karlovic's assistant, though the Alchemy professor would probably have preferred to let him go. Will hung on to the job, however, since he knew he would need every coin he could gather, and the professor didn't have the guts to try and fire him outright.

Likewise, Professor Dulaney continued his private sessions after Spell Theory, and since Will spent most of his free time practicing in his room, he mastered every lesson between one session and the next. He was capable of managing spells up to the second order within two weeks of returning to his studies, and he made a point of learning the silence spell from Arrogan's book. He felt confident he would be capable of the unlocking spell within another week or two.

His first real problem came at the end of his second week after returning to class. He remembered that he still had a piece of armor to pick up from the armor-smith's shop, but when he attempted to leave through the gate, the guard stepped out to block his path.

"What's this?" asked Will.

"I'm afraid you aren't allowed to leave the campus grounds," cautioned the guard. "Chancellor's orders."

Will frowned. "I'm not under arrest. I've been charged with no crime."

The man was sweating nervously in his mail hauberk. *Is he scared of me? He's armed and armored and I'm not even carrying a weapon.* "If you try to leave, I'll be forced to—"

"Do you honestly think you could stop me?" asked Will curiously.

The guard's eyes went wide. "Are you threatening me?" His hand was on his sword now.

Will held up his hands. "No. I'm asking a simple question. You're wearing mail and padding, plus you're at least ten years older. I could just run around you. The gate's pretty wide. I doubt you could catch up."

The guard glared at him, his fear beginning to fade. "As I was saying, if you leave, I'll be forced to report it to the proctors. The chancellor has ordered us to ensure you stay on college grounds, for your own safety. I'm not sure what he'll do if you disobey him."

"All right," said Will, retracing his steps. "I didn't mean to make you nervous. I used to be in the army, you know. I have a lot of respect for men who are just trying to do their jobs and keep order."

The guard didn't say anything as he walked away. On the way back, he considered his problem. If he'd still had friends, he would have simply asked one of them to make the trip for him, but he didn't think that was currently an option. Not unless he was willing to resort to intimidating people.

Shaking his head in disgust, he returned to his room and resumed his new favorite activity, practicing his spellcraft. The lessons Professor Dulaney gave him weren't particularly interesting. All the spells involved practical tasks needed for artificers, etching turyn-sensitive runes in objects, polishing metal, annealing steel, or increasing the hardness of alloys. The only spell he'd found remotely useful for him in the present was one that sharpened knives, but he'd already taken care of the maintenance on his sword the old-fashioned way by the time he learned it.

The one thing the spells did do for him, however, was improve his precision and skill, helping him to gain the experience he needed to attempt ever more complex spell constructs.

Back in his room, Will summoned Arrogan's *Practical Magic* and resumed his work on mastering the unlocking spell. After a few hours of that, he grew tired and examined his ring. Two weeks without meaningful conversation had left him feeling lonely, but he wasn't sure he was ready to face the ring's harsh criticism.

"Are you there?" he asked.

"That's a stupid question, as usual," responded the ring.

Will smiled, feeling grateful for the ring's rough response. *I really am losing it. I'm starting to like abuse,* he thought. "I survived the duel," he informed his inanimate partner.

"I already knew that, oh master of the obvious. How is it working out for you? Never mind. I just remembered—I don't give a damn."

"Not so well," he admitted. "I wasn't expelled, but they won't let me leave the grounds and no one will talk to me anymore."

"Ah, to be so lucky," sighed the ring.

"What do you mean?"

"I have this idiot who talks to me incessantly," explained the ring. "I'd kill to have your problem."

"Killing is what got me this problem."

"And I warned you, didn't I?" replied the ring sourly.

"Besides," said Will. "I'm starting to go crazy without anyone to talk to. Don't you get bored being trapped in there without any conversation?"

"I don't experience time," said the ring.

"Huh?"

"Listen, dumbass, don't you think it would be exceptionally cruel to trap an intelligent mind in an object and then force it to wait in darkness and isolation for days or weeks? Even Aislinn isn't that cruel. The magic is such that I basically cease to exist when you aren't talking to me. You should do more of that, by the way."

"Oh." Now that he thought about it, it made sense.

"So, what did you want?"

"Conversation," said Will. "I'm getting lonely."

"Fuck me," swore the ring. "Please melt me down. I can't take any more of this slow torture."

Will laughed. "Maybe you can help me with a problem."

"I'm afraid to ask."

"I already mentioned they won't let me leave the grounds, and I don't have any friends to make the trip for me, so—"

The ring finished his sentence, "You want to sneak out. How original."

"Well? Can you help?"

"You've already got Arrogan's book," reminded the ring. "Why don't you look through it? There's a spell in there for climbing if I remember correctly."

"How complex is it?" asked Will.

"It isn't too hard."

"I mean what order is it," Will clarified.

"Order? What the hell does that mean?"

"And here I thought you held all the knowledge of a master wizard," Will teased. "They classify spells by their complexity here. Currently I'm able to handle up to second-order spells, but I think I'm close to managing third."

"What kind of fussy, ostentatious bullshit are they teaching wizards these days?" exclaimed the ring. "Back in Arrogan's day you just worked until you could do something. Nobody wasted time *classifying* spells. You kept at it until you could do what you needed, whether it was complicated or not."

"It's just a way of categorizing—"

"It's a load of shit is what it is. Take my advice. Don't just sneak out. Get out and keep going. If you stay in this place too long, they'll fill your head with so much crap you might as well cut your own balls off as soon as try to cast a *real* spell."

Will shook his head. "Well, how did they teach spellcraft back in the day? Surely you didn't take a new apprentice and expect him to start with something like the unlocking spell right away, did you?"

"Of course not! We started with easy spells, but we didn't have to make up fancy systems to classify them."

"Then what did you call them?"

"Well, there's very easy, easy, average, sort of hard, really hard, and please-kill-me-now-since-no-one-should-ever-be-forced-to-try-this-because-it's-so-fucking-difficult."

Will started laughing so hard it took him a minute before he could catch his breath. "All right. I concede. Your system is better."

"Damn right it is. What does 'second order' even mean?"

"The silent thief spell in Arrogan's book is what they consider a second-order spell these days," explained Will. "The unlocking spell is in the range of third-order, I think."

"Then the climbing spell should be no problem. It's easy, like the silence spell."

"I'll look it up then."

"Are we done?" asked the ring hopefully.

"Yes," said Will. "And thanks, I feel better now."

"You're making me sick. I'd vomit if I had a mouth—or a stomach."

Will was still chuckling as he took out *Practical Magic* again and began thumbing through the pages. After the unlocking spell came a variety of cleaning spells, some for laundry, others for floors, and one interesting one that was labeled 'Instant Bath.' As Dulaney had previously said, it appeared that most wizards did use individual spells to clean specific things. He hoped he would someday be good enough to learn Selene's masterpiece so he could forego the others. As it stood currently, if he wanted to clean himself, he'd have to disrobe, use one or two spells to clean his clothing, and then a separate spell to bathe himself.

Even so, he would have killed to have such an ability when he'd been in the army.

Turning another page, he found the spell the ring had mentioned. It was simply titled, 'Climbing, for Fun and Profit.' Will climbed into bed and began to study the page.

CHAPTER 17

Fencing class the next morning followed the same pattern that it had since he'd returned from his injury. Will did exercises to stretch out his body and particularly his thigh, while everyone else avoided him. He hadn't been up to sparring during the first two weeks, but his body was recovered enough for it now. Even so, no one wanted to engage with him. No surprise there.

Composition was a disaster. Professor Conrad gave him terrible marks for his latest essay, as usual. The only bright spot was that she said nothing to him in front of the other students, so he was spared from embarrassment.

History was rather interesting that day, however, as Professor Fontenot got diverted down a tangent during the lecture. "I would like to stress that you must read the historical documents we have with a certain degree of skepticism," she said.

"In particular, the birth and death dates of some historically significant wizards are simply impossible. Many of them claimed to have lived for centuries, and while the writings that we have confirm this, it was very likely that the writers of the period simply believed what everyone believed, that it was true.

"Given our modern understanding, and the dissipation of the myths and ignorance surrounding the use of magic, we know without a doubt that the claims of extreme longevity, or perhaps immortality, were nothing more than a show of smoke and mirrors. Very likely, the wizards of the time wanted to protect themselves by obscuring their most obvious weakness, the fact that magic use shortened their lives. In fact, they may have been desperate to believe their own stories, in order to avoid the very real fear of dying.

"Further evidence of these deliberate acts of obfuscation can be seen in many of the spells that have been passed down from that time. As many of you know—or should know—if you've been paying attention in Spell Theory—we do not include very many ancient spells in our curriculum. The reason for that is very simple. A large number of the spells we have from that time would significantly shorten your life. A select few might kill the person attempting them with the very first cast.

"In years past, we lost a few students every year when they attempted to 'rediscover' the glory of the past, and because of that we keep many historical texts under lock and key now, to protect the foolish and unwary," she finished. Melinda Fontenot shook her head. "I've gotten off topic. Returning to our discussion for today, can someone tell me what started the Terabinian War for Independence?"

A girl near the front, Heather Nelson, raised her hand. "The Betrayer wanted power and killed his teacher, Valemon."

His teacher? thought Will. *Valemon was his student, not the other way around.*

Professor Fontenot shook her head. "That's a popular theory among the less educated, but it ignores the context of the time. The rise of the Prophet and the cult that followed him were definitely factors that led to the split between our nations today, but the underlying pressures of the period were what led to the Prophet's popularity.

"The deeper cause can be traced back almost a hundred years before that, to the beginnings of demon worship in what we now call Shimera, though at the time it was considered part of Barsta. By the time the Prophet emerged, the cult of Madrok had pushed the barbarians out of Shimera to where they now reside, in modern Barsta. The cult had begun to move outward, and since they found the lands of Faresh to be inhospitable, they were starting to make inroads into Greater Darrow.

"While the wizards of that time had convinced the masses that they were powerful and near-immortal, they were in fact quite weak. No lone mage could hope to stand against a demon whose slightest touch was fatal," explained the professor.

Bullshit, thought Will, wishing he could argue openly.

"When Valemon first discovered the elementals and created the heart-stone enchantment, Greater Darrow was already in a state of crisis. While none of us would wish to be subject to his aberrant religious doctrines, the fact remains that without his discovery we would all likely be serving as slaves to Madrok by now, whether as adherents or as sacrifices."

Will couldn't take it anymore. He didn't know how it was done, but from what Arrogan and Aislinn had both told him, elementals hadn't been *discovered*, they were created. He raised his hand.

Professor Fontenot glanced at him and then started to move on, but he was too stubborn to be ignored. "I have a question," he announced loudly.

She gave him a look of long suffering. "Yes, Mister Cartwright?"

"You said Valemon discovered elementals. Where did he find them? Are there congruence points that lead to elemental planes?"

The teacher gave him an angry glare. "No one knows. After Arrogan murdered the Prophet, the War for Independence began, and once that was over, he made a very determined effort to eliminate every one of his former friends and allies in this country who might have preserved that knowledge. Some have even suggested that the Betrayer was in fact an agent of Madrok and that by eliminating sorcery he hoped to strip our nations of their protection against the demon worshippers."

"My point," said Will, "is that we don't know where the elementals come from. You're making a leap of faith in assuming they came from elsewhere and weren't simply created in some fashion. If they came from another plane, surely we would have found evidence of it by now."

Professor Fontenot closed her eyes and took a deep breath before responding. "I can't fault your logic, but the same applies to the idea that they were created whole cloth from nothing."

"Not from nothing," argued Will. "According to the records of the time, wizards traveled through congruences and had a less antagonistic relationship with the fae. That's no longer true. Isn't it possible that Valemon was stealing the materials he used to create elementals? Or that perhaps he was using spirits or creatures from Faerie to produce them? That would explain both the current antagonism between us and the fae as well as provide a motive for Arrogan's actions."

The professor's face reddened. "What could possibly justify his murder of both his monarch and his fellow colleagues, the wizards and sorcerers of the time? Do you think such violence can be excused?"

Will was on his feet now. "Speaking from personal experience, I believe that there are absolutely circumstances that might force someone to violent action. Whether such is justified or not is a matter for laws and courts to decide."

"And yet Arrogan was never caught and judged," said the professor. "Those with power must be doubly wary, for it is harder for them to be brought before the courts." Her eyes were piercing as she stared at Will. "Indeed, some killers are never brought before a judge."

"Not if they haven't broken any laws," answered Will, acid in his voice. "Especially not when my supposed victim was the one who was abusing his power and the law to avoid justice."

"Get out," snapped Melinda Fontenot.

Will left, and the class released a collective sigh of relief as the tension in the room finally began to dissipate.

He was angry, with himself, with the teacher, with the world. *I shouldn't have spoken up in class,* he told himself. *I knew no good would come of it.* He went back to his room and worked on the climbing spell until it was time for lunch.

After that he forced himself to go to his Math and Spell Theory classes. The thought of skipping was attractive, but he knew if he started, he wouldn't be likely to stop. The only way to deal with the negative pressure bearing down on him was to keep showing up.

He spent more time on his spellcraft after his classes were done, feeling a sense of pride in the fact that he was already able to reliably put the climbing spell together. He hadn't actually released it and tested it out yet, nor could he remember it completely without referring to the book, but he was definitely improving.

After supper he headed to the Alchemy building for his evening's work with Professor Karlovic. The work was still new, but it was only mildly interesting. Some of it was manual labor, and the rest was planning the next stages of whatever project the professor wanted to pursue, as well as double-checking his math. It was thoroughly practical, and good experience, but he wasn't learning anything new.

The Alchemy professor was one of the few teachers who didn't seem to care about what he had done. Or perhaps he was simply too pragmatic to bother thinking about it.

"Our numbers don't agree," said Karlovic as Will showed him his check result. "Do it again."

"I don't think I made a mistake," said Will. "Maybe you should redo yours."

The professor tsked at him. "That's why I'm paying you. If you get the same answer a second time then I'll redo mine, but only then."

Will couldn't argue with that logic. Especially when he spotted his mistake a few minutes later. Their answers matched after that.

"That's a relief," said Karlovic. "I really didn't want to do it all over again."

Feeling almost relaxed in the presence of another human being, Will let down his guard and began to talk. "Professor?"

"Mm-hmm?"

"They tell me that I'll probably have to pay a blood-price for Dennis Spry's death, a thousand crowns."

"It's a safe bet," agreed his teacher.

"And I don't have that sort of coin," added Will.

"Then you'll need a rich patron if you want to stay out of prison," observed the professor dryly. "I heard Princess Selene visited you."

"I can't ask her," said Will. "I can't even see her." He didn't want to explain the complicated relationship he had with King Lognion's daughter. "Is there anyone in the college who might help? Professor Courtney seemed interested in getting my help for his research."

"Very few at Wurthaven could afford that kind of outlay without bankrupting themselves, and those that could—won't. And Alfie, for all his success, certainly doesn't have that sort of money," Karlovic informed him.

"Isn't there a way I could earn the money?"

The professor's eyes narrowed. "What are you suggesting?"

"You told me before that there are potions we don't make because there's no way to produce them just by concentrating natural essences, old-fashioned recipes. Some of those must be pretty valuable."

His teacher sighed. "You're asking me to help you burn some of your life in exchange for money."

Will couldn't tell the man it wouldn't be dangerous for him, but then he didn't need to. "It's either that or live a very short life in Count Spry's prison."

"Even if you are a natural transducer, as Professor Dulaney has been telling me, you'll still pay a significant price. If a normal person was lucky enough to have a fifty-percent efficiency from their affinity, some of those potions can cost a person the equivalent of a week or two of their life. If you really can manage it with nearly a hundred-percent efficiency, you'd still be using up half that much of yourself."

"What's the most valuable potion that people still make and sell?" asked Will.

"I don't know what other people are willing to sacrifice in their own labs—"

Will shook his head. "I mean a potion that still has a market. One that's common enough that there's regular buyers."

His teacher rubbed his chin. "I guess that would be either a potion of blood cleansing, or a universal antidote."

"What are those?"

"A blood cleanse is used when a patient has a septic wound or a serious infection. The universal antidote is a potion that nullifies the effects of most poisons and drugs. There's not as much of a market for the antidote, however. It's mainly bought by wealthy merchants or rich nobility."

"Do the healers here buy the blood-cleanse potion?"

Karlovic nodded. "They do. Every year there's a few Alchemy students who are desperate enough to make them to pay their tuition. Just one dose costs a person roughly two weeks of their life, though, or one week for you, assuming Dulaney is right."

Correction, none, thought Will. "How much do they pay for it?" asked Will.

"Usually about nine gold crowns."

Will did the math. He'd need to make a hundred and twelve potions to earn a thousand gold. "Will you give me the formula for it?"

His teacher had done his own math. "Will, you're talking about using up two to four years of healthy life for this."

"You said other students do it sometimes," Will countered.

"Two or three times," said Karlovic in exasperation. "I'm not even comfortable with that. Using students to produce such things is an abuse of power. Even if they want to do it. As a teacher, I'm against leveraging the alchemists of the future to satisfy the demands of the wealthy in the present. That's the whole point of my effort here. Producing potions that don't cost young men and women their life's blood to create."

Will returned his teacher's gaze evenly. "I'm against people abusing their power too. That's how I wound up in this situation. If I don't do something soon, I won't have much of a life left to waste."

"And what about the next time?" challenged Karlovic. "Sure. Let's say you solve your problem this way once. What happens later when you need money again? And trust me, it will happen. You'll do the same thing. Then, before you know it, you're twenty-five in a body that feels sixty."

"That's my choice," said Will. "At least I'll have made something that helps people."

His teacher rubbed his face, then got up and left the room. He returned five minutes later with three pages in his hands. The ink was still drying. "Here. I copied them out for you."

"Thank you."

"One is for the blood-cleanse, the second is the antidote potion, and the third is just for men."

"For men?" Will was confused.

Karlovic nodded. "For men who have trouble in bed. It's quite popular. I'm fairly sure it could be adapted to take advantage of my methods, but I haven't done so yet, so the demand is still fairly high. It also takes less of your own turyn to produce."

"Trouble in bed?" asked Will. "You mean…" He made a rude gesture with his arm and fist.

"Exactly," chuckled Karlovic. "It's a more common problem than you probably realize at your age."

"How much does it sell for?"

"A gold crown each."

He whistled, trying to imagine who would pay so much money for a single night of—he stopped there. He already knew the sort of people who were willing to pay that and more. People like Chris Burnham. His classmate hadn't had a physical problem—that he knew of, anyway—but he'd been willing to pay much more for access to sex. He hoped the men buying the potion were using it with their wives, or at least with someone willing. Will decided he would save that one for last, if he couldn't sell enough of the others.

"How much will you charge me to use the equipment in one of the smaller workshops?" asked Will.

"Nothing," said his teacher.

"That doesn't seem fair."

"You've already paid a fee to use the lab here, and what you're doing will help others. I won't be a party to exploiting you by increasing your cost. You will have to pay for materials and ingredients, however, or any glassware if you break it."

"I'll make sure you don't regret this, sir," said Will gratefully.

Karlovic sighed. "Just don't kill anyone else."

Will smiled. "I'll keep that in mind." *But I won't promise it.* Thus far, life had put him in violent situations too often to believe it wouldn't happen again eventually.

Chapter 18

Will returned that evening with both the formulas and several lists of materials and their respective prices. He spent a little over two hours calculating his costs and what his profit would be on each potion if he was able to sell them at the expected price.

The blood-cleansing potion seemed to be the most reliable source of income. The materials would cost roughly a gold crown for each potion, which meant his initial estimate had been slightly optimistic. He would actually need to make around a hundred and twenty-five of them to pay the blood-price, and that was assuming that the price didn't drop when he tried to sell so many potions.

The excitement of having found a solution to his problem made it impossible for him to sleep, however. So, he spent a half an hour practicing his spellcraft, then went downstairs. It was still an hour before Dianne would lock the doors—enough time for a walk.

A stroll along the wall that the entrance was in would fill the time nicely. He wanted to see if there were other guards or watchers, and the easiest time to do that without being seen was at night. His visual advantage made the task almost trivial.

Will returned to the dorm just in time. He hadn't found any guards, patrols, or watchers. Aside from the guard at the gate, Wurthaven's perimeter was completely unguarded. Will guessed he should have expected as much though, it was a school after all, not a military camp or a lord's fortress. A thirty-foot wall was enough to discourage all but the most reckless of souls.

Back in his room, he decided to test the climbing spell. With the book open, he managed to construct the spell in under half a minute, and when he released it, he felt the turyn sweep over him, causing his hands, knees, and feet to tingle.

He put both hands against the wall where they stuck with incredible force. Try as he might, he couldn't pull them free. In the end he was forced to dismiss the spell so he could consult the description in the book, where he quickly discovered his mistake.

In order to facilitate climbing and simultaneously prevent falls, the spell required three points of contact at all times, two hands plus a knee or foot, or two knees and one hand, etc.… There were multiple possible combinations. As soon as a fourth contact point was achieved, one of the others would be released according to a given order. If the climber had two hands and one of the lower contact points attached, as soon as the other leg was brought into contact one of the hands would be released, according to whichever had been in contact with the climbing surface longest.

It wasn't the most elegant way to implement such a spell, but Will could understand that trying to create a spell that relied on a more complicated system would likewise have been much more difficult to cast. Selene's cleaning spell was a perfect example—the more intelligent a spell was in its behavior, the more its complexity increased.

He cast the spell again and put his hands on the wall of his room. Then he brought his leg up and felt his knee stick. It wasn't until he had brought his other leg up and it had made contact that one of his hands came free, enabling him to reach upward. Once it was in place, his first knee came loose. Once he had gotten the knack of it, he could ascend fairly quickly, and even if he went too fast and tried to move the wrong limb, he couldn't fall. He had to move the correct body part to continue.

Working his way upward, he reached the ceiling and kept going. Will grinned as he looked down. He was hanging upside down now. Moving on, he reached the opposite wall and started down headfirst. Things didn't get awkward until he reached the floor. At that point his options were to continue climbing or to reposition himself until his feet were beneath him. He chose the latter and then dismissed the spell.

"Not bad," he told himself, feeling a sense of pride.

He practiced constructing the spell several more times, then went to bed.

The next morning, he went to Fencing practice, and feeling positive, he managed to convince one of his classmates, Matthew Holmgren, to spar with him. His leg was stiff, which cost him most of the points, but he still felt good about it.

Composition class went horribly, as usual, and History was an exercise in frustration. Once it was over, though, he left the building and set out for his adventure. Skipping lunch, he would have three hours to get to the armor smith's shop and return. Will kept an eye out for observers as he passed the dorms and headed on to the place he planned to cross the wall.

There were several hundred yards between him and the nearest building, as well as numerous trees and bushes, so being seen wasn't a concern, so long as he wasn't followed and no one else happened to be walking nearby. He cast the climbing spell without having to resort to double-checking the book, then made his way to the top of the wall.

One the other side was the lane that would eventually pass the college gate before continuing on toward the royal palace. Beyond it were more buildings. Will waited until the road was clear before descending the other side of the wall. Whistling a merry tune, he began heading for his destination.

He was almost to the city market when he felt something that made him stop. Will studied the people around him but saw nothing unusual. He was surrounded by the usual townsfolk, a mixture of citizens, merchants, sellers, buyers, men, and women. They all seemed ordinary, but he couldn't shake the feeling of *wrongness.* Squinting, he looked again, paying close attention to the turyn in the air.

His eyes were drawn to a wooden post that held up the awning of a building ahead. Will moved closer and adjusted his vision, increasing its sensitivity to turyn. There was a handprint on the wood. *No, not a handprint, a paw print,* he realized. Faint scratches marred the wood where the tips of the claws would have rested. His newly sensitized eyes could just barely make out the shape, which was composed of traces of black turyn. *A demon?* "How can that be?" Will muttered.

He was in the middle of Cerria, the capital city of Terabinia. Warlockry was outlawed, and Priests of Madrok were even less welcome, if that was possible. Who would dare bring a demon into the city?

"Are you looking to buy rushlights, sir?"

The man addressing him was looking out from the door beneath the awning. He wore an ordinary cloth cap over his head and had a round, friendly face. Since learning the light spell Will had no need of cheap lighting, but he was curious about the mark he had found. "Not today, but if you don't mind, I'll see the quality of them. I may need some in the near future," Will answered. He followed the man through the door.

Inside he saw what he'd expected, bundles of dried rushes that had been soaked in fat. They were commonly used in place of candles, due to their cheap price. Will pretended to examine them while he used his turyn-sensitive vision to search for more traces of demonic essence. He found none.

"Thanks for letting me look," he told the stranger, staring at the man's shoulder. He wondered if there might be a dark tattoo on the skin underneath the man's doublet.

Resuming his journey to the armorer's shop, he reminded himself that he had no reason to suspect the trader, aside from the claw print outside, and that might have come from a demon that had merely passed by the man's shop. Will kept his eyes open the rest of the way, alert to any further signs.

Byron Waters was happy to see him when he stepped into the shop. "I thought perhaps you'd decided not to pay," said the heavily bearded man.

Will shook his head. "I apologize for worrying you. I was injured and forced to stay abed for quite a while."

"You're still alive, so I presume it was somewhere other than where the brigandine would have covered."

Will patted his thigh with one hand. "I got a saber point through the meat and into the bone."

"You're the duelist from Wurthaven!" exclaimed Byron. "The story's been all over the city."

Will grimaced, then gave a weak smile, holding up both hands. "That's me."

"You came to order that armor far too late for your duel I, think," said Byron.

He shrugged. "Actually, I really wanted it for now."

The armorer nodded in understanding. "You expect Count Spry will send men after you in an alleyway one of these days." He walked toward the other room. "It's in here."

The brigandine vest was smaller than most of the others in the room, since it was made to go under his clothes. The exterior was covered in navy blue linen with silvery metal rivets showing through every inch or so. Turning it inside out, Will saw that the linen padding beneath was slightly thinner than his gambeson, but it would probably be enough to prevent the small plates from being driven into his skin.

"Again, I want to warn you," said Byron. "This isn't proper armor. If you really want to be safe, you'll get a proper brigandine and wear it over a full gambeson, or better yet, a gambeson and a mail shirt. And you'd have to have another made, because this one will fit too closely to go over anything else."

"That's fine," said Will. "This is exactly what I wanted." He took off his tunic and tried his new piece of armor on, testing the fit. "I have a gambeson and mail shirt, but I can't wear them at Wurthaven. Plus, I want something hidden. If I'm attacked it will probably be by surprise. If they don't know I'm wearing it, they're more likely to aim for a vital spot, which is what this covers."

"As long as they're stabbing you with a dagger or something light. If someone hits you with an axe or something big, you're going to regret it," replied Byron.

"If they're sneaking up on me it's almost certain to be something small," replied Will.

"Fair enough," said Byron. "Have you heard the news today?"

"What news?"

"The Patriarch is suing for peace. Apparently, what we did to his army in Barrowden has left them in a terrible position. Lognion's moved more soldiers there and they're afraid we'll invade them next."

Of course, Will knew what had happened, but he hadn't heard much about the aftermath, so he decided to fish for details. "I heard we pushed them out of Barrowden, but it wasn't that bad, was it?"

The shopkeeper whistled. "What rock have you been hiding under? Our army sacked their main camp in Barrowden and set fire to the entire thing. Thousands died trying to get out, and then Lognion kept them bottled up for weeks there while the survivors starved. By the time they tried to break out, they were too weak to fight. We slaughtered them. Not many made it back to Darrow. It will be years before they can field an army like that again."

Things hadn't happened exactly like that, and Will was sure the Terabinian army hadn't reached Barrowden for days if not weeks after he had set fire to the camp, but if even half of what Byron had said about the death toll was true, it was big news. *But I did the right thing,* he told himself silently. *Didn't I?*

No, he was sure he hadn't been wrong. If he hadn't done it the Patriarch's army would have pushed past Branscombe and the war would be raging on Terabinian soil. But would more people have died, or fewer? Was the highest good defined by what path led to the lowest cost in human lives, or was it more important that they were enemy lives, rather than Terabinians?

But they started it, he reminded himself. *They attacked us.* It would have been easy if he knew for certain that were true, but his recent study of history, even the skewed history taught at Wurthaven, had shown him that every event had deep roots. Every war led to more wars later on, and it was inevitably the soldiers and civilians who paid the price in blood, while those who instigated the conflict hid behind stone walls.

Will handed over the ten crowns he owed the man and put his tunic back on, over his new armor. Twisting and turning, he took note of the noise it made, but he left the shop and found a place out of view before casting the silence spell on himself. He was pleased with the result. Other than being slightly thicker around the chest, it would be nearly impossible for someone to know what he had on beneath his clothing without touching him.

He supposed that a particularly acute observer might notice the fact that his clothing didn't rustle or make any noise, but he figured that was unlikely. Satisfied, he began his return journey to Wurthaven.

Once again, he waited until there was a clear space on the road before casting the climb spell and ascending the wall. He immediately noticed a difference in his movement. While walking, the armor hadn't affected him, but it made his torso noticeably stiffer as he climbed. Not enough to be a problem, but it was something to consider in the future. His mail and gambeson wouldn't have interfered at all, aside from their weight; both items were extremely flexible.

At the top of the wall he noticed a couple below him, kissing. Sitting on top of the wall was conspicuous, so he climbed back down to the street and waited half an hour, feeling foolish. Thankfully the lovers were gone when he made his second attempt, and he was able to return to his dorm room without incident.

He only had a few minutes left before his Math class, so he summoned some bread from his limnthal and ate half of a large bun before storing the rest once more. Then he went to class.

When his classes were finally over, he returned to the dorm, but Dianne stopped him as he was heading for the stairs. She had a package for him. He was afraid it might be a notice from Count Spry, but when she handed it to him, he knew that couldn't be it. It was a heavy parcel wrapped in brown paper.

He took it to his room before opening it, whereupon he found a study journal inside. He pulled back the cover and saw the pages were covered in neat, delicate handwriting. Scanning the lines, he realized it was the notes for his Composition class. He thumbed through the journal and found that farther on, it reached the current point in their lectures. Past that was a similar copy of the notes from his History class.

There was no note from the giver, but he thought he recognized the handwriting as that of Janice Edelman. *Maybe she doesn't hate me. It must have taken days to make a copy.* The journal hadn't been cheap either.

Chapter 19

The rest of the week went about as expected. Janice's notes helped, but Will's Composition class was still brutal. Even when he managed to turn in a decent essay, Professor Conrad refused to consider its merit because his penmanship was so terrible. He felt like he was improving, but it seemed impossible he'd ever manage to meet her expectations.

His other classes were all right, though. Even his History professor treated him fairly, although she clearly didn't like him. Professor Karlovic released him from his duties as an assistant temporarily, in order to give him more time for his private projects.

When Will had asked about his class credit, Professor Karlovic had given him an interesting answer, "If you can make these potions and pay off a thousand-crown debt, then you've more than exceeded my expectations. Let me know when you can come back to work."

It was the end of the week and Will was currently staring at the glassware he'd set up for the first step of his personal salvation. On the left were two vessels stacked one on top of the other. The bottom one held water while the one above it contained crushed borage leaves. From the top of that vessel a glass column emerged and then connected to a condenser—a double-walled glass tube—that descended at a forty-five-degree angle to the right. The outer layer of the condenser connected to tubes that fed water in and out, keeping the inner wall of the condenser cool.

The bottom of the condenser connected to a separator, a short glass column that had a valve at the bottom that opened into the final receiving vessel. Once the water in the first vessel began to boil, steam would rise through the borage leaves, releasing and vaporizing the oils and carrying them along to the condenser, where both would condense and drip into the separator. The oils would form one layer and the water, or hydrosol, would form a second layer. The valve on the separator could open to allow the layers to drain into the receiving vessel separately.

The entire process would take him several hours, especially once he factored in cleaning all the glassware afterward. He'd also have to repeat the process several times, since he needed extracts from not just borage, but also garlic, nasturtium, and verbena. In each case, once the oil was collected, he would have to reinforce the turyn naturally present until it was sufficiently potent.

The recipe that Professor Karlovic gave him included descriptions of simple spell constructs that would essentially filter and constrain the turyn he produced to match that of the essential oil, but when he'd asked his ring about it, he had received a different answer.

"They're idiots," said the ring. "Although I'm amazed that they've found methods for overcoming their handicaps."

"Handicaps?"

"They're using transducers in their artifice, and spell constructs in their alchemy, all to get around the fact that they haven't been trained to convert turyn properly. You don't need to bother with that silliness. You just need to pay attention and match your turyn to the resonance of the turyn in the extract. It's a hell of a lot easier than going through the rest of that rigmarole. You'll get better results too. An artificial method like a transducer or a spell construct is unlikely to perfectly match the turyn in the extract."

"How will I know when it's enough?"

"A substrate can only contain so much turyn before it either starts to bleed away or the substrate explodes," said the ring. "You just keep pushing until it stops absorbing turyn."

"Explodes?" exclaimed Will.

"Don't worry, most oils don't react violently if you go too far, but be careful with the metal salts."

The final step of producing the blood-cleansing potion did involve one salt, silver bromide, but Will would just have to take his chances and hope he didn't damage any glassware.

That evening he finished his first extraction and then began infusing the borage oil with turyn. It took most of an hour, as he repeatedly exhausted himself and then waited on his body to recover by absorbing more turyn from the environment. He went through the process eleven times before the borage oil stopped accepting more turyn, then he stored it inside the limnthal.

Storing it there had also been the ring's suggestion. Karlovic's recipe had called for using an airtight brown bottle to prevent the oil's potency from degrading, but even then, it would only stay good for a few days.

The time constraint made the procedure difficult, because the other oils had similar stability problems.

A single alchemist had to limit the amount of each ingredient they produced, because they were limited by the time they needed to produce the other ingredients, infuse them, and then combine them all for the final potion.

"The limnthal solves that problem neatly," said the ring. "That's one of the reasons it was prized and considered the mark of a true wizard in my day."

"Does it stop time?" asked Will.

The ring laughed. "Don't be ridiculous. Nothing can stop time, not completely. The limnthal serves as a type of congruence point between you and a different plane, one where time moves a thousand times slower than it does here. The knowledge was a gift from the elves."

Will gaped. "Elves are real?"

"You've met Arrogan's daughter, you've had to pour troll piss around Arrogan's garden, and you have to ask if elves are real?" The ring laughed at his ignorance. "They live on a different plane, just like trolls do."

"Can I go there?" asked Will. "Are there congruence points to travel there?"

"Yes and no," said the ring. "There's only one known congruence, and they keep it a closely guarded secret. In my day it was thought that the congruence must be at sea somewhere, because the elves always arrive on ships."

"Why haven't I ever heard of them?"

"They don't come often. Time moves more slowly where they live, probably at about half the speed of time here. In my day their ships would show up only rarely, perhaps once every four or five years. But they don't dock in Terabinia or Darrow anymore. If you want to see one of them, you'd have to go to Trendham. They still trade at the port of Bondgren every few years."

"But not here. What happened?" asked Will.

"Guess."

"How should I know?"

"I'll give you a hint, lackwit, it's the same reason the fae hate us these days."

"Sorcery?" Will should have known. "When are you going to explain that to me?"

"When you're dead."

"That's not much help," said Will.

"It's not meant to be. The knowledge of how elementals are created would do you no good and might potentially do the world a great deal of harm. Arrogan worked hard to destroy that knowledge."

"He kept telling me it was evil, but it would be easier to understand if I knew *why* it was so evil."

"And it would also make you a target of anyone with power. Not that I care if you get tortured for being stupid. I won't tell you because then there'd be the possibility that you or some other idiot would use the information. As long as no one knows I don't have to worry. Anyway, we've gotten off topic. Lythia is one of the few planes that connects to ours with a slower rate of time."

"Lythia, as in the Lythial Sea?" asked Will.

"Why do you think it was named that?" replied the ring. "They called it the Lythial Sea because that's where they thought the elves came from. The elven kingdom is named Lythia."

"Oh."

"Incidentally, it's also one of the roots in the name 'limnthal.' Personally, I think it was a poor choice, though, since the limnthal connects to a more distant plane, one we'd never have discovered if it weren't for the elves. There are probably congruences from their world to the one that the limnthal uses."

In any case, the limnthal was incredibly useful for alchemy. Since time moved much slower there, Will could produce as much as he needed of each ingredient without having to do them in small batches and continually repeat the process. He finished the borage oil that evening and then used the weekend to do the rest.

Monday, once his classes were done, he completed the final step. Each potion had to be done individually and imbued with one last bit of turyn to activate it before it was stoppered and stored. Although he had produced enough of the oils and silver bromide to create nearly two hundred doses, the final activation process took him an hour for each potion, so he only had enough time to finish four blood-cleansing potions. He felt confident, however, since he could produce two to four each day from that point on, depending on his available time.

On Tuesday he finished lunch and went to the Healing and Psyche building to see if he could sell them. A young man behind a desk just inside the front entry greeted him. "Back so soon? Are you hurt again?"

Will didn't know the man's name, so he didn't attempt pleasantries. "Is Doctor Morris here? I'd like to see if he's interested in some potions."

The receptionist gave him a look of resignation. "Desperate for coin?"

"Is it that obvious?"

"Everyone knows you've got an axe over your head. It was only a matter of time before you came here. Doctor Morris doesn't take care of this sort of thing. You need to talk to Ilona Fretz. She handles supplies and logistics for the Healing department."

"Where can I find her?"

The receptionist pointed. "Down that hall. Last door on the left."

Will took the path indicated and found himself in front of a white door with a nameplate above it. He knocked and entered after hearing a response, "Come in."

The room was a stark contrast to the orderly appearance of the front lobby and just about every other part of the Healing and Psyche building. It was cluttered, with floor-to-ceiling shelves surrounding a wooden desk. The shelves were crammed with ledgers and papers, while the desk itself was barely visible. Behind it sat a dowdy woman with brown hair tied into something resembling a bun. "Can I help you?" she asked.

"I was told you handle the purchasing of potions for the hospital wing."

She looked him up and down, her face emotionless. "I do. You must be the latest sacrifice."

"That's what I'm told," said Will.

"You're the one who killed the count's son, right?" He nodded, and she continued, "You're never going to make enough to pay that blood-price."

"I intend to try. How much will you pay?"

"I'm assuming you made blood-cleansing potions." Then she stopped. "I'm Ilona Fretz, by the way."

"Will Cartwright."

"Call me Ilona," she replied. "I can offer nine crowns for a blood-cleansing potion. How many do you have?"

"Four, but I can make as many as you'll buy."

She gave him a sad look. "I wish I could say no, but if it wasn't for people like you, we wouldn't have any for our patients. Let's see the ones you've made."

The potions were in his pouch. Will drew them out and placed them on the desk, or attempted to—there wasn't enough empty space to set them down. Ilona solved his crisis by taking them from him directly and then storing them in a drawer. "You can collect the crowns from the Bursar's Office tomorrow. I'll send them a notice of credit."

"Don't you want to make sure they're properly made?"

"I will," she said. "If they aren't, you'll find out when you go to collect."

"I'll bring more at the end of the week," Will told her.

Ilona sighed. "I shouldn't say this, but it won't matter how many you bring. You'll never get the thousand crowns you need selling potions to us."

"Why not?"

"Because our budget for such purposes is limited."

Will felt his stomach clench. "How limited? Would it help if I take a lower price?"

She gave him a look of pity. "Lower it all you want, but we can't spend more than six hundred crowns on potions. That's my budget for the year. Normally, though we'd like more, there aren't enough potions coming in to come close to that figure."

"Can't you get your budget increased? I can make at least two hundred if you can buy them."

Ilona shook her head. "I don't have that sort of authority."

"If I sell them to you at a decreased cost the department could consider it an investment for the future. I'd be willing to sell them for four gold a piece if you'll buy enough to get me to the total I need," said Will desperately.

Her expression was sympathetic. "You could wind up taking ten years off your life doing something like that. Are you sure?"

He nodded.

"I'll talk to Doctor Morris about it. If he's interested, he might take it to the Chancellor's Office and see if he can get them to agree. I can't make any promises, though."

"Thank you," said Will. He left after that, unsure how he should feel. On the one hand, he had pretty much secured more than half of the thousand crowns, but on the other, he had no idea how he'd make the other four hundred crowns. Could he sell the other potions that Professor Karlovic had given him instructions for? He didn't think he could find several hundred paranoid nobles to buy the universal antidote, and even if he could, would they deal with the killer of Count Spry's son?

What about the potion for men? How would he go about selling hundreds and hundreds of those? He'd have to make nearly five hundred to cover the materials and have enough profit left over to leave him with four hundred crowns.

"One day at a time," he told himself. "Something will come up." He started snickering to himself. *That would be a good sales line for the virility potion, 'something will come up.'*

Chapter 20

He stuck to his plan during the next few days, going to classes and spending most of his free time in the evenings finishing blood-cleansing potions. By Thursday he had twelve more finished and he was already sick of making them. His classes that day were uneventful, until he met with Professor Dulaney for his private spellcraft session.

The professor was walking him through the structure of a complex transducing spell construct, something that was widely used, and which also served as the basis for the transducers that artificers used in their enchantments. The entire thing was worse than useless for Will, since he was able to transform turyn as needed, but Dulaney insisted that he needed to learn it as part of his foundation in modern spellcraft.

During a brief pause, Will asked a question that had been on his mind. “Are there demons in Cerria?”

The professor sat back, staring at him in surprise. “I should hope not. Why would you ask that?”

“I saw some black turyn,” said Will. When Dulaney frowned, he corrected himself, “I saw some turyn that possessed a void polarity.”

“You’re referring to when you saw the demon in Barrowden?”

“No, sir. I saw it in the city.”

“You’re restricted to the campus, aren’t you?”

“Well—”

The professor shook his head. “I should have known. So, you snuck out. When was this?”

“A little over a week ago,” he admitted.

“And where did you see this void turyn?”

“It was on a post holding up a shop awning. It looked like a paw print.”

Dulaney looked at him oddly. “You saw a trace left on an object?”

He nodded.

“It should have been too faint to see. There are spells to detect such things, but I don’t think a person could just spot it without some sort of aid unless the source of the turyn was right there in front of them.”

Will cursed himself. He'd forgotten that he'd amplified his vision in order to see the traces. *Nothing to do but double down, I guess.* "I can see trace amounts, if I try hard," he insisted.

The professor seemed doubtful. "Let's do a test then." He held up his hand. "You step out of the room. I'll put my hand on something in the room and channel a bit of turyn into it. If you can come in and tell me what I touched, I'll consider it proof."

"Fine," said Will, then he rose and went into the hall, closing the door behind him. After a few minutes Professor Dulaney called for him to come back in.

"Let's see what you can do."

Will glanced around the room with his normal eyesight first. As always, there were wisps of turyn floating through the air, currents that moved around and past himself and the professor. He thought there was a hint of something stronger on the bookcase, but he couldn't pinpoint it exactly where.

Dulaney studiously ignored him as he walked to the bookcase, giving away nothing. Will stared at the shelves, then adjusted his vision until the wisps of turyn around him began to glow brightly. A thumbprint appeared on the spine of one of the volumes. Will pointed to the spot. "Here. You put your thumb right there."

"Interesting!" exclaimed Dulaney. "If I hadn't just seen you do that, I wouldn't have believed it. How long will the mark remain visible to you?"

"Huh?"

"Raw turyn traces like that diffuse at a predictable rate, losing about half their intensity every thirty minutes or so. The question in my mind now is how sensitive your sight is. What's your limit? If you knew that, you could estimate how long it had been since the trace you saw in the city was left there, or at the very least you could put a rough limit on how long it had been."

Will was confused. "Wouldn't that depend on how strong the initial trace was?"

"The diffusion follows an exponential curve," said Dulaney. "Even if the initial application of turyn was very intense, it would dim quickly. If you figure out how sensitive your ability to see is, you can still get an estimate. You might be off by a few hours if the source was much stronger than expected, but even that would be helpful to know."

"Should I stay here and watch until I can't see the thumbprint any longer?"

The professor laughed. "Do it in your room. I have things to do later. I can't have you hanging around my office for however long it takes. Back to your original question, there should be no demons in Cerria. If one did somehow get in, it would be big news. Are you certain of what you saw?"

He nodded. "Very sure. Are there other things that could have produced it besides a demon?"

"None that would be any less alarming than a demon in the capital. The undead use void-polarized turyn, but necromancy is forbidden, and there hasn't been a confirmed case of anyone practicing necromancy in decades."

"What should we do?"

Dulaney gave him a direct stare. "*You* should do nothing. I'll report this to the proctors. If you do happen to see anything else like this, let me know immediately. As for sneaking out, you do understand why the chancellor ordered that you be kept within the confines of Wurthaven, don't you?"

"To punish me."

"No, to protect you," corrected his teacher. "The college can't do anything about your monetary problems, but we can try to keep you safe. Count Spry may not be patient enough to wait for you to fail to pay his blood-price, in which case he may have hired people to waylay you in the city. You should consider that before you recklessly go around disobeying the chancellor's rules."

"You're not going to report me, sir?"

Dulaney shook his head. "No. I've explained the 'why' of it. It's up to you to show some sense."

Will went back to his room after that. He didn't feel like making potions, so he decided to relax after supper. Of course, after sitting in his room for an hour or two, he got bored. His complete lack of a social life was beginning to grate on his nerves. So, he worked on the unlocking spell some more. The feeling of constructing so many runes and connecting them together was a strange one; as he got close to completing it, the spell the construct would begin to wobble, as slight imperfections in the earlier runes began to add up, making the entire thing unstable. Each time he tried it got better, but eventually it would grow too unwieldy and collapse, sending glowing sparks onto his lap where they winked and vanished.

I'm getting close, he told himself. It was just a matter of refining his control. Each time as he neared his limit, he imagined it must be similar to the feeling a juggler got when trying to add another ball to the number he could keep in the air.

He remembered Selene building her signature spell, the 'princess purification,' in front of him. At the time he hadn't known how difficult her feat was, but she had done it flawlessly. *How long did she practice to have that kind of control?* he wondered. At the time he had only been concerned with showing off his ability to take someone else's spell from their control, and he had overlooked the magnificence of her achievement.

At the moment, his highest aspiration was to be able to master her spell, to be capable of creating an eighth-order spell construct, as she had done. Lately he'd begun using some of the cleaning spells in *Practical Magic* to clean his clothes, his armor, and even his room, but having a spell like hers, one that could do it all, seemed extraordinary.

Tired of trying the same spell over and over, he turned to the next page. "Wind Wall," he read the title aloud. Then he studied the description and realized it was the spell his grandfather had used to protect himself from the crossbow bolts fired at him on the day that he died. *Almost worked,* Will reminded himself. Arrogan hadn't accounted for the fact that one of the crossbowmen would fire early, striking him before the order to fire.

Judging by the complexity, it seemed to be third-order, similar in difficulty to the unlocking spell, so he turned to the next page. "Demon Armor," read Will. "What's this?" At a glance, the spell was simpler than the previous one, probably second-order. The description said that it produced a defensive flame that encapsulated the caster's body. As he read further on, it also stated that the flames wouldn't harm people or objects. In short, it wouldn't burn anything.

Will activated the limnthal so he could talk to the ring. "What's this spell, demon armor, supposed to do?"

The ring chuckled darkly. "It looks awesome."

"That's it? It looks scary?"

"Well, it had a practical purpose once, but nobody really needs it these days."

"So, what was the purpose?"

The ring barked, "Moron, did you read the name? It's demon armor, what do you think it does?"

"Make me look like a demon?"

"Somebody give me hands so I can smack myself in the face," said the ring. "No, it protects the caster from demons! You said you saw one once, right? Did you see flames around it?"

Will shook his head. "No, it was all teeth and black smoke."

"Well, they take different forms, but one thing is true of all of them. They use a type of turyn that is the antithesis of living creatures. Do you know why most of the elementals you see are fire elementals?" asked the ring.

"I just assumed it was because fire is so destructive."

"All elementals are destructive," said the ring. "No, the reason is that at that time, when Valemon was chopping up—" the ring stopped speaking for a moment, then resumed. "I mean, when he was starting to create elementals, he had a desperate cause. The Cult of Madrok was infiltrating the Empire, what you call 'Greater Darrow' these days. They had demons, and they were damned hard to fight. Fire was the best weapon against them."

"Why?"

"It's high in energy and low in order, or physicality. That means it's one of the best types of turyn to counter demonic essence. It burns them far better than it burns people. If he'd been making elementals to fight wizards, he'd have chosen earth or water—those have a high degree of order and consequently use a lot of physical matter. Even air would be better against a human."

Will was confused. From what he had seen, fire elementals were incredibly destructive. He couldn't think of anything so terrifying as being burned alive. "Fire seems just as dangerous to me," he opined.

"To regular people, sure," said the ring. "But to a true wizard, it's the easiest type of elemental attack to nullify, because it's almost entirely pure energy. Sure, there's a little bit of plasma in there, but once you absorb or convert the turyn, it doesn't do much. You've defended yourself from fire attacks. You should remember how easy it was."

"Well, yeah," said Will, still uncertain.

"Think about what would happen if an earth elemental attacked you with a stone spike from the ground," said the ring. "If you absorb the turyn from the attack that's wonderful, but what's left? You still wind up with a goddamn piece of obsidian up your ass. So, what if the elemental can no longer control it? You're dead."

Will nodded. "I guess that makes sense, but what about demons? Why is fire so bad for them?"

"Are you really that stupid? I just explained it to you."

He sighed. "Rephrase it for me then."

"Demons have a very loose association with what we think of as physical matter. Their bodies are sometimes solid, but more often they're a loose collection of nasty things. What connects those pieces is the foul turyn they produce. Since fire is very close to its exact opposite, it destroys their essence very effectively. Think about it this way—what happened when your girlfriend fought the demon?"

"She's not my girlfriend," said Will.

"Lover, whatever you want to call her, it doesn't matter. So, when—"

"She wasn't my lover," he interjected, his face turning red.

"Fuck-friend?"

"What's wrong with you?" Will exclaimed. "No! She's a princess and I'm—no one."

"You're the last goddamn true wizard in the world," corrected the ring. "As much as I hate to admit that, you're pretty fucking important. I'd say you're worth at least three or four useless sorcerer princesses. Didn't you save her life?"

"We saved each other a few times," said Will indignantly.

"And you didn't even get laid? Tell me the truth, Will. I don't have eyes, so answer my next question honestly."

He was beginning to regret starting the entire conversation, but he played along. "What's the question?"

"Are you ugly? I don't mean regular ugly—I mean horse's ass ugly. Like the kind of ugly only a mother would love but she still wouldn't take you out in public."

Will ground his teeth together but remained silent.

"You can be truthful. It doesn't matter to me, since I can't see or smell you. Do people run screaming in the other direction when they see you on the street?"

"Are you done?"

"Almost. I'm just glad I finally understand why you don't have any friends. They're probably scared the ugly might be contagious."

Will sighed audibly.

"All right. Back to the topic at hand," said the ring. "So, when your *platonic* princess friend with the tolerance and compassion of a saint fought the demon to protect your indescribably grotesque person from the demon, she was using earth and water, right?"

"I have some objections to your description, but yes," said Will.

"And how did that work out for her?"

"It got in close and sort of covered her, then it started prying apart her stone armor and got inside."

"If she'd had a fire elemental protecting her, that wouldn't have happened. It could have surrounded her and there wouldn't be anything to pry apart. Any time the demon touched the flames it would be burned to ash. Now do you understand?"

"I see your point," said Will. "But this demon armor spell says it doesn't burn things."

"That spell predates the use of fire elementals. It was made by wizards to protect themselves. The flames would be very inconvenient if they hurt one's allies or set fire to someone's home. Trust me, they still work just as well on demons, though. The one thing to remember, though, is even though the spell has 'armor' in the name, it won't stop swords, arrows, or pretty much anything else."

"So, it isn't really a battle spell, then," said Will.

"It damn well is if you're staring down a demon," said the ring. "Other than that, it just looks wicked."

"There *are* battle magics, though, aren't there?"

"Another stupid question," answered the ring. "Of course, there are. But you won't find them in that book. There's a few other spells that are good for demons, though."

"Why aren't there some in the book?"

"Because it's titled *Practical Magic.* It's full of things you'll actually use. The climbing and unlocking spells, for example, are incredibly useful. It isn't often you need to kill someone. If that's what you want, go back home. There's a book there that has some handy spells in it for dismembering people."

"Then why are there spells for demons in the book?"

The ring paused. "Demons were a much bigger problem back then. Arrogan killed quite a few people near the end, sure, but most of his early fights were against Madrok's spawn. The only wizard who fought more demons than Arrogan was his friend, Syllanus."

The name sounded familiar. "Who was Syllanus?"

"A wizard," said the ring. "A good friend of Arrogan's. One that didn't truck with sorcerers and compromise his principles like so many of the others did. Why? Did they mention him in your history class?"

"No. I don't think so," said Will. "But it seems like I heard the name somewhere before."

Their conversation ended after that and Will packed it in for the night. He was tired, but tomorrow would be a new day.

CHAPTER 21

Will went to Fencing practice the next morning. The others were now sparring with him regularly, though no one showed any interest in talking to him. After they finished, he went to the Bursar's Office and collected his thirty-six crowns before taking the twelve potions he had made over to Ilona Fretz.

Then he returned to the dorm to clean up before his History class. Dianne Young stopped him when he came in. "There's mail for you, Cartwright."

The cold formality she treated him with still stung, but he accepted the envelopes with equanimity and took them to his room to read. One of them was simply a quick note from Professor Karlovic telling him that someone had expressed interest in acquiring some universal antidote potions. Will would need to talk to him later to find out the details.

The second letter was the one Will had been dreading. It came from the head magistrate's office rather than from Count Spry himself and it spelled out in legal terms that he'd been named as the cause of Dennis Spry's death and would be required to pay a one thousand crown blood-price. It also gave him two weeks to respond, whether by petitioning the court if he felt he wasn't at fault or notifying them that he would pay the fine.

Will went over the math in his head once more. Ilona had told him the college would only pay for another fifty blood-cleansing potions. After collecting the gold for that, he'd have just over six hundred crowns to his name. If he worked on those potions over the weekend and devoted the first two evenings of the next week, he could finish all fifty, leaving him just twelve days to figure out how to raise the other four hundred crowns.

"There has to be a way," he told himself.

The last envelope was different from the others, being smaller and carmine in color. A wax seal bearing the royal crest sealed it. Curious, Will broke the seal and removed an elegant invitation.

You are cordially invited to attend the Royal Winter Ball, which will take place in Geimhreadh, on the 24th day of Nollag, in the Year of our Lord, 460.

It went on to detail the type of attire, which was beyond his means unless he continued making money after paying off his blood-price. That didn't bother him, though. If he could manage to pull together a thousand crowns, he could find a way to come up with another twenty or thirty to pay for a fancy ball. He wouldn't have been interested at all, if it weren't for the fact that the event was being thrown by the king, which meant that Selene would almost certainly be there.

"I'm a fool for thinking of her," Will muttered. "I've got bigger problems and there's absolutely no way we could ever marry." He wanted to kick himself. *Marry?* She was a sorceress. Even if she wasn't a princess, he shouldn't be considering such a thing.

He couldn't help himself though. His mind was continually concocting fantasies in which they ran away together. He'd convince her to give up the elementals and he'd learn enough to train her in the fundamentals of wizardry that Arrogan had taught him. *That's the stupidest idea I've ever had,* he told himself, *and there are a hundred reasons why it could never happen.*

If he was smart, he'd forget about her and start thinking about women who weren't completely out of reach, such as Janice Edelman. Sure, she was probably still angry with him, but the notes she had given him proved she didn't hate him. He found her very attractive too.

Will spent several minutes trying to construct a similar fantasy involving Janice, but every time his attention wandered, her face transformed into Selene's.

He was wasting time. Stripping off his clothes and the brigandine he wore beneath them, he used a spell to give himself a bath. It wasn't as satisfying as an actual bath with water and soap, but the end result was the same. Then he used a different spell to clean his clothing before a knock on his door distracted him. It had been so long since anyone had visited him that he found himself frozen for a moment as he pondered who it could be.

Will pulled on his trousers and padded on bare feet to the door before throwing it open. "Hello?"

Janice stood in the hall, and her eyes traveled over his bare chest for a second before coming to rest on his face. Her cheeks colored as she struggled to regain her composure. "I w-wanted to tell you—" She stopped and turned away. "Could you put something on?"

He grinned gleefully. "Sorry, I didn't expect to be entertaining guests." Turning back, he snatched up his tunic and pulled it over his head. "Come in."

She shook her head. "Oh, I couldn't. I just came to apologize."

Will caught her wrist and tugged her through the doorframe before closing the door. "You don't have to apologize. We only have a few minutes before we have to leave for class anyway." He gestured to the chair while he sat down to put on his socks and boots.

"I shouldn't have come in," she said. "People might talk."

"No one saw you come in anyway," he replied. "Thank you for the notes. I recognized the handwriting."

"I feel bad for how you've been treated," she told him. "I shouldn't have avoided you. I got a letter from my parents, by the way."

"Are they well?"

Janice nodded. "It seems that Dennis' father didn't get word of the cause of your duel, or if he did, he didn't take it out on them. Unfortunately, he told them he wouldn't be sponsoring me after this semester."

"That's terrible!" exclaimed Will. "Wait, then why is he no longer sponsoring you?"

"Dennis isn't here anymore, so he doesn't need anyone to clean up after the little monster. In any case, I'll have to leave, so it was pretty pointless of me to avoid you," said Janice. "I thought maybe I could help you with Composition, at least until then." Her gaze fell on the brigandine vest. "What's that?"

"I'll show you," said Will. He needed to put it on before he could finish dressing anyway. He started removing his tunic once more and she closed her eyes. Will laughed as he picked up the armored vest and slipped it on. "I'm not bare-chested anymore," he told her. "It's safe."

Of course, the brigandine vest was still open in the front, but he was already closing it as he fastened the buckles in the front. That done, he pulled his tunic back on and cinched it around his waist with his belt. He rapped on his chest with one fist so she could hear the metallic sound of the plates inside.

"Armor? Why are you wearing armor?"

"Just being cautious." He handed her the letter he had just gotten from the magistrate.

Her eyes went wide when she saw the sum he was required to pay. "By the Holy Mother! What are you going to do?"

He explained his potion-making scheme, then added, "I can come up with six hundred, but I'm sure I'll find a way to make the rest."

She shook her head. "I still don't understand."

"Understand what?"

"Why you did it."

"You said your parents would get tossed out if Dennis started telling lies to—"

Janice sighed. "No. Why *you* did it. I had every reason to do something like that, if I'd had a way to get away with it, but you didn't. Now you're being forced to pay that enormous sum of gold. You barely know me."

Will nodded. "I'm a little stupid, my grandfather used to tell me that all the time."

"And because of me you're—"

He held up his hand. "No, you're missing the point. It wasn't because of you. It could have been anyone and I probably would have done the same thing. I have a penchant for bad decisions."

She stared at him for a moment. "I don't have much, but I still have a few crowns left over. I'll try to figure out if there's another way to get more. Maybe I could help you with the potions. You shouldn't bear the cost alone. How many years will that take off your life?"

"None," said Will. He wanted to lie about it, as he had with everyone else, but that would only make her guilt worse.

"Don't be ridiculous," she responded. "You might be stupid, but I certainly am not, and I've been paying attention in class."

"Listen," said Will. "I have quite a few secrets and I can't share most of them, for one reason or another. Maybe I can later, but all I can say right now is that using magic doesn't use up my life the way it does for everyone else."

"Are you a sorcerer? Do you have a secret elemental hidden away somewhere?"

"No. Never that," he said emphatically. "Come on. We need to leave, or we'll be late to class."

***

After his classes were done Will went to the Alchemy building and found Professor Karlovic in his office. "I got your message."

The professor smiled. "We had an inquiry and I thought you might be interested."

"How much are they paying?"

"Twenty crowns each, and they want five. Can you have them ready by Tuesday?"

Will nodded. "Definitely." He could put off finishing the blood-cleansing potions and spend Sunday working on the universal antidote. The material cost for the antidote potion was higher, but even so he would make a profit of seventy-five crowns. After that it would only take a little over three hundred to reach his goal. It seemed as though his luck was finally taking a turn for the better.

He spent the rest of the evening making preparations to create the universal antidotes, paying for the materials with some of the coin he had already made and setting up the equipment for the first steps. With that done, he went to bed at his usual time and started early the next day.

There was some time involved in the procedure, so he wouldn't be able to finish them until the next day, so once the first steps were completed, he worked on the finishing steps for more of the blood-cleansing potions. By planning his time carefully, he finished all five of the antidotes over the weekend and still managed to complete ten more of the blood-cleansing potions.

He had the workshop to himself Sunday afternoon as he worked, so during a break he woke up the ring for a conversation.

"What is it now?" asked the ring.

He told it about his latest project, but before he could finish it interrupted him. "And you need my help for that? Can't you do anything on your own?"

"That's not it," said Will. "I was just wondering if you can think of anything else I can do to earn money. I'm still going to be about three hundred crowns short and my time is running out."

The ring thought about it for a while before answering, "Actually, I was wondering why your dabbler of a professor didn't ask you to do a potion of regeneration. Back in Arrogan's day those were pretty valuable and considering the amount of turyn that goes into one I'd guess they'd be almost unheard of now."

"What does it do?" asked Will.

"I'd think it would be self-explanatory, given the name."

Will sighed. "Regeneration could mean a lot or just a little. Give me an idea how much it can do."

"Well, it won't cure a bad case of the piles," snickered the ring. "It won't help with brain injuries, disease, or poisons, but as long as a person is breathing, it'll damn near fix anything else."

"Can it grow something back?"

"Why? Did someone bite off your little *friend*?"

"You know what I mean. Can it regrow and arm or a leg?"

"Sort of?"

Exasperated, Will let his impatience show in his voice. "Can you just explain it? Don't make me keep fishing for answers."

"Where's the fun in that? All right, fine. No, it won't grow back lost limbs. It's also slow. It lasts about an hour and if you've got a serious wound it'll incapacitate you while it's working. Say for example you had a friend with a spear through his belly, if you get the spear out and give it to him before he bleeds to death, he'll be right as rain. The potion will knock him out, of course, and he probably won't wake up for a day or two, but that's a small price for not dying."

Will couldn't help but think that the potion sounded more like a miracle than magic. "What's the downside?"

"It tastes bad," said the ring. "But anyone who's taken medicine before should expect that."

"That's it?"

"It tastes really bad, and the smell is awful enough to make you wish you'd been sprayed by a skunk so you could forget the rotten stench you just got a whiff of. One of the ingredients is a little difficult to acquire too, which was the main reason it was rare in Arrogan's day."

I knew there'd be a catch, thought Will. "What is it?"

"Troll piss."

"Are you swearing, or was that a joke?"

The ring chuckled. "Neither, no wait, actually all of the above plus one. It's a great swear, it's funny, and it's also the damn truth."

Will growled. "Troll piss!"

"I just said that a second ago. You can't help but repeat the obvious, can you?"

"No, I was swearing," snapped Will. "Why'd you bother telling me about regeneration potions if there's no way I can get the ingredients? Actually, while we're at it—why did Grandfather have me waste something so valuable? Do you know he used to make me pour the stuff around his garden?"

The ring sighed contentedly. "It works great for keeping deer and other vermin out of a garden too. It lasts for *months*!"

"But it was a waste," insisted Will. "Think of the lives that he could have saved. Or if that wasn't enough motivation, he could have made the potions and sold them! It would have really been nice if there had been some sort of inheritance stored in the limnthal!"

"There was an inheritance," argued the ring.

"Butter does not count."

"Say that again the next time you are days from civilization and you're on the verge of starving to death. You'll never want for fresh bread and butter, you ungrateful wretch."

Will sulked silently.

The ring said nothing for a minute, but finally it relented. "Fine. You're such a sour puss. I wouldn't have mentioned it if there wasn't a way for you to acquire the liquid gold you require."

"I've never seen a troll. No one I know has ever seen a troll, and the only congruence point to Muskeglun that Arrogan ever told me about is back in his basement in Barrowden," said Will. "So exactly how do you propose I find a troll and persuade him to pee in a jar for me?" A sudden realization hit him then. "Wait! Did he have some stored in his workshop?"

"Definitely," answered the ring. "But I believe you just told me he had you pour it around his garden."

"Wouldn't he have had more?"

"Not likely. He hated Muskeglun. You will too. It's a terrible place."

It took Will a moment to process the ring's words. "I will too—wait, you want *me* to go there?"

"Why not? He used to make regular trips there. If he could do it, you could too."

"But I don't know enough magic to survive in a place like that," protested Will.

The ring began to laugh. "Magic isn't very much use in Muskeglun. In fact, it's almost better to not be a wizard than to be one."

"Why?"

"A normal wizard is used to using magic. Actually, let me clarify that. A *proper* wizard, of the sort Arrogan trained you to be, is used to using magic. Not only that, but a proper wizard has his source compressed, so he doesn't generate very much turyn of his own. Muskeglun is almost the exact opposite of Faerie—there's very little ambient turyn. For a regular human, that's not a problem, because they generate the proper amount of turyn to sustain themselves, but for someone like you, you have two options."

"Which are?"

"You either release your grip on your source while you're there, or you bring elixir of turyn with you and use it to keep from dying. That's not too bad on its own, but it also means you have to avoid using magic, which if you've gotten in the habit of relying on it, can be difficult," explained the ring. After a short pause, it added, "As much as I hate to admit this, being a sorcerer is something of an advantage there, especially if you have a fire elemental. Not only do they have an additional source of turyn, but trolls are very afraid of fire."

Will thought about it for a minute, then summed everything up. "So, you want me to go to Muskeglun, refrain from using magic while I'm there, and somehow fight a troll using nothing but my normal fighting prowess? The more you say, the less this sounds like a possible solution and the more it sounds like an unpleasant way to commit suicide."

The ring replied, "First, you should probably remove the word 'prowess' from your dictionary as I doubt it will ever apply to you in any context, much less in fighting. Second, even though Arrogan was a badass in every sense of the word, even he wouldn't think about taking on a troll in single combat unless it was absolutely necessary. Trolls are fast, strong, somewhat intelligent, and they can recover from nearly any injury. Did I mention claws? Yeah, they have claws too. In fact, the only reason there are still humans is that trolls seem to be utterly incapable of using magic, otherwise we'd have gone extinct."

Will frowned. "Are you saying there are trolls in our world, or that there used to be?"

"Someone decided to bring a few over a long time ago. It didn't work out well. They multiply quickly and they'll eat almost anything. Trendham almost wound up being named Trollheim instead."

"Was Arrogan around back then?"

"No, this was long before his time. The trolls ate everyone they came across. Armies failed against them. It was a bad time to be human. The only reason we're still here today is that the wizards of the time got over their differences and made a concerted effort to burn them all to ashes. In fact, they'd have gotten rid of trolls entirely, but for the fact that going to Muskeglun and repeating that effort was simply impossible, due to the problems I mentioned a minute ago."

"You realize that everything you've said just reinforces the fact that I shouldn't go looking for trolls," Will pointed out.

"Rest easy my young fool, for I will share with you the secrets to a successful holiday in the gloomy, disease-infested swamps of Muskeglun. You already have everything you need: desperation, a notable lack of common sense, and me, your trusty guide." The ring continued, explaining a plan of action that sounded almost reasonable.

Chapter 22

By Tuesday, Will was ready to meet his new customer. The meeting place was at an upscale tavern named the Lazy Pony, and Will left after Composition since that gave him three hours until he had to be back for Math class.

He was still largely unfamiliar with the streets of Cerria, so having a little extra time to find the tavern was a good thing, but despite his worry about getting lost, he found the place easily. The district the tavern was in was only a half-mile from the market where he had sold his peppercorns and the sign was visible from more than a block away. The sign pictured a sleeping horse, which made it fairly distinctive.

Given the speed of his trip, Will figured that the midday bells wouldn't ring for at least a half an hour, so he was early for his meeting. The street outside the tavern had a number of people in it, most of whom seemed to be heading one way or another, though a few were loitering near the tavern. For the most part everything seemed normal, although Will took notice of one man who stood a short way down, staring at the tavern itself.

Or is it me he's looking at? Will wondered. The fellow didn't seem dangerous. He was older and hunched over, as though his back could no longer quite manage a fully erect posture. Will watched the man for a few seconds, until the stranger looked away and began walking in the opposite direction.

Will headed inside and looked around. The interior was clean and well maintained, with woodwork that was neat and well made. The tables and furniture were all similar, and most notably, they all matched. While he didn't have much experience with common houses and pubs, Will had never been in one where the furniture wasn't a hodgepodge of different styles.

The place wasn't empty, but neither was it crowded, as it likely would be later in the day. Unsure where to sit, Will went to the bar and found a stool. As there was only one other customer at the bar, it was only a minute before the bartender came over to wait on him.

"You seem a little young," said the man.

Will grinned. "I'm here to meet someone."

The bartender nodded. "That's your business. Can I get you something?"

"Small beer," answered Will. The barkeep stepped away and returned a few moments later with a metal cup.

"Two pennies," said the man. After Will had slid the coins across the bar, the bartender added, "I'm Max if you need anything else."

Will nodded.

"Who are you waiting for?"

"I don't know what he looks like," said Will. "But his name is Roger Barlow. He'll probably ask for me when he comes in. My name is William Cartwright."

"He'll probably spot you right away," said Max. "The crowd is small, you're young, and he'll check the bar first."

Will had been worried about that, but the bartender's observation was probably correct. He relaxed a little and nursed his cup, watching the door. He didn't have to wait long.

The man who entered spotted him almost immediately, meeting his eyes and heading straight for him. The newcomer was dressed in a rich doublet with fur trim. The man's face was freshly shaved, except for a neat, square-cut goatee. "Are you William?" he asked as soon as he came near.

"William Cartwright," he answered with a nod.

"Roger Barlow," said the man, extending his hand. Will's buyer spent a few minutes with the bartender, ordering a glass of wine. Once it had arrived, he turned back to Will. "Do you have the universal antidote potions?"

"I do," said Will. He untied a small bag from his belt and started to open it. "If you'd like to examine—"

"No need," said Roger, waving a hand at Will dismissively. "I trust Karlovic's judgment, and honestly, I wouldn't know how to tell if they were real or not." He pulled a small pouch from the side of his doublet and passed it over. "Feel free to count it."

The weight was enough to suggest the pouch contained gold, but Will opened the top and caught a glimpse of yellow metal before closing it again. He didn't particularly want to count so much money in a public place. He decided to offer his buyer the same courtesy. "I guess I'll trust you as well. Are there any other potions you might be interested in?"

Roger shook his head. "These aren't for me. I'm buying them on behalf of a friend."

Curious, Will asked, "Might I ask who your friend is?"

"No," said Roger flatly.

"I understand." Will finished his beer and stood up. "I'll get going then. Just let Professor Karlovic know if you need anything else."

The man nodded, and Will headed for the door. The entire exchange had felt strange to him. Was this how smugglers and spies felt? It hadn't exactly been a shady deal, but the anonymity of the buyer made him feel sneaky. As Will stepped into the street, he played along with the cloak-and-dagger feeling and surreptitiously checked his surroundings.

Then he saw something that snapped him out of his boyish mood. The old man he had seen before entering was back, but now he was standing on the other end of the street, away from the direction he had headed in previously. *Why did he come back? Is he really watching the tavern, or me?*

Will glanced around one more time, trying to note the faces of those nearby, then he set off toward the old man. It wasn't the direction that would take him back to Wurthaven, but he felt a need to get a closer look at his potential stalker. The old man noted his approach and turned around, suddenly interested in something on the ground and coincidentally hiding his face. *That's definitely suspicious,* thought Will, *but it could just be paranoia on my part.*

He took a right at the next intersection of roads and walked casually, fighting the urge to speed up. Will wanted to look back, but if someone was following him that would be a giveaway, so he kept his face forward.

But his efforts to appear unaware backfired on him. He spent too much time thinking about his outward appearance and too little keeping track of his turns as he meandered along. Ten minutes and a multitude of cross-sections later, Will realized he was thoroughly lost. Worse, he had left the nicer part of the city he had been in and had wandered into a slum. The buildings around him were dirty and in disrepair. There were fewer people on the road as well.

He heard a whistle from somewhere ahead. *Is that a signal?* Unable to help himself, he looked back. The old man was there, almost a full block behind, but there were two younger men much closer, within thirty feet. Their eyes were cold and unfriendly.

Will stopped, turning to face them. *Going forward will only take me into whoever they have waiting ahead.* The street was almost empty now, and he noticed that the other random townsfolk who remained were all moving indoors. They knew something was about to happen.

Will summoned the limnthal and stored the bag of gold in it as he began walking toward the two men. He doubted they noticed the action, since they probably couldn't see turyn. He didn't dismiss the limnthal, since he might have to summon something else from it. The two bravos smiled as they saw him heading their way. They knew the game was almost over and they seemed anxious to start the fun.

The distance closed quickly, and at fifteen feet one of the two pulled a long, curved knife from his coat, while the other produced a wicked baton with iron nails driven through the business end. Will's heart was pounding in his ears, but he kept his cool and started to summon his saber. There was a sound behind him, a boot sole against stone, and he was driven forward as something slammed into his back with enough force to make him stumble. It felt like someone had punched him in the kidney.

The man with the club leapt forward, swinging at his head, and Will barely managed to dodge the blow, falling into the man with the knife instead. A second blow struck his belly, as the man's companion stabbed him.

Will caught the knife-wielder's arm. The fellow seemed surprised as he lost his grip on the knife after its unexpected encounter with his brigandine, and Will slammed his right elbow into the assassin's face.

The unseen man that had attacked him from behind exclaimed, "He's wearing some sort of armor!"

Will jumped back from the man with the club and then ran, heading straight for the old man, who was holding back in the distance. The old man's eyes widened and then he started fleeing, while the two ambushers who were still on their feet began to give chase.

Focusing his turyn, Will outpaced his pursuers and rapidly caught up to the old man, then passed him. "I'll be back for you," he threatened as he raced by.

One of the men behind him whistled. *Another signal,* thought Will. That meant there were probably more of them ahead of him. *How many could there be?* Rather than go straight, he ducked around the corner of the next building, then stopped and summoned his saber while pressing himself close to the wall.

The first pursuer that rounded the corner ran straight into a horizontal slash that opened his shirt and spilled his intestines onto the ground. The man screamed and staggered sideways, trying to hold his guts in, while the second pulled up short. Will didn't give the second man time to recover, though. Lunging forward, he rammed the point of his sword into the man's belly, driving it hard enough that the tip emerged from the man's back.

At the same time, he felt a terrible pain in his left shoulder—the club had found his flesh there. Will struggled to pull his sword free while the dying man swung at him again. The blade wouldn't move, though, and he was forced to release the hilt as he leapt back.

Then the third man arrived, knife in hand.

Will dodged around the man with the sword through him, who was only now beginning to sink to the ground, crying, "He's killed me, Davy!"

The third killer advanced cautiously, aware that he was facing an unarmed opponent. Will caught him with the source-link spell and injected a portion of his turyn. The man's face took on a look of distress, and a second later he began to vomit.

Stepping back, Will kicked the man with his sword still stuck in his chest. The assassin fell sideways to the ground and flailed helplessly at him as Will stepped on the man's chest and jerked the saber free.

Two more were closing in, coming from the direction Will had been running toward. He still had a few seconds before they arrived, so Will used them to slash the vomiting bandit across the back and legs as he drunkenly staggered about, trying to avoid the blows while emptying his stomach.

All three of his original assailants were down now, though two of them were still crying out in pain. The one who'd had his belly opened was particularly loud, while the other was too busy retching to say much. The two new criminals stopped a few feet away, sizing up their prey.

"You made a big mistake, kid," said one of them. Both of them held formidable clubs.

"How? Are you going to kill me twice now that I've hurt your friends? Why don't you think before you make threats that don't make sense." He talked to buy time, as his source-link spell connected with both of his opponents.

"Smart ass. You'll find out. It could have been quick and easy, but I'll make sure you suffer. We'll take our time with you." The thug whirled his club as he spoke, demonstrating his prowess.

Will backed away, taking a second to make sure the street was still clear behind him. He couldn't afford any more surprises. His left shoulder was throbbing, and he could feel blood dripping from his fingertips. He was steadily pulling turyn from the two men as he stayed out of their range. "Why are you doing this?" he asked.

His two enemies separated, moving to the sides so he couldn't escape. "Same as always. Someone wants you dead." The man's words slurred as they came out, and his movements grew sluggish.

The other one lunged forward, swinging, but he stumbled and fell to the ground as his strength faded. A few seconds later they were both on the ground, unconscious.

Will stared at them. The adrenaline surging through his veins made him want to do something terrible. The terror and violence were clouding his thoughts. His first instinct was to kill both of them. It would be easy enough. Two quick thrusts and he could leave both of them to bleed to death. Clenching his jaw, he looked around. No one was watching, and there didn't seem to be any more assassins coming.

With an effort of self-control, he dismissed his sword. Then he picked up a knife one of the earlier men had dropped and used it to hamstring both of them. It was a bloody and vicious act. If they recovered, they'd be lucky to walk again, and if they did it would be with a permanent limp. He felt an ugly sense of satisfaction. *I didn't kill them,* he thought, trying to convince himself he'd done the right thing, but was maiming them any better?

Will tried to clear his thoughts. What was the best thing to do next? Run? Wait for the city patrol? There was still no one visible in either direction. He summoned his cloak from the limnthal and put it on, using the hood to cover his head, then he began rifling through the ruffians' purses.

The dead man and the two unconscious ones were simple enough. The one who was moaning and holding his stomach together cursed him the entire time. Will used the man's own knife to cut his purse free and stored the entire thing in his limnthal. "Who paid you to do this?" he asked.

"I'm dying. Leave me alone," moaned the assassin.

Will examined the man's open belly with expert eyes. There wasn't much blood, which meant the fellow wasn't likely to bleed to death. "It might take you several days to die," he said. "If someone wraps you up tightly you might last until the fever takes you."

"I'll tell them it was you," spat the thug. "When the guards get here. I'll tell them you did this."

"Are you asking me to finish you off?" Will threatened.

Despite his mortal wound, the man tried to scoot away. "I take it back. I won't. I don't even know your name!"

"Someone knows me, otherwise you wouldn't have ambushed me," said Will. "Who?"

"Remi," answered the dying man. "It was Remi that gave us the job."

"Who's that?"

"The greybeard, you were chasing him."

"The old man?"

The thug nodded.

"How do I find him?" asked Will.

"I don't know," said the man fearfully. "Honest, I don't. He found us."

"Where did he find you then?"

"At the Mangy Dog, near the south gate," said the man.

"Mangy Dog?"

"It's a tavern. It's supposed to be the Green Dog, but that's what everyone calls it. Remi and a few like him come there when they want to hire men for a job."

Will stared into the man's eyes. "How do I know you're telling the truth?"

"Please, I don't want to die. I've got a family," begged the thug.

Will winced. *I really didn't want to know that.* How many people would go hungry because of what he had done? Did the men he had crippled have families too? His anger had faded, and now it was slowly being replaced by remorse. *Damn it.*

Despite his better sense, he produced a blood-cleanse potion from his limnthal. "If someone stitches you up properly, you might live. Wait until the fever starts and take this. It will stop the sickness from killing you."

"Really?" A faint hope was dawning on the disemboweled man's face.

Maybe, thought Will, but he kept his doubt to himself. He stood up and looked around. "Where are the city patrollers?"

"They don't come around here very often," said the wounded man. "We thought we'd gotten lucky when you came this way."

Will was torn. He'd been considering waiting for the patrollers. They would ask him some difficult questions, but he was clearly the victim. Leaving the scene would be a crime, but then again, none of the men knew his name, and he doubted the man who had hired them would go to the authorities.

But if he left, the man he'd interrogated might die before anyone helped him. "Is there anyone around here who would help you?" asked Will.

The man nodded.

"Why aren't they coming?"

"They're all indoors. Probably scared you'll kill them," admitted the wounded man.

That made up his mind for him. "I guess I should leave then."

He started to walk away but the wounded man called after him, "My name's Cedric. If I don't die, I'll remember you."

Will looked back in disbelief. "Is that a threat?"

"A debt," said Cedric, holding up the vial Will had given him.

Will studied the man for a moment, his expression blank, then he nodded.

Chapter 23

Will walked a short distance, then took the first right turn he came across. There were some people in the cross street, so he kept going until he saw an alley he could duck into. Once he was sure he wasn't being observed, he cast the climbing spell and made his way up to the roof of the two-story building. The climb was agonizing, for his shoulder protested every time he lifted his left arm.

He tried to make himself comfortable on the roof, then used his belt knife to cut off his left sleeve so he could use it as a bandage. The wound was ugly, but not serious. The biggest danger was that it would turn septic. Getting it properly cleaned and treated would minimize that risk, but he was too tired to move.

Once he had bandaged it to stop the bleeding, he lay back on the roof to rest. The sun was shining on his face, turning the world orange even through the lids of his eyes, but he fell asleep anyway. When he woke, the sun was still up and he was uncomfortably warm. His armor and tunic were damp with sweat—the blood on his clothes had already dried.

Everything seemed fine, until Will started to move. His back was in agony and his left arm vigorously protested when he tried to use it to assist in sitting up. *I should have gone back to the dorm before resting,* he realized.

He half-grunted, half-laughed in pain as he struggled to get to his knees. Climbing down was going to be a nightmare. Will eased his way down until he could look over the edge and make sure the alleyway was clear. It was, but the street beyond it had gotten busier.

Without the climbing spell, he would never have made it down without falling, and even with it there were several moments that forced painful cries from his lips. Will flexed his knees once he was down, grateful that at least his legs were still in good shape. Then he set off to find his way back to Wurthaven.

He walked almost a mile east along one street before stopping to ask for directions, since he wanted to avoid talking to anyone who might have seen his fight. The sooner they forgot his face the better. An old washerwoman pointed out the way he needed to go, and after a mile in that direction he found an intersection he recognized. Will found another alley and removed his cloak, then he switched out his tunic with a more common one that he kept in the limnthal.

By the time he reached the wall that separated Wurthaven from the city, his muscles had loosened up, but the climb was still painful. He was glad when it was finally over. One more modest walk and he would be back to his room.

Will was almost to the entrance when someone called out to him, "Will!" Turning his head, he saw Rob walking toward him. *No one's spoken to me in weeks, and now today of all days...*

"Rob," he said simply.

"How have you been?" asked his one-time friend.

"Not bad."

"I wanted to apologize for not being around. I had to leave for a week, so you probably thought I've been avoiding you. Well, I did for a little while. I didn't know what to think. I know you've probably had a hard—what's that on your face?" Rob's expression turned to one of concern.

"Probably just dirt—"

Rob leaned closer, examining his cheek. "That's blood. There's dried blood all over the right side of your face. What the hell happened?"

"I took a bad fall earlier," said Will weakly.

"Don't go inside like that. Wait over there." Rob pointed to the side of the dorm. "Keep your right side toward the building. I'll be back soon." He left, heading toward the bath houses on the other side of the dormitory. He returned a few minutes later, a wet towel in his hand.

Will used the towel to wipe the crusted blood from his face, and when that wasn't enough to satisfy his friend, Rob took the towel into his own hands to finish the job properly. "There," said his friend. "I think you can go in without scaring anyone to death now."

Rob followed him inside and stayed with him all the way to his door. Will stopped there and looked back. "I'd invite you in, but I have a lot of work to do."

"Oh," said Rob. "Don't worry about it. Are you sure you're all right, though?"

He nodded. "I'm fine."

"You were a little stiff coming up the stairs, and your complexion is off. You still haven't told me what happened to you. That blood didn't come from nowhere."

"I just had a fall," repeated Will. "I didn't even realize I was bleeding."

"It didn't look like it came from your scalp," countered Rob.

"I'll figure it out when I wash up. I'm fine, Rob. We can talk tomorrow."

Rob gave him a dubious look. "You still remember where my room is, right? Come find me if you need anything."

"I will."

After Rob left, Will stripped off his clothing, making a pile on the floor. Then he examined his left arm. There were several ugly punctures in the skin and muscle close to where it met his shoulder. The skin was red and crusted with blood, and Will didn't like the look of it. He could see a mild bruise around the punctures, but he was mainly worried about the wound turning sour.

His brigandine was in fair shape, however. One of the plates in the back was dented and a rivet had popped loose, but otherwise it seemed fine. *I'd have died if hadn't been wearing it,* he observed silently, remembering the two knife attacks it had stopped, one to his kidney and the other to his gut. Will resolved to never leave the room without it on in the future.

His grandfather would probably still be alive if he'd been wearing something similar the day he'd been shot with the crossbow.

Will didn't feel like using the bathhouse. Not only did it cost money that he couldn't afford, but he didn't want to explain his injury. So, as he had done so many other days over the past two weeks, he used the personal bathing spell.

The scream that ripped free from his throat probably scared his nearest neighbors. Afterward, Will hopped around the room, intermittently swearing and gasping for breath. Apparently, the personal cleaning spell hadn't been designed with injuries in mind. While his body was now clean, his shoulder throbbed with hot agony and blood dripped from the puncture wounds. The spell had removed the scabs and dirt in the un-gentlest way possible.

"Why am I always goddamned stupid?" Will swore at himself. He could hear footsteps outside. Someone had probably gone to fetch Dianne. He had to hurry.

Ignoring his pain, he cast another spell to clean his clothes and then stored his brigandine in the limnthal. When a knock came at his door, he was ready. "Mister Cartwright? Are you in there?"

Will opened the door wide, making sure Dianne could see his empty room. *No bodies here,* he thought. "I'm sorry," he said sheepishly. "I stubbed my toe."

"They said it sounded like someone was being murdered," said Dianne suspiciously, her eyes roving across the innocent-seeming interior of his room.

"I overreacted," explained Will. "I'm not very good with pain."

Dianne's eyes met his. She seemed unconvinced. "Somehow, I doubt that, William." She turned away. "Try to keep it down."

He shut the door and sank to the floor with relief. Blood was already seeping through the fabric of his hastily donned tunic. He'd have to clean it again. Fortunately, he'd kept his left side away from Dianne while she looked in. He removed the tunic and re-bandaged his shoulder.

With that done, he removed the purses he had taken from the street bravos and examined their contents. There was a mixture of coins that when added up didn't quite total ten crowns in value. He also counted the purse of gold his buyer had given him, and he was happy to see that it did indeed contain a hundred gold crowns.

Adding up everything he had, plus the remaining gold he could make from selling blood-cleansing potions to the college, he would need to earn another two-hundred and seventy crowns to pay the blood-price. "And I've got the rest of this week, plus next week, in which to do so," he muttered. "How hard could it be?"

A year before he couldn't have imagined having ten crowns, much less a thousand. If he could just get past his current difficulty, he could easily make enough money in the future to take care of his family indefinitely. It was a sobering thought.

The ring's plan was looking more appealing the closer he got to the deadline. *But do I dare?* There were good reasons that no one tried to do what he was considering.

"Then again," he muttered. "Very few people are willing to make powerful potions anymore, given the cost to their futures. If there were more people like me, there might also be more who were willing to risk going to Muskeglun as well."

Will tried out the demon armor spell before going to bed. It wasn't particularly difficult for him now, though he still needed practice to ensure he had it memorized. "Damn, this looks wicked," he said to himself, watching as red and orange flames flickered over his body. Hopefully he would never need it for its intended purpose, but he could see himself using it to intimidate someone. It might have even been handy during his fight earlier, if he'd been able to cast it without referring to the book first.

Chapter 23

Practice and repetition. Aislinn had been right. A wizard's greatest asset was knowledge, and Will was determined to do his best to make it his own.

He didn't wake in time for his classes the next day. The sun was shining through his window at a steep angle by the time Will turned his head to look, and a shiver ran through him as his blanket fell away. He was freezing.

"It can't be that cold," he said, sitting up. The ache in his bones confirmed that idea. It wasn't cold—he had come down with a terrible fever. Will checked his arm and saw that the flesh was red and inflamed. "Great," he said dourly, "just great."

With some effort, he got to his feet. He needed to relieve himself, but a trip outside was too much, so he slid the chamber pot out from beneath the bed. His urine was a pink color as it emerged. *Definitely bruised my kidney too,* he observed.

He drank some water, courtesy of a jar stored in the limnthal, and then he returned to bed. His sleep was troubled by fever dreams that were only interrupted when his shivering got so bad that it woke him. At some point during the day he drank some more water and made use of the chamber pot again, but the rest of the time he stayed in bed.

Someone was beating a drum, but the beat was inconsistent. "They'll never make good music like that," he mumbled. It was a while before he realized the sound was actually that of someone knocking on his door.

"Will, are you in there?"

"No," he croaked, feeling amused by the genius of his humor. He must have stumbled to the door, for he found his hand on the door handle. Opening it, he looked out. Janice stood in the hallway. "Hi."

"Holy Mother! What happened to you?" she asked.

"Just the usual," he said. His teeth chattered as he waved his hand dismissively. For some reason the floor swayed beneath him, as though he was at sea. Will smiled. "Don't worry. I'm an excellent sailor. Watch." He navigated back to his bed despite the rolling of the waves.

When he opened his eyes again, he was on the bottom bunk. Someone leaned over him. "Are you awake?" asked a feminine voice.

It was Selene. Will stared up at her, feeling grateful for her presence. "You have to stop coming here," he muttered. "You'll get in trouble."

"You weren't in class for two days," she replied. "And from what I heard, you missed your afternoon classes the day before that. I was worried." She removed a towel from his forehead and replaced it with a fresh one. "Your fever isn't getting better."

"That's all right. They were going to kill me anyway."

"Is that how you injured your shoulder? Were you in a fight?"

He shook his head. "Not a fight really, more of a slaughter. I killed one, maybe two. The others are probably alive, cursing me somewhere. It wasn't nearly as bad as the demon we fought."

"Demon?"

"Yeah, remember? You killed the priest and then the demon attacked me. You nearly died saving me."

Selene's expression grew worried. "Will, do you recognize me?"

He smirked. "No. You won't trick me that easily."

"You aren't making any sense. Do you know who I am?"

"No," he said stubbornly. "If I did, I couldn't love you." Reaching out, he tried to pull her closer for a kiss, but she slipped his grasp and pulled away.

"You're hallucinating. You need a doctor."

"Love isn't a disease," he responded sagely. "Don't believe what your father tells you. Besides, I took a blood-cleanse potion. I'll be fine."

She held up a glass vial. "Is that what this is?"

He nodded. "I made a bunch of them."

"There was only one on your desk, and it's still full."

"I'm pretty sure I took it," he argued.

She gave him a serious look. "You need to take this." She unstopped the vial and put one hand behind his head to help him sit up.

Will was feeling petulant. "Not without a kiss."

"I'm not kissing you, Will. You don't even know who I am," she told him.

He chuckled. "I'll pay. I have money."

She was glaring at him. "If I didn't know you were out of your gourd, I'd make you regret saying that."

He grinned. "That's the going rate, six clima for a kiss from a princess."

"I can't decide if you're delusional or whether you've got a story to tell. I'll be asking for an explanation when you're better." She held the vial up to his lips. "Here, drink it."

Will closed his mouth stubbornly. "Uhn-uhn." When she pulled her hand away, he insisted, "Kiss, or no medicine."

She seemed uncertain, then her eyes filled with determination. "You're going to be embarrassed later, but you asked for this." Her head leaned in and her lips met his.

He took the potion after that and she helped him back down. He couldn't help but note the flush on her cheeks. "I won't tell your father," he added reassuringly. "There's money in my pouch."

"I appreciate that," she said dryly. After a second, she asked, "Wait, you really paid her for kisses?"

"You paid me first, thief," he shot back. Something seemed different about Selene, though. "Did you change your hair?"

Her eyes narrowed, and she sighed. "More than that."

Chapter 24

"Wake up, Will. You need to eat."

He sat up with a start. His clothes were damp with cold sweat. Seth sat in a chair beside the bed, a steaming bowl in his hands. Will stared at his old roommate suspiciously. "How long have you been here?"

"A while."

"What day is it?"

"Friday. You were ranting and raving all night."

Will felt his cheeks blush. "Did I do anything—unusual?"

"Aside from talking about fighting demons and thinking I was a girl, no."

Will grew still. "That's it?"

Seth nodded. "That's it. Don't worry."

He doesn't want to embarrass me, Will realized. "You're a true friend, Seth. Thank you."

"Don't thank me too much," said the other boy. "I'm not moving back in. Besides, it was Janice who found you."

"Janice?"

"She came to bring you her class notes and said she found you out of your mind," Seth explained. "She asked me to watch over you today."

Which one did I kiss? Will wondered, *Seth or Janice?* He decided it didn't matter, either way he had embarrassed one of his friends. Sitting cross-legged, he accepted the warm soup and began to eat.

Seth stayed for another hour, then left. That evening Janice returned, bringing more soup and a pitcher of watered pear cider. Seeing that he was getting around and that his mind was clear, she didn't stay very long.

Will made it to the dining hall for every meal over the weekend, and by Sunday afternoon he was feeling much more himself, though his shoulder was still stiff and sore. What worried him most, however, was that he had lost a significant amount of time. He had to appear before the magistrate on Friday, either to show proof that he had paid the fine, or that he had the means to do so.

He hadn't even had a chance to confer with Professor Karlovic regarding the regeneration potion. If the professor didn't have a copy of the old formula, or if there was no way to sell the potion, Will would be in serious trouble. But he didn't have time to wait.

Will put on his brigandine and the one of his intact tunics, then he left the dormitory and headed for his favorite wall-crossing spot. The climb wasn't as painful as it had been the last time, but it was still uncomfortable. From there he made his way to the southern gate. Unlike some of his previous destinations it was easy to find. He merely had to follow the road outside Wurthaven until it met the main street that bisected the city and follow it southward. The walk took almost two hours, but soon enough he was outside the capital and heading into the open countryside.

He considered putting on his gambeson and mail, but they might complicate the next part of his plan, so he stuck with what he was wearing. Stopping beside a shade tree near the road, Will sat down for a rest. "Tailtiu, Tailtiu, Tailtiu, thrice called, come to me," he said quietly. Deep within, he could feel a connection as his message reached his fae aunt.

A strange subliminal knowledge came with the connection. "East," he said aloud, naming the direction that was tugging at him. The congruence point she would emerge from was somewhere in that direction. Will left the road and set off across a field of barley, hoping he wouldn't upset any farmers if they saw him.

He walked for half an hour before he spotted a familiar figure coming toward him from the opposite direction. He waved.

There was a sly smirk on Tailtiu's lips as she came close and looked him up and down. "It took you long enough to call me."

I missed you, thought Will, but he didn't dare voice such an opinion. "I have a problem."

His aunt ran a hand along her side and down one hip, turning languorously to give him a good view of her attributes. "And I'm sure I have what you need," she answered in a sultry voice.

"I see you haven't changed."

Tailtiu's expression didn't change. "I'm immortal. That should go without saying."

"I need to use another unbounded favor."

She smiled. "What do you require?"

"Ten days of service," he said quickly.

"Ten?" Her brow furrowed. "Last time you only required three days for one favor."

"I could ask for a lot more than that," said Will. "Do you have an objection?"

"A counteroffer," she replied. "I'll give you thirty days of service if you sweeten the deal. I want an hour of your time and I'll promise that you survive without permanent harm." Tailtiu drew closer, her eyes hungry.

"No," Will said firmly, fighting his instinctive urge to back away. He had learned from past experience. Any sign of weakness and her predatory instincts would grow stronger, making Tailtiu even more difficult to deal with. "I could ask for a year. Would you prefer that?"

His aunt pouted. "I wouldn't agree to it. Length of service is negotiable."

"Then I'll require a limited task if that's not amenable to you. Would you like to go to Muskeglun for me?" He already knew what her answer would be. Traveling to the turyn-starved realm was a near certain death sentence for the fae.

She sighed. "Fine, ten days then."

"I've changed my mind. I'll need fifteen days."

"Is this how you haggle?" she asked curiously. "You wanted ten a moment ago."

Will took a step closer, until their noses were almost touching. There was anger in his eyes. "No. This is how I demand. Next time I make a generous offer you would do well not to irritate me."

Tailtiu licked her lips and her stance shifted, bringing her closer, until her body just barely brushed against his. "Every time we meet, you get better," she said softly, her breath caressing his cheek. "I look forward to the day you blunder into my grasp." She looked down, drawing his eyes to her hands, which were far too close to Will's vulnerable regions.

A second later her attitude changed, transforming in an instant. Tailtiu laughed. "Very well, fifteen days, and you won't ask me to enter Muskeglun—ever."

"Deal."

"What do you need?"

"How quickly can you get me home?"

She frowned. "I can't use the same route I took to get here. Parts of it would be too dangerous for you."

"Fine. How quickly can you get me home—safely?" amended Will.

"A few hours, but you need to take off the armor. You stink of iron."

"It's under my clothes. It won't burn you."

"Unless you wish the trip to take a day or more, you'll remove it. Some of the beings we'll be traveling near wouldn't take kindly to the presence of so much iron." Her tone indicated she wouldn't budge on the issue, and since they had finalized their bargain Will knew she wouldn't try to deceive him.

"Fine," he said at last. He pulled off his tunic and removed the brigandine, baring his chest.

As he stored his armor in the limnthal she commented, "You should get rid of the trousers too. They look uncomfortable."

He shook his head, putting the tunic back on and belting it around his waist.

"The buckle is iron," observed his aunt. "Put that away too."

"You were never this particular before."

"If you want to get there quickly, and in one piece, you'll do as I ask," she warned him. "There are places in Faerie that are far more dangerous than those you've been through before."

Will relented, removing his belt and storing it as well. He replaced it with a short length of rope that he tied in its place. Tailtiu shifted, becoming a giant doe, and she knelt to make it easier for him to mount. "Hold on tightly," she cautioned.

"If we're going to do this frequently maybe we should have a saddle made."

Her head turned to the side and she fixed him with one eye. "You're not putting a saddle on me unless you start mounting me in other ways." She took off before he could reply, forcing him to lean forward and throw his arms around her neck.

After a short run, she stopped near a farmhouse. Will could see a congruence point beside a tree in front of the house. "Do you think they'll see us?" he asked.

"Who cares?" responded his aunt. She walked to the congruence and shifted them to Faerie. "I couldn't care less what they think."

Fair point, he thought. Will examined their surroundings. They were in a rough, stony desert that was far different than any of the other places he had seen in Faerie previously. Before he could ask about it, she began running again, and a few minutes later they crossed through another congruence point into what he thought was probably his world. "Where are we now?" he asked.

"Some place in Shimera," said Tailtiu. "I don't keep up with the human names of places. There's a city to the north of us, but we won't be going near it."

"Shimera?" said Will with some alarm. "Are there demons here?"

She snorted. "If we went to one of their temples, probably, not out here in the countryside."

They traveled through Shimera for a quarter of an hour before entering another congruence. When they entered Faerie this time, Will was shocked by the cold. Snow was everywhere and the sky was black. "Wasn't it daytime in Faerie?" he asked.

"My world is not like yours," she reminded him. "This is the land of night. The sun never shines here. Try not to speak until we pass back into your world."

She moved forward slowly, finding her way through drifts that rose as high as her belly. Will adjusted his eyesight to see better, for the stars above were dim. He noticed dark shapes moving across the white snow, flitting between the trees.

Tailtiu kept going, until suddenly a pair of dark shadowy figures blocked her path. They were vaguely humanoid in shape, but Will could make out nothing of their features. "Why do you interfere?" she asked. "Would you risk the wrath of the Forest Fae?"

One of the figures pointed at Will. "Give him to us," pronounced a thick, raspy voice.

Tailtiu turned her head to look at Will. "Show them the limnthal."

He did as she asked, nervously holding out his hand and summoning the glowing enchantment. The two figures backed away at the sight of it and Tailtiu said, "He is a wizard. The accord still holds. Do not interfere with us again."

The shadows vanished.

"What were those things?" he asked.

"Not here." Tailtiu resumed her pace, taking them through a copse of snow-covered trees. The land descended, sloping and then rolling gently upward again, interrupted only by white-capped stones and scrubby bushes. Will could hear strange noises in the distance, unearthly howls that were nothing like anything he had heard before. Tailtiu increased her speed as the ground leveled out.

Glancing back, Will saw something on four legs behind them. It was some fifty yards behind, but it was coming closer. "There's something following us," he said quietly.

"Shhh." His aunt kept her pace steady.

The thing behind them broke into a ground-eating lope, closing quickly. Tailtiu broke into a run and the beast snarled, racing after them. "I thought the accord protected us," said Will.

Tailtiu yelled back. "The next congruence is close. When I shift, keep going. Don't stop. I'll follow when I can!"

"What are you planning to—" Will found himself flying as Tailtiu shifted into another form, causing him to tumble across the snow-covered ground. In a panic, he scrambled to his feet and looked back.

The beast following them was roughly canine in shape and features, though it was hard to say for certain as its body was covered with shifting shadows. It slammed headfirst into a massive brown monster that rose up where Tailtiu had been only moments before.

A bear? Claws and teeth raged as the two beasts tore into each other. Will was paralyzed for a moment, torn between doing as he had been told and his desire to help his companion. Blood, both red and black, sprayed across the pristine white snow. If he'd been wearing his mail he might have gone back, but the sight of the blood and claws made up his mind for him. He'd be shredded in an instant if he tried to interfere.

Will took note of their trail and turned to run in a straight line along the course Tailtiu had been following. He fell repeatedly as he tripped over limbs and rocks hidden by the snowfall, but he clambered to his feet each time and rushed on. Behind him the air was filled with a cacophony of grotesque growls and unearthly screams. Worse, he heard more howls in the distance, as friends of whatever it was that Tailtiu was fighting began to answer the dark beast's cries for aid.

He almost missed the congruence as he ran, spotting the telltale shimmer just as he went past it. Fighting his fear, Will stopped and turned around. "I found it!" he shouted, hoping she could break away and follow. His only answer was a horrifying collection of snapping cracks, as though something massive had been broken. Silence followed. "Tailtiu!"

There was nothing to be seen, until a moment later a large, brown form broke through the nearest clump of bushes. Tailtiu limped toward him on three legs, leaving a trail of blood behind. Her face was terrible to look on, for the flesh had been ripped away on one side, revealing vicious teeth covered in blood. She stumbled as she moved, staggering on unsteady paws.

Forgetting his terror, Will ran in her direction, closing the distance. He had just reached her side when he heard branches breaking as something massive moved through the trees somewhere nearby. "You're almost there," he told her, but the bear collapsed.

She was too big for him to carry. "Shift," he told her. "Let me help you."

Her one good eye focused on him. "Fool." Then her flesh melted and flowed, changing into the familiar shape of his aunt. One of her arms was limp, a bloody mush of flesh and broken bones, but her face was worse. The skin was gone on one side, hanging down from her chin, exposing her teeth and jawbone. Ignoring the gory vision, Will knelt and picked her up, then ran for the congruence point.

He could hear the heavy breathing of something behind him as he ran. He covered the last ten feet and shifted them through the congruence point without ever looking back. Warm air washed over him, and they fell onto soft earth covered in dry leaves. They were back in his world, though he had no idea where they were.

"Will you be all right? Can you heal?" he asked.

Tailtiu used her good arm to lift her torn cheek, pressing it back into place. After a few seconds it seemed to reattach itself, though it was still a bloody mess. "It's too slow here," she told him. "I need to go back to Faerie."

"Can I help?"

A wicked look appeared in her one good eye and she pointed to her torn lips. Will nodded and leaned forward, keeping his lips pressed firmly together to avoid getting any of her blood in his mouth. Fatigue washed over him as she drew strongly on his turyn, draining the life from his body, but he didn't fight it. He worked with her, offering up as much of his energy as she could take.

Just before he collapsed, she pushed him away. "Enough."

Will lay beside her, expanding the outer shell of his turyn to enable him to recover his energy faster. He watched as she sat up, her body slowly healing. "Where are we?" he asked.

"I don't know," she answered. "I only know that the next congruence leads to a place in Faerie that's close to the one near your house."

"I don't understand how you plan a route when you don't know where anything is."

"I know Faerie," she said simply. "I know all the places where our worlds touch, where they are in Faerie. As long as I know which one I wish to reach, I can get there by moving back and forth, but I don't know where all those places are in your world. Very few of them are important to me."

Her answer made a certain strange sense, and he was too tired to question her further about it. There were other things that were more important. "What were those things?"

"The ones we spoke to were darklings. The creatures I fought were fel-wolves."

"Why did you have to fight them? The first ones listened to you."

"Why don't you talk to dogs?" she said, answering his question with one of her own. "You talk to people but not animals. The darklings are intelligent, they're part of the accord. Most of the beasts in Faerie don't talk, therefore they aren't bound by contracts. They live according to only their appetites."

"So the darklings are fae?" he asked.

"In a sense, as is everything living in my world," she replied. "My people are closer to your kind—they were human once. The darklings came from somewhere else. They're fae now, but they are not like us."

That got him to thinking. "Were they demons then? Demons that moved to Faerie and transformed?"

She shook her head. "No. Demons can't survive there. Their essence is inimical to ours, but you have the right idea. The darklings came from a place of shadow and they made their part of Faerie into something similar, a place of cold and dark things. That's why the fel-wolves like it near them."

"The more I learn, the less I know."

"You've barely begun to drink from the cup of knowledge," said his aunt sagely. "You know nothing, and yet, even if you knew everything I do, you would realize that your knowledge was but an insignificant drop in an infinite sea of mysteries."

That was pretty profound, coming from a merciless, sex-starved, psychopathic killer, thought Will. "I think I like your people better than the darklings," he said.

Tailtiu laughed. "That's why we're more dangerous for your kind. Beauty does not equal kindness. Whether you're dealing with the Forest Fae, or the darklings, it's the same. Both are driven by hunger, and neither have any sense of mercy or kindness."

"I still like you better," he said stubbornly.

His aunt gave him a sly look. "Keep thinking that way. It will only make it easier for me to get what I want, and afterward, I'll devour your heart."

The deadly cold in her eyes made him shiver involuntarily. *Maybe she's right.* He decided to change the topic. "What would have happened to you if you hadn't escaped, if I had left you there?"

"It would have been unpleasant. I cannot die. They'd have torn me apart and eaten their fill. Recovering could have taken a long time. I wouldn't have been able to complete my service to you for many years." Slowly, she got to her feet. Her arm was still a mess and she was favoring one leg, but she lifted her chin proudly. "Still, I bested two of them. It was their numbers that made the fight impossible."

Will's turyn had recovered, so he stood as well, moving closer so he could offer his shoulder. Tailtiu draped her good arm around his neck. "How long will it take you to heal?" he asked.

"Here? Far too long. Better that we go to the next crossing. It will take us to a place close to my home. I can recover quickly there."

They resumed their journey, limited only by her limping pace.

CHAPTER 25

The rest of the journey didn't take long. The next portion of Faerie they entered was green and heavily forested, a reflection of the Glenwood that Will had grown up in. Tailtiu began to move more easily within minutes of their crossing, and by the time they reached the final congruence point back to his world she seemed to almost be back to her old self.

"This congruence leads to the forest near your home," she told him. "I can go partway with you, but as you know, I can't approach the house itself."

Because of the Cath Bawlg, the goddamn cat, he thought quietly. "Stay here," he replied. "You should finish healing."

"You should let me heal you before you leave," she informed him.

"I wasn't injured."

"You were already hurt when you called me. It's a small wound. Let me take care of it."

He nodded. "Fine."

She reached out her hand, then paused. "You won't burn me again?"

Will remembered the first time she had healed him. He'd had severe frostbite and had been close to death. She had put him to sleep, and while he was unconscious his body had turned her magic against her. "As long as I'm awake, you're safe," he told her.

She put her hand on his shoulder, and power trickled through her fingertips, moving through his wound and causing his flesh to burn and itch. The sensation was painful at first, but as his wound healed it became first pleasant, then pleasurable. Her turyn continued onward, coursing through his veins and quickening his heart rate. His eyes widened and his lips parted with an involuntary gasp. "That's enough," he said, struggling to control himself.

"Are you sure?" she whispered, her eyes ranging downward. "You seem to be enjoying it."

He pushed her hand away. "I said, enough!"

"So testy," she replied. "I only did as you required."

"You were doing more than that," he accused.

"And how do you know?"

"I've helped people before. None of them started writhing and moaning." He turned his back on her, hoping to hide the more physical aspects of his condition.

"Maybe you weren't doing it right," she teased. "I could teach you the trick to it."

"No, thank you."

"Are you sure? That human girl you like might appreciate it. Wouldn't you like to please her?"

"I need to get going." His face was beginning to turn red.

"Part of it is blood flow, sending it to the right places. The other part is in the brain. Find that center within yourself and you'll be on the right track. It's much the same, whether you're dealing with men or women," she advised.

Will started walking; he knew the way home.

"If you do decide to experiment, be careful. A rough touch could kill the one you wish to pleasure," she called after him. "It's best to practice on yourself until you get the hang of it."

Will walked faster, wishing he could plug up his ears. Tailtiu's laughter followed him, ringing through the woods like silver bells as he made his escape through the congruence.

***

Sammy jumped to her feet when he crossed the threshold. "Will!"

He caught her as she charged into him. "How have you been, Sammy?"

"Bored. Nothing ever happens. Auntie won't let me leave the house."

Will pushed her out and held her at arm's length. He'd only been gone a few months, but his cousin seemed to have grown almost an inch. "It's dangerous out there."

She shook her head. "Not anymore. They're building a fort in Barrowden. Eric's there now. He's been here to visit several times now, but Auntie still won't let me go to town."

He should have realized. He hadn't thought about the fact that Barrowden was now back in Terabinian control. Still, he agreed with his mother. "Sammy, listen, the town is full of soldiers. I wouldn't want you there by yourself."

"*Our* soldiers," she argued. "It's perfectly safe."

"It's a place full of nothing but men. Until things settle down more, you should listen to her."

She looked up at him, batting her eyes innocently. "Why?"

Will grimaced. "You know why."

"Are you saying I'm pretty?" There was mischief in her eyes.

"I just know how men are."

"Do you mean how *you* are?"

"Huh?"

She stared hard at him, her eyes like green agate. "Is that what happened with Annabelle?"

Will stepped back in alarm. "What are you talking about?"

"She's pregnant."

It took him a moment to process her words and the accusation in her glare. "Wait! You don't seriously think it was me, do you?"

Sammy shrugged.

"Where's Mom?"

"In the bedroom."

"What about Uncle Johnathan and Annabelle?"

"They went to trade in Barrowden," she answered.

Will went to the bedroom door and opened it. Erisa looked up from where she sat at the desk. "William!"

"Mom."

He crossed the room to greet her, giving his mother a big hug. Before he could say anything, she asked, "Where have you been? We got worried when the army showed up and Eric came to visit. He told us you were imprisoned."

"There was a misunderstanding. They thought I had kidnapped the king's daughter."

"What? How?" Erisa was confused.

Sammy figured it out first. "Selene! Great goat tits! She's a princess?"

Erisa glared at her niece. "Samantha, language!"

Will's cousin looked defiant. "Teats isn't a swear word."

"It is when you say it like that," said Erisa sharply.

Will wanted to laugh, but he had more important things on his mind. "Mom, Sammy told me about Annabelle. It isn't my baby."

His mother looked at him seriously. "I had my doubts, but your uncle said he saw the two of you together."

Sammy's eyes lit up. "He did!" Then she wagged a finger at Will. "For shame."

Will ran a hand across his face in frustration. "That wasn't what he thought." Will explained how Annabelle had snuck into his bed, and how he had rejected her advances.

"The truth would have come out anyway," said Erisa. "She began to show not long after you left. So, unless she was carrying twins, it didn't seem possible."

Will breathed a sigh of relief. "It's not that I don't want to help her. I just don't want to take the blame for something I didn't do."

"I'll take care of it," said his mother, her voice cool.

"You won't kick her out, will you?" asked Will worriedly. "She still needs our help."

Erisa gave him a hard look. "William, you know our history. Do you really think I would turn the girl out? I just don't appreciate her lies."

"I don't think she's all there," suggested Sammy.

"That goes without saying," said Erisa. "Still, the girl's been through hell."

"What will you do?"

"She's a hard worker," said his mother. "I can't deny she's been a big help, but she's lost her family. We'll make her part of ours, so long as she can behave herself."

Will gave his mother a panicked look, waving his hands. "Oh, hell no!"

Erisa shook her head. "Not like that, William. We'll adopt her. I wouldn't mind having a grandchild."

"Oh." Will paused. "Wait, would that make her my sister?"

His mother scratched her head. "I don't know. We'll figure it out later. First I want you tell me where you've been and what you've been doing."

Will gave them an abbreviated version of what had happened to him after his last visit. He glossed over his time in the royal dungeon, making it sound as though the misunderstanding had been resolved as soon as he got to the capital. He also played up positive side of his time at Wurthaven, omitting his duel with Dennis Spry and the fact that he had to come up with a colossal sum of money.

"So, why are you here now?" asked Erisa. "You could have sent a letter. Is it all right for you to miss your classes?"

Will dissembled, "I wasn't sure a letter could reach you. I didn't know you'd made contact with the town."

His mother appeared suspicious. "You still should have waited. You must have needed something to come all this way."

"It only took me a few hours to get here," Will bragged. "With Tailtiu's help long journeys are easier than you might think."

"I'm not sure that makes it any better," said Erisa. "I know how dangerous the fae are. I don't think your grandfather would have approved of you using their help for something so minor either."

Will played his final card, completing his lie. "Well, actually I did have another reason for coming."

"I knew it," said his mother.

"I need to use Arrogan's workshop."

"They don't have workshops at Wurthaven?"

"It's a class project. I have to bring something back from another plane," he lied, praying that his mother didn't know enough to know that wizards no longer traveled to other worlds voluntarily.

"What does that have to do with the workshop?"

"There's a crossing point in the workshop. I want to use it to bring something back from Muskeglun."

"What's Muskeglun?"

Will felt the tension leave him. If she didn't know that, then she wouldn't know the danger. "It's another plane, like Faerie, but much less dangerous. I want to collect some plants there."

Erisa's eyes narrowed. "*Less* dangerous? A pit of snakes is less dangerous than Faerie, but I still wouldn't let you jump in one. Be specific."

He got creative. "Well, it's a swamp from what I've heard. So, it isn't completely safe, but I don't have to stay very long. Don't worry, though. I've done a lot of reading and I'm prepared for the worst. There aren't any monsters, though, if that's what you're thinking."

Sammy had been listening with interest. "If it's that safe, maybe I can come with you!" she interjected.

Will and his mother responded simultaneously, "No."

"Why can he go, and I can't?" demanded his cousin.

"For one, he's almost reached the age of majority," said Erisa.

Will finished for her, "And for another, I'm the only one who can move through congruences, and I won't take anyone else."

Erisa turned back to him. "How long will you be over there?"

He had no idea of course, but he hedged on the long side to keep her from worrying. "A few days, a week at most."

"Will you have dinner first?" asked his mother.

Sammy's eyes lit up. "Maybe you'll cook?"

"The sooner I finish this the better," said Will. They sighed as he opened up the trap door that led to Arrogan's workshop. He started down, then stopped partway. "It's possible I may take another way back after I'm done. I'll send a letter to Barrowden if I do, so don't worry about me."

Erisa's mouth dropped. "How can I *not* worry? It could be weeks before I find out if you're all right!"

Will smiled apologetically. "Sorry, Mom." Then he pulled the trapdoor down over himself. "Be sure to lock up. I'll knock if I come back this way!" he shouted.

He had planned to don his mail before crossing, but he could hear his mother's steps across the floor above. "William Cartwright!" Not wanting to drag things out, he went to the corner and crossed over into Muskeglun.

Chapter 26

The first thing that Will became aware of was the smell. It assaulted his nose and seemed to press in against his skin like a heavy blanket. The air was warm and muggy, and the sky above was a dim yellow, as though the sun was being filtered through a yellow mist. He was surrounded by thick foliage, and his feet had already sunk an inch or two into the soft muddy ground.

He brought out the limnthal and summoned his gambeson and mail, but even as he shrugged his way into the armor, he regretted it. The heat was oppressive, and the padded coat would only make it worse. *I should move quickly then,* he thought.

Calling to the ring, he announced, "I'm here."

"Where?"

"Muskeglun. I took the congruence in Arrogan's old workshop."

"Did you make the preparations I suggested?"

"I brought plenty of cheap ale," said Will.

"Good. How about the elixir of turyn?"

"I just have what grandfather stored in the limnthal. I didn't have time to make more."

"Idiot. That stuff is probably old, not to mention you'll have to convert it. Making your own is always better, especially if things get tricky. Weren't you listening to me?"

"Yes, I was listening, but things happened. I spent several days in bed. I didn't have enough time left."

"Lazy bastard, you'll have no time left if a troll rips your liver out and makes a snack out of it," swore the ring.

Will looked through the nearest bushes. Beyond them was a shallow lake with tall, graceful trees lining its shores. Other than the stagnant smell of decay, the scenery was pleasant. "What's done is done," he told the ring. "Where do we go from here?"

"If things haven't changed too much then Clegg's village should be to the east."

"Which way is that?" asked Will. "I can't see the sun. The sky is hazy."

"Do you see water?"

"Yeah."

"Go the opposite direction. The closest water is to the west of where you came in. Are you wearing the antlers?"

Will paused. "I thought you were joking about that."

"No! You fucking nitwit! Do you at least have it with you?"

"Yes, it's in the limnthal."

"Well get it out and put it on."

Will balked. "It's hot here. My armor is already making me sweat buckets, and the cap will just make it worse. What's so important about the antlers? There are no fae here to piss off."

"It's not about the fae," said the ring. "It's about recognition. Trolls can't tell us apart; we all look the same to them. Clegg will recognize the antlers. If he thinks you're me—err, if he thinks you're Arrogan, he'll be less likely to do something stupid."

"You just admitted you're Arrogan," Will pointed out.

"It's hard to get used to referring to him in the third person," said the ring. "I'm really not him, so don't get your hopes up. I'm just part of what used to be him."

"Why don't you just use his name? It will be easier for both of us."

"I don't think it would be right."

"Would you prefer me to give you a name? I think Amos would suit you."

"Don't you fucking dare!"

Will chuckled. "Then I guess we'll stick with Arrogan."

"Fine," said the ring sullenly. "But if you start calling me Grandfather, I'll—"

"You'll what? Cuss me to death?"

"You think I can't?"

"Knowing you, you probably could, Arrogan," said Will, trying out the name.

"Have you put the cap on yet?"

"One second." Will summoned the antlers and put the cap over his head, tying the attached strap beneath his chin. "There. All set." Facing away from the stagnant lake, he set off through the ferns and bushes.

He began to get tired within minutes. "I don't feel very good."

"Your turyn is getting low."

"This fast?"

"You're spoiled. You've gotten so used to absorbing whatever you need you've forgotten what it's like to run out," said Arrogan. "Get one of the elixirs out, but just sip it as needed."

Will did, and though the taste made him gag, he began to feel better.

"Another thing you can do is expand your area of absorption, like you do when you're about to cast something big. It won't do much, but you'll absorb slightly more, even here. Every little bit helps," suggested the ring.

Will took its advice. He summoned his saber as well, using it to cut a path through the dense undergrowth. It wasn't strictly necessary—the foliage wasn't too thick to pass through—but he figured it would be easier to find his way back later if there was a clear trail. Using a dueling sword in such a fashion wasn't something most would do, since it would rapidly dull the edge, but now that he knew the spell to quickly sharpen a blade, he wasn't worried.

Fifteen minutes later, he took another sip of the elixir. It cured his fatigue, but did nothing for the heat. His gambeson was beginning to show sweat stains under his armpits, despite the fact that the sweat had to soak through multiple layers of linen. "How far is it to his village?"

"About an hour's walk."

"Ugh." He wondered if the armor was a mistake. "The heat is killing me."

"You haven't even been here that long," said Arrogan.

"I'm wearing a mail shirt."

"Did I tell you to do that? You'll sweat to death."

"It seemed reasonable," said Will defensively. "They have claws, remember?"

"So it will take them a few minutes longer to rip you to pieces. Listen, if it comes to a fight, run. And if you're running, the mail will only slow you down. Are you sure you were really my apprentice? I'm allergic to stupidity."

That was all the encouragement Will needed. He started to shimmy out of the armor, but he paused as something rustled in the brush to his right. "I heard something," he whispered. Before he could say anything else, a tall figure came into view, striding toward him.

Will's mouth went dry as the creature stepped over the closest ferns, stopping in front of him. It was humanoid in shape, standing somewhere close to nine feet tall. Its skin was a mottled grey and looked to be covered in lichen or some similar growth. Though it was standing erect, its arms were impossibly long, such that its hands hung almost to its knees. The fingers were tipped with long, green claws, which matched the thing's teeth when it opened its mouth to gape at him. "Grhllk!"

He held up his hands, then pointed to himself. "Friend!"

"I don't remember agreeing to that," quipped the ring. "I'd say we're acquaintances at best."

The troll's eyes were small, black beads set deeply within a heavy brow. It bent forward to examine him, inhaling deeply to get his scent. Then it growled.

"It's a troll," said Will, trying to keep his voice calm.

"Where?" asked Arrogan.

"In front of me. It's smelling me now."

"Point to the antlers, then show him the ale."

Will lifted one hand to point at the antlers on his head. Then he summoned the ale cask he had bought. It wasn't large, being only a rundlet that held perhaps eighteen gallons of cheap ale, but he hoped it would be sufficient.

The troll took a step back in alarm when the wooden cask appeared. Will pointed at it and said the word, "Ale." Then he pointed to the troll.

The creature seemed to understand. "Lrmeg reth," it pronounced, pointing to itself.

Will nodded, then pointed at the knotted, gnarly protuberance between the troll's legs. "I'll trade for that."

The troll turned its head to one side, then uttered a long string of nonsensical syllables, followed by a series of strange coughing sounds.

"Will, are you making gestures?" asked Arrogan.

"Yeah, I'm trying to explain what I want."

"Well, you're confusing him. Lrmeg seems to think you want to have sex with him. You should let me do the talking."

"You can speak troll?"

"I thought I explained that earlier. By the way, that coughing sound you heard was Lrmeg laughing. You're lucky he doesn't fancy humans." The ring went on to utter an unholy collection of bizarre grunts and sounds. After listening a moment, the troll answered.

"Back away from the ale now," suggested the ring. "Maybe make a sweeping gesture with your arm. Oh! And give him the empty jar you brought."

Will summoned the jar. "Will he know how to use it?"

"I'll explain. And again, I told you already, they aren't like you."

"What does that mean?" asked Will.

"They aren't stupid," said Arrogan. The ring began speaking in troll again, and after a short while the troll took both the ale cask and the empty jar. Then it left.

"He left," said Will. "But he didn't pee in the jar."

"Did you expect him to do it in front of you?"

Will paused, unsure what he had been expecting. "Well, no, but—"

"Listen, trolls aren't like humans, but they're not stupid and they do have their own culture. Urinating is a very private thing for them. They don't do it very often since their bodies are very efficient in reusing waste. I guess you could say they're shy."

"Shy?" Will was dumbfounded. "How can they be shy? The troll was naked. I saw way more than I ever wanted to see of his anatomy. If he can walk around like that, why couldn't he just pee right then and there?"

"There are several erroneous assumptions in that rock that you pretend is a brain," said Arrogan. "First, trolls don't have gender. Second, the thing you saw between his legs isn't where they urinate from. They only have one orifice, so they have to vomit it up from their mouths."

Will felt nauseous just imagining it, but another question entered his mind. "Then how do they reproduce?"

"Two ways," said the ring. "The simplest is when some part of them gets cut off. They regenerate like starfish, so if you cut off an arm it will grow back, but the dismembered arm also recovers, growing an entirely new troll. That's one reason they got out of control when they entered the human realm long ago. Cutting them up just made matters worse."

"That's disgusting."

"Wait until I tell you how they reproduce sexually—"

"Please don't."

"—one troll jams his thing into another troll. It's got a sharp point on it when they're aroused. Once he's inside, it breaks off and recombines with the flesh of the other troll, then it grows for a few weeks before clawing its way out."

Will's stomach turned over. The smell of the swamp wasn't helping either.

"So, you're lucky Lrmeg knew enough to realize you weren't seriously trying to solicit him for sex, otherwise he might have given you a fatal wound."

His stomach heaved, and he began to retch.

"Yeah, that's pretty close to the sound they make when they're going at it," said Arrogan. "You're a natural." Then he laughed. "I just realized you're more similar to them than I thought, since in a way, they're all a bunch of giant dicks."

The ring laughed maniacally while Will fought to get his rebellious stomach to quiet down. Eventually it calmed and he focused on his breathing. Once he felt better, he asked, "How long do you think we'll have to wait?"

"Somewhere between five or six hours and a full day."

"Why so long?"

"I already told you they don't pee very often. It's a lucky thing that they like ale. They'll throw a party, get drunk, and afterward they'll hopefully be sober enough to deposit the recycled liquids in the jar you gave them."

A fresh wave of nausea washed over him and he started to feel faint. It wasn't like him to be so easily nauseated, and he eventually realized, it was the lack of turyn that was making him so sensitive. He took another sip from the elixir of turyn, finishing the vial, and immediately began to feel better. There were twenty-two more vials left, and he'd used one in less than an hour. *I'll run out if they take a full day,* he observed silently.

While he waited, Will took off his armor and stored it in the limnthal. It was simply too hot to continue wearing it. He kept his saber out, though, just in case. It might be a futile gesture, but if he was attacked, he didn't intend to die without a fight.

Arrogan laughed when he mentioned the sword. "At the very best you'll just leave a few new baby trolls behind, assuming you manage to cut anything off before they eat you."

"You aren't very encouraging," said Will sourly.

"You don't have to worry. I came here quite a few times. These trolls are well behaved. There won't be any trouble."

The heat was miserable. Even without the gambeson, Will was sure he would die of dehydration from sweating so much. One by one, he sipped at the elixirs of turyn, storing the empty vials as he finished them. When he wasn't drinking those, he drank the water stored in the limnthal. His thirst seemed unending, and he wondered which would run out first, the water or the elixirs.

It wasn't just sweating that made him uncomfortable, though; the air was filled with insects, all of which seemed to think he was a tasty treat. At one point he asked, "Isn't there a spell to keep flies away?"

"There is," answered the ring, "but you couldn't use it here."

"Why not?"

"Are you getting dumber? Or has the heat cooked the wet noodle that serves as your brain?"

Oh, the turyn expenditure, Will realized. "Couldn't I just drink more of the elixir?"

"You could, but keeping a spell active eats up a lot more power than you might think. Something that would seem insignificant in our world would cause you to run through those elixirs every few minutes."

"I think it would be worth it," he grumbled. "I've probably lost a quart of blood already."

He was on the tenth vial of turyn when a rustling announced the return of Lrmeg. Will saw the large clay jar in the troll's hands. Lrmeg placed the jar on the ground in front of him and Will opened the lid for a brief second to check the contents. He regretted it immediately as the smell assaulted his nose. He jammed the lid back in place and stored the jar in the limnthal before the stench could overwhelm him.

"He just brought the jar back," said Will, for Arrogan's benefit. "Can you thank him for me?"

A short string of guttural noises issued from the ring, and Lrmeg nodded. Will started to turn away, thinking it was time to head back home, but the troll barked a command of some sort. "What was that?" he asked.

"He said you haven't given him the reward," responded the ring. "Didn't you give him the second cask?"

Will's mouth went dry. "There is no second cask."

"I told you to bring two quarter casks," said Arrogan. "Which part of that were you too stupid to understand?"

"They didn't have quarter casks, so I got a rundlet cask. It's almost twice as much so I thought it would be fine," explained Will.

"Then you should have gotten two rundlets, idiot! They expect one to drink right away and a second one when they return with the product of their festivities."

"Oh. Well, that's unfortunate."

"I can't believe you're really this stupid," said Arrogan. The troll was beginning to growl as its suspicion grew. "He sounds really angry."

"What do I do?"

"Can you ask them to melt down the ring after they finish with you? I don't really fancy being stuck in Muskeglun until the end of time."

"This isn't the time for jokes," Will hissed.

"That wasn't a joke."

Will's mind was racing. "I have an idea. Tell him I have his ale."

"They really dislike liars," the ring warned.

"Just do it!"

Another string of unintelligible gibberish emerged from the ring, and Will summoned the water jar. It was still more than half full, so it was fairly heavy, which Will hoped would help with the lie. He backed away as Lrmeg stepped forward to claim his prize.

Will summoned another elixir of turyn and drank the vial in a single gulp. He continued to back away, and when he saw Lrmeg reach for the lid of the jar, he turned and ran. A blood-curdling scream rang out behind him, urging him to greater speed. Will focused his turyn in his legs and ran for all he was worth.

"What did you give him?" asked the ring. "He's calling for your head. Every troll in the area is going to be hot on your trail."

"Water!" Will blurted out as he ran. He could hear Lrmeg crashing through the foliage close behind him. "How fast can they run?"

"Faster than you."

The ground ahead was clear and level for a short distance, so Will risked a look back. Lrmeg was just ten feet behind and closing quickly. *Shit, shit, shit!* Somehow, he managed to run faster, but it still wouldn't be enough.

"If you still have that sword out, I have a piece of advice," said the ring. "They don't feel much pain and you can't really hurt a troll permanently, but there is one spot you can aim for that will slow them down."

"Where?" yelled Will.

"The dick," said Arrogan. "Not the dick itself mind you, but inside the body behind it. That's where the brain is."

Will was dodging around trees and heavy bushes, trying to maintain his lead against the larger heavier troll. "I'm about to die and you're still trying to be humorous?"

"I'm serious. Aim for the groin."

He didn't have enough wind to continue the conversation. Will saw a large, dead tree lying across his path. He remembered it from his hike earlier, so he knew the other side of the massive trunk was relatively clear. He slapped his left hand down on top of the horizontal log and vaulted over, then dropped into a crouch on the other side with his sword at the ready.

Lrmeg didn't even have to jump. The troll passed over the fallen tree with nothing more than a wide step, and Will stood up beneath the troll. With both hands he rammed the saber upward, straight into the crux where Lrmeg's legs met.

The troll screeched as a foot and a half of steel entered his body, then twisted violently and fell to one side, his body twitching. Will jerked the sword free and resumed running. "I got him!"

"I guess it's true what they say about fools and luck," said Arrogan.

"How long will he be down?"

"A few minutes. Even if you put it right through his brain, they heal very quickly."

Hooting calls echoed through the trees, making it impossible for Will to tell where they were coming from. It sounded as though they were all around him. He focused his turyn on his legs and lungs and continued his headlong flight. His decision to cut a path turned out to be fortuitous, else he would have quickly lost his way back.

Minutes passed, and he was forced to drink another elixir of turyn. He was beginning to hope that he had lost his pursuers. Hope died when he saw his destination ahead. At least fifteen trolls stood between him and freedom.

"They were waiting for me!" he exclaimed.

"I told you they weren't stupid," Arrogan commented dryly.

The cracking of branches and rustling of leaves announced Lrmeg's approach from the rear. Will saw shadows to his left and right and he knew he would be surrounded within moments.

Desperate, Will attempted a spell he had studied but never practiced, the demon-armor spell. Fear and adrenaline sharpened his mind, and he somehow succeeded in assembling the construct on the first try. He slammed as much turyn into the spell as he dared, then released it.

Heatless, red-orange flames engulfed his body and Will charged into the pack of trolls standing between him and the congruence point, waving his sword and screaming at the top of his lungs. "Burn! Burn, you motherless bastards!"

Surprised at the appearance of a human bonfire, the trolls scrambled back, falling over one another to escape the suicidal human. One of them was knocked prone by his companions as they fled. Will leapt over the fallen troll and reached the congruence, then promptly fell flat on his face as his feet slipped on the muddy, leaf-strewn ground.

He scrambled to his feet—or tried to; his body had become sluggish. The spell was draining his turyn faster than he had expected. The flames around him flickered and died, while the trolls turned and glared at him angrily.

Legs shaking, he managed to stand and took one final step. He was free. Will moved sideways, his body shifting between worlds as the troll he had jumped over swept a long, claw-tipped hand through the place he had been standing.

Will found himself in the dark, lightless interior of Arrogan's workshop and dizziness overtook him. Exhausted, he sat down suddenly.

"Are they eating you yet?" asked Arrogan curiously.

"Shut up," said Will and dismissed the limnthal. He lay down on the cold, stone floor and enjoyed the silence.

CHAPTER 27

After a few minutes, Will's turyn recovered and with it his strength. He sat up and cast a light spell, illuminating the workshop so he could ascend the ladder. He stopped when he noticed he still had the saber in his hand, its blade covered in drying troll ichor.

Two spells later and the blade was clean and newly sharpened, then he stored it in the limnthal. He had given up using the sheath altogether. It was easier to summon it when needed and store it when not needed. Satisfied that he wouldn't frighten his mother with a gore-covered weapon, he went up the ladder and knocked on the trap door.

It opened a few seconds later, accompanied by his mother's face, illuminated by a candle she held in one hand. "William?"

"It's me, Mom," he answered before taking another step and poking his head out.

"Did you find what you needed?" she asked.

Will smiled, emerging the rest of the way into the bedroom. "I did. No trouble at all."

"What was it like—Sweet Mother Temarah! Are you wounded?" Erisa began checking him over. "Take off your tunic."

Belatedly, he realized his mistake. He'd cleaned and put away the sword but neglected the fact that Lrmeg had also bled all over him. There was crusted gore in his hair and dark stains on his tunic. "Don't worry, none of it is mine," he said quickly.

"I should hope not! What is this? It isn't blood. Oh, you smell like rotten meat!" Erisa pointed at the door. "Outside!"

His mother followed him out, giving orders as they went. The sun was just beginning to come up. "Sammy, fetch the tub. Annabelle, I'll need you to help haul water. Where's Johnathan?"

"In the garden," answered Sammy, giving Will a look of disgust as she wrinkled her nose. "What happened to Will?"

Since she was pregnant, Annabelle's reaction was more severe. "Ack! Oh, I think I'm going to be sick!"

"Do it outside," snapped Erisa. "It smells bad enough in here already. Keep moving, William. Don't stop."

Will considered stopping them and using a personal bathing spell, but his mother already had everyone in motion, so he went along with the flow. It had been a while since he'd had a proper bath without using magic anyway.

"Strip," ordered his mother, using a tone that would likely have made even Sergeant Nash jump to obey.

Will looked helplessly at Sammy and Annabelle. "Mom…"

Erisa glanced at the two young women. "Take his clothes around back and wash them in the other tub."

"Awww," said Sammy, though she didn't argue.

Annabelle wasn't so quick to obey. "It's nothing I haven't seen before."

Erisa glared at her. "I'm not done talking to you, young lady. Would you like to continue our conversation with Will present?"

Annabelle made herself scarce.

An hour later, Will was dressed in a warm robe and warming his feet by the fire while his clothes drip-dried on the porch. Sammy sat in a chair nearby. "Will you be cooking?" she asked hopefully.

"I'm a little tired," said Will.

"You can start peeling carrots, Sammy," ordered Erisa. "I'll be cooking."

Johnathan stood in the doorway, and he laughed at the pout Sammy adopted when she heard the news. "Why don't you tell us what happened, Will?"

"Well, I didn't expect any trouble, but there are trolls in Muskeglun," began Will.

"Trolls?" Erisa glared daggers at him. "I swear, William, you're taking years off my life."

"It would have been all right," protested Will. "But I didn't bring a second cask of ale." He explained what had happened while trying and failing to downplay the dangers. It was a futile attempt—the word 'troll' alone made it clear how dangerous his adventure had really been.

When he finished, his uncle spoke first. "Lesson learned. Next time, bring three casks of ale."

Will furrowed his brow. "Three?"

"Two for the trolls and one for me. It's been a while since we had any good ale."

Erisa leaned over and half-heartedly punched her brother's shoulder. "Is that all you have to say? He nearly got himself killed."

Johnathan gave her an unsympathetic look. "It won't do much good to scold him. He's a grown man, and a wizard to boot. It's not like we can stop him from putting himself in danger. At least he's going back to Wurthaven. He should be safe there. I'm still worried about what will happen to Eric if the king decides to prosecute a war with Darrow."

"He's not even eighteen yet," complained Erisa.

"I will be in another month," Will pointed out. Then something occurred to him. "Have you seen Eric recently?"

His uncle nodded. "He came by last week on his day off. He wanted to show us his new armor."

Will grinned. "He got new armor?" He had wondered if Selene would be able to make good on her promise considering the way her father had summoned her back home.

Erisa looked closely at him. "Was that from you?"

He shook his head. "Selene."

His uncle whistled. "A present from the king's daughter herself!"

Annabelle seemed depressed by the news. "Have you seen her?"

"No. I asked her for the favor before we got you out of Barrowden, but I wasn't sure if she would remember it after everything that happened."

Johnathan spoke again. "Well, whatever you told her must have been good. When Eric visited, he had not only a coat of mail but a breastplate and a new helm. Did you know he bought out his conscription?"

"No," said Will.

His uncle nodded. "He's a corporal now, and with some luck he might make sergeant in another year or two."

Will was happy for his cousin, and slightly jealous. He had just made corporal himself when he'd been forced into the circumstances that led to him winding up in Wurthaven. His military career had come to an abrupt end. *And what am I now? A student with few prospects and an axe hanging over my head.* "I wish I had been here to see him."

"He should be back in a week," said Erisa.

"You should see him," put in Sammy. "He's huge now! Even his muscles have muscles. I think he's even stronger than Papa!"

Eric had always tended more to muscle than Will had. Not that he was small by any means. Will had gained more height, and his military time had given him a respectable amount of muscle, but he suspected that Eric had continued to surpass him.

Annabelle patted his forearm. "It's all right, Will, some of us prefer men on the leaner side."

He pulled his arm away hastily and Erisa frowned. "I wish I could stay, but I can't," he informed them. "I have to get back as soon as possible. When Eric comes back, ask him to check on my friends from Company B, Tiny and Dave. I'd like to know how they're doing."

Deep down, Will wished he could leave enough money to afford mail for Tiny and Dave. He had the coin now, but he needed every crown if he was going to have a chance of paying the blood-price he owed.

"You'll stay for a day at least, won't you?" asked his mother.

"I can't."

Erisa scowled. "Your clothes aren't even dry. You should wait a while and by then it will be afternoon. You should wait and leave tomorrow morning."

"The places I'm traveling through have different times of night and day. Some of the journey will be at night no matter when I leave. Besides, darkness isn't really a problem for me anymore." He tapped his temple, next to his eyes. "The sooner I return the better." *I have to make these potions and find a way to sell them before Friday,* he thought, *otherwise my goose is cooked.*

Of course, there was another option available to him. He could run. With Tailtiu's help he could go almost anywhere, places where Count Spry's men could never find him. But that wouldn't keep his family safe. Now that they were meeting with Eric, the secret of their hiding place wasn't so secret anymore. If Count Spry couldn't find him, he might well decide to take revenge on those close to him.

"I should be able to bring money next time," said Will.

"Eric's been helping us lately," said Johnathan. "Don't worry too much. We'll be fine. It can't be easy for you to travel this far."

"It isn't as hard as you might think," said Will, trying not to remember the fel-wolves. He got to his feet. "I need to look at Grandfather's books before I go."

The bookshelves in Arrogan's bedroom were pretty much just as they had been, although Erisa had added a few decorations here and there. Will summoned the limnthal so he could speak to the ring. "I need to find the recipe for the regeneration potion."

"And you think I can help with that?" asked the ring dourly.

"I'm in your old bedroom," clarified Will. "But I don't have time to search through every book for it."

"*Gidding's Apothecary* will have it," said Arrogan.

"Isn't that the first book on alchemy you showed me?"

"It's the main one," the ring informed him. "All the good recipes are in there."

Will scanned the shelves until he found the massive tome, then stored it in his limnthal. "Are there any books with battle spells here?" he asked.

"Not for you," said the ring waspishly.

"Are they too difficult?"

"Most of them are too easy—deceptively so. You're just beginning to learn. You shouldn't mess with things like that until you're able to handle more difficult magic."

"That makes no sense. You just said they were easy," snapped Will.

"A five-year-old has the strength to pick up a knife, but would you hand him a shaving razor? Of course not. You teach him to play ball, you fine-tune his athletic skills. You let him grow up and learn restraint. Battle spells are simple and deadly. With them you could kill or injure dozens with a small mistake. Even worse, you could kill yourself. Grow up first. Learn the hard stuff, hone your skills. Then you can think about picking up spells that kill."

"I'm not a child," said Will, though even to his own ears, he sounded petulant.

"How did you escape the trolls?" asked Arrogan, shifting gears.

"I used the demon-armor spell. You told me they were afraid of fire, so I hoped it would scare them enough so I could get to the crossing point."

"The demon-armor spell is a battle spell, but a relatively safe one. The important thing, though, is that you used it creatively. You need to learn many more spells and gain experience using them in unexpected ways before you jump into something as crude and stupid as simply blowing people up. If you aren't willing to do that, you may as well get a fire elemental and give up on mastering true magic, because you won't be much better than a goddamn sorcerer."

"That's all well and good, but it won't make much difference if I get killed before I gain the sort of mastery you're talking about," argued Will.

"Then it's better if you die," said the ring coldly. "How many times do you think I used battle spells to kill people?"

"Considering all the people you supposedly killed, I'd imagine you used them pretty frequently."

"Wrong. Even if you're trying to kill someone, it's very rare for the best option to be a spell of mass destruction," said Arrogan.

"I don't want mass destruction! *Any* destruction would be good, even something small, or a way to defend myself."

"Listen up, boy. There are a few books in this room with those sorts of spells, but you'll never find them. Not the way you are now, and I'm not going to help you, because those books also contain a few spells that could do things like slaughter everyone in Cerria. I'd rather you meet an unfortunate end than take a risk that a novice like you might stumble across a spell that could cause that sort of havoc. Stick to the book I left you, *Practical Magic.* There's plenty in there to help you."

"Yeah, I can climb walls and open locks," said Will sarcastically.

"Two spells they would *never* teach you in that pig wallow you call a school," snapped the ring angrily. "The same goes for most of the other spells you'll find in *Practical Magic*. And yes, a few of them can be used to lethal effect. Be patient and eventually you might be as much of a wizard as that girl you keep pining for."

"Selene isn't a wizard."

"She's more of a wizard than *you*. You told me about that cleaning spell she created. Assuming you weren't lying, that thing is a work of genius. Her only fault lies in not having been trained properly from the beginning, that and having elementals, of course. You could learn a thing or two from her."

"Could she learn?" asked Will suddenly. "Could I teach her, the way you did me?"

"A muttonhead like you couldn't teach a pig to find mud."

Will ignored the insult, having long ago become used to Arrogan's inflammatory invective. "But is it possible?"

"It's possible, if you ever figure out how to find your head from your asshole. The spell-cage spell is in the book I left you as well, not that you're close to being able to use it. If you ever become skilled enough to use that cleaning spell of hers, then you might consider trying it."

"Is the spell-cage spell that hard?"

"No. The point here is that you need to learn finesse before you start putting other people's lives at risk."

"William?" It was his mother's voice.

Will dismissed the limnthal and turned around. "I think I found it."

"Were you talking to someone?" asked Erisa.

How could he explain the Ring of Vile and Unspeakable Knowledge and Power to her? It wasn't impossible, but it was a long conversation he didn't really feel like having. "Just talking out loud," he told her. "How are my clothes?"

"Damp. You shouldn't wear them yet. You'll catch cold."

"I have an idea." He went out the front door to examine his clothes, which were draped across the porch rail. With a moment's concentration, he assembled the spell he had been using to clean his clothes for the past few weeks. He'd never used it on already clean clothes, but he reasoned that a relative lack of dirt wouldn't stop it from working. Sammy followed him out to see what he was doing.

A cloud of water vapor appeared, then rapidly dissipated, leaving his tunic and trousers bone dry. Will smiled and turned toward Sammy, who was staring at him with wide eyes. "They're dry now."

"That was amazing," said Sammy in awe. She tentatively reached out to feel the fabric. "Are you sure you won't move back home? You could save me so much time."

He ran his hand down Sammy's coppery curls. "Sorry, little fox, I can't stay."

"Little fox?" His cousin's eyes studied him as she tried to decide if the term was an attempt to tease her.

"Little fox," repeated Will, tapping the end of her nose. "Red hair, pointy nose—you remind me of a fox kit."

"Hmmm." Sammy looked thoughtful. "I guess I'll allow it." She gave him a quick hug, then Will took the clothes to the bedroom and swapped them for the robe he was wearing.

Suitably dressed, Will said his goodbyes and went back outside. Everyone stood on the porch and waved to him as he left. Will gave them a return wave and marched resolutely into the forest. Despite his resolve, he really didn't want to leave. The world that waited on him was lonely and full of danger.

Chapter 28

The return trip with Tailtiu was similar, but this time they took a longer route, avoiding the region of Faerie where the darklings lived. It added a few hours to the trip, but Will felt it was worth it. Now that he had acquired what he needed, he felt less uncertainty about the future. He had a rough idea of how long it would take to make the potions, so the remaining variable was whether he would be able to sell them before Friday and whether they would fetch a price high enough to solve his problem.

It was early Monday afternoon when he finally got back to Wurthaven. Will even managed to make it to his last class, Spell Theory. As soon as that was done, he wanted to start on the regeneration potions, but lack of sleep was making it difficult to focus, so he went back to the dorm and went to bed early.

He woke several hours before dawn and made use of his time by going to the Alchemy building and arranging the initial setup for the regeneration potions. He wouldn't have enough time to start the first phase, but he wanted to have everything ready for the next evening once he was done with Spell Theory.

That done, he went to his Fencing class. It was his first appearance in almost a week, so he had some explaining to do, which he glossed over by claiming to have been ill for most of the previous week. It wasn't too far from the truth, aside from omitting the reason he had been so ill.

After that was Composition, in which Janice shot questioning glances at him, though she didn't have a chance to ask where he'd been the previous day. She caught him in the hall after class since they both had half an hour before History would start. "Where were you yesterday? I thought you were well enough for class."

"I had to run some errands."

She looked suspiciously at him. "What errands?"

"I had to get an ingredient for a potion I'm making," he answered truthfully.

Janice looked him up and down. "You didn't get banged up this time, or are you hiding new wounds?"

Will looked away, feigning innocence. "I'm not sure what you're referring to."

"You still haven't told me what happened to you last week. Were you in a fight? I saw the wounds on your shoulder." She paused, then lowered her voice, "Did you kill someone?"

He closed his eyes, taking a deep breath. *Actually, yes, I did kill someone, or possibly two someones,* he thought. Opening them again, he fixed her with a level stare. "Is that what you think of me?"

Janice didn't flinch. "Well, did you?"

He looked around to make certain no one was close by. "Actually, I went into the city to sell some potions. I was ambushed on the way back. I had to defend myself."

Her eyes narrowed. "And?"

"And I may have killed someone. I definitely wounded each of them. I didn't wait around to see how they fared afterward," he told her. It wasn't quite the truth, but it was close enough.

"*Them?* How many were there?" she hissed.

"Several," he said sullenly. "The less you know the better."

"Bull," she said angrily. "It was because of me, wasn't it? Did Count Spry set them on you?"

He shook his head, then lied, "Probably not. I think they saw me getting paid when I sold the potions. They were just regular ruffians."

"I don't know why I bother asking. You never give me straight answers anyway," she huffed. After a brief pause, she added, "Tell me about Selene."

His cheeks reddened, and he asked tentatively, "Was that you?"

"What do you think?"

"Well, Seth didn't seem very flustered, so—" Janice's gaze hardened as he spoke, so he quickly changed tactics. "I'm sorry. I wasn't myself. Thank you for taking care of me, in spite of my strange behavior."

Her features softened. "I wasn't mad, until you mentioned Seth. Being mistaken for a princess is one thing, being confused with your ex-roommate is another thing entirely. Just don't let it happen again."

"Thanks," he said humbly. "And once again, sorry."

"Don't be. You were delirious. I'm still worried about you, though. You realize you're heading for disaster, don't you?"

Which one? he wondered. "How so?"

"You've made an enemy of one of the most powerful noblemen in Terabinia and you're in love with the king's daughter. I don't see this ending well for you."

Will tried to laugh it off. "I've been told I make poor choices."

"Well, at least one of them is my fault, so depending on who kills you, I may feel responsible."

"I'll try to make sure it's the king that kills me then," he joked.

"That isn't funny."

He gave up on humor. "In any case, Dennis wasn't your fault. He chose to do what he did, and I chose to take the law into my own hands. You weren't responsible for either one of those things." Anxious to end the conversation, he looked around. "I think it's almost time for History."

The rest of the day passed without event, and after supper that evening, he returned to the Alchemy building. The first stage of the regeneration potion involved bringing the troll urine to a boil under high pressure. Apparently, this was necessary to ensure that no living matter from the troll donor survived within the fluid. While he waited on that to finish, he used his time to activate more of the blood-cleanse potions.

He worked until almost midnight, finishing the sterilization and setting up the next stage of the process. During the dead time while he waited on the second stage to finish, he finished a total of five of the blood-cleanse potions. By the time he had cleaned up and made his way to bed, he was dead tired and ready for sleep.

The next day he followed the same pattern, completing five more of the blood-cleanse potions and finishing the purification of the final ingredients in the regeneration potions. His yield had been good, and given the amount of urine he had started with, it appeared he would be able to make nearly ten of the regeneration potions.

Professor Karlovic stopped by the workshop where Will was working as he was leaving for the night. "I see you're hard at work."

Will looked up and nodded. "Yes, sir. I didn't see you yesterday, but I have something I think you'll be interested in."

"Which is?"

"I'm working on regeneration potions," said Will. "I should have some ready tomorrow, but I need to sell them quickly."

The professor's brows rose in amazement. "How? The main ingredient is impossible to get."

"I went to Muskeglun. I traded ale for urine."

Karlovic was shaking his head in disbelief. "But you don't speak their language, do you? No, of course you don't. No one does anymore. How did you make yourself understood?"

"I found some notes and advice left behind in an old journal from my master," said Will, bending the truth. "That and some luck got me what I needed."

"I'd like to see that journal," said the professor. "Your old teacher obviously had a lot of secrets."

"Sorry, Professor. I promised not to share his work. Perhaps someday, when I'm older and I've understood it all. Maybe I could become a teacher. I think there's a lot of old knowledge that the world could benefit from."

Professor Karlovic frowned. "Where did you get the recipe for the regeneration potion? Was that in his journal as well?"

"He had a copy of *Gidding's Apothecary.* I copied the recipe from there."

"That's a restricted book," said the professor. "The recipes are dangerous and inappropriate for modern alchemy. That's why I've worked so hard to find new methods to produce alchemical products. How did your former teacher come to possess a copy?"

"He wasn't a modern wizard," said Will simply.

"Do you have the book?"

Karlovic's sudden interest made Will cautious. "No. But I can get to it when need be."

"What does that mean?"

"It's hidden."

Irritated, the professor responded, "You certainly keep your secrets close to your chest. I've gone out of my way to help you, even going as far as lending you this workshop. Don't you think you should trust me a little more?"

"I appreciate it, sir. I really do, but I've gotten more paranoid of late. Did you know I was attacked after I met the buyer for the universal antidote?"

"Attacked?"

"Ambushed," said Will. "Right after I left the tavern, several men started following me. I barely escaped with my skin intact."

"Are you suggesting I had something to do with that?"

Will shook his head. "No, sir. Personally, I think it was done at the behest of Count Spry, but I really don't know enough to say. Until I can pay off the blood-price I can't afford to let my guard down."

Karlovic coughed. "Well, I suppose I can't blame you. When do you have to pay?"

"Day after tomorrow. That's why I need to find a buyer quickly."

"Friday? That's absurd! There's no way I can find a buyer that soon. Those regeneration potions might be worth five hundred crowns a piece, but finding someone that can afford them won't be easy. What about a loan?"

"A loan?"

The professor nodded. "How much do you lack? With the potions in hand, and a little help from me, you might be able to get a loan to cover the difference until you can sell those potions."

"After I turn in the rest of the blood-cleanse potions and collect from the Bursar's Office, almost three hundred crowns."

"Three hundred?" Karlovic seemed as though he was about to choke. "That won't be easy. Let me talk to the chancellor in the morning. There may be something he can do."

"Thanks, Professor."

"If I can find a way for you to get the gold, will you let me see the book?"

"*Gidding's Apothecary,* doesn't the college have a copy?" asked Will.

The professor nodded. "It's very old and some of it has been damaged. I'd very much like to compare the two and see if I can fill in the blanks."

Will thought about it a moment. "I can't sell it."

"I just want to examine it. You can stay with me the entire time. I wouldn't dream of stealing it. In fact, if you'll let me, I could have scribes make copies. I'd be willing to let you have a new copy so you wouldn't have to risk damaging your original in the future."

Arrogan's copy was in excellent condition, a result of whatever preservation magic the old man had used on his library, but Will didn't feel like explaining that. "I think that would be satisfactory."

"Come find me at lunch tomorrow. I may have good news by then," said Karlovic.

The professor left after that, and Will finished cleaning up. He went to bed that night feeling more hopeful than he had in weeks.

The next day he dropped by the Healing and Psyche building to give Ilona Fretz his latest blood-cleanse potions. He also inquired about the regeneration potions.

"You've really made them?" she asked, her eyes lighting up with interest.

Will nodded. "After I finish them this evening, I should have seven or eight."

"We'd love to have them, but there could be some difficulties. How much would you be willing to sell them for?"

"I don't know how much they're worth," said Will slowly. "Professor Karlovic tells me they might go for as much as five hundred gold apiece.

Ilona visibly winced. "That makes it even more problematic. I've already used up my expense budget for the year buying the blood-cleanse potions. I'll have to talk to Doctor Morris. He might be willing to rearrange our budget for something like this." She paused. "But I don't know if I can get him to agree to a price like that."

"I need at least three hundred crowns," said Will. "Otherwise they're going to lock me up tomorrow."

She frowned. "I'll see what I can do. Come see me in the morning."

Will left, feeling nervous. His optimism from the night before was fading. He hoped Professor Karlovic would have something good to tell him at lunch.

Composition was a disaster. He'd missed almost a week of classes and he'd been so focused on his alchemy projects that he hadn't put any time into making up the essay he had missed. Professor Conrad wasn't shy about pointing out his deficiencies in front of the rest of the class. "You've missed two essays, Mister Cartwright, and that's on top of the fact that your earlier work was abysmal. Do you really think I'll give you pass for this class at the end of the year?"

If I'm even here, Will thought. "No, ma'am. I'll try to do better."

Janice caught up to him in the hall. "I could help."

He gave her a despondent look. "How?"

"Let me do a few of your essays. All you have to do is recopy them."

"I'm not Dennis," he said flatly.

She flinched as though he had slapped her, but she didn't back down. "I didn't deserve that."

Will deflated. "You're right. I'm sorry. But it really won't work. Professor Conrad has seen my previous essays. She wouldn't be fooled if I turned in something you wrote."

She pursed her lips. "Then let me help you. You write it, and I'll help you revise it. We can work on it Saturday."

He wasn't sure he would still be a free man on Saturday, but sharing his anxiety wouldn't help. "Sure," he answered, "and thank you."

Everything changed in History class, however. Midway through the lecture the double doors to the auditorium banged open. The professor turned in annoyance to address whoever had interrupted, but her angry response died in mid-sentence. "I don't know who you think—"

There were four armed and armored city constables in the doorway. One of them held a rolled-up piece of paper. "We have an arrest warrant for William Cartwright. Is he present?"

Will wanted to melt into the floor, but there was no avoiding the situation. Every face in the auditorium turned to him, and Melissa Fontenot raised her arm silently to point at him. Grimly, Will stood and looked down at the men who had come to claim him. "I'm not due to see the magistrate until tomorrow."

"Given the considerable size of the sum you owe, an order has been given to detain you a day early to ensure that you do appear," said the lead constable. "I'd advise you to come quietly."

His heart was pounding, and he could feel a cold sweat break out on his skin. Unconsciously, Will clenched his fists. There were only four of them. *I've dealt with worse odds.* A hand on his arm brought him back to reality.

"Violence will only make things worse," said Janice.

Will lowered his eyes. If he let them take him, it was all over. He'd never be able to finish raising the money. He glanced around the room, seeing a mixture of curiosity, worry, and excitement on the faces of his fellow students. They were wondering if the man who had murdered Dennis Spry would put up a fight.

He made his way to the aisle and descended to the floor of the auditorium, where the constables waited on him. One of them held a pair of iron shackles in his hands. "Those aren't necessary," said Will. "I'll come quietly."

"Turn around," barked the lead constable. "Give me your hands."

Cheeks burning with shame, Will did as he was told, and the constables bound his arms together behind his back. Once he was restrained, they started to leave, but one of the men shoved him from behind, causing him to stumble. Unable to catch himself, his head slammed into the wood floor, bloodying his lip.

"Get up, you clumsy lout!" ordered one of the constables.

Will tried to do as commanded, but the two men hauling him up by his shoulders only made things more difficult. He stumbled again and was rewarded with a boot to his ribs before he finally managed to get back on his feet.

He thought the worst of the shame was past, but as they left the building a crowd of curious onlookers formed to see who was being arrested. If felt as though every single student who wasn't currently in class came to watch his forcible departure.

"You didn't have to arrest me," complained Will as they walked him down the path that led to the main gate. "I would have been there tomorrow."

"Stop bitching," said the lead constable. "This is just the beginning. After they hand you over to the count's men tomorrow, you'll be dreaming of being back in our custody."

Will couldn't help but agree, though he wouldn't give them the satisfaction of doing so out loud.

Chapter 29

The city jail in Cerria was much larger than the one he had been in back in Branscombe. It had not just one holding cell, but an entire floor of them, each large enough to hold ten men, whether they liked it or not. The main headquarters for the city constabulary was three stories high, with the first floor reserved for the front desk, admitting, and other rooms that the officers used during their daily duties. The second floor was where the human trash was kept, as Constable Allen had been kind enough to explain to him, making sure that Will knew he was definitely included in that category. The third floor was administrative offices.

The residents of the holding cells were also more varied. The one that Will was currently in held six other men, two petty thieves, a man who had murdered his wife, another who had been caught sleeping with someone else's wife, a drunk who had been found sleeping on the street, and a beggar. Apparently extreme poverty was a crime in Cerria, and while Will had money, he couldn't help but think the vagrancy laws were unfair. Though he wasn't poor, he was about to be sentenced for not having enough coin, so he felt a certain amount of solidarity with the beggar.

After he was brought in, the constables relieved him of his under-armor and his belt knife, but the rest of his clothes were left on his person.

Unfortunately, for all its size—or perhaps because of it—the cell in the Cerria jail was dirtier and smellier than the one he had spent time in back in Branscombe. *I'm becoming an expert in jail cells,* thought Will ruefully. *At least it's better than the king's dungeon.*

The front wall of the cell was iron bars, while the other three walls were solid stone with built-in stone benches. If any of the occupants had to relieve themselves, there was an open drain in the center of the floor.

The benches were long enough to hold three or four men apiece, though currently there were three men on one bench, two on the second, and a solitary fellow occupying one all to himself. Will could smell trouble when he looked at the fellow, but he wasn't in a mood to care. He walked toward the bench with only one occupant.

"Fuck off, mate. I don't like company," said the man stretched out on the bench.

His good sense was telling him to go sit at the bench with only two men, but Will's irritation overrode his caution. "We'll get along well, then, I don't either. Go sit over there." He pointed at the other bench.

The other man stood up. Will didn't waste time, however; he cast the source-link spell and connected it to his new companion as he was rising. That accomplished, he examined the man he was almost certainly about to fight. The fellow was slightly taller, though not quite as well muscled as Will. His clothes were dirty but in good repair.

"What did you get put in here for, boy?" asked the stranger.

"The name is Will, and I'm here for killing a man in a duel."

"A duel? How honorable! You must feel very special!" said the other man mockingly. "But I don't see a sword now. You don't think that fancy crap will get you anywhere in this place, do you?"

Will smiled coldly. "Perhaps you could teach me?" He saw the other man's body began to tense and immediately injected a healthy dose of turyn into his opponent. A look of confusion crossed the man's face, and then Will slammed his fist into the poor bastard's upset stomach. With his other hand, he turned the fellow toward the center of the room just before he began to vomit, spraying his last meal onto the floor.

The man fell to his knees and managed to direct the rest of his stomach's contents into the drain. Will sat down on the now-empty bench. "Clean it up when you're done," he ordered. "It smells terrible."

"Asshole," gasped the sick man. "What did you do to me?"

"Nothing compared to what I'll do if you don't scrape the rest of your vomit into that hole," said Will, leaning back against the wall. The man started to argue, but his stomach began heaving again. Will glanced at the bench with three men on it. "If one of you wants more room, you're welcome to join me over here."

One of them answered, "But Jax—" The man stopped a second later and pointed at the man still vomiting on the floor.

"I'm allergic to assholes," said Will. "I don't mind sharing a bench with someone polite."

At first no one moved, until at last the drunkard staggered across the room and sat down on the other end of Will's bench. "Don't mind if I do," he slurred. "I'm Ben, by the way."

"Nice to meet you," said Will, trying not to flinch away from the smell of stale beer on the man's breath. He pointed at the man who was almost done retching. "He's Jax, right?"

"Yeah," said Ben. Several of the others in the room nodded in agreement.

Jax was finally getting back to his feet. He turned and glared at Will. "You'll regret—"

Will's expression was hard and uncaring. "Clean it up. If I have to repeat myself again, you'll be sleeping in the mess you made."

Jax said nothing for a few tense seconds, then got down on his knees and began scraping the rest of the vomit into the hole. Will closed his eyes and tried to nap. He figured he had a few hours before Jax felt well enough to start something again and he wanted to be rested before then.

***

Will ignored the food the guards brought that evening. He had two reasons for doing so, one being that the food looked disgusting. His other reason was simply that he didn't want anything solid in his stomach that might result in him needing to squat over the drain hole in the middle of the cell. Peeing with six spectators was bad enough. He figured if he got hungry enough, he would eat some of the bread stored in his limnthal, but missing one or two meals wouldn't kill him.

The rest of the evening and the night that followed were miserable for Will. Jax never worked up the courage to have another go at him, but the stone benches were not designed with sleep in mind. He dozed off in short stretches of a few minutes at a time and at one point woke when Ben slumped over and landed with his head in Will's lap.

Will eased out from under the snoring drunk and stood for a few hours rather than wake the man. Jax stared at him, confused by his seeming kindness toward the drunk.

Will stared back. "Try not being a jackass and maybe you wouldn't have to get your ass kicked all the time."

"Fuck off," said the thief, but he made no move to get up and start another fight.

Morning couldn't come soon enough, and when the guards came by with breakfast, Will greeted them with a smile. "None for me, thanks," he told them.

One of them unlocked the door. "You weren't getting any anyway. Come out."

Will did as he was told. "Am I already going to see the magistrate?"

"No, you're being released. Count Spry has dropped his petition. You're free to go," said the guard.

"What? How can that be?"

"His man went to the magistrate this morning, said he'd received the blood-price you owed him. That's all I know."

Will didn't know how to respond. He followed the guard numbly, and a few minutes later he found himself standing in the street, holding his brigandine and belt knife in one hand. "What just happened?" he muttered to himself. He turned back to the constable who was about to leave. "Where is the magistrate's office?"

The guard stopped and pointed at a large, slate-grey building directly opposite the jail, "That's the courthouse. You can ask the clerks in there, but if you actually want to see the magistrate, you'll have to make an appointment. It's hard to see him unless you have a case brought before him."

Will thanked the man and studied the street. He couldn't believe that Count Spry had simply given up on extracting his pound of flesh. *And his men would know I'm here and that I'm being released.* There were a lot of people moving through the street, but he made note of the faces of those who seemed to be loitering, then crossed over and went up the steps of the courthouse.

The interior was wide and spacious. Numerous doors let out from the main lobby, and most of them bore labels with the name of the court they served. It took Will a couple of minutes before he noticed a door labeled simply, 'General Inquiry.' Stepping in, he found a small, neat man seated at a desk.

"Can I help you?"

"I have a question," said Will. "I was supposed to see the magistrate today about a blood-price I owed to Count Spry, but I've been told the petition was dropped."

The man nodded. "For future reference, you should know the name of the magistrate if you hope to find the right court, but in your case, I happen to know. Magistrate Tumfrey was the one who was overseeing your case."

"Oh. How many magistrates are there?"

"Seven currently. Your case was pretty well known, though. It isn't often someone kills a nobleman. If you go across the lobby, you'll see the door for Magistrate Tumfrey's clerk. He can tell you more."

Will thanked the clerk and followed his advice. The door for Tumfrey's office was taller and framed by an impressively carved doorframe. He stepped inside and saw several people waiting in chairs. A long desk divided the room with a rather portly, red-faced man on the other side. Someone was already speaking to the man, so Will took a seat.

It was half an hour before Will got a chance to speak to the clerk. "I'm here to ask about what happened with my case," he told the man behind the desk.

"Name?"

"William Cartwright. I was supposed to appear before Magister Tumfrey about a blood-price."

"The case was dropped by Count Spry. You needn't worry about it," said the clerk immediately.

"Can I ask why?"

The clerk seemed bored. He propped his double-chin atop a plump hand as he answered, "I wouldn't presume to know. Most probably someone paid the blood-price—either that or someone convinced the good count to forego his due."

"Is there a way I can find out?"

The chubby clerk waved his hand dismissively. "I wouldn't know. You'd have to ask the count himself."

Will shifted uncertainly on his feet. "Is there a chance he'll change his mind? Could he ask me to pay the fine later?"

"No need to worry. The petition was formally registered and then dismissed. The count can't legally bring it up again now that it has been dropped."

"Thank you." Will left the office and went back to the street. He felt considerably relieved, at least in the financial sense, but the place between his shoulders itched. *Someone's bound to try and stick a knife in me,* he thought. He needed to put his armor back on, but the street was no place to undress.

He spotted two men at opposite ends of the street who were still there from his previous study. One of them glanced away when Will's eyes fell on him. Two buildings down from the courthouse was a large public house that probably did a brisk business serving the constables and those who frequented the courts. Rather than head for Wurthaven, Will decided it would be wise to get a meal and make a plan before risking the streets.

The inn was named The Hanged Man, probably by someone with a strong sense of irony, but despite the grim label, it was large and well kept. It offered a small number of rooms for visitors, but it was obvious as soon as Will entered that its main business was feeding the people who worked at the courthouse. A quick glance at the tables showed him that at least half the patrons were either clerks, constables, or other professionals. The remainder were probably those who either had a case to be heard that day or possibly people who lived nearby.

Will approached the bar, and when the tall, lanky man who was serving drinks came over, he asked, "Do you have any private spots to drink?"

"You mean a snug?"

"I haven't heard that term before."

The bartender smiled knowingly. "Private booths. We have a lot of customers who don't want to be seen drinking. Wait a second and Lynn will show you."

Will watched the entrance while he waited and saw one of the men he had noticed in the street enter and find a small table close to the door. He didn't have any more doubts about the man's purpose now.

A few minutes later, a serving maid returned, her tray laden with empty cups. The bartender spoke to her briefly, and she walked over to Will. "Follow me."

She led him down the bar and turned a corner through an open archway that led into another large room separate from the front room. It was lined with small, box-like, wood-paneled alcoves with curtains that kept the identities of the occupants private. Will was seated in one and he marveled when he saw that the exterior wall had a small window with frosted glass to let in sunlight. A small table sat between two padded benches, and wood panels covered the walls on both sides. He had never seen anything like it before.

"This is amazing," he said in awe.

Lynn smiled. "A lot of high-ranking officials like them, whether because they don't want to be seen drinking, or when they're here to meet a mistress. It costs one clima per hour, plus whatever you order."

"I'm actually very hungry," Will admitted. "What do you have?"

"Today it's shepherd's pie," she answered. "That and a pint of ale will set you back five pennies. Are you eating alone?"

"Pardon?" Will was confused, since there was clearly no one else with him.

She laughed. "It's a question with two meanings. Most who rent a snug either have a friend they're meeting with or they want a lady to keep them company."

"I don't have either."

Lynn laughed again. "I meant, sometimes they want us to *provide* a companion—for dinner or—" She rolled her eyes upward meaningfully, staring at the ceiling.

Her meaning dawned on him, though he still wasn't sure what she was looking at. He stared upward. "What's up there?"

"Rooms."

His cheeks warmed suddenly. "I don't think I need a companion."

"Too bad." She winked at him. "You look like you could use one. I'll put your order in. Ale and pie for one." Then she left, making sure to close the curtain behind her.

Will was so flustered that it took him a moment to remember why he had wanted privacy to begin with. "Armor, right," he reminded himself out loud. He quickly pulled his tunic over his head and then sorted out the brigandine so he could put it on.

The curtain opened behind him, and Lynn stepped in with a wooden tankard. "Oh."

Will blushed again. "Sorry, I needed to change." Hurriedly, he got the brigandine on and began working on the buckles.

Lynn put the tankard down and stared at him dubiously for a second. Then she stepped over. "Let me help. It will be quicker." Her fingers nimbly threaded the straps through the buckles and tightened them one by one. "So, why are you putting armor on? It seems like a strange thing to do in a tavern." She finished and moved back a step.

Will grabbed his tunic and pulled it over his head. "I'm worried someone is about to put something sharp between my ribs—or try to."

"They'd best think twice if they're planning to try something in here," she warned.

"Not here," he said quickly. "I just left court, but someone is following me. I wanted a chance to prepare before they catch me in the street."

"Ah," she said. "So, you ducked in here."

He nodded.

"Who's after you?"

Will hesitated, but something about the barmaid made him want to trust her. "Count Spry. One of the men he hired is already out front, sitting at a table by the door." A shocked expression crossed her face and he began to regret his decision.

After a second she responded, "We have a private back door. It costs a silver if you want to use it when you leave."

"Thank you!"

"Don't thank me yet. Let me talk to Jared. I'll be back with your food in a few minutes." A second later she was gone. She returned a short while later with a platter containing his food. "Bad news. Jared's already taken coin to keep them informed," she told him.

"How much? I'll double it," offered Will.

Lynn shook her head. "Jared doesn't work like that. He's got principles. Once he's bought, he stays bought. If you'd paid him first, he wouldn't have accepted their coin."

"That's very trustworthy of him," said Will. "But it doesn't make me feel better."

She patted his shoulder sympathetically. "I'm not as principled. I shouldn't have told you."

"Is there anything else you can do?"

"Just advice. Don't bother with the back exit. They'll be waiting for you."

I'm screwed, thought Will. *The best I can hope for is a bloodbath, and the worst involves me being gutted or kidnapped.*

"Eat your food. They can't do anything until you leave. Jared won't permit violence inside the inn. Maybe you can wait them out. I'll be back to check on you in a little while." With that, she left him alone.

CHAPTER 30

Will ate the food and sipped his ale, politely refusing a refill. He needed his wits about him. An hour passed, and he paid Lynn for a second hour in the snug. Then he asked, "If I wanted to rent a room, where's the entrance?"

She pointed across the room. "There's a private staircase from this room to the second floor where the rooms are. There's another going up from the front room too, but usually the people who rent a snug don't want to be seen going upstairs. Are you thinking about renting one?"

Will shook his head. "No. I'm going to use the back exit once my hour is up." He passed her a second clima. "For the use of the back door."

Lynn frowned. "I warned you about the back already."

He winked. "I know. Make sure Jared knows I plan to leave that way."

Her eyes lit with understanding. "Ahh, I'll do that." She started to leave, then looked back. "Good luck."

He waited until she had been gone a minute, then peeked out through the curtain. Some of the other snugs were occupied, but all of them had drawn curtains, so there was no one observing the open part of the room. Will cast the silent armor spell on his clothing, then went across the room to the stairs and ascended carefully.

At the top of the stairs he found a long hallway with doors leading off at regular intervals on either side. He went to the first door and listened for a moment, increasing the sensitivity of his hearing as much as possible. Someone was breathing inside, though it sounded as though they were asleep. He moved on to the next door.

He heard nothing, so he tried the handle and discovered the door was locked. Then he cast the unlocking spell, or tried to. At some point he misremembered the runes and his construct fell apart. Summoning the book from the limnthal, he studied the spell for a second, then tried again. This time he succeeded. Opening the door, he hurried inside just in time, for someone had started to open one of the other doors down the hall.

Will breathed a sigh of relief, for the room was indeed empty. He was alone. His relief was short-lived, however, for it only took a second for him to note that there was no exterior window. He had chosen the wrong side of the hall. He spent a minute or two thinking about the layout of the building. *I'm an idiot!* he swore silently. *Of course, the other side is the one with the outside wall.*

He listened for a brief minute to make sure the hall was empty before exiting again, then he crossed the hall and went down a few doors to listen outside the room that he thought the last guest had stepped out from. He heard breathing. Someone was sleeping inside. *Damn it.*

He tried two more doors before he found nothing but silence. Casting his spell once more, he unlocked the door and went inside, then he relocked the door behind himself. Thankfully, this room did have a small window. If he had been given to fat, he wouldn't have been able to use it, but it appeared to be just large enough to fit his frame.

The style of the window was unfamiliar to him. He was used to curtains and shutters, but behind the curtain he found a wooden latticework containing glass squares. It took him a moment to figure out how to unlatch it and push the doors apart. Looking out, he saw wooden shutters lying against the exterior of the building, presumably to protect the glass in stormy weather. Beneath him was a side alley that was empty aside from a beggar sleeping against one wall.

Will cast the climbing spell and descended to the ground, then crossed to the neighboring building and went up the wall as quickly as he could manage. Once he was on the roof, he moved to the backside of the building where he could survey the back alley. From there, he was able to observe the back entrance of the tavern he had left.

Two men waited by the door, and four more stood ten feet further down the alley. All of them seemed to know one another, for they were talking back and forth. Will scooted as far back as he could, until he was just barely able to see them without exposing himself. He was prepared to wait.

Half an hour went by before another man appeared, one who he recognized. It was the greybeard, Remi, the man who had hired the first group of thugs that had nearly killed him. Remi began loudly haranguing the men waiting in the alley.

"What are you so upset about, Remi?" Will whispered to himself with a grin. "Did you lose something?"

Remi finished scolding his hirelings and they separated, taking separate paths to search the alleys and streets around The Hanged Man. Will continued to watch, hoping he would get lucky.

After a few minutes most of the men returned and Remi sent them out again, instructing them to search further afield. Once they were gone, he was left alone.

Will summoned the rope from his limnthal and tied it around a heavy brick chimney emerging from the side of the building beside the side alley. Then he slid down it as gracefully as possible, which in his case wasn't graceful at all, but at least he made very little noise, thanks to his silent armor spell. Once down, he hurried to the corner and looked around it. Remi was only fifteen feet away.

For once, luck favored him. Remi was facing the other direction. Will advanced five or six feet and cast the source-link spell, then drained his target until the man collapsed unconscious. Rushing forward, the got his arms around the old man's chest and dragged him back to his rope. He made a large loop around Remi's chest, just beneath his arms, then tightened it up and tied it off.

Using the climbing spell, he went back to the roof and then began dragging the old man up after him. Hauling on the rope hand over hand turned out to be harder than he expected. A year or two before and he might not have succeeded, but his time in the army had served him well. Will did have a brief moment when the old man was almost to the top when he considered just letting the old bastard drop. *It would serve him right.* But he persisted, and eventually managed to get the man up onto the roof with him.

With that accomplished, he took hold of Remi's legs and moved him toward the center of the roof where they couldn't be observed from the ground. Taking his rope from the chimney, he used it to truss up his captive then went through the old man's purse and pockets.

He found seventeen gold, which he stored away in the limnthal, along with an assortment of daggers and blades that the wily old man had secreted all over his person. Will found the man's wrist sheaths and boot knives particularly interesting. *That's me. Always ready to learn.*

The prospect of waiting hours and hours for the man to recover wasn't appealing, so Will re-cast the source-link spell and studied his captive thoroughly. Once he thought he had a good feel for the man's turyn, he tried to match it and slowly injected a tiny amount of his own turyn into the older man. *The last thing I want is for him to start retching up here.*

Remi finally came around, his eyes opening slowly to stare at Will in confusion. "What?"

Will loomed over him, his shadow keeping the sun out of the other man's eyes. "I heard you were looking for me. Here I am."

A sense of alarm passed across Remi's features, but he didn't have the energy to sustain it. "What did you do to me?"

"Very little, thus far," said Will. "What happens from here depends on you."

"What do you want?"

"Not being hounded by you and your dogs is rising to the top of my list lately. I didn't enjoy hurting your men a few weeks ago, which is why this time I decided to cut the head off the snake. Tell me, Remi, are you the head? I don't think so, and if not, it isn't your neck that needs to bleed."

Will could see fear growing on the other man's face. "I won't bother you anymore. This was just a job for me. I won't take it on again."

"If you sincerely mean that, then I need to know the name of the man hunting me."

Remi winced. "I don't know who it is."

Will rolled the helpless man onto his side so he could see the slope of the roof leading downward. "If that's really all you know, then I may as well dispose of you and try again with the next crew that comes after me."

"Wait! I haven't finished," begged Remi. "I don't know who he works for, but I know the man who does. I can help you find him."

He rolled Remi onto his back again. "How can I trust you, Remi? You don't seem like the trustworthy sort."

"I wouldn't dare double-cross you," said the gang leader. "Not after this."

Will rubbed his chin thoughtfully. "I don't think that's enough. You might try to run or hide." Then he slapped his knee dramatically. "I have it!" He moved away from the prone man and turned his back on him.

"What are you doing?" asked Remi worriedly.

Will called up the limnthal then summoned one of his empty potion vials. Then he summoned the waterskin he had stored to replace the water jar. He filled the vial three-quarters of the way, then dismissed the waterskin and brought out the spice box. He added ground anise to the vial then re-stopped it and shook the vial vigorously.

He turned back to Remi and showed him the clear vial, then he began a nonsensical chant and cast the color-changing spell on the water within, turning it a virulent green color. Remi's cheeks paled. "Given that you've been hunting me, I'm sure you know that I'm an accomplished alchemist, don't you?"

The old man nodded anxiously.

Will held up the vial. "This contains a magical poison, but don't worry, it works very slowly."

"I'm not drinking that," said Remi firmly, struggling to lift himself on shaky arms. Will recast the source-link spell and paralyzed the man, causing him to fall back. He caught Remi before he could start to roll.

Remi's eyes darted back and forth fearfully as Will pried his jaws apart and poured the anise-flavored water into his mouth. Then he released the paralysis of the man's throat muscles while holding his mouth shut and blowing on his face, as though he was giving medicine to a dog. The old man gagged and choked, but eventually he was forced to swallow.

Will smiled at him maliciously. "That's a good boy." He gradually injected a tiny portion of his turyn into the man, enough to make him nauseous and reinforce the illusion of his ruse. "You might feel sick for a little while, but it will pass. You'll probably start to regain your strength soon, but don't let that fool you. The poison you've taken will start to kill you in a week's time. I promise you that it will be a slow and painful death."

The greybeard's eyes were filled with hate. "Why should I help you then? I'm going to die anyway."

Will summoned one of his blood-cleanse potions from storage, making sure the man saw it appear from thin air. "This is the antidote. As long as you take it within six days, you'll be fine."

"Give it to me!"

He wagged his finger playfully in front of Remi's face. "That would defeat the purpose, wouldn't it? I need a faithful dog, but you won't be very loyal if I give you your treat before you do your job, will you?"

"What's the job?"

"I want to see the man who's been paying you. How that happens depends on you."

"You want to meet him? He wasn't going to see me again. I'm just supposed to leave a note informing him after you've been disposed of."

"Tell him that I've killed your men again and that you need additional money to hire more," suggested Will.

"He'll be furious!"

Will's expression was cold and unsympathetic. "Not my problem. You want to keep breathing, don't you?"

"I'll be ruined if I take another payment and still don't deliver," whined Remi.

"I'd suggest taking the money and finding a new place to live." Will held up Remi's empty purse. "You'll probably need it, since I suspect you're broke now."

"You're evil!" spat the rogue. "I thought you were just a student."

"My teacher was far more spiteful than you could ever imagine, Remi. It's only natural that I would strive to emulate him."

"How do I contact you after he replies?" asked Remi sourly.

"Leave a note for me with Jared at The Hanged Man," answered Will. "You seem to be on good terms with him already. Make sure you include the time and place you'll be meeting the target. I'll also need you to mark him, so I know for certain who he is."

"Mark him?"

"I'll be watching your meeting. You just need to give some sort of sign, so I know for certain it's the right man. After that, I'll follow him."

Remi nodded. "Ah, I get you. He'll probably want to meet at The Mangy Dog. I'll scratch my head while I'm talking to him. But what about afterward? How do I know you'll give me the antidote?"

"Unfortunately for you, you don't have a choice," Will answered plainly. "But you might take note of the fact that I only killed one of your men last time."

"After today, that's cold comfort."

Will chuckled. "Too bad." He moved away to the other side of the roof.

"How do I get down?"

"Wait a few hours," advised Will. "Your strength will come back. The rest is up to you." He cast the climbing spell and descended into the side alley then began making his way back to Wurthaven.

Along the way, he found another place to hide and changed into his gambeson and mail, adding his steel cap to further confuse any spotters who might be watching for him. He made it to the college wall without incident, and once he was back within the campus he changed back into his brigandine and tunic.

It wasn't yet noon, so he was able to make it to his afternoon classes.

CHAPTER 31

All eyes were on him during his classes, but Will was beyond embarrassment. He'd come to accept his reputation and so he kept his head up, boldly meeting the gazes of any who dared stare too openly. Without exception, they all looked away as soon as he met their eyes.

After Spell Theory, he had his one-on-one with Professor Dulaney. "Your improvement is surprising, Mister Cartwright. I've never had a student gain proficiency so quickly."

Will had just completed yet another near-useless spell construct, at least in his opinion. He'd frequently complained about what he was being taught, so Dulaney had complied by teaching him a reinforcement spell meant to strengthen stone by reordering its inner matrix.

According to his teacher, reinforcement spells were important, but seldom used because of the cost to the user. Since Will had continually stated that he didn't care about costs and wanted to learn real magic, the professor had consented to teaching them to him. Now that he'd finished learning the version for stone, he would next learn a similar spell to alter the properties of steel.

"Probably because your students are afraid to practice," said Will acerbically. "I spend most of my free time perfecting what you've shown me." *Or other spells,* he thought to himself.

Dulaney didn't say anything, but his expression was that of a man who thought his student thought too highly of himself. "Be that as it may. Next week I'd like to start you on a fifth-order spell."

Will frowned. "You said it would be the steel reinforcement spell."

"It will, but not the fourth-order form. There's a more complex version that allows you to choose whether you're increasing tensile strength or hardness. It's a much more flexible spell and it has the additional benefit of being able to work with anything from wrought iron to high-quality steel."

Fifth-order sounded like it would be much more difficult to use. He was only barely able to handle the fourth-order constructs that the teacher had given him. "Won't it take a long time to cast a spell like that? It might be easier to learn separate fourth-order versions."

"Challenging you will help your skill grow faster," said the professor. "Besides, once you get beyond a certain level of ability it won't matter. A spell that you use frequently can be reflex cast, even if the complexity is high."

"Reflex cast? What's that?"

"It's like muscle memory. You don't have to think about walking or running. You've done them for so long your body remembers. Magic becomes like that over time. It happens more with simple spells, but if you use a higher-order spell frequently it will eventually get to the point where you don't even have to think about it. You'll have done it so often that you'll be able to form the construct in the blink of an eye," explained the professor.

Doubtful, Will replied, "I don't think I'll ever need to cast a reinforcement spell often enough for that to happen."

"True, unless you become an engineer. But your overall speed and accuracy with all spell constructs will improve as you get better. Reflex casting will happen naturally with spells that you use often. I can't help but be curious about what you'll be capable of in a year or two."

"Why?"

"As I said, you're learning faster than any student I've had, except perhaps for some of the sorcerers, and most of them weren't as dedicated to spellcraft."

"Like Selene?" Will asked idly.

Dulaney's eyes lit up. "If you really do know her, then you know what I mean. She was nothing like most of the privileged twits who I've tutored over the years. She was diligent and talented."

"I'll do my best to live up to her example," said Will. He rose to leave.

"Hang on a moment."

"Sir?"

"I heard about your arrest yesterday. May I inquire what happened?"

"The blood-price was paid," said Will, leaving his answer ambiguous. "I'm a free man. Were you worried about me?"

"Call it professional interest. Master Courtney has been asking about you as well. He'll be glad to hear you won't be going to waste in a prison cell."

"He still wants me as a test subject, I suppose."

"He's mentioned it a few times," admitted the professor.

"In the spring," said Will. "This term has been too busy for me."

"I'll pass that along."

Will left. It was too soon to check for a message at The Hanged Man, so he went straight to the Alchemy building. He still had a lot of work to do.

He was just setting up to complete the regeneration potions when Professor Karlovic stepped into the workshop. "I see you came back in one piece."

Will shrugged. "For now."

"I found someone willing to offer you a loan."

"I won't need it," Will answered abruptly. "My debt is paid."

"Then we just need to find buyers for your regeneration potions," said the professor happily.

Will had been thinking on that very topic all afternoon. Between the blood-cleanse potions, his sale of the universal antidotes, and what he had taken from thieves, he would soon have well over seven hundred crowns to his name. Not only that, but he could make more in the future, once the Healing Department's budget reset next year. Money was no longer a problem for him, and the regeneration potions seemed incredibly precious. Too precious to sell.

"I've decided not to sell them," he told Karlovic.

The professor was stunned. "You can't be serious!"

"I am. If you do happen across someone desperate enough, I might consider it for a thousand crowns, but not less, and I'll want to know the buyer's name in advance. There are quite a few people I'd rather not help, for any price."

His teacher looked unhappy. "I've been loaning you the use of this workshop for free. Have you considered that?"

Will raised his brows. "Would you like me to pay for the privilege? I'll be happy to do so."

Karlovic was taken aback. "I wasn't trying to extort you. We're friends, are we not?"

"You were planning to get a broker's fee, weren't you?" he asked pointedly. The Alchemy professor's face reddened, but Will continued, "I'm not angry. You should get paid for helping me. I just prefer it if we're honest with one another. You can ask for a rental fee, or you can hope to make a profit finding buyers if I decide to sell more potions in the future. Either way is fine with me."

"Let's just leave things as they are," said Karlovic sourly. Then he added, "You've gotten awfully jaded for one so young."

"It had to happen sooner or later," said Will uncaringly. "I'm just beginning to see the world for what it is."

The professor left, and Will returned to his work. That evening, he finished activating the regeneration potions. He had hoped for eight, but after accounting for losses during the previous stages he only managed to get seven completed potions. With that done he returned to the dorm with several hours to spare before bedtime.

He settled down at the desk in his room and called up the limnthal, then turned over his hand and looked at the Ring of Vile and Unspeakable Knowledge. "I need some advice."

"Wolfsbane," answered the ring immediately. "It isn't a pretty death, but it's quick. You'll save yourself and everyone else a lot of time and trouble if you take some. Just be sure to melt me down first."

Will sighed at first, then found himself chuckling. "You never change."

"I don't have much opportunity," said the ring. "I'm a piece of jewelry, jackass."

"Let me tell you about my day."

"Please no," begged Arrogan. "Not that. Anything but that."

Will ignored the ring's plaintive cries and launched into a retelling of his arrest and subsequent adventure. It took several minutes and when he finished, he asked, "What do you think?"

"Well, for starters, your storytelling skills could empty a tavern of patrons, but despite that, I have to admit you had a somewhat interesting day."

"I was hoping for some practical advice," said Will dryly.

"Your solution for that Remi fellow was creative. You surprised me with that. I would have just used a chameleon spell and followed him, but I think you actually have a better chance of finding out what you want to know by doing it the way that you did," said the ring.

"A chameleon spell, what's that?"

"It's in the book. Try reading it sometime."

Will took out *Practical Magic* and thumbed through the pages until he found the spell Arrogan had mentioned. His jaw dropped. "This has to be at least sixth-order! I'm not even close to being able to use this."

"Cry me a river."

He was still curious. "What does it do?"

"I guess you've never heard of a chameleon," said Arrogan. "How about the cuttlefish, or maybe the octopus?"

"I've heard of the octopus," said Will indignantly.

"Well, then maybe I should have named it the octopus spell."

"That doesn't tell me anything. Does it make the caster grow extra arms?"

Arrogan laughed. "No, lackwit, it's a camouflage spell. It's for hiding. It helps your body to blend into its surroundings. It will even change as you move, which is a large part of the reason it's so difficult."

"Octopuses can do that?"

"And chameleons and cuttlefish to varying degrees," answered Arrogan.

Will thought about it for a minute. "It would be handy, if I could cast it. But I can't learn it in time."

"What do you want to do?"

"Follow the man that Remi identifies for me."

"There's a tracking spell in there too. It's a lot easier," suggested the ring. "But you have to touch your target. It puts a magical beacon on them that leaves a trail you can follow for hours afterward."

"Thanks. I'll look it up." He dismissed the limnthal and returned to the book.

In the past, he had spent most of his time studying one spell at a time, trying to master each in a linear fashion, but he had come to understand that the book wasn't really a primer for learning. It was a collection of spells that Arrogan had found useful, and as such, there wasn't any order or planning to how they had been organized in the book.

He began leafing through the pages, skimming over the titles and trying to get a larger view of what it contained. On the next page past the chameleon spell, he found a fire-starter spell that was just as simple as the basic light spell, consisting of only three runes. "How many times have I needed this?" he wondered aloud.

Beyond that he found the spell for repelling insects. It was fourth-order, so it was just within his means and he vowed he would put some time into learning it. He might not be able to use it Muskeglun, but his time in the army had made him wish for such an ability hundreds of times in the past.

On the next page he found a spell that sounded interesting. "Force-lance," he muttered. It was a simple spell, being only second-order, so it would be simple to learn. From the description, it sounded as though the spell created something like a spear of magical force that he could use to impale opponents. Will felt like hitting himself. "I should have found this sooner."

Of course, being second-order, it would still take him several precious seconds to cast, unlike the source-link, which he was already reflex casting. Even so, if he had learned it sooner, he might be able to reflex cast it by then. He was close to being able to do so with the climb spell, and it was of a similar difficulty. "All right. Forget insects for now, I'll work on this one next."

He turned the page and found the tracking spell that Arrogan had mentioned. It appeared to be third-order, so it would take him a bit of effort to learn. Reading through it he wasn't sure he would be able to cast it quickly enough to use in a high-pressure situation like he might encounter when Remi identified the man who had been hiring him. "Maybe I should work on this first."

After that was a spell that promised to shatter glass or anything brittle. Will kept turning the pages. Next was a spell to blur the caster's form, making him or her more difficult to hit in combat. It was a second-order spell as well, and from his past experiences he could see himself needing it frequently. "Stay focused," he told himself. "I should learn the force-lance before this."

Then he came across the darkvision spell and he had to laugh. It was fifth-order in difficulty, but given his far superior ability to adjust his eyesight, it was utterly pointless for him to learn. He turned the page and found a spell he had wished for since the day he had seen Selene use it.

"Renders up to four active enemies unconscious, causing them to fall into a deep slumber," Will said, reading from the description. He despaired when he looked at the spell diagram, however, for it was firmly within the sixth order of difficulty. *It's much easier just to kill people than disable them,* he realized. He couldn't hope to learn it yet, but he promised himself that when he was capable enough, he would practice the spell until he could reflex cast it. Anything to stop leaving a trail of dead or maimed bodies in his wake.

There was a warning at the bottom of the page, "Not suitable for use against other wizards." He wondered if that meant other wizards as Arrogan had known them, or simply anyone able to see and use turyn. It was obvious to him that most spells would fail against a properly trained wizard, but the warning might also mean that practiced casters developed a will strong enough to fend off the effect.

He moved on to the next page. "Wind-wall," Will read aloud. He started to skip over the page, but then he paused to look over the description. His excitement grew as he realized he had found the spell that Arrogan had once used against the soldiers attacking Barrowden. It was a fourth-order spell, so he could manage it, just barely, though he would need to be able to cast it instantly the way his grandfather had if he wanted to use it in combat.

The spell was extremely flexible. It could be used to create an updraft or a downdraft that would divert arrows or even sling stones. There was also a way to shape it into a cyclone that surrounded the user. The only downside was that it used an extreme amount of turyn, so sustaining the spell was nearly impossible without a way to quickly replenish one's energy.

Will thought about the day Arrogan had died. The old man had used the spell at the last possible moment to deflect the crossbowmen's quarrels. As a result, he had been struck with a bolt when one of the soldiers fired early. Even so, it was a testament to Arrogan's skill and reflexes that he had been able to time the spell so perfectly. The second time his grandfather had used the spell, he'd formed it into a cyclone, and Will still remembered the devastating effect it had produced. All the men within several feet of him had been torn to pieces.

He imagined how things would have gone when he was ambushed if he had been capable of using the wind-wall spell at the time, and an evil grin spread across his face. *Of course, I'd have wound up killing most of them instead of just one,* he realized. Still, he had to learn it.

His mind was made up, and he spent the rest of his time before bed practicing the wind-wall spell construct, though he didn't dare actually cast the spell in his room. He also decided he needed to make some elixirs of turyn of his own. In a combat situation he might not be able to afford a few minutes to recover after using the spell, and using Arrogan's old elixirs was less efficient.

He fell asleep with a smile on his face.

CHAPTER 32

Will was glad for the weekend, since he was able to sleep an hour later, but he still had a lot to accomplish. He started by dressing and arming himself. Remi's wrist sheaths seemed imminently practical, so he wore those and made sure the knives that came with them were properly sharpened. Then he put on his brigandine and covered it all with his one undamaged tunic. He was quickly running out of clothes, but he intended to remedy that.

Once he was dressed, he spent half an hour practicing the wind-wall spell construct, though its complexity made him despair of ever being able to reflex cast it. When he was almost done, he summoned the limnthal and asked Arrogan a question. "There are so many spells to learn. How many did you manage to get good enough to reflex cast them?"

"What's that?" asked the ring.

"A spell you can cast without thinking about it."

"Oh! We called those instinctive spells in my day," said Arrogan. "To answer your question, I have no idea. I never counted them, but it was quite a few."

"How much is a lot?"

"Hundreds."

"Hundreds?" Will was stunned. "How could you possibly get that good at so many?"

"When you live for several centuries, it just happens."

"But how do you remember them all?"

"You don't. That's the whole point. By the time you can instinctively cast a spell, you don't remember it anymore. It just happens. That's one reason for recording them in books. If I had to teach you a spell that I had learned to reflex cast, I'd have to look it up."

"That makes no sense. Don't you have to have it memorized to be able to cast it that way?"

"It isn't a matter of memory or knowledge. It's similar to learning to juggle. Once you learn, you never forget; your hands just move on their own. If you tried to think about what each hand was doing, when to catch, when to throw, you'd fail. Instinctive casting is the same, except it isn't matter of muscles, it's a memory engraved in your soul. Live long enough and every spell you use often will become a matter of instinct."

Will frowned. "What about combat spells? You can't use most of them in a practical manner if you have to slowly construct them, but you can't get good enough to cast them that way unless you cast them often. Do you just have to practice them continually?"

"Practice is best for spells like that," agreed the ring. "But you can still use them in combat, you just have to prepare the spell ahead of time."

"Huh?"

"Construct it and hold it until you need it."

"No one ever mentioned that," said Will. "How do you do it?"

"I would have taught you that from the beginning. What are your instructors doing?"

"Well, they don't teach combat magic to begin with," Will reminded him.

"I suppose that makes sense. There's no point in worrying about it if you never intend to really use magic on a regular basis, much less quickly. Still, it isn't a separate skill. It's just a matter of preparation. Unlike instinctive casting, the strength of both your will and memory are important if you expect to hold more than one spell, however."

"So what do you do?"

"The same thing you always do," said the ring. "You construct the spell but rather than cast it, you hold it. When you're ready, all you have to do is invest the turyn and release it."

Understanding hit Will like a carpenter's mallet, and he felt stupid. "So it's just like practice. It never occurred to me you could hang onto a construct for very long."

"For as long as your patience lasts. If you've developed a strong will, you can manage more than one at a time, though it requires a keen mind as well, so you're probably already disqualified."

Will chuckled. He still missed his grandfather, but when the ring insulted him it almost felt like the old man was still with him. *I'm warped,* he thought. "So how many could you do, when you were alive?"

"Three, and I was one of the best."

"So, someone was able to do more than that?"

"None that I ever heard of, other than Aislinn. She could manage four at a time, so long as none of them were extremely complex."

"She was better than you?"

Arrogan grunted. "There's a reason she was known as the goddess of magic, even before she became one of the fae. But I had my own special talents."

"Such as?"

"Pure spitefulness," said the ring. "She was kinder than me, though not by much."

He laughed, then dismissed the limnthal. In one conversation, a whole new world of possibilities had opened up for him. He could manage to construct any spell in the book he had, so long as it was fourth-order or less. Up until then, he had thought he would need to have perfectly memorized a spell to be able to use it in a real-world situation, but if he prepared one ahead of time and held onto it, he could choose anything he was capable of.

As a test, he constructed the light spell, held onto it, then attempted to construct the fire-starting spell. He lost both constructs almost immediately. Given that the two spells were the simplest he knew, he would need a lot more practice before he could manage two at a time. He tried again, this time constructing the wind-wall spell while consulting the book. Once it was complete, he left the room, holding it in one hand.

He made it downstairs, out the door, and halfway to the college wall before his concentration slipped and the construct crumbled. He took out the book and assembled it once more, then resumed his walk.

Once he was close to the wall and out of sight of the college buildings, he decided to test it out, picking a spot well away from any trees or bushes. Investing his turyn, he felt a wave of fatigue wash over him as a powerful wind whipped around him.

That was underwhelming, he thought, but he knew what he'd done wrong. He hadn't prepared by creating a larger reserve of turyn before releasing the spell. Starting again, he expanded his outer shell and let it fill with as much turyn as he could hold, then he constructed the spell. Taking a deep breath, he injected his turyn into the construct and released it.

A vast, roaring wind encompassed him, tearing through the open space and ripping up the lawn around him for ten feet in every direction. The spell took everything he had, and he stayed on his feet only from stubbornness and long practice functioning while turyn-deprived. His grandfather's cruel teaching practices made more sense to him now.

Arrogan cast this, then fought several soldiers until the sorcerer refilled his turyn, thinking he was helpless. Damn!

His turyn was recovering quickly, but knowing what the old man had done still impressed him. *I've got a long way to go.*

Will continued on to the wall, cast his climb spell, then went up and over. He had a lot of places to visit that day. He reconstructed the wind-wall spell and practiced holding it while he walked, stopping to redo it whenever his concentration wavered. His first stop was at The Hanged Man. He entered and went to the bar and waited until Jared came over. "Did anyone leave a message for me?"

The bartender nodded, then walked down the bar and reached under it. He returned with a small slip of paper in hand, which he passed to Will.

The Mangy Dog, tomorrow evening at sixth bell. I'll be inside at a corner table.

~R

"Thanks," said Will, passing the bartender a single clima for his trouble. "Do you know a good tailor?"

"Just normal clothing?"

"Mainly," answered Will, "but I also need something for a palace function in a month."

"If you've got the coin, you should go to Branstowe's on High Street."

Will took Jared's advice and sought out the tailor he had mentioned. As before, he paid close attention to the street as he left, but he saw nothing that made him suspicious. A short ten-minute walk brought him to Branstowe's.

He was taken by the smell of fresh linen and wool with a subtle underlayer of leather when he entered the tailor's shop. "Can I help you?" asked a well-dressed man with a cloth tape measure draped around his neck.

"I need new clothes," Will announced.

The man smiled. "That's what I'm here for. What do you need in particular?"

"Everything. I'm a student at Wurthaven, so I need several new tunics and matching trousers, but I also have to attend a palace function."

"The Winter Ball?"

Will nodded. "The king invited me."

The tailor whistled, then held out his hand. "I'm Bryan by the way, Bryan Branstowe. What sort of budget do you have?"

"I want to look good and I'm not afraid of the cost," said Will.

"And you need everything?"

Will nodded.

Bryan looked him up and down. "So, new shoes, paned hose, a linen shirt, doublet, and a jerkin," said the tailor. "Oh, and a hat. Come over here and let me show you the fabrics we have to work with."

He followed the man around the shop for several minutes, and soon his head was spinning. "Can't you just choose for me?" he asked.

Bryan smiled. "I'd never hear that from a nobleman, but if you trust me, I'll have you dressed better than the proudest count or baron. Even so, tell me what colors you prefer."

They eventually settled on a dark grey doublet with a burgundy jerkin and hose. Bryan spent several minutes measuring Will from head to toe and making notes in a small journal. After he was done, Will asked, "How much will all this cost?"

The tailor spent a moment adding, then answered, "Fourteen gold crowns. That's including the regular clothes."

Will tried to hide his shock. He'd expected a high price, but actually hearing it was another thing. "How much should I pay now?"

"Most of my customers would be insulted if I asked for a deposit, but since you're not a nobleman—five crowns?"

Will handed over the coins.

"Come back in two weeks and I should have it all ready."

He asked for advice on a good cobbler and left the shop. By the time he had left High Street, he had purchased two pairs of boots and a pair of shoes for the ball. He summoned the oilskin bag with his mail in it, and then he went to see the armorer, Byron Waters.

"Back again?" said the amiable armorer, stroking his beard. "What do you need?"

Will got straight to the point. "This is my mail, but it needs a few repairs. I'd also like to have greaves and a breastplate made."

Byron nodded. "A wise choice. Where's your helm?"

He hadn't thought to summon it before entering the shop and he was loathe to do so in front of the man. "I have a steel cap, but I didn't bring it."

"Do you use a mail coif with it?"

Will shook his head, "Just linen padding."

"If you'd like a new helm then I'd recommend getting a new cap with an aventail."

"Aventail?"

"It will save you some weight. Rather than wearing a padded cap, mail over that, and a steel cap on top, you just have the padding and the helm. The mail is attached directly to the helm itself."

"Wouldn't it be loose around the neck?"

"There's a strap so you can buckle it tightly around the chin. Are you returning to the army?"

Will shook his head. "No, but I have a bad tendency to get into situations where I need more protection than just the brigandine you made me."

"You'll draw stares if you walk around town in that much armor," said Byron with a chuckle.

"I only plan to use it when I know I'll need it. Do you sell shields?"

"You're definitely planning to go to war," the armorer declared with a wink. "I don't make shields, but I can recommend a reliable smith that does."

"I appreciate that," said Will. "Also, I wonder if you can give me some advice."

"Ask away."

"I have two friends in Barrowden. When I was there, someone paid to have this mail made for me. Is there a way to do that for my friends?"

Byron opened his arms wide. "Look no further. It's not an uncommon request. Most go to the military headquarters first, but you'll be sent to a dozen different people before you find the right logistics officer. I can accept a payment and send a letter to Master Harless in Branscombe. We have a system of credit we've worked out over the years."

"You'll make the mail here?"

The armorer shook his head. "I can't get their measurements. Harless will do that, as well as have his apprentices produce the mail."

In the end, Will handed over a hundred crowns for Dave and Tiny's mail shirts, though he also received a promise that he would be refunded the extra coins once the final cost was determined. It would be a few weeks before he received the refund, though. He paid another sixty-three crowns for his own armor purchases, then went to the shops that Byron recommended.

He bought a new shield, a falchion to replace the one he had lost, a spear, and a crossbow with ten bodkin-tipped bolts. The weaponsmith warned him several times not to carry the crossbow inside the city, since they were outlawed for civilians within Cerria.

As soon as he was away from the weaponsmith, he stored his new weapons in the limnthal. The crossbow he loaded and cocked before putting it in storage. Ordinarily that would have been a bad idea, but since time moved so slowly inside the limnthal he wasn't worried about damage to the weapon.

All told, he'd spent a hundred and eighty-one crowns, and he was still flush with money. *I could get used to this,* he thought wryly. *I need to give some to Mom the next time I make a trip home.* Once he finished the blood-cleanse potions and collected his due from the Bursar's Office he would still have well over five hundred gold to his name.

Another thought came to him, Janice's tuition. She had lost her sponsor because of him, but he could certainly afford to pay for her expenses. The thought made him smile. Life was looking up.

From there, Will returned to the main street and made for the south gate. He needed to talk to Tailtiu. Once he was outside the city, he made for the congruence point he had met her at previously. He whispered her name as he walked so she could start her journey.

It was half an hour after he arrived before she appeared. "You need to travel again?" she asked.

"No. I need you to do something different this time. Are you able to enter the city?" He jerked his head in the direction of the capital.

She gave him an odd look, then gestured to her legs. "I have feet."

"Without becoming a spectacle," he clarified, eyeing her naked form. "During the daytime."

"You wish me to be seen or unseen? At night I could manage either, but during the day I would have to use a disguise."

As he watched, her form shifted, becoming that of an unremarkable middle-aged woman. Her ethereal beauty vanished, replaced by a face that could pass unnoticed in almost any crowd. The disguise was perfect, except for a complete lack of clothing and breasts that had grown to incredible proportions.

"Are those really necessary?" he asked, looking away.

She laughed. "A lot of farmwives have these. I thought it would be fun."

"Except they generally wear clothing."

The illusion of a thick wool dress covered her body, though Will could still see through it to a certain degree. "Such as this?" she asked.

"What if a mage sees you?"

"If you're that worried, I can steal a dress. I also have other forms."

Inspiration struck him. "Like a mouse, or maybe a bird?"

"Not here. Back in Faerie I can use smaller forms, but in your world it's impractical unless the form is of a similar or larger size."

He remembered how large her owl form had been in Barrowden. "Why is that?"

"Creating extra pseudo-flesh is much easier than removing actual flesh to become smaller. In Faerie my turyn is almost unlimited, but here I have to use my magic with care," she explained.

Will thought over what she had said for a second. It made sense, but it raised further questions in his mind. Did human wizardry have spells to change the user's form? If so, they were probably extremely complex. He resolved to ask Arrogan later.

He handed Tailtiu a gold crown. "Find a dress, but leave the coin to compensate the victim."

"You wish me to do so now?"

"As long as it doesn't take you more than an hour. I'll wait."

She transformed into a massive wolf and broke into a run, vanishing through the barley field. She returned less than half an hour later with a dress in her mouth. Will then watched her go through the unsettling process of transforming back into a human woman, awkwardly putting on the dress, and adjusting her size and proportions to fit the clothes.

He glanced at her feet. "You forgot shoes."

"I don't like them."

Will sighed but didn't feel like fighting her over the issue. Being barefoot in the city would make her a little unusual but he didn't doubt that she would be able to compensate for that when it came to following the target. "Let's go," he told her.

He took her into Cerria and led her to The Mangy Dog. "Two men will be meeting here today at sixth bell."

"What bell?"

He took a moment to explain the city's bell tower that rang at specific times to notify the citizens of the current time. The tower had a complex water clock within that tracked time and activated a mechanism to ring the bells a specified number of times at different points throughout the day and night. "When the bell rings six times, it means that it's six o'clock in the evening. They should be meeting sometime close to then."

"I see."

He described Remi to her, then went on, "He'll be sitting at a corner table inside the tavern. I want you to watch him. When he meets the man I'm interested in, he will scratch his head. After that, I want you to follow the person and find out where he goes. Stay with him until you're sure he's stopped for the night, then report back to me."

"Where will you be?" she asked.

"I'll be here with you at fifth bell, so I can point Remi out to you. I want to make sure you're watching the right man. After that I'll wait on top of one of the buildings near here."

Tailtiu looked unhappy. "I'll have to be within the city for hours and hours."

"What's wrong with that?"

"It smells, and there's iron everywhere. It's extremely unpleasant."

"But you can do this, right?" asked Will.

She lifted her chin. "Of course. Following a human is simple. Your kind are almost blind and deaf."

"Excellent. I'll meet you back here at fifth bell."

"I'm not waiting inside the city until then," she said firmly. "Call me when it is time. I'll return then."

CHAPTER 33

After a nice lunch at The Hanged Man, Will returned to Wurthaven and spent the next several hours finishing up a few more blood-cleanse potions. When he got tired of that, he practiced constructing the wind-wall spell. He was able to put it together without referring to the book now, but it was still a slow process that took nearly half a minute.

When the time came, he returned to the city proper and made his way to The Mangy Dog, stopping in the street half a block from the tavern. He called Tailtiu and waited, though not for long—she appeared within a span of ten minutes.

He handed her five silver clima. "You can use these to pay when they ask for money."

She sniffed. "I wouldn't drink anything in that place."

"You don't have to drink it. Just order a cup of ale and pretend to sip it. You'll look strange if you don't seem like you're drinking."

"If you insist."

They waited, and half an hour later Will spotted Remi entering the tavern. "That's him."

His aunt seemed disgusted. "Couldn't you find a tastier specimen for me to watch? That one's gone rotten already."

Will laughed. "He's just old. Go inside and find a table. Make sure you can watch him easily without seeming obvious."

She looked down her nose at him. "Have you forgotten my age? This isn't my first time in a human public house."

"Fine. Just don't prey on any of the humans. You're supposed to be a normal woman. Remember that."

"Be specific. By 'prey' you mean what exactly?"

"Don't kiss anyone or drain their turyn. No sex."

"I couldn't do that anyway. Did you forget the accord?" she reminded him. "May I defend myself at least?"

Will's eyes narrowed. "From what?"

Tailtiu ran her hands downward, framing her chest and sliding them along her hips. "You underestimate my appeal."

"Oh! Well, if something like that happens, of course you should defend yourself, but don't start any trouble. Remember, the whole point of this is to discreetly follow the man that Remi meets with."

"No fornication, no fighting." Tailtiu shook her head sadly. "I think you've deeply misunderstood my basic nature."

"I have faith that you will control your urges," said Will.

She winked back at him. "It's not mine you should worry over, nephew." Then she left, heading toward the front door of The Mangy Dog.

Will walked farther down the street, until he reached the side alley he had picked out. Moving into its shadowy recess, he cast the climb spell and made his way to the roof, where he settled in for a long wait. The building he had chosen was half a block from the tavern, but he could easily observe its front door from where he was.

People came and went, but he had no way of knowing which of them might be going in to meet with Remi. There really wasn't much point in him watching at all, since he was sure Tailtiu could handle her job with ease. He merely needed to be somewhere close by to hear her report when she was done, and that might be much later.

He heard a crash, and when he looked up, he saw a man tumble into the street. *Did he get thrown out of the tavern?* Will wondered. A second later someone screamed, and another man *flew* through the tavern entrance, as though he'd been launched by a catapult. More screams echoed down the street, and the pub's patrons began spilling through the doors as they tried to escape the chaos inside.

What the hell is happening? thought Will, feeling a sense of panic. Another body flew through a window that had been firmly shuttered, sending fragments of wood spinning outward. Smoke billowed out through the opening.

He started for the edge of the roof so he could descend and see if Tailtiu needed help, but just then a dark streak of black fur darted through the doors and disappeared down a cross street. *A wolf? She's crazy.*

Leaning back down on the rooftop, Will closed his eyes. Everything was ruined. He didn't know what had happened, but he was dead certain that a massive brawl followed by a fire meant that Tailtiu wouldn't be able to follow his target. *And I thought it was a brilliant idea to have her do the stalking for me.*

He stayed where he was. The plan was for her to meet him when she was done, and since the job was already spoiled, he didn't think it would be long. After an hour had passed and she still hadn't appeared he began to worry. What was taking her so long? *I saw her escape. Surely, she didn't get caught after that, did she?* He wondered if he should descend and look for her, but he wouldn't know where to begin.

He whispered her name three times and felt the connection, along with a certain emotion from her end, *not yet.*

"She's alive, but what is she doing?" he muttered in frustration. Looking down the street, he was glad to see that the bucket brigade had succeeded in putting out the fire before the tavern had suffered too much damage.

Another hour passed and he saw a dark form overhead, obscuring the stars. After a moment a giant owl descended, then transformed into his aunt. She smiled as she walked across the sloping slate tiles toward him. Her steps were confident and balanced, as though she was crossing over nothing more dangerous than level ground.

"What happened?" he said flatly, not bothering to look at her.

"I found his home," she answered brightly. "I'll show you."

Will lifted his head and looked at her in surprise. "How? I saw what happened back at the tavern. You didn't follow him, you destroyed the place."

Her features showed confusion. "Nothing happened. Who says I didn't follow him?" She paused, then she realized what he meant. "Oh, that! That was nothing. I had already marked him before that. He was well gone before all the fighting started."

"There wasn't supposed to be *any* fighting," spat Will. "You should have left right after your target did."

"I didn't want to seem to obvious. Trust me. I've been stalking prey for far longer than you've been alive. And you said I could defend myself," she answered with the air of someone who had been offended.

Will got to his knees carefully to avoid sliding off the roof. "What happened then?"

"I was attacked," she said huffily.

"You need to be a little more explicit for me."

"Oh, it was explicit. One of the men there grabbed me." She groped her breast to illustrate her point. "Then he tried to kiss me."

Will's mouth dropped. His aunt was practically the avatar of sexual assault. In fact, her service to him was in payment for one of several occasions that she had kissed him without permission. The idea that she would be offended by someone doing the same to her seemed ridiculous. "I'm not sure you should be the one to judge people for things like that," he began.

"You told me not to prey on them," she reminded him. "Besides, I was trying to stay in character. A human woman would have taken great offense, so I merely played my part."

He stared at her in frank disbelief. "So what did this *human* woman you were pretending to be do, once she was insulted so rudely?"

"Not much," she said with a pout. "I threw him over the bar, but then the bartender started yelling because some of his crude glassware broke, and one of the man's friends decided to try and grab my hair. I tried to respect the bartender's complaints, so I threw that man across the room. He landed on another table, though, and the people there weren't too happy about it."

Will covered his face with his hands. "What about the ones you tossed into the street?"

She grinned mischievously. "That was a bit later. I warned them to leave me alone, but no one wanted to listen, so I had to be a little firm with them. I didn't lose my temper until one of them tried to stab me with a nasty piece of iron. After that I had to get rough. Still, I don't *think* any of them died."

"And the fire?"

"Some fool knocked over an oil lamp."

"He knocked it over, or you threw him into it?"

She pouted. "Is there a difference? Besides, I didn't throw that one. I broke his leg while maneuvering him onto the bar, then I gave him a push. He landed on the lantern when he slid off the far end."

"What about the ones you threw into the street, or the one you tossed through a window?"

His aunt shrugged. "There were so many. It's hard to remember all the details. The important thing is that the bartender decided to escalate the situation when he pulled out a crossbow and pointed it at me. That's when I decided to take the high road and leave."

"You call *that* taking the high road? You'd already destroyed the place!"

"I didn't kill him, though I should have, and the tavern is still there. Look, see?" She pointed down the street to where the blackened building still smoked.

Will gave up. "You said you still managed to follow the target?"

She nodded happily. "Shall I show you where he lives?"

Will nodded, and she walked to the edge of the roof and casually stepped off. He followed more carefully, easing himself to the edge and casting the climb spell so he could get down safely. She was waiting for him. "You're so slow. Why didn't you jump?"

He stared upward. The drop was at least twenty feet. "A fall like that might kill me. At the very least I'd probably break my ankles."

She shook her head. "Your people are too fragile. It's a wonder you manage to live as long as you do."

He didn't bother responding. Tailtiu led him through the alley and up one street, turning when they came to High Street. She had lost her dress and given up on appearing human, but her body seemed almost translucent. Under the dim streetlamps she was difficult to see. He followed her down High Street until she turned left and went north into one of the wealthy districts.

The houses here were still crowded tightly together, but their quality and size were far removed from the structures in most of the rest of Cerria. Most of the houses were three stories tall, with brick or stone fronts and gated entrances. Will wasn't too surprised, though. He had expected that the man paying Remi would be among the elite and powerful citizens of the capital.

"That one," said Tailtiu, pointing to a red brick house that was fronted by a tiny green garden surrounded by a wrought iron fence. An ornate carriage was parked in front of the gate. "The carriage wasn't here when I left," she observed.

Will took note of the house number so he could find out who owned it later. Then he moved back a short distance to take advantage of a tiny gap between two buildings. He wanted to watch the house for a while. The owner of the carriage might be important.

"Do you know whose house it is?" asked his aunt.

Will shook his head.

"We should go inside and see," she suggested.

"I don't want them to know I've found them yet."

"Why?"

"Because whoever it is might do something desperate, like try to kill me again."

"Again? If they've tried once you should just get rid of them. Should I do it for you?"

Considering what she had just done back at the tavern, he had no doubt she could make good on her offer, but Will had a strict policy about allowing the fae to kill humans. It was a road he didn't want to start down. "I don't know who is in that house. It might be that most of the residents aren't my enemies. There could be women and children."

"That's foolish," she replied. "Children grow up to be enemies, especially if you kill their parents, and women—they could be just as deadly, if not more so. Your values are warped."

"I don't want to be lectured on my morals by an immortal and immoral fae, who kills without the slightest hesitation." She started to reply, but he waved his hand at her to shush her. "Someone's coming out," he whispered.

A servant had opened the door and a lady exited, escorted by a gentleman that Will didn't recognize. He knew the lady, though. Her face was engraved on his heart. He watched wordlessly as a footman opened the carriage and the woman got inside. His body was frozen, and it seemed as if even his heart had stopped. He didn't move or speak until the carriage had disappeared from view. "That was Selene," he said in a hushed tone.

"The girl who abandoned you in Barrowden? See! You should have just let me kill them all," said Tailtiu helpfully.

Will turned on her. "Tailtiu! Listen to my words. You are *never* to harm that woman. Do you understand? No matter what happens, whether I'm alive or dead. I don't care if you see her stick a knife in my chest with your own eyes, she is to remain untouched. Is that clear?"

Tailtiu's eyes darkened until they seemed to eat the light. "Once you are gone, I will do as I please. Have you forgotten the accord? Your death will erase it. I will kill whoever I choose when that day comes."

"Not her," said Will. "Please."

She leaned forward to whisper in his ear. "So long as you live, I will abide by that, but once you are gone, I will make only one promise. Since that woman is so dear to you, I will devour her without fail. She will be my first."

Dread filled his heart, but it was quickly replaced by fury. His hand moved on its own, and Will caught the fae woman by the throat and shoved her violently against the closest building. "Say that again and I will use my last favor to demand your life," he hissed, grinding out the words one by one between clenched teeth. "Is that what you want?"

Her cheeks colored but there was no fear in her eyes, only a twisted vision of enjoyment. "Such passion! Surprising in such a meek lamb. Very well, I will withdraw the promise, but if you expect me to reverse it and guarantee her protection you will have to bind me with your last favor. Are you willing to spend it so carelessly?"

Will's anger began to subside, but he was tempted to give the order, just to be safe. He closed his eyes and tried to clear his head. He wasn't thinking rationally. *I've let her get to me. She's trying to force me to spend my last unbound favor.*

"Say the word," she urged. "I am yours to command, after all."

"Go," he ordered. "I have no further need of you tonight."

Tailtiu looked disappointed. He released her and she walked away, glancing back only once. "Until then."

Chapter 34

He left the fake antidote with Jared at The Hanged Man, along with a note for Remi expressing his sincere desire to never need to find the man again. He doubted Remi would need another lesson, though. Will had scared the rogue pretty badly during their last encounter.

Will's next week went by without trouble. Rather than ask around in town, he found Rob and asked him how to send a letter to Count Spry. His friend immediately brought up the fact that the count was still in the city and that a letter should be delivered to his city house. With a small amount of digging, Rob found the address for him.

As he had suspected, the house number and street name were a match for the place Tailtiu had found. *But why was Selene there?* he wondered. It was possible that she had merely had some innocuous reason for visiting the man. She was a princess after all, and the count was one of the most highly ranked noblemen in the nation. She might have been there to socialize or even for some political purpose, but the timing was suspicious.

Knowing for certain that Count Spry was still hiring killers to catch him didn't feel like much of an improvement over merely suspecting the man. He still couldn't do anything about it. Not unless he was willing to do something along the lines of what Tailtiu had suggested. It had a certain practical appeal, but Will had two big reasons not to take such a course. One, he wasn't sure he could manage such a feat. He had no idea what type of protections or defenses the count had. Two, he wasn't calloused enough to be willing to kill the man in cold blood. *I'm not an assassin,* he told himself. *No matter what some people seem to think.*

With no clear options, he put his heart and effort into his classes and personal projects. With Janice's help, he began to make tangible progress in Composition. His penmanship was gradually improving, and his writing skills went from terrible to merely poor. When he had informed Janice of his plan to finance her remaining years at Wurthaven she had been skeptical, but over time she warmed to the idea.

As their friendship deepened, she also warmed to him in tiny ways that made him nervous. She sat closer, and he caught her looking at him with an odd look in her eyes now and then. He couldn't be sure, though. It was possible he was misreading her intentions, but on several occasions she mentioned how futile his romantic feelings for Selene were, and he took that as a warning.

His friendship with Seth also improved with time. The other boy began to visit him once in a while, and eventually they started studying together. Seth made it clear that he had no intention of moving back in with Will, but beyond that he no longer seemed so wary.

Having several friends and no longer failing any of his classes, Will began to feel like a real student. The next few years at Wurthaven seemed like they might not be so bad after all. Not if they were like his present.

Will also picked up the new pieces of armor he had commissioned. Byron Waters' workmanship was excellent, and he had no complaints. He didn't know if he would ever need the extra armor, but he felt better knowing he had it if the need arose.

During his free time in the evenings and on weekends, he finished up the blood-cleanse potions and then went about replacing Arrogan's old elixirs of turyn with newer potions that contained his own turyn. Once that was out of the way, he devoted himself to improving his spellcraft. With Professor Dulaney's tutelage, he eventually succeeded in becoming competent enough to cast fifth-order spells and he looked forward to the day he would be able to cast sixth-order spells. Having the use of the sleep spell would greatly improve his non-lethal options the next time he was attacked in the street.

Dulaney taught him a variety of spells for altering the material properties of various substances ranging from metals to things like ropes and even fabric, but when he was on his own Will dedicated himself to the spells in *Practical Magic.* By the time the month was done, he had memorized all the spells within it that he was capable of casting, with the exception of darkvision.

He separated his spellcraft training into three distinct parts. The first was memorization of spells he could already cast and making sure he could do so without resorting to a book or his notes. The second was repetitive casting, to enable him to reflex cast, and for that he chose to focus on the wind-wall spell. The third part was training himself to hold a prepared spell for long periods of time. He practiced that with the wind-wall spell construct also, reasoning that it might help him learn to reflex cast it sooner.

A month passed in relative peace and quiet, until one day he made the mistake of stepping into Professor Dulaney's Spell Theory class with a wind-wall spell in hand. He had gotten so used to carrying the prepared spell that he had forgotten to dismiss it, and while the first-year students couldn't see turyn yet, his teacher certainly could.

"Mister Cartwright, what is that?" asked Dulaney in front of the class.

"What sir?"

"The spell in your hand."

"Oh!" He quickly dismissed the construct. "Sorry, sir. I was practicing and forgot I had it with me."

Dulaney frowned, but class resumed. During their private tutoring session afterward, though, he mentioned it again. "You're practicing holding a prepared spell?"

"Yes, sir."

"Why?"

"I thought it would be handy to be able to do so."

"There are only a few reasons to practice such a skill, and most of them are highly questionable," said Dulaney.

Will looked at his teacher innocently. "Then you've never practiced it?"

Professor Dulaney's lips formed a thin line. "I didn't say that. Everyone does eventually, even if only by happenstance during normal practice. Either way, it's extremely disconcerting to see someone walking around with who-knows-what ready to go off at any moment. Surely you can see why that would make people nervous."

"I didn't mean to bring it into class, sir. I forgot I had it."

His teacher rubbed his chin. "Then you've made significant progress. That was a fourth-order spell if I'm not mistaken. If you're going to keep doing it, though, put it somewhere it won't make the people around you feel threatened."

Will's brows furrowed. "Pardon? How do I do that?"

"I meant that you shouldn't walk around with it in your hand. It's more polite to store it inside your body," said Dulaney.

Will's mouth formed an 'o.' He already knew he didn't have to keep spells strictly in his hand, and in fact he'd played around with using different areas to attach them, such as his shoulders, but he'd never considered putting it *inside* himself. "You can do that?"

"Of course. The spell construct is intangible. Observe." Dulaney held up one palm and Selene's eighth-order cleaning spell appeared above his hand in a matter of seconds. Will was impressed by how quickly his teacher assembled the complex spell. Once it was whole, the man turned his hand and pressed it to his chest. The spell construct disappeared from view. "Keeping it here, no one would suspect that I'm ready to clean virtually anything with just a thought," he said dryly.

Will caught the sarcasm but didn't respond.

The professor leaned forward across the desk and stared at Will with interest. "So, what was the spell you were practicing with? It wasn't one that I've shown you."

"It wasn't anything special," said Will weakly.

"It looked like some sort of elemental wind spell."

Will knew he was caught, so he decided to come clean. "It was a wind-wall spell."

Dulaney nodded knowingly. "I thought so. Hopefully you understand how destructive that spell is."

"Yes, sir. I've tried it in places where there's a lot of room and nothing to damage."

"I'd heard a rumor that the groundskeepers were looking to find whoever was destroying parts of the lawn." Dulaney chuckled. "The bigger problem is this. That spell is a combat spell. Where did you learn it?"

Will abandoned honesty. "I found it in the library, sir."

"That seems unlikely. Those spells are kept in a restricted section. Only teachers and researchers with special permission are permitted to examine them."

He racked his brain for an explanation. "I found it on a folded note stuffed inside one of the older books. I didn't realize it was restricted."

Dulaney's eyes clearly said he didn't believe his young student, but he didn't challenge the lie. Instead, he gave advice. "I hope you realize that if you're ever caught breaking into the restricted section that the consequences are severe."

"I've never been there, sir. Honestly. But I will keep your advice in mind. You don't need to worry."

"Make sure no one sees you practicing that spell. I won't take the blame if you're caught."

Will promised he would be careful. He left feeling that he had narrowly dodged serious trouble and vowed to find a better place to practice the spell.

A few days later, he was surprised when Dianne, the resident assistant, stopped him on his way to his room. "You have a letter, William."

Her attitude toward him was no longer quite so frosty, but there had been no sign she would ever show him the same warmth she previously shown. Will accepted the folded envelope and took it upstairs to read.

Your father's wife suspects the truth and may have shared her suspicion with the duchess. Be careful.

There was no signature or other indication as to who had left the message, but Will recognized Selene's flowing script. He pondered the meaning of it. His father, the Baron Mark Nerrow, was married to the sister of Duke Arenata. The duke was also the Royal Marshal, in charge of Terabinia's military and probably the single most powerful nobleman in the country.

King Lognion had already warned Will that if the baroness learned of his bastard heritage, she might do almost anything to eliminate a possible challenger to her heirs.

But how could she have learned the truth? Will had had no contact with his father since their single meeting in Branscombe. Had she somehow learned of the care package his father had sent when he started studying at Wurthaven? It seemed unlikely. Mark Nerrow had been scrupulously careful for the entirety of Will's life, otherwise his wife would have discovered the truth long ago.

Could it have been Count Spry's doing? That made little sense, as the Count knew even less about Will beyond recent events. Speculation was getting him nowhere. *If she knows then I'll have even more people out for my blood.*

Thinking about it made him anxious. He was already doing everything he could to keep himself in one piece, so he pushed the matter to the back of his mind. It was beginning to get crowded back there, with his questions about Count Spry, and his further concern about why Selene had been visiting the man.

Nothing was ever simple.

The Winter Ball was only two weeks away, and Will realized he still hadn't picked up his new clothes from the tailor. It was Friday and he'd just finished his classes for the day, so he decided to head into the city.

With the blood-price no longer hanging over his head the chancellor had rescinded the ban on him leaving the college grounds, but he still didn't want to announce his departure to whoever might be watching the gates, so he left by climbing the wall. From there he made his way through the streets to Branstowe's tailoring shop.

As always, he kept an eye on his surroundings. Paranoia was becoming a habit for him and he had no intention of changing his ways any time soon. He was wearing his brigandine beneath his tunic, as he had done for several months now, and he also had Remi's special knives strapped to his wrists. Combined with the fact that he could summon a variety of weapons at a moment's notice he couldn't see any way he could be better prepared, short of wearing all of his armor in public. If his life got any more dangerous, he'd have to resort to hiring guards to escort him everywhere.

Bryan Branstowe seemed relieved to see him. "I expected you a few weeks ago. I was starting to wonder if you wouldn't come."

The tailor's work was exceptional, though Will found himself feeling embarrassed at just the thought of wearing such finery. At Bryan's insistence, he tried everything on. The fit was perfect, but the close-fitting hose made Will's legs feel naked. *It's just one day. I can do this,* he told himself.

Bryan admired his handiwork. "If you had a gold chain and some rings, I'd think you were a duke," he announced. "You must have a lot of admirers already, though. Several people stopped in to ask about you."

Will frowned. "Who?"

"I don't know. Both were women, noble ladies of course. They came on different days and neither seemed to want me to know their identities."

"Considering your clientele, shouldn't you have recognized them?"

"Most of my customers are men, or the servants of such men."

"Can you describe them to me?"

"One was older, with dark blond hair. The other was a young woman, about your age," said the tailor. "Both were well dressed but they had removed anything that might identify their houses."

"Did the younger one have dark hair?"

"Yes. She was striking. Long, dark hair and blue eyes. Do you know her?"

Will nodded.

Bryan's eyes twinkled. "Is she special to you? She asked for you by name."

"Maybe. What did she want to know?"

"She was curious about what sort of attire you were purchasing, the colors and fabrics. I suspect she might have planned to place an order on your behalf, but she seemed satisfied with your choices."

"And the other woman?"

"She wasn't as curious. She merely wanted to know how long it would be before your clothes would be ready." Bryan noticed a look of irritation on Will's face. "Privacy isn't usually a concern in tailoring. Should I have said nothing?"

"I've made quite a few enemies," admitted Will. "There's a good chance anyone asking about my affairs doesn't have my best interests at heart."

The tailor nodded. "I apologize then. People don't normally ask about these things, so I was caught off-guard, plus clothing usually isn't a sensitive matter."

Will was more curious as to how so many people knew he'd visited the tailor in the first place. Since he'd returned several weeks later than expected, he wasn't too worried about being ambushed, though. He was too far off schedule. He removed the new clothes, changed back into his usual attire, and then paid the tailor his due. As he was about to leave, he stored his new purchases in the limnthal.

Stepping into the street, he immediately noticed something odd. The lane was entirely empty but for a few exceptions. Directly across from the tailor's shop stood three men with long, grey cloaks. Will started to glance to his sides when his peripheral vision picked up movement, but it was too late.

Something hit him square in the chest, *hard*, knocking him back and driving the wind from his lungs. Two crossbow bolts stood out, tangled in the fabric of his tunic. A third had gone deeper, piercing his brigandine and penetrating his abdomen by perhaps an inch or two. He stumbled and fell, feeling a sharp pain as the bodkin point tore at his belly.

As he dropped, he noticed that the three men across the way had thrown back their cloaks to reveal now-empty crossbows. From the sides, two men were closing on him with flanged maces in hand. Apparently, they had been waiting a short distance away from either side of the door, and it was obvious that their task was to make sure he couldn't get back up if the crossbows failed to do the job. "He's wearing body armor of some kind," one of them called to his accomplices.

He saw all this as he fell, and by the time he struck the ground he knew he was in far over his head. The two side men were already standing over him, raising their maces to strike. The armor he wore wouldn't do much against impact weapons, if they even bothered to aim for his body. His head was too tempting a target.

There was only one thing he could do. He channeled all the turyn in his body into the spell he was holding and released it. A blast of wind erupted around him, throwing his mace-wielding enemies off their feet and causing them to tumble. Without preparing a greater amount of turyn, the wind-wall spell wasn't powerful enough to cause them greater harm.

Still unable to draw breath, he could see the men across the road were already winching back their crossbows to reload. Will scrabbled backward, grabbing the door handle and hurrying into the shop before slamming the door shut. Bryan looked at him in alarm, his eyes spotting the quarrels sticking out of Will's clothing.

Almost completely bereft of turyn, Will was only able to move because of his training and extreme stubbornness. "They're coming," he croaked to warn the tailor. Then he reached down and pulled out the bolt that had partially penetrated. There wasn't much blood to be seen.

To his credit, Bryan recovered from his shock quickly and rushed forward to lock the door. "There's a door in back."

Will nodded weakly and staggered in that direction. As he went, he summoned an elixir of turyn from the limnthal and drank it in one gulp, feeling his strength return in a rush. Then he expanded his outer shell and began absorbing more turyn from the environment.

His mind raced through the possibilities. Given some time, he'd have put on his armor, but the shop door didn't look that substantial. He decided his best option was to wait on the men to break through the door since there might be others covering the rear exit. Will summoned the crossbow from his limnthal and prepared a simple spell. He positioned himself at the back of the main room, some fifteen feet away from the door and slightly to the left, where he wouldn't be in direct line of sight for the enemy crossbowmen when the door opened.

Several heavy mace blows shattered the wood holding the door's bolt, and it flew open. As the first assassin stepped inside, Will fired, hitting the man square in the chest, close to the heart. The man dropped the mace and clutched at the shaft as he staggered to one side and his companion entered. Will's force-lance struck that one, blowing a hole through his midsection and sending the man falling backward into the street.

Will stored his crossbow again. He couldn't afford the time to reload it. Moving forward, he summoned his falchion and put the still-living assassin out of his misery. He prepared a second force-lance spell. He was too nervous to look out the door to use it, though, but he had an idea.

Reaching down, he grabbed the man he had just killed by the chest and heaved him to his feet with strength born of fear and adrenaline, then shoved the man through the open door ahead of him.

Quarrels thudded into the body. Will released his body shield and unleashed his force-lance on one of the crossbowmen. The man died instantly, and his companions started to run, for they knew they couldn't reload in time. Will charged at them but stopped at a distance of ten feet and caught both with his source-link. He pumped enough turyn into them to overwhelm them with nausea, then slew them each in turn with his falchion.

Everything had happened in less than the span of a couple of minutes. Will looked down the street and spotted the men who were diverting traffic. There were two at each intersection, and though they saw him, none of them made a move to approach. *They're still confident the kill team will finish me,* he realized. *But why?* A scream from the tailor's shop answered his question. *The back door!*

Will ran back inside, where he was greeted by a scene from a horror story. Bryan was thrashing on the floor, covered by *something.* It was all black smoke and teeth. Will recognized it as a demon from his previous experience. Standing in the doorway to the back portion of the shop was a black-robed man.

He didn't stop to think. He cast the demon-armor spell and his body was engulfed in heatless flames. Something flew from the robed man's hands, a streak of turyn, and Will felt the man's spell slam into his chest. His half-empty outer shell absorbed some of the power before it struck his chest, but the spell still had enough power to throw him against the wall when it landed.

The demon was rising from what was left of Bryan's torn remains. Will chose to focus on the caster first, though. He didn't attempt to get back to his feet, but instead formed another force-lance. It took a few seconds, but he released it before the dark-robed priest could cast again, and his spell shattered the man's ribs, flinging him into the back room. Then the demon landed on top of him.

It screamed as the flames ate into it, emitting an unearthly wail. Will gave it a bloody smile. "That's right, you bastard. Burn!" With its master dead, the demon attempted to flee, but Will dropped his sword and wrapped flaming arms around it. It writhed and tore at him, shredding his clothes and tearing the flesh on his arms and legs, but it couldn't escape. Will felt his turyn pour out as his spell and the demon's essences destroyed each other.

The sizzling carnage went on for almost thirty seconds before the demon finally sagged, collapsing as its body fell apart into black blood and loose claws. Will got to his feet and drank another elixir of turyn to replenish his strength. Then he surveyed the damage to himself and the shop.

He was in surprisingly good shape. His arms and legs had numerous cuts and scrapes, but nothing serious. The wound in his belly was shallow and didn't seem to be bleeding much. His clothes were ruined, and the brigandine would need serious repair, but overall, he was functional. The same could not be said of poor Bryan Branstowe. The tailor would never produce another garment.

Will tried to think. It wouldn't be long before either the remaining soldiers came to get him, or the city guard appeared. He needed to be gone. Taking several long strides, he crossed the room and went behind the small counter. Bryan had put the gold he had received back there, and Will was rewarded when he spotted a heavy iron cash box. He stored it within the limnthal with a touch. *No point in not making the best of a bad situation,* he thought. Bryan wouldn't be needing the money anymore.

He considered the back door, but decided it was too risky. There might be more men waiting outside. He already knew the situation on the street in front. Walking boldly, he exited the front door. The street was still empty, and he waved at the men blocking the intersections. They stared at him in confusion. Before they could react, he crossed the road and went between the two closest buildings, then he cast his climb spell and made his way to the roof.

He moved until he was safe from observation and then worked his way over so he could observe the scene of his recent calamity. Several minutes passed, and then the men who had been blocking the intersection moved in. A cart and horse came soon after, and the bodies were loaded and covered with a tarp. Sand was thrown over the blood on the street, and then the men and the cart left. Their actions were calm and unhurried as though they were doing nothing out of the ordinary. Not long after that, pedestrians and foot traffic began to traverse the street. Will wondered how long it would be before someone tried to pay a visit to the deceased tailor. The entire thing was surreal. *They didn't even bother searching for me. They just cleaned up once the plan was an obvious failure.*

The calm professionalism and complete lack of regard for the law or other repercussions chilled him to the bone. The men who had attacked him had operated with confidence that no one would interfere. They'd already had a plan to dispose of the bodies, whether his or their own. It was obvious that someone with considerable power was behind the entire thing. Someone who had connections with the Priests of Madrok.

Was it Duke Arenata acting on behalf of his sister, or Count Spry? It was even possible that Selene was behind it, though Will refused to believe it. *Otherwise why would she have warned me? Could there even be a third party after me, one I have no knowledge of?*

Will removed his torn tunic and used it to wipe away the blood. He tore off a large piece and made a ball out of it, which he stuffed between his brigandine and the wound on his abdomen. He used more strips torn from it to bandage the worst cuts on his arms and legs, then summoned one of his new tunics and put it on.

Confident that he no longer looked like a war refugee, he descended to the ground of one of the side alleys then confidently walked out, heading for the armorer's shop.

CHAPTER 35

Will commissioned two more of his peculiar innerwear brigandines and promised he would bring his damaged one in for repair when they were done. He had no intention of surrendering it until he had a replacement. Then he returned to Wurthaven. He didn't bother with the wall, but entered through the main gate since it was only when leaving that he felt he needed to conceal his movements.

He was tempted to go to the Healing and Psyche building for treatment of his cuts and bruises but decided against it. The only people who knew he had been at the tailor's shop were either dead or unlikely to talk about it. Seeking medical assistance would only serve to build a case against him if someone did accuse him of being involved in the fight.

He ran into Seth in the hallway as he headed for his room. The other boy greeted him warmly. "Hi, Will." His eyes narrowed as he noted the haggard look in Will's eyes. "Are you all right?"

Will nodded. "Yeah, I'm fine. Just tired."

Seth studied his face. "Is that blood?" he asked hesitantly.

Will smiled nonchalantly. "Probably. I fell during saber practice a bit ago."

"Isn't your saber practice in the morning?"

He brushed past his friend. "I'll see you later. I need to get cleaned up." He unlocked his door and shut it quickly behind him before Seth could ask any more questions. It wouldn't help his newly rekindled friendship if Seth found out he'd massacred another group of would-be assassins.

Finally alone, he stripped completely, then braced himself before using a spell to clean his body. As before, the pain was intense as the spell stripped away both dirt and scabs, and an involuntary grunt of pain escaped his lips. "Damn! That hurts!"

He used another spell to clean his impromptu linen bandages and then set about properly binding his wounds. For good measure, he drank one of the extra blood-cleanse potions he had saved. He wasn't sure if it would work if used prophylactically, but he wanted to avoid another bad fever. He had more if the wound in his belly still turned septic.

Studying his brigandine, he discovered that several of the rivets had popped loose and some of the plates were badly bent. He used the hilt of one of his daggers to pound them roughly back into shape so they wouldn't poke into him while wearing it. He'd have to continue using it until the new ones were ready. As long as he didn't get shot again in the same places, it would protect him. "Better than nothing," he muttered.

He cleaned and re-sharpened his sword, reloaded his crossbow, and then put them both back in storage. "It's a good thing my sleeves are long, otherwise everyone would be wondering about the cuts and bruises on Monday," he observed.

The combat had left his muscles sore and his body tired in a way that only happened after a fight. It felt as though he'd strained his back too. *Probably when I picked up the dead man, or maybe when that spell threw me against the wall.*

He lay down for a nap, even though it was still afternoon. Normally he would dismiss the spell he was holding before getting into bed, but this time he decided to see if he could maintain it while asleep. It was worth a try at least.

Will awoke a few hours later, and while his body was stiff and sore, his mind was clear. He called up the limnthal and addressed his ring. "Something happened today," he began.

"You're going to tell me about it, aren't you? What did I ever do to you?" said Arrogan.

He ignored the remarks. "I went to a tailor to pay for some clothes and I was ambushed."

"Before you go any further, let me ask you a question. Were you ambushed by people you annoyed by continually talking to them about things in which they had absolutely no interest? If so, I'd like to say that I empathize with their suffering."

Will found himself smirking. "Stop trying to cheer me up."

"I truly and honestly am not trying to cheer you up," insisted the ring. When Will didn't respond the ring spoke again. "Well, go ahead. Don't drag this out. Punish me with your story."

He explained what had happened, including some pertinent past information about how he had dealt with Remi and seeing Selene leaving Count Spry's city home. He also mentioned the note he had received. When he finished, he asked, "What do you think?"

"Are you expecting praise for surviving such an elaborate ambush?"

Will frowned. That hadn't been his purpose, but he did feel somewhat proud of his tenacity. He'd not only survived a surprise attack with five armed attackers, a spell caster, *and* a demon, but he had soundly beaten them. "I only wanted your advice about what to do next, but since you mention it, I *did* do rather well, didn't I?"

"Fucking idiot!" swore Arrogan. "You do something stupid then expect a compliment? If this keeps happening, you *will* die. You won't get many chances to learn from mistakes like this, because the final lesson is getting your life snuffed out."

"I did the best I could with what I had!"

"That isn't the point, you wooden-headed dolt!"

"Then what is?"

"The first thing you should realize is that if you've been ambushed, you screwed up. The whole point of an ambush is catching you in a situation where you aren't prepared and eliminating you with an attack you can't defend against. They very nearly succeeded this time, even if you did survive. If they get another chance, they'll do their best to make damn sure there's no way you can get out of it alive. What you should be thinking about now is how *not* to be ambushed again."

Frustrated, Will said the first thing that came to mind, "Is there a spell for that?" There was a long pause, during which he realized how silly the question was.

But then Arrogan replied, "You'll find it in *Practical Magic* on the page titled 'Of course not, idiot!' It's right after the one titled, 'How could anyone ask such a dumb question?' and right before the page titled, 'How to arrange your own funeral if you're too stupid to live.'"

For the first time in a while, Arrogan's words found their mark and Will felt his cheeks color. "Professor Dulaney says there are no stupid questions," he replied sourly.

"Until you come along and infect a perfectly innocent question with your idiocy," said Arrogan. "You need to stop massaging your Professor Dulaney's feet, or sucking his toes, or whatever the hell it is you're doing, and learn to think for yourself. Stop asking questions you know the answers to and start figuring out what the important questions are. Knowing the right questions is the biggest part of not being stupid."

"Are you done?" asked Will sourly.

"Maybe. I think I have one more." After a pause, he went on, "No, that was it."

"How do I keep from being ambushed again?"

“Finally,” said the ring. “The first thing to do is stop being predictable. As overwhelming as it is having so many people trying to kill you, you have to think about it from their perspective. Setting an ambush isn’t easy. You have to know where your target is going to be and get there first. You have to have enough time to set up for him. That means that whenever possible, you have to make sure no one knows where you’re going to be at any given time.”

That made sense to Will, though he thought he’d been doing that much of the time anyway. “I’ve been leaving unobserved by climbing the wall, and I was supposed to pick up those clothes two weeks ago. They couldn’t have known when I was coming.”

“That shows just how badly they want to get you,” said Arrogan. “They only knew the place, but they were willing to set up and wait for weeks until you arrived. In the future you need to think about any place that someone knows you have to appear at, particularly if there’s a specific time.”

“I’m a student,” said Will. “I have a set schedule of classes every week.”

“You should drop out of this crappy school anyway.”

“I’m not doing that. Not yet, anyway. Is there anything else?”

“Obviously there are times when you can’t avoid being predictable. Like your class schedule, or this dance you mentioned a while back—”

“I also have to pick up some armor I commissioned in a few weeks,” Will interrupted.

“Or that,” agreed the ring. “When you’re faced with something unavoidable, you have to work under the assumption that someone is going to try again. Think about how they’ll do it. Depending on the place, there are usually only a few good options for ambushing someone. Let’s use your armorer as an example. They can’t be sure what direction you’ll come from, which limits your enemy. He has to choose the shop itself for his ambush, either when you enter or leave. He can kill the armorer and wait inside, or plan on taking you in the street.”

“All I can think to do is try to be more aware of the surroundings when I go, but I’ve been doing that anyway.”

Arrogan sighed. “You’ve missed the simplest answer.”

“Which is?”

“Send someone else to fetch it for you.”

Will’s chin dropped, but a moment later he recovered. “Wait, I can’t send a friend into danger.”

“Then send a stranger. It’s unlikely they’ll attack someone other than you anyway. Just don’t send someone they could use to gain leverage.”

He frowned. "Even if it was a complete stranger, I'd feel compelled to help if they were kidnapped."

"Your enemies don't know that. They assume everyone is just as cold hearted as they are," said the ring.

"How about my classes then? I can't send someone in my place."

"The best solution would be to drop out, but if you're unwilling to do that then you need to at least plan an exit strategy for every class in advance. The school is probably safe, but there's always a chance they'll find a way. You should also pick a safe haven to retreat to in the event that they try something really over the top, like invading the campus with an army."

"That's not possible."

"Don't be too sure. You won't live to be six hundred years old if you don't assume that you'll see something at least that crazy every hundred years or so. Trust me."

"Is that why you lived in a shack in the woods with a bolt hole in the basement and a cat keeping the fae away?" asked Will.

"You figured that out, eh?"

"I know its name now too," said Will. "But I still don't understand what it is or why it was protecting you."

"The goddamn cat is a demigod," Arrogan replied. "And he helped me mainly because we had the same enemies."

"And those were?"

"Demons, the fae, and sorcerers," answered the ring. "At least those were the ones that the cat hates as much as I did."

"He's still helping me," said Will suddenly. "At least, he's still protecting the house."

"Really? That's surprising. Does the house need protecting, though? Barrowden is secure now and the fae aren't a problem for normal people."

"What are you suggesting?"

"If you know his name, you can call him. If you can offer him something he wants, he might agree to relocate. He can be a valuable ally, particularly if you've got demons hunting you."

Will scratched his head. "You think he'd move just to get fresh eggs?"

"Idiot! The eggs were just a courtesy! Demigods don't help anyone for something that stupid."

"If I make a bargain with him, wouldn't that make me a warlock?"

"I thought you'd figured that part out already. Are you a warlock because of your dealings with the fae?"

"Oh, right." Will felt dumb. *Don't deal in things that shouldn't be sold and I'll be fine.* "But what could I possibly offer him?"

"You've already killed several sorcerers and two demons," pointed out Arrogan, "so he's likely kindly disposed toward you. That will make it easier, but as to what he wants? You'll have to ask."

"What if he wants me to do something bad? Or asks for favors in the future?"

"If he asks you to kill sorcerers, that's easy. Just say yes." Arrogan's voice was cold and unfeeling.

"I won't be ordered to kill, not even sorcerers," said Will stubbornly.

"Talk to him and see. He's more reasonable than you might expect. Just make sure you tell him that elves are off the table before you bargain," suggested the ring.

"Elves?"

"Yeah, he hates them too. I think he originally lived in their realm, but you don't want to get involved in that feud. Humans and elves are still on somewhat amicable terms, at least in Trendham. You don't want to mess that up."

"Fine, I'll do it."

"Make sure you have an egg ready when you call him."

"I thought you said—"

"Courtesy? Remember?" interrupted Arrogan.

"All right. I won't forget," said Will. "There's something else I want to ask you about." He explained how he had seen Selene leaving Count Spry's city home.

"This is the girl you've been moaning about, right?" asked Arrogan. "I don't know. You haven't told me enough about her, other than that she's a sorceress and the king's daughter, and frankly that's enough to avoid her like the plague."

Will thought back on their past conversations and realized that he hadn't really said much. He'd left Selene out of most of his past descriptions, partly because he didn't want to hear Arrogan bitching about sorcerers, and partly because he was embarrassed. With that in mind, he braced himself for criticism and started at the beginning, explaining everything he knew. Arrogan listened quietly until Will got close to the end of his adventure in Barrowden.

The ring exploded in a furious stream of expletives when Will mentioned Selene being pulled away by some strange magic of the king's making. Will's ears turned red and his cheeks colored as he heard phrases that would have shocked a sailor. Arrogan ended with, "You need to kill him! Him and the girl both! Then you need to find out if he has any friends and kill them too." The last line was laden with such cold malice that Will knew it wasn't a joke.

"I don't understand."

"You said you saw it when she was talking to him outside your house too, didn't you?"

"Saw what?"

"The heart-stone enchantment, you dimwit!"

Confused, Will answered, "It wasn't the enchantment that controls her elementals—"

"No, fool! It's the one that her father uses to control *her*! When you mentioned it the first time, I though it must be some other spell, but now that you've said he summoned her—that changes everything." The ring began swearing again. "What kind of sick bastard does that to his own child?"

Will felt a cold dread begin to creep over him. He didn't want to believe it. "What has he done to her, exactly? Is there a way to fix it?"

But the ring was ignoring him as it ranted on, "How did he learn it? No one should know how it's done. I killed them all."

Will waited patiently until the ring slowed down and ran out of steam. Then he asked again, "What has he done to Selene?"

"I'll only tell you on one condition," said Arrogan. "You have to promise to do something for me."

"What do you want me to do?"

"Promise first."

"No. I need to know what it is you want me to do," insisted Will.

"Then I won't tell you what you want to know," answered Arrogan. "And your girlfriend will die in agony before spending a possible eternity serving the needs of unscrupulous men."

Will already had a feeling he knew the answer to his question. "He's bound her with the heart-stone enchantment, hasn't he? Just like if she was an elemental."

The ring remained silent.

"But I can undo it. Like I did with the elementals after I killed those sorcerers."

"She'll die," said Arrogan cruelly. "Attempt to unbind her and she'll die instantly."

"It didn't kill the elementals when I undid it," insisted Will.

"Because you undid the sorcerer's end of it. If the sorcerer had still been alive, he would have died shortly after what you did. It binds souls, and the bearer of whichever end you unravel will die."

He was horrified. "That's horrible."

"Promise me and I'll tell you the rest. There's more you need to know."

"I won't kill Selene," said Will. "If that's part of it, then you can forget it."

The ring thought about it a while, then answered, "Fine. I won't force you to kill her. Will you promise then?"

"If I promise, will you help me save her?"

A growling sound issued from the ring. "Why do you care so much about that man's cursed spawn?"

Will answered the question with one of his own. "Why did you cut the horns off of one of the Lords of the Fae?"

"This isn't the same," insisted Arrogan. "You hardly know her. You can find someone else to fawn over."

"Promise me that and I'll do anything," said Will earnestly. "Promise me that you'll help me free her and I'll do anything you want."

"She won't thank you," warned the ring. "In fact, she'll probably hate you for it."

"I don't care."

"Fine. We have a deal. You honor your promise to me, and I'll honor mine," announced Arrogan.

"I'll swear to it," agreed Will.

"You have to kill the king."

"What?" Will yelped in alarm.

"You'd have figured it out if you had half a brain," said the ring. "I already mentioned that the person attached to the end you unravel dies. The only way to free her is to kill the king and unravel his end of the heart-stone enchantment. You also need to kill anyone else who knows the secret of the enchantment, be they man, woman, or child."

"Why?"

"Because you swore to," said Arrogan. "The knowledge has to die."

"I won't kill Selene," insisted Will.

"She's your only exception. And if she won't agree to hide the knowledge with you, then I'd advise you to kill her anyway."

"The heart-stone enchantment sounds pretty nasty, but I'm not sure you should overreact. It's not as if—" He stopped mid-sentence. "Wait, is that how it's done?"

"You're starting to think. That's precisely how it's done. Once she dies, either by natural causes or the command of her father, her soul will remain bound. Flesh and mind will pass away, but her spirit will remain, ready to be shaped into whatever elemental form her twisted father desires."

His eyes grew wide. "So every elemental I've seen is—"

"The soul of some poor bastard who was forced into magical slavery," finished Arrogan.

Will remembered something Selene had once said about lesser and greater elementals. "Does the person's soul affect the power of the elemental created?"

"Very much so," said the ring. "The first ones created by Valemon were made with captured fae, but they were too hard to catch. He soon discovered that the souls of wizards were just as good. A wizard like you would produce a greater elemental, while those of the second-rate chumps they train these days would only produce lesser elementals."

Will had an epiphany. "That's why her elemental could restore itself by absorbing turyn from the environment."

"That's right. The mind and body may be gone, but the soul remembers the lessons of its owner's lifetime."

Chapter 36

Will spent the rest of the evening thinking about what he had learned, and the more he thought, the less he liked it. *How can the world be this messed up? What will Selene think of me if I kill her father?* He felt ill just thinking about it.

He tossed and turned in his sleep that night. In his dreams he was alternately the hunter and the hunted. In both cases it was awful, as he was either forced to kill or suffered an agonizing death when his pursuer inevitably caught him. When he woke in the morning, his body was covered by a cold sheen of sweat.

"At least it's Saturday," he told himself, sitting up. His back complained loudly as the muscles he had strained the day before reminded him of the abuse they'd received. He stood and stretched, then began his morning spell exercises.

Will started by constructing each spell he had memorized in turn, forming one then dismissing it so he could create the next. The purpose of the exercise was simply to make sure he didn't forget the spells, but it also served to improve his speed in creating the constructs. For some reason he found it more difficult.

"I must be tired," he told himself. Then he remembered that he hadn't dismissed the wind-wall spell before his nap the day before. "Surely not," he muttered. Turning his attention inward, he felt the spell still within his chest. With one hand, he reached up and pulled the spell out. It was still in perfect shape.

It was the first time he'd kept a prepared spell intact while sleeping, but even more surprising, he'd been able to form new spells without dismissing it. Keeping the wind-wall spell above his right palm, he ran through his exercises again, forming fresh spell constructs above his left hand. A smile crept across his features as the wind-wall construct remained solidly in place.

Two at once! He wanted to shout for joy, but he refrained, staying silent instead while he did a happy jig in his room. Then he dismissed both spells and tried his exercises again. He found them much easier this time. *So, keeping a spell prepared slows me down a little.*

He recreated the wind-wall spell, stored it, then constructed a blur spell and did the same, storing it within his chest beside the other spell. *Should I try for a third?* He tried and felt both of his previous spells fall apart. Two was his limit currently.

But did that include active spells?

To test the idea, he prepared a wind-wall and stored it, then cast the blur spell on himself. The blur spell was an illusion that smeared his appearance across an extra foot of space to either side, making him more difficult to hit, but after casting it only required him to keep feeding it turyn. With blur active, and wind-wall prepared, he tried to construct a third spell, force lance.

The simple construct came together above his palm without much difficulty. *So active spells don't affect how many spell constructs I can have prepared,* he noted. He guessed that active spells were only limited by how much turyn they drew and how long he could sustain the cost.

The Winter Ball was thirteen days away. Will took stock of himself in light of his new training breakthrough. What would benefit him most at the ball? Being able to reflex cast a spell or improving his spellcraft until he could cast sixth-order spells? An even more important question was which of the two he could accomplish in the time remaining to him.

Wind-wall wasn't the best spell for reflex casting. He had realized that after the last assault. He'd had it prepared, but without taking the time to inflate his turyn before the cast it hadn't been at its full force. By default, that would almost always be the case if he was reflex casting it as well. If he was going to start practicing a different spell in the hopes of being able to reflex cast, he would probably take longer than two weeks.

That clinched the decision for him. If he could succeed at sixth-order spells then he could add the chameleon and sleep spells to his repertoire, and both might be handy if something happened at the ball.

Will set out to find a new place to practice. Working on his spellcraft didn't really require a practice environment, since he wouldn't be actually casting the spells, merely constructing them repeatedly, but he wanted some sunshine.

He ran into Rob almost as soon as he left the dorm. "Will!" called his friend. "I haven't seen you in days. Where are you off to?"

"I'm going to practice my spell construction, but I was tired of being cooped up indoors."

Rob took a step back. "Color me shocked. On a Saturday?"

"My life is a little strange," Will admitted. "I try not to waste it. I think Count Spry is still after me."

"After all those potions you made, how much life can you have left?" asked Rob. "You should take time to smell the roses."

Will gave his friend a dour look. "What roses?"

"Ever heard of girls?"

"I doubt any of them are interested in me, and if they were, I'd suggest they look elsewhere. Being around me doesn't seem very beneficial."

"And yet Janice always asks me about you," Rob replied with a smirk.

"She's smart enough to know I'm bad news," countered Will. "Now, I really need to practice."

Rob followed him. "I'll tag along. I should probably practice a little too."

Not wanting to give away the fact that he preferred secluded places at the edge of the campus, Will instead found a bench in a less-traveled area near some of the manicured hedges. It was fairly private and not nearly as suspicious as his usual spots. Will sat and began forming a fifth-order spell meant for softening steel.

Rob started to follow suit, then stopped. "Wow. Isn't that fifth-order?"

Will nodded, finishing his construction then dismissing it to start again.

"I knew you were ahead, since you came here already able to see turyn, but isn't that a bit much?"

He raised a brow. "You're a second-year. You should be doing the same."

"I'm just starting third-order spells," Rob admitted grimly. "I just started on spellcraft this year, so I figured we'd be around the same place."

Will practiced constantly, when he awoke, between classes, after classes, in the evenings—pretty much anytime he had a spare moment. "I practice a lot, and I don't waste my Saturdays smelling roses."

"Gosh, I bet that makes you popular," said Rob sarcastically. "What's the point?"

"The better I get, the better my chances of surviving another day."

"Magic won't help you survive," began Rob, then he stopped. "Wait, are you learning restricted spells?" His eyes were round.

Will said nothing.

"Did Professor Dulaney authorize that? Because of your problem with Count Spry?"

He looked away. "Not exactly."

Rob gasped. "You stole them?"

"No!" stated Will firmly. "My old master left me some books."

"Show me one of the spells."

Will constructed the force-lance spell. "This one is fairly simple if you want to learn it."

"What does it do?" Rob's eyes were full of enthusiasm.

Will explained the spell then fired it off, aiming in a direction where it wouldn't hit anything before it dissipated. The force-lance traveled for almost fifty yards before vanishing.

"What would that do if it hit something?"

He pursed his lips. "Depends on what it hits. It's similar to a physical spear, but with a lot more power behind it. A stone wall would probably stop it cold, but against furniture, doors, or people, it's pretty devastating. It will tear a hole clean through a person's chest."

Rob stared at him accusingly.

Will gave up. He wanted to talk anyway. "I was ambushed yesterday in the city." Of course, after that sentence Rob wouldn't relent until he had relayed the entire tale.

When he finished, his friend asked, "Why didn't I hear about it? An attack on the street in broad daylight, everyone should be talking about it by now."

"They had the street blocked off and they cleaned everything up afterward," said Will.

"So that's why you're practicing so hard," said Rob.

Will nodded. "If I can master sixth-order, I can use a sleep spell instead of slaughtering people every time something happens. I'm trying to get there within two weeks."

"Two weeks? What happens in two weeks?" He gasped. "The Winter Ball? You have an invitation?"

"Unfortunately," said Will. "But I'm worried what may happen. I'm almost certain Count Spry will be there." *And Baroness Nerrow,* he added silently.

"I never know whether to feel sorry for you or envy you," observed Rob. "Do you know how to dance?"

A lance of fear shot through Will's heart. *Dance?* He hadn't even thought about it.

Rob laughed at the expression on his face. "I guess not. You'd better start learning. They call it a 'ball' for a reason. Who are you taking?"

"No one," Will answered.

Rob tutted at him. "That won't do. You have to bring a partner. They'll frown on it if you don't."

"But…"

"I'm sure Janice would go if you ask. I doubt any of the other girls will let you within ten feet before they start running."

Will wanted to curl into a ball and hide. He covered his face with his hands and groaned loudly.

Rob stood up and pulled Will to his feet. "C'mon. I know someone who can help."

"Who?"

"Mom."

It took Will a moment to realize that Rob was referring to the resident assistant, Dianne Young. "She's not very fond of me these days."

"She doesn't have to like you to help. Besides, she'll have to forgive you eventually. This might speed things up."

Will wasn't sure that was true, but he let his friend drag him along. A few minutes later and they were back at the boys' dorm. Rob found Dianne and launched into a quick explanation of the problem.

Dianne looked at Rob, then studied Will with a faint look of reproval in her eyes. He was sure she would refuse, but after a moment she said, "He'll need a partner."

Rob winked at the resident assistant. "You're a woman. Or so I've heard."

"For the ball," clarified Dianne. "Whoever goes with him will need to learn as well."

"Oh!" exclaimed Rob.

"Thank you, Dianne," said Will humbly.

She gave him a stern glance. "I'm doing this to save whoever goes with you from embarrassment."

"I appreciate it anyway."

"Figure out who is going with you. I can help you in the evenings after supper," she told them before returning to her desk.

Rob smiled at Will. "Told you. Now all you have to do is ask Janice. Want to go find her?"

Will waved his hands. "Not now. I need to practice." He was too nervous to think about it then. He needed time to prepare himself mentally. Backing away, he headed for the stairs. Sunshine was overrated; he could practice spellcraft in his room.

Chapter 37

He practiced the rest of Saturday with a feverish intensity. Will liked to believe it was because of his dedication and diligence, but the truth was probably that he was trying not to think about what Rob had suggested. Asking someone to accompany him shouldn't have made him nervous. He was already in love with Selene anyway. Finding a partner for the ball shouldn't cause him any more anxiety than finding a sparring partner during saber practice.

At least that's what he told himself, but going into Cerria and being ambushed by assassins and demons was starting to seem like the preferable option. *What kind of life have I led that I'm more scared of a girl than being attacked?* he wondered.

Sunday found him still unprepared to approach her, but he had plenty of tasks to distract him. After practicing for most of the morning, he went to lunch in the dining hall and when that was finished, he walked back to the kitchen where he paid one of the scullery lads a penny for a fresh egg.

As he walked across the college grounds with the egg in hand, he started chuckling at his actions. "Calling a demigod is easier than asking a girl to a dance. That's what I've come to learn about myself. I'm an idiot."

He found a distant corner of the campus where the groundskeepers had let the trees grow thick and dense, forming a park of sorts, though it was more of a tiny forest. Will circled the area and then spiraled inward, making sure the area was empty before he began. Once he was sure there was no one nearby, he went to the center of the trees and sat down, placing the egg on the ground before him. He repeated the goddamn cat's name three times. "Cath Bawlg…" After the third repetition it felt as though his mind touched something, but it was so faint he might have imagined it.

Will was patient and he put his worries aside, enjoying the sunlight as it played through the leaves above. It reminded him of home and his days playing in the Glenwood. He missed those days. After a while, he became so wrapped up in his memories that he almost didn't notice the approach of a grey tom. The goddamn cat had come.

He stopped in front of Will and sat back on his haunches.

Will produced a small wooden bowl and cracked the egg into it. "I thought you might like this," he said. "It's been a while."

The cat stared at him for a long minute, and when he finally decided the cat was going to ignore the egg, the Cath Bawlg bent and began to lap at the yolk. Will waited until he had finished before he spoke. "I need your help."

The goddamn cat looked up at him and though his mouth didn't move, a voice found his ears. "I wondered if you would be bold enough to call me."

"I wasn't sure if I should," he admitted.

"I am no demon that you should fear to call. So long as you offer respect, I will do you no harm, whether we make a bargain or not."

"I wasn't sure since I have little experience. In the past calling someone was always risky—"

"Because you called the fae," growled the cat. "A human calling one of them is like a mouse calling a cat. We are not enemies."

"We may have much in common," suggested Will.

The cat's ears flicked forward with interest. "Don't dance around the subject, boy. You wish to suggest that you are like Arrogan, but you are not. He and I shared three enemies, but you frequently consort with the fae, and you are friends with a sorceress, so we share only one. Arrogan spilled enough blood to fill a river before he dared to call my name, though I never asked it of him. I owed him a debt before we ever met."

"I've slain a handful of sorcerers and two demons," said Will.

"One demon," corrected the goddamn cat. "Your sorceress mate killed the other one."

His cheeks flushed. "She isn't my mate."

"You're foolish, like most of your kind. Neither of you will admit the truth until it's impossible to deny. My eyes see more clearly. You brought her through my home, risking your own life when faced with my wrath."

"I didn't know."

"Because of her, our arrangement will be limited. Demons are the only enemy we fully share."

"I've already promised to eliminate sorcerers," said Will. "Except for her."

"There are others I bear grudges against," suggested the cat.

Will shook his head. "I won't act against the elves either."

"If Arrogan weren't dead, I would think he was still advising you."

"He is," Will admitted. "His knowledge is still with me, though his spirit has gone."

"More fae tricks," hissed the goddamn cat. "You would do well to rid yourself of them. Arrogan knew better than to accept their aid."

"He did once," countered Will.

"And his wife paid the price for it. You'll learn a similar lesson eventually, and then we'll have more in common." The cat began cleaning egg from one of his paws.

He didn't know how to respond to that, so he decided to move on to practical matters. "If we strike a bargain, what can you—"

The goddamn cat interrupted, "I'm not your fae dog. I come and go as I please. For the demon you have slain I may help you, but only as I decide. I do not deal in favors."

"Then what—"

"Tonight, at midnight, leave your room and come outside. I will show you your greatest desire. That is all I will give." The cat moved forward and bumped his head against Will's knee. "I've marked you. In the future I will watch. Please me and I might aid you another time. Don't call me again. I answer only once." Then he turned and walked away.

Will stared after the cat, unsure what to think. After a moment he summoned the limnthal and told the ring about his conversation.

Arrogan laughed. "I told you not to worry. Bargaining with the cat isn't like dealing with demons, or the fae for that matter."

"But I'm not sure if he's going to help me or not," complained Will.

"Usually the answer is 'not,'" said the ring. "Meet him tonight, though. He never lies. Now that you've called him, he'll watch you."

"What does that *mean* though?"

"It means if he likes what you're doing, he might help. Most of the time it means you're on your own. He never shows up when you want him to," said Arrogan. "It's like having a guardian spirit that doesn't care if you fall and break your neck."

"Then what good is he?"

"What good are cats generally? They don't come when you call, they don't care if you hurt yourself, and they do what they want regardless of what you need. But sometimes, you find a dead snake in a place you might have stepped. The goddamn cat is like that. Trust me, he might not do what you want, but when he does do something, you'll usually discover it was important."

With a sigh, Will dismissed the limnthal and left. He couldn't decide if he had gained an ally or not. He walked back to the dorm, and since he had nothing better to do, he started practicing his spellcraft again.

That evening at the appointed time, Will left his room and walked away from the lamp light that illuminated the areas around the larger buildings of Wurthaven, adjusting his vision as he entered the deeper darkness. It wasn't long before he felt another presence, and a small shadow stepped into his path—the goddamn cat.

The cat said nothing, simply walking away and leaving it to him whether he would follow or not. He led him to the wall on the side of the college that was closest to the royal palace. Will never saw the cat climb, but when he got to the base, he saw him sitting at the top, looking down at him. He sighed and cast the climb spell. On the other side was a small lane that was seldom used, for it led between the college and the palace to the city's northern gate which was kept closed to public traffic.

Across the road was the outer wall of the palace grounds, though unlike Wurthaven's wall, which was set close to the road, it was fifty yards back from the verge. Will had never dared approach it for fear that there might be watchers atop the wall. The cat stopped and a voice found Will's ear, "Adjust your vision. With the heart-light, you can see where the sentries are."

Will did and was surprised to see that the guards atop the wall were spread few and far between, with hundreds of yards between them.

"The king relies on the fact that this place is well within the city's defenses, as well as that no one knows where the watchers are at any given time. Make note of the section directly across from us. If you ever return on your own, that is the best place to cross." The cat moved off the road into the shadows and turned right, following the road north.

"Where are we going?" asked Will, but he didn't get an answer. They traveled for half a mile, until the city wall loomed in the distance, and then the cat began angling his path to track closer to the palace. Eventually they came to an unpaved path that was only a path in the sense that there were no trees or rocks to impede a rider. They followed it to the palace wall, where Will saw a door set in the palace's outer wall. It was open.

"This door should be locked and guarded," said the cat. "Today is an exception, but never come here on your own. In the future it will be even more strongly protected."

Passing through the door, Will was shocked to see bodies strewn about with gaping wounds. *Surely the goddamn cat didn't do this, did he?* Blood stained the ground and was splattered on the stone archway within the gate. A sense of evil seeped into his bones, making him feel cold. Will increased his turyn sensitivity and saw black traces left on the bodies. "Demons," he hissed.

The cat stopped beside one corpse. "This one was a sorcerer."

Will understood. Bending down he put his hand against the man's chest. It was still warm. He pulled the heart-stone enchantment free and picked it apart. A massive elemental spirit appeared and then faded away. The cat walked on, leading him through the wall and into the sculpted gardens of the palace grounds. "What does all of this mean?" he whispered, but again, the cat didn't respond.

The garden was quiet and still, unsettling Will since he knew so much violence had just occurred. Where had the demons gone? Why weren't there soldiers combing the grounds to find the intruders? Had no one raised an alarm?

The palace itself wasn't a fortress or keep as so many lords lived within. It relied on the city's defenses and the wall that surrounded it. Its main concession to defense was that it was built of stone and that the lowest level had narrow windows too slim for a man to pass through. It was defensible, but not against an army. The upper levels had broader windows with glass panes to let in more light. Will followed the cat to the northern corner of the building.

"Directly above us is what you desire. The demons entered through the eastern entrance, to the south of where we are now. They've slain everyone they encountered, so the palace is unaware of their presence."

Will looked south and saw light spilling out from an open door. Cold dread clutched at his heart. *Selene is in there somewhere.* He started in that direction, but the goddamn cat spoke again. "Go that way and you will be too late." The cat stared upward. "Her room is above, on the fifth floor." After a moment the cat turned and began to walk away, back toward the postern gate they had entered through.

"Where are you going?" Will asked desperately.

"I've done what I desired," said the goddamn cat. "What you do from here is your own affair."

Will went to the wall of the palace without pausing to think, then cast the climbing spell. He dismissed the wind-wall spell he had prepared and replaced it with a demon-armor spell. Then he started climbing as rapidly as he could manage, counting the floors as he went.

In less than a minute, he reached the window that was his target. A faint light was emanating from within, likely from a candle. *If it's Selene's room, why wouldn't she use a light spell?* he wondered. Candles were far inferior. He looked in, readjusting his eyesight to make the most of the dim light.

It appeared to be a parlor or sitting room, for it was appointed with cushioned chairs and low tables. A candelabra on a sideboard was providing the illumination, but the room was empty. On the far side of the room was an archway that led to a bedroom, for he could just see the footboard of the bed to the right. A lady's table with a mirror and a stool was directly within his view, and Selene was sitting there, holding something in her hand.

It glinted in the dim light, and Will realized it was a dagger. She was holding it in front of her, with the point against her breast. He could see her expression reflected in the mirror; it was one of desperate resolve. *No!*

He tried the window and found it locked. He began constructing an unlocking spell, but before he could finish, Selene stood and threw the dagger across the room. Her head was down, her face obscured by unbound tresses that badly needed a comb. The sight of her desolation broke his concentration, and the spell construct in his hand dissolved, so he was forced to begin again.

He had just completed the spell when a loud crash emanated from the room, followed by the sound of wood cracking and splintering. Selene looked up, and Will could see dark streaks on her cheeks, but she was no longer crying. Her face showed fear and anger.

Casting his spell he heard the distinctive click as the latch opened and he pushed the window in. He climbed inside just as something dark and massive ran through the parlor. To his left he could see another door, the one that had been destroyed.

A cry of rage filled his ears—Selene—and a blue jet streaked through the air, destroying a chair next to where he was standing. Something evil stood between them, though he could see a hole had been blown through its midsection. If the wound bothered the demon, it showed no sign of it, for it launched itself at Selene anyway.

Will expanded his outer shell to increase his turyn absorption and activated the demon-armor spell, then he charged forward.

CHAPTER 38

The demon was unlike the ones Will had seen before. Where those had been smoke, blood, teeth and claws, this one was a massive bulk of black muscle and scales that glittered in the light. Its attention was firmly on the sorceress in front of it, so it failed to note his arrival as he leapt onto its back.

He had no real plan. His only hope was that the demon armor would do the job. He was mistaken.

For a brief moment he saw Selene, clad once more in her stone armor with blue water blades gripped in each fist, and then, as his spell began to burn into the flesh of the monster, it reached over its back and plucked him loose before flinging him at the wall. Something cracked when his body met stone, and it wasn't the wall.

Pain shot through his back and legs as he slid to the floor. Meanwhile the demon had turned its attention back to its main target, Selene. Her water blades had transformed into spinning circles that surrounded her body, and when the creature tried to catch her in its claws, it screamed with rage, for the water cut away talons and sent black ichor flying whenever it got too close.

Her eyes fell on Will for a moment and he saw fear in them, not for herself, for him. He could almost hear her foremost thought, *Why are you here?*

The distraction cost her, as the demon stepped back and something dark formed in the air in front of it—a spell.

They can cast spells? thought Will. He'd never considered the idea, but it probably should have been self-evident if he'd thought about it. Black tentacles shot forth, dodging between Selene's water blades and grappling with her stone armor. They seized her body and began to pull, but she didn't move. It was then that Will noticed that her stone boots had fused with the floor, anchoring her in place.

To his left, Will saw two more demons of the more common variety enter through the archway, gliding masses of smoke and claws. They spread out to either side, moving to flank the lone sorceress. He tried to rise, but his legs refused to respond.

"Get out, Will," yelled Selene. "Go!"

Fuck that, he thought. He couldn't run if he wanted to, and if he could it wouldn't be to leave. His demon-armor spell had vanished when he struck the wall, but his expanded shell was still absorbing turyn at a prodigious rate. It would be full soon. He studied Selene's stone armor and hoped it would be strong enough.

A water drill tore through one of the smoke demons, causing it to scream in pain, but it didn't stop advancing. Will began constructing his next spell, hoping he could finish it in time.

All three demons were on top of Selene now, pulling and tearing at the stone armor that protected her. Her water elemental had gone wild, ripping through them and sending gouts of viscous, black fluid across the room, but it wasn't enough to stop them. Will could see the stone beginning to crack.

He finished his spell and began to pull himself across the floor. He wanted to be closer, but the floor melted around him, flowing up and covering him in a stone cocoon. *She's trying to protect me. Not now!* He wanted to scream with frustration.

Placing his hands against the stone, he *pulled,* drawing in the turyn the elemental used to sustain its creation. After a moment the cocoon crumbled, and he dragged himself out.

"You idiot!" yelled Selene. "They'll kill you."

Worry about yourself, he thought. He was at the feet of the big demon now. It glanced down and grinned at him with a mouthful of rotten fangs. A few feet away, Will saw red blood beginning to trickle down the outside of Selene's stone armor.

A clawed hand caught him with such speed that he hardly saw it move, and Will felt a searing pain as black talons punctured his chest and back, punching through the plates of his brigandine as though they were made of paper rather than steel.

It lifted Will into the air, and he saw the demon's maw open wider than should have been physically possible. "Go fuck yourself," he muttered, and then he pushed everything he had into the wind-wall and released it.

The room exploded as a furious wind ripped through it, destroying the furniture, the bed, and shredding the demons. The only thing left untouched was Will himself, who dropped to the floor, still gripped within a now-severed demon hand. Selene's armor had shattered, and her body was covered in small cuts and lacerations as the last of the wind sent fragments of wood, glass, and stone across her body, but she was otherwise unharmed.

Will could see some of the demon turyn beneath her skin, though, where it showed through her tattered dressing gown. She stared at him with an undecipherable expression, even as she shivered with pain.

Reaching out, Will caught her ankle and began drawing the turyn from her, draining her of everything, demon essence and normal turyn alike. Gradually, she sank to the floor beside him.

The demonic turyn burned, but his body rapidly converted it and his strength returned. Glancing around, he saw the central portion of the greater demon begin to shift and move. It wasn't dead.

"You jerk," said Selene weakly. "You should have run. Now we're both going to die."

Will gave her a stubborn look, then summoned three potions from the limnthal. He handed a regeneration potion to Selene, then drank one himself, followed by an elixir of turyn.

Under normal circumstances, his disgust at knowing the main ingredient of the regeneration potions would have stopped him from drinking one, but he was beyond caring. The acrid taste was only marginally worse than the flavor of the turyn elixir, and he felt his legs begin to tingle.

The demon was starting to rise on the stumps of its limbs as Will crawled over and recast his demon-armor spell. Its body was regenerating, but not quickly enough to escape as it shuffled and crawled away. He crawled faster, and when he reached it he put his arms around the foul body and pulled it close.

The stench as its body burned was unbearable, but he bore it anyway. The thing writhed and screamed in agony, but eventually its strength ebbed. Pushing it to the floor, Will pulled himself on top and pressed his hands into a gaping wound in the creature's chest. Flesh sizzled and ichor boiled around his wrists as he pushed deeper, until his burning fingers found the monster's heart.

He was absorbing turyn as fast as he could, but the reaction with the demon's body devoured it more quickly than he could replace it. Will concentrated, forcing everything he had into his hands, until he felt the demon's heart disintegrate. Then he sank to the floor beside the corpse.

Holding up his hands, he could see that the skin had burned away, but before his eyes it was beginning to regrow. Testing his legs, he found that he could wiggle his toes again.

Selene was already up again, drawing from her elementals to replace what he had taken, and she shuffled over and sat down beside him with a thump. "I don't know whether to be mad at you or to thank you."

Will smiled. "Just don't kill yourself."

She grimaced. "You saw that?" A dark chuckle issued from her throat. "Don't worry. I didn't have the courage. I'm too much of a coward."

Will tried to sit up and failed. His turyn was recovering, but the regeneration potion was wreaking havoc on his senses. The room was swaying beneath him and his muscles felt weak. On the far side of the room his eyes lit on something familiar on Selene's dressing table.

Five potion vials sat there, and while he couldn't see the labels, he knew what was in them, for he had chosen distinct, fluted glass vials when he had made them. It was his universal antidote potions. *She was the one who bought them.*

Booted feet echoed through the chamber as five guards stormed into the room, accompanied by a well-dressed man in a bloodied doublet. The leader's hair was red, which matched the flames crackling around him, for he was surrounded by a fire elemental. His eyes took in the scene, lingering over Selene for a second before focusing on Will. "Assassin!" The lord's sword came up and darted toward Will.

"No!" yelled Selene, her voice cracking with authority. "He slew the demons! Stay your wrath, Lord Spry." A stone shield shot up from the floor to keep the nobleman's sword from reaching its target.

Ignoring his dizziness through sheer stubbornness, Will got slowly to his feet. He had never seen Dennis Spry's father, but he wouldn't show weakness in front of the man.

"Who is this man?" demanded Count Spry. Selene's stone shield sank slowly into the floor now that the threat had passed.

Selene started to answer, "No one of importance—"

But Will wasn't having it. The blood and terror had left him in a strange state. With a twisted grin, he answered, "William Cartwright, at your service, milord."

The count's eyes widened with surprise. Quicker than thought, his sword snapped up and he thrust it at Will. The point entered where one of the demon's claws had torn his brigandine apart, passing through Will's right shoulder and pushing against his armor in the back.

Selene stared at the scene with horrified eyes, but Will merely grimaced. The pain was intense, but his anger was greater still. Catching the count's wrist with his left hand, he balled his other into a fist and launched a wide haymaker at the count's head.

Count Spry fell back, his sword going with him, and he landed on the floor with a stunned expression. His guards began to rush forward, but another stone barrier sprang up, blocking their path. "Get out of my chambers, now!" ordered Selene.

The count stared up at Will with hate-filled eyes. "You murdered my son, and now you dare come here, into *her* room?"

Will could feel the flesh in his chest beginning to knit together once more, but he had to cough to bring up the blood from his ruptured lung. He smiled at the count with blood-stained teeth. A fresh wave of fatigue washed over him as the regeneration took its toll, but he still replied with a coarse gurgle, "Someone had to protect what you could not." His legs began to give out, but Selene caught him.

Another figure appeared, King Lognion, flanked by two of his personal guards. His sharp eyes took in the scene and then he addressed Count Spry, "I see you take your duties seriously, Lord Spry."

"Your Majesty." The count scrambled to his feet and bowed deeply.

"Lord Spry, return to your chambers. I will call for you shortly as I begin to unravel this mess." The king then glanced at his daughter. "Take your pet wizard to see Doctor Rhalish. If he doesn't die, I would very much like to hear what he has to say. Return to me once he's settled."

Selene began to help Will out, but the count protested, "My liege! You cannot allow—"

Lognion's stern gaze landed on the count with the force of a hammer. "What I allow is entirely within my purview, Lord Spry. I have given you what you wanted. Do not test my patience further."

Selene pulled him along, draping his arm over one shoulder, and soon they were out of the room. "Is the potion still working?" she asked softly.

"I think so," Will answered, feeling fuzzy. "But it's hard to keep my eyes open."

"If you die, I'll be sorely disappointed," she said sternly.

His legs gave out and he began to sag toward the floor, but Selene hauled him upward and slipped her other arm beneath his legs, lifting him like a child. Given their size difference, she was forced to lean sharply back to maintain her balance as she continued walking.

"I can die happily in your arms," said Will, his eyes closing.

"Keep dreaming," she replied.

"Your arms and back are going to hurt like hell tomorrow."

She chuckled. "Unlike you, I don't have to push my body past its limits. I have other options."

Cracking one eye open, Will saw stone encasing her upper arms and shoulders. She was using her earth elemental to reinforce her body. *Nice trick,* he thought.

"It only took you ten seconds to nearly undo all my work of the past few weeks," she intoned sadly.

"What work?"

"Keeping you safe, fool."

"I wasn't worried," said Will. "He didn't know about the potion."

"That's not what I meant, although for a moment I wondered if it would be better if you died. Then I could—" She stopped herself with a shake of her head.

"I hear that a lot," said Will.

"You don't have to worry about Count Spry any longer," she informed him.

Will smiled. "I thought you might have had something to do with the blood-price being lifted."

"Give some of the credit to my father. It was his idea, and without his support the count would not have agreed. There will be no more attempts on your life."

"I saw you at the count's house," said Will.

She stiffened. "Oh."

"I tracked the man hiring the killers back to him and you were there."

"That was the day we came to an understanding," she responded, her voice empty of emotion.

"What understanding?"

"The one in which you get to live," she said acerbically. "Assuming you can keep from goading him into stabbing you again."

"All I did was introduce myself," said Will innocently. "Besides, your *understanding* must not be very good. I was ambushed a few days ago by assassins and a demon." His consciousness began to fade.

The last thing he heard was her question, "What? Where?"

Chapter 39

He awoke a short time later, or so he hoped. He couldn't be entirely sure, but the window in the room showed a dark sky outside, so unless he had slept until the next night it could only have been a few hours. Glancing down, he saw that his chest was bare. Will lifted the blanket covering his lower half and saw that the rest of his clothes had been removed as well.

His skin was smooth and unblemished. *At least the potion did a good job on me,* he thought.

A grey-haired man who he hadn't yet noticed stood up from a chair beside the bed. "You're awake. I'll fetch His Majesty. He will want to speak with you." The old man left the room before Will could reply.

"Great," muttered Will. He sat up and searched the room with his eyes. His clothes, tunic, brigandine, trousers, none of them were anywhere to be seen. "Every time I come here, they steal my clothes."

He was tempted to summon a change of clothes from the limnthal, but he knew Lognion wouldn't miss such a detail, and the less that man knew the better.

The door opened and Lognion Maligant, King of Terabinia, stepped inside. He shut the door behind him and took a seat on the stool beside Will's bed. "Care to explain how you came to be in my daughter's chambers this evening?"

"I was following a demon," said Will. "Or so I thought. It turns out there were three."

"Actually, there were twelve," said the king. "Only three made it that far. There were also twenty soldiers." He held out a scrap of fabric that looked as though it had been cut from a uniform. The crest of Darrow was stitched onto it. "What do you think of this?"

Will frowned. "It seems too obvious."

"Unless they didn't care if we knew who it was," said Lognion, "but I agree. In light of the fact that the Patriarch is currently suing for peace, it seems counterproductive to announce their identities."

"What will you do?"

The king turned his piercing eyes on Will. "You'll find out when the time comes, William Cartwright, for I intend to make good use of you."

Will swallowed. As he stared back at the king, he thought about his promise to kill the man. They were alone, without guards or other obstacles. If he'd had a force-lance prepared in advance, he might have been tempted. But there were four elementals floating above Lognion's shoulders and he had a strong feeling the man was likely to be a formidable spellcaster as well. Even with the element of surprise, Will might fail. He wondered if the king could sense the treachery in his heart, and cold perspiration broke out on his temples.

Lognion smiled coldly. "No need to be so nervous, William. I am your king, not your enemy. However, there is one thing that troubles me. If you followed the demons in, how did you get ahead of them? Count Spry and the others were held back by the fighting, yet you were already in Selene's room."

His mouth felt dry. "I didn't follow them all the way. When I found the dead guards at the postern gate, I followed them to the palace, then climbed the wall to Selene's window."

"Honesty suits you, William," said Lognion. "But how did you know which window was hers?"

He had no good reason for such knowledge, and yet he couldn't tell the king that he'd consulted a demigod—that would only make the man more suspicious of his motives. "I wasn't completely sure, but I've been watching the palace."

"Spying on her? Is that what you're trying to say?"

I'm dead. "Yes, Your Majesty."

The king's eyes lit with gleeful malice. "You display entirely too much attachment to my daughter, Mister Cartwright. We've already discussed this, yet here we are."

"She might be dead if I hadn't," reminded Will.

Lognion leaned over, then hammered Will into the wall with a blinding jab. "Whether my daughter lives or dies is my concern, William, *not* yours. Her life's purpose is to serve me, in life or in death. There might even come a day when I require her death. If that were the case now, then your intervention would be treason."

Will could barely see out of one eye, and his head felt fuzzy from the impact with the wall. Even so, he could hardly believe the words he was hearing. *He's her father!*

"Although you are not as close to me, William, *your* life is also mine, for weal or woe. I am the one who decides whether your heart's blood is of more use to me inside your body, or whether it would be better pooling on the floor at my feet. Do you understand?"

"Yes, Your Majesty."

The king's demeanor changed, and his voice took on a cheerful tone. "However, it is your good fortune that I did not, in fact, desire my daughter's death at this time. Therefore you have done me a service. I should probably reward you." The king smiled broadly. "Is there anything you desire? Speak freely. I am willing to give you almost anything within my power."

The sudden change of mood, so suddenly after the violence, had Will feeling as though he was standing above a pit full of vipers. "I'm not sure."

"I imagine you'd like to marry Selene, wouldn't you?" Lognion winked knowingly.

Will was afraid to answer, but his feelings must have shown on his face.

"Don't worry. I won't punish you for admitting the truth."

"I wouldn't dream of such a gift, Your Majesty, unless she also desired such a thing. For me it would be sufficient if you allow me to be her friend."

"It's good that you know your place, for I will not give you her hand, not for something so mundane as saving her life. I would require something much greater from you first." The king leaned back, seeming to relax. "Very well. I will allow you to be her friend, however letters and words are all you may exchange. This doesn't seem like much of a reward, though. I would prefer to give you land and a title. Fulstrom's place is still vacant. Would that interest you?"

Suspicious, Will responded carefully, "I'm not sure I'm worthy of such a thing."

"Of course, you aren't," said the king. "I only allow men of power to hold title in my kingdom. You would have to accept an elemental first."

"Then I will have to decline, Your Majesty," answered Will nervously, "though I mean no insult in so doing."

"Whether you intend it or not, I *am* insulted, William. I am tempted to have you whipped for your presumption. Does this change your answer?"

"No, Your Majesty. My old master was against the practice of sorcery. It would dishonor his memory if I became a sorcerer." He spoke slowly, and each word felt like a nail being hammered into his coffin.

"Arrogan, you mean," said Lognion flatly. "You think honoring the Betrayer's memory is more important than serving your king?"

Will shook his head. "Can't I do both? Honor my dead master and serve my king? They don't seem mutually exclusive to me."

The king rose to his feet, disappointment written on his face. "You can try, but eventually you will fail. In the end you will likely die tied to a whipping post." Lognion sighed. "Not that I mind. Watching a proud man be whipped to death is good entertainment. Just remember this conversation when that day comes, William. You could have had much more, if not for your pride."

Lognion headed for the door, then turned back. "Not to worry, William. I won't kill you today, but let me remind you, you are in my debt. You would already be dead or in prison if Count Spry were allowed to have his way. Buying his forbearance was expensive, and I will extract the cost from you in service. Only once that has been repaid in full will I consider entertaining myself with your death."

Will waited until the king had left and the door clicked shut before he exhaled explosively, releasing the tension in his chest. *What the hell did that mean?* He spent the next quarter of an hour trying to decide whether he was in trouble or was being rewarded. *At least I can talk to Selene without her getting in trouble. Assuming I ever see her. Or I can send letters. That's good, right?*

He waited in the room for an hour, unsure what to do. He wasn't wounded, aside from his newly acquired black eye. He was fully recovered, and other than being slightly fatigued and sleep deprived, he felt perfectly capable of returning to the dorm.

But he hadn't been dismissed. So he continued to wait. Secretly he hoped that he would see Selene again.

Will felt cheated when he was rewarded only by the appearance of one of the palace servants, an old man carrying a fresh tunic, trousers, and Will's boots. "Your clothes were ruined so His Majesty ordered that we replace them. Your boots have been cleaned and oiled."

"And my armor?" Will knew the brigandine was probably not worth saving. It had been badly in need of repair before his fight with the demon and he doubted it was worth salvaging now.

"It couldn't be saved. I'm sorry, Mister Cartwright. His majesty sent this as a reward and to compensate you." The old man produced a heavy coin pouch.

Will nodded. "Thank you. Am I free to leave now?"

The servant nodded, then backed out of the room. Will waited until the door closed before examining the pouch. It was packed with gold crowns. He hefted it with one hand. He'd gotten accustomed to large amounts of gold lately, and he judged there were probably around a hundred coins within. He felt grateful for a moment, until he considered that he'd used two regeneration potions worth at least a thousand crowns. Potions he might never be able to replace.

"It was worth it, though," he told himself. He'd have used them all if it was necessary and getting to see the look on Count Spry's face after the man thought he had killed him had been worth the cost. Will dressed and departed the palace.

Back in his dorm room, Will consulted the ring. "You won't believe what happened."

"Did your balls finally drop?"

Will ignored the remark. "The goddamn cat took me to the palace. Demons and soldiers had broken in and they were after Selene." He launched into an impromptu description of what had occurred, putting particular emphasis on his face-off with Count Spry and his ambiguous conversation with the king afterward.

Arrogan crowed with glee. "I bet the bastard count was crestfallen when you didn't die."

Will grinned. "I hit him so hard he fell on his ass."

"Why did you turn down the king's offer?"

Surprised, Will responded, "Because I won't be a sorcerer. I thought you'd agree with my decision."

"I appreciate your sincerity, but was that the only reason?"

"It was the main one. Plus, if he gives me land and a title, I'll have to swear fealty."

"Technically you owe fealty anyway, whether you're a landed lord or a lowly peasant."

"I've never sworn it with my own mouth," said Will stubbornly. "Besides, I've promised to kill him. I've been wondering if I wasted my opportunity."

"You might not be as stupid as I thought," said Arrogan.

"Say that again?"

The ring growled. "You heard me the first time. I know what I made you promise, but we haven't discussed a plan. You aren't ready for regicide yet. First you have to discover who knows the secret. If you jump straight to killing Lognion, you'll have the entire kingdom after you. It's hard to gather information under those sorts of circumstances. All that aside, from what you've told me, that psychotic man would take you apart like a joint of beef at a butcher shop."

"I don't know if I'll ever be ready," Will admitted. "I don't like killing."

"Nobody does at first," said Arrogan solemnly. "And hopefully you won't like it even after you're good at it. The task ahead of you will test your soul, but even if it turns you into a monster, you can't back out. Your humanity is a small price to pay to rid the world of such an evil."

"How long is this going to take?"

"Years? A decade? Who knows?"

"Years! I don't want to live like that."

"Patience is a friend to those plotting betrayal."

"I don't want to be a betrayer. If I have to do this, I'd rather be honest and up front about it."

"You think it was easy for me, boy?" said the ring. "The minute you start, every hand turns against you, but I knew that would happen. So I was forced to bide my time until I was sure I had them all. Only when I was ready, only when I was sure, did I spill the first blood. I killed the strongest first, so that only the weak would be left to face me once my plan was known."

"And yet you still didn't succeed," said Will acidly. "Maybe you should have tried something different."

"Don't lecture me, you little shit! You weren't there. You didn't have to kill your friends!"

"Friends?"

"Why do you think they gave me that name? It wasn't just because I killed the Prophet and then later my own king. Half the wizards I purged were men and women who trusted me. I simply couldn't abide what they had become."

It was the first time Will had heard Arrogan go into any detail about the things he had done, and he wasn't about to lose his chance to learn more. "I don't understand. I know why sorcery is evil now, but how was it that you were friends with so many of them?"

"They weren't sorcerers at first," said Arrogan, his voice taking on a sad tone. "The demons from Shimera had become a serious threat, not just to Greater Darrow, but to mankind as a whole. It was that desperation that led to Valemon's popular appeal as the Prophet, and it was that desperation that caused many of my colleagues to despair of winning the fight against Madrok. Sorcery seemed like a necessary solution to many of them, the lesser of two evils."

"I've fought several demons now, and I'm not even much of a wizard yet. What could the wizards of your time have been afraid of?"

An audible sigh came from the ring. "Numbers. Training a wizard, the way you were trained, takes longer. At the very least it takes a couple of years of preparation before you even get to learning spellcraft and practical magic. Mastery takes many years more. A lesser fire elemental can be forged from the soul of anyone; give that elemental to even an untrained novice and you have a sorcerer capable of handling most demons.

"In the beginning there were many with moral objections, but the premise was that the souls of those who became elementals would be released when the danger was past. Then some wizards began cannibalizing their apprentices to create greater elementals, and again they claimed it was for the greater good. But there was never an end in sight. Madrok would never be completely defeated. We're still fighting him today. Once the world was mostly safe, they still wanted to keep the elementals. There was always another excuse, and even those who I considered friends, those who had objected in the beginning, even they wouldn't let go of their elementals.

"There was no persuading them, so in the end, when I was ready, I quietly got rid of the strongest. Death came to them with a smile, a dagger hidden in the hand of a friend. By the time they realized what I was doing, those who could stop me were gone. The inexperienced wizards and novice sorcerers who remained were no match for me. There were too many for me to kill them all, but I eliminated everyone who knew the secret to creating elementals, or so I thought."

The ring fell silent and Will was left to his thoughts. He didn't want to wind up like Arrogan. King Lognion was just one man. If he was the only one who possessed the secret, perhaps he wouldn't have to go as far as his teacher had.

Yet he could see the parallels. He had seen a Priest of Madrok in the Darrowan camp, and now there were demons in Cerria. King Lognion was obviously conserving his elementals, putting them in the hands of his nobles, but was he actively creating more? If not, would he begin doing so if he felt threatened?

Even if the king didn't make more, was it morally acceptable to keep the souls of those already enslaved in eternal bondage to protect the status quo? Arrogan obviously didn't think so, but was he right? If Will kept his promise and eventually succeeded in killing the king, what would be the repercussions? If the demon threat continued to grow, would Terabinia be left unable to defend itself?

Arrogan spoke once more. "I know what you're thinking, boy. I had the same doubts. Better to die human, than to become as twisted and corrupt as the demons we fight. That's the answer I chose."

Chapter 40

Will slept fitfully on Sunday morning, making up for some of the sleep he had missed. After lunch he resumed his personal training for an hour, then went out for a walk to clear his head.

He'd only been outside for a short time before he ran into Janice. She smiled for a second when she saw him, then frowned. Walking over to him, she asked, "What happened this time?"

The regeneration potion had healed all of his wounds, so it took him a moment to remember his black eye. Touching his face, Will grimaced, "Oh, this. I almost forgot."

"Only you would forget getting a black eye."

My back was broken, a demon almost ate me, and then I was run through with a sword. A black eye is rather easy to forget after all that, thought Will. "This wasn't from a fight."

"Are you going to explain?" asked Janice, arching one brow.

Embarrassed, Will replied, "I'd rather not."

"Figures. Fine, I won't ask. Have you finished your essay for Monday?"

"Sort of…"

"Let's go have a look at it."

A short while later they were back in Will's room. Janice sat back and pushed the paper away. "You've improved a lot, but this won't do." She spent the next fifteen minutes pointing out errors and marking paragraphs that needed to be rewritten.

Will despaired of ever being able to earn her approval, much less that of his teacher. Pulling his courage together, he said the words he had been dreading, "I need a partner for a dance."

"Pardon?"

"I thought maybe, if you weren't too busy—"

Janice watched him silently, a strange look on her face.

Will felt as though he was flailing about, but he kept talking anyway. "The Winter Ball is next week."

"At the palace?" Her expression showed surprise.

He nodded. "I'm supposed to bring someone, but if it's too much trouble I understand."

Janice reached out and shook his shoulder. "Get ahold of yourself. Are you asking me to be your date to the ball?"

"Well, it occurred to me. I don't really know any—g—" His mouth froze as he tried to figure out what he meant to say.

"Girls?" asked Janice, trying to help.

He nodded.

"If you want a firm answer, you're going to have to ask a firm question," she replied, a faint warning in her eyes.

Red-faced, Will spat out the words in a rush. "Will you accompany me to the ball?"

There was mirth in her eyes. "I would love to, but there are a few problems."

Will's ears weren't working properly. "I'm sorry. I shouldn't have asked, but you were the—wait, what?" His brain started to catch up. "What problems? Did you say yes?"

She laughed. "I would say yes, but I don't have a dress for it. My family is almost as poor as yours."

He stared at her blankly for a full thirty seconds. "I have money." Jumping up from his chair, he went to his bed and pretended to rummage under the mattress while summoning the purse the king had given him from the limnthal. He handed it to her, feeling awkward.

Janice's hand dropped as the weight of the gold landed on her palm. With a frown she opened the purse and glanced inside. "This is a fortune!"

"It should be enough to buy a dress, right?"

"You could outfit a harem with this," said Janice wryly. "You aren't trying to buy more than a dress, are you?"

Will held up his hands. "No! No, no, no, I just happened to have that much in the purse."

She narrowed her eyes. "You didn't kill anyone for this, did you?" His mouth fell open, and she laughed at his reaction. "I'm just teasing. This is from the potions you've been making, isn't it?"

"Yeah," he answered, feeling a sense of relief.

"Do you trust me with all of this? How much should I spend?"

"As much as you need," said Will. He still had more than five hundred crowns stored in the limnthal.

"Do you know how to dance?" she asked suddenly.

"No."

She frowned. "Me either, at least not the sort of dances they'll be doing at a royal ball."

"Dianne said she could teach us," said Will.

"Problem solved then, but if I'm to have a dress made, I need to go into the city today. There's less than two weeks left until the Winter Ball. Will you go with me? I can't go alone with this much money."

Will started to say yes, but then he remembered his conversation with Arrogan about ambushes. Escorting Janice would only make things more dangerous. "I can't. You won't be safe if I go with you."

"They're still after you?"

He looked away. "Something happens almost every time I go into the city. Maybe Seth or Rob can go."

She gave him a severe look. "How many times have you been attacked?"

"It's not worth thinking about."

She pursed her lips disapprovingly. "Let's go see who we can find."

As it turned out, they ran into Seth and Rob together in the hallway. Both agreed to escort her, claiming to have their own reasons for going into the city. Will suspected they just wanted to pump Janice for information about him while they were away.

After they left, he returned to his favorite activity, practicing his spellcraft, though in truth he was beginning to get sick of it. His desire to survive was stronger than his distaste for boring repetition, however, so he devoted himself to his training.

Two hours of mindless repetition wore him down, however, and his survival instinct began to wane in the face of endless boredom. He called up the limnthal and started a conversation with the ring. "I'm sick of practicing," he began.

"Cry me a river," said Arrogan. "Are you tired of breathing too?"

"I'm sick of practicing the same spells over and over," whined Will.

The ring was unsympathetic. "So, learn some new ones. There's no shortage."

"I've learned them all," said Will. "Except for the chameleon spell and the sleep spell. I can almost cast those too, but I'm tired of working on them."

"Ever heard of a library?"

Will grimaced. "They keep all the good stuff in the restricted sections here."

"And you're suddenly allergic to breaking the rules?"

"No, but I want to wait until I can use the chameleon spell first. Just in case someone shows up."

"Make a new spell then," suggested the ring.

"They haven't taught us how yet," said Will. "It's all theory in the first year. New spell construction isn't part of the curriculum until the second year."

"Bunch of prissy fancy pants mumble-bums!" swore Arrogan. "It isn't that hard."

"They said you can kill yourself if you don't know what you're doing."

"Of course, it's dangerous! So is taking a piss in the dark, but you aren't going to wet the bed, are you? Start with something small and be cautious and you'll probably be fine."

"I don't even know where to start."

"Well, as I said before, I can't really teach you anything since I can't see what you're doing and I don't remember the specifics of most of the spells I used without being able to read." The ring paused, then added, "But I'm full of ideas." There was an evil tone in Arrogan's voice.

"Such as?"

"You've mastered the force-lance and demon-armor spells, right?"

"Yeah."

"There are variations of those that you should be able to figure out. I used to use a spell I lovingly called a 'death-lance.'"

His interest was piqued. "What did it do?"

"Well, the force-lance uses turyn in a form that produces a physical force. But suppose you were fighting demons again and you would rather use something more effective against them. The death lance spell was similar, but a bit more complicated. It allows the caster to substitute a different type of turyn. The version I used was antithetical to living beings, so even a grazing shot could kill someone. I can't show you the formula for that, but you could do something similar with the turyn output formula built into the demon-armor spell. If you combined that with the base form of a force-lance spell you could produce an attack that would be lethal to demons."

"Ooh," said Will with a gasp.

"Conversely, you could use the turyn type output from a force-lance spell to create a version of the demon-armor spell that would protect you from physical blows. I'd wait until you have more experience to try that, though. There are some complications involved in shaping it. It's not as simple as plugging one piece into the other. Get it wrong and you'll suffocate yourself."

"Ouch."

"The death-lance was dangerous too, since the energy involved could kill the caster as easily as an opponent, but if you try it with the sort that's inimical to demons you should be relatively safe."

Will summoned *Practical Magic* from the limnthal and began studying the diagrams for force-lance and demon-armor. With some advice from the ring, he gradually figured out which parts of each performed which functions. Using a blank sheet torn from one of his school journals, he wrote down the parts he needed, then began trying to figure out how to link them together.

He was so engrossed in the exercise that hours passed without him realizing it. He was startled when a knock roused him from his concentration on the task before him. "Who is it?"

"It's me, Rob."

"Come in, the door's open."

His friend stepped in and grabbed the other chair, spinning it around so he could sit and put his arms over the back. "I never want to do that again."

"You seemed excited when you left."

"Oh, I was! But you have no idea how long we stayed at the dressmaker's. Just the measurements took forever. Seth and I could have left, gone to eat, and come back and they would've still been at it. And all the talk about fabrics—I was sure I was dying."

Will chuckled. "I think you're exaggerating a bit."

Rob looked wounded. "I'm not! Poor Seth almost didn't make it. He fell asleep in one corner of the shop and almost dislocated his neck. I thought we'd have to take him to see a doctor when we got back. I return to you a changed man."

"How so?"

Rob straightened and assumed an air of maturity. "I have seen things, my friend. I have walked the long road and suffered."

"Seen things?"

"Yeah, a whole lot of nothing. We weren't allowed anywhere near while she was changing or being measured. I'm a young man. I'm not meant to sit still and stare at yards of fabric for hours on end. My mind traveled to distant places, and I'm not sure all of it returned."

"So you've attained a higher level of consciousness now? Is that what you're telling me?" asked Will with a grin.

"Long is the road and torturous the journey, young petitioner. The mind of man is not meant for such wisdom."

"And what did you learn?"

Rob slouched in his chair. "I used to think women were exciting, but now I know they can be boring as hell. If I never see another dress again, it will be too soon. You owe me one for today. In fact, you should probably let me take her to the ball. I deserve a reward for my suffering."

"Oh, so you fancy Janice?"

"I'm not blind, Will, though what the girl sees in you makes me wonder if she is."

"Hey now!"

Rob switched subjects, pointing at his eye. "When are you going to tell me how you got that shiner?"

"I'm not."

"Such a good friend you aren't," said Rob sarcastically. "Fine, don't share. Janice told us you don't dare walk the streets, though. Is it Count Spry?"

Will shook his head. "I don't think so. Not anymore at least. I might need to beg you for another favor early next week." He was thinking about when his new brigandine would be ready for pick-up.

"If it involves the dressmaker again, you can go straight to hell my friend. Anything else I'll consider."

"I have some armor being made."

"What happened to your fancy secret armor?" asked Rob. When Will's face showed surprise, he added, "Seth told me about it after your last misadventure."

"Do you want the truth? I'll tell you, but I won't explain the details."

Rob clapped his hands together as though praying. "Please, master, I wait on your wisdom!"

Will began counting off attacks with his fingers. "Two knife attacks, three crossbow bolts, a sword thrust, and five talons." He paused for a moment. "I think that's everything, unless I missed something. In any case, my old armor is no longer usable."

"Holy Mother!" swore Rob. "Are you serious?" He reached forward to tentatively probe Will's chest. "And you're still in one piece? Did someone sew you back together? Tell the truth. You're one of the undead now, aren't you? I bet if you take that tunic off, you're nothing but stitched-together body parts."

Feeling bold, Will stood and pulled up his tunic, showing off his unblemished skin. "I'm all of a piece."

"How the hell? Are you even human?" Then Rob's eyes grew round. "Wait, did you say *talons*? What talons?"

"I already told you, I'm not sharing the details. Just trust me when I say it's not a good idea to go into the city with me. That's why I needed you to go with Janice, and why I need someone to pick up the armor for me next week. I'm not sure I'd make it alive if I went myself."

Rob grimaced and the humor left his face. "I feel like a terrible friend. I want to force the details out of you, but I'm honestly scared to know more. I'll get the armor, and if there's anything else I can do, just let me know." He leaned over and looked at Will's desk. "What are you working on?"

"A new spell."

"You're learning a new spell?"

"No, I'm trying to make a new one, or recreate one at least," said Will.

"Damn, Will. You shouldn't be trying that sort of thing for at least another year."

Will shrugged. "I don't have a lot of time to spend waiting around for what the school curriculum thinks is best for me."

Rob frowned. "I know you already have some spells the school wouldn't approve of. What more do you need?"

"A spell to kill demons."

Rob's face paled, then he held up one hand, flexing his fingers as though they were claws. "Talons," he muttered.

"Or claws," said Will. "I'm not sure. Are talons just on birds?"

Rob reached out and took Will by the shoulders, turning him so they were face to face. "Listen to me, Will. You should stick with hunting girls. It's safer and a lot more rewarding."

Will returned a lopsided grin. "I think I'm more scared of girls."

"Than demons? Don't expect me to come to your funeral. You're a wizard, Will. Leave the demons to sorcerers. We don't have the power for that sort of thing."

Will sat back down in his chair. "I didn't choose this, but I'm not going to run from it." He looked up at Rob. "And you're wrong. We do have the power for this, or we should have."

CHAPTER 41

The next day after his classes were over, Will tried out his cobbled-together spell. The result was less than spectacular. What had looked workable on paper didn't line up when he actually tried to construct the spell. He was forced to go back over his design and adjust several elements before he had something that could actually form a coherent structure. And when he actually tried casting his newly revised spell, it promptly blew up in his face.

Arrogan had a good laugh when he described what had happened. "It's a good thing you're working with a type of turyn harmless to humans or you might have blown your face off. Not that that is necessarily a bad thing. It probably would have improved your looks."

Will was beginning to understand why designing new spells was considered dangerous.

"Next time, don't invest the full amount of turyn in it," advised the ring. "It might not be dangerous with this spell, but it's a good habit to get into for future spell designs. Start with a fraction of the power needed to activate it and then work your way up slowly. Once you're sure the construct is stable, you can test it at full strength."

"You knew that would happen, didn't you?" accused Will.

"It was a fair bet, but this was a safe spell for accidents, and accidents are the best way to learn."

After that Will went over the entire design again, paying particular attention to balancing each element so the construct wouldn't have excessive strain at any given point. He thought it was perfect, but one thing bothered him, so he asked the ring, "The new spell is more complex. It's definitely third-order."

"That's to be expected," said Arrogan.

"Why?" asked Will. "The original force-lance is only second order. This is the same thing, just with a different type of turyn output."

"You just built it and you don't know why?"

Exasperated, Will sighed. "Well, I can *see* that it has an extra layer for the positive chaos turyn, but I don't understand why it has to be that way."

"Force effects are the simplest, as well as the most powerful effects," explained the ring. "That gives them excellent properties for a lot of battle magics, but in this case, you're modulating it to produce a different type. While that makes it immensely effective for demons, it complicates the spell construct."

Curious, Will asked, "What are these excellent properties you mentioned?"

"For force effects? There are several. Aside from being the simplest type to produce, they create the most physical force of any type of spell, better even than earth, considering there's no actual matter involved. They also ignore basic principles that spells incorporating physical matter normally have to obey. For example, one of the staple defense spells, the point-defense shield, relies on it because force spells ignore momentum and inertia."

"What does that spell do?"

"It creates a tiny shield of pure force," explained Arrogan. "It's usually the size of a buckler, maybe a foot in diameter."

"It doesn't sound very handy," opined Will. "It's too small to block much."

"Well, you don't use it to stop a hail of arrows, numbskull. It requires skill and precision, but it will stop anything it gets in front of dead in its tracks, assuming it doesn't block something so absurdly powerful that it overloads the spell, and that's rare."

"That sounds sort of useful, but not extremely so. I must be missing something."

The ring snorted. "Nothing new there. The reason it's so beloved and well used—"

"By who?" interrupted Will.

"By wizards in my time. People who knew what the fuck they were doing," replied Arrogan. "Are you going to let me finish?"

"Go ahead."

"As I was saying, the reason it *was* so beloved is because of its efficiency and extreme durability. For a tiny input of turyn, you get a shield that can block almost anything, from a charging bull to a devastating death-lance. You can use it in all sorts of situations, both defensively and as an offensive trick depending on where you place it."

"Why not make it bigger then?"

"Force effects use turyn on an exponential curve."

"What the hell does that mean?"

"It means that the turyn required goes up drastically as the size of the spell effect increases. It also drops rapidly as the spell-effect size decreases. So for small things, like a force-lance, or a small shield, you can get a lot of bang for very little turyn, but if you try to do something big, like create a force-dome, you'll exhaust yourself in seconds. Turyn used to manipulate elemental effects follows a nearly linear power curve. That's why large-scale effects are generally done with it, like the wind-wall spell for example. Wind is one of the best elemental types for destruction on a wide scale—it has the physicality that fire lacks, while at the same time it isn't as dense as water or earth."

Will remembered his Math professor putting special emphasis on exponential and linear graphs, but at the time he had only thought about it as a graphing problem. It hadn't really *meant* anything to him in a practical sense. He'd also heard Dulaney mention the differences in turyn cost based on the type of turyn used, but again, it hadn't impacted him directly.

Now it was beginning to mean something. "I think I'm starting to see what you're driving at," said Will slowly.

"It will mean more as time goes on," said Arrogan. "A true wizard is a master of magic, a master of turyn in all its forms. Spells are the means we use to effect our will, to impress our desires on the universe, but they aren't everything. We also ride the currents of free turyn around us. To be effective in combat you have to learn to balance all of it, the turyn you're absorbing, the turyn you're using, and what's going on around you. At times you'll want to be empty, to better improve your ability to take your opponent's magic away from him. At other times you want as much as you can hold, so you can fuel a larger spell."

"It sounds complicated."

"It is, when you *think* about it. Practice and training will make it natural and instinctive. It's similar to dancing. You practice so that when you get on the dance floor you don't have to think about what your feet are doing. You just flow with the music. Sorcery has ruined the practice of magic these days. Most sorcerers are idiots with big hammers, lacking all skill and finesse. Because of them, the modern wizards are lackluster as well. They've retained much of the technical knowledge, but their inability to use magic regularly has stripped them of the art. What you're becoming is so different from both of them that they won't be able to believe what you can do."

"We'll see," said Will neutrally. The mention of dancing had dampened his spirits and provoked a new round of anxiety. He dismissed the limnthal so he could focus on trying out his newly revised spell.

This time it worked, firing off a red-orange beam that struck a nearby tree without doing any harm to it. Hopefully it would have a far different effect if he ever had to use it on a demon.

With a deep sigh, he put away his papers and walked back to the dorm. It was time to meet Dianne and Janice for their first dance lesson.

They were standing outside the dormitory when he arrived, and Will thought Dianne seemed particularly energetic. Her face was alight with barely concealed enthusiasm. *Either she really loves dancing, or she's looking forward to seeing me embarrass myself,* he thought sourly.

Together the three of them went to the gym. Since it was evening, the building wasn't being used for much, making it a perfect place to practice. Dianne started them with a waltz, taking each of them in turn through the steps as she alternated her role between leading and being led.

Will tromped all over Dianne's feet, and once she pronounced him ready to attempt the dance with his partner, he did the same to Janice. After an hour of clumsiness, it felt as though the only thing he had mastered was discovering new ways to apologize.

Poor Janice did her best to hide a faint limp as they left afterward.

"I really am sorry," said Will for the hundredth time.

"It's all right," Janice responded mildly. "You'll get better."

He wasn't sure about that. They met again at the same time the next day, and he repeated his performance, putting new bruises on top of the ones he had given them the day before.

"Ow!" yelped Janice after a particularly painful assault on her toes. She released him and hopped backward on her other foot. "Shit! Are you *trying* to lame me for life?"

Will was already apologizing, while his face felt as though it had gotten even redder. Dianne stared at Janice in surprise. Neither of them had ever heard Janice swear before. She seemed to have finally lost her patience.

"Take a rest, Janice," said Dianne. "I'll practice with him for a bit." She had a look on her face that said she knew she was risking her life for her the good of her fellow woman. Will stepped forward, but Dianne held up one hand. "Take off your boots. You aren't allowed to wear footwear until you improve—considerably."

Things went better after that. Deprived of their weapons, Will's feet couldn't inflict as much damage, and Dianne was more adept at avoiding his trampling attacks. Will was starting to feel more confident, so much so that when the next turn came, he attempted to lead Dianne into a twirl. It went well, until he kicked the older woman's legs out from under her.

The resident assistant's derriere met the gym floor with a resounding thump as she crashed to the ground. She lay there for a moment staring up at him with an angry expression. "William," she said quietly, her voice thrumming with barely concealed malice, "are you trying to kill me?"

"No, ma'am! I'm sorry. I'm not sure what happened."

"You *kicked* me! Why?"

"It was a spin so—"

"No. You don't kick. You never kick. *I'm* the one twirling. All you have to do is keep your goddamn legs in one place and hold my hand." She gingerly got up from the ground, rubbing her posterior with one hand. "Were you dropped on your head as a baby?"

Will hung his head in shame. "Probably." He glanced up at Janice, hoping for support, but she refused to meet his eyes.

As the week progressed, he gradually got better, but both Janice and Dianne remained wary whenever they began practicing with him. *Once stomped, twice shy,* thought Will.

In his free time, he found that his spellcraft was developing quickly. The effort of developing a new spell had brought about more improvement than he had seen in the weeks prior. He wasn't sure why, but Arrogan didn't seem surprised at all.

"To create a new spell, you had to break apart two others and learn their constituent parts in a new way. Your overall understanding of how they work is better now. Of course, that would lead to you being able to cast the original spells with greater alacrity and efficiency," said the ring.

His improvement was such that on Saturday morning he finally managed to successfully put together a sixth-order construct, the chameleon spell. Naturally, he tried it out immediately and was amazed as his arms shifted color, almost fading from sight.

The turyn drain was light, so he felt sure he could keep the spell up almost indefinitely once cast. He experimented by walking around his dorm room. While moving he could spot the motion of his limbs, but whenever he stopped his body faded almost completely from sight. "This is wild," he muttered.

Not content to stay inside, he ventured into the hall. Two other students were walking along and they glanced in his direction, then stopped. He could tell they had seen something when he stepped out. They seemed confused. He held still for a minute and eventually they must have decided that they were imagining things, for they moved on and went to the stairs. They passed right by him on their way.

Wanting to test it further, he went to Seth's door and knocked. "Who is it?" asked his friend, but Will didn't answer.

After a moment the door opened, and Seth looked out. Will was standing directly in front of him, but Seth's eyes didn't focus on him at first. The other boy looked from side to side, frowning, and then he stared at the space directly in front of him. A few seconds later he jumped and fell against the doorframe with a scream. "What the hell?"

Will began to giggle. "It's me, Seth."

Seth was scrambling backward across the floor, staring in Will's direction while squinting. He gave the impression of someone who had lost his glasses. "What is that? Why can't I see you properly?"

"A chameleon spell," said Will proudly. "I just mastered it. I've been working on it all week."

"Turn it off. You're freaking me out!" whined his friend. Will did, and Seth breathed a sigh of relief. "Where did you learn a spell like that?"

"It was something my old master left me."

"He must have been a pervert."

Will snorted. "Possibly." Then a thought occurred to him. "Don't mention this to Rob. He'll be begging me to sneak him into the girls' dorm if he finds out."

A funny look entered Seth's eyes, but he shook his head after a moment. "Yeah. That would be really wrong."

Will gave his friend a knowing look. "Clearly, Rob isn't the only pervert around here."

"Shut up," said Seth. "It just crossed my mind for a second."

His eyes narrowed to slits. "I'll be watching you."

Seth laughed. "Seriously, though. You probably shouldn't mention this to anyone, not just Rob. Otherwise people will suspect you anytime something comes up missing."

"I hadn't thought about that."

"You never think first. That's why you're always in trouble," opined Seth. "Now go away. I need to finish this essay." He pushed Will out of the room.

Will stood in the hall for a minute, trying to decide what he should do. He couldn't just go back to his room. He was too excited. He constructed the spell again and cast it on himself, then made for the stairs.

Exiting the dorm without being seen was even easier than he'd expected. He had to stop twice on the stairs as other people came up, but as long as he stayed to one side and kept still whenever someone got close, no one noticed him.

The front door was the only real challenge, and he quickly realized there were only two strategies that might work. He could either wait until no one was around to notice the door opening, along with the strange blur pushing it, or he could try and sneak along behind someone going his direction.

Not feeling patient, he chose the latter course and nearly got caught by the door. The boy ahead of him, Chris Burnham, never knew he was being shadowed. Will scuffed his shoe once they were outside, though, and he thought he would be caught, but Chris merely glanced back then went on his way.

Will fixed the noise problem by casting the silent-armor spell on himself. He felt the turyn drain increase, but it was still manageable. To offset the drain, he increased his outer shell to take in turyn at a greater rate, then he headed for the wall. It was time to explore the city again.

The addition of an active climbing spell significantly increased the drain on his turyn. "I could probably keep this up for fifteen or twenty minutes," he told himself. It was something to keep in mind if he ever had to hide while suspended on a wall, though.

Free of the confines of Wurthaven, Will began to wander. He had no particular destination in mind, being more interested in seeing just how effective the chameleon spell would be in crowded areas.

He kept his eyes on the people around him, watching to see if they noticed him. Moving was constantly a risk, as people frequently looked to see what had caught their eye, but as long as he grew still immediately after, they generally gave up and moved on. Staying close to walls and buildings seemed to help as well, while standing in the middle of an open space caused people to glance in his direction more frequently. At one point he nearly dropped the spell to run, certain that a suspicious pedestrian was about to call him out. Fortunately, the man gave up after a minute of confused staring and moved on.

Since he had no appointment or particular place to be, he wasn't worried about another ambush, and being nearly impossible to observe made him feel even safer. He continued to wander, and half an hour later he found himself staring at the main entrance to the royal palace.

He hadn't consciously made his way there, but seeing the place, he realized it was where he wanted to be. Selene was inside. *I'm a fool,* he thought.

The main gate was tempting, but there were four guards posted within the arch. Walking past them would be difficult with no distractions, plus there was the near certainty that at least one magic user would be hidden somewhere close by. Will suspected the flow of turyn around his body would be even more noticeable with two spells active.

He moved on, heading back toward Wurthaven before turning north along the lane between the two. The goddamn cat had pointed out the best place to cross the wall, and he was determined to try it out.

The climbing spell made scaling the wall easy, and although a guard happened to walk by as he neared the top, the man never even paused. Will waited until the soldier was almost to the other end, then crossed over the merlons and stepped onto the walkway. He descended to the palace garden immediately after.

Crossing the wide-open spaces of the garden worried him the most, so he took his time, moving slowly and stopping near bushes to reassess whether anyone was looking down from the wall or from one of the palace windows. It took nearly half an hour to get to the spot directly beneath Selene's window.

Recasting the climb spell, he made a slow ascent to avoid drawing the eyes of the guards on the distant outer wall. He found something new when he neared Selene's window. A warding spell had been placed on the stone around it. He stopped there, unsure how to proceed.

Will studied the runes woven into it for several minutes, but he couldn't remember the first ward he had encountered—the one around her tent—well enough to know if it was the same ward. He had inadvertently absorbed that ward without immediately alerting her, but it was possible this magic worked differently.

He simply didn't know, and he hadn't studied wards at all in school. *I need to make up my mind soon. I can't hang here forever.* Eventually his turyn would run out from the drain of maintaining three spells at the same time. Then an idea came to him.

First he prepared the unlocking spell and tucked it away so he could quickly cast it if his idea worked. That done, he held out his free hand and put it close to the ward, so that his skin was just an inch away while he studied the turyn of the ward. Concentrating, he matched his turyn with the ward until he couldn't tell the difference between them. Then he placed his hand against the stone.

Nothing happened, and a slow grin spread across Will's face. Keeping his hand on the ward he cast the unlocking spell, then matched the turyn in his other hand before pushing the window open. Moving slowly, he did the same with his legs as he crept over the sill and entered the room. He shut the window and stepped back before letting the turyn covering his body return to normal, then he dismissed the climbing spell and breathed a sigh of relief.

The parlor was empty, so he listened intently for a minute to see if she was in the bedchamber. He heard nothing. Walking slowly, he crossed the room and looked in to be sure. He was alone.

"Well that's disappointing," he whispered to himself. "What should I do with myself?"

He did a slow circuit of the parlor, finding little of interest, though he noted that the sideboard was stocked with both a fresh pitcher of water and a decanter of wine. He poured himself a cup of water and drank it in two long swallows.

Unable to resist any longer, he went to the bedroom. *Not to go through her things,* he reminded himself. *I'm just curious, that's all.*

The bed was a work of art. It had four massive posts carved with flowers and vines, while the headboard depicted an idyllic landscape. Gauzy curtains were drawn back at the corners and he wondered if she used them to keep flies out while she slept. He'd never seen such a luxury before, not even on Arrogan's ornate bed.

Turning away, he examined the dressing table, which held an array of mysterious objects. The only thing he recognized there were his antidote potions, which held a special place in the center. It surprised him that she hadn't just put them away in a drawer out of sight. *Does she just look at them?*

There were three large wardrobes and two massive wooden chests. He opened one of the wardrobes and glanced inside. As expected, it held numerous dresses and gowns, and while some were what one would expect of a princess, quite a few were of common fabrics and unassuming appearance. *Probably because she likes to go out and pretend to be a commoner,* he thought.

He shut the doors and didn't bother looking in the others. *I'm not here to snoop.* He turned back to the bed, noting the depression on one of the pillows. It must have been the one she slept on. Mind blank, he took a step toward it, unsure of what moved him.

He paused as he spotted something on the floor in one corner of the room, a small wooden box. It was lying on its side as though it had fallen there. Will walked over and picked it up, then opened it.

He drew in a sharp breath as he saw the ring within, a delicate gold band shaped into the form of roses. Set in the center was vibrant, clear stone that sparkled as he turned it in the light. He'd never seen one before, but he was almost certain it was a diamond. *It's huge. Why was it over here on the floor?* Not wanting to leave it there, Will closed the box and put it on the dressing table.

The pillow was calling to him. With two long strides he crossed the room and picked it up, pressing it against his face and inhaling. He could smell her hair, along with a faint scent of lavender. After a few seconds he started to put it back in its place, feeling guilty.

A loud click from the other room announced the opening of the outer door.

Chapter 42

A surge of panic shot through him, as it took a moment for his rational mind to remind him that he was still hidden by the chameleon spell. Will stood still, waiting, and after a moment he saw Selene enter the bedroom. He didn't say anything at first, wanting to be sure she was alone.

Her actions confirmed that a second later, when she began removing her dress. As he realized what she was doing he felt the blood rush to his cheeks, and he fought a short but fierce internal battle. His better nature won out.

"Selene, wait, I'm in here with you," he said, trying to make his voice as calm and unthreatening as possible.

Selene's reaction was far more severe than he had hoped for. The sound that came from her throat was more of a yip than a scream, reminiscent of a puppy that's had its tail stepped on. She straightened up, fighting to escape the dress that was tangled around her head and arms. Twisting her body to throw it off, she stepped forward and one foot landed on the stool beside her dressing table.

Will was too far away to catch her, but he called out again. "It's Will. Don't panic!"

She caught her balance somehow, though her rough struggles ripped the seam along one side of her dress. Selene straightened up and managed to get her head back through the neck of the dress to peer in his direction. Despite her ridiculous situation and near fall, she had the dignified air of a cat after an awkward fall. Her demeanor denied the existence of any such event. "Will?"

"I'm right here," he answered. He dismissed the chameleon spell and her eyes focused on him.

"How did you get in here—again?" she demanded, then she noticed the pillow still in his hands. "And why are you holding my pillow?"

He tossed the pillow onto the bed as though it had suddenly caught fire. "No reason."

An evil light appeared in her eyes. "Did you sneak in here to cuddle with my pillow?" she teased.

"No! I just—I hadn't seen material like that before. I was curious about the fabric," he sputtered.

Walking over to him, she stuck one arm through the ripped side seam and took the pillow from the bed. Lifting it to her face, she sniffed. "Too bad. It doesn't smell at all. You must have been disappointed."

"Lavender," he retorted, giving her a wink.

She smiled faintly, then dropped the pillow and poked him in the chest with her one free arm. "Pervert. How did you get in this time?"

Will's eyes locked onto hers, and for a moment he forgot to breath. *Why are her eyes red? Was she crying again?* She betrayed no sorrow or depression in her behavior, but he asked anyway, "Are you all right?"

Selene blinked. "Of course." She twirled in place, her free arm sticking out like the stem of some deformed fruit. "Why wouldn't I be? This is the new rage amongst fashionable dressers."

Will laughed at her performance, but he couldn't help but feel she was forcing herself to be more cheerful than she actually felt. He started to sidle around her. "I'll go into the other room so you can change."

"No need." Bending at the waist, she shook herself twice then pulled the dress away and dropped it to the floor. Her eyes were challenging as she looked back at him, covered only by a thin, linen shift. "I'm not ashamed to be seen like this," she added. "Not by you."

He kept his eyes firmly on her face. "Your father—"

"Is not here," she finished for him. "Are you worried? There's no one here to protect you."

"Worried?"

She nodded. "You once accused me of planning to make you into my pet or slave. Something like that. Remember?"

He grinned. "I know you better now." Moving to the other side, he tried to get past her, but she moved again, blocking his way.

Selene glared at him. "Don't you dare try to run away. Last time we hardly had a chance to speak. I've caught you fair and square. You're my prisoner until I decide otherwise."

Will put his wrists together. "Will there be chains this time?"

"I haven't decided yet." Turning away, she went to her dressing table and glanced at herself in the mirror, grimacing when she saw the tangled mess her hair had become. Her eyes looked down, and he saw her spot the ring box. Without saying a word, she opened a drawer and dropped the box into it.

Something about the way she had held it bothered him, as though she didn't even want to touch the box. "What was that?" he asked.

"Something unfortunate," she replied simply. "I don't want to talk about it. I'd rather hear how you got into my room again. This is turning into a habit of yours. What is this, the third time?"

"If you count the tent," said Will.

"I do. One second." Moving to the wardrobe, she opened it and pulled out a thick quilted dressing gown, which she pulled around her shoulders. Then she left the room and went to the outer door in the other room. Opening it, she spoke to the guards outside. "I'm tired and I don't wish to be disturbed. Tell the maids to stay out. Unless it's the king himself I don't even want to hear a knock on this door. Understood?" She closed and locked it then, and not content with just that, she dropped the wooden bar that made it impossible to open from the outside.

Her orders, combined with the way she had sealed the door, made Will strangely nervous when she returned. "I came in through the window," he said, to answer her earlier question.

Selene went and examined it. "The ward is still intact."

"I was worried that it might be different from the one before," explained Will. "So I matched my turyn to that of the ward. I wasn't sure if it would work."

She gave him a disapproving look. "If it hadn't, you'd be dead. If the lightning shock didn't kill you, the fall afterward would have finished the job. You're insane. Was it that important for you to see me?" As she spoke, she was approaching step by step.

"Yes."

"Why?"

He gazed at her helplessly. "For the life of me, I don't know. I might have had a reason, but I can't remember it."

Selene removed the dressing gown without looking away, tossing it over the chair beside the dressing table. Will could think of no reason for removing it, unless she was making a statement of some kind. His willpower failed him, and his eyes drifted down, then up again, studying her figure through the linen shift as she walked closer. A hunger was building in him.

But he knew it couldn't happen. Shouldn't happen. He turned his head to one side and tried to warn her, "I know you trust me, but you should put something else on."

She stopped, her face just inches from his. Then he felt her arms sliding around his waist, pulling him close. Unable to stop himself, he returned the gesture, crushing her shoulders within his arms, holding her tightly. He was afraid to let go. Given any space, any room to maneuver, he would do far worse.

"I want you to see me, Will," she said, speaking into his shoulder. "Do you understand?"

Yes! "No," he said stubbornly. "You know that can't happen. I'm no one."

"Let me go," she said firmly. He did, and she took a few steps back and opened one of the wood chests at the foot of her bed. Will heard the sound of coins, then she straightened and closed the chest. Reaching down, she grasped the hem of her shift and lifted it over her head.

She was utterly nude, and when her face turned back, he could see that her eyes were glistening. Selene held out her hand. On her palm were six silver clima. "I want a kiss."

He never remembered taking the first step toward her, but when he reached her, the coins went flying and a moment later, they fell awkwardly onto the bed, a tangle of arms and legs. They half-kissed, half-wrestled for several minutes, until at last he rolled onto his back and Selene began unlacing his jerkin. He tried to help, but his clumsy fingers only slowed things down; she slapped his hands away.

The jerkin came off, then she started on his trouser laces while he tugged and pulled to get his tunic off. Once his chest was bare, he paused, staring at her. Selene met his gaze, and he asked, "Why?"

She blinked, but her determination didn't fade. "Don't ask me why." Then she backed away and jerked at his trouser legs as though they had done something terrible to offend her. A triumphant smile flashed across her face and then he was naked. Climbing back into the bed she settled beside him and their lips met again.

Youth and passion made them impatient, but before they lost control of themselves, he heard her whisper, "I want you to be my first. It has to be you."

The next quarter of an hour passed in a blur. Being the first time, it was frequently awkward, sometimes painful, and yet still poignantly wonderful. Will felt sad and slightly embarrassed that it came to an end so soon, primarily because of him.

They lay staring at each other for several minutes. "I can't believe that happened," said Selene, echoing his thoughts.

"It was too quick," said Will sourly.

"The first time always is," she responded sagely.

He gave her a suspicious look. "Where'd you hear that?"

"The servants. They gossip a lot, and some of it is pretty randy," she admitted. "Only half my education is from books; the rest is from listening around corners." Will tried to sit up, but she caught his hair and pulled him back down. "You're not getting away that easily."

He gave her another kiss. "How long do we have?"

"You can leave tomorrow—maybe."

"Tomorrow is Sunday, but I have classes on Monday," he warned her.

"I know most of your instructors. I'll see to it that you get extra credit if you aren't able to make it to class," she responded, gazing at him with molten eyes.

Looking at her, he felt the beginnings of a ravenous hunger, as though the he had only imagined their previous adventure. Rolling over, he pinned her beneath him, relishing the smile on her lips. "I'll do my best to earn it," he growled.

"You'd better," she threatened. "Or you'll have to retake the test again."

"How many times can I retake it?"

"That depends on you."

Chapter 43

Saturday evening passed like an impossible dream, one Will wished he might never awaken from. They slept in short stretches, waking occasionally to fight new battles and struggle against the inevitable progress of time. Eventually they grew hungry, and Selene went to the door to request a tray of food be brought up.

Will kept himself camouflaged and hidden each time the door opened, just to be safe, though Selene repeatedly assured him no one would enter without her permission.

After the food arrived, she returned to the bedroom with a tray in her hands, then stopped to glare at him. He was tugging on his trousers. "What are you doing?"

"I'm cold," he complained.

She put the tray down, tutting at him. "No clothes."

"I'll freeze to death."

Selene tossed her dressing gown aside and gave him an arch look. "Don't be such a baby. You don't see me complaining." She glanced around, then went to the wardrobe before returning with a rose-colored housecoat. "This is all you're allowed."

Will laughed, then pulled on the garment. It was too small for him, stretching at the shoulders and refusing to meet at the middle. "I can't even button it."

"Perfect," she declared. "Let's eat."

They did, but between bites they talked. First on Will's agenda was the ever-present possibility of his death. "How can you be sure no one will come up here?" he asked.

"I've ordered them not to."

"Won't that seem suspicious?"

Selene sniffed, then took another bite of her lemon tart. "It's actually within character for me right now. I am currently in the midst of a tantrum according to Father."

"A tantrum?"

She nodded. "We've had a few fights lately. I'm sure he thinks I'm up here sulking."

For as long as he had known her, he'd never seen anything remotely like a sulk from Selene. Anger maybe, but she wasn't the type one could apply childish terms to. "Won't he come try to make up with you?"

"He hasn't stepped foot in my room since I was six," she said matter-of-factly. "When he decides it's time to make up, he'll order me to come to him. Then he'll probably order me to apologize." Her words were filled with bitterness.

That was the most absurd sort of parent-child relationship that Will had ever heard of, but given what he had seen of King Lognion, it was believable. "What are you fighting about?"

Selene paused, her eyes remaining fixed on the food, as though she was afraid to look elsewhere. After a moment she swallowed, then answered, "I don't want to think about it. Now is all that's important."

Will frowned. "You can trust me. You know that. Just tell me what's—"

She leaned across and put a finger to his lips, a haunted look in her eyes. "Please, Will. Just this once, let's pretend we're the only people in the world."

"But," he mumbled around her finger.

"No buts. It's just us. There's no one else and no tomorrow," she said, failing to hide the desperation in her voice. "Just us."

Will relented, unwilling to spoil the mood. He nodded and then nipped her finger. Selene jerked her hand back and smiled.

They finished the food then Selene brought up a new topic. "I want to learn those spells of yours. They didn't teach anything like that at Wurthaven when I was there."

"Which ones?"

"The flame thing you used to burn the demon for starters. Oh, and definitely the chameleon spell. I can't tell you how many times I've wished no one could find me."

He laughed. "Being a princess is rough." Holding up one hand, he slowly assembled the demon-armor spell for her.

She made him do it twice more, studying the runes closely as they came together. Then she replicated the spell on her first try, constructing it perfectly. Will stared at her enviously. "You make it look too easy. Do you know how long it took me to learn that?"

"The more you learn, the easier it is to learn more," she replied. "Even so, I should write this down so I can remember it later." She went to a small writing desk at one end of the parlor and began making notes. A few minutes later she returned. "Now let's see the chameleon spell."

Being a sixth-order spell, that one took considerably longer, but he was still impressed with the ease at which she absorbed the knowledge necessary to replicate the complicated spell. In less than an hour, she had mastered constructing it and then she recorded it in her notes alongside the demon-armor spell. *She did create an eighth-order spell while she was still at Wurthaven,* Will reminded himself.

That gave him an idea. "I want to learn a spell too," he told her.

"What spell?"

"The Princess Purification," he said with a grin.

Her mouth went wide with shock. "Is that what they're calling it? How embarrassing. That isn't what I named it."

"What did you call it?" asked Will.

"Selene's Solution," she said proudly.

It didn't sound right to him. "Solution? There's no solution involved."

She shook her head. "You've been making potions too long. Solution as in 'answer,' not a chemical solution."

"Oh, that makes more sense."

"Why are you asking me? You can't cast eighth-order spells yet, can you? Even if you could, the school has a copy. It isn't a restricted spell, after all."

Will called up the limnthal and summoned *Practical Magic*, then opened it and flipped through until he reached the blank portion near the back. "I want *you* to write it out for me and sign it too. That way I'll have your autograph."

Despite her maturity, Selene blushed, but her eyes had also noted the appearance of the limnthal. "Can I ask what that was?"

"Trade secret," said Will. "Someday I'll teach it to you," he promised.

She sighed, then examined the book in her hands. "This looks rather old. Where did you get it?"

"It belonged to my grandfather. It was his favorite spell journal from when he was younger. He left it to me when he died." Actually, it had been Aislinn who had passed it on to him, but he didn't want to start another conversation about dealing with the fae.

Selene's eyes softened. "This must be very precious to you. I shouldn't write in this. Let me get something else. I have a few blank journals over here."

She started to rise, but Will caught her hand. "It is precious to me, just like you. That's why I want your spell in there, written in your own hand." Selene blinked, and her eyes began to water. "Whoa!" said Will. "I didn't mean to make you cry. What's wrong?"

She shook her head, then wiped her eyes. "I'm fine. Don't worry about it. I'm just feeling sentimental." She went to the desk and took her time carefully inscribing the spell in the book. After she finished, she sanded the page to prevent smearing, then closed it and returned the book to him. When he started to open it and read, she stopped him. "Look at it later."

"But I want to look at it now," he insisted.

"Later. It will give you something to look forward to." Leaning forward, she kissed him. "I think I'm hungry again."

Will smirked. "But we just ate."

"That's not what I mean," she said.

He stood and sauntered toward the bed, then glanced back. "It's the pink housecoat, isn't it?"

"Definitely," she replied. A moment later, she grimaced when she looked at the bed. The sheets and coverlet were in disarray, and there was also the embarrassing evidence of just how new they both were to adult pursuits. "Close your eyes," she told him.

Will did but cracked one lid slightly, so he could watch what she was doing. Selene's signature spell came together rapidly above her palm and then she released it, letting it expand to encompass the entire room. A gentle wind came up, tickling his skin as the spell performed its magic.

After a minute, she said, "You can open them now." The room looked as though a team of maids had come through. The bed was made, pillows fluffed, and Will felt as though he had taken a bath. Idly he wondered if Selene's spell would be less painful for cleaning wounds. He couldn't be sure, but it had to be better than the rough personal bathing spell he had used in the past.

"Damn, that's handy," he crooned. "You know, that spell of yours is the whole reason I wanted to learn magic."

"Oh, really?"

"Most certainly," he lied with a wink.

"Let me show you some real magic, then."

Sometime later, they fell asleep, and they continued to sleep through the rest of the night and much of Sunday morning. They enjoyed the rest of Sunday from the confines of her rooms, never wanting for more, and by the time night arrived, Will was devoutly wishing he could spend the rest of his days there. *To hell with magic. To hell with demons. Screw all of it. Just let me stay here, with her.* He no longer wanted anything, not even sex—his body was exhausted and his heart content. In fact, he was pretty sure he would be happy to just spend his days idly talking with her.

At the moment she was lying on her side, head propped on one hand. "I'm still curious," she said.

"About what?"

"The enchantment you pulled the book out of. It looked a lot like the graduation seal."

"Graduation seal?" He was thoroughly confused.

Selene pointed at a point just above her left breast. "You remember it. The enchantment that allows me to communicate with my father."

Something heavy formed in the pit of his stomach. She was referring to the heart-stone enchantment her father had put on her like some perverse slave collar. "The one he summoned you with that time?"

"Yes," she said simply. "The enchantment you had looked similar."

He couldn't take it any longer. He had to tell her. "Let's put me aside for a moment. You need to know the truth about that enchantment he put on you."

She sat up, pulling the sheets up beneath her arms. "You didn't even know what it was originally, but now you're going to reveal some hidden truth?"

"It's a heart-stone enchantment," he said, rushing to the end before she could cut him off. "He's bound you just like one of your elementals."

Selene looked at him as though he had grown a second head. "It's a graduation seal. Everyone gets one. You'll get yours after you finish the fourth year. It doesn't even look like the heart-stone enchantment." To illustrate her point, she pulled the seal that held one of her elementals to the surface, along with the enchantment that bound her to her father. "See? They're completely different."

"One end is the master, the other is the slave," said Will. "He could make you do anything, and if you die, you'll remain bound."

"You're talking nonsense. Father is overbearing, and sometimes cruel, but he's never controlled me, not the way you suggest. I've always obeyed him because I must. He's the king."

"Are you sure?" asked Will, his features showing disbelief.

Selene was beginning to grow angry. She put her hands firmly down on either side of her. "Yes, I'm sure! I argue with him all the time. If he had some hidden power built into this enchantment he would have used it by now." She studied Will's face, and when she saw he still doubted her she snapped. "Why won't you believe me?"

He held up his hands in a peaceful gesture. "I want to believe you, but I learned this from someone I trust."

"And you don't trust me? Should I remind you which one of us knows more about spellcraft? There's several hundred people with these. All of them respected wizards and sorcerers, all well trained in their craft. Do you think my father controls all of them? Who's feeding you lies?"

He barely heard her though. In his mind he was replaying her earlier words, *"You'll get yours after you finish the fourth year."* The enormity of that statement stunned him. *He's using Wurthaven like a farm to create an endless supply of elementals. He doesn't even have to kill them. Just wait for them to die from their abnormally short lifespans.*

"Are you listening? I asked who it is that's feeding you this rubbish," she demanded.

Will looked at her sadly. "My grandfather. He told me about it. That enchantment, what you call a graduation seal, is the method for creating elementals."

Understanding dawned in her eyes. "That's why you called me evil, why you think sorcerers are evil. You think they're all souls of people who were enslaved."

"That was wrong of me," admitted Will. "For evil you have to have the intent, but you were innocent. I didn't realize that then, nor did I fully know *why* using elementals was wrong, but I know now."

Selene scooted farther away, incensed. "So I'm a fool. Why do you put so much stock in what that crazy old man taught you? He was obviously crazy."

"He's been right about everything so far. Remember when you made that bet with me about whether it was possible to steal someone's spell? He was the one that taught me that."

She climbed out of bed and grabbed the dressing gown. "That's why you keep refusing to accept an elemental? Father told me he made you an offer. Don't you realize what you could have had?"

"I don't give two figs about being a lord," said Will acidly.

"No, you idiot!" she said, her voice rising. "Me! You could have married me! Did that ever occur to you? Then none of this would have happened!"

She was on the verge of outright screaming. Will had never seen Selene lose her temper like that before, and while he knew she was under a lot of stress it didn't make sense to him now. He was missing something. "Then none of what would have happened?" he asked.

"Just go," she told him, her voice empty. "You won't believe anything I say anyway, since I'm evil."

"I don't think you're evil."

"No? Just a fool then, spewing lies my father twisted my mind with. Do you have any idea the lengths he's gone to, the lengths *I've* gone to, to keep you safe? Do you think Count Spry would be satisfied with any amount of gold for the death of his son? But you won't accept anything. You refused *your* father when he tried to help you, and you refused mine, even though he's the *king*!"

Frustrated by his ignorance of whatever was going on, Will lashed out, "Did I ask either of them to help me? Why would they?"

"Why do you think Mark Nerrow kept going to that tiny village you grew up in? You won't admit it. You're too busy blaming him for leaving your mother, too busy hating him. He did it because he loves you."

Will didn't hate Mark Nerrow. He was too confused about the man to hate him, but the point was academic. It wasn't what he really wanted to know just then. "And your father? Are you claiming he has some noble motive?"

Selene marched toward him, angry tears in her eyes. "No." She punctuated the word and all those that followed with a shove. "He did it because *I love you*. Idiot!"

He'd wanted to hear those words, but not like that. Will couldn't accept her explanation. Accepting it would mean he'd been wrong about everything. It would mean he should have accepted and become a sorcerer from the very beginning. "So, you think I should go find your father and tell him I want an elemental? Is that what you're saying?"

Anger spent, she turned away. "No. It's too late for that. That ship has sailed. Yesterday was our first day together and today will be the last."

"Fine." Will gathered up his scattered clothes and began putting them on. Once he was dressed, he headed for the parlor and the window.

Selene followed. "You don't have to do anything strange to get past the ward. It has a simple password."

"What is it?" he asked, feeling a combination of anger and sadness.

"William. The password is William." The glow of the ward dimmed, and she opened the window for him.

It was already dark outside, but he cast the chameleon spell on himself just to be safe. He was so rattled that he botched two attempts to construct the spell properly. He looked at Selene one last time. “I’m going to save you. Even if you wind up hating me in the process.”

“You can’t save me, Will. I’m not being controlled by anyone,” she said sadly. “You can’t save someone from their own decisions, and I’ve already made mine.” He started to cast the chameleon spell again, but she put her hand over his to stop him. “Wait.” She pressed her lips to his. “I love you. Remember that later, no matter what happens.”

He frowned, tears leaking from the corners of his eyes. “I love you too.” Then he cast the chameleon spell and followed it with the climbing spell before swinging his legs over the windowsill.

The climb down seemed to take forever, but he refused to look up. He didn’t want to know if she was watching. His eyes continued to betray him, and the stones were blurry in front of his face. All he could do was chant to himself, “Stupid, stupid, stupid…” though he wasn’t sure who he meant, himself or the woman in the room above.

Chapter 44

Will stared at the ceiling. He was on the top bunk, which he preferred even though the room was all his. The sun was coming up outside, which meant he was late for saber practice, but he couldn't muster the enthusiasm to care. He'd spent most of the night staring at the ceiling without finding any better answers than the ones he already had.

He had slept a little, but he hadn't needed much, due to his long nap on Sunday morning. The entire weekend seemed like it had been a dream, and contrary to his old fantasies, finally confessing his love hadn't made him feel better.

He was miserable.

Things were clear between them. He had no more doubts about Selene's feelings or intentions, and yet one basic thing stood between them—sorcery. She was both a victim and an unwitting perpetuator of the practice and to get closer to her either he would have to sacrifice his principles, or she would have to learn the truth. From the cold feeling in the pit of his stomach, neither seemed likely.

Eventually he rose and went to his classes, where he ran across all three of his various friends at different points. He declined attempts at conversation, though, beyond simple greetings. Janice seemed most sensitive to his dark mood, but she didn't say anything.

When the time came for their dance lessons, he managed to get through the entire hour without crushing anyone's toes. Dianne even complimented him. "I was beginning to despair of you ever learning last week, but you're starting to get there."

"Thanks, Mom," he responded quietly. It was the first time he had used her familiar appellation since his duel with Dennis Spry, but she let it pass. He should have felt good about that, but it failed to penetrate his dour spirits.

Janice caught up to him as he was leaving. "Will. You seem down."

He nodded; there was no point in denying it.

"Want to talk about it?"

She really doesn't want to hear about my weekend in Selene's arms, he thought soberly. He was sometimes dense, but even he knew better than that. "Not really."

She was watching him carefully. "That's not true. You do want to talk about it."

"It isn't something I should talk to you about," he admitted.

"Why not?"

A cruel impulse overwhelmed his usual consideration. "Because you like me. It's about a girl."

Janice winced visibly, but she didn't try to deny his observation. "Oh. Selene?"

"Yeah."

Ignoring her own discomfort with the topic, she pressed on, "Did you get a letter?"

"I saw her. We talked."

"She rejected you?"

His eyes flashed angrily, but he bit back his first response. *You'd like that, wouldn't you?* "Not exactly," he said instead. "More of a forbidden love and irreconcilable differences sort of thing."

Janice's visage showed surprise and concern. "She confessed to you?" she asked in disbelief.

"We both did. But there's something else going on as well."

"You're a commoner," she stated.

"It's partly that. I've had opportunities to raise my station, but I've rejected them on personal principles. Apparently, that was also a rejection of her," he said bluntly.

Her eyes widened. "Wow. You turned down an offer from the king?"

He nodded.

"And yet you're still alive," she said in a tone of wonder. "That's a miracle considering your other problems. She must be furious."

"That I'm alive?"

"No. That you would rather stand on principle. It's almost like you'd rather be dead than rise to a rank that would make you a possible match for her."

Despite knowing little of the details, Janice had summed it up pretty neatly. "That's pretty much what she said. I've never seen her lose her temper before."

Janice sighed. "She's probably angrier with the situation than with you, but I can't blame her. From where I'm standing, your decision doesn't seem very wise. Can I ask what this principle of yours is?"

"Sorcery is evil."

"Ouch," said Janice. "I change my verdict. She has to be at least a little angry about that. It doesn't help that you're wrong."

"I'm not wrong," he said stubbornly.

"Prove it then. You can't make a bold statement like that without offering some proof."

"I don't have any proof. I just believe what my old master taught me."

Janice shook her head sadly. "Accusations without evidence are merely insults."

"That's essentially what the king said."

"Holy Mother! You told the king that too?"

"Last week. I didn't say it that way exactly, but I did let him know that I thought sorcery was the equivalent of magical slavery. That's how I got the black eye."

Janice took a step back, covering her mouth with both hands.

Will smirked. "Having second thoughts about the ball? Being seen with me might not be the wisest course of action."

She nodded.

His lips formed a firm line, then Will turned and walked away, keeping his spine straight and his shoulders square. *Going alone would be better,* he told himself. *That's how I've dealt with most of this anyway.*

Back in his room, he returned to practicing his spellcraft, though his zeal and enthusiasm were gone. The walls felt as though they were closing in on him. The more he thought about it, the surer he was that going to see Selene had been a mistake. He had promised to kill her father, and whether that was in a month, or years in the future, it would destroy any feelings between them. Falling in love with her was pure folly.

He wasn't in the mood to talk to Arrogan, but he called up the limnthal anyway. *If I'm going to kill a king and however many others it takes, then I need to forge myself into the best weapon possible,* he thought. *That's all I have left.* "I need to learn that point-defense shield you told me about," he said without preamble. "It isn't in your book. Is there a copy at home in your library?"

"Not as far as I recall," said the ring.

That wasn't what he had expected to hear. "I thought you had all the rare spells in those books of yours."

"Ha!" said Arrogan. "My library was a lot less stupendous than you assumed, then. I did have a collection of things you aren't likely to find being taught these days, but there were only a few actual volumes of spells on the shelves, and most of them were things I wouldn't want anyone to learn."

"Like the city killer you mentioned? You knew a lot more spells than those," countered Will.

"Hundreds, maybe thousands," agreed Arrogan. "A lot of them I could reflex cast and I would have been hard put to remember them well enough to put them on paper. The others were memorized. I could have written those out for you, but it would be impossible now."

"What if you needed something different? Isn't that the whole point of having a library?"

"I was a genius, boy, a master of the craft. If I needed something special, I'd create it. After a few hundred years I was pretty good at cobbling together new spells if I didn't have one to do the trick already."

"That's great for you, but it doesn't help me much now."

"Isn't that what your fancy ass college is supposed to be good for? They have a massive library here," suggested the ring.

Will had only visited it a few times. The first time had been in hopes of finding useful spells, but he had left disappointed. The other times had been to do research for essays. None of his experience within the library made him hopeful that he could find what he wanted there. "Anything remotely useable in battle would be in the restricted sections," said Will. "Hell, they put anything that might be potentially used for criminal purposes in there, not just the dangerous stuff."

"Too bad you can't use the chameleon spell yet," said Arrogan.

"I can," Will said simply. "I managed it a few days ago."

"Oh? What did you do first?"

"Nothing," said Will in a sullen tone.

"You're a terrible liar. It was the girls' dorm, wasn't it? You sleazy little bastard."

Will's cheeks reddened. "No!"

"You're seventeen and there's a whole bundle of stupid stuck between your legs. Don't try to tell me you were mature and responsible."

"Not everyone is as twisted as you were at this age," argued Will. He didn't bother mentioning that his birthday had come and gone more than a week prior without anyone knowing.

"If you were stubborn enough to convince me to take you as an apprentice, I doubt you're a goody-goody. You'd probably be in prison by now if you hadn't met me," said Arrogan. "So, just fess up and tell me where you went. It's probably the first interesting story you've had since you started tormenting me with your questions."

"It's none of your business," said Will stubbornly.

"Hmm, so it wasn't the girls' dorm and you're sensitive about it—let me just think about what I know about you already." After a brief pause, the ring gasped, "You didn't!"

"Didn't what?" asked Will warily.

"Sneak into a brothel and watch the ladies going about their work. That's just disgusting. I would have thought my living self would have taught you better than that."

Will was appalled. "I did no such thing. Why would you even think that?"

"I'm just getting under your skin. It's obvious what you did. You went and found that girl you're always mooning about."

Will remained silent.

The ring went on. "The real question is whether you talked to her or not. Since you're here now and not on top of a pike at the city gate, I can only assume you weren't caught."

He refused to be goaded into participating in the conversation.

"Since you're too embarrassed to say anything, you probably just snuck in and watched her undressing. That's just sick. You should be ashamed."

"I didn't!" Will exclaimed.

"So you talked to her, and then—tell me you didn't."

"I didn't," Will lied.

"Didn't talk, or didn't share her bed?"

"Either! Wait, I meant we talked, but that's all."

"You really are a bad liar. I bet you're red as a beet right now," said Arrogan.

Desperate to change the direction of the conversation, Will volunteered some information. "I tried to tell her what you told me, about the heart-stone enchantment."

"Ninny, and how did that work out for you?"

"Not well. She didn't believe me."

"Of course she didn't. Now I understand why you didn't get laid. She probably tossed your ass out after you started preaching to her about being enslaved by her father."

"No, I didn't mention it until later," said Will.

"Hah! So you did defile her!" accused the ring.

"No! That's enough! I'm not talking about this with you."

Arrogan sighed. "Fine. Let me share some wisdom then. You're never going to convince her of the truth regarding the heart-stone enchantment. Would you like to know why?"

"I'd rather know *how* to convince her."

"You can't. People don't like being told they're fools. They simply reject anything that suggests it. Take yourself as a prime example. I've been telling you how stupid you are since day one and you still refuse to accept it. I'm sure my living self did the same, and yet here you are, too dumb to realize your idiocy. Normal people are like that too, just not quite as obvious about it. What you were trying to tell her contradicts everything she knows about herself, her father, and her magic. There's no way she could accept it. All you accomplished is that you probably pissed her off."

"I've figured out that much already," said Will sourly.

"Really? What got the message across? Was it a frying pan to that big stupid noggin of yours, or did she try to put a knife through you?"

He chuckled in spite of himself. "No, but she was definitely mad. Since you're so *wise*, why don't you tell me how I can convince her?"

"You can't. She'll have to figure it out herself, and that won't happen until she dies, or her father uses the enchantment to force her to do something that's obviously contrary to her true self."

"I doubt he could do that," said Will. "She believes in obedience to the king. She'd do anything he told her. Even if she didn't want to, she'd probably think she was obeying out of loyalty."

"You really know how to pick 'em," said Arrogan sarcastically. "But even if she's that mixed up there's a few things no sane person will do."

"Such as?"

"Hurt themselves or hurt their family and loved ones. For example, if he told her to kill herself, she'd realize the truth as she was driving a knife through her own heart. The same would be true if he ordered her to kill him, which isn't likely to happen. Is she in love with you?"

Will didn't answer.

"Then you have three possibilities," said the ring, ignoring his silence. "If he ordered her to kill him, or herself, or you. While the first of those would rather neatly solve two of your problems, it won't ever happen. The other two would also solve your problems, but you wouldn't enjoy the resolution."

"Isn't it possible she could resist a command like that?"

"I suppose anything is possible, but I never saw it happen. At best, it would tear her soul apart and kill her. I doubt anyone is that stubborn."

"I always feel so uplifted after our little chats," said Will dryly.

"That warms my heart. Glad I could help."

He dismissed the limnthal and got to his feet. Then he prepared the chameleon spell and tucked it away for quick use later. It was time to visit the library.

CHAPTER 45

The Wurthaven library was a massive stone building that predated Terabinia, having been constructed in the early days of Cerria, when it had still been part of Greater Darrow. According to the history of the college, it wasn't entirely certain whether the library had been built to serve the college, or whether the college had been built near it as a matter of convenience.

Either way, it was well over a thousand years old and the stonework on the exterior didn't quite match that of the other buildings on the campus. Will approached the main entrance.

The library kept late hours compared to the rest of the college, as it didn't officially close until an hour before midnight. Will walked up the long, stone steps and went inside, greeting the library clerk that manned the massive front desk.

"You're coming in late," said the young man sitting behind the desk. Will didn't recognize him but given his age, the fellow was probably one of the senior students. "You only have a couple of hours before we lock up."

"I'll probably be done by then," said Will, signing the entry register. "If not, I'll come back tomorrow."

"Need help finding anything?"

"No. I'm just finishing a book I started last week," said Will. The library didn't allow any of its books to be removed, so it was usual for students to return on multiple days to read a single tome. He headed for the stairs.

The library had four floors, and beyond the main desk he was unlikely to meet anyone aside from other students that late in the evening. There were assistants to help locate books during the earlier hours, but not after eighth bell.

The ground floor held mainly general materials and books covering various mundane subjects. The second floor was populated with historical texts, genealogical tomes, and a large section of biographies.

The fourth was smaller and the head librarian's office was located there, along with technical sections covering a wide range of engineering texts, alchemical texts, and materials relating to research done by different departments.

It was the third floor he wanted, where the spell archives resided. He made a slow circuit of the floor, checking to see how many people were there. He saw no one in the shelves, but along one end of the floor there were rows of semi-private study cubicles. He spotted two students within those, one asleep and the other reading.

Will returned to the stacks and began walking through them, paying more attention to the organization. As expected, he saw nothing of interest, but the restricted area was easy to see, for it was cordoned off with brass chains.

The chains were mostly a symbolic barrier, since anyone could slip beneath them or step over if they had long legs. It was the wards that lined the floor behind them that were the true obstacle. Will kept walking until he had reached the stairs, then he went down to the second floor. He had time to kill, so he thought he might as well use it working on his next essay for Composition.

The few remaining students left over the course of the next two hours, and once Will thought most of them had gone, he returned to the front desk and signed out, giving a nod to the sleepy clerk. The entrance was some twenty feet away and he walked to it, glancing back just as he put his hand on the door handle.

The clerk was looking down at something he had been reading. Will opened the door and cast the chameleon spell. Then he remained still, watching to see if the clerk would glance up.

The clerk did look up, but only for a split second as he noted the door closing. Then he returned to reading whatever it was that had captured his interest. Will slowly backed away from the door and made his way to the far corner where a few chairs and low tables were set out for students. He took a seat and kept his eyes on the clerk.

When the eleventh bell rang, the man got up and locked the doors before returning to the desk and his beloved book. Will silently cursed. *Why doesn't he leave?*

Since the man showed no sign of moving, Will closed his eyes and tried to nap. He'd be locked in all night anyway, so he figured he'd use his time productively. Almost an hour passed before he heard a sound and opened his eyes. The clerk had finally risen from his seat and was walking to the stairs. *Why is he going up there?*

Twenty minutes went by before the man finally returned and let himself out. Will waited until he was gone, then waited another couple of minutes just to be sure the fellow wouldn't return.

Finally, sure he was alone, Will headed for the stairs and went back up to the third floor. The glass lanterns that hung from the ceiling were out, so it was nearly pitch black. *He must have put out the lights.* It didn't inconvenience him at all, though. He'd adjusted his vision to compensate without even thinking about it. The library was now well lit in shades of grey. *I'll have to make a light to read anything though.* He knew from prior experience that reading was nearly impossible using heart-light.

He stopped in front of the chain that marked off the restricted section. The wards that protected it extended for almost ten feet beyond the boundary line, covering the floor in blue-limned symbols and runes. Dulaney had warned him not to sneak in previously, which meant the professor suspected that others might have done so before him. *What method did they use?* Will wondered. *Did they climb along the shelves, or maybe they had some spell for levitating?*

He was tempted to try climbing, just to see if it would work, but he couldn't afford a failed experiment. It was better to stick with a method he was sure of. Crouching down, he eased his body forward beneath the chain, then held his hand out to hover above the ward while he matched its turyn. Once he had the feel of it, he gingerly placed his hand against the runes.

Nothing happened, and a wicked smile crept across his face. *William Cartwright, plunderer of archives and cat burglar extraordinaire.* He extended his false aura to include the rest of his body and then crawled forward until he could stand up. The restricted section was his to explore.

As expected, he couldn't read most of the titles, but there were a few that stood out. He wondered why. Conjuring a light spell, he readjusted his vision and looked again. Some of the spines were stamped with metallic gold lettering. *Interesting. I can see metallic paint with heart-light but not ordinary inks.*

He walked along the shelves for a short distance before realizing he'd made a major error. There were too many books and his goal was very specific. He needed to check the index, but it was located outside the restricted area. With a sigh he made his way back, carefully bypassing the ward again so he could get out. Then he crossed the floor until he found the long cabinets that held the card index.

Searching for 'battle magic' turned out to be a waste of time, as did searching for 'point defense.' He needed a title or an author name. *I really am an idiot.* Calling up the limnthal, he queried his foul-mouthed companion. "I'm looking for the point-defense spell you told me about."

"You're in the library?" asked the ring.

"Yeah, but I don't have a way to search by spell. I need a title or an author."

"Shit, I don't know who created it. Can't you just go to the section on force spells?"

Will sighed. "I don't know where the sections are, or how they're organized."

"Hmmm. Look for something by Todd Martin."

"Did he create the spell?"

"Nah, he was a total prat, but he fancied himself an expert on force effects. He wrote a few pretentious books on the subject. They should be in the same area where the force spells are."

Will moved down to the M's and pulled out several drawers until he found the right one, then he thumbed through the cards. "Here it is," he announced. "Martin, Todd. *Force Spells for the Refined Mind.*"

"What a git," said Arrogan. "You should burn that one while you're in that section. Do the world a favor."

Will took note of the aisle letter and index number, then put the card back in place and closed the drawer. Returning to the restricted section, he walked along the outside until he found the correct aisle, then carefully made his way past the wards. After a few minutes of searching he found the book. "Here it is. Do you think the spell is inside?"

"Don't even open it. That book is a waste of time. See what's nearby. Just read the titles and authors out to me."

Will moved to the left until he found the beginning of the force-effects section and began reading titles and authors out loud. Arrogan made derogatory comments whenever he recognized a name. Eventually Will got tired. "Is there anyone you didn't hate?"

"My mother," said Arrogan. "She was nice—sometimes."

"What about this one? *Force Effects and Practical Applications* by Lacy Holmberg."

The ring didn't reply for several seconds. "Really? I knew her. Never expected you to find something written by her."

"Think it might be good?"

"No. She couldn't spell her way out of a bad date. Not that she would need to. I'm honestly surprised she could string enough words together to write a sentence, much less a book."

Will chuckled as he moved on. "How about *Breaking Things* by Greg Stone?"

"Yes! I remember that one!"

"Did you know him?"

"No," said the ring. "He was before my time, but I feel like I would have liked him. He had flair."

Will took the book down and thumbed through the pages. There were handwritten notes on some of the margins. Looking closely, he recognized the handwriting. "I think you wrote in this book," he observed.

"Wow," said the ring. "They still have the same copy? You'd think they'd have had it recopied by now."

Will read from the introduction page:

'Force spells are often derided for their simplicity and basic nature, but no class of spells can compare for efficiency and flexibility. Properly utilized force effects can accomplish amazing feats with a minimum of wasted turyn, maximizing the practitioner's intended result with an efficiency that can rarely be matched by elemental spells outside of their specific and limited niches.'

Arrogan's handwritten note on the margin commented:

Except you can only use one at a time, numbskull!

Will frowned, then read the note aloud for the ring's benefit. "I thought you liked this book?"

"It wasn't until I got further in that my thinking evolved on the topic. I was rather opinionated back then," said Arrogan. "Flip to the back. There's an index. You'll be here all night if you want to read through and find the good spells."

Opinionated back then? Doesn't seem like he's changed at all, noted Will. "What did you mean by 'you can only use one at a time?'"

"Oh, that. You can't have more than one force spell active at any given time. No one really has a good notion of why that is, though I'm sure Todd Martin had some overblown and unsupported theory on the matter. Personally, I think it's simply that force spells are linked directly to the caster's will, so you can't divide your attention."

Will tucked that tidbit of information in the back of his mind to think about later. In the index he was amazed by the variety of spells listed. Most of them were differentiated by the shapes of the force effect—there were cages, domes, walls, invisible hands, and all manner of other forms listed. He didn't find anything listed under 'point defense.' "I don't see the spell you mentioned," said Will.

"Read them off to me," said Arrogan.

Will did, and after just a few names Arrogan stopped him. "That's it, 'force buckler.'"

"Why doesn't it have a standard name? It's as though everyone just makes up their own name for whatever they like," complained Will.

"Most force spells are pretty old," explained the ring. "Everyone tends to just call them by whatever makes sense to them. Hell, you could just call it the dinner plate spell and it would fit just as well."

"Dinner plate? Really?"

"You could eat off of it if you wanted to. It's about the right size and shape."

"What would you name it then?"

"Well, assuming I was conceited enough to try and claim credit for it, I would have named it Arrogan's Asskicker."

Will laughed. "How does that make sense? It's a defensive spell."

"And that just shows how limited your imagination is," observed the ring. "Trust me, once you learn it you'll find it's easily the most useful spell in your arsenal. Not only is it handy as an impromptu dinner plate, but it's great for kicking people's teeth in. Master it and you'll be able to spit in almost anyone's eye without fear."

He didn't see how that could be true, so he asked, "Even the king?"

"I wouldn't go that far," said Arrogan. "He probably has an air elemental."

"What does that have to do with it?"

"The point-defense spell won't do you much good if you're dealing with air attacks. It's great for earth and water, since their attacks tend to be more focused. Think about the wind-wall spell, then imagine it as a ranged attack. What would you do?"

"There's a force-dome spell in here," pointed out Will.

"Sure, and you'll be exhausted. Remember what I told you about force effects and size. Forget the big stuff, I'm talking about the point-defense spell. It's nearly useless against air type attacks. That was the point I was making. However, for everything else, it really shines."

"What about fire?" asked Will. "You didn't mention it."

"What about it? You don't need anything to deal with fire. How many sorcerers with fire elementals have you killed now?"

Will nodded. "I see what you mean."

"Water and earth are the worst to deal with, but this spell goes a long way toward bridging the gap. For air you need to hit first and hit hard, otherwise they'll tear you to shreds before you can do anything."

"Even you?"

"I'm dead."

He sighed. "I meant before, when you were alive."

"A master wizard fears little, but you have a long way to go before you're that good. Dealing with air requires a larger repertoire of spells, as well as plenty of experience."

"Well, what would you do if you were faced with an air elemental?" asked Will curiously.

"It depends. Probably an iron-skin transmutation. Then I'd get close and take the sorcerer apart. There's not a lot you can do to an air elemental itself," explained Arrogan.

"Iron skin, that sounds useful."

"It's not nearly as good as it sounds," observed Arrogan. "It'll stop arrows and make you virtually immune to air attacks, but it's useless against water and earth. Rely on it and you'll have a hole through your midsection big enough to put your fist through. It's only your skin that is transformed."

Will remembered Selene's water drill attack and winced.

"That made me remember something. Remind me to tell you about Leonard Kaspar and his iron cock one day."

"Now I have to know."

"It's a cautionary tale. Long story short, he was obsessed with enhancing himself, so he devised a limited version of the iron-skin spell that would only affect his little friend. Unfortunately, it also denied him any sensation, so he removed some of the protective features thinking that if more of his anatomy changed it might produce the desired effect. Instead, he wound up transforming the entire thing into solid iron."

"Oh wow," said Will. "Was it permanent?"

"No, he managed to reverse the effect, but removing the inherent protections exposed him to unsafe levels of the metal. He wound up dying of iron poisoning a few days later."

"That's not very funny," said Will.

"I haven't finished. Although he did manage to get the desired effect for a time, complete with sensation, his partner was apparently so disgusted by the thing she wouldn't let him near her. So the poor bastard died for nothing."

"Still not funny." Will sat down and began copying the spells he wanted, beginning with the point-defense spell. Despite Arrogan's disparagement, he also copied the force-dome, wall, and cage spells. After a moment's consideration he also added the force-fingers spell to his journal. That done, he put his supplies back in the limnthal and returned the book to its place.

Several hours had passed by then, and Will knew he should probably try to sleep some, since he would still need to go to class after leaving the library in the morning, but he was too wound up to think about rest yet. So he wandered the stacks for a bit, picking out books at random and examining the contents.

He passed another hour that way, until he happened across a spell that seemed interesting. "Grasping shadows. I wonder what this does." Reading through the description, he found that it was meant to immobilize and opponent by creating shadows that held their feet to the ground. Unsure whether it was really useful, he asked the ring.

"Possibly," said Arrogan. "There are more effective force spells that do the same thing, but I'll let you tell me why the spell uses shadows instead."

"Because they're scarier?" offered Will.

"No. It's because you can only use one force effect at a time. If you use one for immobilizing your opponent you can't use others, like the shield, or a force-lance. You really have to start paying attention."

"Ahh."

"Coincidentally, earth-type spells work better for that sort of thing. It's also one of the most common ways you'll be attacked by someone using an earth elemental. They always want to either encase you in stone, snare your feet, or just drop you in a pit. Keep that in mind."

Will copied the spell down anyway. Then he moved on, working his way through the aisles until he came to the corner of the third floor, where two walls met. An iron door was set in one wall, its surface covered with dark runes. "What's this?" he muttered.

The strangest thing about the door was the fact that it didn't seem to have any magic imbued within it or the runes that covered it. The runes themselves were physically engraved in the metal, and while there were odd black scorch marks on the door, it seemed magically inert. He studied it carefully with his eyes for several minutes, adjusting his turyn sensitivity to make sure he wasn't missing anything, but he couldn't find any trace of magic.

Gingerly, he reached out and touched it nervously. A wave of relief passed over him when nothing happened.

There was a large, circular wheel and lever mounted in the center of the door, which seemed to control a mechanism to open it, but when he tried to move either of them, they refused to budge. It seemed to be locked.

Unable to contain his curiosity, he constructed the unlocking spell and cast it. It sank into the metal, and a long groan issued from the door as something inside it began to move. The wheel turned, and he saw the door shiver slightly. Reaching out, he pulled on the lever and the door swung slowly open.

"That was easy," he observed.

Inside, he was shocked to see that the walls of the room were uniformly composed of black iron. Even the ceiling and floor were iron, as though the door opened into a sealed box. On either side of the room were iron shelves with rows of books. "It's a vault," he said to himself.

He looked at the first book to his right, which was titled, *A Primer of the Undead.* Will's eyes widened. Surely the undead weren't real? He lifted the dusty tome from the shelf and opened it. Thumbing through the pages, he found fantastic illustrations of horrific monsters with all manner of names: wights, ghouls, zombies, vampires, and liches. He had no idea what a lich was, but it looked unpleasant. He hurriedly closed the book and put it back.

Overcoming Mortal Frailty was the title of the next book. Opening it, he found a spell written on the first page immediately after the introduction. At a glance he could see that it was well beyond anything he could cast. He couldn't even begin to guess at what order of complexity it fell within. Some of the requirements listed beside it seemed impossible. "Vampire blood? How would anyone get that?"

He closed it and moved on, skipping past titles such as *Serving the Dark Lord, Wisdom of the Void,* and *Sacrifice and Power*. "This is some seriously evil shit," muttered Will. His fingers stopped above a less intimidating title, *Modern Necromancy, Bringing Light out of Darkness.*

"Modern," he chuckled. The book had to be hundreds of years old at the very least, but he supposed it had been modern when it was written. He opened it and found the table of contents. The first few chapters seemed to be involved in the healing arts, but the ninth chapter had a frightening title. 'Desecration of nations, a practical examination.'

Overcome with curiosity, he flipped through to that chapter. What he found boggled his imagination. The rituals described seemed incomprehensible and involved things he had never heard of. *Ley lines?* He returned to the beginning of the book.

The second chapter held a number of spells supposedly used in healing, so he went to that chapter and began to peruse them. Most were beyond his understanding, but one in particular stood out to him. He wondered if he could find a way to put it to use.

Arrogan would probably disagree, but if there's even a chance... He wasted no time copying it down.

That done he looked at the next book, *Demonic Deliverance.* "Nope!" he declared. The spot next to it was empty, but it looked as though there had definitely been a book there until recently. The shelf was almost clear of dust in that place, while a thick coating lay on everything around it. *Someone removed one of the books? Who?*

A feeling of dread began to creep along his spine. It was time to leave.

Stepping out, he shut the heavy door and spun the wheel until he heard a series of clicks. The lever would no longer move, and the door seemed to be locked, so he left, heading for the other end of the aisle. It took him a minute to calm himself enough to concentrate so he could bypass the ward again, then he was free.

Returning to the ground floor, he found his previous resting spot and hid himself with the chameleon spell. He couldn't wait to leave. The metal vault had left a chill in his bones that was hard to shake.

Chapter 46

He struggled to get through his classes without falling asleep, and in truth, he was only partly successful. Fortunately, most of the teachers in his morning classes had gotten to the point where they actively ignored him, whether he was asleep or paying attention. *The perks of being unpopular,* he thought raggedly during lunch.

Will was more awake for the afternoon classes, but he still rushed out after his private session with Dulaney, anxious to get back to his room and take a nap. His eyelids felt as though they had lead weights attached to them.

He might have slept through his dance lesson, but Janice came and knocked on his door until he woke and answered it. She looked remorseful when he opened the door, but then she fixed her eyes on his face. "Were you asleep?"

"Mmhmm," he answered. "I was busy last night."

"Was it dangerous?" she asked with a tone of disapproval.

He shrugged. "Maybe a little. Not compared to some days."

"It worries me that you're getting used to things like that," she remarked. "Come on. We're going to be late."

Will didn't move. "I thought you weren't going to the ball."

She glanced back at him. "I've had a chance to sleep on it. I probably shouldn't, but I'm not going to abandon you just yet."

"Thanks."

Their dance lesson went even better than the day before. Will was finally beginning to move beyond not laming his partner and on to trying to appear as though he wasn't having a bizarrely slow-moving seizure. Dianne even complimented him. "I wouldn't have believed it last week, but there may be hope."

Afterward, Will returned to his room and began going over the spells he had gathered the night before. Most of the force spells were a little more complicated than he felt like tackling, so he focused on the point-defense spell that Arrogan had recommended. It was only a third-order spell, so he was able to commit it to memory in less than an hour, and after that he spent a short while practicing with it.

He spent the remainder of his time before bed working on the necromancy spell he had acquired. It was a fifth-order spell, so it would take him another day or two to gain enough confidence to cast it without relying on his notes, but he hoped it would be worth it in the end.

Before falling asleep, he decided to consult with Arrogan about some of the things he had seen in the vault. He gave a brief description of the door and what he had found within. Arrogan was not pleased.

"You could be dead, or worse, insane!"

Will sighed. "Don't be dramatic. It wasn't that bad."

"You said one of the books you saw was named *Wisdom of the Void,* didn't you?"

"Yeah."

"Just opening that one drives some men insane."

"Is there some sort of curse on it? Or a spell?"

"Not at all," said the ring. "It's simply the fact that some knowledge is so corrosive, so detrimental, that simply being exposed to it can undermine the foundations of decency and sanity. They should have had that volume chained up. Better still, it should be burned."

"What about the other books I mentioned?"

"Most of those are just fucking dangerous. I hope you didn't do more than read the titles."

"I skimmed a few pages in some of them," admitted Will, telling a half-truth. "Have you read them?"

"One or two," said Arrogan. "Most of them aren't particularly useful if you're looking to continue existing in a world full of healthy, living, breathing human beings. Some of the information is handy if you wish to be forewarned. You shouldn't even think of approaching most of those topics until you've fully matured, and maybe not even then."

"I'm eighteen now," said Will.

"You were seventeen before," said Arrogan suspiciously. "When did this happen?"

"A couple of weeks ago."

"Well happy belated fucking birthday," said the ring sourly. "And no, when I said matured, I meant as a wizard."

"How long does that take?" asked Will.

"Considering how much stupid you have to work out of your system, you might be mature by the time you're a hundred, but I wouldn't count on it."

"Well, I wasn't planning on going back," said Will reassuringly. "I do have some questions, though."

"Such as?"

"Are vampires real?"

"Not anymore, as far as I know."

"So they *were*?"

"Sorcery isn't the first magic to nearly ruin humanity," said Arrogan. "Necromancy leads down some very dark paths. Some, like liches, aren't too bad, at least not for humankind as a whole."

"I've never heard of liches," said Will. "So vampires are worse?"

"Yes and no. A lich is a singular entity, essentially a type of undead wizard. They're powerful in the extreme and usually evil beyond belief. Vampires don't have anything on liches, but the problem with vampires is that they're infectious, like a disease."

"Ahh, I see," said Will. He moved on to his next question, "What's a ley line?"

"You rotten little shit! You did more than just skim. Don't even think about getting involved in anything that manipulates ley lines. You'll either kill yourself, or kill a lot of other people. The former possibility being the best outcome."

"So they're bad?"

"No, but they aren't often used for anything that isn't bad. Not these days anyway. They're like rivers of magic that flow beneath the earth. Wizards used to tap into them to empower vast spells or rituals. Imagine someone trying to put a ward around an entire city. They'd need to tap into a ley line to do that. Most of the time, however, it's some crazed maniac trying to create a plague or wipe out a city. Either way, you don't need to think about things like that for a long, long time."

"What about necromancy?" asked Will, changing topics again. "Can it really be used for healing?"

"I swear to the all the gods, boy, if I wasn't dead already, you'd put me in an early grave. Did you read every book in there?"

"No, but I saw this one titled *Modern Necromancy, Bringing Light from the Darkness,* and I looked through it a little. The first half seemed to be mainly about healing," explained Will.

"Healing is necromancy, though most healers hate hearing it described that way," said Arrogan. "Healing and necromancy are two sides of the same type of magic. I haven't heard of that book before, though."

"It was interesting," said Will mildly.

"You didn't copy anything out of it, did you?"

"No, of course not," Will lied.

"Will!" growled the ring.

"I didn't!"

"I hope you're telling the truth. Stick to whatever watered-down bullshit they teach at Wurthaven on the subject. The risks aren't worth it. I haven't wasted all this time listening to you cry about that girl to have you run off and become a necromancer trying to raise an army of the dead, or worse, try to turn yourself into a lich or something equally distasteful."

Will didn't say anything.

"Are you listening to me?" demanded the ring.

"I am. I was just distracted."

"Devote yourself to mastering the point-defense spell. The sooner you can instinctively cast it, the better. That's when it really begins to shine."

Will pursed his lips. "It's pretty simple. I think I could cast it in just a second or two with a little practice. Would reflex casting really make it that much better?"

"Infinitely," said the ring. "Force spells are tied to your will. I think I mentioned that before. That makes them different in a few key respects."

"Yeah, you mentioned it. I can't have more than one active at a time."

"That's not the important thing here," said Arrogan. "Because they're tied to your will, they can't be taken or altered by another caster. They're essentially immutable. Did I ever give you the *talk*? About your stick?"

Will snickered. "Mom told me about the birds and bees a long time ago."

"Not that stick."

"Yeah, you did, then you beat the crap out of me." He could still vividly remember the day Arrogan had given him the lesson about taking spells away from other magic users when it was advantageous. He had illustrated the point by using sticks and had subsequently chased Will around with one.

"Good," said the ring. "I wish I could repeat that lesson every day. Anyway, the point here is that force spells are excluded from that lesson. If someone fires a force lance at you, you won't be able to absorb any of it. Or if they put a shield in front of you, you won't be able to wrest it from their control. Force spells are intimately tied to the caster. They also, pay attention to this part, they also manifest and operate at the speed of the soul."

"Huh? You mean as fast as thought?"

"Faster than that, I said the speed of the *soul*."

"What does that mean?" asked Will, utterly confused.

"It means that if you learn to instinctively cast it, you'll be able to react to things faster than you can think. The shield will appear wherever you wish it to and far faster than you could ever decide to put it in place deliberately. Crucially, since it doesn't rely on thinking, even a moron like you can use it with instantaneous speed even though the rest of you is as dumb as a stump."

Will began to nod, though he was still uncertain. "So being able to cast it without constructing the spell does sound a little better."

"I wasn't exaggerating when I said infinitely better, numbskull," shot back Arrogan. "Not just a little better, almost immeasurably better. Since the force effect is small, it uses almost no turyn, so you can cast it all day long. As a force effect there's no travel time, so if you cast it in front of someone at the limit of your range, it appears there immediately, not a half second later. If you're being attacked by a rapid succession of spells, you can stop each one, dismiss the spell, and recast it to stop the next one faster than your opponent can even decide what he'll do next. The only thing you can't do is stop area-effect spells, or multiple simultaneous attacks, like a hail of arrows."

He was beginning to see the light.

"Now that you have it, you should practice it exclusively until you can use it instinctively. Forget about everything else until you can do that."

"What about the force-lance?"

"Did I stutter?"

"Well…"

"The force-lance is wonderful, and once you can do the same with that, you'll be dangerous as hell, but you have to stay alive first. It shocks me that I have to even say that. Keeping your body intact so you can keep breathing is always your first priority."

"Fine. I understand. You don't have to rub it in," Will responded.

Chapter 47

Wednesday passed without event. Will practiced the point-defense spell every chance he got, and while he was reasonably quick casting it, he was sure it would probably be weeks before he was able to reflex cast the spell. In truth, he had no idea how long it would take, for he still couldn't reflex any of the spells he had practiced previously.

On Thursday he continued working on it, but after a successful dance lesson with Dianne and Janice he was feeling anxious and too nervous to sit still in his room. The dance was the next evening, and while he was no longer worried about making a fool of himself during the ball, he still felt worried.

Rob had returned earlier in the day with his two new brigandines, so he put one on under his tunic and dressed to go into the city to get some fresh air. There wasn't anything he needed, and he didn't have any appointments, so no one would be expecting him to leave or to go anywhere in particular. He figured he would be relatively safe. Still, he used the chameleon spell and climbed the wall rather than leaving by the college gate.

Too much caution never hurt, whereas not enough had nearly gotten him killed several times in the past. Once he was away from the school, he slipped into a dark alley and dropped the chameleon spell so he could walk more easily among the crowds.

Will was still wary, though. He kept a close eye on the road behind him and made note of anyone who gave him more than a glance, and he had a sleep spell prepared in case someone did come after him.

It was refreshing to walk the streets openly. He had once taken the privilege for granted. He wandered through the market and examined the various wares for sale. While initially he was just idly browsing, it occurred to him that he had not once bought a present for his mother or Sammy. *Or Selene,* his inner observer reminded him snidely.

There wasn't anything he could buy for Selene, though. As the daughter of a king, she had everything a woman could want. Even with all the gold he possessed, it was highly unlikely he could ever buy anything she would desire.

Sammy was easy, though. One seller had a variety of colored ribbons for decorating women's hair. They could be tied into bows or woven into a braid. Will picked out a bright blue one to go with Sammy's red hair and a yellow one for his mother. On impulse, he picked up a green one as well. He got the third one because he thought one of them might like it, not because he had a brief vision of how the vivid green would look against Selene's dark locks.

Then he remembered Janice. "Should I get something for her too?" he muttered. It seemed only proper, especially since she was risking her own reputation by going to the ball with him the next day.

A ribbon didn't seem appropriate for a formal occasion. *It should be jewelry.* She was relatively poor, so he doubted she had anything to wear with the dress she had bought. After Will asked around for a while, one of the vendors suggested he go look at the jewelers on High Street.

A bell on the door tinkled as he entered, and a prim looking older woman greeted him as he stepped inside. "Good evening, young sir. Can I help you?"

"I need something for a friend. She's going to the Winter Ball but I don't think she has any jewelry to wear."

"A lady friend?" The woman smiled. "I can certainly help you with that. How about a ring, the eternal symbol of love?"

Love? He shook his head. "She's just my partner for the evening. There's nothing like that between us." A vision flashed in his head of the diamond and gold roses that had adorned the ring he'd discovered in Selene's bedroom. It hadn't been a signet or some more officious type of ring. It had looked exactly like the sort of ring a man would give a woman. He closed his eyes for a moment. *She's a princess. She probably has a hundred rings. It could have been an heirloom from her mother or grandmother.*

An heirloom left on the floor, as though it had been thrown there. He remembered the look on her face when she had put it in the drawer. What had she told him when he asked her about it? *"Something unfortunate."* Will felt a tightness growing in his chest.

"Sir?"

Will's eyes snapped into focus. The shopkeeper was looking at him curiously. "Excuse me?" he asked.

"I asked if you might be interested in a necklace or some earrings."

"Oh! Sure."

The woman seemed a little exasperated. "Which?"

A necklace might be too much. "Earrings I think."

In the end he selected a modest pair of pearl drop earrings mounted with gold, which set him back a full nine crowns. The shopkeeper wrapped them in a box with a bow. He stored it within the limnthal the moment his hands were unobserved, pretending to tuck the box into his belt pouch. Then he thanked the woman and left.

It took everything he had to keep from heading to the royal palace. More than anything he wanted to sneak in, climb the wall, and ask Selene about the ring. *I was so stupid!* There had been a dozen hints. Someone had to have given her the ring, someone she didn't care for. Was her father forcing her to meet with suitors?

The tension built within him until he wanted to jump and scream out his frustration. He didn't have enough information and he'd look like a fool if he broke into her bedroom again. He had no right to even ask.

Looking up, he realized he had been wandering aimlessly again. Anxiety struck and he glanced back. *Am I being followed?* He'd let his thoughts carry him away. It was the sort of carelessness that could easily get him killed. He could just imagine what Arrogan would say.

He didn't see anyone following him, but that didn't mean there wasn't. He hadn't been watching faces for a while, which meant any of the seemingly random people moving in the same direction as he was could have been deliberately shadowing him.

Will sped up to surprise his imaginary tail, then ducked into the first alley that came up on his left. As soon as he was out of view, he cast a climb spell and went up the wall. A chameleon spell would have been better, but it took too long to cast the sixth-order spell from scratch. He wanted to be out of sight if someone looked around the corner.

Sitting atop the roof, he took a couple of minutes to cast the chameleon spell and then he breathed a sigh of relief. No one had explored the alley, and while watching the street he didn't see anyone stop or act suspicious, as someone would if they had lost sight of their target.

Glancing down, he saw something dark on the roof slates. He stared at it for a moment before realizing it wasn't an ordinary stain, then he adjusted his turyn sensitivity so he could see it clearly. It was a claw print composed of residual turyn, demonic essence.

Slowly he turned his head, surveying the rooftops around him in every direction. As he had learned previously, such a faint residual sign would only remain visible to him for a few hours at most, which meant the demon had been there recently.

He worked his way around the room, looking for more tracks, until he finally spotted what appeared to be one on the roof of the next building over. He climbed down and moved to that roof to examine it. He couldn't make up his mind whether that one was newer or older, so he repeated the process until he found a mark on the next roof over.

That one was definitely slightly newer, so he knew he was heading in the correct direction. Will painstakingly made his way from building to building and then across the street to the next block. The traces were getting stronger, but eventually the trail ended. Will checked the nearest buildings but found no additional tracks.

It was dark now, so he readjusted his vision to allow him to see easily by starlight, then he studied the houses in the area. After a moment, he realized that Count Spry's house was directly across from the building he was crouching on top of. A whole host of thoughts ran through his mind.

Could the count be the one behind the demon attacks? What if it had been him or one of his agents that had stolen the book from the vault in the Wurthaven library? The book had been kept among books on demonology. Could the man be so insane as to be dabbling in such an evil art to exact his revenge?

But why would he try to kill Selene? Was it because she and her father wanted him to give up on his revenge? That didn't make a lot of sense to him. Killing Selene wouldn't help the man, and the soldiers in the attack had worn Darrowan uniforms. It would make more sense that the perpetrator wanted to incite a war, but would Spry benefit from such a thing?

Will waited, trying to adopt the patience of a hunter, and an hour later his patience was rewarded. Something moved on the roof of Count Spry's house, drawing his eyes. He watched carefully until it moved again.

Whatever it was appeared to be small and of an approximately humanoid shape. Will doubted a five-year-old child would be on top of the count's roof. *It's positioned such that it can see the front entrance,* he observed. If it was a demon, it was either guarding the house, or spying on it.

He continued watching, and by the time midnight arrived he had almost despaired of learning anything else, but then a second shape appeared. It hopped from roof to roof and passed within fifteen feet of where Will sat before crossing the road and climbing up to meet the demon on Count Spry's roof.

Will got a good look at it as it passed by him. The thing was shaped like a small, reptilian ape. In some ways it resembled a bat, though it had no wings, relying instead on clawed feet and dexterous paws to climb and jump. After a few seconds, the one that had been on the count's house left its position and returned along the same route. *It's reporting back to its master,* he decided.

He waited until it was out of sight, then climbed down and began walking. He didn't dare follow the thing closely, as he had no idea how acute its senses were, but he didn't need to. Walking briskly, he returned to the place where he had found the first track hours before, then climbed to the roof. The demonic traces were fresh and easy to find. He began following them in the opposite direction.

Will cloaked himself once again with the chameleon spell and began moving more slowly. It took him almost an hour to follow the tracks to where they ended, two blocks away at yet another expensive city house. He couldn't get to the roof of that building without taking a larger risk, though. Like Spry's home, it had an exterior gate guarding the front entrance along with several human guards.

Whoever lived there was obviously not only rich, but also important. He waited across the street, leaning against a different building while he watched the house, but nothing of interest happened.

It was two hours past midnight by then and he was getting tired. He doubted anything of note would happen and he knew he'd need his sleep for the ball the next day, so Will gave up and returned to Wurthaven after taking careful note of the address.

He slept fitfully, and his dreams were plagued by visions of Selene and mysterious villains that summoned demons whenever he tried to get near her. When he awoke the sun was already up and he knew he'd missed saber practice. It was a price he was willing to pay. Sleep was more important if he was to be alert that evening.

His classes went as usual, but all he could think about was the Winter Ball. It was supposed to be a purely social occasion, but given his history he couldn't help but worry that he would wind up in a fight. *Killing someone important in the royal palace is almost certain to piss off the king, isn't it?* he thought wryly. The joke might have been funny if it wasn't a real risk, and worse, it wasn't just himself in danger. Any major blunders on his part might well put Janice's future, or even her life in danger.

His anxiety only grew stronger as the day progressed, until finally his classes were done. He returned to his room and dressed in his new finery. Unfortunately, he couldn't wear his special brigandine with his expensive clothes. Even as slim as it was, it was too bulky to wear both a thick doublet and his leather jerkin over the top.

Going without armor made the spot between his shoulder blades itch, but there was no avoiding it. With time to spare before he needed to pick up Janice, he checked and rechecked the weapons and gear he had stored in the limnthal. *You'd think I was going to war,* he chuckled nervously. *Hopefully I won't need any of it.*

At half past the sixth bell, he went to the girls' dorm and waited in the front lobby for Janice to come down. He didn't wait long; however, when she appeared, he almost didn't recognize her. If it hadn't been for the fact that no one else would be dressed in such a gown, he might have mistaken her for someone else.

Janice glanced up shyly at him as he stared open-mouthed at her. Her hair had been worked and fashioned into an elaborate braid that dropped to her slender neck before rising to form twin spirals atop her head. The dress was a work of art in two different shades of blue. It stopped after just barely topping her shoulders, showing off her neck and delicate collarbones. His eyes rose from her face to her hair, then down to the dress, before stopping at the focal point of the entire assemblage, her décolletage. Will's cheeks colored.

"You'll embarrass me if you keep staring," said Janice demurely.

"Pardon me?" Will sputtered, then he apologized. "I'm sorry. You're just—" *What am I trying to say?* "You look lovely. I didn't expect, I mean I didn't realize—err, you're stunning." He struggled for a moment to figure out what to do with his hands as he became overly self-conscious. Then he realized he was still holding his present for her. "Here, this is for you."

Her eyes lit with surprise. "For me? Should I open it now?"

"I think so. Yes. It's for tonight."

She untied the ribbon with graceful fingers. He'd seen her hands at work countless times before, usually as she was writing or taking notes. *How did I not notice how pretty they are?* Janice's face glowed as she saw the contents of the box. "Oh! Thank you! They're perfect." She removed the earrings and set about replacing the unassuming pair she wore with the ones he had given her. "How do they look?"

"Beautiful," was all he could manage.

"Thank you." She stretched up onto her toes and kissed him lightly on the cheek, and he felt a warm flush rise from his neck to his ears. Janice took note of the look on his face and laughed, her eyes twinkling with merriment. "No need to be so bashful. I know I'm not the one that occupies your thoughts, but it's nice to see I can still make you blush."

"Umm." He had no idea what to say. Glancing around, he noticed that they were drawing a crowd as the other female students gathered to study them in their finery. "We should probably go."

Janice draped her hand across his arm, and he escorted her from the building, feeling more confident with each step. Once outside they started down the walkway, but when they reached the wider lane, she asked him, "Where do we meet the carriage?"

Chapter 48

Fortunately, the royal palace was relatively close to the college, though walking down the lane to the street, then across, and back up to the entrance of the palace took a little more than fifteen minutes. They kept their pace restrained and dignified, but Will felt like a fool the entire time. It simply hadn't occurred to him that he needed to arrange for a carriage. The palace was *right* there, next door.

His mistake became more apparent as they strolled up the palace drive, past a line of carriages that were disgorging their occupants one by one. Will and Janice were the only ones on foot, and they drew stares as they went by.

"Keep your chin up," said Janice from the side of her mouth. "These people are wolves. If they sense embarrassment, they'll go to great lengths to make it worse for you. Smile and pretend you don't give a damn, that it's a lark. They'll wonder if the joke is on them."

He took her advice to heart, smiling and giving a nod whenever someone stared too long. Those watching them seemed more curious than hostile. "You seem like you know what you're doing," Will noted.

She smiled faintly. "I've been dealing with these people all my life. You have to learn quickly, especially when they could ruin you or your family on a whim." For the first time, Will felt lucky he had grown up in a backwater village.

Since they skipped the line of carriages, they were some of the first to enter and the doorman announced their names to an almost empty room, "Mister William Cartwright and Miss Janice Edelman." Arm in arm they entered the massive ballroom, and Will's interest was immediately drawn by a long array of tables on either side of the room. Food. He glanced at Janice, and they began heading toward the nearest table.

"Look at all the food!" said Will happily. "I don't understand why there's so few people here yet. The ball is supposed to start now."

She lectured him as they went, "Ordinarily aristocrats will do their best to avoid arriving early as we did. It's part of how they establish the pecking order. The most important arrive last. Don't worry, though, since we're nobodies, arriving early won't affect us. In fact, we might have attracted negative attention if we'd tried to show up too late."

"More food for us," said Will, already busy packing finger foods into his mouth.

"You're supposed to use the little plates, not eat right off the table," said Janice.

Will smirked, his cheeks stuffed full. "That's what they get for letting pigs into a buffet."

She demonstrated the proper etiquette, loading a small saucer with a light selection of tidbits. With her first two fingers she lifted a tiny quail leg to her lips and removed the meat in a single, efficient bite. Will noticed that she kept her pinky finger out straight the entire time.

"What are you doing with your finger like that?" he asked. He'd seen Selene do the same when she was sipping from a cup, but he hadn't noticed it while eating.

She wiggled her pinky at him. "This is your salt finger. Don't ever let it touch your food or anything dirty."

"Huh?"

Janice pointed to the salt and pepper bowls, which he had just used a moment before. "If someone saw you reach into those with your other fingers, as you just did, you'd be mocked." She demonstrated by dipping the nail of her little finger into the salt bowl and scooping out a tiny portion, which she sprinkled over her plate. "Salt finger, understand?"

"What about pepper? Do I use the other pinky?"

"No. Same finger for all the spices."

"Got it."

"It's lucky for you that the food is being served informally like this. You'd need a few days to learn all the rules for a banquet."

"At least I wouldn't have to injure anyone," remarked Will ruefully. "I still have a lot of sympathy for what your feet went through last week."

She grimaced. "Don't remind me."

They meandered a bit, enjoying the scenery and listening to the doorman announce guests as the room slowly began to fill. Will was surprised when he recognized several of the guests who arrived. Duncan Fisher had come with Rebecca Swafford as his guest, while Craig Larkin arrived with Stephanie Beresford. All four were students that Will had met at various points at Wurthaven, and Rebecca was in his Spell Theory class.

He should have expected it, though, since they were sons and daughters of noblemen. A little while later the chancellor, Lord Bradshaw, and his wife arrived, followed shortly after by both of the college vice-chancellors, Lord Courtney and Lord Connolly.

Will's ears grew numb from the tedium of the constant litany of names, but they perked up when he heard one in particular being announced. "The Baron, Mark Nerrow and his wife, Baroness Agnes Nerrow, accompanied by their daughters, Laina and Tabitha Nerrow." He felt a strange emotion as they entered the room, for three of the four were his blood-relatives, and yet they were almost complete strangers to him.

The Baron's wife, Agnes, was thin and had a severe face composed of sharp lines, but her daughters were a beautiful melding of her features with Mark Nerrow's broader jawline. Laina was almost grown now, with a full figure and light, almost blond hair, while Tabitha was younger, with darker brown tresses and a kind smile. Tabitha reminded him a little of Sammy with her youthful exuberance. *My sisters,* thought Will, feeling his chest tighten.

It had never bothered him before. In fact, he had almost never thought about them, but seeing them then, dressed up and smiling at one another as they followed their mother and father, Will suddenly felt as though he was lacking something. *I'm the dirty secret of the family.* Staring at them, he wondered if they were really related. Laina and Tabitha were refined and ethereal in their beauty, while he—well, he knew his features were coarse. The scar on his cheek was just the icing on the cake, declaring his rough upbringing for all to see.

Janice nudged him with her elbow. "What's with the face? Do you know them? You look like someone just stole the dessert off your plate."

"No," he said somberly. "I don't know them at all."

"Whoa," hissed Janice. Lifting one arm, she wiped his cheek with her sleeve. "Are you crying?"

"Huh? No," said Will, shaking himself slightly to rid himself of his melancholy. "I think I had something in my eye."

"Sure," said Janice. "Try to keep it together. The princess isn't even here yet and you're already getting sentimental.

More people arrived, and the pace began to slow with pauses between entrants. When the doorman announced the Duke and Duchess Arenata, it seemed to be all but over. "That's probably it except for the royals."

Will wasn't sure how he felt about that, and he was also surprised and perhaps relieved that Count Spry hadn't made an appearance, but then the doors opened again. "Her Highness, Princess Selene Maligant with her escort Count Malcolm Spry."

Will froze, and a strange vibration echoed through his chest. He'd begun growling without realizing it. "What the hell?" he muttered. "Why is he here with her?"

Janice put her hand on his arm. "Calm down. You won't win any points by showing your teeth."

He glared at Janice. "Shouldn't he be here with his wife?"

"She died a few weeks ago," she responded matter-of-factly. "Didn't you hear? Apparently, she had a bad case of indigestion."

"What?" A look of horror spread slowly across his face.

"You should try going outside more often," said Janice dryly. "It was the only thing people were talking about for days. She was still young, and of course there have been dark rumors that her demise wasn't entirely natural."

"I go outside plenty," said Will in irritation. "I just don't talk much. People keep trying to stick sharp things in me. Do you really think he had her killed?"

"Shhh, lower your voice," warned his date. "Some things are meant to be thought but not spoken, or at least, spoken very softly."

A hush fell over the room, and the string musicians stopped as King Lognion Maligant entered from the second-floor balcony on the opposite end of the ballroom. The gathered lords and ladies dropped into deep bows and curtseys and remained that way until his voice rang out across the room.

"Noble guests, raise your heads. Welcome to the Winter Ball. Our beloved nation has survived yet another year and we find ourselves here again to celebrate the turning of the seasons and our rest from the labors of the spring, summer, and fall."

As if any of them were out planting or harvesting, though Will sourly.

The king continued, "This year we have even more to be thankful for, as our gallant soldiers successfully pushed the invader from our eastern borders and even now the Patriarch begs us for peace and leniency in the wake of his defeat." Lognion lowered his head and voice menacingly. "Though whether I will grant them such mercy is yet to be seen!"

He paused, and a brief applause broke out in the room. Then the king held up his hands again. "But despite all of that, I have yet another surprise for the people of our land, a small bit of joy I would like to share. As most of you are aware, Lord Spry suffered two great tragedies this year, first the loss of his son and then the loss of his beloved wife

Frya. While such crushing sorrow might destroy lesser men, Malcolm Spry has proved once again what strong stuff he is made of, for he has continued to move forward despite his losses."

Selene and Count Spry were climbing the stairs on one side of the room, moving to join the King where he addressed the crowd. Will began to mumble to himself. "No, no, no, no…" Janice dug her fingers into his arm, warning him to stay silent.

"Without wife or heir, Lord Spry has been left wondering if his house would pass away entirely, but as his liege I could not stand idly by and watch such a friend to the crown suffer. My daughter has always had great affection for Lord Spry and she has recently consented to become his wife. I was only too pleased to grant them my blessing! I ask all of you to do the same, as a month from today they will be wed in the great chapel. Please greet the future bride and groom." The king stepped back from the railing and gestured toward Selene and Malcolm Spry with open arms, inviting them to stand beside him.

With the speech over cheers and applause filled the air and some of the guests called out their congratulations. Will simply stood and stared, and a line he'd once heard from his grandfather tumbled out of his lips. "That needle-dicked bug fucker!"

A lady nearby heard his words and she gasped and moved away, while Janice's face grew pale. A heavy hand landed on Will's shoulder and he turned angrily to see who had dared.

"Mister Cartwright! It's a pleasure to see you hale and hearty! Try to keep my nickname away from the ears of the delicate ladies of this gathering," exclaimed the heavily muscled man. He appeared to be in his thirties with an impressively large mustache and mirthful brown eyes. It took Will a second to recognize the man.

"Captain Barrentine?"

The knight-captain dipped his head in acknowledgment, a smile on his face. "Please, though, call me Sir Kyle here. Military titles are out of place in this company. Will you introduce me to your lovely companion?"

Will awkwardly made the introduction. "May I present Miss Janice Edelman, a fellow student at Wurthaven. Janice, this is Sir Kyle Barrentine. He was my commanding officer during the fight against the Darrowan invasion." He stared at the big knight in wonder. "I'm surprised you even remember me, Sir Kyle, much less know my name."

"How could I forget the single biggest source of trouble in Company B?" said Sir Kyle with a laugh. He winked at Janice. "Miss Edelman,

I don't know how you came to be an acquaintance of this rogue, but you must love excitement. There's rarely a dull moment with this one around." He punctuated the remark by clapping Will on the shoulder so hard that he staggered.

Janice showed a brief flash of white teeth. "I cannot argue with your appraisal, Sir Kyle. He has been a handful, even at Wurthaven."

"Sir Kyle," began Will, "could I trouble you for news of the men in Company B? You probably don't know them but…"

"Let's go get some air," suggested the knight. "We can talk on the veranda, rather than bore the ears of these notables with war stories." There was a warning in his eyes.

They followed Sir Kyle across the room to a wall that held several sets of broad, glass-paned double doors that had been thrown open to allow air into the crowded ballroom. There were already some people milling around outside, but the knight led them to a quiet spot where they could speak without being overheard. The knight's demeanor became less jovial as they gained privacy. "Mister Cartwright, I see some things never change. You looked as though you were about to bring out a barrel of lamp oil and set fire to the place."

Will looked to one side uneasily. "I wouldn't go that far."

"You're lucky I spotted and you and came over to say hello. If I hadn't been close enough to cover for you, that remark would have put you in dire straits."

"I can't communicate how grateful I am for your intervention, Sir Kyle," said Janice with absolute sincerity.

Will scowled, still angry inside. "I can't help the truth."

The knight stared at him disapprovingly for a full thirty seconds before his face began to crack into a smile. "Needle dick—what was the rest? I don't think I've ever heard that one."

"Bug fucker," said Will helpfully.

Sir Kyle chuckled. "It probably is true. Where did you hear such a thing? Were you a sailor in the past?"

"My grandfather was—colorful," said Will reluctantly. "Pardon me, Sir Kyle, but are you really the same man who commanded Company B? I don't remember you being so—"

"Friendly? Easygoing?" supplied the knight.

Will nodded.

"You'll understand if you ever feel the burden of command, especially when you're certain that you're leading a hundred men who trust you into certain death."

"You're right," said Will. "Maybe I was too self-centered back then. I never thought about the stress you were under."

"Don't blame yourself. That's an officer's job."

Will's eyes snapped up to the man's face. "Blaming me, or yourself?"

"Both," said Sir Kyle soberly. Then he held out his hand. Will stared at it for a moment, confused. "You're supposed to shake it," said the knight.

Will did, still confused, but the military man continued, "I want to thank you for what you did in Barrowden, Mister Cartwright. You saved a lot of lives, mine included, but most importantly you saved those I was responsible for."

"I'm not sure what you mean, sir. I don't think I was a very good soldier."

The knight laughed. "You were a terrible soldier, but fortunately, you didn't let that, or anyone else, stop you from doing what needed to be done. The men know what you did. I made sure of that."

"Sir?"

"I knew before then, after you took out all the sentries and killed the camp commander in the pass, but there was no room for commendations or medals at that time. I had discipline to enforce. Plus, there were the rumors of black magic, but after you were sent to the capital and later exonerated, we got word. We also discovered some of what you did in Barrowden. It's good to see that His Majesty has seen fit to reward you."

Janice and Will exchanged a knowing glance. "I'm not sure I'd call it a reward," said Will. "I've had some rather ugly disagreements with the king."

"About what?" asked the knight, displaying genuine concern.

"I can't really talk about it, sir."

"Is it the princess, or Count Spry? I've heard the tale of your duel."

Will didn't know what to say, but Janice answered for him, "Both."

Sir Kyle shook his head, then put a friendly hand on Will's shoulder. "You should turn your eyes elsewhere, William. At the very least, if you can't control your temper, you should leave before you get yourself into a situation you can't escape from. I'd hate to see you whipped and dishonored after everything you did."

"Thank you for the advice, sir. I'll keep that in mind," said Will in a neutral tone.

"He's stubborn," offered Janice.

Sir Kyle nodded. "I'm well aware." He glanced back toward the ballroom. "I should return and mingle. If you get tired of the college you should think about coming back to help us, William. There's a good chance we'll be going to war and I could use a good officer."

Shocked, Will asked, "Officer?" He pointed at himself. "Me?"

"You don't think you could return as a wizard and be put in the rank and file, do you? I'd be a fool to put you back on the line."

"But I'm not licensed yet," explained Will. "It will be three and a half more years. Five if I want to graduate."

Sir Kyle chuffed. "As if I give a damn! I only know a little of what you did when you were with Company B, and I'm sure there's a lot I didn't hear about—and that was before you had any training. There will be a place for you. Keep that in mind if things get too hot for you in Cerria." The knight stepped away and gave a brief wave. "I'm off."

"He seemed to like you," observed Janice.

"He could have fooled me," said Will. "He was nothing like that when I was in the army."

"Being an officer is no small thing. You'd have a career, a stable income, and eventually a stipend when you retired. It might be better than staying in Cerria."

Something in her eyes suggested more. That perhaps he wouldn't have to go alone. Will shook his head. "You have to finish college, even if I don't. And I don't plan on giving up on Selene."

"I wasn't suggesting that. I know how you feel, but you need to remember she's getting married and there isn't much you can do about it."

Will thought about the necromantic spell he had learned, the same spell he currently had prepared and tucked away. He hadn't planned on doing anything with it, not so soon, but was tonight the right time? Would there ever be a right time? He'd be gambling with his life. *No, not with Janice here,* he told himself. *Who knows what would happen to her in the middle of that kind of chaos?* "Let's go back inside," he told her.

"Will you be able to behave?"

He nodded. "I'll be good. I promise."

CHAPTER 49

The ball was in full swing when they reentered, and couples swayed and swirled back and forth across the dance floor while musicians played from one end of the room. Will was dazed by the sight of so many colorfully dressed men and women moving back and forth. His eyes automatically searched the crowd, looking for a dark-haired woman with blue eyes.

He spotted Selene a minute later, as Malcolm Spry led her through an elegant series of turns across the floor. The man was an excellent dancer, which did nothing to assuage Will's frustration.

Janice took his hand. "Shall we?"

Will felt guilty when he looked at her. No one should be forced to attend such an event with a shoddy partner filled with jealousy and eyes for another woman. He resolved to be more attentive. With a smile he answered, "I think we should."

They joined the flow, and after adjusting their pace, Will found himself enjoying the dance. He'd improved considerably over the past two weeks, and while he was still a novice compared to most of those who graced the floor, he had nothing to be ashamed of. Janice positively glowed in his arms, attracting jealous gazes from many of the other ladies in the room. Wealth couldn't compete with natural beauty, and Janice had that in spades.

They went through the paces several times, and Will felt his shoulders begin to relax, though he tensed again when Selene and the count passed by a few feet from them. Selene met his eyes and he saw curiosity, frustration, and possibly jealousy reflected in them. She was studying Janice carefully.

Janice moved closer, putting her lips next to his ear. "I think she's jealous."

So am I, thought Will. "Should we take a break?" he asked.

"Admit defeat? I thought you were a warrior," she challenged.

"We're dancing, not fighting."

Janice gave him a sultry smile, then breathed into his ear, "The dance floor is a battleground too. Why not give her something to think about?"

From the corner of his eye he saw Count Spry's hand, pressing firmly against the small of Selene's back. Will's blood was rising again, and he whispered back, "I'm game."

"Put your hand a little lower," said Janice. "Hold me tighter."

"Are you sure?" asked Will hesitantly. If his hand went any lower, it would rest against the curve of her posterior in a rather scandalous manner.

"Confidence," she responded. "Don't be timid."

He lowered his hand and they moved on, their bodies close together. Janice smiled at him. "A little more." She leaned in, pressing herself into him.

Will let his hand slide a few inches lower, surprised by his own boldness. After a few minutes they passed Selene and her fiancé again and he was gratified to see Selene miss a step. Her eyes were boring into them.

The song ended, and he and Janice moved to the side to make room for other dancers while they caught their breath. His partner's face was flushed and her eyes bright. Janice gave him a grin full of mischief. "I think I enjoyed that a little too much," she admitted.

An older couple approached them from one side and the gentleman nodded at them. Will felt a chill when he recognized the man's face. It was the Royal Marshal, the man who had sent him to the dungeon in Cerria, Duke Vincent Arenata. "I believe we've met before, Mister Cartwright."

"Your Grace," returned Will, giving a shallow bow. "May I introduce my companion, Miss Janice Edelman?"

The duchess stepped forward, interrupting her husband's advance. "You may," she answered.

The Duke seemed slightly uncomfortable. "This is my wife, the Duchess Arenata."

"Lady Arlen will do," said the duchess.

Janice bowed and Will followed suit. "Your Grace, it's a pleasure to meet you," said Janice.

Arlen Arenata smiled. "Would you mind if I borrowed your young man for a dance Miss Edelman?"

"Not at all," she replied.

The duke stepped in. "I'll be happy to take you around the floor in the meantime."

Will watched helplessly for a moment as the duke whisked Janice away, then realized he was about to dance with the duchess. *Please don't let me screw this up,* he thought desperately. He held out his hand and tried to imagine it was Dianne he was dancing with.

He stiffened slightly as she touched his hand, for he felt something strange. Will forced himself to relax and recovered from a near blunder, and they began to dance. But he still felt it, an odd, alien quality in her turyn. Every person's turyn was slightly different, but something about Arlen Arenata's was beyond the norm, as though she wasn't quite human.

"Count Spry seems very happy," said the duchess idly, her eyes watching him.

Will nodded slightly. "I'm sure any man would be, if he could marry the king's daughter."

"Especially you," she observed. "Vincent told me about your adventure with her. You must have become very close."

"I consider her a dear friend," Will answered in a neutral tone.

The duchess smiled sadly. "It's a pity you aren't of higher station. So many things would be easier for you if you were. It seems unfair that a man of your talents has been given so little."

"I'm content with my life."

"Have you met Baron Nerrow? I saw him and his daughters a minute ago," said Arlen. "They're beautiful girls, blessed with everything they could wish for, and their father dotes on them terribly. It's a wonder they aren't spoiled."

Will struggled to keep his face blank. "I've seen them. They do seem very fortunate."

The duchess leaned in and whispered in his ear, "There's a rumor that Mark Nerrow had a bastard. Have you heard that?"

"I don't circulate in such high company often," Will responded. "So I don't really hear rumors or gossip."

"I find it a sad story. It isn't the son's fault. My husband's sister is Mark's wife, in case you didn't know."

"I think I'd heard that somewhere."

Arlen nodded. "I'm sure you did. I couldn't help but think, though. If that bastard child had wealth and power of his own, a title independent of his father's, they'd probably welcome him in with open arms. He'd be a blessing, rather than a threat, don't you think?"

What the hell is she suggesting? Will wondered. *Is she pushing me to accept an offer like the king did? If so, why?* "I couldn't speculate on that, Your Grace."

"Oh, of course not!" said the duchess. "I wasn't suggesting that you should. Is it true that you refuse to accept an elemental?"

Will was beginning to panic. *How did she hear that?* He decided not to deny it, though. "It is true."

"Would it be rude of me to ask why?"

Selene passed by, dancing now with Will's father, and he saw the look of concern on her face as she glanced at him and the duchess. She caught his attention for so long that he almost stumbled.

"Am I making you uncomfortable, Mister Cartwright?" asked the duchess.

Yes, very, he wanted to shout. "Not at all. I've refused an elemental because I think the practice is wrong."

"Have you ever considered that there might be other routes to power?" There was something dark and hungry in the noblewoman's eyes. "Power that might make you an attractive suitor in the king's eyes?"

Startled, Will let his surprise show. "The princess is already engaged."

"Count Spry isn't a young man. It's not beyond the realm of possibility that something might happen to him. Think of his poor wife! She was quite young, and yet he's a widower."

The dance was almost over, and Will couldn't wait to free himself from the duchess' cold touch. He was beginning to feel nauseous. "I'm not sure what you're suggesting."

"If you're curious you should call on me one day," said the duchess. "Preferably this coming week. My husband is busy with his work during the day, so we could converse without disturbing him."

The music faded away, and they stepped away from the dance floor. Will bowed to his partner and she smiled, then reached out and took his hand. "Think about it." Then she moved on to find other diversions.

Will looked down at the card she had left in his palm. It was a beautifully written calling card bearing the duchess' name and address. He stared at it for a moment, wondering what it could mean, then he took note of the address and a cold chill shot through him. It was the address of the house he had been watching the night before.

He needed to think, but before he could collect his thoughts Mark Nerrow approached with his younger daughter in tow. "Mister Cartwright, we meet again."

"Your Excellency," said Will, bowing again.

"Have you met my daughter, Tabitha?"

"I haven't had the pleasure, sir."

"This is her first year coming to the Winter Ball, but she's been looking forward to it for quite some time," said the baron. "She's been practicing all year to prepare." There was a not so subtle hint in Will's father's eyes.

For once, he wanted to comply. He gave Tabitha a warm look that was entirely genuine and bowed in deference. "Would you give me the honor of a dance, milady?"

Tabitha blushed, putting one hand over her mouth. "I'm not a lady, yet."

"May I call you Tabitha then?" asked Will.

"Please do, Mister Cartwright, if you'll let me call you William, that is."

He nodded and Mark Nerrow passed his daughter's hand to Will. "Enjoy yourselves. I've been needing a rest."

They took to the floor and Will did his best, though it was clear that Tabitha was far more experienced and agile. "I'm sorry if I'm not quite up to your expectations," he apologized.

"Nonsense," said Tabitha with a happy smile. "I'm just happy to dance with someone who isn't my father!"

Will found himself staring at her in wonder, searching her face for familiar features. *This is my half-sister,* he told himself, wishing he could share the knowledge with her.

Tabitha noticed his attention but misunderstood the reason. She glanced away with a faint smile. "William, you shouldn't stare."

"Pardon me, Tabitha. I was simply smitten by your grace and elegance. Your father must be very proud to have you for a daughter." He stretched out his hand and led her through a quick twirl.

"I wouldn't know about that," deferred the young girl. "But he's a good father, all things considered."

Will nodded. "You must love your family."

She gave him an odd look. "What a strange question. Doesn't everyone?"

"Most do," admitted Will. "But not everyone is so blessed."

"Like Selene?" suggested his sister with a coy smile. When she saw his surprise, she added, "Laina told me that you were close friends, so you probably know what I mean."

"N—not really," stuttered Will.

"I didn't mean anything serious. Just that it's been hard on her, what with having a king for a father."

Will nodded. "I can see that."

"Just between you and me, I think he's scary," said Tabitha secretively.

Will had no intention of being drawn into that line of discussion. Instead he asked a different question, "What do you think of Count Spry?"

"Oh, he's very nice!" she responded immediately. "Their entire family visited us a few years ago. I feel badly for him, losing both his son and his wife. Dennis was kind."

Will felt grateful that apparently Tabitha didn't know he was the one who had cut Dennis Spry's life short. "Hopefully Selene will be happy with him," said Will, fishing a little more.

"I'm sure she likes him, though it must be strange since he's around father's age," said Tabitha. "She never does anything unless she really wants to." His sister lowered her voice. "She was always fighting with her father because of that."

The dance came to an end, and Will felt someone tap on his shoulder. Glancing behind himself, his eyes widened when he saw Selene standing there. She smiled at Tabitha. "I see you've met my friend."

Tabitha nodded and gave the princess a grin, then moved forward to embrace her. "It's so good to see you, Selene! Why don't you ever visit us anymore? It's so dull with just Mother, Father, and Laina there."

"Sorry, Tabbycat," said Selene affectionately. "Life just keeps getting in the way. I promise I'll come see you someday soon—after the wedding."

Tabbycat, Will noted, feeling even more like an outsider. Selene shared more familiarity with his sisters than he ever would.

"Are you going to ask?" said Selene. "Or should I keep standing here? The music is starting again."

His eyes snapped into focus. "Would you like to dance?"

Selene flowed toward him, and Will's breath caught in his throat as they moved onto the floor. It took him a moment to get his breathing under control, but once he had, the first words that dropped from his lips were, "I'm sorry."

"No, you're not," she said without bitterness. "You believe what you believe. I disagree, but I won't hate you for it. I can't."

Will was amazed by her calm demeanor. "You seem remarkably accepting," he noted.

Her eyes met his for a moment, flashing an array of hidden emotions, then she looked away. "The past week has helped me find some perspective. Life is too short to bear grudges. Things are as they are. It's no use bemoaning what I can't change."

Selene's cool wisdom tore at his heart. *I don't want you to accept things as they are,* he cried internally. His arm tightened and he pulled her closer. "We could run away," he whispered.

"And do what?" she replied. "There's nowhere we could hide."

"I could take you anywhere. Trendham, maybe."

"If I gave up the elementals. Is that what you mean?" said Selene.

"I don't care anymore," said Will, letting his desperation show.

She pulled away, creating a little space between them. "You forget that I'm a slave," she remarked, a challenge in her voice.

"Prove me wrong. If you're right he can't stop us, and if you're wrong, I'll come back and free you, even if I have to move mountains to do it."

Selene's face held a look of resignation. "I've already made my decision, Will. No one's forcing me. Malcolm is a decent man, despite how his son turned out. It isn't as bad as you think, and if this will appease his need for vengeance, then it's worth it to me."

He wanted to scream, but he kept his calm. "It isn't worth it to me."

"You'll get over it," she said quietly. "There are other women. Your partner tonight is beautiful, and from what I've seen, intelligent as well. She comports herself well."

Despite her smooth words, Will could sense the jealousy hidden behind them. *How can she be so cool and collected?* he wondered. *Is it something they train into aristocrats from birth?* His jaw clenched. "Whatever you think is going to happen, won't," he warned.

"What does that mean?"

"I'm not going to quietly accept this. They'll have to drag me away from your wedding in chains, so forget about protecting me. I'll just ruin all your hard work," he told her.

She scowled at him. "Don't ruin our only dance."

"Can't we have another?"

"I'm expected to move around," she said sadly. "It's a fact of life for me. Everyone wants a moment."

"I'll visit you tomorrow," said Will, abandoning his pride.

"I won't be there," said Selene. "My future husband and I are attending a social at Lord Courtney's home."

"Then the next day," he suggested.

"Father expects me to entertain foreign dignitaries."

"The day after that?"

She gave him a sad look. "Give up, Will." Then she began listing her itinerary for the next week, just to show him how hopeless it was. He listened in despair, until one particular name caught his attention. "—and Friday we're attending a party hosted by Duchess Arenata," she finished.

His heart sped up and his mind began to race.

Selene went on, "Besides, what happened was a mistake. I don't intend to meet you again. I'll honor my promise, now as well as after the wedding."

"Don't go to the party," said Will, ignoring her declaration.

"Which party?"

"Arenata's," he clarified. "She's up to something. I felt something strange from her, and yesterday I—"

"May I cut in?" asked a male voice.

Will turned and looked in irritation at the man standing behind him. It was his father. "I'm not done—"

Mark Nerrow leaned in, speaking softly, "The music has already stopped. Don't be so obvious." Then he smiled at Selene and offered her his hand. "Would you do this poor old man the honor of a dance?"

Will was forced to accept the inevitable, so he gathered up the remnants of his dignity and moved to the side of the room. He spotted Janice across the floor, already dancing with yet another nobleman he didn't recognize, so he had a moment to himself.

Thinking back over Duchess Arenata's words, he felt certain that the woman was up to something, and the timing of her request for him to visit her was ominous. It was clear she wanted him to visit her before the party. That combined with the strange aura that surrounded her, and the fact that the demon trail had ended at her home, set off alarm bells in his mind.

He needed more information, and quickly.

Glancing around, he saw Sir Kyle talking to a lady. Will thought it was the knight's wife, but he wasn't entirely certain. He began making his way over, but Sir Kyle stepped away for a dance with another woman before he reached them. With a sigh, he approached the lady instead. "Excuse me, milady," said Will.

The woman was close to thirty, if Will had to guess her age, and she was tiny as well. She looked at him with friendly eyes. "Good evening—Mister Cartwright? Did I get that right?"

He nodded. "You know my name?"

"You're the young gentleman my husband was telling me about," she replied. "I'm Alice Barrentine." She stretched out her hand.

Will bowed over it for a moment, holding it close to his lips. "Lady Alice, it's a pleasure to meet you."

Her eyes darted toward the dancers. "Shall we?"

He gave her an apologetic look. "Forgive me, Lady Alice. I came to ask a favor of you and your husband."

"Oh?"

"Something has come up and I need to leave suddenly," he explained. "I wanted to ask if you'd be willing to give my companion a ride home later. I feel terrible for abandoning her." He took a moment to point out Janice, who was still dancing.

Lady Alice nodded, but gave him a curious look. "Have you at least told her you're leaving?"

"It's rather urgent." He backed away and headed for the exit, while Lady Alice scowled at his back.

As soon as he was outside, he increased his pace to a brisk walk, muttering quietly to himself, "Tailtiu, Tailtiu, Tailtiu…"

CHAPTER 50

As soon as he was away from the palace, he cast the chameleon spell, then headed for Wurthaven. He didn't bother using the gate but climbed the nearest portion of the wall and used the relative privacy within the campus ground to remove his jerkin, doublet, and hose, replacing them with his brigandine, a tunic, and trousers.

Feeling more comfortable, he recast the chameleon spell and crossed the wall again, heading into the city and plotting his course for the area where the Arenata home was located.

"Janice is going to kill me," he muttered to himself. "Not that I can blame her." Abandoning a lady at a ball was the height of discourtesy, but he couldn't afford to waste the opportunity. The ball would continue for several more hours, meaning that the duke and duchess would be out of their home for some time. There was even a fair chance they might have given their servants the night off since they wouldn't be back until late.

Without having any better knowledge of the Arenatas, he likely wouldn't be able to pick a better time to try and enter the house. He waited against a building close to their home, leaning against a wall and remaining still to get the best effect from his camouflage. While there he took a moment to put a silent armor spell on his clothing and then dropped his prepared spell, replacing it with a sleep spell.

Tailtiu arrived a quarter of an hour later. She was naked, as usual, but she had transformed into the form of an abundantly endowed human woman and had covered her nudity with an illusory dress. Despite his magics, she walked straight up to him. "You've gotten better," she said without preamble.

"How did you spot me?"

"Your spell isn't perfect. You're quite visible in heart-light," said his aunt. Then she grinned. "You smell delicious too."

All the polite discourse at the ball combined with the stress of the situation to put Will's head in a weird place. Without thinking, he replied, "Thanks, you smell nice too."

She grinned lasciviously. "Would you like a taste?"

His gears finally connected, and his brain snapped into motion. "Oh! No! I'm here to break into that house." Will pointed at the Arenata residence.

She looked him over. "With those magics you don't seem like you would need my help for this." Tailtiu examined the house for a moment, then asked, "Is it the demons?"

Will nodded. "I'm not sure how good their senses are, and I'm also worried there might be more inside. I thought I'd call an expert."

Tailtiu seemed pleased. "I'm touched that you think so highly of me," she said. "Most demons' senses are no better than those of humans, but there are exceptions. Give me a few minutes and I'll be back." She strolled away, her body becoming vague and indistinct as she went. Will struggled to keep his eyes focused on her as she crossed the road and walked to the side of the house, then went over the front wall so quickly that it was hard to tell if she jumped or climbed.

Will waited, and she returned a quarter of an hour later. "It's relatively safe. The ones on the roof are no better than humans, and I detected none inside."

"You went inside?"

She nodded. "A window on the second floor was open. The upstairs was empty, and the ground floor is occupied by two humans, a man and a woman in a room behind the kitchen. There's also a guard just inside the gate."

He was amazed by her nonchalant report, especially given the small amount of time it had taken. "Did you scout the entire house?"

Tailtiu shook her head. "You should experiment with your vision more. There are more kinds of light than just sunlight, starlight, and heart-light. It can be confusing, but with practice you can find people through walls and some barriers. I just looked around upstairs, made a quick peek downstairs, and then left the way I entered. I recommend you go to the back. There's a heavy door there, locked but unguarded. If you wish to use the front, you'll have to disable the guard."

He took her advice, moving slowly to avoid being spotted. Will passed down the narrow alley between the Arenatas' house and their neighbors' and entered the back alley. There was a heavy, ironbound door there with an impressive lock. It was a simple matter for his spell to open it, and then he was inside. Tailtiu followed him in.

He tried what she had mentioned, adjusting his vision to extremes that made it hard to see ordinary objects. Walls became diaphanous, and he feared that if he tried to walk, he might stumble into the furniture, but by remaining still and studying what he saw he could indeed spot the ghostly figures of two people in a nearby room. They were lying down, possibly sleeping.

Will began to get a headache, so he returned his vision to something close to normal with a heightened sensitivity to light so he could easily see in dim areas. Moving through the kitchen quietly, he made a quick circuit of the ground floor, but there wasn't anything to draw his attention.

Tailtiu tapped him on the shoulder. "Are you looking for demons or were you just wanting to avoid them?"

"Both."

They were standing beside the central staircase and she pointed at the wall that descended from the edge of the stairs to the ground. "There's a door there, and the stink of demons."

It took him a few minutes to find the hidden latch that released the door, allowing a section of the wall to swing out. A heavier door stood behind it, secured by a chain and padlock. Will used his unlocking spell again and removed them, keeping his eyes open in case there was a ward involved, but he saw no sign of magic. "I don't see any traces of demonic essence," he remarked.

"Not turyn," said Tailtiu. "Their smell. It lingers in the air behind the door."

Will prepared a demon-lance spell and opened the door, but nothing leaped out. A stone stair led downward to what must be a cellar or basement of some sort. "Should we go down?" Will asked nervously.

"That depends on you," said his aunt. "There might be demons below, or it may just be the smell left from their passing."

"If it comes to a fight, how many can you handle?"

"Without knowing the type and strength, it's impossible to say. A dozen of some, but there are others too powerful for me to face even one on one," she admitted. "Shall I scout ahead?"

He didn't want to keep relying on her or put her in situations he was afraid to face himself. "No, we'll go together." Stepping forward, he began to descend, grateful that his silent armor spell made his footfalls on the stone steps inaudible.

The stairs went down a considerable distance, much too far to be built for a simple cellar. They twisted around a central column, as though they were built into a tower, and when they finally stopped it was in a small room with a wide stone arch opening into a larger area. The archway was carved with runes, and turyn glowed and pulsed around its perimeter as well as in the air itself. Tailtiu frowned. "I cannot enter."

Will studied the wards, though as usual, he knew little of their function. Still, he believed he could bypass them in the same way he had the ward in the library. "I think I can get past," said Will. "Can't you do the same?"

She shook her head. "This is no ordinary magic. Look at the runes. Do you see the inlay? They're done in both silver and iron. The magic is infused with the properties of the metals. Very few beings not of this world could pass. In particular, demons and fae would not survive. You might, so long as you don't trigger the ward."

He'd started to worry as he listened to her. "Are you sure?"

Tailtiu shrugged. "You're a true wizard, though young. Unless my father gave the limnthal to someone unworthy, you should be able. Passive magics were never very effective against well-trained wizards."

Will had made up his mind. "Wait for me here. I won't stay long." He took a minute to attune himself to the ward, then stepped through while holding his breath. Nothing happened.

Inside, his eyes took in a vast chamber and he exhaled loudly. The area was circular, perhaps fifty feet in diameter, with a vaulted ceiling that sloped gradually up to a point in the center. A massive crystal jutted up from the center of the floor, and ten feet from it were circular channels laid out on the stone, forming a protective circle of some kind.

On the left side of the room was a stone pedestal with a human-shaped depression carved into its surface, as though it was meant for someone to lie upon. Iron rings protruded from the stone on each end, and chains ran through them and piled up on the floor. After a moment he realized their purpose. They were shackles, to bind the victim to the top of what must be a sacrificial altar.

He moved closer and noted small openings at the base of the altar, openings that were probably meant to direct blood into the channels on the floor. Will's stomach twisted, for there were already dark stains on the stone.

Copper runes decorated the entire circumference of the stone channels, and while he recognized the individual runes he couldn't guess at their purpose. He called up the limnthal and extracted an empty journal and a piece of charcoal. Then he began to make a rough sketch of the scene.

His drawing skills weren't the best, but he got the layout of the room, altar, and circle down, then began writing out the runes. It took a while, since the circle was so large. The charcoal wasn't well suited for writing, so he had to make the runes larger than the circle he had drawn, and he had to continue writing them out on the second page.

As far as notes went, his were a mess, but he had enough to reconstruct it in better detail later. He put the journal and charcoal away and then stepped forward to examine the crystal in the center. Will felt a vibration that started in his feet and went completely through him, making his teeth tingle. The crystal pulsed with turyn, as though it was reacting to his presence.

Will stretched out his hand toward it and felt a buzzing in his fingertips. As they got closer to the crystal, he felt pain and his skin began to smoke. Hastily, he withdrew, blowing on his hand. It was as though he had touched a hot stove.

The buzzing and vibrating stopped once he removed himself from the circle entirely. *What the hell is that thing?* he wondered. He was wise enough to guess that he shouldn't touch it, and there was nothing else to examine, so he decided it was time to leave. Will made one more visual inspection of the room as he made for the exit and noticed something he had missed before. Just beyond the altar was a tall iron stand. He'd mistaken it for some sort of lamp or sconce holder the first time, but in fact it supported a leather-bound book.

He took a few steps closer and read the name on its spine, *The Book of Seals*. For a moment he considered stealing it. *That would surely put a kink in their plans.* But if he did, it would be apparent that someone had broken in, and he wasn't ready to warn his potential enemy yet, so he left it alone.

Will returned to the antechamber where Tailtiu waited. "Let's go."

At the top of the stairs they heard a tinkling as the guard at the front gate pulled on a bellpull to alert the servants in the house. Fighting panic, Will put the chain back on the door and snapped the padlock into place, then shut the secret door. They hurried into the kitchen just before the two servants came hurrying out of their quarters to attend the arrival of their masters.

He felt a sense of accomplishment as they went out the back door and shut it behind them. Unfortunately, without the key he had no way of relocking the door, but hopefully when the servants discovered it they would assume they had forgotten to secure it. Most likely they would be afraid to report the oversight to the duke or duchess. Will made a mental note to see if there was a spell for locking doors the next time he went to the library.

Will let Tailtiu retire and returned to the college. As it happened, he saw a carriage pass down the lane as he walked back to his dorm. *Janice,* he thought. He quickened his step and managed to reach the entrance to the girls' dorm before she went inside.

The look she gave him was one of extreme displeasure coupled with concern. "You!" exclaimed his spurned dance partner.

Abashed, Will studied the ground. "I can explain—"

"Why bother?" she responded, irritation plain in her voice. "I already know what you'll say."

That surprised him. "You do?"

"Shall I make the excuses for you?" asked Janice. She didn't wait for a response. "I'm sorry, Janice. I had to do something dangerous and it couldn't wait, so I snuck off. No, I can't tell you what it is, it would only put you in danger as well. Oh, and by the way, someone stabbed me twelve times, but I'll be better in a few days, don't mind the blood on my clothes."

"I didn't get stabbed," said Will defensively.

She stepped forward aggressively. "You didn't? Maybe I should fix that for you."

Will stood his ground. "I really am sorry."

Janice deflated, then reached up to remove her earrings. "Do you need to return these?"

"They were a gift, not a rental," said Will. "Did you have fun tonight?"

Her eyes seemed to shoot flame for a second. "You really have the gall to ask me that?"

He shrugged, not knowing how to answer.

She sighed. "The first two hours were grand, until Lady Alice explained that you had abandoned the palace—and me. After that I pretended that you were still there, somewhere. I figured it might benefit you if no one knew you were actually gone. With me there they might not have realized."

He hadn't thought of that. *Damn, she's quick.* Will felt another surge of guilt, since he didn't deserve such a friend. He apologized again, earning himself yet another glare.

"Are you going to tell me what happened? Or will you really leave me in the dark—again?" she groused.

"Tomorrow," promised Will. He was beginning to realize he needed more opinions and Janice was definitely sharp enough to offer some insights he might have missed.

As soon as he was alone in his room, he consulted the ring. "I'm in over my head," he announced.

"Nothing new there," said the ring. "The miracle is that you haven't drowned yet, but then I suppose since you're already brain dead you don't need air."

Will felt a grin creep across his face. "I snuck into the Arenatas' home."

"I presume you had a reason," said Arrogan, "unless you've decided to start a new career as a housebreaker."

He relayed the tale of how he had tracked the demons, then added his talk with Duchess Arenata at the ball. "I found a book in her cellar too."

"What was it called?"

"*The Book of Seals.*"

A loud groan came from the ring. "Oh, please, not that one."

Will winced. "Is it bad?"

"The name is misleading," said Arrogan. "It's one of the hidden texts of the Priests of Madrok."

"It's their holy book?"

"There's nothing holy about it, but no, it's not their main religious text. *The Book of Madrok* is mostly useless gibberish. *The Book of Seals* deals in far more practical information."

Will's anxiety was increasing. "Practical how?"

"It details the rituals and rites necessary to summon many of the greater demons and generals who serve Madrok. The only bright side is that this duchess of yours couldn't possibly use it. The power requirements for those rituals are too high. She'll just wind up killing herself," Arrogan explained with a note of satisfaction.

"Maybe," replied Will. "I haven't told you what else I found in her house." He described the strange chamber beneath the manor, with its crystal outcropping and copper-inscribed ring. Will ended by detailing the altar and chains.

The ring said nothing for a moment, then began to speak in a somber tone. "Will, I want you to listen carefully. You need to leave Cerria. Go home and get your mother, then find a new place to live. Darrow isn't as bad as it sounds, or you could go to Trendham, they've got a very enlightened government if you like making money."

"Why?"

"Don't ask why. Just do it. Take that girl with you if you like her. What did you say her name was?"

"Selene."

"No, not her, the other one. Your princess is a lost cause."

"Janice?"

"Yeah, Janice. She sounds like she's got a level head on her shoulders. Take her, go get your family, and move to Trendham. Make some babies. If you're lucky, her good looks will offset your crippling ugliness and they won't turn out too bad. You can even finish mastering magic there. Maybe someday you can lead a magical revolution and start a new age of proper wizardry. Just don't stay in Cerria."

"I'm not leaving," said Will firmly. "So, you might as well tell me what's going to happen so I can do something about it."

"First, I don't know what will happen," said Arrogan, "not without seeing the circle you described firsthand, but I do know that it will be bad. Second, you aren't equipped to interfere with a strategic-class ritual. You'll only get yourself killed and the people in the city will still wind up suffering some awful catastrophe. The best thing you can do is go somewhere else."

"Strategic-class ritual? What does that mean?"

"Remember when you asked me about ley lines?"

"Yeah."

"Cerria sits atop the crossing point of two major ley lines. It's one of the reasons the city was built here. Back in my day, there was a chamber just like the one you described. I thought it was buried, but apparently someone figured out where it was and excavated the damned thing. The crystal you saw was the contact point, a device used to tap into the ley lines. Are you beginning to see where I'm going with this?"

"You think she's going to destroy the city?"

"Not necessarily, but if you go in there and try to stop her you almost certainly will. You can't stop a ritual like that without causing feedback."

Will repeated himself. "I'm not leaving, so tell me what *you* would do if you were alive, because I know you wouldn't just sit back and watch everything go to hell."

"You don't know that. I was stubborn, not stupid," said the ring in a grouchy tone.

"I *do* know that. You ruined your life and your marriage just to get rid of sorcery. Stop trying to make me do the wise thing and tell me what I can do."

Arrogan sighed. "I don't know. I can't *see* the ritual that you sketched out. The only person who could decipher it would be Aislinn. Does she owe you a favor?"

Will knew the answer to that. "No."

"Then get out of town. You can't afford her price whatever it might be."

"She's my grandmother," Will reminded him.

"She's *fae*! Whatever hidden sentiment there is in her heart doesn't mean a damn to her. Trust me, I know!"

"If that's all you're going to say then we're done talking," said Will.

"Listen up, you little shit! If you think you can shut me—" Arrogan's voice ended abruptly as Will dismissed the limnthal.

He stared at the wall for half an hour while he thought about everything he had learned. He knew Arrogan was right. He didn't know enough. He didn't have the power necessary. He was inadequate in every way, but he didn't have to do it alone.

He still wasn't ready for sleep, so he practiced with the point-defense spell until his mind was numb and his body was tired enough to rest.

CHAPTER 51

The next morning Will ran through his spellcraft exercises then set about recopying his hastily made sketch of the chamber beneath the Arenata home. He redid the drawing of the room, including the central crystal and circle, then made a separate drawing of the circle with the runes inscribed around it. He used pen and ink this time and took his time so he could actually fit the runes around the circle.

It still wasn't perfect, but he hoped it would be enough for Aislinn to sort out what the circle was meant to do. With his preparations made, Will dressed in his brigandine and a simple tunic, then set out. He headed out of the city and made his way to the congruence point that Tailtiu had met him at once before. Once there he called Aislinn.

He felt a connection after he uttered her name, but it wasn't a positive response. Will waited anyway. An hour later he called her name again. While he waited, he practiced the point-defense spell, and when that became too boring, he ran through his other spells once more. Since he was in an open field, he also took the opportunity to actually practice casting the wind-wall spell so he could get a better feel for its effects as well as how quickly he could recover from using virtually all of his turyn at once.

He couldn't say for sure, but it felt like he was getting better at it, both in his ability to draw in a large amount of turyn quickly, as well as the sheer quantity he could hold and use at once. He wondered what his limit was, or if there was one. *There has to be,* he told himself, *otherwise there'd be no reason for people to create rituals to tap into ley lines.*

Another hour passed and despite the winter sun, his body was growing cold in the constant wind that blew across the field. He called again, and this time he could feel annoyance from Aislinn's end of the connection. *Too bad,* he thought. *This is too important for me to leave you be.*

Will went back to practicing the point-defense spell and another hour passed. Just as he was about to call again, he saw a figure walking toward him across the field. It was Tailtiu. He waved and waited until she had reached him.

"This is counting against the time you bargained for," she stipulated as soon as she was within earshot.

"Fine. Where's your mother? I need to speak with her."

"She's busy. She told me to warn you that if you keep calling her she may lose her temper."

Will arched one brow. "I wasn't aware of self-restraint being a thing for the fae."

"You're still alive, aren't you?" said his aunt.

"Point taken. Can you give her a message for me?"

"I am at your service after all," she responded. "What's your message?"

"Someone is planning to tap into the ley lines and enact a strategic-class ritual in the city. I think they're planning to summon a demon lord or something similar." He summoned his journal and showed Tailtiu his drawings. "I was hoping she could tell me what this will do. These are the drawings I made after our scouting mission last night."

His aunt sneered. "Why do you think she would care?"

Will stared at her for a moment, thinking carefully. *Why indeed?* "Aren't demons and fae enemies?"

"Demons are inimical to all living beings," returned Tailtiu. "But we have no particular concern for what they may do to humankind."

"Tell her I plan to stop the ritual, one way or another," said Will, remembering what Arrogan had told him. *If she has any concern for me at all, she'll want to see what it will do.*

Tailtiu shrugged. "I'll pass your message to her." Then she left.

Will waited another hour, continuing his practice, before giving up. He sat down in the grass and stared at his knees. He felt lost. The whole world was going to hell and no one knew or cared enough to help. *That's not true,* he reminded himself. *You just want to wallow in self-pity.*

He thought about his options again. The one that made the most sense was contacting the king. As much as he disliked the man, he doubted King Lognion would turn a blind eye to even his most trusted retainer trying to use such a ritual within the city.

He didn't trust the king, however, and he suspected that Selene's engagement to Count Spry was partly to punish him. It was ridiculous to think that, since he was completely beneath consideration, but it felt that way no matter what his logical mind told him.

Will got up and dusted off his trousers. Janice was probably looking for him, anticipating his explanation. No one else wanted to listen to him anyway. *Besides, she understands the politics of the nobility far better than I do.*

Back at Wurthaven, he discovered that Janice wasn't in the girls' dorm, so he went back to his room. Dianne caught him before he went upstairs and told him that Janice had been by twice looking for him.

"I'll be in my room if she returns," he told the resident assistant. Will went upstairs and did what he did best, mindlessly practice. After a while he got so bored that he fell asleep sitting on the bottom bunk.

When he woke, it was to the sound of someone knocking on the door. He rose and found Janice standing in the hall. "Where have you been?" she demanded.

"Trying to talk to the goddess of magic," he snapped.

That set Janice back on her heels. She slipped around him and went inside while he closed the door. "I never know when you're joking," she told him.

"I rarely do. It's just that my life is so laughably absurd that the plain truth usually sounds like a joke when I try to explain it."

She gave him a serious look. "Are you saying you really were trying to talk to the goddess of magic?"

He nodded. "She isn't really a goddess, though, just a fae wizard from antiquity."

"And you think she might respond to you?"

"She's my grandmother, sort of."

Janice held up her hands. "Let me sit down. The more you talk the less sense you make."

"I have a lot of secrets," Will warned.

She nodded and scooted back on the bottom bunk so she could rest her back against the wall. "There's no class today and I've got plenty of time."

He debated with himself, wondering how much he should tell her. Almost no one had heard everything, and he tended to keep things even from those who knew most of his story. Arrogan and Aislinn were the only ones that he hadn't kept anything significant from. Could he tell Janice all of it, when he hadn't even shared as much with Selene? *Well, Janice isn't bound by an enchantment for one thing,* he observed, *and she doesn't owe fealty to anyone.*

She had the added advantage of not being biased in any way regarding the various supernatural factions he dealt with. She probably knew next to nothing about the fae, the goddamn cat, or demons. Janice wasn't a sorcerer, or connected with any political factions—she was just his friend. *And she fancies me,* he reminded himself. *So, she's probably as loyal as anyone could possibly be.* That could be a problem later, though, if jealousy caused her to become scornful of him.

He decided to be honest. It was far past time to find someone he could trust. "I have a question for you first."

"All right."

"I know you have some feelings for me. I worry that later you might become resentful. You already know where I stand, but some of these secrets could be used against me—"

Janice cut him off. "I've spent most of my life with an axe over my head, in one form or another. The Spry family always had my family in the palm of their hands. Coming to Wurthaven was just the latest example of their generosity, generosity that could be taken away at a moment's notice. Even if I came to hate you, I wouldn't betray your trust."

"Here goes then," said Will, and he began his story, starting from the beginning. He told her about his first meeting with Selene, his training with Arrogan, the invasion of Darrow, and his complicated relationship with the fae. He even included the goddamn cat, which was something very few people knew about. With that background, he moved on to his time at Wurthaven and gave her the details of the attempts on his life and some of his activities that were outside of the law. The only thing he restrained himself on was his time in Selene's room. He only shared enough so that she would know his relationship was more than an unrequited love. His break-in at the library and at the Arenata house were what he finished with.

Janice's face went through a variety of transformations during his story, but she managed to wait for him to finish—somehow. When he eventually ended, she asked, "Are you done?"

He nodded.

"Sweet Holy Mother Temarah!" she exploded. "Was all of that true?"

"As far as I remember it."

"You slept with the princess? What were you thinking?"

He held up his hand. "I never *said* we slept together."

She goggled at him. "Do you expect me to believe you didn't?"

"Only if you're going to throw things," he said jokingly.

Janice didn't laugh. "She might be pregnant. Have you thought about that? How careful were you?"

"It was my first time," he said defensively. After a second he added, "Hers too."

Her eyes narrowed. "Did she ask you to be careful?"

That was a question that hadn't occurred to him. "No. It was in the heat of the moment. I don't think either of us were thinking clearly."

"She was thinking clearly, you dimwit. Women don't forget something like that! Hell, she practically ambushed you. So, I'll ask again, how careful were you?"

Will was blushing several shades of red by then. "The first time caught me by surprise, but after that—"

Janice covered her face with one hand. "This is so fucked up," she muttered. "She was trying to get pregnant, or at the very least, she didn't care."

"I don't think so," said Will.

"She's getting married," spat Janice. "Consciously or not, she was trying to take some part of you with her, or maybe she wanted some sort of revenge against her future husband. It's the same either way, though, whether she was motivated by love or hate."

It made a pretty big difference in Will's mind, but he held his tongue. Janice's perspective was already helping him to see things that had never occurred to him.

Janice gasped again. "Your child could be the next king!"

Will frowned. "I don't think so. Selene can't take the throne, so if Lognion dies it would go to the closest male—"

"That's Malcolm Spry," Janice informed him. "He's a distant cousin from several generations back."

"Isn't there anyone more closely related?"

"The throne has been passed through a single line of fathers and sons since Terabinia was founded. None of the other children survived. That's why Selene doesn't have any uncles or close relatives. Her brother should have inherited, though I suppose it's no surprise since he wasn't named Lognion."

"Why would he be given his father's name?"

She shrugged. "All the surviving heirs were named Lognion. That's why all our kings have had the same name. I guess it's tradition."

Will felt a strange sense of foreboding. He hadn't thought about it before, but if Selene's older brother had died, then his father had probably made an elemental out of him. Had his death been deliberate or accidental? Would Lognion mark his eventual heir with his own name and kill all his other children?

Janice went on. "Anyway, the point here is that if the king dies, Malcolm will become king and his son, if Selene bears one, would be the next king. Do you see what I mean now?"

It was a sobering thought, except Will had no intention of letting the marriage occur unchallenged. That was something he couldn't bear to think about. "I think so."

"No, I don't think you do. Let's consider different scenarios. Suppose the count finds out she's pregnant with your child. He'll most likely kill it. If the king found out instead, who knows what he'd do. He might hide the fact for her sake, or kill it for Spry's."

"This is all assuming she's pregnant," said Will. "That's still a big if."

"You're both eighteen," countered Janice. "It's not a big if, and the consequences are so big you should keep it in mind."

The entire conversation made Will think of his own father, and he wondered if Mark Nerrow had been forced to deal with similar circumstances. For the first time he felt a small portion of sympathy for the man.

"There's something else to think about," said Janice. "Do you know who's third in line for the crown, if Lognion doesn't have an heir?"

Will had no idea and said as much.

"It's Vincent Arenata."

"Shouldn't it be the other way around?" asked Will. "The duke is the higher ranked of the two."

She shook her head. "Their relative power and rank doesn't matter at all. For inheriting the throne it's only the strength of their relationship to the royal line that matters."

A sinister picture was beginning to come together in Will's head. If the king died suddenly, Malcolm Spry would inherit, but if the king and Spry both died, it would be Vincent Arenata. A demonic catastrophe that could be blamed on Darrow would be the perfect cover. One thing didn't fit, though. "If Arlen Arenata is trying to set up a situation in which her husband becomes king, why would she want to talk to me? She's bound to offer me what I want, which is Selene, but leaving her alive would mess things up."

"You're misunderstanding," Janice corrected him. "Selene can't inherit. It's only Count Spry she has to worry about, or his child. If Selene doesn't marry him, or if she's shown to have your child in her womb, then the throne is free and clear, so long as Malcolm dies. She probably wants to enlist your aid in getting rid of Spry, since you have a clear motive. You want Selene."

"What about the ritual?"

She shrugged. "I don't have any idea."

"She's probably planning something big to get rid of both at once," Will speculated. "She might need help making sure Count Spry is in the right place when it happens." Another thought occurred to him. "The marriage to Spry makes more sense now too. If Selene marries him and has a child, then Lognion knows Arenata can't kill him to get power. The child would be the main target."

Janice nodded. "If Selene had a son he would be next in line, even if Spry and Arenata were both alive. She can't inherit, but her child would have a stronger claim than either of them."

"The assassination attempt on the palace makes sense now too," Will pointed out. "If the Arenatas knew about the impending marriage, they'd want to nip it in the bud."

"And Spry was there the same day, so they could kill two birds with one stone," agreed Janice. "You stopping the assassination is probably what made them desperate enough to try this ritual."

It all fit together, and it led to an answer that Will didn't like. To save Cerria, he would have to save Count Spry. If he left matters as they were, then the king, who he'd already promised to kill, would die. If Lognion and Spry both died, there would be no serious obstacles left to him marrying Selene. He could fulfill his promise to Arrogan without personally killing Selene's father. It was a double win for him.

How bad could this ritual be? he wondered. Obviously, the Arenatas expected to survive whatever was coming. Arrogan's advice was looking better with each passing moment.

The only problem was his conscience. Will had no love for King Lognion—the man was psychotic, and he was using Wurthaven as a farm for human souls to produce elementals—but the alternative looked worse. The Arenatas were willing to resort to using demons to gain power, and they weren't shy about furthering the war with Darrow either, if it covered their motives.

Will wasn't quite sure which was worse, but if he chose to side with the king it might destroy his chances to stop Selene's wedding. Could he sacrifice his own heart's desire if it was better for the people?

The door to his room opened without warning, surprising Will. He was sure he'd locked it. When he looked up, he saw Aislinn standing in the doorframe, her presence filling the room. Will turned to Janice, who he was sure must be worried, but he saw that she was already asleep.

Aislinn gave him a murderous smile. "Grandson."

CHAPTER 52

"Grandmother," said Will, momentarily lost for words. His brain caught up a second later. "I thought you weren't coming."

"After your incessant calling, and that message from my daughter, how could I not?" responded the fae lady. "At the very least I need to make sure you learn a lesson for your rash actions."

Will knew she couldn't harm him directly. He hadn't early on, but after learning about the accord he knew he had less to fear than she intimated. "The accord—"

Aislinn's hand was around his throat, her nails digging in. He wasn't sure when she had moved, but she was right in front of him now. "You're right. I wouldn't dare snap your neck with this hand, or tear open your veins to watch you bleed to death in front of me. You're perfectly safe from that."

Will was struggling to breathe, and for some reason his grandmother's words weren't comforting.

She went on, "But do you think any of that would stop me? If I desired it, you would have been dead long ago, perhaps not by my hand, but you would be dead all the same." Aislinn released him and took a second to smooth out his tunic, her face the very picture of motherly concern. She stepped back and smiled, admiring her work. "There, that's better. I simply abhor wrinkles."

He wasted no time apologizing. "I'm sorry, Grandmother. I was afraid and you were the only one who could help me."

Her eyes were cold as death. "As it will always be, my pet. In the future be sure to show proper respect and I won't be tempted to do something rash."

"May I speak with you for a short time? The usual terms?"

Aislinn shook her head. "Not today. I'm afraid you've become spoiled. You will have to pay in advance if you wish to receive my advice."

Will tried to think of something he could safely offer her. He already knew an egg wouldn't suffice. *If only the fae were a little more like the goddamn cat,* he thought.

"I want the girl," said Aislinn.

He shook his head. "You can't have Janice."

Aislinn showed her teeth. "I meant the princess."

"No."

The Mistress of Magic gave him an odd look. "I haven't even told you what I would do with her. Are you certain?"

I'm not going to wind up like Grandfather. "I won't make that bargain. Ask for something else."

"A single year," said his grandmother, holding up one finger. "You can have her back then."

He scowled. "It wouldn't matter. She'd be like you."

"I'll return her with her humanity intact."

Will didn't believe it. Maybe she would still be human, but he couldn't imagine a year with the fae wouldn't cause some kind of irreparable harm. "You can't promise she wouldn't be changed somehow."

"She would certainly be changed," agreed Aislinn, "but she would be human."

And what if she is pregnant? thought Will. The child would be born fae if Selene was living on the other side. He shook his head. It was all a moot point anyway. "I'm not bargaining with someone else's life, certainly not Selene's. All I want is some advice. It isn't worth the price."

Aislinn smiled. "Then I have only one other offer. Grant me one unbound favor and I will give you my advice."

"What if you don't know anything useful?" suggested Will. "It's a very obscure ritual. Do you want me to risk such a valuable thing for an uncertain gain?"

His grandmother frowned. "Who knew you would be such a vexatious child. Very well, let me see this ritual and I will give you my judgment. If I deem the information vital, I will tell you so and you will grant me the favor. If it isn't, I will tell you such and we can come to different agreement if you wish to know what I know. You know that I cannot lie."

He mulled it over. It was true that she couldn't lie. If she saw the ritual and discovered something that he desperately needed to know, she would tell him, and the reverse was also true. Reluctantly, he answered, "Deal."

She held out her palm and Will produced his journal. "I sketched this from a chamber I discovered under the Arenatas' home. The ring says it's the old contact point for the ley lines beneath Cerria.

The circle is laid with copper runes and stone channels for blood." He pointed out the altar and showed her his separate inscription of the runes.

Aislinn studied it for several minutes. "This is more worrisome than I anticipated, but I must be honest. You do not need to understand this ritual. You could simply leave the city and you wouldn't suffer. In fact, your personal situation might improve if you allow this to proceed without interfering."

"I don't plan on leaving the city."

"Then you desperately need my knowledge, otherwise you are likely to die."

"Why?"

"Will you pay the price?" His grandmother lifted one brow questioningly.

"One favor," he said, nodding.

"One *unbound* favor," clarified Aislinn. "There will be no conditions on it. If I ask you to die, you will die. Are we clear?"

"Could I trade you the one Tailtiu owes me?"

"What use would I have for such a favor from her?" said Aislinn with a snort. "There is nothing she can give me that I do not already have. A favor from you is much more valuable."

"Then I guess we have a deal. One unbound favor."

Aislinn's laughter rang out, filling the room and sending chills up his spine. She leaned close and whispered in his ear, "You will come to regret this choice. When I claim this favor you will learn the greatest pain that the human heart can experience." Her breath tingled against his neck. "Look forward to it," she murmured.

Will closed his eyes and clenched his teeth, then relaxed. What was done was done. "Tell me what I need to know."

"So dramatic, Grandson. Relax. I will make certain you have the knowledge necessary to save your people, your friends, and your lover. The first thing you must be made aware of is the fact that this ritual has already begun. It began roughly three weeks before you entered the chamber."

"How do you know?"

"That was the last time the moon was full," said Aislinn, her voice full of certainty. "It must be completed on the night of the next full moon, this Friday. Otherwise the consequences to the city will be severe. The feedback might destroy much of the city center."

He blanched. "How do I stop it?"

"Stopping it is simple," she replied. "Kill the one who initiated the ritual and wait for Friday to pass. If the second step isn't completed, the ritual magic will crumble."

"That sounds fairly simple."

"It is, if you don't mind the contact point overloading with magic that has no outlet or purpose. I believe I already mentioned that such an event would lead to the catastrophic destruction of a substantial portion of the city."

Will held up his hands. "All right. Let me be more specific. How do I stop the ritual without destroying anything?"

"You don't."

He sighed in exasperation. Sometimes his grandmother could be so blunt and straightforward that she became cryptic even in honesty. He knew she understood what he wanted to know, but she was going to force him to tease it out of her bit by bit. "So, supposing that I don't stop the ritual from being completed, what will happen?"

"Whoever initiated this did so with a blood sacrifice. They will end it with another sacrifice, so one thing to consider is that someone will be murdered, though it doesn't matter too much who they choose. Once the dying blood enters the channels in the floor the final phase will begin."

Will stopped her there. "Dying blood? Why did you phrase it that way?"

Aislinn gave him a wicked smile. "Since you are paying so well, I'll include a lesson in magic. Everyone assumes that blood sacrifice is about harvesting a soul, or that the blood itself has some special property. It doesn't. Blood sacrifice merely requires blood from a living being, even an animal will do. The crucial point is that the blood is alive, and that after its removal it begins to die. This death, spread out across a ritual circle, facilitates one of the simplest and most efficient types of turyn conversion. In this case it will be used to convert the vital turyn of the ley line into void turyn that can be used to create a gate between your world and the demonic realm that Madrok resides in."

"So, the ritual circle is acting like a transducer," said Will.

She nodded. "I believe that is the term the wizards today prefer."

"What if the second phase was started using a different catalyst?"

His grandmother gave him a look of approval. "An interesting idea, but one that would likely prove to be even more catastrophic. The contact point is already filled with a large amount of void turyn. Finishing the process with a vital type would produce an even larger explosion."

"Hmm. So I need to continue with blood, or at least something that produces the same type of turyn."

"Indeed."

"What will happen when this gate opens?"

"It will be large enough for a major demon to enter, likely whichever one the creator of the ritual named. There will also almost certainly be an army of lesser demons that come with their master. If the circle master has made a bargain with the demons, they'll kill whatever targets he or she has stipulated, along with whoever else they encounter."

Will thought about it for a moment. His frequent bargains with the fae gave him a certain amount of experience with difficult deals and that brought him to another question. "What things would these demons be interested in? More specifically, what would the ritual master have likely bargained with?"

"An excellent question. Demons are primarily interested in souls. They cannot survive in this world indefinitely, but they can use the souls they take to create more demons or to power their infernal creations back in their own world."

A certain parallel became apparent to him. "Sort of like how sorcerers use them to create elementals."

"Exactly. Except they use them to create sources of void turyn, either by creating more demons or incorporating them into vile machines or enchantments," said Aislinn. "Now let me finish. A major demon would either desire a large number of sacrifices up front, which doesn't seem to be the case here, or the promise of a period of freedom in which to harvest souls themselves. Very likely, your enemy has chosen to offer the demons the latter in exchange for killing certain specific people first."

King Lognion and Count Spry, thought Will. "What about those the ritual master doesn't want killed?"

"That number would necessarily be small, otherwise the demons won't agree to it," said Aislinn, "but probably there will be a mark of some sort to be given to those who will be granted protection."

He was beginning to get a clear picture of what the duchess probably intended to do, but he had more questions. "You've explained the blood channels, but what about the copper inlay? That portion of the circle appears to have a different purpose."

"There are always two ways to motivate, the carrot and the stick. Copper is an efficient metal when creating enchantments involving fire," noted his grandmother. "The person who created the ritual is probably not well versed in this fact. I doubt they intend to use the punitive portion of the circle at all. They may have copied it there simply because it was included in the original instructions in the book."

Will frowned. "So the copper part is for punishing the demons?"

"If one doesn't wish to pay them in souls, the other option is to torture them into submission. The rewards are far more limited, however."

"Could I simply punish them until they go back home?"

"It's possible, though you would incur a very deep and personal grudge. Consider this: the Shimerans pay a high price for the aid they receive from Madrok's minions, but if you incite his wrath he may well begin offering them his aid for a lower cost if they agree to destroy Terabinia and you with it."

"That's an awfully specific outcome."

"It's what I would do," Aislinn said sweetly. "Angering a demon lord might achieve your short-term goal but result in greater death and suffering in the long term as they seek vengeance against you."

Will chewed his lip. None of his options sounded particularly appealing. "Could I direct the demons to kill enemies of Terabinia, like the Patriarch?"

"One man would hardly be enough to satisfy them, but the short answer is no. Darrow is too far from where the ritual is located. Otherwise the Shimerans would have already taken over the world using similar tactics. Demons can't survive here for long periods, so the targets need to be in Cerria or close by."

He was a little relieved to hear that. The idea of sending a demon army off to slaughter innocents in another nation wasn't very appealing to him, though it was obviously better than letting them kill his countrymen.

Will had his answers. He knew what he would need to do. Now he only needed to learn the specifics. "Can you teach me how to control the ritual?"

Aislinn's smile was laced with venom. "I thought you'd never ask. It will take some time to educate you in the specifics."

"How long will Janice sleep?" asked Will.

"As long as we need, an hour or two."

"Let's get started then."

Chapter 53

Janice woke with a yawn and stretched. After a second, she sat up with a start when she realized she was still in Will's room. Her eyes locked onto him. "How did I fall asleep?"

"It probably had something to do with my brilliant conversational skills," said Will.

His friend got to her feet and surreptitiously checked her clothing. Will presumed it was for signs of tampering. "Really?" he asked. "You know me better than that."

"Think about what I've been through," she reminded him. "I'm always a little suspicious, even if I know you wouldn't do anything like that. I can't help it." Satisfied that nothing had happened to her, she resumed a casual tone. "So, where were we?"

"You corrected a lot of my ignorance regarding the nobility and we sorted out the motivations of the Arenatas. I have to thank you," said Will. "I never would have understood things so clearly without your help."

She squinted at him. "You sound as if we're done."

Will nodded. "I know what I need to do now, or at least I have a better idea."

Janice motioned for him to continue. "And that would be…?"

He adopted an apologetic countenance. "I'm afraid that my forthrightness ends here. The past I have shared, but the future remains my own."

"You sound like a poet," observed Janice. "I'm not sure it suits you. Are you telling me that you've made a plan, but you aren't going to share?"

"Calling it a plan would be giving me too much credit," said Will with a smirk. "But I've got a rough idea of what I'll do."

"Then why won't you explain?"

To keep you from trying to stop me, he thought. "There's not much you can do to help and knowing would only put you at risk."

"I'd rather judge that for myself."

"Too bad," he responded cheerfully. Taking her hand, he led her to the door. "You've already been a huge help to me."

She glared at him. "And now you're tossing me out?"

"Yep."

She left after a few minutes of growling and complaints, and Will settled in for more practice at his spellcraft. As usual he focused on the point-defense spell, though he didn't expect to improve enough for him to be able to reflex cast in within a week. *Still, if I survive this week, I'll need it in the future.*

And he definitely intended to survive, at least until the wedding. Beyond that nothing was certain.

The rest of the weekend was boring in the extreme, as he did nothing but practice. Occasionally he ran through his other spells, but he spent most of his time on the defense spell as Arrogan had advised him.

He'd considered going to the king with what he had learned, but after hearing Aislinn's explanation he felt it was a bad idea. King Lognion was corrupt and power hungry. The man would likely choose to try and manipulate the ritual to his own ends if it couldn't be stopped. Will couldn't allow that any more than what he anticipated the duchess would do with it.

Selene was one of the few he trusted to do the right thing, but she was still firmly under her father's control, so he was limited in how much he could share with her. He would try to contact her after his meeting with the duchess. Only then would he be sure of all his options.

Monday finally came and he went through the motions of attending his morning classes, but once it was time for lunch, he made his way to the school gate and walked into the city. Will didn't bother sneaking out or otherwise trying to hide his exit. The one who had been trying to kill him was waiting for his visit. She wasn't likely to attempt to kill him again until she had heard his answer.

When he was just a block from the Arenata residence, he noticed a stray cat had begun following in his wake. He stopped and looked back at the grey tom. "I didn't expect to see you."

The goddamn cat didn't answer, as usual. With a shrug, Will went on, ignoring his presence. The cat followed him all the way to the front gate and sat patiently while he rang the bell. A guard appeared and inquired, "And you would be?"

"William Cartwright. I'm here to see Duchess Arenata if she isn't otherwise engaged," he responded.

"One moment," said the man. He left and went into the house but returned a few minutes later. "If you will follow me." The gate swung open.

Will followed the guard to the front door, where he was greeted by a manservant who ushered him inside. From there he was led to the front parlor and asked to wait. As he sat down, he noticed the cat was lounging on the floor across from him. "She's going to see you," he warned, keeping his voice to a whisper.

The cat ignored him, seemingly only interested in bathing himself.

After a few minutes, Duchess Arenata appeared, followed by a maidservant carrying a tray set with a silver teapot and two cups. She gestured to the table and waited until the tray was deposited. "See that we're not disturbed, Miriam," ordered the duchess. Duchess Arenata studied Will with a pleased look, and it was only after a second that he realized he had committed his first faux pas.

Will jumped up and gave a short bow. "It's a pleasure to see you, Your Grace. I'm honored you would let me call on you in your home."

Arlen Arenata's lips stretched into a thin smile. "I am glad you chose to come. Please, do sit." She gestured to the chair he had just been sitting on a moment before. She followed suit, sitting across from him.

Will's eyes darted to the cat, but he was no longer where he had been. He started to relax, then noticed the goddamn cat was now sitting directly beneath the duchess' chair. *When did he move to there?*

"Are you all right, Mister Cartwright? You seem somewhat distracted," observed the duchess.

"Yes, Your Grace. To be honest, I'm nervous. This is the first time I've been invited to the home of someone so austere."

"Hopefully you find my home pleasant."

He nodded. "I do, though I'm curious as to what you wish to speak with me about."

"Shall I be blunt?" she asked.

"If you wish. I'm not well experienced with courtly graces," admitted Will.

"When you first came to Cerria, there were rumors that you engaged in certain illegal practices, warlockry to be specific."

Will showed surprise. "The king knows I'm innocent of those charges. It's why he had me released."

She smiled knowingly. "Let's be honest with one another. We're both initiates in forbidden arts. I heard you were quite gallant in your defense of the princess when demons came to take her."

Why would she bring that up? She was the one that sent the demons. "I'm not sure what you're driving at, Your Grace."

"You slew a fairly powerful demon, Mister Cartwright, without the use of an elemental. You don't expect me to believe you're simply a wizard, do you?"

"Her Highness had two elementals with her," stated Will.

"Neither of them were fire elementals. Earth and water are ill suited to dealing with demons," countered Arlen. "The fact that the two of you survived, not to mention your other interesting exploits, leads me to believe you are receiving help from other powers. Am I wrong?"

She thinks I'm a warlock, he realized. "It wouldn't be wrong to suggest that," he dissembled.

"Then I'm also sure you are probably familiar with the art of bargaining."

He nodded. "I am." It was then that he noticed the duchess had no elemental with her. He had gotten so used to seeing them with nobles that he had simply assumed she had one. He knew her husband had several. *Did she take up demonology to fill a perceived lack?* "What are you proposing?"

"I'm offering you quite a substantial reward, in exchange for almost nothing on your part. I simply want your promise not to interfere in my affairs. A pledge of neutrality if you prefer to think of it that way."

"I don't think I've ever interfered in your affairs, Your Grace."

Her eyes flashed. "Don't play dumb, Mister Cartwright. You know far more about current circumstances than you let on. How else do you explain your presence the day the princess and Count Spry nearly died?"

Dumb luck? he thought, but then he corrected himself. *No, it was the goddamn cat.* The same cat that was currently washing itself beneath her chair. *She thinks I figured out her plans a long time ago, at least before the assassination attempt.* He wanted to laugh. He wished he had known so much back then. He decided to take a risk. "Very well, I won't insult your intelligence. I presume you want to make sure nothing goes wrong on Friday. Am I correct?" A faint look of alarm crossed over the duchess' features, then vanished. *She didn't think I knew that much,* he noted.

Covering her surprise, she responded, "I see I wasn't wrong about you. That's why I'm willing to offer you something you seem to greatly desire."

"What would that be?" he asked blandly, affecting disinterest.

"Princess Selene, not to mention the possible gratitude of a king."

"And by king you are of course referring to the new one to take Lognion's place," he added.

The duchess nodded.

"Demons aren't known for their discretion," Will observed. "How can you promise her safety in the event that something terrible happens to the inhabitants of the palace?"

"And your safety," corrected the duchess.

He laughed. "I've dealt with demons on several occasions now. If what you're planning is as big as I think, I'd make certain I wasn't anywhere in the vicinity."

It was obvious that the duchess didn't like his tone, but she kept herself in check. "If not for yourself, at least safety for her and a few others."

"How many?"

"Ten," she answered immediately.

"Make it twenty," Will demanded. "I have quite a few friends."

She sighed. "Twenty then. I will provide you with a vial of special ink, as well as the symbol you must inscribe. The only stipulation is that you must not provide Count Spry or the king with this mark, otherwise my plan will be for naught."

"It will seem rather strange if I ask Selene to let me draw upon her."

"Give her a gift, almost anything will do, small or large. So long as you inscribe my mark upon it and do so with a portion of the ink, it will protect her. Just make sure it's something she will keep with her."

"And all you want in exchange is my pledge?"

The duchess smiled.

"Very well," said Will. "I pledge on my soul that I will not stop your ritual."

She rose and left the room, returning a moment later with a vial and a slip of paper with the symbol marked on it. After that, she bade him goodbye and stepped out. The servant, Miriam, escorted him to the door. Will watched the cat follow the maid with some amusement—no one had noticed the creature the entire time.

Shortly thereafter he was on the street, walking back to the college. Away from the house he felt his stress subside, and fatigue washed over him. He hadn't realized until then just how nervous he had been.

Something bumped up against his legs and he looked down to see the goddamn cat. The cat circled him once and then began walking with something approaching purpose. Will followed. *This is my life now, following a stray cat demigod.*

He led Will to the college but kept going until he had reached the lane that led between the college and the palace. He turned onto that road and Will followed him north. *Is he telling me to see Selene now?*

As expected, the goddamn cat moved off the road in the direction of the palace at approximately the same place he had before, the area that he had told Will was best for crossing the wall. He stopped in the tall grass and stared up at him. "You have done well," came its voice, emanating as usual from some place that didn't quite match up with the cat in front of him.

"Today?"

"The demon that attacked the palace last time," responded the cat. "I had doubts about whether you would survive."

"Thanks for your confidence in me," said Will wryly.

"You have decided on your course of action this Friday," stated the cat. It wasn't a question.

Will grimaced. "I'm not sure it's the right thing to do. According to Aislinn it might be the worst option."

The goddamn cat licked one paw. "It is, but I approve. A cat never worries about the future, that will take care of itself."

"So you agree with her?"

The cat hissed. "Never accuse me of agreeing with one of the fae. Her assessment was correct, but it lacked an important element."

"Which is?"

"Me."

Will felt hope rise in his chest. "Will you help me?"

"No. I want only revenge. You belong to the fae bitch until your debt is resolved."

"And yet you led me here," Will pointed out.

"Don't mistake self-service for assistance. She is alone and your next conversation serves my interests."

"What should I tell her?"

"Enough that she trusts you, not enough for her to stop you." There was a brief pause, then the voice added, "She will kill you."

That surprised him. "You mean if she finds out what I intend to do? That doesn't make sense. I'm trying to help—"

"Verb tense is important, human. If I can make the effort to utilize your frustrating language, you should at least master it well enough to understand the difference between will and would."

"You're saying she will kill me if I say too much?"

"There is no 'if.' She will kill you."

Will was confused, as always seemed to be the case when he spoke with the Cath Bawlg. “I don’t understand.”

The cat got to his feet and began to walk away, but the voice continued, “Remember this if you need comfort. The dead do not fear revenge, nor can they seek it. Don’t forget to say your goodbyes.”

Will stared after him long after the cat had disappeared. “What the fuck does that mean?” he said finally, struggling not to shout.

CHAPTER 54

Will was worried about what sort of reception he would receive, but when he said his name and deactivated the ward protecting the window, Selene appeared just seconds later and helped him through. The held each other for a long minute afterward, knowing that words would only spoil their reunion, for there was nothing good in the facts that lay between them.

"You shouldn't have come," she said at last, when they broke apart. "You can't stay either."

"I didn't intend to," Will snapped, regretting the tone of his voice immediately. "I came to warn you."

"Why did you vanish from the ball?" she asked, ignoring his statement.

"Did you think I might do something stupid?" Her face answered his question. *I guess I deserved that look,* he told himself. "I was looking for evidence about the warning I'm here to give you." As she continued to stare, he felt the need to add, "And yes, it was dangerous."

"You need to show some concern for yourself, Will," she warned. "I can't look after you. Not anymore."

"I didn't ask you to," he said grumpily.

"No, I'm asking you to take care of yourself. How do you think I'll feel if something happens in the future? Just because I'll be married doesn't mean it won't torture me if I find out you've gotten yourself killed. I'm asking you to be careful for my sake, if you won't do it for yourself."

He understood her feeling, but his frustration at the situation made him angry anyway. "Too damned bad," he spat. "If you want to protect me, you'll have to do it yourself. If you're not in it, I'll spend my life however I choose. Don't put the responsibility for your guilty feelings on my shoulders."

Her eyes narrowed. "How did I fall in love with someone so selfish?"

"Selfish is taking it upon yourself to get married without consulting the person you're supposedly saving," Will shot back. "I don't think I've got a monopoly on selfishness here."

Selene's nostrils flared as his words registered and he could see she was breathing heavily. Will supposed he must look the same. He fought the urge to seize her in his arms, though whether he wanted to kiss her or strangle her was unclear to him. "Do you want to hear my warning or not?" he asked.

"Not really," she said sullenly.

"The Duchess, Arlen Arenata, is planning to kill Count Spry and your father," said Will without preamble.

Selene's politically inclined mind understood immediately. "She thinks she can make her husband king? A murderer can't inherit. Not only that, she couldn't possibly succeed."

"She could. And she'll kill a lot more people along the way."

"How?"

"I'm not going to share that, but I intend to make sure it doesn't happen. All you have to do is make certain that you and your fiancé don't show up at her little get-together on Friday."

"If you don't tell me the details, I won't let you leave," threatened Selene. "I'll call the guards." As she spoke, her earth elemental pulsed and a stone barrier grew up from the floor to block the window.

"If you do that, your father will have me in the dungeon, if he doesn't choose to execute me immediately," countered Will. In his mind he could still hear the goddamn cat's warning, *"She will kill you."*

"That option is starting to sound better all the time," Selene challenged.

Will called her bluff. "Do it then."

They stared at each other for what seemed an eternity, until finally she gave a long sigh of exasperation. The impromptu wall of stone slowly disappeared. "I hate you sometimes."

Will couldn't look away. "The feeling is mutual."

Reluctantly, he took a step toward the window, but her voice stopped him in his tracks. "I have fifteen minutes before I have to appear downstairs."

He met her gaze. "That's not much time."

Selene agreed, "It isn't."

By the time his brain caught up with his body, he was already carrying her into the bedroom. They wrestled with each other and their clothes, filling the next quarter of an hour with frantic desperation. Somewhere in the back of Will's mind he remembered Janice's observation, and as the end arrived, he hesitated. Selene urged him on. "Don't stop. This is the last time."

A minute or two later his breathing slowed, and reason returned. "I thought last time was the last time," he muttered.

"This time it really is. It has to be," she declared, though Will thought he saw doubt on her face. Then she pushed him away. "I'm going to be late!"

They hurriedly reassembled themselves, and Will headed for the window. Selene was standing at the outer door of her bedroom when he turned back to add, "Don't give the duchess any warning. Don't give anyone time to consider. Cancel at the last minute."

She nodded, frustration still showing in her visage. Then he defenestrated himself and she exited through the door.

When Will finally arrived back on campus, he was still shaking his head in disbelief. *My life just keeps getting stranger*. The bell tower rang once, denoting the end of the lunch hour, and he was shocked to realize he still had time to make it to his first afternoon class.

The thought of sitting through classes, not just then, but for the rest of the week, seemed intolerable. How could he concentrate when wasn't even sure he would live to see the weekend? By the time his last session with Professor Dulaney ended, he was ready to jump up and run from the room.

Being back in his dorm room wasn't much better, though. He sat at his desk and endlessly rehearsed the scenario in his mind, trying to imagine the best way to accomplish his goal. Then he began experimenting with the spells he knew, to see if he could produce them quickly enough. Unhappy with the results, he revised which spell he would have ready in advance and then ran through the sequence he expected to need when Friday arrived.

After two or three hours of that, he was too exhausted to think anymore, so he switched to mindlessly practicing the point-defense spell. It was a relief when it was finally time for bed, but he immediately found that he couldn't sleep.

It was going to be a rough week.

The next day passed in similar fashion, and it was a relief when Rob showed up at his door that evening. Will was desperate for anything to take his mind off the future. "How was the ball?" asked his friend.

"The food was amazing," said Will. "There were tables and tables of it. I don't even think it was all eaten."

Rob laughed. "You went to a royal ball and all you can talk about is the food?"

"What am I supposed to talk about?" asked Will, nonplussed.

"The ladies, the dancing! Who did you meet? Come on, I want details!"

Will gave his friend a sly look. "Oh, that."

"Of course, that! Did you step on anyone's feet?"

"No!" said Will, immediately feeling defensive.

Rob didn't seem convinced. "Really? Last week Janice told me she was certain you would mangle some noble lady and cause a major incident."

"Well, I improved quite a bit before the ball," Will huffed. "I assure you that no ladies were mangled through my efforts."

"Crippled? Lamed? Moderately impaired?" teased Rob with a grin. "You can tell me. I'll only laugh."

Will couldn't help but laugh. He gave his friend a modest account of his time at the ball, including the fact that he had danced with Tabitha Nerrow, the Duchess Arenata, and the princess. Rob was particularly impressed with the last one. "You danced with the princess? Did you reminisce about your times together, fighting against the Darrowans?"

"I wouldn't say that, exactly."

"Two old war buddies, rediscovering their unbreakable bond forged during time of war…" Rob swept his hand across the air in front of him as he set the stage for his delusional play.

Will frowned. "War buddies?"

Rob wasn't done. "And of course, as they gaze into one another's eyes, they realize that their feelings haven't changed, despite the differences in their rank and station."

It sounded as though Rob was just getting warmed up to the topic, so Will stepped in to intervene. "The king announced her engagement to Count Spry," he announced dryly.

"Oof!" exclaimed Rob, who then doubled over as though someone had knocked the wind out of him. Then he straightened up suddenly. "Wait, did you say Count Spry? Dennis' father? Oh, dear lord! That had to sting."

"Don't remind me."

Rob's eyes fluttered and he fanned himself dramatically with one hand. "Give me a second. I'll have to revise this scenario." He took several deep breaths, the resumed, "All right. So the two war buddies stare into each other's eyes, realizing their love in undiminished—"

"War buddies makes it sound like I'm in love with a grizzled veteran," commented Will.

His friend smiled. "That could happen too. In fact, it would make a great love triangle. There you are, torn between your love for the princess, and your love for your squad mate, the noble, but very hairy Gregory. But alas, Gregory is already married, so your love can never be. Spurned by your bearded lover, you turn to your other war buddy, Selene, only to discover she has been betrothed to your archnemesis, the evil Count Spry!"

Will snorted. "You're really having fun with this, aren't you?"

"I haven't gotten to the best part yet," said Rob, "when Selene discovers that the count is secretly making sordid assignations with your old lover Gregory. Then, the two of you, both spurned by the men you love, return to one another for romantic revenge!"

"As twisted as all of that is, I think I would prefer it to reality at this point."

Rob lifted his chin proudly. "My stories are always preferable to reality. Perhaps someday I shall write a play. *The Tragic Love of William, Sir Gregory, Count Shitstain, and Some Princess or Other.* How's that for a name?"

"It sounds wonderful."

They continued to chat for another hour or so, then went downstairs for supper, meeting Seth along the way. The banter and company of friends did a lot to ease the tension Will had been suffering under. When they finally separated and returned to their rooms, he felt much better and he was able to return to his practice with a clear head.

CHAPTER 55

Will spent the next couple of days preparing a few alchemical mixtures that he thought would come in handy, and by the time Friday arrived he felt as ready as he could possibly be. According to Aislinn's information, the ritual would need to resume some time after the sun set but before midnight. Will intended to make sure he was there before that happened.

He had no idea whether the duchess had invited other guests, aside from Selene and the count. Ordinarily, for similar socials the host would include a small circle of friends, but given that the duchess intended to kidnap then murder one of her guests, he hoped that wouldn't be the case. The more people he had to deal with, the more difficult his job would be.

It largely depended on how Arlen Arenata intended to carry out her plan. When Will arrived, he found the worst-case scenario, for there were four empty carriages parked on the lane in front of the Arenata residence. *That's at least eight guests, and hopefully Selene and the count aren't among them,* he noted. With that many people, the duchess had either planned to wait until some or most had left, or she intended to drug or otherwise incapacitate them.

Will couldn't wait to find out which was the case. He glanced down at himself, double-checking that everything was in place. He was wearing his mail and gambeson along with the addition of his newer pieces of armor, greaves, breastplate, and his improved steel cap with aventail. If things went well he wouldn't need any of it, but it was better to be prepared than dead, if things didn't go as planned.

The chameleon and silence spells made it easy to approach the carriages, each of which still had a driver waiting. The drivers were bored, naturally, and had gathered together near the gate to the house where they could banter with one another to pass the time. Will moved to within fifteen feet, using one of the carriages to provide extra cover. Then he painstakingly constructed a sleep spell and unleashed it on them. Slowly, all four of the drivers collapsed to the ground.

The guard at the gate was understandably alarmed. Will caught him with a second sleep spell, the one he had kept prepared in reserve. Once all five were down, he spent a couple of minutes preparing another sleep spell, as he wasn't sure how soon he would need the spell again. Then he used a spell to unlock the gate.

Leaving the guard and the drivers asleep in front of the house wasn't a good option, but he feared that moving them might shake them from their magical slumber, so Will used the source-link spell to drain each of them before he dragged them inside and laid them in the grass near the front door. Afterward he closed and relocked the front gate before going to the door and ringing the bell.

When it opened, he used his newly prepared sleep spell to render the maid unconscious. He caught her as she slumped and carried her down the steps, then returned to the door. From the doorway he could hear voices inside, engaged in a lively banter within the parlor. No one had noticed the maid's disappearance yet. Working as quickly as he could, Will prepared another sleep spell. Nervousness almost made him fail, as he worried someone would come to check on the door before he was ready, which might force him to use more violent methods. His practice paid off, though, and he kept his calm long enough to finish the spell construct. That done, he stepped inside and shut the door behind him, making sure to lock it.

Before leaving the entry hall, he shifted his vision into that strange spectrum that would allow him to see through walls and confirmed the positions of the inhabitants. There were three people in the kitchen, presumably servants, and ten people in the front parlor. He grimaced. Ten would be chancy, especially since at least five of them were sorcerers.

Will returned his vision to normal and revised his plan. Moving slowly, he slipped past the parlor and into the back hallway that ran to the kitchen. He entered there and put the three servants to sleep, then prepared the spell again. Tucking that sleep spell away, he got a second one ready, holding it in his hand. *With luck I can get eight,* he told himself, but he knew the odds weren't good. Magic users of whatever variety were likely to resist the spell.

He returned to the hallway and watched the door leading from the parlor. Eventually someone would come to see what had happened to the maid. With luck, he could winnow a few more people from the main group and make his task easier.

He didn't have to wait long. Arlen Arenata appeared after a minute. "Miriam! Where have you gone?" The duchess approached the door and seemed surprised to find her maid nowhere in sight. She glanced around. "Where has that useless girl run off to?"

Will began to sweat. If the duchess opened the front door, she would see the unconscious bodies and the jig would be up. Arlen seemed to debate which way to go for a moment, then turned toward the kitchen, passing right by William, who was leaning against the wall.

He released the sleep spell, hoping it would work. The turyn swirled around the duchess for a moment, then dissipated. She swayed for a moment but stayed upright. "Who did that?" she demanded.

Damn it, Will swore silently. Stepping forward, he moved in. Arlen Arenata's eyes widened in alarm as she saw the strange blurring produced by his chameleon-cloaked body, then her head snapped sideways as his gloved fist slammed into the side of her head. She would have fallen against the wall, but he caught her shoulders.

Ideally, as he had envisioned it, he would ease her to the floor then move on, but the duchess wasn't unconscious. She was stunned and badly hurt, but still struggling. She started to scream but he clapped his hand over her mouth, whereupon she promptly bit him. He jerked his hand away and hit her again, causing her head to bounce off the floor.

That should have been it, but no, she was still moving. Her mouth opened again, and this time he punched her in the belly, driving the wind from her lungs. While she gasped for breath, he tried the source-link spell and was relieved when it connected. Will drained the turyn from her until she finally succumbed and fell unconscious.

Wasting no time, he dragged her from the hall and around to the side of the stairs. He opened the hidden door there and dragged her body inside before closing the door. As he exited, he spotted a streak of blood on the floor. *Was her nose bleeding?* he wondered. It had happened so quickly that he hadn't noticed.

Will felt thoroughly disgusted, not only with the violence, but with himself. Hitting a woman, especially an older one, felt wrong to him. To be fair, it always felt wrong, but beating a middle-aged woman senseless felt exceptionally repulsive. *She was going to summon a demon lord and kill who knows how many people,* he reminded himself. *Plus, she's already murdered at least one person. Never mind all the assassination attempts.*

Rationalizing didn't help. He still felt the sickening crunch as his fist had connected. *How am I going to finish this if I'm already having trouble?* he thought. He was snapped back to the present when he heard a male voice call from the parlor. "Arlen! Get back in here, you're missing out!"

Seven more to go. It seemed impossible. Most of those remaining were sorcerers, but despite that fact Will didn't want to kill them. He didn't think any of them knew the true evil of sorcery and their only crime that he was aware of was that of showing up at the wrong party. He prepared a sleep spell and tried to decide whether he should wait or storm in.

The decision was taken from him when a man stepped out. Will waited to see if anyone else would join the man, but then against all luck, the newcomer's eyes focused on Will. The man shouted an alarm and his fire elemental began to swell.

Shit! Will released the sleep spell, which failed, then he rushed forward, ignoring the fire elemental. He slipped past it and lifted one leg in a front kick, planting his boot in the man's chest and sending him flying back into the parlor to crash atop a table laid out with tea and cakes. Chaos ensued.

A man at the far end of the room began a spell, drawing on his elemental, but Will was faster. He completed a point-defense shield in less than a second and put it directly in front of the man, whereupon the spell the man cast struck it and blew back, knocking Will's enemy prone.

Will called up the limnthal and summoned his last resort, a vial that he hoped would turn the tide in his favor. He tossed it forward and the vial broke in the middle of the room, sending an acrid wave of choking gas outward.

The gas had its intended effect, but it was at that point that Will realized his plan had a fatal flaw. While his opponents were indeed struggling to breathe, their elementals were just fine. He wasn't just fighting five human sorcerers, he was fighting seven elementals, five of fire, and two of earth.

I'm about to die.

He ducked out of the doorway and prepared a spell he was intimately familiar with, though he felt remorse even as he did. *I didn't want it to happen like this.*

That cost him several seconds, and one man ran out of the smoke just as he finished. Will began a second spell and smiled as his attacker made the mistake of swinging a fist in his direction. The man hadn't taken stock of the armor Will was wearing. What had been meant as a jab to Will's stomach turned into swearing as the man jerked back his wounded and possibly broken hand. Will released the force lance he had just constructed, and the nobleman's torso exploded, sending blood and gore spraying back into the room.

Taking a deep breath, Will started into the smoke that only he could see clearly through, or so he thought. Something like a battering ram struck him in the chest, sending him flying into the wall beside the door. Looking down, he saw that the front of his breastplate had crumpled inward from the force of the blow. Fragments of stone dusted the front of him and fell to the floor.

I'd have died right there, he realized. As it was, he was struggling to get up from the ground. One of the fire elementals was almost on top of him, and he guessed that its owner had panicked, for it leveled a massive blast wave of fire at him. It was almost guaranteed to turn the house into a blazing tinderbox.

He expanded his outer shell of turyn and absorbed the flame attack, grateful for the turyn. Then he pushed himself away from the wall and released the spell he had prepared, putting everything he had into it.

A raging wind exploded outward from his body, and for a moment the Arenata living room was exposed to the full force of a tornado. The world around him disintegrated as people and furniture were tossed together in a destructive dance. When the wind died away a few seconds later, the parlor had become a bloody abattoir of flesh, bone, splintered wood, and offal.

Will struggled to keep his stomach from emptying itself at the sight. The elementals of the dead men and women rose from the debris and stood looming around him. They were waiting for the inevitable, for the victor to claim them as his own.

"I'm going to free you. Wait a few minutes." He staggered out of the room and opened the front door. Then he began dragging the coach drivers, the guard, and the maid inside. He lined them up on the floor of the kitchen where the other servants were sleeping, then he drained the turyn from the maid to ensure she wouldn't waken.

After that he straightened up and stretched his back. He was already tired and sore. *And the main event hasn't even started yet,* he reminded himself. Will went to the blood-spattered parlor and spent fifteen minutes locating the heart-stone enchantments that controlled the elementals, releasing them one by one. "Go in peace," he told them each in turn. He phrased his final words in that manner for two reasons, one being to say farewell, and the second being that he didn't want them to set fire to the city before fading away.

The house was secure, at least until someone came looking for the people who wouldn't be going home. There was also the possibility of a late-arriving guest. Will double-checked to make sure he'd locked the front door. Anyone that wanted to come in would have to deal with both the locked outer gate and the door. That left one entrance. Will went through the kitchen and locked and barred the back door.

He stepped carefully through the sleeping servants and returned to his hostage, the unconscious Duchess Arenata. Will was surprised to see that despite the fact that he'd drained her of turyn only a few minutes ago, she was already beginning to come around. For a sorceress he wouldn't have been surprised, but for a normal wizard or warlock he found it strange. *Does she have some hidden source of vitality?* He didn't know. He drained her again, then unchained the door leading to the ritual chamber below.

As he bent to lift the unconscious woman, he saw the goddamn cat sitting beside her, sniffing the woman's shoulder. Its nose wrinkled in disgust. "I wondered if you would show up," Will remarked. "I could have used some help."

The cat's golden eyes fixed on him but there wasn't a verbal reply. Will could imagine one, however. *"I serve my interests, not yours."*

The journey down the long, winding stairs was miserable. Will was already sore and aching from the battering he had received. His breastplate had deformed enough that it pinched uncomfortably, and carrying a grown woman in his arms only made things worse. He hoped he would have the strength necessary to deal with what would come next. *If not, I just murdered a bunch of people for nothing.*

He glanced down and addressed the unconscious duchess. "Except you, but you're not dead—yet."

At the bottom of the stairs he faced the ward once again. This was a major turning point in his plan. He could bypass the ward, but he had no idea if the duchess could. It might be attuned to her person, which was what he hoped, but it might also require a password. If the latter was the case, she might die. *And if she dies, I'll have to use my own blood.*

For a moment he considered simply absorbing the ward's power and nullifying it. He stretched out his hand to do so but stopped when the goddamn cat hissed. "Don't," said the voice of the Cath Bawlg. "The ward is an annoyance for you but a much greater one for the demons. It must remain—for now."

"I'm not sure the woman can pass," explained Will.

"She can," replied the cat. "I am the only one who will not."

"You're not coming in with me?" Will felt as though a cold rock had settled in his stomach. "Then what the hell is the point of you showing up at all? You're just going to watch? You can't even see through this ward!"

The cat ignored him, then began cleaning his butt with keen interest. It was easy to see where Will ranked on his list of priorities.

"Fuck you too," snapped Will. Cursing a demigod probably wasn't wise, but he was beyond caring. Making an effort that was becoming familiar to him, he adjusted the turyn that surrounded him and walked through the ward. The duchess survived without apparent harm, though Will wasn't sure if it was because enough of his turyn had covered her, or whether it was simply that she was attuned already.

"Either way, it worked," he said aloud before examining the chamber. It had visibly changed since his previous visit. The crystal in the center was humming, and a vibration filled the entire chamber. The copper runes on the floor were glowing with turyn, while the empty blood channels seemed dead and vacant of power.

Will crossed the chamber and deposited his burden. Then he arranged the duchess on the pedestal so that her body fit properly within the human-shaped depressions. He removed her shoes then chained her ankles before moving to the other end and chaining her wrists. Doing so made him feel sick. *I can't believe I'm doing this.*

From the limnthal he summoned two sheets of paper, the notes he had made while discussing what he would do with Aislinn. They included very particular instructions for the final preparation. Will scanned over the first page, then grimaced. He had forgotten one thing. *This just makes it worse,* he thought. Removing his belt knife, he began cutting away the duchess' clothing.

Aislinn had explained that removing the clothes had less to do with symbolism, and more to do with making sure that none of the victim's blood was wasted. The cloth and fabric would absorb a significant portion and that might prevent enough from reaching the stone channels. Will closed his eyes at times as he pulled and tugged away the pieces of her dress. He didn't want to see what he was doing, though it was somewhat unavoidable.

Amazingly, the duchess regained consciousness once again, prompted perhaps by the feel of cold stone against the skin of her back. She stared up at him in horror. "What are you doing?" she murmured weakly.

Will clenched his jaw. *This just makes it so much worse.* But he couldn't allow himself to follow his normal inclination to mercy. "You know what I'm doing. This is what you planned for Count Spry."

"He's your enemy. Why would you do this?"

"Because I'd rather protect those you would have killed than satisfy my personal grudges," said Will.

"You swore an oath," she hissed, more energy returning to her by the second.

"I swore to see to it that the ritual wasn't stopped," corrected Will. "I never said I'd let you be the one to finish it."

"Treacherous fool!" spat the duchess. "If you stop me, you'll never have the king's daughter for your own."

"If your way was the only way, I still wouldn't do it."

"Bastard! What do you hope to gain? Who will you kill to pay the price for this?"

Will's eyes were hard. "I'm not a warlock. I won't kill anyone. I don't bargain with the lives of others."

"Yet you'll spill my blood!"

"A balance must be found. You began this by taking the life of another. You'll pay for that crime with your own."

"And who are you to judge me?" she said angrily, desperation in her voice.

"The last true wizard." It felt strange as he said it, but he felt the truth of it in his bones. Most might look on him as a vigilante, taking justice in his own hands, but the reality was that he was the last member of the order that in times past would have been responsible for her punishment.

He lifted his knife one last time, choosing where to make the first and final cut.

CHAPTER 56

Aislinn's instructions had been explicit. *"Choose a place that will bleed freely and at length. If she dies too quickly enough blood won't be spilled. The heart must remain active to pump her living blood into the channels."*

Will knew plenty about human vasculature, though he never thought he'd be using that knowledge for something like this. The veins in her neck were tempting, but if he nicked the artery there, she would die too rapidly. Rather than risk that, he chose the wrists. He could cut through both veins and arteries there since they were smaller.

Arlen Arenata's eyes bulged as she saw him bring the knife to bear, and she screamed long and loud, thrashing hopelessly against the chains that held her. Will made the cut quickly, drawing hard and pressing down on the blade firmly, severing the flesh of her wrists until the blade found bone.

The duchess screamed as though hell itself had come to claim her. *Which perhaps it has,* thought Will. He moved to the other side of her body and repeated his action. Then he turned away, unable to bear the sight of what he had done, but he couldn't stop the sound of her screams from penetrating his ears.

With the cuts already made, it wasn't intensely painful, he knew that, but the mewling curses that Arlen Arenata hurled at him would have made anyone believe she was in excruciating torment. She swore and cursed, but then, as she began to grow gradually weaker, she switched to begging, pleading with him for mercy.

Will moved to the far side of the chamber and vomited up what little food was in his stomach. He hadn't eaten well at lunch because of his anxiety, knowing what he would have to do later, but even so he retched and heaved, bringing up pure bile once his stomach was empty. When he finally recovered Arlen's voice had become faint.

Will did his best to ignore her, consulting his notes instead and examining the circle so he could identify the control points that Aislinn had told him about. The circle was controlled not by incantations as the stories so often claimed, but by simple, spell-like functions. To alter its function required the controller to move to the appropriate point and create a simple rune that he or she would then connect to the matching rune in the circle. The resulting connection between caster and circle would alter the flow of turyn within the ritual, activating and deactivating different functions.

He found the points he needed and made a mental note of their locations so he could find them quickly when the need arose. Thus prepared, he checked the progress of the blood through the channels. It had almost reached the end, where it would complete the circle, but the duchess' wrists had stopped producing blood.

Steeling his heart, he went and checked his victim. She was unconscious but still alive. Fighting back a fresh wave of nausea, he took out his knife again and made a deep cut on the inside of her thigh. That produced the desired effect.

By this point Will wanted nothing more than to run screaming from the chamber. He'd had enough. He'd done enough, and he doubted he could ever expunge the horror of those actions from his memory.

It was then that the sanguine circle finally reached completion. The crystal in the center of the room changed, its light vanishing, being replaced by a fluid darkness that flowed upward to form a massive black orb in the center of the circle. Will fought down a surge of panic. He'd forgotten to prepare his spells. He quickly constructed the spell he wanted and stored it. He wished he could prepare a second one as well, but he needed to be free to form the control runes for the circle.

A sickening miasma filled the air as a form emerged from the ebon orb. Will thought it was a smell at first, but after a moment he realized it was simply demonic turyn, so potent and concentrated that it threatened to overwhelm his senses. The man-shaped being who stood in front of the orb was powerful in the extreme.

Will formed the demon-armor spell and cast it. He didn't hope to protect himself from the demon lord with it, merely offset the effect of its sickening aura. It worked and he moved to the control point he needed.

"You are not the one who made the compact with me," declared a silky voice.

Bracing himself, Will raised his eyes and gazed on the being that had come. What he saw was a man with sharp, cruel features and skin that seemed alternately a deep green or a dark green. The color shimmered back and forth as he studied it. The demon lord was clothed in plate armor constructed from some strange bluish metal. Will responded to his statement. "No, I am not. What is your name?"

The demon laughed. "What is this?" Then his eyes scanned the room before falling on the still form of Arlen Arenata. "A petty betrayal, what a lovely scene!"

"Your name, demon," insisted Will.

"I am Leykachak, third in rank beneath Madrok himself. I am at your service, assuming the original terms of the compact still hold."

Will knelt beside the rune he needed and formed its complementary control rune above his palm. "They do not," he replied.

"Ahh, what an adorable warlock you are," said Leykachak. "Do you wish to renegotiate then?"

"I think not," returned Will. "I am not a warlock. I will have no dealings with your kind."

"Then you will die," warned the demon lord. A second form was beginning to emerge from the orb behind it.

Will activated his rune and the blood circle sizzled, sending up plumes of acrid smoke as it ceased to function. The ebon orb vanished, leaving an arm and leg to fall twitching to the chamber floor, a testament to the unlucky demon that had been about to cross.

Leykachak glared at him with seething hatred. "Why would you do that? As powerful as I am, more could be accomplished with my underlings' aid."

"I don't seek your aid," explained Will, standing and moving to the next control point.

"Then you should have fled rather than open the gate," the demon informed him. "Now that I am here you cannot hope to stop me. This circle will not hold."

Will felt strangely calm. After the terrible slaughter above and the horror he had just committed, he couldn't muster enough emotional energy to be afraid of the creature that was threatening him. He almost didn't care if he died. Almost. Will formed the next control rune and linked it to the copper rune he had selected. Flames flared within the circle, identical in nature to the ones that covered Will's body.

The circle was now drawing power from the ley lines and converting it into the same vital turyn that was deadly to demon-kind. Leykachak screamed in rage as his face and skin began to bubble and boil. "You would punish *me*? I will tear out your heart! You cannot hope to succeed." The demon lord began to press forward, pressing his hands against the invisible barrier that held him within the circle.

Will felt the pressure build through his connection, but he refused to stop. This was the crucial moment. He stared boldly back at the demon lord, unwilling to give up. In his mind he was replaying Aislinn's advice. *"Theoretically you could destroy him there, but you won't. Any demon lord brought by such a ritual will be too powerful. Eventually your strength will fail, and it will break free. You must hold it as long as possible. Every second the circle's punishment lasts will greatly weaken the demon."*

He had asked her what to do once the circle failed, and she had further counseled, *"Run. If you weaken the demon enough, it won't last long in our world before it must retreat. If you can escape its grasp long enough, you might survive. Though it isn't likely."*

Leykachak was screaming out a constant litany of curses in some language Will couldn't understand. The floor shook as it pounded against the barrier, but he kept up his link with the circle. Though most of the power came from the ley lines, he still felt his strength fading. A quiet desperation crept over him as he stared at the demon lord, whose power didn't seem to have diminished in the slightest.

Keeping up his concentration, he called up the limnthal and summoned his vials of turyn. He had twenty left and the day before he had been confident they would be enough. Now he was having doubts. He drank one and felt his strength return.

It didn't last long. Leykachak's efforts to free himself seemed to be growing in power rather than diminishing. Sweat ran down Will's cheeks and neck, soaking into the padded gambeson beneath his armor. He drank another elixir and found himself struggling to maintain his concentration. The elixirs weren't meant to be taken in such quick succession, nor had he expected to be using his power so quickly.

He took the fourth barely a minute later and felt a wave of nausea rise from his gut. *My own turyn shouldn't make me sick,* he thought. *Is it spirit sickness or is my will about to break?* He didn't have enough experience to be sure of the difference, but either way the end result would be bad. The one time his will had broken in the past, it had left him unable to practice magic for weeks.

Today it would mean his death.

Will's hands began to shake and at last he realized the problem. Some of the turyn from the circle was leaking into him through the link. No matter how much pressure he put forth, it swirled and seeped into him, like freshwater from an estuary mixing with the sea at its outlet.

He downed a fifth elixir, but it was no use. The problem wasn't his turyn, it was his control—he simply couldn't maintain the purity of a one-directional flow. Bile rose in the back of his throat and his stomach threatened to rebel once again. *Not now!*

The floor buckled and cracks began to form, causing the copper runes to shift. Any more and the circle's integrity would fail. Will was faced with a terrible decision. Should he continue to push on or stop while he could still run? He feared that if he waited too long his body would fail him.

Leykachak leered at him, sensing his weakness. "Your fragile mortal body can't last much longer, child. You're failing. In a moment you'll break and then I'll take my time with you. Death is too good for you. I'll rip your soul free and fashion a toy from it, an ornament of endless agony with which to amuse myself."

Will felt despair, and tears of frustration began to form in the corners of his eyes. He didn't want to die, or whatever it was that was about to happen to him. He'd given everything he had, done everything that was required, no matter how much he had hated it. He'd done it all, not for himself, but for people who didn't even know his name, much less that there was a terrible evil about to erupt in the midst of their city.

And for Selene, he told himself, though he knew she would be furious when she learned how he had died.

He lifted his head and stared back at the embodiment of evil. It terrified him to his core, but when his lips opened the only thing he could think to say came straight from his memory of his grandfather. "First, you can go fuck yourself, then you can wipe your ass with a porcupine, you ugly son of a bitch!" He wasn't sure if he'd ever heard Arrogan use that exact phrase, but he was sure the old man would have approved.

Another pressure wave shook the room, and the circle failed. Will fell, tumbling backward and landing on his backside. Leykachak raced forward with a grace that made his frightening speed seem almost languid. The demon lord's skin and features healed themselves almost instantly.

Let's fix that, thought Will, and he released the demon-lance spell he had prepared earlier, overloading it with half of his remaining strength.

The blazing red beam shot forth and struck Leykachak full in the face as he was reaching for the wizard who had tormented him. It blasted away part of the demon's head and sent him falling back, ass over head.

Will scrambled to his feet and tried to run. The exit was his only hope, but Leykachak recovered almost instantly. A black line of power raced from the demon's hand, wrapping around Will's ankle, searing his skin and dragging him back. "Not so quickly, my pet," crooned the demon lord.

Looking back in horror, Will saw another spell forming above the demon's hand. Without thinking, he formed a point defense shield and put it directly in front of Leykachak's hands. The demon's spell exploded harmlessly against it and Will released his spell.

The demon lord seemed surprised, and Will turned to look back at the exit. He knew he wouldn't make it. Ignoring his enemy, he formed a force-lance spell and tried to aim for the archway that led to freedom.

Leykachak laughed. "Idiot. Destroy the ward. You'll only make my escape from here easier, but don't expect me to thank you for the favor."

Will released the spell, firing it directly at the arch. The distance wasn't great, but it was far enough that he could conceivably miss.

His long hours of practice paid off, and the stone arch exploded as the lance of power struck the keystone at the top of the arch. Will turned back to Leykachak. "I'd like you to meet the goddamn cat. He's a friend of mine." The air seemed to shake as a low growl reverberated through the room.

Will barely managed to erect a second shield in time to prevent the demon lord's next spell from obliterating him. Then the Cath Bawlg flew past him, no longer in the form of a grey tomcat. The beast that filled Will's vision was beyond anything he had expected. It was a cat of enormous dimensions, with deep, shadowy fur and burning gold eyes.

The Cath Bawlg landed on the demon lord, and the fight that ensued was almost entirely one sided. The demon that had seemed unbeatably powerful just a moment before crumpled under the goddamn cat's ferocious assault. Black ichor sprayed the walls, followed shortly after by entrails as the mighty cat disemboweled his prey.

Will stood back, watching in awe. It was a scene that would have horrified him an hour before, but his mind and body were numb. All he could feel now was a sense of amazement as the Cath Bawlg quite literally tore Leykachak limb from limb.

The demon's body continued to struggle feebly, until the goddamn cat pulled his heart free and devoured it in a single massive bite. Only then was the fight over. Will remembered Tailtiu's words about the cat from long ago, *"whatever it eats does not return; its prey remains dead—forever—including us."*

"Good riddance, asshole," Will remarked.

The giant cat left the ruined carcass and walked over to sit down in front of him. "I was beginning to think you had decided on suicide," observed the cat's deep voice.

"Aislinn told me to keep him contained as long as possible to weaken him," explained Will.

"Did she also tell you to use potions to extend your strength? The demon was weak enough for me to easily destroy after the first minute of punishment you subjected him to. The rest of your effort was merely an exercise in self-torture."

Will gaped at the massive cat. *Son of a bitch!* "You mean I was wasting my time?"

"Not entirely. I was impressed by your stubbornness."

Feeling angry and foolish, Will turned toward the metal book-stand. He wanted to finish cleaning up the scene and go back to the dorm, but his leg collapsed under his weight. When he looked down, he realized that the demon's spell had done him far greater harm than he had known.

The Cath Bawlg wandered over and gave his lower leg a long, slow, and excruciatingly painful lick, but after the tongue came away Will found his leg whole once more. *That saved me a regeneration potion,* he thought. "Thank you."

The cat turned one eye to regard him solemnly. "It is I who should thank you. You have brought me a great gift. Today's vengeance was sweeter than I imagined."

"Does that mean I can call on you for a favor?"

"Do not insult me. I do not deal in favors and gifts as your accursed fae do. I will repay you in time, as I choose." The great cat padded toward the stairs, diminishing in size with each step. "Remember, do not call me." Then it was gone.

I should have expected that, thought Will sourly. Getting back up on his newly restored leg, he went and collected the book the duchess had used and stored it in the limnthal. A moment later he recovered what remained of his elixirs of turyn.

After that he surveyed the chamber, wondering whether he should try and remove any of the evidence of what had happened. As things currently stood, it appeared as though someone had broken into the house, murdered most of the guests, then used the duchess to initiate a dark ritual. "Then again," Will muttered, "I guess that's exactly what did happen, though they'll likely misunderstand the purpose."

He wondered what the king would think if he found out that Will was the culprit. Based on past experience Will figured he'd either be beaten and told he deserved a reward or executed. King Lognion's personality was too bizarre to guess which option the man would choose.

Will was too tired to care. "Fuck him. I have to kill him eventually anyway." On that positive note, he headed for the exit. He stopped when he noticed something bulky lying in his path. It was the breastplate that Leykachak had worn. Whatever it was made of had remarkable strength, for while the Cath Bawlg's claws had left scratches in it, the piece of armor was still in one piece. The inner straps had failed, allowing the goddamn cat to pry the backplate away and extract his prey, but the dark bluish metal had held its shape.

He stored it in the limnthal, thinking it might be useful someday. Then he went up the stairs. For a brief moment he considered searching the house, since it probably held a fortune in valuables, but he was too tired. He wanted out, and he had no idea how long it would be before the city guard descended on the place. It might be hours or minutes. He had no way of knowing. It depended on whether anyone came calling and got suspicious when no one answered at the gate or door.

With that in mind, he chose to exit via the kitchen door. Will covered himself with a chameleon spell, then added a silence spell. He didn't have a key for the door and didn't feel like constructing the unlocking spell, so he used a force lance instead, blowing the heavy wooden timbers apart. The noise might draw attention, but he was done, and no one was likely to spot him now.

Outside, he made his way around the house and down the street. As he went, he saw another carriage come down the road, one of particularly extravagant construction. He realized it was one of the king's personal carriages as it passed by. *Damn, that was fast,* thought Will.

He quickened his step so he would reach the next side alley sooner. He wanted to be away. When he looked back, however, it wasn't the king who emerged from the carriage, but Selene. *I told her to stay away,* he thought with some irritation. *What will she think if she sees the interior?*

For a second he was tempted to return. Perhaps he could explain, but then he saw a second figure emerge from the carriage, his old friend Count Spry. Will turned his back and kept walking. *I don't care anymore,* he lied to himself.

Chapter 57

Despite everything he had been through, Will slept without dreams that night. The tension and anxiety that had been building for a week was finally over. His last thought as he closed his eyes was simply to wonder whether armed men would show up in the middle of the night, beat down his door, and arrest him, but when he opened them again, it was morning.

He was beginning to develop a certain fatalism. Will's life was such that he was convinced he would die soon, so he woke with few expectations. He was simply glad to see the sun once more. He opened the window and let the sunshine warm his face. For a moment, he was at peace.

Until a vision flashed through his mind, that of the duchess bleeding slowly to death. Will's stomach knotted and he tried to get to the chamber pot before it emptied itself. He didn't make it. When the heaving finally passed, he was forced to use a cleaning spell to get rid of the vomitus.

Will dressed, and he tried to ignore the fact that his hands were trembling as he struggled to lace up his trousers. Then he went downstairs to find breakfast. He was ravenously hungry.

In the dining hall he found a table where he could sit alone, but Rob spotted him and came over to join him, followed a few seconds later by Janice, who seemed strangely subdued.

As usual, Rob failed to read the mood. After shoveling several sausages down, he paused to announce the news of the day. "Did you hear about what happened last night?"

Will focused on his porridge, but he felt Janice's eyes on him.

"Someone broke into a party at the Arenatas' home! Everyone was murdered! Well, except the servants, who somehow don't have a clue what happened. They said the front room of the house was ankle deep in blood and guts. The duke had a hole the size of man's fist all the way through his chest."

More images flashed through Will's mind and he found his food refusing to go down his throat. He stifled a gag and put his spoon down.

Janice gave Rob a cool look. "Would you mind if we saved such talk for another time? We're eating."

"Oh! Sorry." Rob glanced at Will. "Are you all right? I didn't mean to make you gag."

Will shook his head. "It wasn't you. I think I'm coming down with a stomach bug." He got up to leave. Janice rose to follow him, but Will held up a hand. "Don't worry about me. I'll be fine in a day or two."

The look on her face made it apparent she would be along to see him shortly, but Will shook his head. "Tomorrow." He went back to the dorm.

Will stepped into his room and shut the door, grateful to be alone again. Then he walked to the bed, sat down, and put his face in his hands. He felt like crying, but that pleasure was denied him for some reason. Instead he let out a long, low groan that seemed to resonate with the ache in his chest.

"What's happened to you, Will?" came a woman's voice, thick with disappointment.

His head shot up and the force-lance spell that he'd prepared before bed appeared in his hands, but his eyes found no one. *That was Selene's voice.* He put the spell away and scanned the corners of the room carefully, assuming that she had used the chameleon spell.

Before he could spot her, Selene dismissed the spell and her body came into view, standing beside the window. She was staring out at the campus.

"Nothing," he responded. "As you can see, I'm doing well. I never expected you to show up here."

"I wanted to try the spell out," she replied evenly, her voice dead. "You shouldn't be the only one who gets to sneak into people's rooms."

He scratched his head. "I've often dreamed about you appearing like this. I just wish it was on a better day."

"Feeling guilty?"

Will nodded. "That's a reasonable diagnosis. Is there a treatment for it?"

He could see the muscles in her jaw working. After a few seconds, she replied, "Depends on who you ask. The most popular remedy for your condition would be a public execution."

"Are you here to deliver the treatment?"

Selene's head snapped around and she fixed him with a red-eyed gaze. "Is that what you think? I'm worried. I saw the inside of that house. At first, I was worried that you might be among those who died in the front room. They're still trying to figure out if the duchess' body is among them, but the parts they've recovered don't add up properly."

"She isn't there."

"I know. I found her, but no one else will."

Will felt a strange sensation, but he had no name for it. Was it hope, companionship, or simply relief? "You saw that?" he asked.

She nodded. "I sealed the top of the stairs with stone. No one will even know there was a passage there."

"Why would you do that?"

"At the time I told myself the chamber should be hidden, so that no one else would try to misuse it, but I was lying to myself. I didn't want anyone to see what you did."

"The only one I really care about is you. If you've seen it, then I could care less what anyone else thinks."

She moved closer and sat down beside him. "What I saw was horrific. Tell me what happened. Some of it I understand already, having seen the circle and the remains, but there's a lot that doesn't make sense."

Will felt as though the world was crashing down on his head. He wanted to tell her, but one fear lay underneath everything else. *She won't love me once she knows what I've done.* He took a deep breath and held her gaze for a moment. "I kept most of what I knew from you, but now that it's over, there's no reason not to tell you, other than my own selfishness. You deserve the truth."

"Selfishness? You think I—"

"Let me tell it, then I'll accept whatever you think of me afterward." And with that, he launched into a retelling of the night before. He began with what he had learned from Aislinn, for that was his only justification. As usual, he didn't mention the ring. That was a secret he didn't intend to share until Selene was free of her father's control, assuming such a day ever came.

He described his reasoning and his plans, then went on to explain the parts that had gone wrong, leading to the massacre in the parlor. The ending was the part he dreaded most, for it had gone exactly as he had planned. Perhaps it had been necessary, but what he had done to the duchess still horrified him. It was a dark stain in the back of his mind that he avoided looking at.

Except that now he had to tell it to Selene.

Somehow he did, and then he fell silent. A miserable cold filled him then, as he knew the knowledge would stand between them. Until a shocking sensation swept over him, Selene's arm moved across his shoulders and she embraced him.

"Before you get the wrong idea," she warned, "I'm furious with you, but probably not for the reasons you think. This is so you'll stop thinking stupid thoughts." He felt her lips brush his cheek. "I could never hate you."

He turned his head to stare at her in surprise. "But the duchess—"

"I don't give two figs about what you did to that woman," she interrupted coldly. "She deserved it. I care much more about how you hurt yourself to do it. What I'm truly angry about is the people who died because of your *accident* in the parlor."

A terrible thought came to him then. *What if some of them were friends of hers?*

She read his mind. "No, I didn't particularly care for any of them. The Arenatas were unpleasant to say the least, and they kept similar company. That isn't to say those people deserved it. I'm fairly certain most of them were innocent of her plot."

Will nodded.

Then she added, "Next time tell me so I can help you. Maybe we can prevent such accidents, and if not, at least I'll share the blame. I would rather carry the burden with you than see you suffer like this."

"Next time?"

She arched one brow. "Knowing you, there will be a next time. Don't forget who my father is. I've been raised with unpleasant choices. Part of the reason I continually feel compelled to help people is to make up for my own guilty feelings."

The knot in his chest was beginning to relax, and a question that had been bothering him came to his lips. "I chose not to tell the king, but if I had—"

Selene pursed her lips. "I love my father, but I'll make a confession to you now. He's cruel and callous when it comes to ruling and decisions of power. I like to think his choices are correct, even when they're distasteful, but in this case I'm glad you didn't tell him."

"What do you think he'd have done?" asked Will.

"The same thing, up to a point," she replied instantly. "Except he would have only minimized the deaths and given some of his enemies and detractors to the demon lord to mollify it. Overall, I think your answer was the best one, other than what happened in the parlor. Although, if I'd known what you planned, I would have insisted on helping. I won't let you off easily if you cut me out like this again."

Will shrugged. "Well, you are getting married. I can't drag you into my affairs."

"It was my fiancé and my father who were to be murdered. Even if our lives were entirely separated, it would still be my business."

"Point taken. Next time I have to kill a demon lord I'll only keep it a secret from you if it doesn't involve your family."

Her eyes narrowed. "You'd better tell me anyway."

"What about your husband?"

"Future husband," she corrected. "I'll do whatever's necessary and we'll figure it out afterward. He saw the ritual circle, by the way, and the duchess' body. I had to tell him that that was the reason I tried to avoid attending the party."

Will winced. "Does he know that I was the one?"

She shook her head. "I didn't know the details, but I did tell him that he was probably the one meant to be sacrificed. He doesn't know for a fact that you were there, but he's not unintelligent. He probably suspects."

"How much do you think he suspects?" asked Will, sliding his hand up her back and lightly touching her neck. He smiled as a shiver ran up her spine.

Selene gave him a serious look. "I don't think he suspects *that*." Then she frowned. "But I'm pretty sure he knows there's something between us." She turned her head and kissed him slowly. Then she stood and walked toward the door. "I should get going."

Will couldn't bear to see her leave so soon. "I have to go to class," he announced.

Selene looked back, puzzlement on her features. It was Saturday, so his remark didn't make much sense. After a pause, she asked, "When?"

"Day after tomorrow."

She laughed as his game became apparent. "That isn't much time."

"It isn't."

Selene's countenance took on a predatory look as she walked back toward him. A moment later she pounced, and Will found himself on his back looking up at her. "This is the last time," she said firmly after their first long kiss.

"Of course," he replied.

Sometime that afternoon they woke from what had been a long and pleasant nap. Despite the fact that Will was free until Monday, Selene insisted that she had to return. Reluctantly, Will let her go, as he had no other choice.

Before she stepped out the door she turned back. "I forgot to warn you."

"About what?"

"Father is going to know it was you."

He stared at her blankly, then realized why. "The elementals."

She nodded. "You'd never make it as a serial killer. That's your big giveaway every time. You always free the elementals."

Will felt a new anxiety take hold, destroying the peace he had felt a moment before. "Any advice if he summons me?"

"Be honest. He hates liars. Don't beg or plead either. The only thing he admires is strength. If you're lucky he might even reward you."

Will shook his head sadly. "I've already turned down the only reward that means anything to me."

It took a second, but then she realized he meant the duchess' offer. "If you had accepted that one then I wouldn't love you the way I do." She kissed him again, recast her chameleon spell, then slipped out the door.

Will closed it behind her. "And yet you're getting married anyway," he muttered. "What a stupid world."

CHAPTER 58

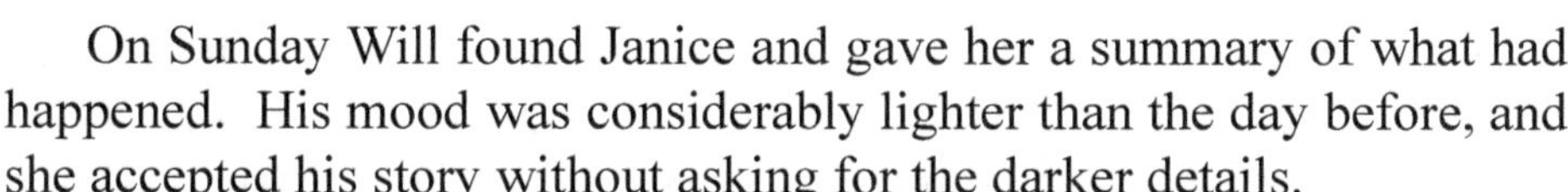

On Sunday Will found Janice and gave her a summary of what had happened. His mood was considerably lighter than the day before, and she accepted his story without asking for the darker details.

After that he resumed his obsessive training schedule. The worst might be behind him, but there was still one more obstacle looming before him in the future, and he was even more determined not to let it pass unchallenged.

The goddamn cat's warning still bothered him too. *"She will kill you."* He had thought perhaps that the cat's warning referred to her reaction to how he had stopped the ritual disaster, but clearly that wasn't the case.

He wanted to dismiss the warning, but after seeing the Cath Bawlg's power in action, he was even more convinced that he couldn't ignore it. As he thought about the upcoming wedding and what he intended to do, however, it fit into a certain dark logic.

During one of his breaks he called up the limnthal and told Arrogan about recent events. The ring was angrier than usual.

"You cut me off in mid-sentence!"

"You were getting repetitive," said Will.

After the inevitable shitstorm of swearing that ensued, the ring eventually calmed down. "So, you successfully stopped the ritual, and everyone was saved. I'm so damned happy for you," finished Arrogan acidly.

Not everyone, thought Will. He still had bad moments when he thought about the people he'd had to kill. "I have a question," he announced.

"Why don't you bargain away another favor to Aislinn then? I'm sure she'll be happy to answer you."

"This is a human question."

"You realize I'm a piece of talking jewelry, right?"

"But you used to be human, and you're probably one of the few who ever suffered enough to know the answer to this one."

"Color me interested," said the ring. "What's this question?"

"After all the terrible things you had to do, the killing and betrayals, did you ever get better?"

Arrogan huffed. "I was the best."

"No, I mean—" He was at a loss for words. "Were you able to sleep at night? Did you have nightmares?"

The ring's tone turned somber. "Oh, that."

"Yeah—that."

"I don't have a good answer for you. From what I saw there are four basic types of people in the world when it comes to how these things work out. The first kind usually can't function, as in they'll get themselves killed before doing what's necessary. They're usually kind, generous, wonderful people and they die horribly. The second kind will leap at the chance to do what you did, and they'll never look back. In fact, they may enjoy it and start looking for excuses to kill again. Luckily, those types are rare. This king of yours is probably one of those. Anyway, you're definitely neither of those. You fall into the third or fourth category, same as most people."

"And what are those?" asked Will.

"They're similar. Both will do what's necessary, and both will be miserable about it afterward the only difference is that some people get over it and some don't. If you throw enough shit at anyone they'll eventually crack, but let's assume you don't suffer that kind of continual misery. From here, you'll either get past this, or you won't, and it isn't really up to you. You'll either have nightmares about it the rest of your life, or you won't. There's no good way to know how it will turn out for you."

"How did it turn out for you?"

Arrogan didn't answer for a while, but eventually he broke his silence. "I was all right through most of it, until Aislinn was taken from me. I don't think I ever got over that. She was the last one that believed in me. Once she was gone, that's when I gave up on everything."

"You never told me how it happened."

The ring sighed. "I was desperate and couldn't find a better solution, so I made a bargain with the stump-lord. I offered him an unbound favor for his assistance."

"So he took Aislinn for the favor? That doesn't make sense."

"He wanted her, but he couldn't have her. Since she was a wizard and bore the limnthal, she was a party to the accord. If she had been an ordinary human, he could have compelled me to turn her over."

"But they can't harm humans."

"Because we represent them. They don't have any rights of their own except through our agreement with the fae. The fae can't touch them, that's true, unless they have leverage over one of us. Anyway, that didn't matter, because Aislinn was a wizard too."

"So what happened?"

"He showed up when we were together and told me he was ready to claim his favor. I assumed it would be something unpleasant, or maybe even some form of slavery, but it was worse than that. He asked me to die."

"What, just die, for no reason?"

"Oh, he had a reason, and Aislinn fell for it. She begged for my life, and his response was that she could offer herself to him instead."

Will felt a chill run up his spine. "And she was pregnant..."

"We didn't know that at the time. If Aislinn had known she would probably have let him kill me. Hell, I would have slit my own wrists before she had a chance to choose."

"That's horrible."

"The worst part is that I'm sure he knew. He knew she was pregnant with my child. He took her because it was twice the bargain, and my suffering would be all the greater when it became known."

Will shook his head. "That's just sick. How could anyone be that cruel?"

"The fae are cruel, down to their very bones," said the ring. "That's how I learned the lesson. Up until then the forest lord had always seemed like a friend to me. Even though I knew I shouldn't, I trusted him just a tiny bit. I think he must have been human once."

"What do you mean?"

"Well, as you know, the fae are all of human origin, but some are born there, like Tailtiu, while others are humans who were changed, like Aislinn. Immortality is a hard burden to bear, and my personal theory is that the ones who were once mortals can't quite handle it. They go slightly insane. I think what the rotten prick wanted was for me to kill him."

"Couldn't he just ask you then? Making you hate him seems extreme."

"Suicide isn't in their nature. They can't die in Faerie, and coming here is something they can only do for short periods. Eventually the call of Faerie drags them back."

"Could you have killed him?"

"Damn right I could have! I was furious. When I found out about Tailtiu I went and found him. That's when I took his horns, but I realized what he really wanted at the end. I had planned to imprison him and bring him back so I could watch him slowly wither away. When I figured out that's what he wanted, I left. Afterward I tried to console myself by imagining that he was suffering, but it was never enough to satisfy me. I nursed the grudge for the rest of my life, and now I'm still holding onto it, at least until you melt me down."

Will didn't know what to say.

"Now you understand why I get so frustrated when I think you're getting sentimental about Aislinn. Don't be confused. Even if she has some maternal feeling toward you, in the end she's one of them and her feelings, whatever they are, will only drive her insane."

Will was properly worried by then. Aislinn had already asked for Selene once, and now he owed her an unbound favor. Selene wouldn't even have the option of choosing for herself. If Will gave her over, Aislinn would simply take her. "Can you refuse to honor a bargain with the fae?" he asked.

"Choice is the foundation of mortality," said the ring. "Unlike the fae, humans can always make choices, as long as they're willing to bear the consequences. If you refuse to honor an unbound favor, the consequence is death."

"Would I just fall over dead?"

"Oh no. Nothing like that. Aislinn would kill you, but it's just as inevitable. She's too powerful to fight and her nature is such that she couldn't let you live even if she wanted to. The fae are bound by their rules."

"Is there a way to hide from them?" Will was beginning to feel desperate.

"From some of them, maybe, from Aislinn I doubt it. She's not just fae, she's the most skilled wizard I've ever known. There are probably gods that would think twice before pissing her off. The only place she wouldn't go is Muskeglun. The lack of turyn really hurts the fae, but she's clever. The trolls would likely catch you and turn you over."

"What can I do?"

"You're worried she might really want the girl, eh?"

"Of course."

"All you can do is hope she actually has your best interest at heart, or at least that she isn't that cruel. Maybe she'll ask for something small. Either way, you'll know better than to ever bargain an unbound favor again. Some lessons are hard but unavoidable."

CHAPTER 59

Another week went by, filled only by classes and Will's near-constant efforts to fill every spare moment with practice. In other words, he was intensely bored, but refused to let himself find anything more interesting to do. The wedding was only a couple of weeks away and he needed to be ready.

The only thing that interrupted his quiet insanity came on Friday afternoon, when a carriage arrived bearing two sorcerers and a squad of guardsmen. They escorted him from his Spell Theory class, prompting a few interesting comments from his classmates as he voluntarily got up and went with them. "Being arrested again, Will?"

He ignored the remarks and kept his thoughts to himself. It wasn't as though he had a reputation to ruin. During the ride to the palace, he sat between the two sorcerers, a man and a woman who had apparently been born without personalities.

"Did the king seem like he was in a good mood?" Will asked one of them, but there was no response.

In fact, they had said almost nothing, even when they appeared to claim him, other than to inform him that the king desired his attendance. The only positive sign was that he hadn't been put in chains—yet.

Half an hour later, he found himself in a small sitting room, possibly the same one in which he had first met the king after being released from the dungeon months ago. *I've come full circle,* he thought. *This is where I was freed, and where I'll probably be sent back.* He wondered if he should lie down and pretend to sleep, but he doubted King Lognion would see the humor in it.

Will leapt to his feet when the door opened and the king entered, giving a deep bow. "Raise your head, William," said Lognion, before taking a seat. "Sit down."

Will sat, but didn't speak.

"My investigators have finished going through the mess at the Arenata residence, and I have to admit, what you did was impressive," said the king. "I'd like you to tell me about it."

"I did the best I could with the tools I had, Your Majesty."

"Then you admit you killed eight of my subjects?"

Will nodded. "Yes, Your Majesty."

"Including the Duke and Duchess Arenata?"

"Most definitely."

"There were only seven bodies found," said King Lognion. "What happened to the duchess?"

"I sacrificed her, using the same altar on which she planned to place Count Spry," said Will. "She intended to summon Leykachak, one of Madrok's demon generals and use his service to murder you, Your Majesty."

"You did this by yourself?"

"Yes, Your Majesty."

Lognion licked his lips, as though savoring the taste of something pleasant. "You chained Arlen to the table and bled her. Was she conscious?"

"Very conscious. She cursed me loudly in the beginning."

"Did she beg?" asked the king.

Will could see a flush in Lognion's cheeks. *He's enjoying this.* Though the realization disgusted him, he also remembered Selene's advice. *I can use this.* In a neutral tone he answered, "She pled with me for her life."

"I underestimated you, William. I never expected such brutal efficiency. I thought you too soft-hearted. Where did the ritual take place?"

"In a secret chamber beneath her home. The entrance was sealed with stone afterward to prevent anyone from finding it." Will wished he could hide that fact, but since Selene had seen it there was no hiding the information. The king would eventually hear it from her lips, if he hadn't interrogated her already.

King Lognion smiled. "So my daughter helped you."

"I tried to keep her out of it. I only warned her to stay away that day, along with Count Spry. She came later, however, and found the scene before anyone else."

"Why didn't you inform me of the duchess' plan to assassinate me?"

"Interfering with the ritual was extremely dangerous," said Will. "I preferred to handle it myself rather than risk involving you, Your Majesty."

Lognion's eyes narrowed. "You wanted power for yourself."

This is the dangerous part, thought Will. He smiled. "Unfortunately, the demon lord wasn't very useful. His service would only be bought by allowing him to kill a large number of people. I didn't find that very helpful, so I tried to dismiss him."

"But you couldn't, obviously," remarked the king.

Will nodded. "I was forced to destroy Leykachak instead."

That got Lognion's attention. The king's eyes went wide and he leaned forward with an intense expression. "How? Such a thing shouldn't be possible."

"I had previously enlisted the aid of one of the demon's most powerful enemies. When it became apparent that Leykachak wouldn't cooperate, I weakened the demon lord as much as possible and let my ally finish him off."

"Do the fae have such power?"

"I'm not sure. My information came from them, but they were not who assisted me. It was a cat deity of some sort. I don't really understand its intentions," admitted Will.

"You've dealt with both the fae and a demigod, yet you complain that sorcery is immoral. Your reasoning escapes me, warlock."

Will blanched. "I am not a warlock, Your Majesty. I do not bargain with what is not mine."

The king grinned maliciously. "A philosophical definition that wouldn't get very far in court. Your actions would have you sentenced to death by any magister in Terabinia."

Will bowed his head. "Your judgment is the only one that matters to me, Your Majesty."

King Lognion leaned back in his chair. "You present a problem for me, William. Whereas before I thought you an interesting curiosity, you've shown yourself to be in possession of a dangerous amount of competence, along with powerful allies. If you were anyone else, I'd probably have removed you by now, but your actions have continually benefited me, even as they simultaneously annoy me."

Will shrugged. "I am what I am."

"Have you considered killing me?"

That line almost caused Will to choke, but he quickly got control of himself. *How can I answer that question honestly?* "If I ever had such thoughts and confessed to them, you would certainly execute me, Your Majesty."

Lognion smiled, an evil flame showing behind his eyes. "I would, though you've answered the question indirectly. I am intrigued by your honesty. Give me a reason to let you live."

"Our goals are aligned. You are an effective ruler and Terabinia would fall into chaos if someone tried to overthrow you. My own goal is to protect and nurture the people of this nation. Rather than try to take power for myself, I prefer to align myself with stability."

The king frowned. "I don't believe in altruism. You'll have to do better than that."

"I'm in love with your daughter," admitted Will.

Lognion laughed. "And yet I have given her to someone else. It seems our goals don't align well at all."

"I don't have the power to take her. My only hope is to serve you well, since I couldn't dare to oppose you."

The king got to his feet and paced across the room before turning back. "I'm afraid I still don't understand you, William. The ritual was your best opportunity. It probably could have killed me and Count Spry as well. If your goal was my daughter, then you wasted your chance."

"As I said before, Your Majesty, my principles don't allow for the murder of innocents."

"Yet you killed the people in that house, and you sacrificed the duchess herself. Such principles and ruthlessness do not mix."

"I am what I am. My life is in your hands." Will's heart was racing, and tiny droplets of cold sweat were forming on his brow. He had a wind-wall spell prepared, but he doubted he could kill the king, even if he had surprise on his side. His intuition was screaming at him that the man was far more dangerous than he appeared.

King Lognion stood over him, looking down. "Very well. This is my judgment. Kill Count Spry quietly in his home. Make sure that none can trace his murder to you. Do this and I will give you his place as well as my daughter."

Will started to protest, but the king held up his hand. "Silence. This is not mercy or a boon. You have earned my interest. I believe you would make a useful tool, and my daughter seems the only leash capable of ensuring your loyalty. What do you think of my offer?"

Will rose from his seat and knelt, bowing his head. "I won't murder the count."

Lognion sneered at him. "Then you're a fool."

Looking up, Will tried to project a confidence he didn't truly feel. "She won't marry him. Your daughter is in love with me."

Lognion's fist struck suddenly, driving Will to the floor. Stunned, Will counted several seconds before his eyes would focus properly.

"Selene understands filial duty and she obeys my will, as is only right. She will marry whoever I say. Love has nothing to do with it."

He struggled to collect his thoughts, for his brain felt as though someone had stuffed his head full of wool. *Did I go far enough? Maybe I should have taken the offer instead of sticking to this ridiculous plan.* "She won't marry him," he repeated for good measure.

The king dragged him up from the floor and hit him again, knocking him over the chair and causing him to tumble until he fetched up against the wall. "Get out," commanded the king. "If you won't make yourself useful, then I have no need of you. You have until the wedding to consider your options."

King Lognion left and Will tried to stand, but his legs had turned to jelly. Two servants appeared after a minute and half carried him to the waiting carriage. The same complement of sorcerers and guards escorted him back to Wurthaven, where they unceremoniously dumped him on the cobblestones in front of the main gate.

Will managed to sit up as the carriage pulled away. *I think that went rather well,* he thought. He waited a few minutes longer before attempting to walk, and the entire time he could see the Wurthaven gate guard staring at him. He stood and staggered drunkenly past the guard station and then looked over at the guard. "No, it's fine. Don't get up. I'll be all right," he announced sarcastically.

The guard looked away, pretending to study the road in front of the college. *What an asshole,* thought Will. *I liked the other guard better.*

He had almost recovered his balance by the time he reached the dorms, but someone must have spotted him and spread the word when he returned, for Seth, Rob, and Janice were all waiting on him. They accosted him before he could go inside.

"Whoa! Look at your face!" exclaimed Rob. "That's impressive."

Janice was already examining him, holding his head between her hands as she tried to see how badly he'd been hurt. "It's horrible. Who does something like this?"

"He looks like a ring-tailed cat," suggested Seth helpfully.

"Thanks, Seth," said Will.

"I've never seen someone with *two* perfectly matching black eyes," declared Rob. "Don't worry, though. It will probably improve your looks."

"Maybe you'd like a set too," offered Will. "You could definitely use some improvement."

"No thanks," said Rob quickly. "I've given up on looks. I rely on my dazzling personality to impress the ladies."

Janice turned on Rob. "What's that smell? Oh, I see now. It's the bullshit that keeps falling out whenever you open your mouth."

Seth hadn't experienced Janice swearing before, and the shock sent him into a convulsive fit of laughter.

"As much as I'm enjoying our reunion, I think I should go lay down," said Will, pushing past them.

Seth was kind enough to accompany him, offering an arm to make sure he didn't lose his balance on the stairs. Janice and Rob let him go once they saw he was in good hands.

Back in his room, he shooed Seth out and lay down on the bottom bunk. Stress and fatigue had made him sleepy, but before he closed his eyes he summoned a large steak from the limnthal and cut it in half. Then he lay back and put one piece over each eye. The cool meat felt nice on his bruises, and he fell asleep shortly thereafter.

CHAPTER 60

His eyes had become a lovely shade of bluish black the next day, and the swelling made them difficult to open. Will practiced some, but he didn't spend long hours at it. He reasoned that he deserved some rest. *Lognion really throws a mean punch,* he observed when he examined himself in the mirror.

Naturally, there was a considerable amount of whispering when he appeared in the dining hall, though he ignored it. After the first trip for breakfast, he asked Seth to bring him food at mealtimes for the rest of the weekend. He didn't feel like being a spectacle.

On Sunday the swelling went down and he practiced more, but in the afternoon he was bored, so he decided to consult the ring. As usual, Arrogan was in top form.

"It's times like these that I truly regret not being able to see," the ring informed him. "It would be so satisfying to see your ugly face right now."

"I'm glad you worry about me," said Will dryly.

"Mainly I worry about you dying without ever melting me down," admitted Arrogan. "You seem to have a death wish."

"I'm just doing my best."

"This plan of yours is foolish."

Will sighed. "You don't think I can pull it off?"

"There's a lot that could go wrong. You're counting on that sadistic bastard indulging his worst impulses, which is risky. If you've misjudged him, he might do something you don't expect, and even if he does do what you think, you could die. You haven't even mastered the point-defense spell yet."

"I'm close—I think."

"Close won't cut it. Close will get you dead. Even with it, you might cock the whole thing up. Are you really sure this is what you want to accomplish? She'll still wind up married to Count dickhead."

That was the part that bothered Will the most, but he wouldn't admit it. "She might not. Once she knows the truth, she might choose me."

"And you think that monster she calls a father will let her have her way? He's more likely to just put something sharp and pointy right through your middle and call it a day."

Will shook his head. "He's rotten to the core, but he's remarkably consistent about certain things. In the past he's made considerable concessions for her wishes."

"You mean letting you live? He just did that because he thought he could find a way to make use of you. Making his daughter feel like he listened to her was just a bonus," said Arrogan. "Let's look at all the things that can go wrong. First, he might just decide to kill you at the start, what will you do then?"

"I'll switch to Plan B. I'm planning to survey the area. I'll make sure I have a clear exit."

"Second, he might be too good, and you'll die before you escape."

"Well, then I'm dead. Let's move onto what happens if he doesn't try to kill me right away," said Will.

"All right, so supposing that doesn't go ass up, Count Spry is very likely to make an attempt."

"Selene won't let him," Will pronounced confidently.

"You're trusting a girl who has no idea what you plan to do. She'll be embarrassed and stunned. She might not react in time. Hell, she might cheer him on."

"She won't. Say what you will, but I trust her heart."

"Spoken like a fool."

"The plan is simple," argued Will. "It doesn't matter too much *exactly* what happens, or who does what. As long as the basic elements are in place there's a good chance that Selene will be forced to face the truth one way or another. I just need her and her father in the same place. Toss in some murderous intent and the recipe is done. I just have to stay alive long enough for her and her father to go head to head."

"That brings me to the next big thing that could go wrong," said Arrogan. "Your plan works, she has her epiphany, but you die anyway. After that she gets to live miserably ever after with Count wrinkly-dick, knowing the truth but completely unable to do a damn thing about it."

"At least she'll know the truth. She deserves that."

Arrogan wasn't done, however. "And the final thing that might go wrong is she might just tell you to go fuck yourself. You march in there and make a complete ass of yourself and she just says, 'Sorry, no thanks.' Everyone laughs, then they have a murder party and finish the wedding without you annoying them."

"That also falls under Plan B," said Will.

"You damn well better make Plan B good, because I'm sure that's the one you'll wind up using, one way or another," said Arrogan.

Will agreed with him there. In his mind he thought the most likely probability was that he'd expose the truth but still have to abandon the scene. After that he'd have to find some way to return in the future. By then Selene would have fully understood the truth and he could find some way to extricate her from her predicament, likely by killing the king. That she might have to spend a period of time married to Count Spry was distasteful, but he might have to accept it.

"You should just take the king up on his offer and kill Spry," opined Arrogan.

"You're missing the point," insisted Will. "If I do that, she'll never know the truth. We'll get married and then I'll spend the rest of my days running errands for her father since he could use her against me, or simply kill her at any time."

"It's better than being dead. Besides, you promised me you'd kill Lognion, so you'd be free eventually."

"And she would hate me for killing her father," argued Will.

"You want too much. You want to win *and* be happy. You can't have both. Trust me, I was married."

Will couldn't help but snort. "Which did you choose?"

"Being happy, until everything went to hell anyway. In your case though, winning means living, so just kill her father and deal with the consequences. Lots of men are married to women who want them dead and they do just fine."

"I'm going to win and be happy."

"You're going to go in there an humiliate yourself. The only question is whether you'll get out alive."

Will had had enough, so he dismissed the limnthal. *I'll just have to make sure Plan B is as good as I can make it, and if that fails, there's always Plan C.* He hadn't shared his other option with Arrogan, because he knew the ring wouldn't have approved.

On Monday he went to visit the armorer, Byron Waters, and brought out the demon general's breastplate for him to examine. The smith stroked his beard as he stared at the strange metal. "I can't say I've ever seen anything like this. Where did you get it?"

"I'm not really free to discuss that," said Will. "Do you think you can adjust it to fit me?"

"Let's see how close it is," said Byron. The armor-smith opened the breastplate and backplate and tried putting it on Will, making notes as he marked the places where it was too tight or too loose. After a quarter of an hour he gave his answer. "It's close to your size, so if the metal is workable, I can make a good fit for you without having to start from scratch. Leave it with me for a few days."

"How much do I need to pay?"

Byron waved him away. "You've been a good customer. I'll trust you. I won't know until I do the work anyway. It depends on how stubborn the metal is."

Will left, making his way to the southern gate and exiting the city. Once he was near the congruence point, he called Tailtiu and waited. She appeared within just a few minutes. "That was quick," Will noted.

"Since I still owe you many days of service, I thought I would stay close to this crossing," Tailtiu replied.

"How considerate of you," said Will. "I want you to go into the city with me again. I need to examine a building."

"You want me to sneak in for you?"

"Not today. In fact, I can just walk in. It's getting out that concerns me," he explained. "I want you to get familiar with the area. When the day comes, I'll need you to help me escape."

She cocked her head to one side. "The man who defeated a demon lord plans to run?"

He shook his head. "I didn't defeat Leykachak, I just softened him up for—"

Tailtiu held up her hand. "Don't say its name. Just the thought of it ruins my mood."

They walked together into the city, and Tailtiu adopted her overly endowed farmwife disguise. When they eventually reached the great cathedral near the city center, she stared up at it. "What is this?"

"The Church of the Holy Mother," Will replied. "Selene is getting married here."

Tailtiu nodded in understanding. "I see. You plan to murder your former lover on her wedding day. It makes sense that you would want my help escaping. You'll have most of the city on your heels." She was rubbing her hands together with anticipation.

"No," said Will flatly. "That isn't what I intend—not at all."

She arched one brow. "A double murder then, bride and groom?"

"No!"

"Ooh, you're thinking big! Maybe you plan to block the exits and trap everyone inside? A fire would finish them all."

"Sweet Mother, no! Is that all you think about? Killing people?"

Tailtiu licked her lips, fixing her eyes on him. "Of course not. There's one other thing—"

"Don't say it," ordered Will. *I knew better than to ask.*

In front of the cathedral was a large square that featured a statue of the goddess in her fierce warlike aspect, armored and pointing a sword skyward. According to legend, Temarah had been born as a mortal woman in some forgotten age. Raised as a cooper's daughter, she went on to serve in the house of a great lord before eventually having her innate divinity revealed. Will wasn't firm on the details of what happened after that as he'd never paid close attention. He knew she'd eventually married a man who later became the god of the underworld, but it didn't make sense to him. *Why would a goddess of virtue and motherhood marry the god of the dead?*

Two large roads met at the square, though they were diverted around the statue by a circular lane that allowed the carriages of the wealthy to drop off their occupants near the front steps. Taking a leisurely walk around, Will saw that smaller roads also passed along the sides and front of the massive stone building. There were exits on each side of the building.

"No matter which way I leave I'll have to cross at least one street before I can find cover," he muttered out loud. "I'll definitely need your help." The chameleon spell wouldn't be sufficient if he was running across clear ground in broad daylight, but Tailtiu's mist would be enough even by itself. He looked at his companion. "Let's go inside."

His aunt smiled. "I've always wanted to defile a church."

Will sighed. "There will be no defiling today, or any other day for that matter."

"I don't understand why you're so shy," she complained. "It's not as if you're a virgin anymore. I don't ask for much."

He ignored her and walked up the steps to the massive wooden doors that stood open. The church was open to the public most days of the week. The doors were only shut late at night and during official services.

Once inside, he could see that the front entrance led directly into a wide aisle that went straight through the center of two wide rows of benches until it met the main altar at the center. Auxiliary aisles further bisected the benches on either side, allowing the worshipers to move in and out even when the cathedral was filled. On the left and right of the main altar were smaller sections that branched off, giving the layout a cross-like structure. The smaller sections also had benches, though these were cushioned and reserved for the nobility.

Glancing up, he noted that the main section also had a second level that resembled a wooden balcony. It held more seating for important visitors, likely merchants or others with money but no title.

As they walked down the aisle Will noticed that a priest was watching them, which made him feel slightly self-conscious. From one side of his mouth he whispered, "Just act natural."

Tailtiu chuckled. "I'm always natural, speak for yourself."

They spent a few more minutes examining the sides of the room and then exited from the eastern end of the sanctuary so he could take note of any differences in the layout. The smaller sections had no central aisle, which meant anyone leaving had to move along the sides, and the doors were smaller.

Back outside, Will took Tailtiu on a walk of the surrounding neighborhood. Unfortunately, the city in that area featured wide spaces. Both the roads and the areas between the buildings were broad. The buildings were small as well, being only a single story tall. Will guessed there must be a building code to prevent any nearby structures from competing with the cathedral's dominance of the local area.

Tailtiu's mist would be a life saver, but he still wasn't comfortable. He wanted something better, so he returned to the cathedral and walked around the exterior once more, hoping he would spot something helpful.

"You keep looking up," observed his aunt. "What about the sewers?"

Will stopped, then looked down. The wide streets around the cathedral were marked by several large openings into the city's sewer system at their edges. "You're a genius," he exclaimed.

"I already knew that," she replied.

He walked over to the gutter opening nearest to the eastern entrance of the cathedral. It was definitely wide enough lengthwise, but the other dimension was too narrow. He took note of the construction, for the top portion of the gutter was formed of a single long stone that reminded him of a door lintel. "If we weaken the mortar, we might be able to lift the top stone and slip through."

Tailtiu bent down and put one hand on the top edge. In a seemingly effortless exercise of strength she lifted the stone, pulling it free and causing the mortar to fall away. "Like this?"

"Put it down!" hissed Will, glancing around to see if anyone was watching them.

She did and he ushered her down the street at a brisk pace. “You’re freakishly strong,” he remarked. “Have I mentioned that before?”

“Not just my arms either,” she said with a wink.

Will closed his eyes. “Please, stop.”

“The real question,” she continued, “is whether there’s a route from there that’s large enough for a clumsy human to navigate.”

“Can you check it for me later? Preferably at night.”

She nodded. “I do my best work at night.”

Will shook his head. There was no winning with Tailtiu. “I’ll meet you tomorrow to see what you’ve discovered.”

CHAPTER 61

The next day Will went through his paces—classes, practice, and meals—then consulted Arrogan once more. "I need some advice."

"You need to find a better conversation starter," said the ring. "Every time you begin with the same line. I'm getting tired of it."

"How about this one? I don't want to die."

"Better, but I'd prefer one like this, 'Arrogan, I'm tired of tormenting you. I'll be taking you to be melted down today.'"

"If you keep being difficult, I'll start taking you to my classes and activate the limnthal so you have to listen to the lectures," threatened Will.

"Now you're just being nasty," said Arrogan in a wounded tone. "Who taught you to behave like that?"

"You did."

"Fair enough. What did you want to know?"

"I know what I want, but I don't know if it's possible. Is there a way to design a spell to break glass vials on command?"

"Definitely not," pronounced the ring, but there was an odd tone in its voice.

Will sighed. "There's a way. Just tell me. I don't want to play the question game."

"Your question was shit," complained the ring. "But fine, I won't torture you. You can't do something like that with a spell. You need an enchantment."

"I haven't learned much about enchantments yet."

"They're similar to spells, but they're written on something."

"Like the spells in a journal?"

"No, idiot. These are written forms that *do* something. Usually it's to produce a prolonged or permanent effect, but they can also be used for one-time activations. In your case, what you want is something simple. It's similar to the shatter spell you learned, but you inscribe it on something. For a vial you'd probably use a piece of paper or a label. With a command word you could activate it and destroy the vial."

Will felt his excitement growing. "That's exactly what I need. Can you teach it to me?"

Arrogan's sarcasm was thick as he replied, "Sure, I'll just write it out for you."

"Can't you just tell me the runes and the order to write them in?"

"How about you try writing down the chameleon spell you've been using so frequently? Do it without referring to *Practical Magic.* Can you manage that?"

Will frowned. Of course he could. He'd memorized the spell and he practiced it daily. *I'll prove him wrong this time,* he thought. "Give me a few minutes." Going to the desk, he found a blank sheet of paper and began writing.

"Take as long as you want," said the ring.

Halfway through, Will got stuck. Eventually he was forced to construct the spell as if he was planning to cast it. By doing that he figured out what he had forgotten and was able to continue. He got stuck again a few minutes later, and before he was done transcribing the spell onto the page, he had been forced to construct the spell four times. "I did it," he announced.

"And you almost certainly had to create the spell construct to remember how it was done, didn't you?" asked Arrogan.

"Yeah," he admitted.

"Now you understand what I meant before when I said I couldn't teach you spells. It's even worse when you can reflex cast something, because you've stopped consciously creating the construct. In the case of enchantments, there isn't even a construct to refer to. It's something done purely on a material substrate, so unless you use the same enchantment every day, you're unlikely to remember all the details. That's why we have these things called *books.*"

"Sounds like I'll need to make another trip to the library," Will acknowledged. "Do you know what the enchantment I need is called?"

"No clue," said Arrogan. "I just remember it's very simple. Even someone like you should be able to master it fairly quickly. If you can find the information."

"Thanks," said Will. He dismissed the limnthal and considered his options. Professor Dulaney would probably have the knowledge, but whether the teacher would agree to share it with him was another matter. Failing that, he would need to find a third- or fourth-year student and ask them, since they started learning enchantments in the third year. Sadly, he didn't know anyone beyond the second year, not well enough to ask anyway. The only third-year he could name off the top of his head was Craig Larkin, and he was certain that one of Dennis' old friends wouldn't want to help him.

Will ran through his practice exercises a few times and then left. It was time to meet Tailtiu and see what she had discovered. On his way through the lobby he ran across Rob, which gave him an idea. "Rob!"

"Will!" said his friend, responding with a grin and an equal amount of mock enthusiasm.

He laughed. "Do you know any third- or fourth-years well enough to ask them about something?"

"I know a few thirds," said Rob, rubbing his chin as though pondering a deep and serious matter.

Will described what he wanted to know. "Do you think you could find someone who would tell you, or at least point you in the right direction?"

Rob nodded. "Probably. Give me a day or two. Why do you want to know?"

"It's just for an alchemy project I'm working on."

"Sure…" said Rob with obvious disbelief. "I see why you want me to ask. Everyone knows you're up to no good."

Will put on an air of great offense. "You wound me, my friend!"

"Says the man with two black eyes."

He couldn't argue with that. They talked for a few more minutes and then Will went on his way. He met Tailtiu outside the city not long after dusk had settled over the landscape.

"Did you find a way?" he asked.

His aunt nodded. "The sewers under the center of the city are large. You may have to swim for some part of the journey. Also the smell is intense."

"But there's a way out?"

"You won't even need my guidance," answered Tailtiu. "Just follow the flow and you'll wind up at the river outlet. There's an iron grate there, but that won't be much of a problem for you."

At least one thing is working out smoothly, thought Will. "That's great. All I need from you now is for you to wait for me outside the cathedral on the date of the wedding."

"What time?"

"I'm not sure," said Will. "It's going to be on the next Saturday after this coming weekend. I think the ceremony takes place at noon, so I'll probably be running for my life some time shortly after that."

"Probably? Are you not certain?"

He shrugged. "There's a tiny chance that things will go better than I expect. If that happens, I might not need to run at all, but I rather doubt that will be the case."

"Or they might kill you before you can escape," added Tailtiu.

Will grimaced. "Or that. If I don't come out, wait until nightfall. If I haven't sent you a message by then I'm probably dead. There's also a chance I might have been imprisoned. Perhaps you could extract me."

"Human dungeons are full of iron," she responded, wrinkling her nose, "but I will try if you wish me to."

He smirked. "I think I'd like that."

With that settled, he returned to Wurthaven where he spent a short time practicing before heading to the Alchemy building. Assuming he could acquire the enchantment he needed, he would also want to have the alchemical vials ready for use.

The next day passed without much to mark it, although he still caught the other students glancing at him now and then, presumably to get a look at the now-yellow bruises around his eyes. After Spell Theory he took the opportunity to see if Professor Dulaney would share the information he needed. Will explained what he was trying to find out and then waited to see how the teacher responded.

Dulaney frowned at him. "Why the sudden interest in enchantments? Most students don't encounter them until their third year, though I had ideas of starting you on them next year."

"Just curious, sir," said Will innocently. "I'm always looking to expand my knowledge."

His teacher laughed. "Anytime a student says something along the lines of 'I just want to learn,' I know it means trouble. Your request is oddly specific for someone with innocent intentions."

Will decided to try his backup story. "I just want to play a prank on someone, a very harmless prank."

"Mm hmm. How'd you get the black eyes?"

"I'd rather not talk about it, sir."

Dulaney nodded. "Funny, I feel the same way about enchantments. I'll see you tomorrow." Standing, he patted Will on the back as he ushered him out of his office. Will growled in frustration as he left.

I expected as much, he told himself, trying to suppress his disappointment.

On Friday he returned to the armor-smith's shop, where he encountered another piece of disappointing news. "I can't do a damn thing with it," Byron Waters informed him. "I can't even figure out what it's made of. I've never seen anything like it. Where did you get it?"

Will pursed his lips. "Would you believe me if I said it came from another world?"

The smith scratched his beard. "I'd believe anything about now. It's a little bit lighter than regular steel, and the color is strange, but the material properties are what amaze me. I haven't been able to bend it in the slightest, even after annealing. Ordinarily something that hard would be brittle, but it refuses to respond to anything I do to it. I shattered one of my best cold chisels just trying to see if I could put a mark on it."

"Well, damn. I had hoped to use it."

"It would make the finest breastplate anyone could ever hope to own, if it could be shaped," agreed Byron. "You say it came from another world. Do you know what made those scratches?" He pointed to the faint lines that the goddamn cat's claws had left. "It looks like a beast did it, but anything that could scratch this metal would have to be harder and sharper than any weapon ever forged."

"I can't really say," said Will sadly. "But you're right. It was a beast, though from an entirely different world than the one this breastplate came from."

"You move in strange circles, young man," said the smith. "I hope I never meet that beast of yours." He left the room and returned a moment later. "Here's your other breastplate. I was able to knock it back into shape at least."

Will held it up so he could see how the light reflected from it. He couldn't even tell where it had been dented. "You made it look like new. How do you manage that?"

"Practice and patience," said the smith with a proud smile. "A good solid round of buffing and polishing at the end also goes a long way toward hiding any imperfections." He moved closer and put a hand on Will's shoulder. "By the way, I didn't ask, but what hit you? That dent was right in the center, the strongest part of the armor. I'd almost think you were laying down while someone pounded on you with a maul."

"I think it was a stone spike".

"A sorcerer? Who, how—never mind. Probably better that I don't get too nosy. When I first met you, I thought it strange that a young scholar would want so much armor, but I'm starting to think you don't wear enough."

"I can't help but agree with you."

"Well, be careful. I'd hate to lose a good customer."

Will smiled. "It would break my heart if I couldn't keep spending my gold here." He collected his things, paid for the repairs, and soon he was on his way back to Wurthaven.

When he was back in his room he practiced some more, and when he finally grew tired of that he summoned the limnthal so he could ask Arrogan about the breastplate. He described its color and what the smith had said regarding its strength and hardness.

Arrogan stopped him halfway through his explanation. "You don't have to bother telling me all that. If you got it from Leykachak's body I already know what it is. The technical term for it is driktenspal, but no one ever used that name. It was made up by some pretentious ass who liked weird names. We called it demon-steel."

"Is there any way to use it?"

"Sure. You just need to find a mage-smith familiar with the metal and the spells that make it pliable enough to be worked."

"A mage-smith," muttered Will, rolling the term around in his mouth. "Where do you find one of those?"

"You don't, jackass!" spat Arrogan. "I killed the last two a long time ago. A mage-smith is first and foremost a wizard, and they were among those who I had to eliminate."

Will sighed. "Is their knowledge preserved somewhere?"

"There's probably books about their work here in Wurthaven, or in the library in Myrsta, but I doubt there's anyone who has worked with the metal itself in several hundred years."

He thought about it for a minute. A mage-smith was probably Arrogan's equivalent for the modern wizard engineers who trained at Wurthaven. If he was going to find someone with the background to figure out how to work with the metal, or at least put the old knowledge to use, he would probably have to start with the college Engineering Department. *A project for the future, if I'm still around,* he decided.

"Is there anything else you know about demon-steel?" he asked.

"Not really. There were legends about where it came from, of course. Some said it was mined and smelted by Madrok himself from the pits of hell, but I never put much stock in those sorts of myths. More likely it's just a somewhat rare metal found in hell. Most of the more important demon lords wear armor made from it."

"That reminds me of something else. Aislinn warned me before, when I was trying to figure out what to do about the ritual. She said that if I punished the demon lord or refused to give him what he'd been promised that I would become a target. She even said that Madrok might start helping the Shimerans for a lower cost, so they could destroy me or Terabinia."

The ring thought about it for a moment. "She's right, as usual, but you killed Leykachak, so I don't think you have much to worry about."

"The cat killed him," corrected Will.

"Same difference. The thing about demons is that they don't get along. Their hierarchy is held together by fear and power. The revenge you might expect would only be a concern if a humiliated Leykachak had to go home with his tail tucked between his legs. Then he'd use his connections and influence to try and find a way to make you suffer. Since he's dead, the others aren't likely to care. That's assuming they even know who did it. You weren't the one who initiated the ritual after all."

That took one concern off his shoulders. Will dismissed the limnthal and returned to practicing. He went to bed early that night and when he started again the next morning, he noticed a change when he constructed the point-defense spell. After weeks of no discernable change, the construct was beginning to come together almost effortlessly. It still wasn't instantaneous, but he hardly had to think about it. He couldn't help but feel hopeful that he was getting close to his goal.

His excitement was interrupted by a knock on his door. He found Rob waiting in the hall. "I found it," said his friend.

"Found what—oh! The enchantment?" Will ushered Rob into the room. "How did you get the information?"

"Veronica Wellings," said Rob simply.

Will just stared at him blankly, for the name meant nothing to him.

"The redhead," added Rob.

Will shrugged.

"You need to get out more," said his friend with notable disgust. "I'm starting to think you don't even look at girls. She's the third-year with the flaming red hair. All the guys in her class are crazy about her. I've been wanting an excuse to talk to her for ages, and you, my friend, finally gave me one."

He nodded. "You're very welcome."

"Smartass," Rob bit back. "Anyway, after asking around I found out she's planning to focus on Engineering in her fifth and sixth years, so she's been paying close attention to it in her studies *this* year."

Will was beginning to feel impatient. "Did you learn the enchantment from her?"

His friend scowled at his abruptness. "Well no, but I did get a date!"

Will covered his face with his hands.

"Congratulations, Rob. I'm so happy for you. It's amazing that a girl like that would go on a date with you!" said Rob in an overly enthusiastic tone.

"What was all that?"

"What you should say when you're happy for a friend, you knob," replied Rob darkly.

"Oh, I see," said Will. Then he adopted a saccharine smile and repeated the words. "Congratulations, Rob! I'm so damned happy for you! Will I be invited to the wedding?"

Rob ignored his tone and accepted the words as his natural due. "Thank you, Will. I'll introduce you someday, maybe after the wedding."

Will laughed. "So, you didn't learn the enchantment. Are you just here to brag?"

"No. She told me the name. It's called a 'glass trigger,' or more properly a 'destructive trigger.' Apparently, they're used a lot in mining and excavation when they want to release acids or set off explosions without being too close."

"Now I know what to look for. Is it restricted?"

Rob shook his head. "According to Veronica it isn't. Most enchantments aren't, since they aren't usually dangerous or useful for criminal endeavors. Anyway, for whatever reason, this one is so basic and common that there's not much point in trying to put it in the restricted sections."

After that, Will wasted no time before going to visit the library, this time in a legitimate fashion, and just as Rob had said, the enchantment was easy to find in several of the early enchanting primers. Knowing the name of what he was looking for made all the difference in the world.

The simplest version was little more than what amounted to a one-time use enchantment inscribed on a piece of paper and imbued with a small portion of turyn. The user could pick a command word at the time of creation, so it was possible to use different commands if separate activations were desired. The obverse was also true—multiple triggers could be made that used the same command word so that all would activate at the same time.

There were also more complex versions that could incorporate multiple command words, in case the user wanted more flexibility, and there were other types that could be used to trigger spells built into separate enchantments. Will didn't feel ready for any of those, but all he really needed was the simple version. He copied it into his journal and then made notes on the text before leaving the library and heading for the Alchemy building.

He wanted to test the enchantment out on actual vials in a controlled environment, and the Alchemy building had rooms built for just such things.

His tests went well. The enchantment was just about the simplest thing he had ever learned, and it worked exactly as he'd hoped. Will spent a few hours preparing enough triggers for the vials he had already made.

Now I just have to make sure everything is in place for the wedding, he thought.

Chapter 62

Will sat on the end of the last pew in the cathedral. He was wearing his best clothing, the doublet and hose he'd had made for the Winter Ball. It was the only thing he had that was remotely acceptable for a royal wedding, but he still felt uncomfortable about the fact that he had no armor on. His brigandine was too bulky to wear with the doublet and jerkin.

After everything he'd been through, not having at least torso protection made him feel naked and vulnerable. The fact that he was almost certain to face serious threats to life and limb didn't make it any easier. *But the armor might interfere anyway,* he reminded himself, thinking of Plan C. Plan C revolved around the spell he had prepared and tucked away, though if he had to use it, he wasn't sure he would survive.

Best case, I walk out of here with Selene, though there isn't really a snowball's chance in hell of that happening. No, he would almost certainly have to rely on Plan B and hope they couldn't catch him. His main goal was to show Selene the truth. Happily ever after would have to wait for another day.

He had come to the cathedral the day before, so he could surreptitiously prepare the scene, and he had returned early in the morning so he could hide himself with a chameleon spell before the cathedral filled with guests. If he'd had an invitation, he would have just walked in with everyone else, but someone had neglected to send one to the princess' illicit lover. *It's almost as if they don't trust me,* he thought sourly.

Will had secretly hoped the goddamn cat would show himself, but he had seen no sign of that worthy being in attendance. The cat only did was suited him, and since there were no demons or fae involved in a royal wedding, it probably didn't interest the demigod.

Once the church had filled with those commoners lucky enough to be considered worthy of an invitation, Will had dropped his chameleon spell and mixed in with them so he could find his current seat. Trying to stay hidden would have been too risky with so many sorcerers in attendance, which is what most of the nobility were, and they were due to arrive.

The side entrances opened, and the peers of the realm began to enter, filling one of the smaller side sections. Once they were inside, the other section filled with wealthy citizens deemed too important to sit with the other commoners. With everyone seated, the orchestra in the back began to play, and a hush fell over the crowded cathedral.

The huge double doors of the main entrance opened once more and Count Spry marched down the central aisle to take his place in front of the altar, where the high priest waited for him. Will's heart began to speed up in anticipation.

A few minutes later the doors opened again, and Princess Selene Maligant stood between them, flanked by her father and backlit by a sun that seemed to have been created for only that purpose. The light yellow of her dress glowed in the light, and Will forgot to breathe. *She's more beautiful than I could have ever imagined.* He was stunned for a moment, and it wasn't until he felt a tear trickle down one cheek that he realized how utterly taken he was by the moment.

Her dress was a work of art—simple, yet embroidered with lace and flowers that seemed to flow across her shoulders and down her arms. He could only stare as King Lognion began to slowly escort her down the aisle, and doubts began to assail him. *I shouldn't be here. I'm going to ruin everything, and she'll hate me for the rest of her life.*

Selene smiled beatifically as she walked down the aisle, her eyes scanning the crowd of well-wishers. She stumbled when her gaze fell upon Will, and her eyes widened in alarm. He could almost hear her unspoken words: *"Don't do it. Don't you dare. They'll kill you."*

Will smiled reassuringly, though he doubted his expression had the intended effect. Soon she had passed by and he was left staring at her back. The ceremony continued. The high priest opened with his greetings to the assembled crowd, and a lengthy soliloquy about the sanctity of marriage and the hallowed history of the institution. Will only wished it would go more quickly, for his heart was racing a mile a minute and he wanted to get on with his idiocy before he died of a heart attack.

Eventually the priest reached the part Will had been waiting for. "If any man here can show just cause why—" A hush fell over the cathedral and loud gasps sounded from some of the guests as Will rose and began walking down the central aisle.

The guests were understandably confused, and among the wedding party there wasn't a single face that showed anything less than pure malice as they watched Will's approach. Even the priest was furious; he didn't bother asking what Will wanted. The cleric gestured to the wings and ordered, "Take this fool out of here!"

So much for tradition, thought Will as two unarmed guards approached him from either side. Weapons had been forbidden inside, though the soldiers outside the building were well armed. Will caught both men with the source-link spell when they were twenty feet away, and by the time they reached him they were too weak to seize him. They grasped feebly at him and he pushed them away, whereupon they collapsed to the floor. "I think you should hear what I have to say!" he announced loudly.

Selene was staring at him, her face the very picture of a human being in the throes of absolute horror. King Lognion watched him with a bemused expression, but Malcolm Spry's features had transformed to reflect the vast and uncontainable rage that had filled him from head to toe. "You dare?" screamed the count, spittle flying from his lips. He followed his expression of outrage with a hastily constructed bolt of fire, drawing from his elemental too quickly for anyone to react.

Will lifted his hand, though it was an unnecessary gesture, and when the blazing line of flame reached him it flickered and went out as he absorbed its power. "Princess Selene does not love this man," he said, pitching his voice so it could be heard from one end of the cathedral to the other. "She is marrying him against her will."

"Only legal causes can be given at a time like this, young man," said the priest, who seemed to have decided to properly act his part. "Declarations of love are not sufficient to—"

"Marriage is a voluntary act," interrupted Will. "Can one who has been compelled be considered to be a voluntary participant?"

Count Spry appeared on the verge of apoplexy, and a new spell started to appear above his palms. Selene shoved him to interrupt the cast. "Stop it, Malcolm!" She turned her attention back to Will. "I'm doing this of my own free will," she declared.

Will drew steadily closer and they were less than ten feet apart by then. "No, you aren't. You love me. You're doing this because *he* told you it was the only way to protect me." He accompanied the accusation with a finger pointed at the king.

Selene's features were desperate, her eyes full of fear. "William, you have to stop, before it's too late."

"I won't stop," said Will calmly. "There's nothing left for you to fear and nothing to gain. This wedding won't protect me now that I've stood here and made a fool of that man." His eyes darted toward Count Spry. "Tell them the truth."

"William, please," she begged. "You have to—"

Count Spry couldn't take it any longer. He rushed forward. "I'm not going to stand here and listen to this fool prattling on about—"

Selene acted on instinct. As the groom started to pass by, she caught the back of his jacket, pulling him off balance. Though it wasn't quite intentional, she wound up throwing him to the floor in front of the gathered masses. "I said stop!" she shouted. "This is my business, not yours!" Selene stared down in dismay at the man she had just humiliated.

The count wasn't done, however. From the floor he turned his face to the king. "Your Majesty, I call on you to end this travesty and expel this man at once!"

King Lognion's face, which had shown only amusement, slowly changed to an expression of annoyance. "Count Spry, return to your place and be silent. You try my patience." Then he looked at Will. "William, you never cease to amaze. Do you think this will earn my blessing? You cannot be that great a fool."

Will looked from Selene to her father. "No, Your Majesty. I only want the truth to be known. Your daughter is in love with me. She only weds the count because you have ordered her to do so." Deep down he was beginning to worry. Things hadn't gone terribly wrong yet, but neither had they proceeded as he hoped. If they went on much longer, he would have to abandon the attempt and move on to escape before it was too late.

Selene's eyes moved from the count, to Will, to her father in quick succession. Her heart and mind were a mess of emotions. Anger and frustration competed with pure confusion as she tried to decide what to do. The situation was devolving rapidly, and she knew there was no point in continuing with the wedding any longer, but what worried her most was the expression in her father's eyes.

The elementals hovering above the king's shoulders were pulsing brightly, and Will could see lines of turyn being channeled from them into their master. Lognion's eyes stared at him with cold intensity. "You should have listened to my offer, William. This was not the way, and now you will suffer the fate that befalls any man who dares anger me." A spell began to form in front of him.

Will started to react, but Selene stepped in front of him. "No!" she declared loudly. "If you want to kill him, you'll have to kill me first."

A shocked groan came from the audience and King Lognion paused, letting his spell fade. His attention was on his daughter now, and the malice in his gaze was hot enough to melt steel. His voice emerged in a low, menacing tone. “I will say this only once, daughter. Step aside. Your pet has gone too far.”

Selene’s jaw was set in defiance. “I won’t.” Reaching behind her, she took Will’s hand in her own. If she felt any surprise when she felt what he held in his palm, she didn’t show it on her face. She closed her fist around the object and Will wrapped his hand around hers.

That should be enough, thought Will. *He’ll compel her to move with the heart-stone enchantment and then I’ll have to run for my life. She’ll know the truth, though. She’ll know he’s been lying to her all along.* A few more seconds and it would be time for Plan B.

King Lognion addressed the crowd. “Everyone out!” No one moved for a few seconds, but after he repeated his command the people in the benches began to hastily head for the exits. Lognion repeated his order for the benefit of the clergy as well. “I said out! I want everyone but Count Spry, my daughter, and the soon-to-be-dead man out of this cathedral.” It took several minutes for the place to empty, and after it had he looked at the count. “Stand by me if you would, Malcolm, so I can shield you. We wouldn’t want you dying by accident.”

Will’s heart leapt into his throat when the king spoke again. “Very well, my willful daughter. It’s time for you to learn a painful lesson. You have only yourself to blame for this. Please kill the idiot standing beside you.”

Selene almost laughed. “You’re insane—” but then the heart-stone enchantment in her chest pulsed, and her voice stopped suddenly. She released Will’s hand and turned without hesitation, her other hand covered by a stone spike which she drove toward his midsection.

He was too close to dodge and too surprised to move, but a force shield appeared in front of her spike, causing it to shatter. Will took several steps back. *This isn’t what I wanted,* he thought desperately. “Selene, if you can hear me, try to fight it!” he called.

King Lognion stood behind a force dome and laughed, while Count Spry looked on in confusion. Stone from the floor flowed upward to encase Selene’s body in heavy armor, while water condensed around her hands, forming deadly water blades. There was nothing in her eyes but determination.

Will tried to think. This wasn’t one of the situations he had anticipated. But it wasn’t all bad. The king had finally given a command that would destroy her delusion. He just had to survive. It was time to run. He began backing away when a water drill speared toward him. He intercepted it with another force shield. Two more followed it in quick succession, and he stopped those as well, then the floor began to move.

She'll try to trap me, he realized. "Let's start the party!" he yelled, using the phrase he had picked for his enchantments. Tiny explosions rang out at various points throughout the cathedral, as the alchemical smoke bombs he had planted the night before shattered. Worried about both himself and the crowd, he had chosen a formula that would produce a harmless gas to obscure the area. He ran to one side as smoke filled the room, adjusting his vision as he went.

He was the only one who could see now, and all he had to do was get to one of the exits. There was nothing Selene could do to stop him.

Or so he thought.

When he reached the eastern exit, he found nothing but a thick stone wall. Something swept toward him through the smoke, and he only evaded it by dropping down to lie on the floor. It was a twisting, horizontal column of water that tore apart the wooden benches as it passed. *Shit, shit, shit!* He leapt to his feet as it passed and ran toward the main entrance. It was probably blocked too, but it was all he could think to do.

Will was forced to dodge another column of water as he ran, and when he reached the door he found it just as solidly blocked. Keeping his eyes on Selene and the king, he started back toward the center of the cathedral. He dodged several more water columns as he went. Selene was systematically destroying the interior of the cathedral in her efforts to kill her unseen opponent.

Once he was close enough to be sure of his aim, Will unleashed a force bolt at King Lognion. It exploded forcefully against the dome surrounding the monarch. Will saw Lognion stumble for a moment, but he kept his feet and his defense didn't shatter. *How long can he keep that dome up?* wondered Will. Then he realized that with four elementals, the king probably had the turyn to sustain it almost indefinitely.

"That's not very sporting of you, William," laughed Lognion. "I'm not your opponent, Selene is."

He resisted the urge to reply, which would give away his position. Instead, Will fired off several more force lances, pounding the king's defenses, but they seemed to have no effect. Then stones began to rain down from the ceiling, and he was forced to produce shields to block those that came to close to hitting him. *This is ridiculous,* he thought. *I can't win like this.* He kept moving, firing off force lances at irregular intervals, hoping he could force the king to use up his absurd turyn reserves.

"I think we've had enough of this smoke," said Lognion. "It's time for you to die, William." A strong updraft swept through the cathedral, pushing the alchemical smoke up and away from the ground. Within seconds the air was clear, and the ceiling was obscured by a strange-looking indoor cloud as the king's air elemental kept the smoke suspended. "Finish him, Selene!"

Will tried to construct a chameleon spell, but Selene spotted him and sent a water drill in his direction. He was forced to abandon the spell construct and block her assault with a shield. He changed tactics, trying to cast a blur spell, but stones fell from the ceiling, this time with much greater accuracy.

He deflected those with rapid-fire shields, including an occasional shield to stop the water drills that Selene tried to hit him with while he was distracted. But in the end, he knew it would be useless. He could only stop her attacks for so long. Eventually he would miss, or something he didn't see would strike him from a blind spot.

He had to fight back.

Running toward her, he deflected attacks left and right, then somehow managed to find a pause long enough to construct a spell. His force lance struck her dead center, shattering her armor and flinging her backward. *Now!* Before she could recover, he cast his oldest spell, the source-link. If he could drain her turyn, he could end the fight without bloodshed.

It failed to connect, and Will stared at her in horror. He tried again, and still had no luck.

His last gambit had failed. It had never occurred to him that her will was strong enough to resist him. He'd always assumed that Arrogan's training made him superior. He turned to run, but the floor opened up beneath him. He'd gotten too close. Selene's earth elemental had absolute control of the stone in close proximity to her. *"She will kill you,"* the goddamn cat had warned. *It couldn't have been any clearer,* thought Will. *And I thought he was being mysterious.*

The stone closed around him, trapping him in the floor from the waist down. His hands were free, though. He raised them and formed a force-lance. Selene's armor still hadn't reformed. If he released the spell it would blow a hole completely through her chest.

Selene stepped forward, a long, sharp spike of stone in her right hand, pointed at his chest, and their eyes met.

It was a timeless moment. Will knew he couldn't defend himself unless he released the force lance, but as he stared at her, he couldn't do it. Selene drove forward, intent on driving the stone weapon through his heart, but she froze at the last moment.

And then she began to scream.

It was a heart wrenching sound, one that Will wished never to hear again, as if all the despair in Selene's soul was pouring from her tortured throat. Her eyes were locked on him the entire time, and blood began to drip from them, from her nose, and even from her ears. Selene's body shook violently as she struggled against the magic twisting her soul, and her scream went on and on.

She was dying, for her soul was beginning to tear itself apart.

"Release her!" yelled Will. "It's killing her! You have to release her!"

Count Spry had had enough. Running forward, he cried out, "Just kill him already!" There was a long dagger in the man's hand, though he shouldn't have had a weapon given the rules of the church.

Will struggled for a moment. He couldn't create a shield and he couldn't use the force lance with Selene in front of him. It took him a precious second to decide what to do, and as he dismissed the force-lance, Malcolm Spry's dagger slammed into his chest.

Being stabbed was surprisingly painless, relatively speaking. Will tried to say something, but blood emerged instead of air, turning his curse into a gurgle. Then the count pulled his blade free and drove it home again, this time lower, piercing Will's diaphragm. That was when the pain truly began. Will released his final spell, the one he had held in reserve, but nothing happened.

He watched as the count pulled his blade back to strike a third time, but then Malcolm Spry's head vanished. It took him a moment to realize that one of Selene's water blades had decapitated the man. Will's eyes found hers. She was still screaming, still dying. And in the background, he could hear nothing but King Lognion's laughter.

Will choked, bringing up more blood, and then he felt his heart stutter, slowing in chest. His vision grew dark. He wanted to speak. To tell her it would be all right. *If I die, the enchantment won't kill you.* Then his heart finally thudded to a halt.

William Cartwright's muscles relaxed, and his head fell forward, and then at last, he was dead. The last sound that reached his ears was silence, as Selene's screaming finally ceased.

***

Chapter 62

Selene Maligant, only daughter of King Lognion, closed her mouth and let her raw vocal cords rest. She had been trapped in a living nightmare, one in which her father was somehow driving her to kill Will. She blinked, for her vision was blurry and her eyes hurt. Wiping her nose, she found blood on the sleeve of the priceless dress she wore. Her head was filled with pain, and it was difficult to think.

Then she saw the blurry shapes of two bodies on the floor in front of her. The nightmare had been real. "No! No, no, no, no! William! Say something. Please say something!" She fell to her knees, and her dress began to rapidly absorb the pooling blood on the floor.

"I warned you," said a voice from behind, her father. "Hopefully you've learned a lesson from this." Then a dark chuckle emerged from his throat. "It's going to be difficult to find you a husband after this. It appears that your suitors have an unacceptably high mortality rate."

Selene ignored him. Calling on her elemental, she released Will's body from the ground and laid him carefully on the now smooth stone floor. Heedless of the blood, she put her head against his chest, but she heard only silence. "Will, you can't be dead," she told him desperately.

Then she remembered what he had handed her. The vial was still in her hand. Hope sprang up in her chest. It was a miracle she hadn't broken it during the fight. Unstopping the vial, she lifted Will's head and poured most of the regeneration potion down his throat. She saved the last few drops and poured those into the stab wounds in his chest. "Wake up, Will. You're going to be all right," she said softly, tears mixing with blood and making messy tracks down her cheeks.

Lognion nudged Will's body with his toe. "He's dead, Selene. Nothing will bring him back, though I must admit it was clever of him to give you a regeneration potion. You shouldn't have wasted it."

Selene held his head in her hands as she knelt over him. Her face was only inches away as she began to plead, "Will, Will, come on. You're not dead, you know you aren't. This is a trick. Wake up, please wake up. You have to show him that it was just a trick. The potion will heal you. You just have to open your eyes."

"Regeneration potions only work on the living," said Lognion dryly.

"Shut up!" screamed Selene. "It will work, it has to work." She was crying uncontrollably now, her body rocking to and fro as she held William's limp form.

"Get up," ordered the king. "We should leave. They need to come clean up this mess."

"I'm not going anywhere!" Selene hissed, her voice thick and ugly. "He's not dead."

"It was a fun game while it lasted," said Lognion, "but it's over now."

"I won't leave him."

The king sighed. "I never could deny you anything. Fine, we'll wait." Moving off to one side, he located a bench that was still largely intact and righted it so he could sit down.

Half an hour passed while Selene held her dead lover, talking to him softly and crying intermittently, but Will's body failed to move. After an hour the body began to noticeably cool as the cold stone floor drew its warmth away.

King Lognion finally lost his patience and walked away, returning a few minutes later with a group of men. He took his daughter by the arm and dragged her away. Selene didn't resist, for she had lost the will to fight.

"What should we do with the bodies, Your Majesty?" asked one of the men.

"Take the count's remains and have them sewn back together so we can give him a proper burial," said the king.

"And the other one?"

Lognion looked at Will's corpse for a moment, his mind calculating. "Burn it."

CHAPTER 63

Selene sat in the carriage next to her father as they returned to the palace. Inside she felt empty. There was nothing, just black despair. The man who had raised her gave her a smile she knew to be a lie, then he said, "You'll feel better later."

"I'm going to kill you," said Selene evenly.

"I think it's better this way," said her father. "You know how I prefer honesty. You were always a willful child and it was exhausting dealing with your stubbornness. Now I no longer have to pretend."

"This isn't a joke. I'm going to murder you in your sleep," Selene informed him.

"Perhaps you'd like to go on one of your little charity trips? You always liked those. I'll even donate this time so you can feed people, or buy them clothes—whatever it is you like to do for them."

Something snapped inside her. Selene snatched the dagger from her father's belt and thrust it at his chest, but her hand stopped while the point was still inches from his heart. Her arm refused to respond. Clenching her jaw in frustration, she tried to push it home, but her body wouldn't answer her commands.

Lognion smiled. "That won't work I'm afraid. You can't kill me. You'll have to get creative if you expect to do the job, but I have my doubts that it's even possible. Your mind probably won't even let you consider ideas that would potentially succeed." A frustrated groan escaped her lips, but the blade wouldn't move any closer to her father's heart. "Put the knife back in its sheath and behave yourself, Selene."

Tears ran down her cheeks as her traitorous hand did as her father bade. "How can this be real?" she asked. "Was my entire childhood a lie? Is this just a game for you?"

Her father sighed. "It depends on how you define lies and games. I've done my best to keep you content, so long as it didn't interfere with my goals. There's no reason for me not to continue doing so. So long as you don't waste your time struggling against reality, your life can be just as it was."

"Will is dead! Don't you understand? I loved him. Nothing will ever be as it was."

"He was potential breeding stock at best, don't be so sentimental. Now that you've killed off two suitors at once we may have trouble finding a new stud to produce my next heir."

She stared at her father in horror. "You think I would produce a child for you to torture as you have tortured me?"

Lognion chuckled. "Don't be dramatic. You've had a good life."

"Until you decide to turn me into an elemental. Did you think I wouldn't figure that out? Will warned me, but I didn't believe him."

The king arched one brow. "What of it? You can live a normal life. I have no need to kill you early. Worrying about what will happen after you die is pointless. At least you will still be useful to me." He paused, then fixed his eyes on her. "But you *will* produce an heir for me. I have no desire to marry again so soon. There's no reason your womb can't be put to good use."

"I won't."

"You will, and I'll even allow you to select your mate. Be grateful I'm not choosy. So long as you find someone that can give you a healthy child, I care not. If you're stubborn, however, I will make the choice for you. There are plenty of men in the palace, and even a bastard will suffice. Perhaps one of the guards?"

"Go to hell!"

Lognion's face twisted into a sneer. "Anger me, child, and it might be *all* of the guards."

Selene wanted to vomit. She fought down her nausea and asked, "Why do you want a child so badly?"

"That is for me to worry about. Do not fear. I won't make you raise it."

A new thought came to her, one so terrible she hadn't dared to consider it before. "My brother didn't get sick, did he? What did you do to him?"

"He served his purpose." Lognion glanced at her, his eyes devoid of any trace of concern. "Rejoice that you were born female. You need only provide me with sons."

She stared at him with hate filled eyes. "You mean grandsons."

"If you don't take too long. Don't test my patience," said her father. "I have a hundred ways to punish you for defying me, some more humiliating than others."

Disgusted, she moved even farther away, until she was pressed against the side of the carriage. Selene's shock and dismay were so great she couldn't find words to respond.

Lognion laughed. "It was just a hypothetical. Fear not, I have absolutely no interest in you."

Selene had known her father was unusual, but she had spent her life convincing herself that he was merely pragmatic. A man forced to make hard choices for the good of his people. That illusion was shattered. *He's not even human,* she realized. *Even a demon would have more empathy, more emotion, than this creature.*

If she couldn't kill him, there was one other option. Leaping forward, she opened the coach door, but before she could throw herself onto the street, his command rang out. "Stop. You are forbidden from killing yourself. Your womb is far more valuable than gaining another elemental. Return to your seat."

Her body obeyed, but her mind continued to reason. *Why does he need a male child?* she thought. She refused to give up. If all she was allowed were her thoughts, then she would use them as well as she could. *Or is it male children? What did he do to Alex?* She could hardly remember her brother, but she mourned him anew.

***

He was adrift in a sea of lights, or were they stars? Could stars be so bright? He had no idea. A different question came to him. *Who am I?* There was no answer, either from within or from without.

A voice echoed around him. "Are you ready, child?"

He tried to answer, but he had no voice. *Ready for what?* he thought.

"A new life, or none at all. The choice is yours."

Was I alive before?

"You're alive still, if you wish, though great pain awaits you if you return. A new beginning might be better. Your most recent life was ill-fated."

He thought about it a moment, though he had nothing but nebulous empty concepts with which to imagine life. *Will I be loved?*

"Love is ever present. No life is without it, though the same is true of suffering. They are provided in equal measure. Your last life had too much of both."

It must have been interesting.

"Interesting is rarely a good thing. Trust me."

Who are you?

"A part of you, or perhaps it would be better to say you are part of me. I was a fellow traveler once. Now I guide those who need me."

Was your life interesting?

"Far too interesting."

Would you return to it if you could? His only answer was a long silence. *I think I'd like to return. I can always try a new life later, can't I?*

"Very well, you may return, though I will give you one piece of advice. Don't fear pain, for it gives meaning to life. Do not fear love either, for while it will always lead to more pain, it also makes it bearable. Both are inescapable."

***

Will felt a strange shifting, as though his body was being shoved about. After a moment he realized something was rubbing him, rubbing one place in particular. A voice came to his ears. "Will, please wake up. Wake up. Please."

He opened his eyes and found Tailtiu's face looking down on him. Her features took on an odd expression. "You're alive." Her lips quirked into a sly smile and she looked down. "You're *alive*."

"Stop that," ordered Will. "Didn't I tell you never to touch me without permission?"

"Orders given by dead men don't count," she countered.

He pushed her away with a frown. "What were you doing?"

"Since you were dead, I thought I'd test something I once heard about dead men and their members."

Disgusted, he motioned for her to move farther away. "That's sick. What would you have done if it worked?"

"Exactly what you imagine," she said with a grin. "After that I thought I might go on a small killing spree to celebrate your demise."

She never changes, he thought. Will sat up and examined his surroundings. He was sitting in the back of what appeared to be a farmer's cart, partially laden with turnips. Looking over the sides, he saw they were on an empty road that bisected two wide fields of barley. "Why were you saying that to me?"

"I heard Selene saying it over and over. She was quite emphatic, as though it might actually cause you to revive, so I thought perhaps there was some purpose to it."

"Where were you?"

"Watching through one of the cathedral windows. You died in a spectacular fashion. I've never seen anything quite like it." Then she frowned. "That reminds me, how is it that you're alive? I'm quite sure you were dead just a short while ago."

"Plan C," he said flatly. "Though I'm a little surprised it worked. I thought the spell had failed."

"Spell? It was a dagger that killed you," she informed him.

"Necromancy," he explained. "A spell that was supposed to allow me to die and return to life after a short period of time. I wasn't sure how it would work." He inspected his chest, poking fingers through the tears in his doublet and jerkin. "Did you heal me?"

Tailtiu shook her head. "I tried, but nothing worked. The dead don't heal. Selene poured a potion down your throat, though."

"The regeneration potion," said Will. "I guess I'm lucky. It must have started working when I came back, otherwise I probably would have died again."

"You knew you were going to be stabbed?"

He shook his head. "No. I gave the potion to Selene in case she got hurt. I had some small thought she might need it for me if things went really wrong, but I actually thought I would escape without getting hurt." Then he asked, "Where are we?"

"South of the city. I was going to take your body back and show it to Mother."

Will smirked. "How thoughtful of you."

"I am always full of thoughts," Tailtiu remarked. "They were planning to burn your body. I didn't think Mother would approve."

He grimaced. *That would have been really unfortunate.*

"So I waited until they were alone and killed the men carrying you. Then I found this cart, and since it seemed useful, I took it from the man using it. He wasn't very cooperative."

Will stared at her. "You *killed* them?"

She nodded happily, flashing a smile full of white teeth. "Two guards and the old man with this cart."

"You aren't supposed to kill humans. That's against the accord."

Tailtiu tutted at him, waving her finger back and forth. "You were dead. Weren't you listening earlier? I was planning to go back and have some more fun after delivering your corpse to Mother."

"Listen, Tailtiu. I don't want you killing people, even if I'm dead. That's an order."

His aunt laughed. "I'll do whatever I please when you're gone. If it bothers you so much, don't die."

He clambered out of the cart, sighing as he went. There was no use arguing with his psychotic aunt.

"Where are you going?" she asked.

"Back. How long was I dead?"

"A long time. The sun will set in a few hours. When you say 'back,' what do you mean exactly?"

"To wherever Selene is, probably the palace. She's probably stricken with grief. Every minute I delay only makes things worse for her."

It was rare to see the expression on her, but Tailtiu gaped at him in disbelief. "Didn't they *just* murder you? Is dying so fun that you're keen to experience it again?"

Will shrugged. "It actually wasn't very painful at all. Considering what I've been through without dying, I'd say living hurts worse." In his head he remembered a familiar voice, *"Don't fear pain, for it gives meaning to life."* He tried to recall where he had heard the phrase, but his mind came up blank.

"I've never known a mortal that didn't fear death, now I wonder if I'm missing something."

Will was already walking back toward Cerria. "You're dismissed. I'll call you again if I need you." There was nothing in him but calm as he set his feet toward his goal. Whether it was a side effect of dying or some other cause he didn't know, but there was no fear left in him, only clear purpose.

Somehow, he knew that whatever happened, or whenever he did finally die, it would be all right. In the meantime, he intended to act according to his principles. Selene was waiting for him.

CHAPTER 64

At some point during his journey, Will decided to put on his armor. Being unafraid was one thing, but dying recklessly would be the height of foolishness. He discarded his ruined finery and dressed in his arming jacket, mail, and helm. Atop those he wore his greaves and breastplate.

His next consideration was what spell he should prepare, and after a few minutes he decided on the sleep spell. Playing dead wasn't likely to work again, and he had more imminent obstacles likely to appear on his way to the palace.

The first of those obstacles stepped out to challenge him as he started to enter the city, two men dressed as guards. "Hold! State your name and business."

The city guard didn't normally challenge everyone who entered, but a man wearing so much armor was highly unusual. Will cast the sleep spell and watched them slump to the ground, then he walked on.

That was silly, he realized. After he was away from the gate, he took a minute to cover himself with a chameleon spell, then added a silence to his armor. He didn't need to create extra problems for himself. He prepared another sleep spell and with that he felt ready to continue.

The rest of his journey to the palace went without interruption, though he didn't bother moving carefully. If anyone noticed the strange shimmers and distortions as he walked by, they didn't attempt to do anything about them. At the palace gate he walked past the four men standing guard. They stared at him curiously as he passed, but it was the sorcerer that stood inside the gate who reacted first, leveling a fierce blast of fire at the spot where he stood.

The fire exploded almost at its point of origin as it met Will's force shield, killing the sorcerer before the poor man realized what had happened. Will turned and used the spell he had prepared, sending the guards into forced slumber. He took a moment to free the sorcerer's elemental and prepared another sleep spell before moving on.

Apparently, the sorcerer's death hadn't been noticed, for no one came out to block his path. Will kept walking, moving along the paved carriage lane until he reached the main entrance of the palace. He put the guards there to sleep, then refreshed his prepared spell before using an unlocking spell on the doors. Will pushed them open and strode in.

He already knew the layout of most of the palace, since he'd stayed there for almost a week when he first came to Cerria. *Not counting my time in the dungeon,* he thought wryly. His time in Selene's room and the halls outside of it after the demons had come to kill her had also informed his knowledge of some of the upper floors.

The main corridor would take him to the ball room, so he turned into the right-hand corridor since it led most directly toward the living areas. At the end of that corridor he turned left and found the smaller staircase that led up toward Selene's bedroom. *And the king's chambers too, probably.* He wasn't sure where His Majesty's chambers were located, but he knew they were in the same general area.

As he climbed the stairs, he wondered whether he would kill King Lognion or not. He probably wasn't a match for the man yet, but if the opportunity presented itself, he knew he would be a fool not to take it.

Will put the thought from his mind. He was beyond worry. He would do whatever was necessary, nothing more, nothing less.

When he reached the second-floor landing, he encountered the last person he expected to see roaming the halls, King Lognion. The king's sharp eyes noticed the shimmer of his form almost immediately.

Lognion reacted without surprise. "My men told me someone had taken your body. Now I see why."

Will dismissed the chameleon spell. "I didn't feel like being cremated today."

Two overly alert guards started up the stairs from below, having apparently heard their king talking to a stranger. Will waited until they were close, then turned and put them to sleep while almost simultaneously putting a force shield behind himself, just in case Lognion attacked.

The king was smiling when he turned back to face him. "You didn't need to do that. I would have told them to return to their posts."

Will shrugged. "Sorry. I'm feeling a bit on edge. Next time I'll ask first."

"You've come for Selene, I presume," stated the king.

"I thought she might be feeling down, considering how the wedding went."

Lognion nodded, then took a step back, gesturing in the direction of his daughter's room. "She isn't feeling well, but I'm sure she'll be glad to see you."

"I'm taking her with me," Will stated flatly.

"If you wish," the king responded. "Though you're welcome to live here with her. It would probably be more comfortable for the two of you."

That surprised him, but he didn't let it shake his confidence. "You have no objections?"

"I had none two weeks ago, though you chose to create a spectacle rather than handle things in a more circumspect manner," said Lognion. "Now that she's made her position clear and personally removed her fiancé from consideration, I have no reason to stand in your way."

Will stared at the man, unsure if he believed him, though he'd never known the king to lie. He stood frozen for almost a minute, trying to choose his course. He wanted to kill the king. It was perhaps the first time he had honestly *desired* the death of another human being, but all his instincts were warning him against making the attempt.

A look of understanding occupied the king's visage. "I'm sure you're thinking about killing me, William, but I would advise against it. You would only inconvenience both of us. Go claim your prize. I assure you I bear you no ill will. If anything, I'd like to thank you for the sublime entertainment you provided today. In all my years I have rarely encountered such an inspired performance."

The king turned away as though he hadn't a care in the world. Will watched him go, but when he started down the hall toward Selene's bedroom, Lognion spoke once more. "There is a price for my daughter, William. Never forget that. For as long as she binds your heart, you will serve me. Disappoint me and both of you will regret it."

Will's jaw muscles twitched as he ground his teeth together. He fought the urge to attack the monarch then and there. Without looking back, he answered, "You will never have my oath, Lognion."

The king laughed. "I don't need it."

***

The guard who stood outside the princess' door warned him away with a stern look. "Her Highness does not wish to be disturbed."

Will connected a source-link to the man with barely a thought, then responded as he gradually drained the man's strength. "We may meet again in the future. Next time I would advise you never to get between me and the woman in that room. Remember that when you awaken later."

The guard felt his strength begin to ebb and started forward, reaching for his sword, but it was too late. Will caught his hand and held him still for a few more seconds, then helped him gently to the floor.

He knocked, but there was no response, so he knocked again. He waited half a minute before knocking a third time. This time he heard Selene's voice coming from a distance, probably her bedroom. "Go away!"

Will constructed an unlocking spell and used it on the door. There was a satisfying click as the lock disengaged and he was gratified to find that she hadn't also barred it. He swung it open with one hand and stepped into the sitting room.

Her next warning came from the direction of the bedroom. It was accompanied by the rustling of bedsheets. "Step one foot further and even your family won't be able to recognize what's left of you."

"It would be easier for the sun to reverse its course, than for me to leave without seeing your face," said Will.

There was no reply, and even the sounds of the bed linens fell silent.

"Can I come in?" Will asked.

"I don't know who you are, or what magic you're using, but if you speak with that voice again it will be the last thing you do," Selene threatened, her voice low and hoarse.

"This is my voice. I have a lot to tell you." As he spoke, the floor seemed to melt around his feet, and he sank halfway to his knees into the stone. Selene's disheveled face appeared as she stepped out from the other room, and the haunted look in her eyes broke his heart. Her hair was a tangled mess, as though she had yanked and pulled at her braids to free it, then given up halfway. She still wore the remains of her wedding dress, though it was stained with dirt and blood. At some point she had roughly cut away the train and a good portion of the skirt. The sleeves were gone, and what remained was barely more than rags.

The whites of her eyes were red where the blood vessels had ruptured during their last confrontation, and there was crusted blood above her lips and more dried blood marked a trail from her neck to her collarbones. She stared at him with the eyes of one afraid, too fearful to dare to hope that what she beheld was the truth. "What is this?" she asked, her voice coming out in a croak. "Is this a cruel joke?"

"It's me," said Will carefully as his eyes began to tear up. He couldn't bear the sight of her misery.

"You're dead."

He nodded. "I was—for a little while."

Selene's head turned uncertainly from one side the other, as if she was searching for the ones who must be toying with her emotions. "This can't be real. How?"

"I had a spell ready to fake my death. I was planning to use it if I couldn't escape, but I didn't expect I'd get stabbed as well. Fortunately, when it wore off the potion you gave me took care of the rest."

The stone imprisoning his legs flowed upward, encasing his torso and then his arms. He made no attempt to resist, and a few seconds later he was thoroughly trapped with only his head free to move. Selene stepped tentatively forward, then reached out to touch his face. "Prove to me this is really you."

Will smiled, and fat teardrops rolled down his cheeks. "I have six silver clima in my pouch. I can pay, if you're willing to give me a kiss."

Her face crumpled as a weak sob escaped her lips, then the stone holding Will in place crumbled, falling to the floor around him in dusty chunks. Selene's hands latched onto his neck and shoulders in a grip that was painful as she pulled him to her. They stood like that for a minute or so before she pushed him away, though she didn't release her hold on him. She stared at his breastplate. "That thing needs to go," she remarked quietly.

"Your dress is even worse," said Will.

"At least it isn't made of cold metal." They spent the next quarter of an hour removing his armor, as she decided that the mail was also unacceptable. When they finished, he stood dressed only in his tunic and trousers, then she embraced him again.

Selene's arms were so tight they threatened to crush his ribs, but Will couldn't help but wrinkle his nose. "You need a bath," he told her softly.

"Speak for yourself."

Will knew he wasn't dirty. He had cleaned himself before donning the armor and the tunic he had worn beneath it was still fresh. He lifted the collar to his nose and sniffed, noting the smell of stale sweat and acrid iron. The padded gambeson had imparted its characteristic and almost permanent odor to his clothes even though he hadn't worn it more than an hour or so. "Maybe you're right," he admitted.

He dug around in his pouch for a moment, then found the coins he was looking for and held them out. "I still haven't gotten that kiss yet."

She took his head in her hands and gave him a brief but solid kiss before pulling away in disgust. "What is that?"

He had forgotten the terrible taste in his mouth, and his cheeks flushed with embarrassment. “Troll piss.”

“What?”

“The regeneration potions, they’re made with troll piss. The one you gave me must have lingered in my mouth and throat for a few hours before I woke up.”

Selene gagged. “I even drank one of those!” she said, reminding him of the night they had fought the demons in her room. “Why didn’t you tell me?”

“It’s better than dying. No one would take one if they knew,” said Will with a wry smile.

“That is absolutely vile.” She looked down at her tattered dress. “We both need a bath.”

“Spell?” he suggested.

“A real bath, and you need to wash your mouth out with lye.”

He snorted. “That would kill me all over again.”

“If a dagger won’t do it, you ought to be able to handle poisoning.” She paused. “How did you get in here?”

“I’ve already seen your father,” Will said reassuringly. “Apparently he’s willing to hand you over as damaged goods. I told him we would be leaving here soon.”

“Leaving?”

“Unless you want me to live here with you. I assumed you’d rather be somewhere else.”

Selene thought of her father and shuddered. “Anywhere. But first we need to bathe, and you have a lot of explaining to do.” She stepped toward the outer door. “I’ll call for a tub No, never mind. Let’s use the main bath.”

“Main bath?”

She nodded. “It’s much nicer than bathing in a copper tub.”

“Probably for the best,” said Will. “The man outside your door won’t be waking up for a while.” He began storing his armor within the limnthal, then started to move to one of the chairs so he could sit down. Selene’s hand caught the back of his tunic and he heard a strange sound.

Looking back, he saw her face twist as her emotions began to well up again. His arms went around her, and they wound up sitting on the floor together for some time, alternately crying and soothing each other. Strangely, even during the moments when his own tears came, he felt a subtle happiness underlying it. *I’m not alone.*

When they had finally gained a semblance of composure Selene led him to the bath, which turned out to be an expansive tiled room devoted to that singular purpose. It reminded him of a public bathhouse, though it was smaller and entirely reserved for the use of the royal family. As such it was well appointed and far more private. They soaked in a smooth stone pool filled with warm water for more than hour while he shared his recent events with her. Selene also described her conversation with her father for him, and while Will was disgusted, there was little about the king that could shock him any longer.

The revelation of Lognion's desire for male heirs bothered Will more than any other part of her story. It also reminded him of a previous concern. "Selene."

"Yes."

"Is there a chance that—" His words came to a stop, but his eyes drifted down toward her belly.

It took a few seconds, but understanding dawned on her. "Oh, no. Not at all."

"Are you sure? We weren't very careful."

"I'm not pregnant, William. I'm certain of that."

He frowned. "How do you know?"

"There's a spell to prevent surprises of that sort," she told him. "I learned it during my second year at Wurthaven."

"Oh," he said with a sigh that held both relief and a faint disappointment. "I hadn't heard of that." Then his brain began working through her statement. *Did she look it up in the library? If so, why?* As a royal she was expected to bear an heir soon after marriage, and before that—well obviously the things they had been doing were strictly forbidden. Yet he knew she hadn't experimented previously, or at least he was fairly certain. The questions circled in his head, but his mouth was helpless to express them.

Selene laughed at his confusion. "Professor Fontenot taught me. She teaches all the girls at Wurthaven once they're capable of third-order spells."

"She does?" That was news to him.

"It isn't something she talks about in class. Usually she calls them in for a private conference. It's something she feels strongly about," explained Selene. She studied his face as he processed her words. "What exactly were you thinking a few seconds ago?" A malicious grin appeared on her face. "Were you worried? Did you think maybe I'd had a lot of *experience*?"

"No!" he declared firmly. "I mean, it would have been surprising, but what came before isn't any of my concern." His eyes narrowed. "Besides, it was obvious from your amateurish performance that that wasn't the case."

She squinted back at him. "You're going to pay for that remark." When she saw the look of anticipation on his face, she added, "Later. We need to find somewhere to stay. I don't want to spend another night sleeping under this roof."

Mildly disappointed, he responded, "I wasn't in the mood anyway. Those demon eyes of yours are too scary. I have a few more regeneration potions if you want to fix them."

Selene turned her face away. "I'm never using one of those disgusting potions again, now that I know what's in them. My eyes can heal on their own."

Soon after that, they dried and dressed themselves. Selene selected a few things from her room and Will stored them away. "I can send for the rest when we find a place big enough to keep it all," she said firmly.

"Let's use the side entrance," Will suggested. "I had some trouble at the front gate. I'd rather not go out that way."

She frowned, but nodded without asking. They left via the postern gate, and after a short walk down the north road they came to the entrance to Wurthaven. Will started in that direction, but Selene caught his arm. "There's somewhere else we need to go first."

"Where?"

"The cathedral."

"The one you nearly destroyed?" asked Will. "At this hour?"

She nodded. "They don't lock the doors until midnight. We still have time."

"For what?"

"You'll see."

CHAPTER 65

Contrary to her opinion that the cathedral would be open, the doors had been blocked and a guardsman was stationed outside. "I'm sorry. You can't come in," the man informed them. "The sanctuary may be closed for a few weeks until repairs are made."

Selene stepped forward so the guard could see her face clearly in the lantern light. "I am well aware. Open the door for me."

The man's face paled and he dipped into a low bow as he recognized her features. "Your Highness, forgive me."

"Is Father Latimer within?" she asked.

"His Holiness has already returned home, Your Highness."

"Find someone and roust him out of bed. I require his presence."

The guard's face showed dismay. "I can't leave my post, Your—"

"No one will vandalize the interior. We will be here until your return," she said with unyielding authority.

The guard left, and Will and Selene went inside. The interior was worse than he remembered, and Will felt a sudden sense of guilt, as though he were a criminal returning to the scene of a crime. *I suppose I am,* he thought, *though she did most of the damage.*

For her part, Selene showed no sign of discomfort, much less embarrassment. Much like a cat, she surveyed the destruction she had wrought as though it had been caused by a third party, rather than by her own hand.

"I guess it could be worse," offered Will. "Most of the damage is just woodwork—benches and whatnot."

Selene pointed up at the vaulted ceilings. "They'll have to repair the roof as well. I pulled quite a few stones loose when I was trying to smash your head. It's a miracle I didn't damage the arches and cause the entire ceiling to collapse."

"You seem remarkably calm about the matter," said Will in a neutral tone.

She shrugged. "I think I've developed a unique perspective. It probably has something to do with having been raised by a tyrannical lunatic." She paused and looked at him seriously. "I'm probably not quite normal either. Does that bother you?"

"I'd be lying if I said I wasn't worried," said Will. "But I love you anyway. Why?"

"If you marry me, you'll be stuck with me for life," she explained.

He smiled. "I can worry about that later, for now I'm just glad we're both—" His mouth froze as his brain worked out what she was planning. "Wait, is that why you called for the high priest?"

"What else would I call him here for?"

"But—"

"You *do* want to marry me, don't you? It isn't too late to back out."

Will's eyes were as big as saucers. He sputtered, "Well, yes, but I haven't asked you yet. I don't have a ring. People have to be warned. Aren't there a lot of formalities? You're a royal princess."

"I recall you saying just a few hours ago that you would either move into the palace or take me with you. I assumed you meant marriage."

"Well, yeah, I did, but..." Will backpedaled as he tried to sort out his words.

Her gaze was intense, and the effect was only made worse by the fact that the whites of her eyes were stained a vivid red. "William, are you telling me that after storming in here, disrupting my wedding, and destroying most of the interior of this church, that you *don't* intend to marry me?"

All he could do was stare at her blankly.

"After I murdered my groom for you? You died, came back from death itself, marched into my home and confronted my father, and now you're getting cold feet?"

Cold fear clutched at his heart for a moment. *She's insane, just like her father.* Then he saw her lips quirk up at the corners as a mischievous smile threatened to break through her façade. *She's teasing me. But is she serious too?* "Are you serious?" he asked. "Do you really want to get married, right *now*, atop the still-warm ashes of today's catastrophe?"

Selene moved closer, her hand rising to catch the front of his tunic in a tight fist. It might have been a threatening gesture, but the expression on her face said otherwise. Hidden behind her calm determination was a flicker of quiet fear. "You died today," she said. "I almost married the wrong man. My father is insane and may well kill one or both of us at any time. I won't wait any longer. If I don't marry you now, who knows what will happen tomorrow?"

Will's chest tightened.

She looked up at him. "Do you think I'm mad?"

He pulled her close and held her gently. "No. Sometimes I think you're the only sane person in this twisted mess of a world, and I still have no idea why you love me."

She answered, speaking softly into his chest, "Someday I'll explain it to you."

They waited together for almost three quarters of an hour before the high priest appeared, though the man looked none too happy about having been forced from his bed. Will felt sorry for Father Latimer. The man had definitely had a stressful day.

The priest's first responses were of shock and disbelief, followed by excuses. "I can't, Your Highness. Your father, His Majesty, has to approve. This simply can't be done. You aren't some peasant farm girl. There must be witnesses, the banns must be published, there are a—"

Selene cut him off. "My father has already given his approval. Send men to confirm it if you don't trust my word. Witnesses can be found. Bring in the guards if need be. Frankly I don't care. The banns are not a requirement. If you have any other excuses make them quickly, but be warned, my patience is thin."

The High Priest of the Church of the Holy Mother was not so easily browbeaten, and he argued for a while, but it was obvious to Will that the man was hopelessly outmatched. Messengers were sent to inform the palace, and two guards and an acolyte were brought in to serve as witnesses. Father Latimer was steadfast in one regard, however—he wouldn't proceed until either the king appeared, or his written approval was received.

Another full hour passed while they waited, and it was nearing midnight when a runner appeared bearing the king's writ. As Selene had said, Lognion had no objections, though Father Latimer stared at the paper as though trying to decide if he had lost his mind.

While the high priest was muttering to himself, Will pulled Selene aside. "We don't have rings."

"I don't care," said Selene. "We can make them out of string for all I care. Wait, I have an idea. Do you have two gold crowns?"

Will summoned them from his limnthal. She took them from his hand, then her face grew serious. "Will, I didn't believe you before, but now that I know the truth, I can hardly bear the knowledge. You once told me you could never marry a sorceress."

That was true, but at present, he was willing to make an exception. Before he could say as much, though, Selene's two elementals manifested physically, growing into man-sized figures of water and stone on either side of her. She handed a gold coin to each of them. "Hold your hand out so they can see your ring finger," she told Will.

He held his left hand out toward the water elemental, Syllanus. *Arrogan's best friend, the only one who didn't turn against him,* he thought silently.

Selene addressed the elementals verbally, something he had never heard her do before. "This is my last task for you, my friends. Forgive me for keeping you all this time. I didn't understand."

Wait, is she going to give them up? Will couldn't hide his shock. *But she'll be unable to use magic without slowly killing herself.* For once, despite his principles, he wanted to stop her.

The gold coin disappeared into Syllanus, and the water blurred into motion. When the coin reappeared a minute later, a small hole had been bored through the center. The elemental held it up to Will's hand to compare, then withdrew it once more. It repeated the cycle several times, until the hole in the coin would just fit over his finger, then it took the coin one last time. When it returned it a moment after, the outer portion had been ground and buffed down until all that was left was a perfectly polished gold band, one that neatly fit his finger.

On the other side Selene's earth elemental had done the same with her coin. With their tasks accomplished, Selene drew out the knotted enchantments that bound the elementals to her, and for the first time, Will witnessed a sorcerer voluntarily unbinding the enchantment. The elementals bowed in Selene's direction first, then turned and gave a second bow to him. They slowly dissipated after that, and the couple were left standing alone.

"Will you marry me now, Will? I'm not a sorceress any longer."

"You idiot. I was going to marry you anyway," he said quietly. "What will happen to you now?"

"I'll have to make do, just like everyone else does. Fair warning, though, Father will be furious when he finds out. Greater elementals are extremely rare." She smiled as she said it.

A figure approached from one of the side entrances, though it was a moment before Will recognized the newcomer. When he did, he stared at her in horror. It was his grandmother, Aislinn. "How?"

"I keep a close eye on those who owe me favors, William." She then turned her attention to Selene, studying the young woman with careful eyes. "I have no objection," she said at last, as though giving judgment.

"You have much to learn, girl, but as you have sacrificed your ill-gotten power, I will give you my blessing."

A low, hissing growl came from the ground near Will's leg and when he looked down, he saw the goddamn cat. His back was arched, and his hackles raised as he glared at Will's fae grandmother.

Aislinn looked down at the creature, barely disguising her alarm as she realized its presence in the room. She took a half step back, then stopped. "Why are you here?"

"I also have an interest here, fae witch. I would advise you not to interfere," said the Cath Bawlg, his voice coming from everywhere at once.

The tension in the air was palpable, and Will glanced back to see that Father Latimer had taken note of the new arrivals. The High Priest of the Holy Mother was crouched behind the altar, hands clasped in a silent prayer to Temarah to grant him her protection.

Aislinn answered, "I am not here to interfere. I will bear witness to their marriage. My only interest in this is my new granddaughter-in-law."

"Then I will bear witness as well," responded the Cath Bawlg, "to ensure you keep your word."

The high priest peered over the altar at them. "Are we safe to continue?"

The ceremony proceeded from there, and Father Latimer wasted no time on platitudes or lengthy speeches. He moved through the required phrases with remarkable alacrity, and before Will knew it, they were already to the vows and 'I do's.' He felt stiff and awkward until the moment of the kiss, and though it began awkwardly, his heart melted and his body relaxed.

The high priest was anxious to leave, but Selene wouldn't release him until a marriage document had been drawn up and four copies made. All those present signed, including Aislinn and the goddamn cat, who set his paw to the pages and left a blackened print on the papers. Selene took the first copy, and Aislinn took another on her insistence. The other two were reserved for the church and the king. The fae lady gave a final warning to Father Latimer as she took possession of her copy. "Make sure your king knows I was here. If he thinks to interfere or annul this joining, I will not allow it."

The goddamn cat simply walked away, though to Father Latimer's chagrin it stopped to mark the altar on its way out. The high priest was already sending his acolyte to fetch rags and water as the others made their way out. He seemed eminently relieved to see the end of the entire affair.

Aislinn stopped on the steps leading away from the church and then addressed the new couple. "I will claim my favor the day after tomorrow, William. See that you consummate your vows before I return."

Will's arm reflexively went in front of the new bride. "What?"

"The favor you promised," reminded his grandmother. "I will take the girl."

His cheeks flushed with rage. "I told you I wouldn't bargain her. That's why I traded an unbound favor instead!"

Aislinn smiled wickedly. "Perhaps you're unclear on the meaning of an *unbound* favor. It's worth more because it can be anything, including something as mundane as taking your bride. Next time don't be stupid. Any deal is better than offering an unbound favor."

Will's jaw was set. "Then I'll refuse."

Selene grabbed his hand. "Wait. What are we talking about here?"

"She plans to take you away, to Faerie," said Will.

Aislinn had a different answer. "Your husband is about to commit suicide."

"Not 'about to.' I'll say it plainly," declared Will. "I, William Cartwright, will not—"

His words cut off as Selene clapped one hand over his mouth. "Will, not another word!" She faced his grandmother. "What do you mean? Suicide?"

Aislinn's features were set in stone. "If he refuses to honor the favor, I will kill him. Here and now." Then she glanced at Will. "And your name is William Maligant now. When a man marries into royalty, he must give up his own name, not the other way around."

Selene shook her head. "I don't want my name anymore. That's not the point. What do you want from him?"

Will pulled his face away from her hand. "It doesn't matter, I'm not trading you—"

The bride moved closer, wrapping her entire arm around his head. "Will Cartwright, I swear by all the gods we are going to have our first fight right here, in the street, if you—don't—stop—talking!"

The groom was considering what would happen if he knocked Selene's legs out from under her, but Aislinn was already speaking, "I want you, Selene Maligant, and if you will not come with me, my grandson will pay the price with his life."

"You can go to hell!" screamed Will as he twisted around Selene so he could face his grandmother.

"Can I trade you a favor in exchange for his?" asked Selene desperately.

"You don't have any standing," argued Will. "You aren't a true wizard."

Aislinn chuckled. "She doesn't have the *right*, but she doesn't need it if I'm willing to accept her offer, and I will. You have a bargain, Granddaughter."

"Deal," exclaimed Selene.

"No!" shouted Will. "I refuse."

"Too bad," said his grandmother. "You no longer owe me anything." She gave Selene a look of approval. "I made the same choice once, and though I've suffered for it these many centuries, I have never regretted it. You will make an excellent apprentice."

Will struggled to stand up straight, since he and Selene were still entangled. He managed to get free, then promptly tripped and wound up sitting down hard on the steps. "A what?" he asked.

"You are not fit to train her yet," said Aislinn. "And if she is not trained your marriage will be tragically short-lived." Wicked laughter rang out from her lips. "I told you before that I wouldn't take her humanity. You should have listened. Did you think I planned to use her as a sex slave for my depraved husband, or perhaps for his servants?"

Will was furious. "Of course, I did!"

Selene stared at him. "Will, I know she's fae, but isn't she your grandmother? You shouldn't say things like that."

"You don't know her like I do. Wait until you meet her daughter. She's a whore."

Selene's face paled, but Aislinn only laughed louder. "It's true."

"See?" said Will, feeling slightly vindicated. "Even she admits it."

"All fae are to some degree. We're rather proud of it," agreed Aislinn. She looked at Selene. "If you're willing, we could probably teach you things that would keep this choir boy you married blushing well into his second century."

Selene's face regained its color as her cheeks reddened. "I don't think that will be necessary."

"As you choose. I'll come for you day after tomorrow." Aislinn walked away, her figure fading into obscurity long before the distance would have dictated it should.

EPILOGUE

Dianne Young stepped out of her door as Will and Selene entered the front lobby of the boys' dorm at Wurthaven. Her expression turned to disapproval as she realized Will had a woman beside him. "The door was locked, William. It's after hours. How did you get in?"

"Well…"

"Never mind, I don't want to know. What I would like to know is why you think it's appropriate to bring a female student into this building in the middle of the night?" demanded the resident assistant.

Will held up one hand. "First, she isn't a student, she's an alumna. Second—"

"It's nice to see you again, Auntie," said Selene politely.

"Auntie?" Will was utterly confused.

"Since she wasn't our dorm mom, we called her 'auntie' instead. Everyone loved Dianne, at least they did while I was here."

Dianne's eyes were fixed on Selene's face and the slowly widened as recognition came to her. "Selene? Your Highness!" She dipped into a respectful curtsey.

Selene caught her hands, pulling her up to stand straight. "There's no need for that tonight. How have you been?"

"Well," said Dianne. "How have you been? Didn't you get married today? I heard there was an awful disturbance at the cathedral. Where is your husband?" She glared at Will as though he had committed some terrible crime.

"*I'm* her husband," said Will sourly.

Dianne took a step back and stumbled, catching herself on the edge of the front desk. "What?"

Selene merely smiled sweetly, then gave a single nod.

The resident assistant was in shock, but after a moment she asked, "Why are you here?"

"She's homeless," said Will dryly. "I told her she could sleep on the floor."

Selene shot him a dirty look, then answered Dianne's question, "It will only be one night. We'll find other lodgings tomorrow."

Poor Dianne's head seemed about to explode. Her eyes darted back and forth. "Wait! That wasn't a joke?" She stared agape at Selene. "You really married *him*?"

"Hey!" said Will, feeling hurt.

Selene held up the marriage certificate, her eyes twinkling mischievously. "According to this we're married. Do you think it's too late to get out of it?"

Dianne's hand covered her mouth. "Holy Mother!" Then she squinted at the document. "Is that a paw print?"

Selene spread the paper out atop the desk so Dianne could look at it properly. She was obviously enjoying the moment. "One of the witnesses was a cat…"

Will gently slid between the two women, gathering Selene and the document into his arms. "I'll explain everything tomorrow, Mom."

"We're very tired," agreed Selene, affecting a false yawn.

They climbed the stairs together, leaving the astonished resident assistant standing in the lobby. Once they reached the fourth floor, they made their way to his room, and when the door was finally closed and locked, they both sighed in relief.

"I'm exhausted," said Will. He'd only gotten four hours of sleep the night before, and that seemed like a lifetime ago. "Which bunk do you want?"

Selene arched one brow curiously as she looked askance at him.

"The beds are too small for us to both share one," he explained.

The look in her eyes could have blistered paint. "I thought I was supposed to sleep on the floor?"

"If you insist," said Will nonchalantly. When Selene began to advance on him, he hurried to add, "That was a joke." She cornered him on the bottom bunk, and he answered her with a kiss. After time, they came up for air. "Can't we sleep first?" asked Will.

Selene sighed. "I'm not really in the mood either, but I'm not taking any chances."

"Grandma's orders?"

She nodded, and what followed was best described as functionally acceptable. Will was asleep almost before his part was done. Selene watched his face for a while as he slept, but soon she too lost the battle. Her eyes closed, and when they opened again the morning sun was streaming in through the window.

Thankfully it was still the weekend, and they had the entire day to make up for the deficiencies of the night before.

The story continues in:

Scholar of Magic

Stay up to date with my release by signing up for my newsletter at:

Magebornbooks.com

Books by Michael G. Manning:

Mageborn:

The Blacksmith's Son
The Line of Illeniel
The Archmage Unbound
The God-Stone War
The Final Redemption

Embers of Illeniel (a prequel series):

The Mountains Rise
The Silent Tempest
Betrayer's Bane

Champions of the Dawning Dragons:

Thornbear
Centyr Dominance
Demonhome

The Riven Gates:

Mordecai
The Severed Realm
Transcendence and Rebellion

Standalone Novels:

Thomas

About the Author

Michael Manning was born in Cleveland, Texas and spent his formative years there, reading fantasy and science fiction, concocting home grown experiments in his backyard, and generally avoiding schoolwork.

Eventually he went to college, starting at Sam Houston State University, where his love of beer blossomed and his obsession with playing role-playing games led him to what he calls 'his best year ever' and what most of his family calls 'the lost year'.

Several years and a few crappy jobs later, he decided to pursue college again and was somehow accepted into the University of Houston Honors program (we won't get into the particulars of that miracle). This led to a degree in pharmacy and it followed from there that he wound up with a license to practice said profession.

Unfortunately, Michael was not a very good pharmacist. Being relatively lawless and free spirited were not particularly good traits to possess in a career focused on perfection, patient safety, and the letter-of-the-law. Nevertheless, he persisted and after a stint as a hospital pharmacy manager wound up as a pharmacist working in correctional managed care for the State of Texas.

He gave drugs to prisoners.

After a year or two at UTMB he became bored and taught himself entirely too much about networking, programming, and database design and administration. At first his supervisors warned him (repeatedly) to do his assigned tasks and stop designing programs to help his coworkers do theirs, but eventually they gave up and just let him do whatever he liked since it seemed to be generally working out well for them.

Ten or eleven years later and he got bored with that too. So he wrote a book. We won't talk about where he was when he wrote 'The Blacksmith's Son', but let's just assume he was probably supposed to be doing something else at the time.

Some people liked the book and told other people. Now they won't leave him alone.

After another year or two, he decided to just give up and stop pretending to be a pharmacist/programmer, much to the chagrin of his mother (who had only ever wanted him to grow up to be a doctor and had finally become content with the fact that he had settled on pharmacy instead).

Michael's wife supported his decision, even as she stubbornly refused to believe he would make any money at it. It turned out later that she was just telling him this because she knew that nothing made Michael more contrary than his never ending desire to prove her wrong. Once he was able to prove said fact she promptly admitted her tricky ruse and he has since given up on trying to win.

Today he lives at home with his stubborn wife, teenage twins, a giant moose-poodle, two yorkies, a green-cheeked conure, a massive prehistoric tortoise, and a head full of imaginary people. There are also some fish, but he refuses to talk about them.

www.ingramcontent.com/pod-product-compliance
Lightning Source LLC
Chambersburg PA
CBHW060604310726
48982CB00008B/1229/J

* 9 7 8 1 9 4 3 4 8 1 3 6 1 *